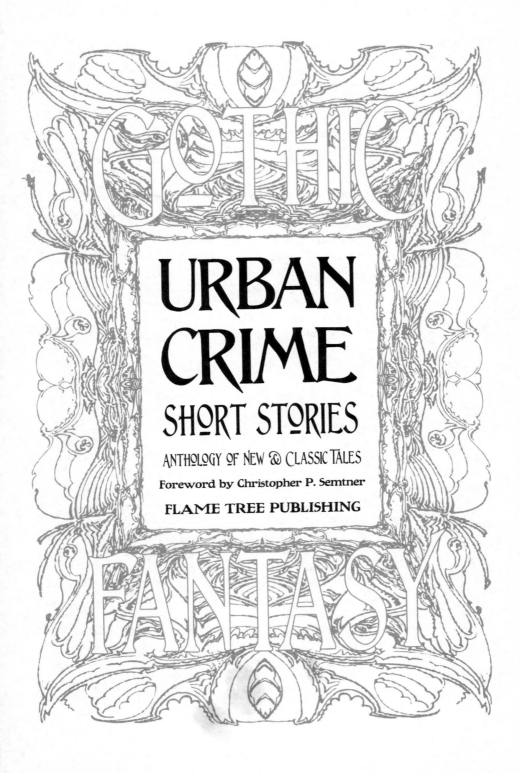

GOTHIC

URBAN CRIME

SHORT STORIES

ANTHOLOGY OF NEW & CLASSIC TALES

Foreword by Christopher P. Semtner

FLAME TREE PUBLISHING

FANTASY

This is a FLAME TREE Book

Publisher & Creative Director: Nick Wells
Senior Project Editor: Josie Mitchell
Editorial Board: Gillian Whitaker, Taylor Bentley, Catherine Taylor

FLAME TREE PUBLISHING
6 Melbray Mews, Fulham,
London SW6 3NS, United Kingdom
www.flametreepublishing.com

First published 2019

ISBN: 978-1-78755-540-2

GOTHIC

URBAN CRIME

SHORT STORIES

ANTHOLOGY OF NEW & CLASSIC TALES

Foreword by Christopher P. Semtner

FLAME TREE PUBLISHING

FANTASY

Contents

Foreword: Urban Crime Short Stories

GROWING UP in the Virginia countryside, we'd all heard of the danger lurking at the other end of the highway. There was a city out there. The few people who'd survived a visit returned with tales of suffocating crowds, rampant crime, drive-by shootings, pickpockets, and other unmentionable terrors. And they all swore they'd never return. I imagined a midnight world where a tourist would be shot dead the second he stepped off the bus. The thought thrilled me. I could not stay away.

This must be what the Victorians felt as populations shifted from farms and villages to the booming cities. During the decades following the Industrial Revolution, the metropolis came to symbolize crime, pollution, disease, and strange foreign immigrants. Cholera, yellow fever, and tuberculosis swept through cramped tenements, leaving horrific death in their wakes. Those who endured the disease, the toxic gas lighting, and the filthy air just might fall victim to thieves, swindlers, or serial killers like Jack the Ripper and H.H. Holmes.

With their fingers always testing the pulse of their times, it seems inevitable that writers would find boundless inspiration in such an environment and its residents. Edgar Allan Poe's narrator encounters 'the type and the genius of deep crime' among the teeming masses of London in his tale 'The Man of the Crowd.' In 'The Traveler's Story of a Terribly Strange Bed,' Wilkie Collins describes the dangers that await a young visitor to a city populated with thieves conspiring to kill and rob him. Fyodor Dostoevsky's *Crime and Punishment* shows just how easily such a visitor can become a murderer. A similar theme is explored in Oscar Wilde's 'Lord Arthur Saville's Crime,' in which the title character is also compelled to kill.

Other authors romanticize the urban criminal, as do E.W. Hornung in his stories of the master criminal Raffles and Maurice Leblanc in his narratives of Arsène Lupin. Master criminals and gangs terrorize entire cities in works like Edgar Wallace's *When the Gangs Came to London* and Jack London's 'Winged Blackmail.'

Just when it seems the thugs and criminals have won the day, the master detective, in the form of Poe's Auguste Dupin or Sir Arthur Conan Doyle's Sherlock Holmes, arrives to expose their nefarious schemes in order to bring them to justice. As the twentieth century city gives birth to new dangers so too arrives another generation of fictional detectives from Melville Davisson Post, Baroness Orczy, and others. In the twenty-first century, the city is larger, darker, and more violent; and its criminals have previously unforeseen weapons and technology. In other words, today's crime writer has more inspiration than ever.

As you read the following stories, which trace the evolution of urban crime fiction from the nineteenth century until today, you just might experience something of the thrill their authors found in the cities they knew. Then you won't be able to stay away.

Christopher P. Semtner
Curator
Edgar Allan Poe Museum, Richmond, Virginia

Publisher's Note

The darker, more gritty types of crime that take place in large cities, are more likely to go unnoticed, perhaps. And the motives for committing such crimes tend to differ from those that take place in the countryside, or even in the suburbs. Early writers of the late nineteenth century such as Fyodor Dostoevsky and Fergus Hume set *Crime and Punishment* and *The Mystery of a Hansom Cab* in Saint Petersburg and Melbourne respectively, exploring how poverty and social class divides can cause motivation for crime. Edgar Allan Poe too was a very early contributor to urban stories, with 'The Man of the Crowd' and 'The Murders in the Rue Morgue' set in London and Paris. We have chosen not to include these stories here because they feature in our book *Edgar Allan Poe Collection of Classic Tales*, but hope that you will endeavor to read them if you haven't. And they were only the beginning of the wealth of stories set in cities that came after them, including bleak depictions of New York from Irvin S. Cobb and Jack London's tales of wealthy businessmen set in and around San Francisco. We hope this collection gives you a sense of the varied nature of urban crime, including some old favourites as well as stories and writers you may not have come across before.

We had a fantastic number of contemporary submissions, and have thoroughly enjoyed delving into authors' stories. Making the final selection is always a tough decision, but ultimately we chose a collection of stories we hope sit alongside each other and with the classic fiction, to provide a fantastic *Urban Crime Short Stories* book for all to enjoy.

GOTHIC

URBAN
CRIME

SHORT STORIES

ANTHOLOGY OF NEW & CLASSIC TALES

Foreword by Christopher P. Semtner

FLAME TREE PUBLISHING

FANTASY

Miss Bracegirdle Does Her Duty

Stacy Aumonier

"THIS IS THE ROOM, MADAME."

"Ah, thank you…thank you."

"Does it appear satisfactory to madame?"

"Oh, yes, thank you…quite."

"Does madame require anything further?"

"Er – if not too late, may I have a hot bath?"

"Parfaitement, madame. The bathroom is at the end of the passage on the left. I will go and prepare it for madame."

"There is one thing more…. I have had a very long journey. I am very tired. Will you please see that I am not disturbed in the morning until I ring."

"Certainly, madame."

Millicent Bracegirdle was speaking the truth – she was tired. In the sleepy cathedral town of Easingstoke, from which she came, it was customary for everyone to speak the truth. It was customary, moreover, for everyone to lead simple, self-denying lives – to give up their time to good works and elevating thoughts. One had only to glance at little Miss Bracegirdle to see that in her were epitomized all the virtues and ideals of Easingstoke. Indeed, it was the pursuit of duty which had brought her to the Hôtel de l'Ouest at Bordeaux on this summer's night. She had traveled from Easingstoke to London, then without a break to Dover, crossed that horrid stretch of sea to Calais, entrained for Paris, where she of necessity had to spend four hours – a terrifying experience – and then had come on to Bordeaux, arriving at midnight. The reason of this journey being that someone had to come to Bordeaux to meet her young sister-in-law, who was arriving the next day from South America. The sister-in-law was married to a missionary in Paraguay, but the climate not agreeing with her, she was returning to England. Her dear brother, the dean, would have come himself, but the claims on his time were so extensive, the parishioners would miss him so; it was clearly Millicent's duty to go.

She had never been out of England before, and she had a horror of travel, and an ingrained distrust of foreigners. She spoke a little French – sufficient for the purposes of travel and for obtaining any modest necessities, but not sufficient for carrying on any kind of conversation. She did not deplore this latter fact, for she was of opinion that French people were not the kind of people that one would naturally want to have conversation with; broadly speaking, they were not quite 'nice,' in spite of their ingratiating manners.

The dear dean had given her endless advice, warning her earnestly not to enter into conversation with strangers, to obtain all information from the police, railway officials – in fact, any one in an official uniform. He deeply regretted to say that he was afraid that France was not a country for a woman to travel about in alone. There were loose, bad people about, always on the look-out…. He really thought perhaps he ought not to let her go. It was only by the utmost persuasion, in which she rather exaggerated her knowledge of the French language and character, her courage, and indifference to discomfort, that she managed to carry the day.

She unpacked her valise, placed her things about the room, tried to thrust back the little stabs of homesickness as she visualized her darling room at the deanery. How strange and hard and unfriendly seemed these foreign hotel bedrooms – heavy and depressing, no chintz and lavender and photographs of…all the dear family, the dean, the nephews and nieces, the interior of the cathedral during harvest festival, no samplers and needlework or coloured reproductions of the paintings by Marcus Stone. Oh dear, how foolish she was! What did she expect?

She disrobed and donned a dressing-gown; then, armed with a sponge-bag and towel, she crept timidly down the passage to the bathroom, after closing her bedroom door and turning out the light. The gay bathroom cheered her. She wallowed luxuriously in the hot water, regarding her slim legs with quiet satisfaction. And for the first time since leaving home there came to her a pleasant moment – a sense of enjoyment in her adventure. After all, it was rather an adventure, and her life had been peculiarly devoid of it. What queer lives some people must live, traveling about, having experiences! How old was she? Not really old – not by any means. Forty-two? Forty-three? She had shut herself up so. She hardly ever regarded the potentialities of age. As the world went, she was a well-preserved woman for her age. A life of self-abnegation, simple living, healthy walking and fresh air, had kept her younger than these hurrying, pampered city people.

Love? Yes, once when she was a young girl… He was a schoolmaster, a most estimable kind gentleman. They were never engaged – not actually, but it was a kind of understood thing. For three years it went on, this pleasant understanding and friendship. He was so gentle, so distinguished and considerate. She would have been happy to have continued in this strain for ever. But there was something lacking. Stephen had curious restless lapses. From the physical aspect of marriage she shrunk – yes, even with Stephen, who was gentleness and kindness itself. And then one day… one day he went away – vanished, and never returned. They told her he had married one of the country girls – a girl who used to work in Mrs. Forbes's dairy – not a very nice girl, she feared, one of these fast, pretty, foolish women. Heigho! Well, she had lived that down, destructive as the blow appeared at the time. One lives everything down in time. There is always work, living for others, faith, duty. …At the same time she could sympathize with people who found satisfaction in unusual experiences.

There would be lots to tell the dear dean when she wrote to him on the morrow; nearly losing her spectacles on the restaurant car; the amusing remarks of an American child on the train to Paris; the curious food everywhere, nothing simple and plain; the two English ladies at the hotel in Paris who told her about the death of their uncle – the poor man being taken ill on Friday and dying on Sunday afternoon, just before tea-time; the kindness of the hotel proprietor who had sat up for her; the prettiness of the chambermaid. Oh, yes, every one was really very kind. The French people, after all, were very nice. She had seen nothing – nothing but was quite nice and decorous. There would be lots to tell the dean tomorrow.

Her body glowed with the friction of the towel. She again donned her night attire and her thick, woollen dressing-gown. She tidied up the bathroom carefully in exactly the same way she was accustomed to do at home, then once more gripping her sponge-bag and towel, and turning out the light, she crept down the passage to her room. Entering the room she switched on the light and shut the door quickly. Then one of those ridiculous things happened – just the kind of thing you would expect to happen in a foreign hotel. The handle of the door came off in her hand.

She ejaculated a quiet 'Bother!' and sought to replace it with one hand, the other being occupied with the towel and sponge-bag. In doing this she behaved foolishly, for thrusting the knob carelessly against the steel pin – without properly securing it – she only succeeded in pushing the pin farther into the door and the knob was not adjusted. She uttered another little 'Bother!' and put her sponge-bag and towel down on the floor. She then tried to recover the pin with her left hand, but it had gone in too far.

"How very foolish!" she thought, "I shall have to ring for the chambermaid – and perhaps the poor girl has gone to bed."

She turned and faced the room, and suddenly the awful horror was upon her. There was a man asleep in her bed!

The sight of that swarthy face on the pillow, with its black tousled hair and heavy moustache, produced in her the most terrible moment of her life. Her heart nearly stopped. For some seconds she could neither think nor scream, and her first thought was: "I mustn't scream!"

She stood there like one paralysed, staring at the man's head and the great curved hunch of his body under the clothes. When she began to think she thought very quickly, and all her thoughts worked together. The first vivid realization was that it wasn't the man's fault; it was her fault. She was in the wrong room. It was the man's room. The rooms were identical, but there were all his things about, his clothes thrown carelessly over chairs, his collar and tie on the wardrobe, his great heavy boots and the strange yellow trunk. She must get out somehow, anyhow.

She clutched once more at the door, feverishly driving her finger-nails into the hole where the elusive pin had vanished. She tried to force her fingers in the crack and open the door that way, but it was of no avail. She was to all intents and purposes locked in – locked in a bedroom in a strange hotel alone with a man...a foreigner...a Frenchman! She must think. She must think. ...She switched off the light. If the light was off he might not wake up. It might give her time to think how to act. It was surprising that he had not awakened. If he did wake up, what would

he do? How could she explain herself? He wouldn't believe her. No one would believe her. In an English hotel it would be difficult enough, but here where she wasn't known, where they were all foreigners and consequently antagonistic ...merciful heavens!

She must get out. Should she wake the man? No, she couldn't do that. He might murder her. He might ...Oh, it was too awful to contemplate! Should she scream? Ring for the chambermaid? But no, it would be the same thing. People would come rushing. They would find her there in the strange man's bedroom after midnight – she, Millicent Bracegirdle, sister of the Dean of Easingstoke!

Visions of Easingstoke flashed through her alarmed mind. Visions of the news arriving, women whispering around tea-tables: 'Have you heard, my dear? ...Really no one would have imagined! Her poor brother! He will of course have to resign, you know, my dear. Have a little more cream, my love.'

Would they put her in prison? She might be in the room for the purpose of stealing or ...She might be in the room for the purpose of breaking every one of the ten commandments. There was no explaining it away. She was a ruined woman, suddenly and irretrievably, unless she could open the door. The chimney? Should she climb up the chimney? But where would that lead to? And then she visualized the man pulling her down by her legs when she was already smothered in soot. Any moment he might wake up….

She thought she heard the chambermaid going along the passage. If she had wanted to scream, she ought to have screamed before. The maid would know she had left the bathroom some minutes ago. Was she going to her room? Suddenly she remembered that she had told the chambermaid that she was not to be disturbed until she rang the next morning. That was something. Nobody would be going to her room to find out that she was not there.

An abrupt and desperate plan formed in her mind. It was already getting on for one o'clock. The man was probably a quite harmless commercial traveler or business man. He would probably get up about seven or eight o'clock, dress quickly, and go out. She would hide under his bed until he went. Only a matter of a few hours. Men don't look under their beds, although she made a religious practice of doing so herself. When he went he would be sure to open the door all right. The handle would be lying on the floor as though it had dropped off in the night. He would probably ring for the chamber-maid or open it with a penknife. Men were so clever at those things. When he had gone she would creep out and steal back to her room, and then there would be no necessity to give any explanation to any one. But heavens! What an experience! Once under the white frill of that bed she would be safe till the morning. In daylight nothing seemed so terrifying.

With feline precaution she went down on her hands and knees and crept toward the bed. What a lucky thing there was that broad white frill! She lifted it at the foot of the bed and crept under. There was just sufficient depth to take her slim body. The floor was fortunately carpeted all over, but it seemed very close and dusty. Suppose she coughed or sneezed! Anything might happen. Of course it would be much more difficult to explain her presence under the bed than to explain her presence just inside the door. She held her breath in suspense. No sound came from above, but under this frill it was difficult to hear anything. It was almost more nerve-racking than hearing everything …listening for signs and portents. This temporary escape in any case would give her time to regard the predicament detachedly. Up to the present she had not been able to visualize the full significance of her action. She had in truth lost her head. She had been like a wild animal, consumed with the sole idea of escape …a mouse or a cat would do this kind of thing – take cover and lie low. If only it hadn't all happened abroad! She tried to frame sentences of explanation in French, but French escaped her. And then – they talked so rapidly, these people. They didn't listen. The situation was intolerable. Would she be able to endure a night of it?

At present she was not altogether uncomfortable, only stuffy and …very, very frightened. But she had to face six or seven or eight hours of it – perhaps even then discovery in the end! The minutes flashed by as she turned the matter over and over in her head. There was no solution. She began to wish she had screamed or awakened the man. She saw now that that would have been the wisest and most politic thing to do; but she had allowed ten minutes or a quarter of an hour to elapse from the moment when the chambermaid would know that she had left the bathroom. They would want an explanation of what she had been doing in the man's bedroom all that time. Why hadn't she screamed before?

She lifted the frill an inch or two and listened. She thought she heard the man breathing but she couldn't be sure. In any case it gave her more air. She became a little bolder, and thrust her face partly through the frill so that she could breathe freely. She tried to steady her nerves by concentrating on the fact that – well, there it was. She had done it. She must make the best of it. Perhaps it would be all right after all.

"Of course I shan't sleep," she kept on thinking, "I shan't be able to. In any case it will be safer not to sleep. I must be on the watch."

She set her teeth and waited grimly. Now that she had made up her mind to see the thing through in this manner she felt a little calmer. She almost smiled as she reflected that there would certainly be something to tell the dear dean when she wrote to him tomorrow. How would he take it? Of course he would believe it – he had never doubted a single word that she had uttered in her life – but the story would sound so ...preposterous. In Easingstoke it would be almost impossible to envisage such an experience. She, Millicent Bracegirdle, spending a night under a strange man's bed in a foreign hotel! What would those women think? Fanny Shields and that garrulous old Mrs Rusbridger? Perhaps ...yes, perhaps it would be advisable to tell the dear dean to let the story go no further. One could hardly expect Mrs Rushbridger to ...not make implications ...exaggerate.

Oh, dear! What were they all doing now? They would be all asleep, everyone in Easingstoke. Her dear brother always retired at ten-fifteen. He would be sleeping calmly and placidly, the sleep of the just ...breathing the clear sweet air of Sussex, not this – oh, it was stuffy! She felt a great desire to cough. She mustn't do that. Yes, at nine- thirty all the servants summoned to the library – a short service – never more than fifteen minutes, her brother didn't believe in a great deal of ritual – then at ten o'clock cocoa for every one. At ten-fifteen bed for every one. The dear sweet bedroom with the narrow white bed, by the side of which she had knelt every night as long as she could remember – even in her dear mother's day – and said her prayers.

Prayers! Yes, that was a curious thing. This was the first night in her life's experience that she had not said her prayers on retiring. The situation was certainly very peculiar ... exceptional, one might call it. God would understand and forgive such a lapse. And yet after all, why ...what was to prevent her saying her prayers? Of course she couldn't kneel in the proper devotional attitude, that would be a physical impossibility; nevertheless, perhaps her prayers might be just as efficacious ...if they came from the heart. So little Miss Bracegirdle curved her body and placed her hands in a devout attitude in front of her face and quite inaudibly murmured her prayers under the strange man's bed.

"Our Father which art in heaven, Hallowed be Thy name. Thy kingdom come. Thy will be done in earth as it is in heaven; Give us this day our daily bread. And forgive us our trespasses...."

Trespasses! Yes, surely she was trespassing on this occasion, but God would understand. She had not wanted to trespass. She was an unwitting sinner. Without uttering a sound she went through her usual prayers in her heart. At the end she added fervently:

"Please God protect me from the dangers and perils of this night."

Then she lay silent and inert, strangely soothed by the effort of praying. "After all," she thought, "it isn't the attitude which matters – it is that which occurs deep down in us."

For the first time she began to meditate – almost to question – church forms and dogma. If an attitude was not indispensable, why a building, a ritual, a church at all? Of course her dear brother couldn't be wrong, the church was so old, so very old, its root deep buried in the story of human life, it was only that ...well, outward forms could be misleading. Her own present position for instance. In the eyes of the world she had, by one silly careless little action, convicted herself of being the breaker of every single one of the ten commandments.

She tried to think of one of which she could not be accused. But no – even to dis-honouring her father and mother, bearing false witness, stealing, coveting her neighbour's …husband! That was the worst thing of all. Poor man! He might be a very pleasant honourable married gentleman with children and she – she was in a position to compromise him! Why hadn't she screamed? Too late! Too late!

It began to get very uncomfortable, stuffy, but at the same time draughty, and the floor was getting harder every minute. She changed her position stealthily and controlled her desire to cough. Her heart was beating rapidly. Over and over again recurred the vivid impression of every little incident and argument that had occurred to her from the moment she left the bathroom. This must, of course, be the room next to her own. So confusing, with perhaps twenty

bedrooms all exactly alike on one side of a passage – how was one to remember whether one's number was 115 or 116?

Her mind began to wander idly off into her school-days. She was always very bad at figures. She disliked Euclid and all those subjects about angles and equations – so unimportant, not leading anywhere. History she liked, and botany, and reading about strange foreign lands, although she had always been too timid to visit them. And the lives of great people, most fascinating – Oliver Cromwell, Lord Beaconsfield, Lincoln, Grace Darling – there was a heroine for you – General Booth, a great, good man, even if a little vulgar. She remembered dear old Miss Trimming talking about him one afternoon at the vicar of St. Bride's garden party. She was so amusing. She …Good heavens!

Almost unwittingly, Millicent Bracegirdle had emitted a violent sneeze!

It was finished! For the second time that night she was conscious of her heart nearly stopping. For the second time that night she was so paralysed with fear that her mentality went to pieces. Now she would hear the man get out of bed. He would walk across to the door, switch on the light, and then lift up the frill. She could almost see that fierce moustached face glaring at her and growling something in French. Then he would thrust out an arm and drag her out. And then? O God in heaven! What then?…

"I shall scream before he does it. Perhaps I had better scream now. If he drags me out he will clap his hand over my mouth. Perhaps chloroform…"

But somehow she could not scream. She was too frightened even for that. She lifted the frill and listened. Was he moving stealthily across the carpet? She thought – no, she couldn't be sure. Anything might be happening. He might strike her from above – with one of those heavy boots perhaps. Nothing seemed to be happening, but the suspense was intolerable. She realized now that she hadn't the power to endure a night of it. Anything would be better than this – disgrace, imprisonment, even death. She would crawl out, wake the man, and try and explain as best she could.

She would switch on the light, cough, and say: "Monsieur!" Then he would start up and stare at her. Then she would say – what should she say? "Pardon, monsieur, mais je—" What on earth was the French for "I have made a mistake." "J'ai tort. C'est la chambre – er – incorrect. Voulez-vous – er—"

What was the French for "door-knob," "let me go?"

It didn't matter. She would turn on the light, cough and trust to luck. If he got out of bed, and came toward her, she would scream the hotel down. …

The resolution formed, she crawled deliberately out at the foot of the bed. She scrambled hastily toward the door – a perilous journey. In a few seconds the room was flooded with light. She turned toward the bed, coughed, and cried out boldly:

"Monsieur!"

Then, for the third time that night, little Miss Bracegirdle's heart all but stopped. In this case the climax of the horror took longer to develop, but when it was reached, it clouded the other two experiences into insignificance.

The man on the bed was dead! She had never beheld death before, but one does not mistake death. She stared at him bewildered, and repeated almost in a whisper: "Monsieur! ...Monsieur!"

Then she tiptoed toward the bed. The hair and moustache looked extraordinarily black in that grey, wax-like setting. The mouth was slightly open, and the face, which in life might have been vicious and sensual, looked incredibly peaceful and far away. It was as though she were regarding the features of a man across some vast passage of time, a being who had always been completely remote from mundane preoccupations.

When the full truth came home to her, little Miss Bracegirdle buried her face in her hands and murmured: "Poor fellow ...poor fellow!"

For the moment her own position seemed an affair of small consequence. She was in the presence of something greater and more all-pervading. Almost instinctively she knelt by the bed and prayed.

For a few moments she seemed to be possessed by an extraordinary calmness and detachment. The burden of her hotel predicament was a gossamer trouble – a silly, trivial, almost comic episode, something that could be explained away.

But this man – he had lived his life, whatever it was like, and now he was in the presence of his Maker. What kind of man had he been?

Her meditations were broken by an abrupt sound. It was that of a pair of heavy boots being thrown down by the door outside. She started, thinking at first it was someone knocking or trying to get in. She heard the 'boots,' however, stumping away down the corridor, and the realization stabbed her with the truth of her own position. She mustn't stop there. The necessity to get out was even more urgent.

To be found in a strange man's bedroom in the night is bad enough, but to be found in a dead man's bedroom was even worse. They could accuse her of murder, perhaps. Yes, that would be it – how could she possibly explain to these foreigners? Good God! they would hang her. No, guillotine her, that's what they do in France. They would chop her head off with a great steel knife. Merciful heavens! She envisaged herself standing blindfold, by a priest and an executioner in a red cap, like that man in the Dickens story – what was his name? ... Sydney Carton, that was it, and before he went on the scaffold he said:

"It is a far, far better thing that I do than I have ever done."

But no, she couldn't say that. It would be a far, far worse thing that she did. What about the dear dean? Her sister-in- law arriving alone from Paraguay tomorrow? All her dear people and friends in Easingstoke? Her darling Tony, the large grey tabby cat? It was her duty not to have her head chopped off if it could possibly be avoided. She could do no good in the room. She could not recall the dead to life. Her only mission was to escape. Any minute people might arrive. The chambermaid, the boots, the manager, the gendarmes. ...Visions of gendarmes arriving armed with swords and note-books vitalized her almost exhausted energies. She was a desperate woman. Fortunately now she had not to worry about the light. She sprang once more at the door and tried to force it open with her fingers. The result hurt her and gave her pause. If she was to escape she must think, and think intensely. She mustn't do anything rash and silly, she must just think and plan calmly.

She examined the lock carefully. There was no keyhole, but there was a slip-bolt, so that the hotel guest could lock the door on the inside, but it couldn't be locked on the outside. Oh, why didn't this poor dear dead man lock his door last night? Then this trouble could not have happened. She could see the end of the steel pin. It was about half an inch down the hole. If any one was passing they must surely notice the handle sticking out foot far the other side! She drew a hairpin out of her hair and tried to coax the pin back, but she only succeeded in pushing it a little farther in. She felt the colour leaving her face, and a strange feeling of faintness come over her.

She was fighting for her life, she mustn't give way. She darted round the room like an animal in a trap, her mind alert for the slightest crevice of escape. The window had no balcony and there was a drop of five stories to the street below. Dawn was breaking. Soon the activities of the hotel and the city would begin. The thing must be accomplished before then.

She went back once more and stared at the lock. She stared at the dead man's property, his razors, and brushes, and writing materials, pens and pencils and rubber and sealing-wax....Sealing-wax!

Necessity is truly the mother of invention. It is in any case quite certain that Millicent Bracegirdle, who had never invented a thing in her life, would never have evolved the ingenious little device she did, had she not believed that her position was utterly desperate. For in the end this is what she did. She got together a box of matches, a candle, a bar of sealing-wax, and a hairpin. She made a little pool of hot sealing-wax, into which she dipped the end of the hairpin. Collecting a small blob on the end of it she thrust it into the hole, and let it adhere to the end of the steel pin. At the seventh attempt she got the thing to move. It took her just an hour and ten minutes to get that steel pin back into the room, and when at length it came far enough through for her to grip it with her finger-nails, she burst into tears through the sheer physical tension of the strain. Very, very carefully she pulled it through, and holding it firmly with her left hand she fixed the knob with her right, then slowly turned it. The door opened!

The temptation to dash out into the corridor and scream with relief was almost irresistible, but she forbore. She listened; she peeped out. No one was about. With beating heart, she went out, closing the door inaudibly. She crept like a little mouse to the room next door, stole in and flung herself on her bed. Immediately she did so it flashed through her mind that she had left her sponge-bag and towel in the dead man's room!

In looking back upon her experience she always considered that that second expedition was the worst of all. She might have left the sponge-bag and towel there, only that the towel – she never used hotel towels – had neatly inscribed in the corner 'M. B.'

With furtive caution she managed to retrace her steps. She re-entered the dead man's room, reclaimed her property, and returned to her own. When this mission was accomplished she was indeed well-nigh spent. She lay on her bed and groaned feebly. At last she fell into a fevered sleep....

It was eleven o'clock when she awoke and no one had been to disturb her. The sun was shining, and the experiences of the night appeared a dubious nightmare. Surely she had dreamt it all?

With dread still burning in her heart she rang the bell. After a short interval of time the chambermaid appeared. The girl's eyes were bright with some uncontrollable excitement. No, she had not been dreaming. This girl had heard something.

"Will you bring me some tea, please?" "Certainly, madame."

The maid drew back the curtains and fussed about the room. She was under a pledge of secrecy, but she could contain herself no longer. Suddenly she approached the bed and whispered excitedly:

"Oh, madame, I have promised not to tell …but a terrible thing has happened. A man, a dead man, has been found in room 117 – a guest. Please not to say I tell you. But they have all been there, the gendarmes, the doctors, the inspectors. Oh, it is terrible …terrible."

The little lady in the bed said nothing. There was indeed nothing to say. But Marie Louise Lancret was too full of emotional excitement to spare her.

"But the terrible thing is – Do you know who he was, madame? They say it is Boldhu, the man wanted for the murder of Jeanne Carreton in the barn at Vincennes. They say he strangled her, and then cut her up in pieces and hid her in two barrels which he threw into the river. …Oh, but he was a bad man, madame, a terrible bad man …and he died in the room next door …suicide, they think; or was it an attack of the heart? …Remorse, some shock perhaps. …Did you say a café complet, madame?"

"No, thank you, my dear …just a cup of tea …strong tea…"

"Parfaitement, madame."

The girl retired, and a little later a waiter entered the room with a tray of tea. She could never get over her surprise at this. It seemed so – well, indecorous for a man – although only a waiter – to enter a lady's bedroom. There was no doubt a great deal in what the dear dean said. They were certainly very peculiar, these French people – they had most peculiar notions. It was not the way they behaved at Easingstoke. She got farther under the sheets, but the waiter appeared quite indifferent to the situation. He put the tray down and retired.

When he had gone she sat up and sipped her tea, which gradually warmed her. She was glad the sun was shining. She would have to get up soon. They said that her sister-in-law's boat was due to berth at one o'clock. That would give her time to dress comfortably, write to her brother, and then go down to the docks. Poor man! So he had been a murderer, a man who cut up the bodies of his victims …and she had spent the night in his bedroom! They were certainly a most – how could she describe it? – people. Nevertheless she felt a little glad that at the end she had been there to kneel and pray by his bedside. Probably nobody else had ever done that. It was very difficult to judge people. …Something at some time might have gone wrong. He might not have murdered the woman after all. People were often wrongly convicted. She herself …If the police had found her in that room at three o'clock that morning …It is that which takes place in the heart which counts. One learns and learns. Had she not learnt that one can pray just as effectively lying under a bed as kneeling beside it? …Poor man!

She washed and dressed herself and walked calmly down to the writing-room. There was no evidence of excitement among the other hotel guests. Probably none of them knew about the tragedy except herself. She went to a writing- table, and after profound meditation wrote as follows:

> *My dear Brother,*
> *I arrived late last night after a very pleasant journey. Every one was very kind and attentive, the manager was sitting up for me. I nearly lost my spectacle case in the restaurant car! But a kind old gentleman found it and returned it to me. There was a most amusing American child on the train. I will tell you about her on my return. The people are very pleasant, but the food is peculiar, nothing*

plain and wholesome. I am going down to meet Annie at one o'clock. How have you been keeping, my dear? I hope you have not had any further return of the bronchial attacks.

   Please tell Lizzie that I remembered in the train on the way here that that large stone jar of marmalade that Mrs. Hunt made is behind those empty tins in the top shelf of the cupboard next to the coach-house. I wonder whether Mrs. Butler was able to come to evensong after all? This is a nice hotel, but I think Annie and I will stay at the 'Grand' tonight, as the bedrooms here are rather noisy. Well, my dear, nothing more till I return. Do take care of yourself.

   Your loving sister,

   Millicent

Yes, she couldn't tell Peter about it, neither in the letter nor when she went back to him. It was her duty not to tell him. It would only distress him; she felt convinced of it In this curious foreign atmosphere the thing appeared possible, but in Easingstoke the mere recounting of the fantastic situations would be positively ...indelicate. There was no escaping that broad general fact – she had spent a night in a strange man's bedroom. Whether he was a gentleman or a criminal, even whether he was dead or alive, did not seem to mitigate the jar upon her sensibilities, or rather it would not mitigate the jar upon the peculiarly sensitive relationship between her brother and herself. To say that she had been to the bathroom, the knob of the door-handle came off in her hand, she was too frightened to awaken the sleeper or scream, she got under the bed – well, it was all perfectly true. Peter would believe her, but – one simply could not conceive such a situation in Easingstoke deanery. It would create a curious little barrier between them, as though she had been dipped in some mysterious solution which alienated her. It was her duty not to tell.

   She put on her hat, and went out to post the letter. She distrusted an hotel letter-box. One never knew who handled these letters. It was not a proper official way of treating them. She walked to the head post office in Bordeaux.

   The sun was shining. It was very pleasant walking about amongst these queer excitable people, so foreign and different-looking – and the cafés already crowded with chattering men and women, and the flower stalls, and the strange odour of – what was it? Salt? Brine? Charcoal? ...A military band was playing in the square ...very gay and moving. It was all life, and movement, and bustle ...thrilling rather.

   "I spent a night in a strange man's bedroom."

   Little Miss Bracegirdle hunched her shoulders, murmured to herself, and walked faster. She reached the post office and found the large metal plate with the slot for letters and 'R.F.' stamped above it. Something official at last! Her face was a little flushed – was it the warmth of the day or the contact of movement and life? – as she put her letter into the slot. After posting it she put her hand into the slot and flicked it round to see that there were no foreign contraptions to impede its safe delivery. No, the letter had dropped safely in. She sighed contentedly and walked off in the direction of the docks to meet her sister- in-law from Paraguay.

The Absent-Minded Coterie

Robert Barr

SOME YEARS AGO I enjoyed the unique experience of pursuing a man for one crime, and getting evidence against him of another. He was innocent of the misdemeanour, the proof of which I sought, but was guilty of another most serious offence, yet he and his confederates escaped scot-free in circumstances which I now purpose to relate.

You may remember that in Rudyard Kipling's story, *Bedalia Herodsfoot*, the unfortunate woman's husband ran the risk of being arrested as a simple drunkard, at a moment when the blood of murder was upon his boots. The case of Ralph Summertrees was rather the reverse of this. The English authorities were trying to fasten upon him a crime almost as important as murder, while I was collecting evidence which proved him guilty of an action much more momentous than that of drunkenness.

The English authorities have always been good enough, when they recognise my existence at all, to look down upon me with amused condescension. If today you ask Spenser Hale, of Scotland Yard, what he thinks of Eugène Valmont, that complacent man will put on the superior smile which so well becomes him, and if you are a very intimate friend of his, he may draw down the lid of his right eye, as he replies –

"Oh, yes, a very decent fellow, Valmont, but he's a Frenchman," as if, that said, there was no need of further inquiry.

Myself, I like the English detective very much, and if I were to be in a *mêlée* tomorrow, there is no man I would rather find beside me than Spenser Hale. In any situation where a fist that can fell an ox is desirable, my friend Hale is a useful companion, but for intellectuality, mental acumen, finesse – ah, well! I am the most modest of men, and will say nothing.

It would amuse you to see this giant come into my room during an evening, on the bluff pretence that he wishes to smoke a pipe with me. There is the same difference between this good-natured giant and myself as exists between that strong black pipe of his and my delicate cigarette, which I smoke feverishly when he is present, to protect myself from the fumes of his terrible tobacco. I look with delight upon the huge man, who, with an air of the utmost good humour, and a twinkle in his eye as he thinks he is twisting me about his finger, vainly endeavours to obtain a hint regarding whatever case is perplexing him at that moment. I baffle him with the ease that an active greyhound eludes the pursuit of a heavy mastiff, then at last I say to him with a laugh –

"Come *mon ami* Hale, tell me all about it, and I will help you if I can."

Once or twice at the beginning he shook his massive head, and replied the secret was not his. The last time he did this I assured him that what he said was quite correct, and then I related full particulars of the situation in which he found himself, excepting the names, for these he had not mentioned. I had pieced together his perplexity from scraps of conversation in his half-hour's fishing for my advice, which, of course, he could have had for the plain asking. Since that time he has not come to me except with cases he feels at liberty to reveal, and one or two complications I have happily been enabled to unravel for him.

But, staunch as Spenser Hale holds the belief that no detective service on earth can excel that centring in Scotland Yard, there is one department of activity in which even he confesses that Frenchmen are his masters, although he somewhat grudgingly qualifies his admission by adding that we in France are constantly allowed to do what is prohibited in England. I refer to the minute search of a house during the owner's absence. If you read that excellent story, entitled *The Purloined Letter*, by Edgar Allan Poe, you will find a record of the kind of thing I mean, which is better than any description I, who have so often taken part in such a search, can set down.

Now, these people among whom I live are proud of their phrase, 'The Englishman's house is his castle,' and into that castle even a policeman cannot penetrate without a legal warrant. This may be all very well in theory, but if you are compelled to march up to a man's house, blowing a trumpet, and rattling a snare drum, you need not be disappointed if you fail to find what you are in search of when all the legal restrictions are complied with. Of course, the English are a very excellent people, a fact to which I am always proud to bear testimony, but it must be admitted that for cold common sense the French are very much their superiors. In Paris, if I wish to obtain an incriminating document, I do not send the possessor a *carte postale* to inform him of my desire, and in this procedure the French people sanely acquiesce. I have known men who, when they go out to spend an evening on the boulevards, toss their bunch of keys to the concierge, saying –

"If you hear the police rummaging about while I'm away, pray assist them, with an expression of my distinguished consideration."

I remember while I was chief detective in the service of the French Government being requested to call at a certain hour at the private hotel of the Minister for Foreign Affairs. It was during the time that Bismarck meditated a second attack upon my country, and I am happy to say that I was then instrumental in supplying the Secret Bureau with documents which mollified that iron man's purpose, a fact which I think entitled me to my country's gratitude, not that I ever even hinted such a claim when a succeeding ministry forgot my services. The memory of a republic, as has been said by a greater man than I, is short. However, all that has nothing to do with the incident I am about to relate. I merely mention the crisis to excuse a momentary forgetfulness on my part which in any other country might have been followed by serious results to myself. But in France—ah, we understand those things, and nothing happened.

I am the last person in the world to give myself away, as they say in the great West. I am usually the calm, collected Eugène Valmont whom nothing can perturb, but this was a time of great tension, and I had become absorbed. I was alone with the minister in his private house, and one of the papers he desired was in his bureau at the Ministry for Foreign Affairs; at least, he thought so, and said –

"Ah, it is in my desk at the bureau. How annoying! I must send for it!"

"No, Excellency," I cried, springing up in a self-oblivion the most complete, "it is here." Touching the spring of a secret drawer, I opened it, and taking out the document he wished, handed it to him.

It was not until I met his searching look, and saw the faint smile on his lips that I realised what I had done.

"Valmont," he said quietly, "on whose behalf did you search my house?"

"Excellency," I replied in tones no less agreeable than his own, "tonight at your orders I pay a domiciliary visit to the mansion of Baron Dumoulaine, who stands high in the estimation of the President of the French Republic. If either of those distinguished gentlemen should learn of my informal call and should ask me in whose interests I made the domiciliary visit, what is it you wish that I should reply?"

"You should reply, Valmont, that you did it in the interests of the Secret Service."

"I shall not fail to do so, Excellency, and in answer to your question just now, I had the honour of searching this mansion in the interests of the Secret Service of France."

The Minister for Foreign Affairs laughed; a hearty laugh that expressed no resentment.

"I merely wished to compliment you, Valmont, on the efficiency of your search, and the excellence of your memory. This is indeed the document which I thought was left in my office."

I wonder what Lord Lansdowne would say if Spenser Hale showed an equal familiarity with his private papers! But now that we have returned to our good friend Hale, we must not keep him waiting any longer.

* * *

I well remember the November day when I first heard of the Summertrees case, because there hung over London a fog so thick that two or three times I lost my way, and no cab was to be had at any price. The few cabmen then in the streets were leading their animals slowly along, making for their stables. It was one of those depressing London days which filled me with ennui and a yearning for my own clear city of Paris, where, if we are ever visited by a slight mist, it is at least clean, white vapour, and not this horrible London mixture saturated with suffocating carbon. The fog was too thick for any passer to read the contents bills of the newspapers plastered on the pavement, and as there were probably no races that day the newsboys were shouting what they considered the next most important event – the election of an American President. I bought a paper and thrust it into my pocket. It was late when I reached my flat, and, after dining there, which was an unusual thing for me to do, I put on my slippers, took an easy-chair before the fire, and began to read my evening journal. I was distressed to learn that the eloquent Mr. Bryan had been defeated. I knew little about the silver question, but the man's oratorical powers had appealed to me, and my sympathy was aroused because he owned many silver mines, and yet the price of the metal was so low that apparently he could not make a living through the operation of them. But, of course, the cry that he was a plutocrat, and a reputed millionaire over and over again, was bound to defeat him in a democracy where the average voter is exceedingly poor and not comfortably well-to-do as is the case with our peasants in France. I always took great interest in the affairs of the huge republic to the west, having been at some pains to inform myself accurately regarding its politics, and although, as my readers know, I seldom quote anything complimentary that is said of me, nevertheless, an American client of mine once admitted that he never knew the true inwardness – I think that was the phrase he used – of American politics until he heard me discourse upon them. But then, he added, he had been a very busy man all his life.

I had allowed my paper to slip to the floor, for in very truth the fog was penetrating even into my flat, and it was becoming difficult to read, notwithstanding the electric light. My man came in, and announced that Mr. Spenser Hale wished to see me, and, indeed, any night, but especially when there is rain or fog outside, I am more pleased to talk with a friend than to read a newspaper.

"*Mon Dieu*, my dear Monsieur Hale, it is a brave man you are to venture out in such a fog as is abroad tonight."

"Ah, Monsieur Valmont," said Hale with pride, "you cannot raise a fog like this in Paris!"

"No. There you are supreme," I admitted, rising and saluting my visitor, then offering him a chair.

"I see you are reading the latest news," he said, indicating my newspaper, "I am very glad that man Bryan is defeated. Now we shall have better times."

I waved my hand as I took my chair again. I will discuss many things with Spenser Hale, but not American politics; he does not understand them. It is a common defect of the English to suffer complete ignorance regarding the internal affairs of other countries.

"It is surely an important thing that brought you out on such a night as this. The fog must be very thick in Scotland Yard."

This delicate shaft of fancy completely missed him, and he answered stolidly –

"It's thick all over London, and, indeed, throughout most of England."

"Yes, it is," I agreed, but he did not see that either.

Still a moment later he made a remark which, if it had come from some people I know, might have indicated a glimmer of comprehension.

"You are a very, very clever man, Monsieur Valmont, so all I need say is that the question which brought me here is the same as that on which the American election was fought. Now, to a countryman, I should be compelled to give further explanation, but to you, monsieur, that will not be necessary."

There are times when I dislike the crafty smile and partial closing of the eyes which always distinguishes Spenser Hale when he places on the table a problem which he expects will baffle me. If I said he never did baffle me, I would be wrong, of course, for sometimes the utter simplicity of the puzzles which trouble him leads me into an intricate involution entirely unnecessary in the circumstances.

I pressed my fingertips together, and gazed for a few moments at the ceiling. Hale had lit his black pipe, and my silent servant placed at his elbow the whisky and soda, then tiptoed out of the room. As the door closed my eyes came from the ceiling to the level of Hale's expansive countenance.

"Have they eluded you?" I asked quietly.

"Who?"

"The coiners."

Hale's pipe dropped from his jaw, but he managed to catch it before it reached the floor. Then he took a gulp from the tumbler.

"That was just a lucky shot," he said.

"*Parfaitement*," I replied carelessly.

"Now, own up, Valmont, wasn't it?"

I shrugged my shoulders. A man cannot contradict a guest in his own house.

"Oh, stow that!" cried Hale impolitely. He is a trifle prone to strong and even slangy expressions when puzzled. "Tell me how you guessed it."

"It is very simple, *mon ami*. The question on which the American election was fought is the price of silver, which is so low that it has ruined Mr. Bryan, and threatens to ruin all the farmers of the west who possess silver mines on their farms. Silver troubled America, ergo silver troubles Scotland Yard.

"Very well, the natural inference is that someone has stolen bars of silver. But such a theft happened three months ago, when the metal was being unloaded from a German steamer at Southampton, and my dear friend Spenser Hale ran down the thieves very cleverly as they were trying to dissolve the marks off the bars with acid. Now crimes do not run in series, like the numbers in roulette at Monte Carlo. The thieves are men of brains.

They say to themselves, 'What chance is there successfully to steal bars of silver while Mr. Hale is at Scotland Yard?' Eh, my good friend?"

"Really, Valmont," said Hale, taking another sip, "sometimes you almost persuade me that you have reasoning powers."

"Thanks, comrade. Then it is not a *theft* of silver we have now to deal with. But the American election was fought on the *price* of silver. If silver had been high in cost, there would have been no silver question. So the crime that is bothering you arises through the low price of silver, and this suggests that it must be a case of illicit coinage, for there the low price of the metal comes in. You have, perhaps, found a more subtle illegitimate act going forward than heretofore. Someone is making your shillings and your half-crowns from real silver, instead of from baser metal, and yet there is a large profit which has not hitherto been possible through the high price of silver. With the old conditions you were familiar, but this new element sets at nought all your previous formulae. That is how I reasoned the matter out."

"Well, Valmont, you have hit it. I'll say that for you; you have hit it. There is a gang of expert coiners who are putting out real silver money, and making a clear shilling on the half-crown. We can find no trace of the coiners, but we know the man who is shoving the stuff."

"That ought to be sufficient," I suggested.

"Yes, it should, but it hasn't proved so up to date. Now I came tonight to see if you would do one of your French tricks for us, right on the quiet."

"What French trick, Monsieur Spenser Hale?" I inquired with some asperity, forgetting for the moment that the man invariably became impolite when he grew excited.

"No offence intended," said this blundering officer, who really is a good-natured fellow, but always puts his foot in it, and then apologises. "I want someone to go through a man's house without a search warrant, spot the evidence, let me know, and then we'll rush the place before he has time to hide his tracks."

"Who is this man, and where does he live?"

"His name is Ralph Summertrees, and he lives in a very natty little bijou residence, as the advertisements call it, situated in no less a fashionable street than Park Lane."

"I see. What has aroused your suspicions against him?"

"Well, you know, that's an expensive district to live in; it takes a bit of money to do the trick. This Summertrees has no ostensible business, yet every Friday he goes to the United Capital Bank in Piccadilly, and deposits a bag of swag, usually all silver coin."

"Yes, and this money?"

"This money, so far as we can learn, contains a good many of these new pieces which never saw the British Mint."

"It's not all the new coinage, then?"

"Oh, no, he's a bit too artful for that. You see, a man can go round London, his pockets filled with new coinage five-shilling pieces, buy this, that, and the other, and come home with his change in legitimate coins of the realm – half-crowns, florins, shillings, sixpences, and all that."

"I see. Then why don't you nab him one day when his pockets are stuffed with illegitimate five-shilling pieces?"

"That could be done, of course, and I've thought of it, but you see, we want to land the whole gang. Once we arrested him, without knowing where the money came from, the real coiners would take flight."

"How do you know he is not the real coiner himself?"

Now poor Hale is as easy to read as a book. He hesitated before answering this question, and looked confused as a culprit caught in some dishonest act.

"You need not be afraid to tell me," I said soothingly after a pause. "You have had one of your men in Mr. Summertrees' house, and so learned that he is not the coiner. But your man has not succeeded in getting you evidence to incriminate other people."

"You've about hit it again, Monsieur Valmont. One of my men has been Summertrees' butler for two weeks, but, as you say, he has found no evidence."

"Is he still butler?"

"Yes."

"Now tell me how far you have got. You know that Summertrees deposits a bag of coin every Friday in the Piccadilly bank, and I suppose the bank has allowed you to examine one or two of the bags."

"Yes, sir, they have, but, you see, banks are very difficult to treat with. They don't like detectives bothering round, and whilst they do not stand out against the law, still they never answer any more questions than they're asked, and Mr. Summertrees has been a good customer at the United Capital for many years."

"Haven't you found out where the money comes from?"

"Yes, we have; it is brought there night after night by a man who looks like a respectable city clerk, and he puts it into a large safe, of which he holds the key, this safe being on the ground floor, in the dining-room."

"Haven't you followed the clerk?"

"Yes. He sleeps in the Park Lane house every night, and goes up in the morning to an old curiosity shop in Tottenham Court Road, where he stays all day, returning with his bag of money in the evening."

"Why don't you arrest and question him?"

"Well, Monsieur Valmont, there is just the same objection to his arrest as to that of Summertrees himself. We could easily arrest both, but we have not the slightest evidence against either of them, and then, although we put the go-betweens in clink, the worst criminals of the lot would escape."

"Nothing suspicious about the old curiosity shop?"

"No. It appears to be perfectly regular."

"This game has been going on under your noses for how long?"

"For about six weeks."

"Is Summertrees a married man?"

"No."

"Are there any women servants in the house?"

"No, except that three charwomen come in every morning to do up the rooms."

"Of what is his household comprised?"

"There is the butler, then the valet, and last, the French cook."

"Ah," cried I, "the French cook! This case interests me. So Summertrees has succeeded in completely disconcerting your man? Has he prevented him going from top to bottom of the house?"

"Oh no, he has rather assisted him than otherwise. On one occasion he went to the safe, took out the money, had Podgers – that's my chap's name – help him to count it, and then actually sent Podgers to the bank with the bag of coin."

"And Podgers has been all over the place?"

"Yes."

"Saw no signs of a coining establishment?"

"No. It is absolutely impossible that any coining can be done there. Besides, as I tell you, that respectable clerk brings him the money."

"I suppose you want me to take Podgers' position?"

"Well, Monsieur Valmont, to tell you the truth, I would rather you didn't. Podgers has done everything a man can do, but I thought if you got into the house, Podgers assisting, you might go through it night after night at your leisure."

"I see. That's just a little dangerous in England. I think I should prefer to assure myself the legitimate standing of being the amiable Podgers' successor. You say that Summertrees has no business?"

"Well, sir, not what you might call a business. He is by the way of being an author, but I don't count that any business."

"Oh, an author, is he? When does he do his writing?"

"He locks himself up most of the day in his study."

"Does he come out for lunch?"

"No; he lights a little spirit lamp inside, Podgers tells me, and makes himself a cup of coffee, which he takes with a sandwich or two."

"That's rather frugal fare for Park Lane."

"Yes, Monsieur Valmont, it is, but he makes it up in the evening, when he has a long dinner with all them foreign kickshaws you people like, done by his French cook."

"Sensible man! Well, Hale, I see I shall look forward with pleasure to making the acquaintance of Mr. Summertrees. Is there any restriction on the going and coming of your man Podgers?"

"None in the least. He can get away either night or day."

"Very good, friend Hale, bring him here tomorrow, as soon as our author locks himself up in his study, or rather, I should say, as soon as the respectable clerk leaves for Tottenham Court Road, which I should guess, as you put it, is about half an hour after his master turns the key of the room in which he writes."

"You are quite right in that guess, Valmont. How did you hit it?"

"Merely a surmise, Hale. There is a good deal of oddity about that Park Lane house, so it doesn't surprise me in the least that the master gets to work earlier in the morning than the man. I have also a suspicion that Ralph Summertrees knows perfectly well what the estimable Podgers is there for."

"What makes you think that?"

"I can give no reason except that my opinion of the acuteness of Summertrees has been gradually rising all the while you were speaking, and at the same time my estimate of Podgers' craft has been as steadily declining. However, bring the man here tomorrow, that I may ask him a few questions."

* * *

Next day, about eleven o'clock, the ponderous Podgers, hat in hand, followed his chief into my room. His broad, impassive, immobile smooth face gave him rather more the air of a genuine butler than I had expected, and this appearance, of course, was enhanced by his livery. His replies to my questions were those of a well-trained servant who will not say too much unless it is made worth his while. All in all, Podgers exceeded my expectations, and really my friend Hale had some justification for regarding him, as he evidently did, a triumph in his line.

"Sit down, Mr. Hale, and you, Podgers."

The man disregarded my invitation, standing like a statue until his chief made a motion; then he dropped into a chair. The English are great on discipline.

"Now, Mr. Hale, I must first congratulate you on the make-up of Podgers. It is excellent. You depend less on artificial assistance than we do in France, and in that I think you are right."

"Oh, we know a bit over here, Monsieur Valmont," said Hale, with pardonable pride.

"Now then, Podgers, I want to ask you about this clerk. What time does he arrive in the evening?"

"At prompt six, sir."

"Does he ring, or let himself in with a latchkey?"

"With a latchkey, sir."

"How does he carry the money?"

"In a little locked leather satchel, sir, flung over his shoulder."

"Does he go direct to the dining-room?"

"Yes, sir."

"Have you seen him unlock the safe and put in the money?"

"Yes, sir."

"Does the safe unlock with a word or a key?"

"With a key, sir. It's one of the old-fashioned kind."

"Then the clerk unlocks his leather money bag?"

"Yes, sir."

"That's three keys used within as many minutes. Are they separate or in a bunch?"

"In a bunch, sir."

"Did you ever see your master with this bunch of keys?"

"No, sir."

"You saw him open the safe once, I am told?"

"Yes, sir."

"Did he use a separate key, or one of a bunch?"

Podgers slowly scratched his head, then said,—

"I don't just remember, sir."

"Ah, Podgers, you are neglecting the big things in that house. Sure you can't remember?"

"No, sir."

"Once the money is in and the safe locked up, what does the clerk do?"

"Goes to his room, sir."

"Where is this room?"

"On the third floor, sir."

"Where do you sleep?"

"On the fourth floor with the rest of the servants, sir."

"Where does the master sleep?"

"On the second floor, adjoining his study."

"The house consists of four stories and a basement, does it?"

"Yes, sir."

"I have somehow arrived at the suspicion that it is a very narrow house. Is that true?"

"Yes, sir."

"Does the clerk ever dine with your master?"

"No, sir. The clerk don't eat in the house at all, sir."

"Does he go away before breakfast?"

"No, sir."

"No one takes breakfast to his room?"

"No, sir."

"What time does he leave the house?"

"At ten o'clock, sir."

"When is breakfast served?"

"At nine o'clock, sir."

"At what hour does your master retire to his study?"

"At half-past nine, sir."

"Locks the door on the inside?"

"Yes, sir."

"Never rings for anything during the day?"

"Not that I know of, sir."

"What sort of a man is he?"

Here Podgers was on familiar ground, and he rattled off a description minute in every particular.

"What I meant was, Podgers, is he silent, or talkative, or does he get angry? Does he seem furtive, suspicious, anxious, terrorised, calm, excitable, or what?"

"Well, sir, he is by way of being very quiet, never has much to say for himself; never saw him angry, or excited."

"Now, Podgers, you've been at Park Lane for a fortnight or more. You are a sharp, alert, observant man. What happens there that strikes you as unusual?"

"Well, I can't exactly say, sir," replied Podgers, looking rather helplessly from his chief to myself, and back again.

"Your professional duties have often compelled you to enact the part of butler before, otherwise you wouldn't do it so well. Isn't that the case."

Podgers did not reply, but glanced at his chief. This was evidently a question pertaining to the service, which a subordinate was not allowed to answer. However, Hale said at once—

"Certainly. Podgers has been in dozens of places."

"Well, Podgers, just call to mind some of the other households where you have been employed, and tell me any particulars in which Mr. Summertrees' establishment differs from them."

Podgers pondered a long time.

"Well, sir, he do stick to writing pretty close."

"Ah, that's his profession, you see, Podgers. Hard at it from half-past nine till towards seven, I imagine?"

"Yes, sir."

"Anything else, Podgers? No matter how trivial."

"Well, sir, he's fond of reading too; leastways, he's fond of newspapers."

"When does he read?"

"I've never seen him read 'em, sir; indeed, so far as I can tell, I never knew the papers to be opened, but he takes them all in, sir."

"What, all the morning papers?"

"Yes, sir, and all the evening papers too."

"Where are the morning papers placed?"

"On the table in his study, sir."

"And the evening papers?"

"Well, sir, when the evening papers come, the study is locked. They are put on a side table in the dining-room, and he takes them upstairs with him to his study."

"This has happened every day since you've been there?"

"Yes, sir."

"You reported that very striking fact to your chief, of course?"

"No, sir, I don't think I did," said Podgers, confused.

"You should have done so. Mr. Hale would have known how to make the most of a point so vital."

"Oh, come now, Valmont," interrupted Hale, "you're chaffing us. Plenty of people take in all the papers!"

"I think not. Even clubs and hotels subscribe to the leading journals only. You said *all*, I think, Podgers?"

"Well, *nearly* all, sir."

"But which is it? There's a vast difference."

"He takes a good many, sir."

"How many?"

"I don't just know, sir."

"That's easily found out, Valmont," cried Hale, with some impatience, "if you think it really important."

"I think it so important that I'm going back with Podgers myself. You can take me into the house, I suppose, when you return?"

"Oh, yes, sir."

"Coming back to these newspapers for a moment, Podgers. What is done with them?"

"They are sold to the ragman, sir, once a week."

"Who takes them from the study?"

"I do, sir."

"Do they appear to have been read very carefully?"

"Well, no, sir; leastways, some of them seem never to have been opened, or else folded up very carefully again."

"Did you notice that extracts have been clipped from any of them?"

"No, sir."

"Does Mr. Summertrees keep a scrapbook?"

"Not that I know of, sir."

"Oh, the case is perfectly plain," said I, leaning back in my chair, and regarding the puzzled Hale with that cherubic expression of self-satisfaction which I know is so annoying to him.

"*What's* perfectly plain?" he demanded, more gruffly perhaps than etiquette would have sanctioned.

"Summertrees is no coiner, nor is he linked with any band of coiners."

"What is he, then?"

"Ah, that opens another avenue of enquiry. For all I know to the contrary, he may be the most honest of men. On the surface it would appear that he is a reasonably industrious tradesman in Tottenham Court Road, who is anxious that there should be no visible connection between a plebian employment and so aristocratic a residence as that in Park Lane."

At this point Spenser Hale gave expression to one of those rare flashes of reason which are always an astonishment to his friends.

"That is nonsense, Monsieur Valmont," he said, "the man who is ashamed of the connection between his business and his house is one who is trying to get into Society, or else the women of his family are trying it, as is usually the case. Now Summertrees has no family. He himself goes nowhere, gives no entertainments, and accepts no invitations. He belongs to no club, therefore to say that he is ashamed of his connection with the Tottenham Court Road shop is absurd. He is concealing the connection for some other reason that will bear looking into."

"My dear Hale, the goddess of Wisdom herself could not have made a more sensible series of remarks. Now, *mon ami*, do you want my assistance, or have you enough to go on with?"

"Enough to go on with? We have nothing more than we had when I called on you last night."

"Last night, my dear Hale, you supposed this man was in league with coiners. Today you know he is not."

"I know you *say* he is not."

I shrugged my shoulders, and raised my eyebrows, smiling at him.

"It is the same thing, Monsieur Hale."

"Well, of all the conceited—" and the good Hale could get no further.

"If you wish my assistance, it is yours."

"Very good. Not to put too fine a point upon it, I do."

"In that case, my dear Podgers, you will return to the residence of our friend Summertrees, and get together for me in a bundle all of yesterday's morning and evening papers, that were delivered to the house. Can you do that, or are they mixed up in a heap in the coal cellar?"

"I can do it, sir. I have instructions to place each day's papers in a pile by itself in case they should be wanted again. There is always one week's supply in the cellar, and we sell the papers of the week before to the rag men."

"Excellent. Well, take the risk of abstracting one day's journals, and have them ready for me. I will call upon you at half-past three o'clock exactly, and then I want you to take me upstairs to the clerk's bedroom in the third story, which I suppose is not locked during the daytime?"

"No, sir, it is not."

With this the patient Podgers took his departure. Spenser Hale rose when his assistant left.

"Anything further I can do?" he asked.

"Yes; give me the address of the shop in Tottenham Court Road. Do you happen to have about you one of those new five-shilling pieces which you believe to be illegally coined?"

He opened his pocket-book, took out the bit of white metal, and handed it to me.

"I'm going to pass this off before evening," I said, putting it in my pocket, "and I hope none of your men will arrest me."

"That's all right," laughed Hale as he took his leave.

At half-past three Podgers was waiting for me, and opened the front door as I came up the steps, thus saving me the necessity of ringing. The house seemed strangely quiet. The French cook was evidently down in the basement, and we had probably all the upper part to ourselves, unless Summertrees was in his study, which I doubted. Podgers led me directly upstairs to the clerk's room on the third floor, walking on tiptoe, with an elephantine air of silence and secrecy combined, which struck me as unnecessary.

"I will make an examination of this room," I said. "Kindly wait for me down by the door of the study."

The bedroom proved to be of respectable size when one considers the smallness of the house. The bed was all nicely made up, and there were two chairs in the room, but the usual washstand and swing-mirror were not visible. However, seeing a curtain at the farther end of the room, I drew it aside, and found, as I expected, a fixed lavatory in an alcove of perhaps four feet deep by five in width. As the room was about fifteen feet wide, this left two-thirds of the space unaccounted for. A moment later, I opened a door which exhibited a closet filled with clothes hanging on hooks. This left a space of five feet between the clothes closet and the lavatory. I thought at first that the entrance to the secret stairway must have issued from the lavatory, but examining the boards closely, although they sounded hollow to the knuckles, they were quite evidently plain matchboarding, and not a concealed door. The entrance to the stairway, therefore, must issue from the clothes closet. The right hand wall proved similar to the matchboarding of the lavatory as far as the casual eye or touch was concerned, but I saw at once it was a door. The latch turned out to be somewhat ingeniously operated by one of the hooks which held a pair of old trousers. I found that the hook, if pressed upward, allowed the door to swing outward, over the stairhead. Descending to the second floor, a similar latch let me in to a similar clothes closet in the room beneath. The two rooms were identical in size, one directly above the other, the only difference being that the lower room door gave into the study, instead of into the hall, as was the case with the upper chamber.

The study was extremely neat, either not much used, or the abode of a very methodical man. There was nothing on the table except a pile of that morning's papers. I walked to the farther end, turned the key in the lock, and came out upon the astonished Podgers.

"Well, I'm blowed!" exclaimed he.

"Quite so," I rejoined, "you've been tiptoeing past an empty room for the last two weeks. Now, if you'll come with me, Podgers, I'll show you how the trick is done."

When he entered the study, I locked the door once more, and led the assumed butler, still tiptoeing through force of habit, up the stair into the top bedroom, and so out again, leaving everything exactly as we found it. We went down the main stair to the front hall, and there Podgers had my parcel of papers all neatly wrapped up. This bundle I carried to my flat, gave one of my assistants some instructions, and left him at work on the papers.

* * *

I took a cab to the foot of Tottenham Court Road, and walked up that street till I came to J. Simpson's old curiosity shop. After gazing at the well-filled windows for some time, I stepped aside, having selected a little iron crucifix displayed behind the pane; the work of some ancient craftsman.

I knew at once from Podgers's description that I was waited upon by the veritable respectable clerk who brought the bag of money each night to Park Lane, and who I was certain was no other than Ralph Summertrees himself.

There was nothing in his manner differing from that of any other quiet salesman. The price of the crucifix proved to be seven-and-six, and I threw down a sovereign to pay for it.

"Do you mind the change being all in silver, sir?" he asked, and I answered without any eagerness, although the question aroused a suspicion that had begun to be allayed –

"Not in the least."

He gave me half-a-crown, three two-shilling pieces, and four separate shillings, all the coins being well-worn silver of the realm, the undoubted inartistic product of the reputable British Mint. This seemed to dispose of the theory that he was palming off illegitimate money. He asked me if I were interested in any particular branch of antiquity, and I replied that my curiosity was merely general, and exceedingly amateurish, whereupon he invited me to look around. This I proceeded to do, while he resumed the addressing and stamping of some wrapped-up pamphlets which I surmised to be copies of his catalogue.

He made no attempt either to watch me or to press his wares upon me. I selected at random a little ink-stand, and asked its price. It was two shillings, he said, whereupon I produced my fraudulent five-shilling piece. He took it, gave me the change without comment, and the last doubt about his connection with coiners flickered from my mind.

At this moment a young man came in, who, I saw at once, was not a customer. He walked briskly to the farther end of the shop, and disappeared behind a partition which had one pane of glass in it that gave an outlook towards the front door.

"Excuse me a moment," said the shopkeeper, and he followed the young man into the private office.

As I examined the curious heterogeneous collection of things for sale, I heard the clink of coins being poured out on the lid of a desk or an uncovered table, and the murmur of voices floated out to me. I was now near the entrance of the shop, and by a sleight-of-hand trick, keeping the corner of my eye on the glass pane of the private office, I removed the key of the front door without a sound, and took an impression of it in wax, returning the key to its place unobserved. At this moment another young man came in, and walked straight past me into the private office. I heard him say,—

"Oh, I beg pardon, Mr. Simpson. How are you, Rogers?"

"Hallo, Macpherson," saluted Rogers, who then came out, bidding good-night to Mr. Simpson, and departed whistling down the street, but not before he had repeated his phrase to another young man entering, to whom he gave the name of Tyrrel.

I noted these three names in my mind. Two others came in together, but I was compelled to content myself with memorising their features, for I did not learn their names. These men were evidently collectors, for I heard the rattle of money in every case; yet here was a small shop, doing apparently very little business, for I had been within it for more than half an hour, and yet remained the only customer. If credit were given, one collector would certainly have been sufficient, yet five had come in, and had poured their contributions into the pile Summertrees was to take home with him that night.

I determined to secure one of the pamphlets which the man had been addressing. They were piled on a shelf behind the counter, but I had no difficulty in reaching across and taking the one on top, which I slipped into my pocket. When the fifth young man went down the street Summertrees himself emerged, and this time he carried in his hand the well-filled locked leather satchel, with the straps dangling. It was now approaching half-past five, and I saw he was eager to close up and get away.

"Anything else you fancy, sir?" he asked me.

"No, or rather yes and no. You have a very interesting collection here, but it's getting so dark I can hardly see."

"I close at half-past five, sir."

"Ah, in that case," I said, consulting my watch, "I shall be pleased to call some other time."

"Thank you, sir," replied Summertrees quietly, and with that I took my leave.

From the corner of an alley on the other side of the street I saw him put up the shutters with his own hands, then he emerged with overcoat on, and the money satchel slung across his shoulder. He locked the door, tested it with his knuckles, and walked down the street, carrying under one arm the pamphlets he had been addressing. I followed him some distance, saw him drop the pamphlets into the box at the first post office he passed, and walk rapidly towards his house in Park Lane.

When I returned to my flat and called in my assistant, he said,—

"After putting to one side the regular advertisements of pills, soap, and what not, here is the only one common to all the newspapers, morning and evening alike. The advertisements are not identical, sir, but they have two points of similarity, or perhaps I should say three. They all profess to furnish a cure for absent-mindedness; they all ask that the applicant's chief hobby shall be stated, and they all bear the same address: Dr. Willoughby, in Tottenham Court Road."

"Thank you," said I, as he placed the scissored advertisements before me.

I read several of the announcements. They were all small, and perhaps that is why I had never noticed one of them in the newspapers, for certainly they were odd enough. Some asked for lists of absent-minded men, with the hobbies of each, and for these lists, prizes of from one shilling to six were offered. In other clippings Dr. Willoughby professed to be able to cure absent-mindedness. There were no fees, and no treatment, but a pamphlet would be sent, which, if it did not benefit the receiver, could do no harm. The doctor was unable to meet patients personally, nor could he enter into correspondence with them. The address was the same as that of the old curiosity shop in Tottenham Court Road. At this juncture I pulled the pamphlet from my pocket, and saw it was entitled *Christian Science and Absent-Mindedness*, by Dr. Stamford Willoughby, and at the end of the article was the statement contained in the advertisements, that Dr. Willoughby would neither see patients nor hold any correspondence with them.

I drew a sheet of paper towards me, wrote to Dr. Willoughby alleging that I was a very absent-minded man, and would be glad of his pamphlet, adding that my special hobby was the collecting of first editions. I then signed myself, 'Alport Webster, Imperial Flats, London, W.'

I may here explain that it is often necessary for me to see people under some other name than the well-known appellation of Eugène Valmont. There are two doors to my flat, and on one of these is painted, 'Eugène Valmont'; on the other there is a receptacle, into which can be slipped a sliding panel bearing any *nom de guerre* I choose. The same device is arranged on the ground floor, where the names of all the occupants of the building appear on the right-hand wall.

I sealed, addressed, and stamped my letter, then told my man to put out the name of Alport Webster, and if I did not happen to be in when anyone called upon that mythical person, he was to make an appointment for me.

It was nearly six o'clock next afternoon when the card of Angus Macpherson was brought in to Mr. Alport Webster. I recognised the young man at once as the second who had entered the little shop carrying his tribute to Mr. Simpson the day before. He held three volumes under his arm, and spoke in such a pleasant, insinuating sort of way, that I knew at once he was an adept in his profession of canvasser.

"Will you be seated, Mr. Macpherson? In what can I serve you?"

He placed the three volumes, backs upward, on my table.

"Are you interested at all in first editions, Mr. Webster?"

"It is the one thing I am interested in," I replied; "but unfortunately they often run into a lot of money."

"That is true," said Macpherson sympathetically, "and I have here three books, one of which is an exemplification of what you say. This one costs a hundred pounds. The last copy that was sold by auction in London brought a hundred and twenty-three pounds. This next one is forty pounds, and the third ten pounds. At these prices I am certain you could not duplicate three such treasures in any book shop in Britain."

I examined them critically, and saw at once that what he said was true. He was still standing on the opposite side of the table.

"Please take a chair, Mr. Macpherson. Do you mean to say you go round London with a hundred and fifty pounds worth of goods under your arm in this careless way?"

The young man laughed.

"I run very little risk, Mr. Webster. I don't suppose anyone I meet imagines for a moment there is more under my arm than perhaps a trio of volumes I have picked up in the fourpenny box to take home with me."

I lingered over the volume for which he asked a hundred pounds, then said, looking across at him:—

"How came you to be possessed of this book, for instance?"

He turned upon me a fine, open countenance, and answered without hesitation in the frankest possible manner,—

"I am not in actual possession of it, Mr. Webster. I am by way of being a connoisseur in rare and valuable books myself, although, of course, I have little money with which to indulge in the collection of them. I am acquainted, however, with the lovers of desirable books in different quarters of London. These three volumes, for instance, are from the library of a private gentleman in the West End. I have sold many books to him, and he knows I am trustworthy. He wishes to dispose of them at something under their real value, and has kindly allowed me to conduct the negotiation. I make it my business to find out those who are interested in rare books, and by such trading I add considerably to my income."

"How, for instance, did you learn that I was a bibliophile?"

Mr. Macpherson laughed genially.

"Well, Mr. Webster, I must confess that I chanced it. I do that very often. I take a flat like this, and send in my card to the name on the door. If I am invited in, I ask the occupant the question I asked you just now: "Are you interested in rare editions?" If he says no, I simply beg pardon and retire. If he says yes, then I show my wares."

"I see," said I, nodding. What a glib young liar he was, with that innocent face of his, and yet my next question brought forth the truth.

"As this is the first time you have called upon me, Mr. Macpherson, you have no objection to my making some further inquiry, I suppose. Would you mind telling me the name of the owner of these books in the West End?"

"His name is Mr. Ralph Summertrees, of Park Lane."

"Of Park Lane? Ah, indeed."

"I shall be glad to leave the books with you, Mr. Webster, and if you care to make an appointment with Mr. Summertrees, I am sure he will not object to say a word in my favour."

"Oh, I do not in the least doubt it, and should not think of troubling the gentleman."

"I was going to tell you," went on the young man, "that I have a friend, a capitalist, who, in a way, is my supporter; for, as I said, I have little money of my own. I find it is often inconvenient for people to pay down any considerable sum. When, however, I strike a bargain, my capitalist buys the book, and I make an arrangement with my customer to pay a certain amount each week, and so even a large purchase is not felt, as I make the instalments small enough to suit my client."

"You are employed during the day, I take it?"

"Yes, I am a clerk in the City."

Again we were in the blissful realms of fiction!

"Suppose I take this book at ten pounds, what instalment should I have to pay each week?"

"Oh, what you like, sir. Would five shillings be too much?"

"I think not."

"Very well, sir, if you pay me five shillings now, I will leave the book with you, and shall have pleasure in calling this day week for the next instalment."

I put my hand into my pocket, and drew out two half-crowns, which I passed over to him.

"Do I need to sign any form or undertaking to pay the rest?"

The young man laughed cordially.

"Oh, no, sir, there is no formality necessary. You see, sir, this is largely a labour of love with me, although I don't deny I have my eye on the future. I am getting together what I hope will be a very valuable connection with gentlemen like yourself who are fond of books, and I trust some day that I may be able to resign my place with the insurance company and set up a choice little business of my own, where my knowledge of values in literature will prove useful."

And then, after making a note in a little book he took from his pocket, he bade me a most graceful good-bye and departed, leaving me cogitating over what it all meant.

Next morning two articles were handed to me. The first came by post and was a pamphlet on *Christian Science and Absent-Mindedness*, exactly similar to the one I had taken away from the old curiosity shop; the second was a small key made from my wax impression that would fit the front door of the same shop—a key fashioned by an excellent anarchist friend of mine in an obscure street near Holborn.

That night at ten o'clock I was inside the old curiosity shop, with a small storage battery in my pocket, and a little electric glow-lamp at my buttonhole, a most useful instrument for either burglar or detective.

I had expected to find the books of the establishment in a safe, which, if it was similar to the one in Park Lane, I was prepared to open with the false keys in my possession or to take an impression of the keyhole and trust to my anarchist friend for the rest. But to my amazement I discovered all the papers pertaining to the concern in a desk which was not even locked. The books, three in number, were the ordinary day book, journal, and ledger referring to the shop; book-keeping of the older fashion; but in a portfolio lay half a dozen foolscap sheets, headed 'Mr. Rogers's List', 'Mr. Macpherson's', 'Mr. Tyrrel's', the names I had already learned, and three others. These lists contained in the first column, names; in the second column, addresses; in the third, sums of money; and then in the small, square places following were amounts ranging from two-and-sixpence to a pound. At the bottom of Mr. Macpherson's list was the name Alport Webster, Imperial Flats, £10; then in the small, square place, five shillings. These six sheets, each headed by a canvasser's name, were evidently the record of current collections, and the innocence of the whole thing was so apparent that if it were not for my fixed rule never to believe that I am at the bottom of any case until I have come on something suspicious, I would have gone out empty-handed as I came in.

The six sheets were loose in a thin portfolio, but standing on a shelf above the desk were a number of fat volumes, one of which I took down, and saw that it contained similar lists running back several years. I noticed on Mr. Macpherson's current list the name of Lord Semptam, an eccentric old nobleman whom I knew slightly. Then turning to the list immediately before the current one the name was still there; I traced it back through list after list until I found the first entry, which was no less than three years previous, and there Lord Semptam was down for a piece of furniture costing fifty pounds, and on that account he had paid a pound a week for more than three years, totalling a hundred and seventy pounds at the least, and instantly the glorious simplicity of the scheme dawned upon me, and I became so interested in the swindle that I lit the gas, fearing my little lamp would be exhausted before my investigation ended, for it promised to be a long one.

In several instances the intended victim proved shrewder than old Simpson had counted upon, and the word 'Settled' had been written on the line carrying the name when the exact number of instalments was paid. But as these shrewd persons dropped out, others took their places, and Simpson's dependence on their absent-mindedness seemed to be justified in nine cases out of ten. His collectors were collecting long after the debt had been paid. In Lord Semptam's case, the payment had evidently become chronic, and the old man was giving away his pound a week to the suave Macpherson two years after his debt had been liquidated.

From the big volume I detached the loose leaf, dated 1893, which recorded Lord Semptam's purchase of a carved table for fifty pounds, and on which he had been paying a pound a week from that time to the date of which I am writing, which was November, 1896. This single document taken from the file of three years previous, was not likely to be missed, as would have been the case if I had selected a current sheet. I nevertheless made a copy of the names and addresses of Macpherson's present clients; then, carefully placing everything exactly as I had found it, I extinguished the gas, and went out of the shop, locking the door behind me. With the 1893 sheet in my pocket I resolved to prepare a pleasant little surprise for my suave friend Macpherson when he called to get his next instalment of five shillings.

Late as was the hour when I reached Trafalgar Square, I could not deprive myself of the felicity of calling on Mr. Spenser Hale, who I knew was then on duty. He never appeared at his best during office hours, because officialism stiffened his stalwart frame. Mentally he was impressed with the importance of his position, and added to this he was not then allowed to smoke his big, black pipe and terrible tobacco. He received me with the curtness I had been taught to expect when I inflicted myself upon him at his office. He greeted me abruptly with –

"I say, Valmont, how long do you expect to be on this job?"

"What job?" I asked mildly.

"Oh, you know what I mean: the Summertrees affair."

"Oh, *that*!" I exclaimed, with surprise. "The Summertrees case is already completed, of course. If I had known you were in a hurry, I should have finished up everything yesterday, but as you and Podgers, and I don't know how many more, have been at it sixteen or seventeen days, if not longer, I thought I might venture to take as many hours, as I am working entirely alone. You said nothing about haste, you know."

"Oh, come now, Valmont, that's a bit thick. Do you mean to say you have already got evidence against the man?"

"Evidence absolute and complete."

"Then who are the coiners?"

"My most estimable friend, how often have I told you not to jump at conclusions? I informed you when you first spoke to me about the matter that Summertrees was neither a coiner nor a confederate of coiners. I secured evidence sufficient to convict him of quite another offence, which is probably unique in the annals of crime. I have penetrated the mystery of the shop, and discovered the reason for all those suspicious actions which quite properly set you on his trail. Now I wish you to come to my flat next Wednesday night at a quarter to six, prepared to make an arrest."

"I must know who I am to arrest, and on what counts."

"Quite so, *mon ami* Hale; I did not say you were to make an arrest, but merely warned you to be prepared. If you have time now to listen to the disclosures, I am quite at your service. I promise you there are some original features in the case. If, however, the present moment is inopportune, drop in on me at your convenience, previously telephoning so that you may know whether I am there or not, and thus your valuable time will not be expended purposelessly."

With this I presented to him my most courteous bow, and although his mystified expression hinted a suspicion that he thought I was chaffing him, as he would call it, official dignity dissolved somewhat, and he intimated his desire to hear all about it then and there. I had succeeded in arousing my friend Hale's curiosity. He listened to the evidence with perplexed brow, and at last ejaculated he would be blessed.

"This young man," I said, in conclusion, "will call upon me at six on Wednesday afternoon, to receive his second five shillings. I propose that you, in your uniform, shall be seated there with me to receive him, and I am anxious to study Mr. Macpherson's countenance when he realises he has walked in to confront a policeman. If you will then allow me to cross-examine him for a few moments, not after the manner of Scotland Yard, with a warning lest he incriminate himself, but in the free and easy fashion we adopt in Paris, I shall afterwards turn the case over to you to be dealt with at your discretion."

"You have a wonderful flow of language, Monsieur Valmont," was the officer's tribute to me. "I shall be on hand at a quarter to six on Wednesday."

"Meanwhile," said I, "kindly say nothing of this to anyone. We must arrange a complete surprise for Macpherson. That is essential. Please make no move in the matter at all until Wednesday night."

Spenser Hale, much impressed, nodded acquiescence, and I took a polite leave of him.

* * *

The question of lighting is an important one in a room such as mine, and electricity offers a good deal of scope to the ingenious. Of this fact I have taken full advantage. I can manipulate the lighting of my room so that any particular spot is bathed in brilliancy, while the rest of the space remains in comparative gloom, and I arranged the lamps so that the full force of their rays impinged against the door that Wednesday evening, while I sat on one side of the table in semi-darkness and Hale sat on the other, with a light beating down on him from above which gave him the odd, sculptured look of a living statue of Justice, stern and triumphant. Anyone entering the room would first be dazzled by the light, and next would see the gigantic form of

Hale in the full uniform of his order.

When Angus Macpherson was shown into this room he was quite visibly taken aback, and paused abruptly on the threshold, his gaze riveted on the huge policeman. I think his first purpose was to turn and run, but the door closed behind him, and he doubtless heard, as we all did, the sound of the bolt being thrust in its place, thus locking him in.

"I—I beg your pardon," he stammered, "I expected to meet Mr. Webster."

As he said this, I pressed the button under my table, and was instantly enshrouded with light. A sickly smile overspread the countenance of Macpherson as he caught sight of me, and he made a very creditable attempt to carry off the situation with nonchalance.

"Oh, there you are, Mr. Webster; I did not notice you at first."

It was a tense moment. I spoke slowly and impressively.

"Sir, perhaps you are not unacquainted with the name of Eugène Valmont."

He replied brazenly,—

"I am sorry to say, sir, I never heard of the gentleman before."

At this came a most inopportune "Haw-haw" from that blockhead Spenser Hale, completely spoiling the dramatic situation I had elaborated with such thought and care. It is little wonder the English possess no drama, for they show scant appreciation of the sensational moments in life.

"Haw-haw," brayed Spenser Hale, and at once reduced the emotional atmosphere to a fog of commonplace. However, what is a man to do? He must handle the tools with which it pleases Providence to provide him. I ignored Hale's untimely laughter.

"Sit down, sir," I said to Macpherson, and he obeyed.

"You have called on Lord Semptam this week," I continued sternly.

"Yes, sir."

"And collected a pound from him?"

"Yes, sir."

"In October, 1893, you sold Lord Semptam a carved antique table for fifty pounds?"

"Quite right, sir."

"When you were here last week you gave me Ralph Summertrees as the name of a gentleman living in Park Lane. You knew at the time that this man was your employer?"

Macpherson was now looking fixedly at me, and on this occasion made no reply. I went on calmly:—

"You also knew that Summertrees, of Park Lane, was identical with Simpson, of Tottenham Court Road?"

"Well, sir," said Macpherson, "I don't exactly see what you're driving at, but it's quite usual for a man to carry on a business under an assumed name. There is nothing illegal about that."

"We will come to the illegality in a moment, Mr. Macpherson. You, and Rogers, and Tyrrel, and three others, are confederates of this man Simpson."

"We are in his employ; yes, sir, but no more confederates than clerks usually are."

"I think, Mr. Macpherson, I have said enough to show you that the game is, what you call, up. You are now in the presence of Mr. Spenser Hale, from Scotland Yard, who is waiting to hear your confession."

Here the stupid Hale broke in with his—

"And remember, sir, that anything you say will be—"

"Excuse me, Mr. Hale," I interrupted hastily, "I shall turn over the case to you in a very few moments, but I ask you to remember our compact, and to leave it for the present entirely in my hands. Now, Mr. Macpherson, I want your confession, and I want it at once."

"Confession? Confederates?" protested Macpherson with admirably simulated surprise. "I must say you use extraordinary terms, Mr.—Mr.—What did you say the name was?"

"Haw-haw," roared Hale. "His name is Monsieur Valmont."

"I implore you, Mr. Hale, to leave this man to me for a very few moments. Now, Macpherson, what have you to say in your defence?"

"Where nothing criminal has been alleged, Monsieur Valmont, I see no necessity for defence. If you wish me to admit that somehow you have acquired a number of details regarding our business, I am perfectly willing to do so, and to subscribe to their accuracy. If you will be good enough to let me know of what you complain, I shall endeavour to make the point clear to you if I can. There has evidently been some misapprehension, but for the life of me, without further explanation, I am as much in a fog as I was on my way coming here, for it is getting a little thick outside."

Macpherson certainly was conducting himself with great discretion, and presented, quite unconsciously, a much more diplomatic figure than my friend, Spenser Hale, sitting stiffly opposite me. His tone was one of mild expostulation, mitigated by the intimation that all misunderstanding speedily would be cleared away. To outward view he offered a perfect picture of innocence, neither protesting too much nor too little. I had, however, another surprise in store for him, a trump card, as it were, and I played it down on the table.

"There!" I cried with vim, "have you ever seen that sheet before?"

He glanced at it without offering to take it in his hand.

"Oh, yes," he said, "that has been abstracted from our file. It is what I call my visiting list."

"Come, come, sir," I cried sternly, "you refuse to confess, but I warn you we know all about it. You never heard of Dr. Willoughby, I suppose?"

"Yes, he is the author of the silly pamphlet on Christian Science."

"You are in the right, Mr. Macpherson; on Christian Science and Absent-Mindedness."

"Possibly. I haven't read it for a long while."

"Have you ever met this learned doctor, Mr. Macpherson?"

"Oh, yes. Dr. Willoughby is the pen-name of Mr. Summertrees. He believes in Christian Science and that sort of thing, and writes about it."

"Ah, really. We are getting your confession bit by bit, Mr. Macpherson. I think it would be better to be quite frank with us."

"I was just going to make the same suggestion to you, Monsieur Valmont. If you will tell me in a few words exactly what is your charge against either Mr. Summertrees or myself, I will know then what to say."

"We charge you, sir, with obtaining money under false pretences, which is a crime that has landed more than one distinguished financier in prison."

Spenser Hale shook his fat forefinger at me, and said,—

"Tut, tut, Valmont; we mustn't threaten, we mustn't threaten, you know;" but I went on without heeding him.

"Take for instance, Lord Semptam. You sold him a table for fifty pounds, on the instalment plan. He was to pay a pound a week, and in less than a year the debt was liquidated. But he is an absent-minded man, as all your clients are. That is why you came to me. I had answered the bogus Willoughby's advertisement. And so you kept on collecting and collecting for something more than three years. Now do you understand the charge?"

Mr. Macpherson's head during this accusation was held slightly inclined to one side. At first his face was clouded by the most clever imitation of anxious concentration of mind I had ever seen, and this was gradually cleared away by the dawn of awakening perception. When I had finished, an ingratiating smile hovered about his lips.

"Really, you know," he said, "that is rather a capital scheme. The absent-minded league, as one might call them. Most ingenious. Summertrees, if he had any sense of humour, which he hasn't, would be rather taken by the idea that his innocent fad for Christian Science had led him to be suspected of obtaining money under false pretences. But, really, there are no pretensions about the matter at all. As I understand it, I simply call and receive the money through the forgetfulness of the persons on my list, but where I think you would have both Summertrees and myself, if there was anything in your audacious theory, would be an indictment for conspiracy. Still, I quite see how the mistake arises. You have jumped to the conclusion that we sold nothing to Lord Semptam except that carved table three years ago. I have pleasure in pointing out to you that his lordship is a frequent customer of ours, and has had many things from us at one time or another. Sometimes he is in our debt; sometimes we are in his. We keep a sort of running contract with him by which he pays us a pound a week. He and several other customers deal on the same plan, and in return for an income that we can count upon, they get the first offer of anything in which they are supposed to be interested. As I have told you, we call these sheets in the office our visiting lists, but to make the visiting lists complete you need what we term our encyclopaedia. We call it that because it is in so many volumes; a volume for each year, running back I don't know how long. You will notice little figures here from time to time above the amount stated on this visiting list. These figures refer to the page of the encyclopaedia for the current year, and on that page is noted the new sale, and the amount of it, as it might be set down, say, in a ledger."

"That is a very entertaining explanation, Mr. Macpherson. I suppose this encyclopaedia, as you call it, is in the shop at Tottenham Court Road?"

"Oh, no, sir. Each volume of the encyclopaedia is self-locking. These books contain the real secret of our business, and they are kept in the safe at Mr. Summertrees' house in Park Lane. Take Lord Semptam's account, for instance. You will find in faint figures under a certain date, 102. If you turn to page 102 of the encyclopaedia for that year, you will then see a list of what Lord Semptam has bought, and the prices he was charged for them. It is really a very simple matter. If you will allow me to use your telephone for a moment, I will ask Mr. Summertrees, who has not yet begun dinner, to bring with him here the volume for 1893, and, within a quarter of an hour, you will be perfectly satisfied that everything is quite legitimate."

I confess that the young man's naturalness and confidence staggered me, the more so as I saw by the sarcastic smile on Hale's lips that he did not believe a single word spoken. A portable telephone stood on the table, and as Macpherson finished his explanation, he reached over and drew it towards him. Then Spenser Hale interfered.

"Excuse *me*," he said, "I'll do the telephoning. What is the call number of Mr. Summertrees?"

"140 Hyde Park."

Hale at once called up Central, and presently was answered from Park Lane. We heard him say—

"Is this the residence of Mr. Summertrees? Oh, is that you, Podgers? Is Mr. Summertrees in? Very well. This is Hale. I am in Valmont's flat – Imperial Flats – you know. Yes, where you went with me the other day. Very well, go to Mr. Summertrees, and say to him that Mr.

Macpherson wants the encyclopaedia for 1893. Do you get that? Yes, encyclopaedia. Oh, he'll understand what it is. Mr. Macpherson. No, don't mention my name at all. Just say Mr. Macpherson wants the encyclopaedia for the year 1893, and that you are to bring it. Yes, you may tell him that Mr. Macpherson is at Imperial Flats, but don't mention my name at all. Exactly. As soon as he gives you the book, get into a cab, and come here as quickly as possible with it. If Summertrees doesn't want to let the book go, then tell him to come with you. If he won't do that, place him under arrest, and bring both him and the book here. All right. Be as quick as you can; we're waiting."

Macpherson made no protest against Hale's use of the telephone; he merely sat back in his chair with a resigned expression on his face which, if painted on canvas, might have been entitled 'The Falsely Accused.' When Hale rang off, Macpherson said –

"Of course you know your own business best, but if your man arrests Summertrees, he will make you the laughing-stock of London. There is such a thing as unjustifiable arrest, as well as getting money under false pretences, and Mr. Summertrees is not the man to forgive an insult. And then, if you will allow me to say so, the more I think over your absent-minded theory, the more absolutely grotesque it seems, and if the case ever gets into the newspapers, I am sure, Mr. Hale, you'll experience an uncomfortable half-hour with your chiefs at Scotland Yard."

"I'll take the risk of that, thank you," said Hale stubbornly.

"Am I to consider myself under arrest?" inquired the young man.

"No, sir."

"Then, if you will pardon me, I shall withdraw. Mr. Summertrees will show you everything you wish to see in his books, and can explain his business much more capably than I, because he knows more about it; therefore, gentlemen, I bid you good-night."

"No you don't. Not just yet awhile," exclaimed Hale, rising to his feet simultaneously with the young man.

"Then I *am* under arrest," protested Macpherson.

"You're not going to leave this room until Podgers brings that book."

"Oh, very well," and he sat down again.

And now, as talking is dry work, I set out something to drink, a box of cigars, and a box of cigarettes. Hale mixed his favourite brew, but Macpherson, shunning the wine of his country, contented himself with a glass of plain mineral water, and lit a cigarette. Then he awoke my high regard by saying pleasantly as if nothing had happened –

"While we are waiting, Monsieur Valmont, may I remind you that you owe me five shillings?"

I laughed, took the coin from my pocket, and paid him, whereupon he thanked me.

"Are you connected with Scotland Yard, Monsieur Valmont?" asked Macpherson, with the air of a man trying to make conversation to bridge over a tedious interval; but before I could reply, Hale blurted out –

"Not likely!"

"You have no official standing as a detective, then, Monsieur Valmont?"

"None whatever," I replied quickly, thus getting in my oar ahead of Hale.

"This is a loss to our country," pursued this admirable young man, with evident sincerity. I began to see I could make a good deal of so clever a fellow if he came under my tuition.

"The blunders of our police", he went on, "are something deplorable. If they would but take lessons in strategy, say, from France, their unpleasant duties would be so much more acceptably performed, with much less discomfort to their victims."

"France," snorted Hale in derision, "why, they call a man guilty there until he's proven innocent."

"Yes, Mr. Hale, and the same seems to be the case in Imperial Flats. You have quite made up your mind that Mr. Summertrees is guilty, and will not be content until he proves his innocence. I venture to predict that you will hear from him before long in a manner that may astonish you."

Hale grunted and looked at his watch. The minutes passed very slowly as we sat there smoking, and at last even I began to get uneasy. Macpherson, seeing our anxiety, said that when he came in the fog was almost as thick as it had been the week before, and that there might be some difficulty in getting a cab. Just as he was speaking the door was unlocked from the outside, and Podgers entered, bearing a thick volume in his hand. This he gave to his superior, who turned over its pages in amazement, and then looked at the back, crying—

"*Encyclopaedia of Sport*, 1893! What sort of a joke is this, Mr. Macpherson?"

There was a pained look on Mr. Macpherson's face as he reached forward and took the book. He said with a sigh—

"If you had allowed me to telephone, Mr. Hale, I should have made it perfectly plain to Summertrees what was wanted. I might have known this mistake was liable to occur. There is an increasing demand for out-of-date books of sport, and no doubt Mr. Summertrees thought this was what I meant. There is nothing for it but to send your man back to Park Lane and tell Mr. Summertrees that what we want is the locked volume of accounts for 1893, which we call the encyclopaedia. Allow me to write an order that will bring it. Oh, I'll show you what I have written before your man takes it," he said, as Hale stood ready to look over his shoulder.

On my notepaper he dashed off a request such as he had outlined, and handed it to Hale, who read it and gave it to Podgers.

"Take that to Summertrees, and get back as quickly as possible. Have you a cab at the door?"

"Yes, sir."

"Is it foggy outside?"

"Not so much, sir, as it was an hour ago. No difficulty about the traffic now, sir."

"Very well, get back as soon as you can."

Podgers saluted, and left with the book under his arm. Again the door was locked, and again we sat smoking in silence until the stillness was broken by the tinkle of the telephone. Hale put the receiver to his ear.

"Yes, this is the Imperial Flats. Yes. Valmont. Oh, yes; Macpherson is here. What? Out of what? Can't hear you. Out of print. What, the encyclopaedia's out of print? Who is that speaking? Dr. Willoughby; thanks."

Macpherson rose as if he would go to the telephone, but instead (and he acted so quietly that I did not notice what he was doing until the thing was done), he picked up the sheet which he called his visiting list, and walking quite without haste, held it in the glowing coals of the fireplace until it disappeared in a flash of flame up the chimney. I sprang to my feet indignant, but too late to make even a motion outwards saving the sheet. Macpherson regarded us both with that self-deprecatory smile which had several times lighted up his face.

"How dared you burn that sheet?" I demanded.

"Because, Monsieur Valmont, it did not belong to you; because you do not belong to Scotland Yard; because you stole it; because you had no right to it; and because you have no official standing in this country. If it had been in Mr. Hale's possession I should not have dared, as you put it, to destroy the sheet, but as this sheet was abstracted from my master's premises by you, an entirely unauthorised person, whom he would have been justified in shooting dead if he had found you housebreaking and you had resisted him on his discovery, I took the liberty of destroying the document. I have always held that these sheets should not have been kept, for, as has been the case, if they fell under the scrutiny of so intelligent a person as Eugène Valmont, improper inferences might have been drawn. Mr. Summertrees, however, persisted in keeping them, but made this concession, that if I ever telegraphed him or telephoned him the word 'Encyclopaedia,' he would at once burn these records, and he, on his part, was to telegraph or telephone to me 'The *Encyclopaedia* is out of print,' whereupon I would know that he had succeeded.

"Now, gentlemen, open this door, which will save me the trouble of forcing it. Either put me formally under arrest, or cease to restrict my liberty. I am very much obliged to Mr. Hale for telephoning, and I have made no protest to so gallant a host as Monsieur Valmont is, because of the locked door. However, the farce is now terminated. The proceedings I have sat through were entirely illegal, and if you will pardon me, Mr. Hale, they have been a little too French to go down here in old England, or to make a report in the newspapers that would be quite satisfactory to your chiefs. I demand either my formal arrest, or the unlocking of that door."

In silence I pressed a button, and my man threw open the door. Macpherson walked to the threshold, paused, and looked back at Spenser Hale, who sat there silent as a sphinx.

"Good-evening, Mr. Hale."

There being no reply, he turned to me with the same ingratiating smile –

"Good-evening, Monsieur Eugène Valmont," he said, "I shall give myself the pleasure of calling next Wednesday at six for my five shillings."

Mickey's Ghost

T.J. Berg

THIS IS a true story – a ghost story – from what seems like long ago, so long ago that my dad can't even remember the girl's name. He claims he has a photo of her somewhere. He claims he remembers it all so well. Perhaps I haven't lived long enough, but I can't think of ever being so old that I would forget the name of a girl that was almost my daughter. Yet still, he says he cannot remember, so I fill in the details from my imagination. I remember nothing of her, of this girl I name Mickey. There are just the bones of her coming into our lives, and the ghost that followed.

I was only a couple years old when my dad brought her home. I can just about picture my dad. He's a composite of photos I've seen as an adult and my earliest memories of him. He has a new sister for me, carried in his arms.

He is a young man then, working in Chicago while my mom raises me and my two older sisters in Wisconsin. He has a mustache covering his whole upper lip, and his hair is a bit shaggy, so dark brown it's almost black. His eyes are just the same, still pale blue, but maybe with a bit more laughter and wildness. I especially imagine his hands being softer then. Not soft, just softer. The years of hard work to follow have yet to crack his skin, tear away his nails, split his cuticles, etch dry white lines between dirt and tan. But they're still hard hands, a working man's hands. He manages property in Chicago.

He takes care of buildings there, mostly in the poor parts of town. He's handy with a hammer and nail, with plumbing and electricity. He's the type that sees the workings of things and knows how to fix them. And he's seen how poor works in Chicago – how people might do anything for a roof over their head, food in their bellies, a few days of work, one last hit, a little sex, or a bottle of booze.

In the many buildings my dad maintains, there are children, some better off, some worse. But Mickey is different. Perhaps only because she lives in the building where he keeps his office, so he sees her often. But then maybe it's her personality. She seems mature, determined, yet able to laugh and be a child. She is boyish, with her dirty fingernails, hair tangled and long, and her odd enjoyment of throwing things – anything, be it balls, pencils, or paperweights. He couldn't have known how old she was, maybe six or seven – close enough to his oldest daughter's age to make it hard to see her unattended, unwashed, unfed. My dad's seen it all, though, and you'd think it would have made him as calloused as his hands.

So Mickey comes by my dad's office a lot. He shares his lunches with her, always asks how she's doing, lets her hang around. Sometimes, she'll take everything off his desk, throw it in the wastebasket in the corner of the room, then bring it all back. But mostly she's quiet, not full of questions and screaming like his girls back home. The only noises she makes are the soft whisperings to herself as she plays with the little rag doll my dad has given her, a doll his own mother made. She won't part with it, even for a washing. The doll's hair and lacy pink dress are as dirty as her now.

And then, my dad realizes she's been around even more than usual. She waits outside his door. A few days of this and he asks her what's wrong.

I try to hear her voice in my head, how she talked. I hear a voice breathy and shy, but articulate enough. No lisp, though her front tooth must be missing. No whine, though she'd have every right. "I can't get inside," she tells him. She is locked out of her apartment.

I can almost feel the anger that was always in my dad. ("Don't tell your father," my mom would say when we broke something. "Let's just fix it.") It had to come at him from his stomach, a hot, tightening fist that pushed up his throat like indigestion and caused him to clench his teeth. This was more than he could stand.

So he finds the ring of keys for this building, each labeled with a piece of masking tape. They take the stairs up because there is no money from the property owner to fix the elevator. He holds her hand until they reach the door. He lets go then, to sort through the keys.

I have a vivid picture of them standing there. Her hand is still suspended, as if waiting to be taken up again. She wears a faded purple dress with yellow flowers, a hand-me-down sent from my mom. Dirty blonde curls are tangled around a rubber band at the back of her neck. On her arms are tiny pink flea bites which she has scratched raw. My dad wears jeans, splattered with paint and grease. A white t-shirt, also full of paint. The hallway is lit through yellowing plastic squares in the ceiling and reeks of curry, incense, and urine. My dad hates all three smells, but the curry is the worst and makes him clench his teeth even harder. He rattles the keys angrily, trying to get Mickey's into the lock. He glances again at the number on the door, written in black marker because the plate fell off months ago.

Finally, the key turns and the door swings open. It's summer, and while the hall was warm, the apartment is oppressively hot and reeks of rotting meat. The stench is so strong the first thing my dad does is cross the room to open the heavy black curtains and the window beneath. A breeze slips in with the sun to stir up dust into the cloying air.

Candles, black and red, mostly without dishes beneath them, perch in wavy pools of cold wax. It seems Mickey's mother has mounted these fire hazards on every available surface. Dirty dishes are stacked on the kitchen counter. The linoleum in the kitchen is covered with crumbs, dust, and sticky-looking spills. An open can of baked beans lies on its side, one dried, brown bean stuck to the sharp-edged top. It looks as if nothing has ever been cleaned and the practical man in my dad can't help but think of the difficulty he always has with roaches.

He feels the brush of fingers against his palm. Mickey turns her eyes up to him as she seeks the comfort of his hand again. He takes it, wanting a little comfort himself as he walks with the girl to the one bedroom in the apartment. The door is closed, and when he opens it he is again accosted by an overwhelming stench. Sweet, cloying incense and rot. It is all he can do not to gag, and yet Mickey only clutches more tightly at his hand. There is no bed, just a mattress pushed against the wall, barely visible in the dark room. He flips the light switch but nothing happens, so he again opens the heavy curtains and the window.

When he turns around bile swells up into his throat. On a table in one corner of the room is an alter. Candles surround an upside down cross, a porcelain bowl, and a dead squirrel. Its tail sticks out of a pool of maggots. He's frozen for a moment. Then he picks up Mickey in his arms, spins away and out of the room, closing the door behind him. All he wants to do is leave the apartment but he must check the bathroom.

The knob is cold, his hand hesitant. My dad has seen dead bodies before. He's even helped coroners move them out of the buildings. He's cleaned out the apartments. He's called families if there were families to call. Yet his hand will not turn the knob. He knows what he will see, a body that is no worse than the others – its nakedness, the bluish cast to the butt and feet, the matted hair, the flies, and the smell. He stands with Mickey, hand tightening on the doorknob but not turning. They are both imagining her mother's body, bloated and sprouting maggots like the squirrel, propped on the toilet, flopped against the wall. The band is still tied around her upper arm, the needle and the spoon are on the floor. My dad covers Mickey's eyes and turns her head toward his chest, then opens the door.

He pulls it shut. The slam is loud in his ears. He backs away, out of the apartment, a numbness spreading over him. It replaces anger and disgust. Now is the time to take care of things, the way my dad has always taken care of things.

He brings Mickey downstairs and tries to make her sit in a chair, but she clings to his neck, so he makes the necessary calls while still holding her in his arms. The police take forever. They arrive in a tired-looking pair with a woman from social services trailing behind. She appears harried, with frizzy black hair and splotchy black skin, but she is warm to Mickey. She clings to my dad's neck, not crying, not doing anything but making a long, high keening noise. It's hard to imagine the conversation that ensues.

My dad making awkward explanations. "I've been feeding her. She's been hanging around my office."

The social worker touching the little girl's shoulder. "You've been kind to her. Would you come down to child services?"

"What will happen to her?" my dad asks.

"Foster care. A group home. She'll be taken care of."

"And if her mother shows up?" Because she hadn't been in the bathroom. She was just gone. Left only a ghost of herself.

The woman shrugs. They both know the mother is probably dead. The woman thinks the hope of her mother will calm Mickey. But Mickey knows the truth. Her mother's gone because she's mad at Mickey, doesn't love her anymore, is disappointed in her. Why else would her mother just be gone, leaving an empty apartment, a ghost to taunt Mickey with her absence, to remind her what a bad daughter she'd been?

"What are her chances of adoption?" my dad asks. He knows the answers to all the questions he asks. He's unsurprised by the social worker's shrug.

And then? How long was the silence? As he held onto Mickey, did he picture her life from this point forward as a ward of the state? Did he picture a building full of unwanted children fighting and scrabbling for love and attention? Did he picture little Mickey growing cold and distant, a withdrawn teenager doomed to walk the same path her mother did?

Whatever went through his head, he made his decision and arranged with social services to take Mickey home. His wife Jo – my mom – is kind, big-hearted but strong, and stern enough to reign in even Mickey. His three daughters would be good company. They'd planned on a fourth anyway. So meetings are arranged, paperwork filled out, and less than a week later my dad drives north with Mickey.

What must it have been like for her? I wonder if she has ever been in a car before, seen open country. It is summer, and Wisconsin is startling in its beauty: trees green and lush, farms with fat grazing cows, a sky so blue and endless she has to press her face against the glass to look up and up into it.

The ride is so long she needs desperately to pee, but when they arrive, finally, her need is forgotten. The house is huge compared to her apartment and seated on an expanse of lawn that must seem to stretch to the ends of the earth, and with a garden full of shiny blobs of vegetables, and a swing-set planted beneath a tall tree with trembling leaves. A creek divides the lawn from a small stretch of wooded land to play in. Raspberries and mulberries grow with wild abandon. Only a ten-minute walk down the road is Lake Como and the beach. I can't help but think this must seem like paradise to Mickey. Yet up here, in Wisconsin, Lake Como is the poor town. Despite their lack of money, my parents are sure the open country and a real family will help Mickey to heal.

Some unhappiness needs more than green grass and creeks and woods and hugs and love to cure, though. Can we fault my parents for their failure? They saw the cure in change and love, because those things have always worked for them before. But Mickey's ghost could not be exorcized with sunshine and love. That bloated, bluish thing followed Mickey all the way north, invisible to those what would help her, stretching its cold fingers toward all that would try.

So I imagine those first days, as my dad described them. He takes a few days off to help my mother. They take Mickey shopping, though they've little enough money. They buy a few new clothes, a new doll. The rest of her wardrobe is filled out with cast-offs from their oldest daughter, Sonja. Although now that they've been given Mickey's papers, my parents find out she's two years older than their eldest daughter.

The girls are introduced. The parents try to explain how they have a new sister. Sonja warms to the idea, takes immediately to the older, mature new friend. The middle child, Michel, seems less sure. She'll surely finds ways to antagonize the older girl. It is her way, and is mostly friendly. Getting Mickey to put a chili pepper in her mouth is Michel's way of making friends.

The first days are a trial. Mickey won't sleep in a bed. She won't eat from dishes and silverware. All she eats is cereal from a box. Every meal is a trial of coaxing the little girl to sit at the table, pick up a piece of silverware, eat something homemade and healthy. When my dad is around, only on weekends after those first few days, she insists on sitting on his lap to eat. Spaghetti sauce sauce slaps her face as her new sisters teach her how to suck a noodle up between her lips, everyone laughing.

Baths are a trial. She is terrified of the water at first, thrashes and screams. Finally mom gives in and gets undressed and steps into the water herself and begins to wash. This doesn't work. The next time she gets Sonja in. Soon they have Mickey bathing. Her skin takes on a healthier glow: pink cheeks, flea bites healing, hair falling in neat ringlets. She takes the rag doll in the bath with her and tries to float her on the plastic soap dish. She learns how to make squirt guns from My Little Ponies by removing their tails. My mom is relieved, even while cleaning the water off the bathroom walls.

Getting her to bed is a trial. Mickey won't stop sleeping on the floor, even though my dad has built bunk beds for her to share with Sonja. She won't even sit on a bed. If my mom sets her on any bed in the house, she screams and bolts immediately to hide in a closet. I don't think she slept once in the bed, though my mom took her out to garage sales to find sheets and blankets she would like: *Star Wars* sheets and a blanket with puppy paw prints. They're still in my mom's linen closet, though now they're faded almost beyond recognition.

It's one trial after another, but Mickey is accepting her new home. My mom is taming the girl. My dad is happy, and looks forward to weekends home with his little girls and his wife. He is proud of them all. Because he doesn't see the ghost, not yet.

Because it is when the entire family is growing the most comfortable, bringing Mickey slowly back to life, that the ghost drags her away. Summer is drawing to an end. Mickey is enrolled in school, the little blue building with the mural painted on it. The school has the same pale, faded tinge of her not-dead mother who follows her everywhere. This frightens Mickey. She sees its walls, its windows closed up with blinds, the monkey bars and merry-go-round in the yard. Her new mom thinks this is a safe place, tells her she'll spend five days each week here. If she was good, they'd let her use paint on the wall, add her own little something to the mural.

"And I'm not far away. You can have anyone call if you want me to come get you."

She is a good mom.

She thinks Mickey is ready.

She's been eating, washing, sleeping – though still in a sleeping bag on the floor. (She has asked for the puppy blanket, but is told she may not have it until she sleeps in the bed.) Mickey agrees to go to school, though she is afraid. She's put in a class with Sonja. They're allowed some time before the rest of the class arrives to explore the room, while my mom discusses Mickey with the teacher out in the hallway.

The inside of Mickey's desk smells of melted crayons and she spends too much time with her head plunged inside, examining the contents. "They won't put me in here, will they?" she asks Sonja. Sonja assures her that no, they only sit at the desks, not inside them. But the closets in the back are worrisome, too. "They won't put us in there, will they?" Mickey wants to know. Sonja doesn't think so, though she remembers – sometimes the older kids are cruel, will make you get inside.

"I won't let them," Mickey tells her. "I'll protect us." But Sonja has her doubts. Mickey's older, but not much bigger than her.

"I have special powers," Mickey says. She gives Sonja a reassuring hug. "I can teach you them if we need them." With the assurance of their shared strength, Mickey starts school for the first time.

The first week my mom receives calls from every teacher. Mickey won't sit in a desk. She stands in the back of the room. Sometimes she starts, her feet making a quick shuffle from side to side: an animal caught in the open, dodging for cover that isn't there. She doesn't talk to the other children. Yet she's quick with lessons. She's protective of and helpful with Sonja, a sweet sister. She painted a lovely rag-doll on the mural. Everyone is hopeful for her. My mother feels such relief, such pride.

She cannot see Mickey's ghost.

But the ghost is there. It is there in the low, late afternoon sun as my mom trudges up the stairs with a basket of laundry. It's in the room with the girls, where my mom finds Mickey and Sonja. It's there with Mickey, who has Sonja's Raggedy Anne doll hanging from the ceiling. A white tuft of stuffing sticks out of Raggedy Anne's stomach. My mom's butcher knife is clutched in one of Mickey's hands, the doll carefully steadied in the other hand.

She is teaching Sonja how to play 'kill.'

Her tone is academic, motherly. She shows how the blade tip should enter the side. "It is most powerful if you cut up, toward heaven," she tells Sonja.

I remember when Raggedy Anne was passed down to me, how I'd always been curious about her stitches. Maybe she'd been jumping on the bed, or fallen from a tree.

Now when I pick up Raggedy Anne I see my mom in the door, her hand going to her mouth. This frightens her more than anything she has seen in her life, because that's *her* little girl, her Sonja, that is watching Mickey, learning from her. And what if Mickey decided one day to turn that knife on something alive? Maybe one of her little girls even?

That instant is frozen in my head, my mom watching the girls with a hand over her mouth. Raggedy Anne hanging from the ceiling. The knife. Mickey's steady, instructive speech. Mickey is trying so hard to be a good big sister.

My mom must have called my dad then, cried, told him to come get her, take Mickey back. And how sad he would have been, how practical, coming for her, taking her back to the city. The long drive silent as the car left the lovely green paradise behind. A hug good bye, a pat on the head, a "be good." These are all sad as I watch them in my imagination, but still I see Mickey, in that room with Sonja, playing kill, playing the big sister as best she could while her mother's ghost stood behind her, the expression on her face unreadable.

Hungry Coyote

Judi Calhoun

"JAKE REDHORSE, from Flagstaff," said the store clerk; he held my driver's license close to his glasses, studying my photo. "You don't look like no Indian." He was the nerdy nosy type, wearing a black sweat-shirt with white bold lettering, *New Hampshire 603 rules.*

"You're a long way from home. At least, you're not one of those Massholes," he glanced at me from over the top of his glasses. "What tribe are you from?"

I felt my chin jut out and my eyes lock onto his. I fought the urge to pound the turd into next week.

"Sorry, I guess I wasn't being politically correct," he said nervously, handing me back my license. His eyes still on me, slowly he lifted the twenty-dollar bill off the top of the twelve-pack of Heineken, and turned to his register.

A wind gust slammed into the sign-covered storefront windows and forced the double doors open enough for some snow to rush inside, along with a strident, high-pitched shrill.

"This is a really bad storm," he said, studying a monitor hanging from the ceiling on the opposite wall, where a female broadcaster was pointing at a weather map. "If this keeps up all night, they just might shut down the interstate. They did last week. You traveling very far?"

I stared him down as I moved my jacket aside to slide my wallet into the back pocket of my jeans, watching him catch a glimpse of my 9 mm Beretta.

"Are… are you a cop?" he stammered, staring at my gun.

I grabbed my beer from the counter, and stepped away feeling his eyes following me out the door. The thick, wet snow struck my face with a raw wind gust. I held onto my Stetson, cursing this east coast misery. I climbed swiftly into my black SUV and opened a beer before starting the engine.

Nosey son of a bitch! Maybe I should have emptied my mag into his scrawny ass. Nah, he wasn't worth the ammo. What the hell was wrong with me? I was used to dealing with punks like him. People sucked no matter where you go, except maybe Flagstaff. Suddenly, I was feeling homesick. Thinking about watching star trails on the Reservation with old friends, beer, and war stories and that damn government housing – I'd never live there again, but still honor my people who do.

I glanced down at the manila file folder on the seat next to me, flipped it open and stared at a bad photo of Chris Stonecryer – unnecessary, since I knew him. He was a Company man, but not a very good one, with a slightly balding head, unshaven round cheeks, very small eyes, and lack of attention to detail. All his information was printed out neatly on official ink-jet paper.

He was thirty-five, born in Somerville, moved to Cambridge. Last year, his wife found nirvana. She shaved her head and left with the loony people for California. He's not the first man to be dumped by a wife who went crackers and joined some doomsday cult, and he probably won't be the last.

None of that mattered because his number was up. He was my next target. I was ten miles outside of Boston, in the burbs, wishing my job was over. Wishing I was sitting at home in front of my fireplace, watching the Broncos beat the Cardinals, slugging down a twelve pack and trying to forget the looks on my victims' faces when they knew they were about to die.

Some days I wondered how many people would be alive if I'd just given up this stinking job and gone into another line of work. The SOBs that I got, would have taken out other innocent people... and maybe I'd even have myself a wife or a family, well... maybe not.

Either way, it didn't matter much. I couldn't quit. I knew the score. Just like my target, Chris – he'd made too many mistakes. He was sloppy. If I got sloppy or tried to run, I'd be terminated next.

The wind slammed against the side of the SUV, rocking and strong-arming the fenders, trying unsuccessfully to lift this two-thousand-pound machine, as if it were a worthy opponent.

I closed my eyes after a moment, enjoying the taste of my Heineken. Navajo drumbeats commenced their tense rhythm inside my brain. I could feel it; an open vision was coming. My Shaman grandfather puffing on that stone pipe, sitting in the lodge on a dream quest. He always had foresights about my dangerous future.

"Foolish Grandson, why must you live and die another man's life? In youth, you are so old, wrinkled before your time."

Shit! He was right. I was ancient. Only thirty years old, but I looked forty-nine. The business of death makes you old. I knew that was true, and yet I would harden my thoughts and do the job. I was the best. That's why they called me.

"Jacob, every new moon Death calls your name...soon Jacob will be dead. Come home Little Mule. The spirits will protect you."

Tap, tap, tap!

I opened my eyes to see the store clerk knocking on the glass. My hand went immediately for my gun. I didn't trust anyone, no matter how harmless they looked, and he didn't look completely harmless. I pushed the button to roll down the window, and I raised the Beretta, pointing the barrel in his face. "What do you want, Squirrel?"

His hands flew up with a gesture of surrender, and he started to tremble.

"I... I saw your eyes closed. I... I thought you were dead."

"Do I look dead?"

"Ah... um, no Sir. Um... you forgot your change." He slowly drew his hand from his outside pocket to take out two one dollar bills and some silver coins.

"Keep it!" I said immediately shutting the window as fast as the damn button would permit. I watched the wide-eyed clerk disappear into the heavy snow, glancing backward way too many times.

I can't even enjoy a beer in peace.

I was about to put it into gear when a white Altima stopped a few parking spots away. A beautiful young woman, maybe in her late twenties, rushed inside. Some kind of long smock or blouse stuck out under her jacket (heavy but too short) and ribbons of deep auburn hair dangled from the pile on top, as if rebels declaring her to be beautiful.

I couldn't stop looking at her as if she were an angel. I did something I never do. I fantasized about what it might be like to be married to that woman.

Jackass! She's probably already married.

I glanced at the clock on the dashboard: three thirty-five a.m. I downed another beer, and slipped the SUV into gear.

The main road was nearly deserted as I maneuvered onto the slick pavement. I thought about that woman and wondered why she was out on a night like this, wondered where she worked, and almost wished I had a normal job.

I've lost my mind or something. Where was this stupid melancholy coming from? *Snap out of it, Redhorse!*

I drew myself up taller in the seat and drove onto the freeway. I ponied-up a safe distance behind a state truck spraying salt and sand from the spreader that hung beneath the massive tailgate. We were going slow enough to keep the law off my back.

I took the exit that would get me over to Route 2 heading south. The snow had let up a little, but the roads were a mess. I pushed the four-wheel drive button and only slid once when I turned onto River Street before making another left onto Franklin.

The lights from a coffee shop, *Anna's Place*, warmed up the cold, falling snow. The blow-up technicolor images of blueberry cakes in the front window made my mouth water just thinking about the smell and taste.

Not now. Business first, that was the Redhorse way. I found Stonecryer's apartment, did a U-turn and thanks to a citywide parking ban, I was able to pull up in front of the building across the street.

Something was wrong. It just didn't feel right. It was too clean – too easy.

Those Navajo drums… wood on leather, mellow music pounding now inside my heart. My dead grandfather wanted to talk… to show me a vision. This was not the time to close my eyes and go into a trance, but his voice broke through my stubborn ignorance. *"Jacob, coyote is always out there waiting, and coyote is always hungry."*

That ancient proverb may have served me well all my life, but *Grandfather just let me go, let me do my job.*

The moment I got out, another blast of wind tried to steal my breath as well as my hat. I struggled with the gale-force squall, wrestled with the back door. I leaned inside and dropped my hat on the seat, unzipped my bag and found my Glock. I made sure it had a full mag, before I screwed on the silencer, then shoved it down the back of my pants. Glancing around the silent snowy streets, I shut and locked the SUV.

I checked my cell. It was 4:01 a.m. I turned off my phone before I shoved the key into the apartment building front door lock, and felt the doorknob turn in my hand. The job always came with keys. It was better than the old days, when you could get arrested for breaking into a place, never mind the murder charge.

Stepping inside, I was grateful to be out of that shitty storm.

Holding my Stetson in my hand shaking it, I wiped my wet hair away from my face and studied the bank of metal mailboxes, confirming Stonecryer's apartment number: C3. I pushed open the inside door and glanced around the dark hallway before I started climbing the stairs.

The plan was simple: I'd find him sleeping. I'd put two rounds into his head, take a quick photo on my smartphone, hit Send, and a check for ten thousand dollars would be deposited in my bank account within ten minutes. Then I'd be on my way to the next job.

Even before I reached the top step I knew there was a problem. The dim light of the hallway reflected brightly on his angled-open door. *Shit!*

I swiftly grabbed my Glock and held it snug against my leg as I moved stealthily toward the open door. *Be invisible,* I told myself, glancing into the darkness. Holding my breath, I leaned against the wall, cursing my luck.

There was no noise coming from any of the apartments. A child's softball and baseball bat were laying in front of apartment C5, just dropped, as if by the child arriving home late. I cringe at the thought of a child sleeping only two doors down, with things going wrong. I moved silently, snatching them, and shoving the gun up under my armpit. I used the bat to push the apartment door slowly, further open, hearing it creak as it moved.

Nothing.

I held my breath and tossed the ball inside.

I heard the pop first, turned to get out of the line of fire. A ripple of small explosions started in the room just behind my back. The percussion and flames sent me flying. I felt my Glock fall somewhere – I cringed at the thought. The loss of my weapon would be considered sloppy work, and the first mark on my record – but I couldn't even try to find it. I went flailing, grabbed for the railing and hauled my ass over, landing hard on the stairs below. I could feel my ankle snap. The pain shot up my leg. My right hand was burned by whatever the hell that was, and it felt as if the fire took all my bones, rendering my hand and ankle useless.

Damn coyote bad luck! I should have known. I had no choice but to lay there for what was probably only a half a minute, but felt like a half hour of vulnerability, laid out, helpless.

Dizzy now from the pain, I rushed down two flights, hearing more explosions ripping through the upstairs apartments. I was out the door and finally able to breathe. I shoved my hand into a snow bank and screamed low from the torturous pain shooting up my arm, watering my eyes.

My SUV was gone. Was I out long enough for it to have been towed? It wasn't the authorities, or the place would be swimming with cops... *shit, how long was I out?* Unless someone with keys – the Company?

Suddenly I understood, Chris *was not* the target. I was. The tables had turned.

If I use my phone, they could easily track me. I hobbled down the dim street, snow and wind slamming into me. I was heading for that coffee shop when a dark figure stepped from beneath the shadowy scaffolding of a half-renovated brownstone.

Immediately, I reached for my Berretta. The pain in my hand nearly brought me to my knees. My fingers refused to bend.

"Redhorse," said Chris, holding a gun on me. "I guess you're not as smart as I was worried you might be."

Hiding my bloody hand behind my leg, I drew closer to faced him down, warrior to warrior. "Why does the Company want me dead?"

He laughed with a deranged look on his fat face. "*They* don't want you dead – I do! I want to make the big money, just like you do. I figured if I killed badass-Jake Redhorse, those Company assholes would have to take me seriously. I hacked into their database and found my name at the top of the list. So yeah, badass-Redhorse, I knew it would be you who came gunning for me."

"You've botched way too many jobs, Chris," I said. "They're never going to promote you or give you more money. You kill me, and an even bigger price tag will be on your head."

"No," he was breathing heavily and nervously wiping sweat from his face with his coat sleeve. "You're wrong, Jake. I'm going to prove it to you, and to them. Bounty boys like you are a dime a freakin' dozen, but a man like me, who can come up with his own resources and even trick a bounty-boy… I'm worth more to them if they put me in management, and I'm dangerous to them if they don't, and with you dead, they'll know it."

He raised his arm, and I watched his finger lightly squeeze the trigger. That's when I rushed him. I might have knocked a smaller man on his ass, but Stonecryer's girth kept him standing.

The gun went off. Blood exploded from my arm.

Son-of-a-bitch! It burned like hell. My Navajo spirit guide kicked me in the ass. All my Ancestors were with me in spirit filling me with this unexpected, awesome rush of adrenaline that spiked through me – a spear-thrust of anger. I pounded him in the nose. Blood gushed and he whined like a baby but didn't go down. We struggled, and I kept trying to get the gun from his hands. It went off again, this time hitting me in the chest.

The pain felt as if my heart was being sliced out of my chest by a machete. I must have been already dead and yet still fighting with a fat man on the snowy streets of Boston.

"What the hell are you made of?" asked Chris. "A normal person would be dead right now! Are you some kind of super machine?"

"Give me that gun, you asshole," my voice heavy, my dizziness growing.

The gun went off again. This time, the force knocked me backward onto the un-shoveled sidewalk. I lay still, feeling the cold flakes as they melted on my face, as the blood pooled and coagulated in the snow.

* * *

Eight years old and I was standing in the woods with my gun-site set on a large Elk doe. Grandfather was holding my elbows to steady my aim, but I lowered the barrel of my gun.

"I can't do it, Grandfather," I said. "I can't kill."

"Jacob, a brave man must die only once, but a coward dies many times. Do you understand?"

I nodded yes, but I really didn't understand, and yet I wanted to, desperately. I took a deep breath and swung my rifle up, pulled the trigger. When the round struck her upper shoulder, the fear in her eyes branded a fire rod in my soul. She staggered some, and then wild panic forced her feet to run… run with fear, perhaps believing she could outrun death. I wondered if in that moment, on the threshold of eternity, did she feel more alive, was there a spark of brilliant clarity right before the light was fully extinguished from her eyes? Yes, just like her, I also believed I could outrun death.

On that warm autumn morning with Grandfather, something died inside of me too. Since then, I have died a thousand times, and now I was bleeding out in a strange land. *"…a coward dies many times. Do you understand?"* I had not understood the question that day…

My eyes opened when a flash lit up the darkness. Chris had taken a photo with his cell phone and was turned away from me, but I could see him smiling as he typed a message with his thumbs. My breath scurried off with the demon wind into the snow-filled night sky.

* * *

"Mr. Redhorse," said a strong female voice. "Can you hear me?"

"Where am I?" I asked into the ether, opening my eyes, taking inventory of my body and surroundings. I saw the bandages on my hand. My chest felt dented and heavy as if coyote himself was standing on top of me all night.

There was a familiar face gazing down at me. *Familiar?* And then I knew why. She was the woman from the quick mart. *Well, well, how ironic. So, this is where she works.*

"Welcome back, Mr. Redhorse," she said, placing my chart on the small table next to me. "You are here at Tufts Medical Center." Taking a warm and firm hold of my wrist, she glanced down at her watch. "You're a very lucky man, a half inch closer to your heart and you'd be dead. As it is, your left lung was grazed and you nearly drown before they stopped the bleeding. Do you know who did this to you?"

"No," I lied. My first words to the owner of that beautiful burnt umber hair, and I lied.

"The fire department found you. They were on a call for an explosion a block away. The police want me to ask you: Do you know anything about that incident? Is that the incident that brought you here?"

"I wish I could answer your questions," I said. "But right now, I just don't know."

I half wondered if she figured out that I was feeding her lies, but she didn't ask any more questions. Nobody did. I'd been holding my breath for the police to come, but they never came. The Company always cleaned up every loose end.

Seven days later when I was strong enough to walk, I found my clothes in the closet, and my cell phone still inside my jacket pocket. I had five missed calls and two text messages. I glanced at the last one. It was under the Company group name, and said two words: *JKR Terminated.*

A *brave man must die but once*...Grandfather's words still rang in my head. They thought I was dead. When that slime, Chris, took my photo and sent it to the Company, they Terminated me.

Chris was supposed to destroy my cell, as it was the only thing on me that could possibly lead back to the Company. A big part of the job was getting rid of *all* evidence. Chris was sloppy and not a good Company man. He never would be. And they would never trust him with a promotion.

All I needed to do was make one phone call, and Chris would be dead, and I'd be back in business. I held my thumb over the number ready to dial.

"*Jacob,*" said Grandfather. "*A warrior recognizes the end of seasons and knows when to lay down his weapons. Remember what I have said many times, your first teacher is your own heart.*"

My heart asked me the question; *do you want to return to this blood profession?*

I leaned on my cane heavily as I turned slowly toward the bathroom. I glanced at my reflection then back down at the cell phone and smiled. What the hell, Chris would be dead soon anyway. My heart was my teacher.

I didn't hesitate – I dropped the phone into the toilet and flushed my old existence away.

See How They Run

Ramsey Campbell

THROUGH THE READING of the charges Foulsham felt as if the man in the dock was watching him. December sunshine like ice transmuted into illumination slanted through the high windows of the courtroom, spotlighting the murderer. With his round slightly pouting face and large dark moist eyes Fishwick resembled a schoolboy caught red-handed, Foulsham thought, except that surely no schoolboy would have confronted the prospect of retribution with such a look of imperfectly concealed amusement mingled with impatience.

The indictment was completed. "How do you plead?"

"Not guilty," Fishwick said in a high clear voice with just a hint of mischievous emphasis on the first word. Foulsham had the impression that he was tempted to take a bow, but instead Fishwick folded his arms and glanced from the prosecuting counsel to the defence, cueing their speeches so deftly that Foulsham felt his own lips twitch.

"…a series of atrocities so cold-blooded that the jury may find it almost impossible to believe that any human being could be capable of them…" "…evidence that a brilliant mind was tragically damaged by a lifetime of abuse…" Fishwick met both submissions with precisely the same attitude, eyebrows slightly raised, a forefinger drumming on his upper arm as though he were commenting in code on the proceedings. His look of lofty patience didn't change as one of the policemen who had arrested him gave evidence, and Foulsham sensed that Fishwick was eager to get to the meat of the case. But the judge adjourned the trial for the day, and Fishwick contented himself with a faint anticipatory smirk.

The jurors were escorted past the horde of reporters and through the business district to their hotel. Rather to Foulsham's surprise, none of his fellow jurors mentioned Fishwick, neither over dinner nor afterwards, when the jury congregated in the cavernous lounge as if they were reluctant to be alone. Few of the jurors showed much enthusiasm for breakfast, so that Foulsham felt slightly guilty for clearing his plate. He was the last to leave the table and the first to reach the door of the hotel, telling himself that he wanted to be done with the day's ordeal. Even the sight of a newsvendor's placard which proclaimed FISHWICK JURY SEE HORROR PICTURES TODAY failed to deter him.

Several of the jurors emitted sounds of distress as the pictures were passed along the front row. A tobacconist shook his head over them, a gesture which seemed on the point of growing uncontrollable. Some of Foulsham's companions on the back row craned forwards for a preview, but Foulsham restrained himself; they were here to be dispassionate, after all. As the pictures came towards him, growls of outrage and murmurs of dismay marking their progress, he began to feel unprepared, in danger of performing clumsily in front of the massed audience. When at last the pictures reached him he gazed at them for some time without looking up.

They weren't as bad as he had secretly feared. Indeed, what struck him most was their economy and skill. With just a few strokes of a black felt-tipped pen, and the occasional embellishment of red, Fishwick had captured everything he wanted to convey about his subjects: the grotesqueness which had overtaken their gait as they attempted to escape once he'd severed a muscle; the way the crippled dance of each victim gradually turned into a crawl – into less than that once Fishwick had dealt with both arms. No doubt he'd been as skilful with the blade as he was with the pen. Foulsham was re-examining the pictures when the optician next to him nudged him. "The rest of us have to look too, you know."

Foulsham waited several seconds before looking up. Everyone in the courtroom was watching the optician now – everyone but Fishwick. This time there was no question that the man in the dock was gazing straight at Foulsham, whose face stiffened into a mask he wanted to believe was expressionless. He was struggling to look away when the last juror gave an appalled cry and began to crumple the pictures. The judge hammered an admonition, the usher rushed to reclaim the evidence, and Fishwick stared at Foulsham as if they were sharing a joke. The flurry of activity let Foulsham look away, and he did his best to copy the judge's expression of rebuke tempered with sympathy for the distressed woman.

That night he couldn't get to sleep for hours. Whenever he closed his eyes he saw the sketches Fishwick had made. The trial wouldn't last forever, he reminded himself; soon his life would return to normal. Every so often, as he lay in the dark that smelled of bath soap and disinfectant and carpet shampoo, the taps in the bathroom released a gout of water with a choking sound. Each time that happened, the pictures in his head lurched closer, and he felt as if he was being watched. Would he feel like that over Christmas if, as seemed likely, the trial were to continue into the new year? But it lacked almost a week to Christmas when Fishwick was called to the witness box, and Fishwick chose that moment, much to the discomfiture of his lawyer, to plead guilty after all.

The development brought gasps from the public gallery, an exodus from the press benches, mutters of disbelief and anger from the jury; but Foulsham experienced only relief. When the court rose as though to celebrate the turn of events he thought the case was over until he saw that the judge was withdrawing to speak to the lawyers. "The swine," the tobacconist whispered fiercely, glaring at Fishwick. "He made all those people testify for nothing."

Soon the judge and the lawyers returned. It had apparently been decided that the defence should call several psychiatrists to state their views of Fishwick's mental condition. The first of them had scarcely opened his mouth, however, when Fishwick began to express impatience as severe as Foulsham sensed more than one of the jurors were suffering. The man in the dock protruded his tongue like a caricature of a madman and emitted a creditable imitation of a jolly banjo which all but drowned out the psychiatrist's voice. Eventually the judge had Fishwick removed from the court, though not without a struggle, and the psychiatrists were heard.

Fishwick's mother had died giving birth to him, and his father had never forgiven him. The boy's first schoolteacher had seen the father tearing up pictures Fishwick had painted for him. There was some evidence that the father had been prone to uncontrollable fits of violence against the child, though the boy had always insisted that he had broken his own leg by falling downstairs. All of Fishwick's achievements as a young man seemed to have antagonised the father – his exercising his leg for years until he was able to conceal his limp, his enrolment in an art college, the praise which his teachers heaped on him and which he valued less than a word of encouragement from his father. He'd been in his twenties, and still living with his father, when a gallery had offered to exhibit his work. Nobody knew what his father had said which had caused Fishwick to destroy all his paintings in despair and to overcome his disgust at working in his father's shop in order to learn the art of butchery. Before long he had been able to rent a bed-sitter, and thirteen months after moving into it he'd tracked down one of his former schoolfellows who used to call him Quasimodo on account of his limp and his dispirited slouch. Four victims later, Fishwick had made away with his father and the law had caught up with him.

Very little of this had been leaked to the press. Foulsham found himself imagining Fishwick brooding sleeplessly in a cheerless room, his creative nature and his need to prove himself festering within him until he was unable to resist the compulsion to carry out an act which would make him feel meaningful. The other jurors were less impressed. "I might have felt some sympathy for him if he'd gone straight for his father," the hairdresser declared once they were in the jury room.

Fishwick had taken pains to refine his technique first, Foulsham thought, and might have said so if the tobacconist hadn't responded. "I've no sympathy for that cold fish," the man said between puffs at a briar. "You can see he's still enjoying himself. He only pleaded not guilty so that all those people would have to be reminded what they went through."

"We can't be sure of that," Foulsham protested.

"More worried about him than about his victims, are you?" the tobacconist demanded, and the optician intervened. "I know it seems incredible that anyone could enjoy doing what he did," she said to Foulsham, "but that creature's not like us."

Foulsham would have liked to be convinced of that. After all, if Fishwick weren't insane, mustn't that mean anyone was capable of such behaviour? "I think he pleaded guilty when he realised that everyone was going to hear all those things about him he wanted to keep secret," he said. "I think he thought that if he pleaded guilty the psychiatrists wouldn't be called."

The eleven stared at him. "You think too much," the tobacconist said.

The hairdresser broke the awkward silence by clearing her throat. "I never thought I'd say this, but I wish they'd bring back hanging just for him."

"That's the Christmas present he deserves," said the veterinarian who had crumpled the evidence.

The foreman of the jury, a bank manager, proposed that it was time to discuss what they'd learned at the trial. "Personally, I don't mind where they lock him up so long as they throw away the key."

His suggestion didn't satisfy most of the jurors. The prosecuting counsel had questioned the significance of the psychiatric evidence, and the judge had hinted broadly in his summing-up that it was inconclusive. It took all the jurors apart from Foulsham less than half an hour to dismiss the notion that Fishwick might have been unable to distinguish right from wrong, and then they gazed expectantly at Foulsham, who had a disconcerting sense that Fishwick was awaiting his decision too. "I don't suppose it matters where they lock him up," he began, and got no further; the rest of the jury responded with cheers and applause, which sounded ironic to him. Five minutes later they'd agreed to recommend a life sentence for each of Fishwick's crimes. "That should keep him out of mischief," the bank manager exulted.

As the jury filed into the courtroom Fishwick leaned forwards to scrutinise their faces. His own was blank. The foreman stood up to announce the verdict, and Foulsham was suddenly grateful to have that done on his behalf. He hoped Fishwick would be put away for good. When the judge confirmed six consecutive life sentences, Foulsham released a breath which he hadn't been aware of holding. Fishwick had shaken his head when asked if he had anything to say before sentence was passed, and his face seemed to lose its definition as he listened to the judge's pronouncement. His gaze trailed across the jury as he was led out of the dock.

Once Foulsham was out of the building, in the crowded streets above which glowing Santas had been strung up, he didn't feel as liberated as he'd hoped. Presumably that would happen when sleep had caught up with him. Just now he was uncomfortably aware how all the mannequins in the store windows had been twisted into posing. Whenever shoppers turned from gazing into a window he thought they were emerging from the display. As he dodged through the shopping precinct, trying to avoid shoppers rendered angular by packages, families mined with small children, clumps of onlookers surrounding the open suitcases of street traders, he felt as if the maze of bodies were crippling his progress.

Foulsham's had obviously been thriving in his absence. The shop was full of people buying Christmas cards and rolled-up posters and framed prints. "Are you glad it's over?" Annette asked him. "He won't ever be let out, will he?"

"Was he as horrible as the papers made out?" Jackie was eager to know.

"I can't say. I didn't see them," Foulsham admitted, experiencing a surge of panic as Jackie produced a pile of tabloids from under the counter. "I'd rather forget," he said hastily.

"You don't need to read about it, Mr Foulsham, you lived through it," Annette said. "You look as though Christmas can't come too soon for you."

"If I oversleep tomorrow I'll be in on Monday," Foulsham promised, and trudged out of the shop.

All the taxis were taken, and so he had to wait almost half an hour for a bus. If he hadn't been so exhausted he might have walked home. As the bus laboured uphill he clung to the dangling strap which was looped around his wrist and stared at a grimacing rubber clown whose limbs were struggling to unbend from the bag into which they'd been forced. Bodies swayed against him like meat in a butcher's lorry, until he was afraid of being trapped out of reach of the doors when the bus came to his stop.

As he climbed his street, where frost glittered as if the tarmac was reflecting the sky, he heard children singing carols in the distance or on television. He let himself into the house on the brow of the hill, and the poodles in the ground-floor flat began to yap as though he was a stranger. They continued barking while he sorted through the mail which had accumulated on the hall table: bills, advertisements, Christmas cards from people he hadn't heard from since last year. "Only me, Mrs Hutton," he called as he heard her and her stick plodding through her rooms towards the clamour. Jingling his keys as further proof of his identity, and feeling unexpectedly like a jailer, he hurried upstairs and unlocked his door.

Landscapes greeted him. Two large framed paintings flanked the window of the main room: a cliff baring strata of ancient stone above a deserted beach, fields spiky with hedgerows and tufted with sheep below a horizon where a spire poked at fat clouds as though to pop them; beyond the window, the glow of streetlamps streamed downhill into a pool of light miles wide from which pairs of headlight beams were flocking. The pleasure and the sense of all-embracing calm which he habitually experienced on coming home seemed to be standing back from him. He dumped his suitcase in the bedroom and hung up his coat, then he took the radio into the kitchen.

He didn't feel like eating much. He finished off a slice of toast laden with baked beans, and wondered whether Fishwick had eaten yet, and what his meal might be. As soon as he'd sluiced plate and fork he made for his armchair with the radio. Before long, however, he'd had enough of the jazz age. Usually the dance music of that era roused his nostalgia for innocence, not least because the music was older than he was, but just now it seemed too good to be true. So did the views on the wall and beyond the window, and the programmes on the television – the redemption of a cartoon Scrooge, commercials chortling "Ho ho ho", an appeal on behalf of people who would be on their own at Christmas, a choir reiterating "Let nothing you display", the syntax of which he couldn't grasp. As his mind fumbled with it, his eyelids drooped. He nodded as though agreeing with himself that he had better switch off the television, and then he was asleep.

Fishwick wakened him. Agony flared through his right leg. As he lurched out of the chair, trying to blink away the blur which coated his eyes, he was afraid the leg would fail him. He collapsed back into the chair, thrusting the leg in front of him, digging his fingers into the calf in an attempt to massage away the cramp. When at last he was able to bend the leg without having to grit his teeth, he set about recalling what had invaded his sleep.

The nine o'clock news had been ending. It must have been a newsreader who had spoken Fishwick's name. Foulsham hadn't been fully awake, after all; no wonder he'd imagined that the voice sounded like the murderer's. Perhaps it had been the hint of amusement which his imagination had seized upon, though would a newsreader have sounded amused? He switched off the television and waited for the news on the local radio station, twinges in his leg ensuring that he stayed awake.

He'd forgotten that there was no ten o'clock news. He attempted to phone the radio station, but five minutes of hanging on brought him only a message like an old record on which the needle had stuck, advising him to try later. By eleven he'd hobbled to bed. The newsreader raced through accounts of violence and drunken driving, then rustled her script. "Some news just in," she said. "Police report that convicted murderer Desmond Fishwick has taken his own life while in custody. Full details in our next bulletin."

That would be at midnight. Foulsham tried to stay awake, not least because he didn't understand how, if the local station had only just received the news, the national network could have broadcast it more than ninety minutes earlier. But when midnight came he was asleep. He wakened in the early hours and heard voices gabbling beside him, insomniacs trying to assert themselves on a phone-in programme before the presenter cut them short. Foulsham switched off the radio and imagined the city riddled with cells in which people lay or paced, listening to the babble of their own caged obsessions. At least one of them – Fishwick – had put himself out of his misery. Foulsham massaged his leg until the ache relented sufficiently to let sleep overtake him.

The morning newscast said that Fishwick had killed himself last night, but little else. The tabloids were less reticent, Foulsham discovered once he'd dressed and hurried to the newsagent's. MANIAC'S BLOODY SUICIDE. SAVAGE KILLER SAVAGES HIMSELF. HE BIT OFF MORE THAN HE COULD CHEW. Fishwick had gnawed the veins out of his arms and died from loss of blood.

He must have been insane to do that to himself, Foulsham thought, clutching his heavy collar shut against a vicious wind as he limped downhill. While bathing he'd been tempted to take the day off, but now he didn't want to be alone with the images which the news had planted in him. Everyone around him on the bus seemed to be reading one or other of the tabloids which displayed Fishwick's face on the front page like posters for the suicide, and he felt as though all the paper eyes were watching him. Once he was off the bus he stuffed his newspaper into the nearest bin.

Annette and Jackie met him with smiles which looked encouraging yet guarded, and he knew they'd heard about the death. The shop was already full of customers buying last-minute cards and presents for people they'd almost forgotten, and it was late morning before the staff had time for a talk. Foulsham braced himself for the onslaught of questions and comments, only to find that Jackie and Annette were avoiding the subject of Fishwick, waiting for him to raise it so that they would know how he felt, not suspecting that he didn't know himself. He tried to lose himself in the business of the shop, to prove to them that they needn't be so careful of him; he'd never realised how much their teasing and joking meant to him. But they hardly spoke to him until the last customer had departed, and then he sensed that they'd discussed what to say to him. "Don't you let it matter to you, Mr Foulsham. He didn't," Annette said.

"Don't you dare let it spoil your evening," Jackie told him.

She was referring to the staff's annual dinner. While he hadn't quite forgotten about it, he seemed to have gained an impression that it hadn't much to do with him. He locked the shop and headed for home to get changed. After twenty minutes of waiting in a bus queue whose disgruntled mutters felt like flies bumbling mindlessly around him he walked home, the climb aggravating his limp.

He put on his dress shirt and bow tie and slipped his dark suit out of the bag in which it had been hanging since its January visit to the cleaners. As soon as he was dressed he went out again, away from the sounds of Mrs Hutton's three-legged trudge and of the dogs, which hadn't stopped barking since he had entered the house. Nor did he care for the way Mrs Hutton had opened her door and peered at him with a suspiciousness which hadn't entirely vanished when she saw him.

He was at the restaurant half an hour before the rest of the parry. He sat at the bar, sipping a scotch and then another, thinking of people who must do so every night in preference to sitting alone at home, though might some of them be trying to avoid doing something worse? He was glad when his party arrived, Annette and her husband, Jackie and her new boyfriend, even though Annette's greeting as he stood up disconcerted him. "Are you all right, Mr Foulsham?" she said, and he felt unpleasantly wary until he realised that she must be referring to his limp.

By the time the turkey arrived at the table the party had opened a third bottle of wine and the conversation had floated loose. "What was he like, Mr Foulsham," Jackie's boyfriend said, "the feller you put away?"

Annette coughed delicately. "Mr Foulsham may not want to talk about it."

"It's all right, Annette. Perhaps I should. He was—" Foulsham said, and trailed off, wishing that he'd taken advantage of the refuge she was offering. "Maybe he was just someone whose mind gave way."

"I hope you've no regrets," Annette's husband said. "You should be proud."

"Of what?"

"Of stopping the killing. He won't kill anyone else."

Foulsham couldn't argue with that, and yet he felt uneasy, especially when Jackie's boyfriend continued to interrogate him. If Fishwick didn't matter, as Annette had insisted when Foulsham was closing the shop, why was everyone so interested in hearing about him? He felt as though they were resurrecting the murderer, in Foulsham's mind if nowhere else. He tried to describe Fishwick, and retailed as much of his own experience of the trial as he judged they could stomach. All that he left unsaid seemed to gather in his mind, especially the thought of Fishwick extracting the veins from his arms.

Annette and her husband gave him a lift home. He meant to invite them up for coffee and brandy, but the poodles started yapping the moment he climbed out of the car. "Me again, Mrs Hutton," he slurred as he hauled himself along the banister. He switched on the light in his main room and gazed at the landscapes on the wall, but his mind couldn't grasp them. He brushed his teeth and drank as much water as he could take, then he huddled under the blankets, willing the poodles to shut up.

He didn't sleep for long. He kept wakening with a stale rusty taste in his mouth. He'd drunk too much, that was why he felt so hot and sticky and closed in. When he eased himself out of bed and tiptoed to the bathroom the dogs began to bark. He rinsed out his mouth but was unable to determine if the water which he spat into the sink was discoloured. He crept out of the bathroom with a glass of water in each hand and crawled shivering into bed, trying not to grind his teeth as pictures which he would have given a good deal not to see rushed at him out of the dark.

In the morning he felt as though he hadn't slept at all. He lay in the creeping sunlight, too exhausted either to sleep or to get up, until he heard the year's sole Sunday delivery sprawl on the doormat. He washed and dressed gingerly, cursing the poodles, whose yapping felt like knives emerging from his skull, and stumbled down to the hall.

He lined up the new cards on his mantelpiece, where there was just enough room for them. Last year he'd had to stick cards onto a length of parcel tape and hang them from the cornice. This year cards from businesses outnumbered those from friends, unless tomorrow restored the balance. He was signing cards in response to some of the Sunday delivery when he heard Mrs Hutton and the poodles leave the house.

He limped to the window and looked down on her. The two leashes were bunched in her left hand, her right was clenched on her stick. She was leaning backwards as the dogs ran her downhill, and he had never seen her look so crippled. He turned away, unsure why he found the spectacle disturbing. Perhaps he should catch up on his sleep while the dogs weren't there to trouble it, except that if he slept now he might be guaranteeing himself another restless night. The prospect of being alone in the early hours and unable to sleep made him so nervous that he grabbed the phone before he had thought who he could ask to visit.

Nobody had time for him today. Of the people ranked on the mantelpiece, two weren't at home, two were fluttery with festive preparations, one was about to drive several hundred miles to collect his parents, one was almost incoherent with a hangover. All of them invited Foulsham to visit them over Christmas, most of them sounding sincere, but that wouldn't take care of Sunday. He put on his overcoat and gloves and hurried downhill by a route designed to avoid Mrs Hutton, and bought his Sunday paper on the way to a pub lunch.

The Bloody Mary wasn't quite the remedy he was hoping for. The sight of the liquid discomforted him, and so did the scraping of the ice cubes against his teeth. Nor was he altogether happy with his lunch; the leg of chicken put him in mind of the process of severing it from the body. When he'd eaten as much as he could hold down, he fled.

The papery sky was smudged with darker clouds, images too nearly erased to be distinguishable. Its light seemed to permeate the city, reducing its fabric to little more than cardboard. He felt more present than anything around him, a sensation which he didn't relish. He closed his eyes until he thought of someone to visit, a couple who'd lived in the house next to his and whose Christmas card invited him to drop in whenever he was passing their new address.

A double-decker bus on which he was the only passenger carried him across town and deposited him at the edge of the new suburb. The streets of squat houses which looked squashed by their tall roofs were deserted, presumably cleared by the Christmas television shows he glimpsed through windows, and his isolation made him feel watched. He limped into the suburb, glancing at the street names.

He hadn't realised the suburb was so extensive. At the end of almost an hour of limping and occasionally resting, he still hadn't found the address. The couple weren't on the phone, or he would have tried to contact them. He might have abandoned the quest if he hadn't felt convinced that he was about to come face to face with the name which, he had to admit, had slipped his mind. He hobbled across an intersection and then across its twin, where a glance to the left halted him. Was that the street he was looking for? Certainly the name seemed familiar. He strolled along the pavement, trying to conceal his limp, and stopped outside a house.

Though he recognised the number, it hadn't been on the card. His gaze crawled up the side of the house and came to rest on the window set into the roof. At once he knew that he'd heard the address read aloud in the courtroom. It was where Fishwick had lived.

As Foulsham gazed fascinated at the small high window he imagined Fishwick gloating over the sketches he'd brought home, knowing that the widow from whom he rented the bed-sitter was downstairs and unaware of his secret. He came to himself with a shudder, and stumbled away, almost falling. He was so anxious to put the city between himself and Fishwick's room that he couldn't bear to wait for one of the infrequent Sunday buses. By the time he reached home he was gritting his teeth so as not to scream at the ache in his leg. "Shut up," he snarled at the alarmed poodles, "or I'll—" and stumbled upstairs.

The lamps of the city were springing alight. Usually he enjoyed the spectacle, but now he felt compelled to look for Fishwick's window among the distant roofs. Though he couldn't locate it, he was certain that the windows were mutually visible. How often might Fishwick have gazed across the city towards him? Foulsham searched for tasks to distract himself – cleaned the oven, dusted the furniture and the tops of the picture-frames, polished all his shoes, lined up the tins on the kitchen shelves in alphabetical order. When he could no longer ignore the barking which his every movement provoked, he went downstairs and rapped on Mrs Hutton's door.

She seemed reluctant to face him. Eventually he heard her shooing the poodles into her kitchen before she came to peer out at him. "Been having a good time, have we?" she demanded.

"It's the season," he said without an inkling of why he should need to justify himself. "Am I bothering your pets somehow?"

"Maybe they don't recognise your walk since you did whatever you did to yourself."

"It happened while I was asleep." He'd meant to engage her in conversation so that she would feel bound to invite him in – he was hoping that would give the dogs a chance to grow used to him again – but he couldn't pursue his intentions when she was so openly hostile, apparently because she felt entitled to the only limp in the building. "Happy Christmas to you and yours," he flung at her, and hobbled back to his floor.

He wrote out his Christmas card list in case he had overlooked anyone, only to discover that he couldn't recall some of the names to which he had already addressed cards. When he began doodling, slashing at the page so as to sketch stick figures whose agonised contortions felt like a revenge he was taking, he turned the sheet over and tried to read a book. The yapping distracted him, as did the sound of Mrs Hutton's limp; he was sure she was exaggerating it to lay claim to the gait or to mock him. He switched on the radio and searched the wavebands, coming to rest at a choir which was wishing the listener a merry Christmas. He turned up the volume to blot out the noise from below, until Mrs Hutton thumped on her ceiling and the yapping of the poodles began to lurch repetitively at him as they leapt, trying to reach the enemy she was identifying with her stick.

Even his bed was no refuge. He felt as though the window on the far side of the city was an eye spying on him out of the dark, reminding him of all that he was trying not to think of before he risked sleep. During the night he found himself surrounded by capering figures which seemed determined to show him how much life was left in them – how vigorously, if unconventionally, they could dance. He managed to struggle awake at last, and lay afraid to move until the rusty taste like a memory of blood had faded from his mouth.

He couldn't go on like this. In the morning he was so tired that he felt as if he was washing someone else's face and hands. He thought he could feel his nerves swarming. He bared his teeth at the yapping of the dogs and tried to recapture a thought he'd glimpsed while lying absolutely still, afraid to move, in the hours before dawn. What had almost occurred to him about Fishwick's death?

The yapping receded as he limped downhill. On the bus a woman eyed him as if she suspected him of feigning the limp in a vain attempt to persuade her to give up her seat. The city streets seemed full of people who were staring at him, though he failed to catch them in the act. When Jackie and Annette converged on the shop as he arrived he prayed they wouldn't mention his limp. They gazed at his face instead, making him feel they were trying to ignore his leg. "We can cope, Mr Foulsham," Annette said, "if you want to start your Christmas early."

"You deserve it," Jackie added.

What were they trying to do to him? They'd reminded him how often he might be on his own during the next few days, a prospect which filled him with dread. How could he ease his mind in the time left to him? "You'll have to put up with another day of me," he told them as he unlocked the door.

Their concern for him made him feel as if his every move was being observed. Even the Christmas Eve crowds failed to occupy his mind, especially once Annette took advantage of a lull in the day's business to approach him. "We thought we'd give you your present now in case you want to change your mind about going home."

"That's thoughtful of you. Thank you both," he said and retreated into the office, wondering if they were doing their best to get rid of him because something about him was playing on their nerves. He used the phone to order them a bouquet each, a present which he gave them every Christmas but which this year he'd almost forgotten, and then he picked at the parcel until he was able to see what it was.

It was a book of detective stories. He couldn't imagine what had led them to conclude that it was an appropriate present, but it did seem to have a message for him. He gazed at the exposed spine and realised what any detective would have established days ago. Hearing Fishwick's name in the night had been the start of his troubles, yet he hadn't ascertained the time of Fishwick's death.

He phoned the radio station and was put through to the newsroom. A reporter gave him all the information which the police had released. Foulsham thanked her dully and called the local newspaper, hoping they might contradict her somehow, but of course they confirmed what she'd told him. Fishwick had died just before 9:30 on the night when his name had wakened Foulsham, and the media hadn't been informed until almost an hour later.

He sat at his bare desk, his cindery eyes glaring at nothing, then he stumbled out of the cell of an office. The sounds and the heat of the shop seemed to rush at him and recede in waves on which the faces of Annette and Jackie and the customers were floating. He felt isolated, singled out – felt as he had throughout the trial.

Yet if he couldn't be certain that he had been singled out then, why should he let himself feel that way now without trying to prove himself wrong? "I think I will go early after all," he told Jackie and Annette.

Some of the shops were already closing. The streets were almost blocked with people who seemed simultaneously distant from him and too close, their insect eyes and neon faces shining. When at last he reached the alley between two office buildings near the courts, he thought he was too late. But though the shop was locked, he was just in time to catch the hairdresser. As she emerged from a back room, adjusting the strap of a shoulder-bag stuffed with presents, he tapped on the glass of the door.

She shook her head and pointed to the sign which hung against the glass. Didn't she recognise him? His reflection seemed clear enough to him, like a photograph of himself holding the sign at his chest, even if the placard looked more real than he did. "Foulsham," he shouted, his voice echoing from the close walls. "I was behind you on the jury. Can I have a word?"

"What about?"

He grimaced and mimed glancing both ways along the alley, and she stepped forward, halting as far from the door as the door was tall. "Well?"

"I don't want to shout."

She hesitated and then came to the door. He felt unexpectedly powerful, the winner of a game they had been playing. "I remember you now," she said as she unbolted the door. "You're the one who claimed to be sharing the thoughts of that monster."

She stepped back as an icy wind cut through the alley, and he felt as though the weather was on his side, almost an extension of himself. "Well, spit it out," she said as he closed the door behind him.

She was ranging about the shop, checking that the electric helmets which made him think of some outdated mental treatment were switched off, opening and closing cabinets in which blades glinted, peering beneath the chairs which put him in mind of a death cell. "Can you remember exactly when you heard what happened?" he said.

She picked up a tuft of bluish hair and dropped it in a pedal bin. "What did?"

"He killed himself."

"Oh, that? I thought you meant something important." The bin snapped shut like a trap. "I heard about it on the news. I really can't say when."

"Heard about it, though, not read it."

"That's what I said. Why should it matter to you?"

He couldn't miss her emphasis on the last word, and he felt that both her contempt and the question had wakened something in him. He'd thought he wanted to reassure himself that he hadn't been alone in sensing Fishwick's death, but suddenly he felt altogether more purposeful. "Because it's part of us," he said.

"It's no part of me, I assure you. And I don't think I was the only member of the jury who thought you were too concerned with that fiend for your own good."

An unfamiliar expression took hold of Foulsham's face. "Who else did?"

"If I were you, Mr Whatever your name is, I'd seek help, and quick. You'll have to excuse me. I'm not about to let that monster spoil my Christmas." She pursed her lips and said "I'm off to meet some normal people."

Either she thought she'd said too much or his expression and his stillness were unnerving her. "Please leave," she said more shrilly. "Leave now or I'll call the police."

She might have been heading for the door so as to open it for him. He only wanted to stay until he'd grasped why he was there. The sight of her striding to the door reminded him that speed was the one advantage she had over him. Pure instinct came to his aid, and all at once he seemed capable of anything. He saw himself opening the nearest cabinet, he felt his finger and thumb slip through the chilly rings of the handles of the scissors, and lunging at her was the completion of these movements. Even then he thought he meant only to drive her away from the door, but he was reckoning without his limp. As he floundered towards her he lost his balance, and the points of the scissors entered her right leg behind the knee.

She gave an outraged scream and cried to hobble to the door, the scissors wagging in the patch of flesh and blood revealed by the growing hole in the leg of her patterned tights. The next moment she let out a wail so despairing that he almost felt sorry for her, and fell to her knees, well out of reach of the door. As she craned her head over her shoulder to see how badly she was injured, her eyes were the eyes of an animal caught in a trap. She extended one shaky hand to pull out the scissors, but he was too quick for her. "Let me," he said, taking hold other thin wrist.

He thought he was going to withdraw the scissors, but as soon as his finger and thumb were through the rings he experienced an overwhelming surge of power which reminded him of how he'd felt as the verdict of the jury was announced. He leaned on the scissors and exerted all the strength he could, and after a while the blades closed with a sound which, though muffled, seemed intensely satisfying.

Either the shock or her struggles and shrieks appeared to have exhausted her. He had time to lower the blinds over the door and windows and to put on one of the plastic aprons which she and her staff must wear. When she saw him returning with the scissors, however, she tried to fight him off while shoving herself with her uninjured leg towards the door. Since he didn't like her watching him – it was his turn to watch – he stopped her doing so, and screaming. She continued moving for some time after he would have expected her to be incapable of movement, though she obviously didn't realise that she was retreating from the door. By the time she finally subsided he had to admit that the game had grown messy and even a little dull.

He washed his hands until they were clean as a baby's, then he parcelled up the apron and the scissors in the wrapping which had contained his present. He let himself out of the shop and limped towards the bus-stops, the book under one arm, the tools of his secret under the other. It wasn't until passers-by smiled in response to him that he realised what his expression was, though it didn't feel like his own smile, any more than he felt personally involved in the incident at the hairdresser's. Even the memory of all the jurors' names didn't feel like his. At least, he thought, he wouldn't be alone over Christmas, and in future he would try to be less hasty. After all, he and whoever he visited next would have more to discuss.

The Escape of Mr. Trimm

Irvin S. Cobb

MR. TRIMM, recently president of the late Thirteenth National Bank, was taking a trip which was different in a number of ways from any he had ever taken. To begin with, he was used to parlor cars and Pullmans and even luxurious private cars when he went anywhere; whereas now he rode with a most mixed company in a dusty, smelly day coach. In the second place, his traveling companion was not such a one as Mr. Trimm would have chosen had the choice been left to him, being a stupid-looking German-American with a drooping, yellow mustache. And in the third place, Mr. Trimm's plump white hands were folded in his lap, held in a close and enforced companionship by a new and shiny pair of Bean's Latest Model Little Giant handcuffs. Mr. Trimm was on his way to the Federal penitentiary to serve twelve years at hard labor for breaking, one way or another, about all the laws that are presumed to govern national banks.

* * *

All the time Mr. Trimm was in the Tombs, fighting for a new trial, a certain question had lain in his mind unasked and unanswered. Through the seven months of his stay in the jail that question had been always at the back part of his head, ticking away there like a little watch that never needed winding. A dozen times a day it would pop into his thoughts and then go away, only to come back again.

When Copley was taken to the penitentiary – Copley being the cashier who got off with a lighter sentence because the judge and jury held him to be no more than a blind accomplice in the wrecking of the Thirteenth National – Mr. Trimm read closely every line that the papers carried about Copley's departure. But none of them had seen fit to give the young cashier more than a short and colorless paragraph. For Copley was only a small figure in the big intrigue that had startled the country; Copley didn't have the money to hire big lawyers to carry his appeal to the higher courts for him; Copley's wife was keeping boarders; and as for Copley himself, he had been wearing stripes several months now.

With Mr. Trimm it had been vastly different. From the very beginning he had held the public eye. His bearing in court when the jury came in with their judgment; his cold defiance when the judge, in pronouncing sentence, mercilessly arraigned him and the system of finance for which he stood; the manner of his life in the Tombs; his spectacular fight to beat the verdict, had all been worth columns of newspaper space. If Mr. Trimm had been a popular poisoner, or a society woman named as co-respondent in a sensational divorce suit, the papers could not have been more generous in their space allotments. And Mr. Trimm in his cell had read all of it with smiling contempt, even to the semi-hysterical outpourings of the lady special writers who called him The Iron Man of Wall Street and undertook to analyze his emotions – and missed the mark by a thousand miles or two.

Things had been smoothed as much as possible for him in the Tombs, for money and the power of it will go far toward ironing out even the corrugated routine of that big jail. He had a large cell to himself in the airiest, brightest corridor. His meals were served by a caterer from outside. Although he ate them without knife or fork, he soon learned that a spoon and the fingers can accomplish a good deal when backed by a good appetite, and Mr. Trimm's appetite was uniformly good. The warden and his underlings had been models of official kindliness; the newspapers had sent their brightest young men to interview him whenever he felt like talking, which wasn't often; and surely his lawyers had done all in his behalf that money – a great deal of money – could do. Perhaps it was because of these things that Mr. Trimm had never been able to bring himself to realize that he was the Hobart W. Trimm who had been sentenced to the Federal prison; it seemed to him, somehow, that he, personally, was merely a spectator standing to one side watching the fight of another man to dodge the penitentiary.

However, he didn't fail to give the other man the advantage of every chance that money would buy. This sense of aloofness to the whole thing had persisted even when his personal lawyer came to him one night in the early fall and told him that the court of last possible resort had denied the last possible motion. Mr. Trimm cut the lawyer short with a shake of his head as the other began saying something about the chances of a pardon from the President. Mr. Trimm wasn't in the habit of letting men deceive him with idle words. No President would pardon him, and he knew it.

"Never mind that, Walling," he said steadily, when the lawyer offered to come to see him again before he started for prison the next day. "If you'll see that a drawing-room on the train is reserved for me – for us, I mean – and all that sort of thing, I'll not detain you any further. I have a good many things to do tonight. Good night."

"Such a man, such a man," said Walling to himself as he climbed into his car; "all chilled steel and brains. And they are going to lock that brain up for twelve years. It's a crime," said Walling, and shook his head. Walling always said it was a crime when they sent a client of his to prison. To his credit be it said, though, they sent very few of them there. Walling made as high as fifty thousand a year at criminal law. Some of it was very criminal law indeed. His specialty was picking holes in the statutes faster than the legislature could make them and provide them and putty them up with amendments. This was the first case he had lost in a good long time.

* * *

When Jerry, the turnkey, came for him in the morning Mr. Trimm had made as careful a toilet as the limited means at his command permitted, and he had eaten a hearty breakfast and was ready to go, all but putting on his hat. Looking the picture of well-groomed, close-buttoned, iron-gray middle age, Mr. Trimm followed the turnkey through the long corridor and down the winding iron stairs to the warden's office. He gave no heed to the curious eyes that followed him through the barred doors of many cells; his feet rang briskly on the flags.

The warden, Hallam, was there in the private office with another man, a tall, raw-boned man with a drooping, straw-colored mustache and the unmistakable look about him of the police officer. Mr. Trimm knew without being told that this was the man who would take him to prison. The stranger was standing at a desk, signing some papers.

"Sit down, please, Mr. Trimm," said the warden with a nervous cordiality. "Be through here in just one minute. This is Deputy Marshal Meyers," he added.

Mr. Trimm started to tell this Mr. Meyers he was glad to meet him, but caught himself and merely nodded. The man stared at him with neither interest nor curiosity in his dull blue eyes. The warden moved over toward the door.

"Mr. Trimm," he said, clearing his throat, "I took the liberty of calling a cab to take you gents up to the Grand Central. It's out front now. But there's a big crowd of reporters and photographers and a lot of other people waiting, and if I was you I'd slip out the back way – one of my men will open the yard gate for you – and jump aboard the subway down at Worth Street. Then you'll miss those fellows."

"Thank you, Warden – very kind of you," said Mr. Trimm in that crisp, businesslike way of his. He had been crisp and businesslike all his life. He heard a door opening softly behind him, and when he turned to look he saw the warden slipping out, furtively, in almost an embarrassed fashion.

"Well," said Meyers, "all ready?"

"Yes," said Mr. Trimm, and he made as if to rise.

"Wait one minute," said Meyers.

He half turned his back on Mr. Trimm and fumbled at the side pocket of his ill-hanging coat. Something inside of Mr. Trimm gave the least little jump, and the question that had ticked away so busily all those months began to buzz, buzz in his ears; but it was only a handkerchief the man was getting out. Doubtless he was going to mop his face.

He didn't mop his face, though. He unrolled the handkerchief slowly, as if it contained something immensely fragile and valuable, and then, thrusting it back in his pocket, he faced Mr. Trimm. He was carrying in his hands a pair of handcuffs that hung open-jawed. The jaws had little notches in them, like teeth that could bite. The question that had ticked in Mr. Trimm's head was answered at last – in the sight of these steel things with their notched jaws.

Mr. Trimm stood up and, with a movement as near to hesitation as he had ever been guilty of in his life, held out his hands, backs upward.

"I guess you're new at this kind of thing," said Meyers, grinning. "This here way – one at a time."

He took hold of Mr. Trimm's right hand, turned it sideways and settled one of the steel cuffs over the top of the wrist, flipping the notched jaw up from beneath and pressing it in so that it locked automatically with a brisk little click. Slipping the locked cuff back and forth on Mr. Trimm's lower arm like a man adjusting a part of machinery, and then bringing the left hand up to meet the right, he treated it the same way. Then he stepped back.

Mr. Trimm hadn't meant to protest. The word came unbidden.

"This—this isn't necessary, is it?" he asked in a voice that was husky and didn't seem to belong to him.

"Yep," said Meyers. "Standin' orders is play no favorites and take no chances. But you won't find them things uncomfortable. Lightest pair there was in the office, and I fixed 'em plenty loose."

For half a minute Mr. Trimm stood like a rooster hypnotized by a chalkmark, his arms extended, his eyes set on his bonds. His hands had fallen perhaps four inches apart, and in the space between his wrists a little chain was stretched taut. In the mounting tumult that filled his brain there sprang before Mr. Trimm's consciousness a phrase he had heard or read somewhere, the title of a story or, perhaps, it was a headline – The Grips of the Law. The Grips of the Law were upon Mr. Trimm – he felt them now for the first time in these shiny wristlets and this bit of chain that bound his wrists and filled his whole body with a strange, sinking feeling that made him physically sick. A sudden sweat beaded out on Mr. Trimm's face, turning it slick and wet.

He had a handkerchief, a fine linen handkerchief with a hemstitched border and a monogram on it, in the upper breast pocket of his buttoned coat. He tried to reach it. His hands went up, twisting awkwardly like crab claws. The fingers of both plucked out the handkerchief. Holding it so, Mr. Trimm mopped the sweat away. The links of the handcuffs fell in upon one another and lengthened out again at each movement, filling the room with a smart little sound.

He got the handkerchief stowed away with the same clumsiness. He raised the manacled hands to his hat brim, gave it a downward pull that brought it over his face and then, letting his short arms slide down upon his plump stomach, he faced the man who had put the fetters upon him, squaring his shoulders back. But it was hard, somehow, for him to square his shoulders – perhaps because of his hands being drawn so closely together. And his eyes would waver and fall upon his wrists. Mr. Trimm had a feeling that the skin must be stretched very tight on his jawbones and his forehead.

"Isn't there some way to hide these—these things?"

He began by blurting and ended by faltering it. His hands shuffled together, one over, then under the other.

"Here's a way," said Meyers. "This'll help."

He bestirred himself, folding one of the chained hands upon the other, tugging at the white linen cuffs and drawing the coat sleeves of his prisoner down over the bonds as far as the chain would let them come.

"There's the notion," he said. "Just do that-a-way and them bracelets won't hardly show a-tall. Ready? Let's be movin', then."

But handcuffs were never meant to be hidden. Merely a pair of steel rings clamped to one's wrists and coupled together with a scrap of chain, but they'll twist your arms and hamper the movements of your body in a way to constantly catch the eye of the passer-by. When a man is coming toward you, you can tell that he is handcuffed before you see the cuffs.

Mr. Trimm was never able to recall afterward exactly how he got out of the Tombs. He had a confused memory of a gate that was swung open by some one whom Mr. Trimm saw only from the feet to the waist; then he and his companion were out on Lafayette Street, speeding south toward the subway entrance at Worth Street, two blocks below, with the marshal's hand cupped under Mr. Trimm's right elbow and Mr. Trimm's plump legs almost trotting in their haste. For a moment it looked as if the warden's well-meant artifice would serve them.

But New York reporters are up to the tricks of people who want to evade them. At the sight of them a sentry reporter on the corner shouted a warning which was instantly caught up and passed on by another picket stationed half-way down the block; and around the wall of the Tombs came pelting a flying mob of newspaper photographers and reporters, with a choice rabble behind them. Foot passengers took up the chase, not knowing what it was about, but sensing a free show. Truckmen halted their teams, jumped down from their wagon seats and joined in. A man-chase is one of the pleasantest outdoor sports that a big city like New York can offer its people.

Fairly running now, the manacled banker and the deputy marshal shot down the winding steps into the subway a good ten yards ahead of the foremost pursuers. But there was one delay, while Meyers skirmished with his free hand in his trousers' pocket for a dime for the tickets, and another before a northbound local rolled into the station. Shouted at, jeered at, shoved this way and that, panting in gulping breaths, for he was stout by nature and staled by lack of exercise, Mr. Trimm, with Meyers clutching him by the arm, was fairly shot aboard one of the cars, at the apex of a human wedge. The astonished guard sensed the situation as the scrooging, shoving, noisy wave rolled across the platform toward the doors which he had opened and, thrusting the officer and his prisoner into the narrow platform space behind him, he tried to form with his body a barrier against those who came jamming in.

It didn't do any good. He was brushed away, protesting and blustering. The excitement spread through the train, and men, and even women, left their seats, overflowing the aisles.

There is no crueler thing than a city crowd, all eyes and morbid curiosity. But Mr. Trimm didn't see the staring eyes on that ride to the Grand Central. What he saw was many shifting feet and a hedge of legs shutting him in closely – those and the things on his wrists. What the eyes of the crowd saw was a small, stout man who, for all his bulk, seemed to have dried up inside his clothes so that they bagged on him some places and bulged others, with his head tucked on his chest, his hat over his face and his fingers straining to hold his coat sleeves down over a pair of steel bracelets.

Mr. Trimm gave mental thanks to a Deity whose existence he thought he had forgotten when the gate of the train-shed clanged behind him, shutting out the mob that had come with them all the way. Cameras had been shoved in his face like gun muzzles, reporters had scuttled alongside him, dodging under Meyers' fending arm to shout questions in his ears. He had neither spoken nor looked at them. The sweat still ran down his face, so that when finally he raised his head in the comparative quiet of the train-shed his skin was a curious gray under the jail paleness like the color of wet wood ashes.

"My lawyer promised to arrange for a compartment – for some private place on the train," he said to Meyers. "The conductor ought to know."

They were the first words he had uttered since he left the Tombs. Meyers spoke to a jaunty Pullman conductor who stood alongside the car where they had halted.

"No such reservation," said the conductor, running through his sheaf of slips, with his eyes shifting from Mr. Trimm's face to Mr. Trimm's hands and back again, as though he couldn't decide which was the more interesting part of him; "must be some mistake. Or else it was for some other train. Too late to change now – we pull out in three minutes."

"I reckon we better git on the smoker," said Meyers, "if there's room there."

Mr. Trimm was steered back again the length of the train through a double row of pop-eyed porters and staring trainmen. At the steps where they stopped the instinct to stretch out one hand and swing himself up by the rail operated automatically and his wrists got a nasty twist. Meyers and a brakeman practically lifted him up the steps and Meyers headed him into a car that was hazy with blue tobacco smoke. He was confused in his gait, almost as if his lower limbs had been fettered, too.

The car was full of shirt-sleeved men who stood up, craning their necks and stumbling over each other in their desire to see him. These men came out into the aisle, so that Meyers had to shove through them.

"This here'll do as well as any, I guess," said Meyers. He drew Mr. Trimm past him into the seat nearer the window and sat down alongside him on the side next the aisle, settling himself on the stuffy plush seat and breathing deeply, like a man who had got through the hardest part of a not easy job.

"Smoke?" he asked.

Mr. Trimm shook his head without raising it.

"Them cuffs feel plenty easy?" was the deputy's next question. He lifted Mr. Trimm's hands as casually as if they had been his hands and not Mr. Trimm's, and looked at them.

"Seem to be all right," he said as he let them fall back. "Don't pinch none, I reckon?" There was no answer.

The deputy tugged a minute at his mustache, searching his arid mind. An idea came to him. He drew a newspaper from his pocket, opened it out flat and spread it over Mr. Trimm's lap so that it covered the chained wrists. Almost instantly the train was in motion, moving through the yards.

* * *

"Be there in two hours more," volunteered Meyers. It was late afternoon. They were sliding through woodlands with occasional openings which showed meadows melting into wide, flat lands.

"Want a drink?" said the deputy, next. "No? Well, I guess I'll have a drop myself. Travelin' fills a feller's throat full of dust." He got up, lurching to the motion of the flying train, and started forward to the water cooler behind the car door. He had gone perhaps two-thirds of the way when Mr. Trimm felt a queer, grinding sensation beneath his feet; it was exactly as though the train were trying to go forward and back at the same time. Almost slowly, it seemed to him, the forward end of the car slued out of its straight course, at the same time tilting up. There was a grinding, roaring, grating sound, and before Mr. Trimm's eyes Meyers vanished, tumbling forward out of sight as the car floor buckled under his feet. Then, as everything – the train, the earth, the sky – all fused together in a great spatter of white and black, Mr. Trimm, plucked from his seat as though a giant hand had him by the collar, shot forward through the air over the seatbacks, his chained hands aloft, clutching wildly. He rolled out of a ragged opening where the smoker had broken in two, flopped gently on the sloping side of the right-of-way and slid easily to the bottom, where he lay quiet and still on his back in a bed of weeds and wild grass, staring straight up.

How many minutes he lay there Mr. Trimm didn't know. It may have been the shrieks of the victims or the glare from the fire that brought him out of the daze. He wriggled his body to a sitting posture, got on his feet, holding his head between his coupled hands, and gazed full-face into the crowning railroad horror of the year.

There were numbers of the passengers who had escaped serious hurt, but for the most part these persons seemed to have gone daft from terror and shock. Some were running aimlessly up and down and some, a few, were pecking feebly with improvised tools at the wreck, an indescribable jumble of ruin, from which there issued cries of mortal agony, and from which, at a point where two locomotives were lying on their sides, jammed together like fighting bucks that had died with locked horns, a tall flame already rippled and spread, sending up a pillar of black smoke that rose straight, poisoning the clear blue of the sky. Nobody paid any attention to Mr. Trimm as he stood swaying upon his feet. There wasn't a scratch on him. His clothes were hardly rumpled, his hat was still on his head. He stood a minute and then, moved by a sudden impulse, he turned round and went running straight away from the railroad at the best speed his pudgy legs could accomplish, with his arms pumping up and down in front of him and his fingers interlaced. It was a grotesque gait, almost like a rabbit hopping on its hindlegs.

Instantly, almost, the friendly woods growing down to the edge of the fill swallowed him up. He dodged and doubled back and forth among the tree trunks, his small, patent-leathered feet skipping nimbly over the irregular turf, until he stopped for lack of wind in his lungs to carry him another rod. When he had got his breath back Mr. Trimm leaned against a tree and bent his head this way and that, listening. No sound came to his ears except the sleepy calls of birds. As well as Mr. Trimm might judge he had come far into the depths of a considerable woodland. Already the shadows under the low limbs were growing thick and confused as the hurried twilight of early September came on.

Mr. Trimm sat down on a natural cushion of thick green moss between two roots of an oak. The place was clean and soft and sweet-scented. For some little time he sat there motionless, in a sort of mental haze. Then his round body slowly slid down flat upon the moss, his head lolled to one side and, the reaction having come, Mr. Trimm's limbs all relaxed and he went to sleep straightway.

After a while, when the woods were black and still, the half-grown moon came up and, sifting through a chink in the canopy of leaves above, shone down full on Mr. Trimm as he lay snoring gently with his mouth open, and his hands rising and falling on his breast. The moonlight struck upon the Little Giant handcuffs, making them look like quicksilver.

Toward daylight it turned off sharp and cool. The dogwoods which had been a solid color at nightfall now showed pink in one light and green in another, like changeable silk, as the first level rays of the sun came up over the rim of the earth and made long, golden lanes between the tree trunks. Mr. Trimm opened his eyes slowly, hardly sensing for the first moment or two how he came to be lying under a canopy of leaves, and gaped, seeking to stretch his arms. At that he remembered everything; he haunched his shoulders against the tree roots and wriggled himself up to a sitting position where he stayed for a while, letting his mind run over the sequence of events that had brought him where he was and taking inventory of the situation.

Of escape he had no thought. The hue and cry must be out for him before now; doubtless men were already searching for him. It would be better for him to walk in and surrender than to be taken in the woods like an animal escaped from a traveling menagerie. But the mere thought of enduring again what he had already gone through – the thought of being tagged by crowds and stared at, with his fetters on – filled him with a nausea. Nothing that the Federal penitentiary might hold in store for him could equal the black, blind shamefulness of yesterday; he knew that. The thought of the new ignominy that faced him made Mr. Trimm desperate. He had a desire to burrow into the thicket yonder and hide his face and his chained hands.

But perhaps he could get the handcuffs off and so go to meet his captors in some manner of dignity. Strange that the idea hadn't occurred to him before! It seemed to Mr. Trimm that he desired to get his two hands apart more than he had ever desired anything in his whole life before.

The hands had begun naturally to adjust themselves to their enforced companionship, and it wasn't such a very hard matter, though it cost him some painful wrenches and much twisting of the fingers, for Mr. Trimm to get his coat unbuttoned and his eyeglasses in their small leather case out of his upper waistcoat pocket. With the glasses on his nose he subjected his bonds to a critical examination. Each rounded steel band ran unbroken except for the smooth, almost jointless hinge and the small lock which sat perched on the back of the wrist in a little rounded excrescence like a steel wart. In the flat center of each lock was a small keyhole and alongside of it a notched nub, the nub being sunk in a minute depression. On the inner side, underneath, the cuffs slid into themselves – two notches on each showing where the jaws might be tightened to fit a smaller hand than his – and right over the large blue veins in the middle of the wrists were swivel links, shackle-bolted to the cuffs and connected by a flat, slightly larger middle link, giving the hands a palm-to-palm play of not more than four or five inches. The cuffs did not hurt – even after so many hours there was no actual discomfort from them and the flesh beneath them was hardly reddened.

But it didn't take Mr. Trimm long to find out that they were not to be got off. He tugged and pulled, trying with his fingers for a purchase. All he did was to chafe his skin and make his wrists throb with pain. The cuffs would go forward just so far, then the little humps of bone above the hands would catch and hold them.

Mr. Trimm was not a man to waste time in the pursuit of the obviously hopeless. Presently he stood up, shook himself and started off at a fair gait through the woods. The sun was up now and the turf was all dappled with lights and shadows, and about him much small, furtive wild life was stirring. He stepped along briskly, a strange figure for that green solitude, with his correct city garb and the glint of the steel at his sleeve ends.

Presently he heard the long-drawn, quavering, banshee wail of a locomotive. The sound came from almost behind him, in an opposite direction from where he supposed the track to be. So he turned around and went back the other way. He crossed a half-dried-up runlet and climbed a small hill, neither of which he remembered having met in his night from the wreck, and in a little while he came out upon the railroad. To the north a little distance the rails ran round a curve. To the south, where the diminishing rails running through the unbroken woodland met in a long, shiny V, he could see a big smoke smudge against the horizon. This smoke Mr. Trimm knew must come from the wreck – which was still burning, evidently. As nearly as he could judge he had come out of cover at least two miles above it. After a moment's consideration he decided to go south toward the wreck. Soon he could distinguish small dots like ants moving in and out about the black spot, and he knew these dots must be men.

A whining, whirring sound came along the rails to him from behind. He faced about just as a handcar shot out around the curve from the north, moving with amazing rapidity under the strokes of four men at the pumps. Other men, laborers to judge by their blue overalls, were sitting on the edges of the car with their feet dangling. For the second time within twelve hours impulse ruled Mr. Trimm, who wasn't given to impulses normally. He made a jump off the right-of-way, and as the handcar flashed by he watched its flight from the covert of a weed tangle.

But even as the handcar was passing him Mr. Trimm regretted his hastiness. He must surrender himself sooner or later; why not to these overalled laborers, since it was a thing that had to be done? He slid out of hiding and came trotting back to the tracks. Already the handcar was a hundred yards away, flitting into distance like some big, wonderfully fast bug, the figures of the men at the pumps rising and falling with a walking-beam regularity. As he stood watching them fade away and minded to try hailing them, yet still hesitating against his judgment, Mr. Trimm saw something white drop from the hands of one of the blue-clad figures on the handcar, unfold into a newspaper and come fluttering back along the tracks toward him. Just as he, starting doggedly ahead, met it, the little ground breeze that had carried it along died out and the paper dropped and flattened right in front of him. The front page was uppermost and he knew it must be of that morning's issue, for across the column tops ran the flaring headline: "Twenty Dead in Frightful Collision."

Squatting on the cindered track, Mr. Trimm patted the crumpled sheet flat with his hands. His eyes dropped from the first of the glaring captions to the second, to the next – and then his heart gave a great bound inside of him and, clutching up the newspaper to his breast, he bounded off the tracks back into another thicket and huddled there with the paper spread on the earth in front of him, reading by gulps while the chain that linked wrist to wrist tinkled to the tremors running through him. What he had seen first, in staring black-face type, was his own name leading the list of known dead, and what he saw now, broken up into choppy paragraphs and done in the nervous English of a trained reporter throwing a great news story together to catch an edition, but telling a clear enough story nevertheless, was a narrative in which his name recurred again and again. The body of the United States deputy marshal, Meyers, frightfully crushed, had been taken from the wreckage of the smoker – so the double-leaded story ran – and near to Meyers another body, with features burned beyond recognition, yet still retaining certain distinguishing marks of measurement and contour, had been found and identified as that of Hobart W. Trimm, the convicted banker. The bodies of these two, with eighteen other mangled dead, had been removed to a town called Westfield, from which town of Westfield the account of the disaster had been telegraphed to the New York paper. In another column farther along was more about Banker Trimm; facts about his soiled, selfish, greedy, successful life, his great fortune, his trial, and a statement that, lacking any close kin to claim his body, his lawyers had been notified.

Mr. Trimm read the account through to the end, and as he read the sense of dominant, masterful self-control came back to him in waves. He got up, taking the paper with him, and went back into the deeper woods, moving warily and watchfully. As he went his mind, trained to take hold of problems and wring the essence out of them, was busy. Of the charred, grisly thing in the improvised morgue at Westfield, wherever that might be, Mr. Trimm took no heed nor wasted any pity. All his life he had used live men to work his will, with no thought of what might come to them afterward. The living had served him, why not the dead?

He had other things to think of than this dead proxy of his. He was as good as free! There would be no hunt for him now; no alarm out, no posses combing every scrap of cover for a famous criminal turned fugitive. He had only to lie quiet a few days, somewhere, then get in secret touch with Walling. Walling would do anything for money. And he had the money – four millions and more, cannily saved from the crash that had ruined so many others.

He would alter his personal appearance, change his name – he thought of Duvall, which was his mother's name – and with Walling's aid he would get out of the country and into some other country where a man might live like a prince on four millions or the fractional part of it. He thought of South America, of South Africa, of a private yacht swinging through the little frequented islands of the South Seas. All that the law had tried to take from him would be given back. Walling would work out the details of the escape – and make it safe and sure – trust Walling for those things. On one side was the prison, with its promise of twelve grinding years sliced out of the very heart of his life; on the other, freedom, ease, security, even power. Through Mr. Trimm's mind tumbled thoughts of concessions, enterprises, privileges – the back corners of the globe were full of possibilities for the right man. And between this prospect and Mr. Trimm there stood nothing in the way, nothing but—

Mr. Trimm's eyes fell upon his bound hands. Snug-fitting, shiny steel bands irked his wrists. The Grips of the Law were still upon him.

But only in a way of speaking. It was preposterous, unbelievable, altogether out of the question that a man with four millions salted down and stored away, a man who all his life had been used to grappling with the big things and wrestling them down into submission, a man whose luck had come to be a byword – and had not it held good even in this last emergency? – would be balked by puny scraps of forged steel and a trumpery lock or two. Why, these cuffs were no thicker than the gold bands that Mr. Trimm had seen on the arms of overdressed women at the opera. The chain that joined them was no larger and, probably, no stronger than the chains which Mr. Trimm's chauffeur wrapped around the tires of the touring car in winter to keep the wheels from skidding on the slush. There would be a way, surely, for Mr. Trimm to free himself from these things. There must be – that was all there was to it.

Mr. Trimm looked himself over. His clothes were not badly rumpled; his patent-leather boots were scarcely scratched. Without the handcuffs he could pass unnoticed anywhere. By night then he must be free of them and on his way to some small inland city, to stay quiet there until the guarded telegram that he would send in cipher had reached Walling. There in the woods by himself Mr. Trimm no longer felt the ignominy of his bonds; he felt only the temporary embarrassment of them and the need of added precaution until he should have mastered them.

He was once more the unemotional man of affairs who had stood Wall Street on its esteemed head and caught the golden streams that trickled from its pockets. First making sure that he was in a well-screened covert of the woods he set about exploring all his pockets. The coat pockets were comparatively easy, now that he had got used to using two hands where one had always served, but it cost him a lot of twisting of his body and some pain to his mistreated wrist bones to bring forth the contents of his trousers' pockets. The chain kinked time and again as he groped with the undermost hand for the openings; his dumpy, pudgy form writhed grotesquely. But finally he finished. The search produced four cigars somewhat crumpled and frayed; some matches in a gun-metal case, a silver cigar cutter, two five-dollar bills, a handful of silver chicken feed, the leather case of the eyeglasses, a couple of quill toothpicks, a gold watch with a dangling fob, a notebook and some papers. Mr. Trimm ranged these things in a neat row upon a log, like a watchmaker setting out his kit, and took swift inventory of them. Some he eliminated from his design, stowing them back in the pockets easiest to reach. He kept for present employment the match safe, the cigar cutter and the watch.

This place where he had halted would suit his present purpose well, he decided. It was where an uprooted tree, fallen across an incurving bank, made a snug little recess that was closed in on three sides. Spreading the newspaper on the turf to save his knees from soiling, he knelt and set to his task. For the time he felt neither hunger nor thirst. He had found out during his earlier experiments that the nails of his little fingers, which were trimmed to a point, could invade the keyholes in the little steel warts on the backs of his wrists and touch the locks. The mechanism had even twitched a little bit under the tickle of the nail ends. So, having already smashed the gun-metal match safe under his heel, Mr. Trimm selected a slender-pointed bit from among its fragments and got to work, the left hand drawn up under the right, the fingers of the right busy with the lock of the left, the chain tightening and slackening with subdued clinking sounds at each movement.

Mr. Trimm didn't know much about picking a lock. He had got his money by a higher form of burglary that did not require a knowledge of lock picking. Nor as a boy had he been one to play at mechanics. He had let other boys make the toy fluttermills and the wooden traps and the like, and then he had traded for them. He was sorry now that he hadn't given more heed to the mechanical side of things when he was growing up.

He worked with a deliberate slowness, steadily. Nevertheless, it was hot work. The sun rose over the bank and shone on him through the limbs of the uprooted tree. His hat was on the ground alongside of him. The sweat ran down his face, streaking it and wilting his collar flat. The scrap of gun metal kept slipping out of his wet fingers. Down would go the chained hands to scrabble in the grass for it, and then the picking would go on again. This happened a good many times. Birds, nervous with the spirit that presages the fall migration, flew back and forth along the creek, almost grazing Mr. Trimm sometimes. A rain crow wove a brown thread in the green warp of the bushes above his head. A chattering red squirrel sat up on a tree limb to scold him. At intervals, distantly, came the cough of laboring trains, showing that the track must have been cleared. There were times when Mr. Trimm thought he felt the lock giving. These times he would work harder.

* * *

Late in the afternoon Mr. Trimm lay back against the bank, panting. His face was splotched with red, and the little hollows at the sides of his forehead pulsed rapidly up and down like the bellies of scared tree frogs. The bent outer case of the watch littered a bare patch on the log; its mainspring had gone the way of the fragments of the gun-metal match safe which were lying all about, each a worn-down, twisted wisp of metal. The spring of the eyeglasses had been confiscated long ago and the broken crystals powdered the earth where Mr. Trimm's toes had scraped a smooth patch. The nails of the two little fingers were worn to the quick and splintered down into the raw flesh. There were countless tiny scratches and mars on the locks of the handcuffs, and the steel wristbands were dulled with blood smears and pale-red tarnishes of new rust; but otherwise they were as stanch and strong a pair of Bean's Latest Model Little Giant handcuffs as you'd find in any hardware store anywhere.

The devilish, stupid malignity of the damned things! With an acid oath Mr. Trimm raised his hands and brought them down on the log violently. There was a double click and the bonds tightened painfully, pressing the chafed red skin white. Mr. Trimm snatched up his hands close to his near-sighted eyes and looked. One of the little notches on the under side of each cuff had disappeared. It was as if they were living things that had turned and bitten him for the blow he gave them.

* * *

From the time the sun went down there was a tingle of frost in the air. Mr. Trimm didn't sleep much. Under the squeeze of the tightened fetters his wrists throbbed steadily and racking cramps ran through his arms. His stomach felt as though it were tied into knots. The water that he drank from the branch only made his hunger sickness worse. His undergarments, that had been wet with perspiration, clung to him clammily. His middle-aged, tenderly-cared-for body called through every pore for clean linen and soap and water and rest, as his empty insides called for food.

After a while he became so chilled that the demand for warmth conquered his instinct for caution. He felt about him in the darkness, gathering scraps of dead wood, and, after breaking several of the matches that had been in the gun-metal match safe, he managed to strike one and with its tiny flame started a fire. He huddled almost over the fire, coughing when the smoke blew into his face and twisting and pulling at his arms in an effort to get relief from the everlasting cramps. It seemed to him that if he could only get an inch or two more of play for his hands he would be ever so much more comfortable. But he couldn't, of course.

He dozed, finally, sitting crosslegged with his head sunk between his hunched shoulders. A pain in a new place woke him. The fire had burned almost through the thin sole of his right shoe, and as he scrambled to his feet and stamped, the clap of the hot leather flat against his blistered foot almost made him cry out.

* * *

Soon after sunrise a boy came riding a horse down a faintly traced footpath along the creek, driving a cow with a bell on her neck ahead of him. Mr. Trimm's ears caught the sound of the clanking bell before either the cow or her herder was in sight, and he limped away, running, skulking through the thick cover. A pendent loop of a wild grapevine, swinging low, caught his hat and flipped it off his head; but Mr. Trimm, imagining pursuit, did not stop to pick it up and went on bareheaded until he had to stop from exhaustion. He saw some dark-red berries on a shrub upon which he had trod, and, stooping, he plucked some of them with his two hands and put three or four in his mouth experimentally. Warned instantly by the acrid, burning taste, he spat the crushed berries out and went on doggedly, following, according to his best judgment, a course parallel to the railroad. It was characteristic of him, a city-raised man, that he took no heed of distances nor of the distinguishing marks of the timber.

Behind a log at the edge of a small clearing in the woods he halted some little time, watching and listening. The clearing had grown up in sumacs and weeds and small saplings and it seemed deserted; certainly it was still. Near the center of it rose the sagging roof of what had been a shack or a shed of some sort. Stooping cautiously, to keep his bare head below the tops of the sumacs, Mr. Trimm made for the ruined shanty and gained it safely. In the midst of the rotted, punky logs that had once formed the walls he began scraping with his feet. Presently he uncovered something. It was a broken-off harrow tooth, scaled like a long, red fish with the crusted rust of years.

Mr. Trimm rested the lower rims of his handcuffs on the edge of an old, broken watering trough, worked the pointed end of the rust-crusted harrow tooth into the flat middle link of the chain as far as it would go, and then with one hand on top of the other he pressed downward with all his might. The pain in his wrists made him stop this at once. The link had not sprung or given in the least, but the twisting pressure had almost broken his wrist bones. He let the harrow tooth fall, knowing that it would never serve as a lever to free him – which, indeed, he had known all along – and sat on the side of the trough, rubbing his wrists and thinking.

He had another idea. It came into his mind as a vague suggestion that fire had certain effects upon certain metals. He kindled a fire of bits of the rotted wood, and when the flames ran together and rose slender and straight in a single red thread he thrust the chain into it, holding his hands as far apart as possible in the attitude of a player about to catch a bounced ball. But immediately the pain of that grew unendurable too, and he leaped back, jerking his hands away. He had succeeded only in blackening the steel and putting a big water blister on one of his wrists right where the shackle bolt would press upon it.

Where he huddled down in the shelter of one of the fallen walls he noticed, presently, a strand of rusted fence wire still held to half-tottering posts by a pair of blackened staples;

it was part of a pen that had been used once for chickens or swine. Mr. Trimm tried the wire with his fingers. It was firm and springy. Rocking and groaning with the pain of it, he nevertheless began sliding the chain back and forth, back and forth along the strand of wire.

Eventually the wire, weakened by age, snapped in two. A tiny shined spot, hardly deep enough to be called a nick, in its tarnished, smudged surface was all the mark that the chain showed.

Staggering a little and putting his feet down unsteadily, Mr. Trimm left the clearing, heading as well as he could tell eastward, away from the railroad. After a mile or two he came to a dusty wood road winding downhill.

To the north of the clearing where Mr. Trimm had halted were a farm and a group of farm buildings. To the southward a mile or so was a cluster of dwellings set in the midst of more farm lands, with a shop or two and a small white church with a green spire in the center. Along a road that ran northward from the hamlet to the solitary farm a ten-year-old boy came, carrying a covered tin pail. A young gray squirrel flirted across the wagon ruts ahead of him and darted up a chestnut sapling. The boy put the pail down at the side of the road and began looking for a stone to throw at the squirrel.

Mr. Trimm slid out from behind a tree. A hemstitched handkerchief, grimed and stained, was loosely twisted around his wrists, partly hiding the handcuffs. He moved along with a queer, sliding gait, keeping as much of his body as he could turned from the youngster. The ears of the little chap caught the faint scuffle of feet and he spun around on his bare heel.

"My boy, would you—" Mr. Trimm began.

The boy's round eyes widened at the apparition that was sidling toward him in so strange a fashion, and then, taking fright, he dodged past Mr. Trimm and ran back the way he had come, as fast as his slim brown legs could take him. In half a minute he was out of sight round a bend.

Had the boy looked back he would have seen a still more curious spectacle than the one that had frightened him. He would have seen a man worth four million dollars down on his knees in the yellow dust, pawing with chained hands at the tight-fitting lid of the tin pail, and then, when he had got the lid off, drinking the fresh, warm milk which the pail held with great, choking gulps, uttering little mewing, animal sounds as he drank, while the white, creamy milk ran over his chin and splashed down his breast in little, spurting streams.

But the boy didn't look back. He ran all the way home and told his mother he had seen a wild man on the road to the village; and later, when his father came in from the fields, he was soundly thrashed for letting the sight of a tramp make him lose a good tin bucket and half a gallon of milk worth six cents a quart.

* * *

The rich, fresh milk put life into Mr. Trimm. He rested the better for it during the early part of that night in a haw thicket. Only the sharp, darting pains in his wrists kept rousing him to temporary wakefulness. In one of those intervals of waking the plan that had been sketchily forming in his mind from the time he had quit the clearing in the woods took on a definite, fixed shape. But how was he with safety to get the sort of aid he needed, and where?

Canvassing tentative plans in his head, he dozed off again.

* * *

On a smooth patch of turf behind the blacksmith shop three yokels were languidly pitching horseshoes – 'quaits' they called them – at a stake driven in the earth. Just beyond, the woods shredded out into a long, yellow and green peninsula which stretched up almost to the back door of the smithy, so that late of afternoons the slanting shadows of the near-most trees fell on its roof of warped shingles. At the extreme end of this point of woods Mr. Trimm was squatted behind a big boulder, squinting warily through a thick-fringed curtain of ripened goldenrod tops and sumacs, heavy-headed with their dark-red tapers. He had been there more than an hour, cautiously waiting his chance to hail the blacksmith, whose figure he could make out in the smoky interior of his shop, passing back and forth in front of a smudgy forge fire and rattling metal against metal in intermittent fits of professional activity.

From where Mr. Trimm watched to where the horseshoe-pitching game went on was not more than sixty feet. He could hear what the players said and even see the little puffs of dust rise when one of them clapped his hands together after a pitch. He judged by the signs of slackening interest that they would be stopping soon and, he hoped, going clear away.

But the smith loafed out of his shop and, after an exchange of bucolic banter with the three of them, he took a hand in their game himself. He wore no coat or waistcoat and, as he poised a horseshoe for his first cast at the stake, Mr. Trimm saw, pinned flat against the broad strap of his suspenders, a shiny, silvery-looking disk. Having pitched the shoe, the smith moved over into the shade, so that he almost touched the clump of undergrowth that half buried Mr. Trimm's protecting boulder. The near-sighted eyes of the fugitive banker could make out then what the flat, silvery disk was, and Mr. Trimm cowered low in his covert behind the rock, holding his hands down between his knees, fearful that a gleam from his burnished wristlets might strike through the screen of weed growth and catch the inquiring eye of the smith. So he stayed, not daring to move, until a dinner horn sounded somewhere in the cluster of cottages beyond, and the smith, closing the doors of his shop, went away with the three yokels.

Then Mr. Trimm, stooping low, stole back into the deep woods again. In his extremity he was ready to risk making a bid for the hire of a blacksmith's aid to rid himself of his bonds, but not a blacksmith who wore a deputy sheriff's badge pinned to his suspenders.

* * *

He caught himself scraping his wrists up and down again against the rough, scrofulous trunk of a shellbark hickory. The irritation was comforting to the swollen skin. The cuffs, which kept catching on the bark and snagging small fragments of it loose, seemed to Mr. Trimm to have been a part and parcel of him for a long time – almost as long a time as he could remember. But the hands which they clasped so close seemed like the hands of somebody else. There was a numbness about them that made them feel as though they were a stranger's hands which never had belonged to him. As he looked at them with a sort of vague curiosity they seemed to swell and grow, these two strange, fettered hands, until they measured yards across, while the steel bands shrunk to the thinness of piano wire, cutting deeper and deeper into the flesh. Then the hands in turn began to shrink down and the cuffs to grow up into great, thick things as cumbersome as the couplings of a freight car. A voice that Mr. Trimm dimly recognized as his own was saying something about four million dollars over and over again.

Mr. Trimm roused up and shook his head angrily to clear it. He rubbed his eyes free of the clouding delusion. It wouldn't do for him to be getting light-headed.

* * *

On a flat, shelving bluff, forty feet above a cut through which the railroad ran at a point about five miles north of where the collision had occurred, a tramp was busy, just before sundown, cooking something in an old washboiler that perched precariously on a fire of wood coals. This tramp was tall and spindle-legged, with reddish hair and a pale, beardless, freckled face with no chin to it and not much forehead, so that it ran out to a peak like the profile of some featherless, unpleasant sort of fowl. The skirts of an old, ragged overcoat dangled grotesquely about his spare shanks.

Desperate as his plight had become, Mr. Trimm felt the old sick shame at the prospect of exposing himself to this knavish-looking vagabond whose help he meant to buy with a bribe. It was the sight of a dainty wisp of smoke from the wood fire curling upward through the cloudy, damp air that had brought him limping cautiously across the right-of-way, to climb the rocky shelf along the cut; but now he hesitated, shielded in the shadows twenty yards away. It was a whiff of something savory in the washboiler, borne to him on the still air and almost making him cry out with eagerness, that drew him forth finally. At the sound of the halting footsteps the tramp stopped stirring the mess in the washboiler and glanced up apprehensively. As he took in the figure of the newcomer his eyes narrowed and his pasty, nasty face spread in a grin of comprehension.

"Well, well, well," he said, leering offensively, "welcome to our city, little stranger."

Mr. Trimm came nearer, dragging his feet, for they were almost out of the wrecks of his patent-leather shoes. His gaze shifted from the tramp's face to the stuff on the fire, his nostrils wrinkling. Then slowly: "I'm in trouble," he said, and held out his hands.

"Wot I'd call a mild way o' puttin' it," said the tramp coolly. "That purticular kind o' joolry ain't gen'lly wore for pleasure."

His eyes took on a nervous squint and roved past Mr. Trimm's stooped figure down the slope of the hillock.

"Say, pal, how fur ahead are you of yore keeper?" he demanded, his manner changing.

"There is no one after me – no one that I know of," explained Mr. Trimm. "I am quite alone – I am certain of it."

"Sure there ain't nobody lookin' fur you?" the other persisted suspiciously.

"I tell you I am all alone," protested Mr. Trimm. "I want your help in getting these – these things off and sending a message to a friend. You'll be well paid, very well paid. I can pay you more money than you ever had in your life, probably, for your help. I can promise—"

He broke off, for the tramp, as if reassured by his words, had stooped again to his cooking and was stirring the bubbling contents of the washboiler with a peeled stick. The smell of the stew, rising strongly, filled Mr. Trimm with such a sharp and an aching hunger that he could not speak for a moment. He mastered himself, but the effort left him shaking and gulping.

"Go on, then, an' tell us somethin' about yourself," said the freckled man. "Wot brings you roamin' round this here railroad cut with them bracelets on?"

"I was in the wreck," obeyed Mr. Trimm. "The man with me – the officer – was killed. I wasn't hurt and I got away into these woods. But they think I'm dead too – my name was among the list of dead."

The other's peaky face lengthened in astonishment.

"Why, say," he began, "I read all about that there wreck – seen the list myself – say, you can't be Trimm, the New York banker? Yes, you are! Wot a streak of luck! Lemme look at you! Trimm, the swell financeer, sportin' 'round with the darbies on him all nice an' snug an' reg'lar! Mister Trimm – well, if this ain't rich!"

"My name is Trimm," said the starving banker miserably. "I've been wandering about here a great many hours – several days, I think it must be – and I need rest and food very much indeed. I don't—don't feel very well," he added, his voice trailing off.

At this his self-control gave way again and he began to quake violently as if with an ague. The smell of the cooking overcame him.

"You don't look so well an' that's a fact, Trimm," sneered the tramp, resuming his malicious, mocking air. "But set down an' make yourself at home, an' after a while, when this is done, we'll have a bite together – you an' me. It'll be a reg'lar tea party fur jest us two."

He broke off to chuckle. His mirth made him appear even more repulsive than before.

"But looky here, you wus sayin' somethin' about money," he said suddenly. "Le's take a look at all this here money."

He came over to him and went through Mr. Trimm's pockets. Mr. Trimm said nothing and stood quietly, making no resistance. The tramp finished a workmanlike search of the banker's pockets. He looked at the result as it lay in his grimy palm – a moist little wad of bills and some chicken-feed change – and spat disgustedly with a nasty oath.

"Well, Trimm," he said, "fur a Wall Street guy seems to me you travel purty light. About how much did you think you'd get done fur all this pile of wealth?"

"You will be well paid," said Mr. Trimm, arguing hard; "my friend will see to that. What I want you to do is to take the money you have there in your hand and buy a cold chisel or a file – any tools that will cut these things off me. And then you will send a telegram to a certain gentleman in New York. And let me stay with you until we get an answer – until he comes here. He will pay you well; I promise it."

He halted, his eyes and his mind again on the bubbling stuff in the rusted washboiler. The freckled vagrant studied him through his red-lidded eyes, kicking some loose embers back into the fire with his toe.

"I've heard a lot about you one way an' another, Trimm," he said. "'Tain't as if you wuz some pore down-an'-out devil tryin' to beat the cops out of doin' his bit in stir. You're the way-up, high-an'-mighty kind of crook. An' from wot I've read an' heard about you, you never toted fair with nobody yet. There wuz that young feller, wot's his name? – the cashier – him that wuz tried with you. He went along with you in yore games an' done yore work fur you an' you let him go over the road to the same place you're tryin' to dodge now. Besides," he added cunningly, "you come here talkin' mighty big about money, yet I notice you ain't carryin' much of it in yore clothes. All I've had to go by is yore word. An' yore word ain't worth much, by all accounts."

"I tell you, man, that you'll profit richly," burst out Mr. Trimm, the words falling over each other in his new panic. "You must help me; I've endured too much – I've gone through too much to give up now." He pleaded fast, his hands shaking in a quiver of fear and eagerness as he stretched them out in entreaty and his linked chain shaking with them. Promises, pledges, commands, orders, arguments poured from him. His tormentor checked him with a gesture.

"You're wot I'd call a bird in the hand," he chuckled, hugging his slack frame, "an' it ain't fur you to be givin' orders – it's fur me. An', anyway, I guess we ain't a-goin' to be able to make a trade – leastwise not on yore terms. But we'll do business all right, all right – anyhow, I will."

"What do you mean?" panted Mr. Trimm, full of terror. "You'll help me?"

"I mean this," said the tramp slowly. He put his hands under his loose-hanging overcoat and began to fumble at a leather strap about his waist. "If I turn you over to the Government I know wot you'll be worth, purty near, by guessin' at the reward; an' besides, it'll maybe help to square me up fur one or two little matters. If I turn you loose I ain't got nothin' only your word – an' I've got an idea how much faith I kin put in that."

Mr. Trimm glanced about him wildly. There was no escape. He was fast in a trap which he himself had sprung. The thought of being led to jail, all foul of body and fettered as he was, by this filthy, smirking wretch made him crazy. He stumbled backward with some insane idea of running away.

"No hurry, no hurry a-tall," gloated the tramp, enjoying the torture of this helpless captive who had walked into his hands. "I ain't goin' to hurt you none – only make sure that you don't wander off an' hurt yourself while I'm gone. Won't do to let you be damagin' yoreself; you're valuable property. Trimm, now, I'll tell you wot we'll do! We'll just back you up agin one of these trees an' then we'll jest slip this here belt through yore elbows an' buckle it around behind at the back; an' I kinder guess you'll stay right there till I go down yonder to that station that I passed comin' up here an' see wot kind of a bargain I kin strike up with the marshal. Come on, now," he threatened with a show of bluster, reading the resolution that was mounting in Mr. Trimm's face. "Come on peaceable, if you don't want to git hurt."

Of a sudden Mr. Trimm became the primitive man. He was filled with those elemental emotions that make a man see in spatters of crimson. Gathering strength from passion out of an exhausted frame, he sprang forward at the tramp. He struck at him with his head, his shoulders, his knees, his manacled wrists, all at once. Not really hurt by the puny assault, but caught by surprise, the freckled man staggered back, clawing at the air, tripped on the washboiler in the fire, and with a yell vanished below the smooth edge of the cut.

Mr. Trimm stole forward and looked over the bluff. Half-way down the cliff on an outcropping shelf of rock the man lay, face downward, motionless. He seemed to have grown smaller and to have shrunk into his clothes. One long, thin leg was bent up under the skirts of the overcoat in a queer, twisted way, and the cloth of the trouser leg looked flattened and empty. As Mr. Trimm peered down at him he saw a red stain spreading on the rock under the still, silent figure's head.

Mr. Trimm turned to the washboiler. It lay on its side, empty, the last of its recent contents sputtering out into the half-drowned fire. He stared at this ruin a minute. Then without another look over the cliff edge he stumbled slowly down the hill, muttering to himself as he went. Just as he struck the level it began to rain, gently at first, then hard, and despite the shelter of the full-leaved forest trees, he was soon wet through to his skin and dripped water as he lurched along without sense of direction or, indeed, without any active realization of what he was doing.

* * *

Late that night it was still raining – a cold, steady, autumnal downpour. A huddled figure slowly climbed upon a low fence running about the house-yard of the little farm where the boy lived who got thrashed for losing a milkpail. On the wet top rail, precariously perching, the figure slipped and sprawled forward in the miry yard. It got up, painfully swaying on its feet. It was Mr.

Trimm, looking for food. He moved slowly toward the house, tottering with weakness and because of the slick mud underfoot; peering near-sightedly this way and that through the murk; starting at every sound and stopping often to listen.

The outlines of a lean-to kitchen at the back of the house were looming dead ahead of him when from the corner of the cottage sprang a small terrier. It made for Mr. Trimm, barking shrilly. He retreated backward, kicking at the little dog and, to hold his balance, striking out with short, dabby jerks of his fettered hands – they were such motions as the terrier itself might make trying to walk on its hindlegs. Still backing away, expecting every instant to feel the terrier's teeth in his flesh, Mr. Trimm put one foot into a hotbed with a great clatter of the breaking glass. He felt the sharp ends of shattered glass tearing and cutting his shin as he jerked free. Recovering himself, he dealt the terrier a lucky kick under the throat that sent it back, yowling, to where it had come from, and then, as a door jerked open and a half-dressed man jumped out into the darkness, Mr. Trimm half hobbled, half fell out of sight behind the woodpile.

Back and forth along the lower edge of his yard the farmer hunted, with the whimpering, cowed terrier to guide him, poking in dark corners with the muzzle of his shotgun for the unseen intruder whose coming had aroused the household. In a brushpile just over the fence to the east Mr. Trimm lay on his face upon the wet earth, with the rain beating down on him, sobbing with choking gulps that wrenched him cruelly, biting at the bonds on his wrists until the sound of breaking teeth gritted in the air. Finally, in the hopeless, helpless frenzy of his agony he beat his arms up and down until the bracelets struck squarely on a flat stone and the force of the blow sent the cuffs home to the last notch so that they pressed harder and faster than ever upon the tortured wrist bones.

When he had wasted ten or fifteen minutes in a vain search the farmer went shivering back indoors to dry out his wet shirt. But the groveling figure in the brushpile lay for a long time where it was, only stirring a little while the rain dripped steadily down on everything.

* * *

The wreck was on a Tuesday evening. Early on the Saturday morning following the chief of police, who was likewise the whole of the day police force in the town of Westfield, nine miles from the place where the collision occurred, heard a peculiar, strangely weak knocking at the front door of his cottage, where he also had his office. The door was a Dutch door, sawed through the middle, so that the top half might be opened independently, leaving the lower panel fast. He swung this top half back.

A face was framed in the opening – an indescribably dirty, unutterably weary face, with matted white hair and a rime of whitish beard stubble on the jaws. It was fallen in and sunken and it drooped on the chest of its owner. The mouth, swollen and pulpy, as if from repeated hard blows, hung agape, and between the purplish parted lips showed the stumps of broken teeth. The eyes blinked weakly at the chief from under lids as colorless as the eyelids of a corpse. The bare white head was filthy with plastered mud and twigs, and dripping wet.

"Hello, there!" said the chief, startled at this apparition. "What do you want?"

With a movement that told of straining effort the lolled head came up off the chest. The thin, corded neck stiffened back, rising from a dirty, collarless neckband. The Adam's apple bulged out prominently, as big as a pigeon's egg.

"I have come," said the specter in a wheezing rasp of a voice which the chief could hardly hear – "I have come to surrender myself. I am Hobart W. Trimm."

"I guess you got another thing comin'," said the chief, who was by way of being a neighborhood wag. "When last seen Hobart W. Trimm was only fifty-two years old. Besides which, he's dead and buried. I guess maybe you'd better think agin, grandpap, and see if you ain't Methus'lah or the Wanderin' Jew."

"I am Hobart W. Trimm, the banker," whispered the stranger with a sort of wan stubbornness.

"Go on and prove it," suggested the chief, more than willing to prolong the enjoyment of the sensation. It wasn't often in Westfield that wandering lunatics came a-calling.

"Got any way to prove it?" he repeated as the visitor stared at him.

"Yes," came the creaking, rusted hinge of a voice, "I have."

Slowly, with struggling attempts, he raised his hands into the chief's sight. They were horribly swollen hands, red with the dried blood where they were not black with the dried dirt; the fingers puffed up out of shape; the nails broken; they were like the skinned paws of a bear. And at the wrists, almost buried in the bloated folds of flesh, blackened, rusted, battered, yet still strong and whole, was a tightly-locked pair of Bean's Latest Model Little Giant handcuffs.

"Great God!" cried the chief, transfixed at the sight. He drew the bolt and jerked open the lower half of the door.

"Come in," he said, "and lemme get them irons off of you – they must hurt something terrible."

"They can wait," said Mr. Trimm very feebly, very slowly and very humbly. "I have worn them a long, long while – I am used to them. Wouldn't you please get me some food first?"

An Occurrence Up A Side Street

Irvin S. Cobb

"SEE IF he's still there, will you?" said the man listlessly, as if knowing in advance what the answer would be.

The woman, who, like the man, was in her stocking feet, crossed the room, closing the door with all softness behind her. She felt her way silently through the darkness of a small hallway, putting first her ear and then her eye to a tiny cranny in some thick curtains at a front window.

She looked downward and outward upon one of those New York side streets that is precisely like forty other New York side streets: two unbroken lines of high-shouldered, narrow-chested brick-and-stone houses, rising in abrupt, straight cliffs; at the bottom of the canyon a narrow river of roadway with manholes and conduit covers dotting its channel intermittently like scattered stepping stones; and on either side wide, flat pavements, as though the stream had fallen to low-water mark and left bare its shallow banks. Daylight would have shown most of the houses boarded up, with diamond-shaped vents, like leering eyes, cut in the painted planking of the windows and doors; but now it was night time – eleven o'clock of a wet, hot, humid night of the late summer – and the street was buttoned down its length in the double-breasted fashion of a bandmaster's coat with twin rows of gas lamps evenly spaced. Under each small circle of lighted space the dripping, black asphalt had a slimy, slick look like the sides of a newly caught catfish. Elsewhere the whole vista lay all in close shadow, black as a cave mouth under every stoop front and blacker still in the hooded basement areas. Only, half a mile to the eastward a dim, distant flicker showed where Broadway ran, a broad, yellow streak down the spine of the city, and high above the broken skyline of eaves and cornices there rolled in cloudy waves the sullen red radiance, born of a million electrics and the flares from gas tanks and chimneys, which is only to be seen on such nights as this, giving to the heaven above New York that same color tone you find in an artist's conception of Babylon falling or Rome burning.

From where the woman stood at the window she could make out the round, white, mushroom top of a policeman's summer helmet as its wearer leaned back, half sheltered under the narrow portico of the stoop just below her; and she could see his uniform sleeve and his hand, covered with a white cotton glove, come up, carrying a handkerchief, and mop the hidden face under the helmet's brim. The squeak of his heavy shoes was plainly audible to her also. While she stayed there, watching and listening, two pedestrians – and only two – passed on her side of the street: a messenger boy in a glistening rubber poncho going west and a man under an umbrella going east. Each was hurrying along until he came just opposite her, and then, as though controlled by the same set of strings, each stopped short and looked up curiously at the blind, dark house and at the figure lounging in the doorway, then hurried on without a word, leaving the silent policeman fretfully mopping his moist face and tugging at the wilted collar about his neck.

After a minute or two at her peephole behind the window curtains above, the woman passed back through the door to the inner, middle room where the man sat.

"Still there," she said lifelessly in the half whisper that she had come to use almost altogether these last few days; "still there and sure to stay there until another one just like him comes to take his place. What else did you expect?"

The man only nodded absently and went on peeling an overripe peach, striking out constantly, with the hand that held the knife, at the flies. They were green flies – huge, shiny-backed, buzzing, persistent vermin. There were a thousand of them; there seemed to be a million of them. They filled the shut-in room with their vile humming; they swarmed everywhere in the half light. They were thickest, though, in a corner at the back, where there was a closed, white door. Here a great knot of them, like an iridescent, shimmering jewel, was clustered about the keyhole. They scrolled the white enameled panels with intricate, shifting patterns, and in pairs and singly they promenaded busily on the white porcelain knob, giving it the appearance of being alive and having a motion of its own.

It was stiflingly hot and sticky in the room. The sweat rolled down the man's face as he peeled his peach and pared some half-rotted spots out of it. He protected it with a cupped palm as he bit into it. One huge green fly flipped nimbly under the fending hand and lit on the peach. With a savage little snarl of disgust and loathing the man shook the clinging insect off and with the knife carved away the place where its feet had touched the soft fruit. Then he went on munching, meanwhile furtively watching the woman. She was on the opposite side of a small center-table from him, with her face in her hands, shaking her head with a little shuddering motion whenever one of the flies settled on her close-cropped hair or brushed her bare neck.

He was a smallish man, with a suggestion of something dapper about him even in his present unkempt disorder; he might have been handsome, in a weakly effeminate way, had not Nature or some mishap given his face a twist that skewed it all to one side, drawing all of his features out of focus, like a reflection viewed in a flawed mirror. He was no heavier than the woman and hardly as tall. She, however, looked less than her real height, seeing that she was dressed, like a half-grown boy, in a soft-collared shirt open at the throat and a pair of loose trousers. She had large but rather regular features, pouting lips, a clear brown skin and full, prominent brown eyes; and one of them had a pronounced cast in it – an imperfection already made familiar by picture and printed description to sundry millions of newspaper readers. For this was Ella Gilmorris, the woman in the case of the Gilmorris murder, about which the continent of North America was now reading and talking. And the little man with the twisted face, who sat across from her, gnawing a peach stone clean, was the notorious 'Doctor' Harris Devine, alias Vanderburg, her accomplice, and worth more now to society in his present untidy state than ever before at any one moment of his whole discreditable life, since for his capture the people of the state of New York stood willing to pay the sum of one thousand dollars, which tidy reward one of the afternoon papers had increased by another thousand.

Everywhere detectives – amateurs and the kind who work for hire – were seeking the pair who at this precise moment faced each other across a little center-table in the last place any searcher would have suspected or expected them to be – on the second floor of the house in which the late Cassius Gilmorris had been killed. This, then, was the situation: inside, these two fugitives, watchful, silent, their eyes red-rimmed for lack of sleep, their nerves raw and tingling as though rasped with files, each busy with certain private plans, each fighting off constantly the touch of the nasty scavenger flies that flickered and flitted iridescently about them; outside, in the steamy, hot drizzle, with his back to the locked and double-locked door, a leg-weary policeman, believing that he guarded a house all empty except for such evidences as yet remained of the Gilmorris murder.

* * *

It was one of those small, chancy things that so often disarrange the best laid plots of murderers that had dished their hope of a clean getaway and brought them back, at the last, to the starting point. If the plumber's helper, who was sent to cure a bathtub of leaking in the house next door, had not made a mistake and come to the wrong number; and if they, in the haste of flight, had not left an area door unfastened; and if this young plumbing apprentice, stumbling his way upstairs on the hunt for the misbehaving drain, had not opened the white enameled door and found inside there what he did find – if this small sequence of incidents had not occurred as it did and when it did, or if only it had been delayed another twenty-four hours, or even twelve, everything might have turned out differently. But fate, to call it by its fancy name – coincidence, to use its garden one – interfered, as it usually does in cases such as this. And so here they were.

The man had been on his way to the steamship office to get the tickets when an eruption of newsboys boiled out of Mail Street into Broadway, with extras on their arms, all shouting out certain words that sent him scurrying back in a panic to the small, obscure family hotel in the lower thirties where the woman waited. From that moment it was she, really, who took the initiative in all the efforts to break through the doubled and tripled lines that the police machinery looped about the five boroughs of the city.

At dark that evening 'Mr. and Mrs. A. Thompson, of Jersey City,' a quiet couple who went closely muffled up, considering that it was August, and carrying heavy valises, took quarters at a dingy furnished room house on a miscalled avenue of Brooklyn not far from the Wall Street ferries and overlooking the East River waterfront from its bleary back windows. Two hours later a very different-looking pair issued quietly from a side entrance of this place and vanished swiftly down toward the docks. The thing was well devised and carried out well too; yet by morning the detectives, already ranging and quartering the town as bird-dogs quarter a brier-field, had caught up again and pieced together the broken ends of the trail; and, thanks to them and the newspapers, a good many thousand wide awake persons were on the lookout for a plump, brown-skinned young woman with a cast in her right eye, wearing a boy's disguise and accompanied by a slender little man carrying his head slightly to one side, who when last seen wore smoked glasses and had his face extensively bandaged, as though suffering from a toothache.

Then had followed days and nights of blind twisting and dodging and hiding, with the hunt growing warmer behind them all the time. Through this they were guided and at times aided by things printed in the very papers that worked the hardest to run them down. Once they ventured as far as the outer entrance of the great, new uptown terminal, and turned away, too far gone and sick with fear to dare run the gauntlet of the waiting room and the train-shed. Once – because they saw a made-up Central Office man in every lounging long-shoreman, and were not so far wrong either – they halted at the street end of one of the smaller piers and from there watched a grimy little foreign boat that carried no wireless masts and that might have taken them to any one of half a dozen obscure banana ports of South America – watched her while she hiccoughed out into midstream and straightened down the river for the open bay – watched her out of sight and then fled again to their newest hiding place in the lower East Side in a cold sweat, with the feeling that every casual eye glance from every chance passer-by carried suspicion and recognition in its flash, that every briskening footstep on the pavement behind them meant pursuit.

Once in that tormented journey there was a sudden jingle of metal, like rattling handcuffs, in the man's ear and a heavy hand fell detainingly on his shoulder – and he squeaked like a caught shore-bird and shrunk away from under the rough grips of a truckman who had yanked him clear of a lurching truck horse tangled in its own traces. Then, finally, had come a growing distrust for their latest landlord, a stolid Russian Jew who read no papers and knew no English, and saw in his pale pair of guests only an American lady and gentleman who kept much to their room and paid well in advance for everything; and after that, in the hot rainy night, the flight afoot across weary miles of soaking cross streets and up through ill-lighted, shabby avenues to the one place of refuge left open to them. They had learned from the newspapers, at once a guide and a bane, a friend and a dogging enemy, that the place was locked up, now that the police had got through searching it, and that the coroner's people held the keys. And the woman knew of a faulty catch on a rear cellar window, and so, in a fit of stark desperation bordering on lunacy, back they ran, like a pair of spent foxes circling to a burrow from which they have been smoked out.

Again it was the woman who picked for her companion the easiest path through the inky-black alley, and with her own hands she pulled down noiselessly the broken slats of the rotting wooden wall at the back of the house. And then, soon, they were inside, with the reeking heat of the boxed-up house and the knowledge that at any moment discovery might come bursting in upon them – inside with their busy thoughts and the busy green flies. How persistent the things were – shake them off a hundred times and back they came buzzing! And where had they all come from? There had been none of them about before, surely, and now their maddening, everlasting droning filled the ear. And what nasty creatures they were, forever cleaning their shiny wings and rubbing the ends of their forelegs together with the loathsome suggestion of little grave-diggers anointing their palms. To the woman, at least, these flies almost made bearable the realization that, at best, this stopping point could be only a temporary one, and that within a few hours a fresh start must somehow be made, with fresh dangers to face at every turning.

* * *

It was during this last hideous day of flight and terror that the thing which had been growing in the back part of the brain of each of them began to assume shape and a definite aspect. The man had the craftier mind, but the woman had a woman's intuition, and she already had read his thoughts while yet he had no clue to hers. For the primal instinct of self-preservation, blazing up high, had burned away the bond of bogus love that held them together while they were putting her drunkard of a husband out of the way, and now there only remained to tie them fast this partnership of a common guilt.

In these last few hours they had both come to know that together there was no chance of ultimate escape; traveling together the very disparity of their compared appearances marked them with a fatal and unmistakable conspicuousness, as though they were daubed with red paint from the same paint brush; staying together meant ruin – certain, sure. Now, then, separated and going singly, there might be a thin strand of hope. Yet the man felt that, parted a single hour from the woman, and she still alive, his woefully small prospect would diminish and shrink to the vanishing point – New York juries being most notoriously easy upon women murderers who give themselves up and turn state's evidence; and, by the same mistaken processes of judgment, notoriously hard upon their male accomplices – half a dozen such instances had been playing in flashes across his memory already.

Neither had so much as hinted at separating. The man didn't speak, because of a certain idea that had worked itself all out hours before within his side-flattened skull. The woman likewise had refrained from putting in words the suggestion that had been uppermost in her brain from the time they broke into the locked house. Some darting look of quick, malignant suspicion from him, some inner warning sense, held her mute at first; and later, as the newborn hate and dread of him grew and mastered her and she began to canvass ways and means to a certain end, she stayed mute still.

Whatever was to be done must be done quietly, without a struggle – the least sound might arouse the policeman at the door below. One thing was in her favour – she knew he was not armed; he had the contempt and the fear of a tried and proved poisoner for cruder lethal tools.

It was characteristic also of the difference between these two that Devine should have had his plan stage-set and put to motion long before the woman dreamed of acting. It was all within his orderly scheme of the thing proposed that he, a shrinking coward, should have set his squirrel teeth hard and risked detection twice in that night: once to buy a basket of overripe fruit from a dripping Italian at a sidewalk stand, taking care to get some peaches – he just must have a peach, he had explained to her; and once again when he entered a dark little store on Second Avenue, where liquors were sold in their original packages, and bought from a sleepy, stupid clerk two bottles of a cheap domestic champagne – "to give us the strength for making a fresh start," he told her glibly, as an excuse for taking this second risk. So, then, with the third essential already resting at the bottom of an inner waistcoat pocket, he was prepared; and he had been waiting for his opportunity from the moment when they crept in through the basement window and felt their way along, she resolutely leading, to the windowless, shrouded middle room here on the second floor.

* * *

How she hated him, feared him too! He could munch his peaches and uncork his warm, cheap wine in this very room, with that bathroom just yonder and these flies all about. From under her fingers, interlaced over her forehead, her eyes roved past him, searching the littered room for the twentieth time in the hour, looking, seeking – and suddenly they fell on something – a crushed and rumpled hat of her own, a milliner's masterpiece, laden with florid plumage, lying almost behind him on a couch end where some prying detective had dropped it, with a big, round black button shining dully from the midst of its damaged tulle crown. She knew that button well. It was the imitation-jet head of a hatpin – a steel hatpin – that was ten inches long and maybe longer.

She looked and looked at the round, dull knob, like a mystic held by a hypnotist's crystal ball, and she began to breathe a little faster; she could feel her resolution tighten within her like a turning screw.

Beneath her brows, heavy and thick for a woman's, her eyes flitted back to the man. With the careful affectation of doing nothing at all, a theatricalism that she detected instantly, but for which she could guess no reason, he was cutting away at the damp, close-gnawed seed of the peach, trying apparently to fashion some little trinket – a toy basket, possibly – from it. His fingers moved deftly over its slick, wet surface. He had already poured out some of the champagne. One of the pint bottles stood empty, with the distorted button-headed cork lying beside it, and in two glasses the yellow wine was fast going flat and dead in that stifling heat. It still spat up a few little bubbles to the surface, as though minute creatures were drowning in it down below. The man was sweating more than ever, so that, under the single, low-turned gas jet, his crooked face had a greasy shine to it. A church clock down in the next block struck twelve slowly. The sleepless flies buzzed evilly.

"Look out again, won't you?" he said for perhaps the tenth time in two hours. "There's a chance, you know, that he might be gone – just a bare chance. And be sure you close the door into the hall behind you," he added as if by an afterthought. "You left it ajar once – this light might show through the window draperies."

At his bidding she rose more willingly than at any time before. To reach the door she passed within a foot of the end of the couch, and watching over her shoulder at his hunched-up back she paused there for the smallest fraction of time. The damaged picture hat slid off on the floor with a soft little thud, but he never turned around.

The instant, though, that the hall door closed behind her the man's hands became briskly active. He fumbled in an inner pocket of his unbuttoned waistcoat; then his right hand, holding a small cylindrical vial of a colorless liquid, passed swiftly over one of the two glasses of slaking champagne and hovered there a second. A few tiny globules fell dimpling into the top of the yellow wine, then vanished; a heavy reek, like the smell of crushed peach kernels, spread through the whole room. In the same motion almost he recorked the little bottle, stowed it out of sight, and with a quick, wrenching thrust that bent the small blade of his penknife in its socket he split the peach seed in two lengthwise and with his thumb-nail bruised the small brown kernel lying snugly within. He dropped the knife and the halved seed and began sipping at the undoctored glass of champagne, not forgetting even then to wave his fingers above it to keep the winged green tormentors out.

The door at the front reopened and the woman came in. Her thoughts were not upon smells, but instinctively she sniffed at the thick scent on the poisoned air.

"I accidentally split this peach seed open," he said quickly, with an elaborate explanatory air. "Stenches up the whole place, don't it? Come, take that other glass of champagne – it will do you good to—"

Perhaps it was some subtle sixth sense that warned him; perhaps the lightning-quick realization that she had moved right alongside him, poised and set to strike. At any rate he started to fling up his head – too late! The needle point of the jet-headed hatpin entered exactly at the outer corner of his right eye and passed backward for nearly its full length into his brain – smoothly, painlessly, swiftly. He gave a little surprised gasp, almost like a sob, and lolled his head back against the chair rest, like a man who has grown suddenly tired. The hand that held the champagne glass relaxed naturally and the glass turned over on its side with a small tinkling sound and spilled its thin contents on the table.

It had been easier than she had thought it would be. She stepped back, still holding the hatpin. She moved around from behind him, and then she saw his face, half upturned, almost directly beneath the low light. There was no blood, no sign even of the wound, but his jaw had dropped down unpleasantly, showing the ends of his lower front teeth, and his eyes stared up unwinkingly with a puzzled, almost a disappointed, look in them. A green fly lit at the outer corner of his right eye; more green flies were coming. And he didn't put up his hand to brush it away. He let it stay – he let it stay there.

With her eyes still fixed on his face, the woman reached out, feeling for her glass of the champagne. She felt that she needed it now, and at a gulp she took a good half of it down her throat.

She put the glass down steadily enough on the table; but into her eyes came the same puzzled, baffled look that his wore, and almost gently she slipped down into the chair facing him.

Then her jaw lolled a little too, and some of the other flies came buzzing toward her.

The Traveler's Story of a Terribly Strange Bed

Wilkie Collins

SHORTLY AFTER my education at college was finished, I happened to be staying at Paris with an English friend. We were both young men then, and lived, I am afraid, rather a wild life, in the delightful city of our sojourn. One night we were idling about the neighborhood of the Palais Royal, doubtful to what amusement we should next betake ourselves. My friend proposed a visit to Frascati's; but his suggestion was not to my taste. I knew Frascati's, as the French saying is, by heart; had lost and won plenty of five-franc pieces there, merely for amusement's sake, until it was amusement no longer, and was thoroughly tired, in fact, of all the ghastly respectabilities of such a social anomaly as a respectable gambling-house. "For Heaven's sake," said I to my friend, "let us go somewhere where we can see a little genuine, blackguard, poverty-stricken gaming with no false gingerbread glitter thrown over it all. Let us get away from fashionable Frascati's, to a house where they don't mind letting in a man with a ragged coat, or a man with no coat, ragged or otherwise." "Very well," said my friend, "we needn't go out of the Palais Royal to find the sort of company you want. Here's the place just before us; as blackguard a place, by all report, as you could possibly wish to see." In another minute we arrived at the door, and entered the house, the back of which you have drawn in your sketch.

When we got upstairs, and had left our hats and sticks with the doorkeeper, we were admitted into the chief gambling-room. We did not find many people assembled there. But, few as the men were who looked up at us on our entrance, they were all types – lamentably true types – of their respective classes.

We had come to see blackguards; but these men were something worse. There is a comic side, more or less appreciable, in all blackguardism – here there was nothing but tragedy – mute, weird tragedy. The quiet in the room was horrible. The thin, haggard, long-haired young man, whose sunken eyes fiercely watched the turning up of the cards, never spoke; the flabby, fat-faced, pimply player, who pricked his piece of pasteboard perseveringly, to register how often black won, and how often red – never spoke; the dirty, wrinkled old man, with the vulture eyes and the darned great-coat, who had lost his last sou, and still looked on desperately, after he could play no longer – never spoke. Even the voice of the croupier sounded as if it were strangely dulled and thickened in the atmosphere of the room. I had entered the place to laugh, but the spectacle before me was something to weep over. I soon found it necessary to take refuge in excitement from the depression of spirits which was fast stealing on me. Unfortunately I sought the nearest excitement, by going to the table and beginning to play. Still more unfortunately, as the event will show, I won – won prodigiously; won incredibly; won at such a rate that the regular players at the table crowded round me; and staring at my stakes with hungry, superstitious eyes, whispered to one another that the English stranger was going to break the bank.

The game was Rouge et Noir. I had played at it in every city in Europe, without, however, the care or the wish to study the Theory of Chances – that philosopher's stone of all gamblers! And a gambler, in the strict sense of the word, I had never been. I was heart-whole from the corroding passion for play. My gaming was a mere idle amusement. I never resorted to it by necessity, because I never knew what it was to want money. I never practiced it so incessantly as to lose more than I could afford, or to gain more than I could cooly pocket without being thrown off my balance by my good luck. In short, I had hitherto frequented gambling-tables – just as I frequented ball-rooms and opera-houses – because they amused me, and because I had nothing better to do with my leisure hours.

But on this occasion it was very different – now, for the first time in my life, I felt what the passion for play really was. My success first bewildered, and then, in the most literal meaning of the word, intoxicated me. Incredible as it may appear, it is nevertheless true, that I only lost when I attempted to estimate chances, and played according to previous calculation. If I left everything to luck, and staked without any care or consideration, I was sure to win – to win in the face of every recognized probability in favor of the bank. At first some of the men present ventured their money safely enough on my color; but I speedily increased my stakes to sums which they dared not risk. One after another they left off playing, and breathlessly looked on at my game.

Still, time after time, I staked higher and higher, and still won. The excitement in the room rose to fever pitch. The silence was interrupted by a deep-muttered chorus of oaths and exclamations in different languages, every time the gold was shoveled across to my side of the table – even the imperturbable croupier dashed his rake on the floor in a (French) fury of astonishment at my success. But one man present preserved his self-possession, and that man was my friend. He came to my side, and whispering in English, begged me to leave the place, satisfied with what I had already gained. I must do him the justice to say that he repeated his warnings and entreaties several times, and only left me and went away after I had rejected his advice (I was to all intents and purposes gambling drunk) in terms which rendered it impossible for him to address me again that night.

Shortly after he had gone, a hoarse voice behind me cried: "Permit me, my dear sir – permit me to restore to their proper place two napoleons which you have dropped. Wonderful luck, sir! I pledge you my word of honor, as an old soldier, in the course of my long experience in this sort of thing, I never saw such luck as yours – never! Go on, sir – Sacre mille bombes! Go on boldly, and break the bank!"

I turned round and saw, nodding and smiling at me with inveterate civility, a tall man, dressed in a frogged and braided surtout.

If I had been in my senses, I should have considered him, personally, as being rather a suspicious specimen of an old soldier. He had goggling, bloodshot eyes, mangy mustaches, and a broken nose. His voice betrayed a barrack-room intonation of the worst order, and he had the dirtiest pair of hands I ever saw – even in France. These little personal peculiarities exercised, however, no repelling influence on me. In the mad excitement, the reckless triumph of that moment, I was ready to "fraternize" with anybody who encouraged me in my game. I accepted the old soldier's offered pinch of snuff; clapped him on the back, and swore he was the honestest fellow in the world – the most glorious relic of the Grand Army that I had ever met with. "Go on!" cried my military friend, snapping his fingers in ecstasy – "Go on, and win! Break the bank – Mille tonnerres! my gallant English comrade, break the bank!"

And I did go on – went on at such a rate, that in another quarter of an hour the croupier called out, "Gentlemen, the bank has discontinued for tonight." All the notes, and all the gold in that 'bank,' now lay in a heap under my hands; the whole floating capital of the gambling-house was waiting to pour into my pockets!

"Tie up the money in your pocket-handkerchief, my worthy sir," said the old soldier, as I wildly plunged my hands into my heap of gold. "Tie it up, as we used to tie up a bit of dinner in the Grand Army; your winnings are too heavy for any breeches-pockets that ever were sewed. There! that's it – shovel them in, notes and all! Credie! what luck! Stop! another napoleon on the floor! Ah! sacre petit polisson de Napoleon! have I found thee at last? Now then, sir – two tight double knots each way with your honorable permission, and the money's safe. Feel it! feel it, fortunate sir! hard and round as a cannon-ball – Ah, bah! if they had only fired such cannon-balls at us at Austerlitz – nom d'une pipe! if they only had! And now, as an ancient grenadier, as an ex-brave of the French army, what remains for me to do? I ask what? Simply this: to entreat my valued English friend to drink a bottle of Champagne with me, and toast the goddess Fortune in foaming goblets before we part!"

Excellent ex-brave! Convivial ancient grenadier! Champagne by all means! An English cheer for an old soldier! Hurrah! hurrah! Another English cheer for the goddess Fortune! Hurrah! hurrah! hurrah!

"Bravo! the Englishman; the amiable, gracious Englishman, in whose veins circulates the vivacious blood of France! Another glass? Ah, bah! – the bottle is empty! Never mind! Vive le vin! I, the old soldier, order another bottle, and half a pound of bonbons with it!"

"No, no, ex-brave; never – ancient grenadier! Your bottle last time; my bottle this. Behold it! Toast away! The French Army! the great Napoleon! the present company! the croupier! the honest croupier's wife and daughters – if he has any! the Ladies generally! everybody in the world!"

By the time the second bottle of Champagne was emptied, I felt as if I had been drinking liquid fire – my brain seemed all aflame. No excess in wine had ever had this effect on me before in my life. Was it the result of a stimulant acting upon my system when I was in a highly excited state? Was my stomach in a particularly disordered condition? Or was the Champagne amazingly strong?

"Ex-brave of the French Army!" cried I, in a mad state of exhilaration, "I am on fire! how are you? You have set me on fire! Do you hear, my hero of Austerlitz? Let us have a third bottle of Champagne to put the flame out!"

The old soldier wagged his head, rolled his goggle-eyes, until I expected to see them slip out of their sockets; placed his dirty forefinger by the side of his broken nose; solemnly ejaculated "Coffee!" and immediately ran off into an inner room.

The word pronounced by the eccentric veteran seemed to have a magical effect on the rest of the company present. With one accord they all rose to depart. Probably they had expected to profit by my intoxication; but finding that my new friend was benevolently bent on preventing me from getting dead drunk, had now abandoned all hope of thriving pleasantly on my winnings. Whatever their motive might be, at any rate they went away in a body. When the old soldier returned, and sat down again opposite to me at the table, we had the room to ourselves. I could see the croupier, in a sort of vestibule which opened out of it, eating his supper in solitude. The silence was now deeper than ever.

A sudden change, too, had come over the 'ex-brave.' He assumed a portentously solemn look; and when he spoke to me again, his speech was ornamented by no oaths, enforced by no finger-snapping, enlivened by no apostrophes or exclamations.

"Listen, my dear sir," said he, in mysteriously confidential tones – "listen to an old soldier's advice. I have been to the mistress of the house (a very charming woman, with a genius for cookery!) to impress on her the necessity of making us some particularly strong and good coffee. You must drink this coffee in order to get rid of your little amiable exaltation of spirits before you think of going home – you must, my good and gracious friend! With all that money to take home tonight, it is a sacred duty to yourself to have your wits about you. You are known to be a winner to an enormous extent by several gentlemen present tonight, who, in a certain point of view, are very worthy and excellent fellows; but they are mortal men, my dear sir, and they have their amiable weaknesses. Need I say more? Ah, no, no! you understand me! Now, this is what you must do – send for a cabriolet when you feel quite well again – draw up all the windows when you get into it – and tell the driver to take you home only through the large and well-lighted thoroughfares. Do this; and you and your money will be safe. Do this; and tomorrow you will thank an old soldier for giving you a word of honest advice."

Just as the ex-brave ended his oration in very lachrymose tones, the coffee came in, ready poured out in two cups. My attentive friend handed me one of the cups with a bow. I was parched with thirst, and drank it off at a draught. Almost instantly afterwards, I was seized with a fit of giddiness, and felt more completely intoxicated than ever. The room whirled round and round furiously; the old soldier seemed to be regularly bobbing up and down before me like the piston of a steam-engine. I was half deafened by a violent singing in my ears; a feeling of utter bewilderment, helplessness, idiocy, overcame me. I rose from my chair, holding on by the table to keep my balance; and stammered out that I felt dreadfully unwell – so unwell that I did not know how I was to get home.

"My dear friend," answered the old soldier – and even his voice seemed to be bobbing up and down as he spoke – "my dear friend, it would be madness to go home in your state; you would be sure to lose your money; you might be robbed and murdered with the greatest ease. I am going to sleep here; do you sleep here, too – they make up capital beds in this house – take one; sleep off the effects of the wine, and go home safely with your winnings tomorrow – tomorrow, in broad daylight."

I had but two ideas left: one, that I must never let go hold of my handkerchief full of money; the other, that I must lie down somewhere immediately, and fall off into a comfortable sleep. So I agreed to the proposal about the bed, and took the offered arm of the old soldier, carrying my money with my disengaged hand. Preceded by the croupier, we passed along some passages and up a flight of stairs into the bedroom which I was to occupy. The ex-brave shook me warmly by the hand, proposed that we should breakfast together, and then, followed by the croupier, left me for the night.

I ran to the wash-hand stand; drank some of the water in my jug; poured the rest out, and plunged my face into it; then sat down in a chair and tried to compose myself. I soon felt better. The change for my lungs, from the fetid atmosphere of the gambling-room to the cool air of the apartment I now occupied, the almost equally refreshing change for my eyes, from the glaring gaslights of the 'salon' to the dim, quiet flicker of one bedroom-candle, aided wonderfully the restorative effects of cold water. The giddiness left me, and I began to feel a little like a reasonable being again. My first thought was of the risk of sleeping all night in a gambling-house; my second, of the still greater risk of trying to get out after the house was closed, and of going home alone at night through the streets of Paris with a large sum of money about me. I had slept in worse places than this on my travels; so I determined to lock, bolt, and barricade my door, and take my chance till the next morning.

Accordingly, I secured myself against all intrusion; looked under the bed, and into the cupboard; tried the fastening of the window; and then, satisfied that I had taken every proper precaution, pulled off my upper clothing, put my light, which was a dim one, on the hearth among a feathery litter of wood-ashes, and got into bed, with the handkerchief full of money under my pillow.

I soon felt not only that I could not go to sleep, but that I could not even close my eyes. I was wide awake, and in a high fever. Every nerve in my body trembled – every one of my senses seemed to be preternaturally sharpened. I tossed and rolled, and tried every kind of position, and perseveringly sought out the cold corners of the bed, and all to no purpose. Now I thrust my arms over the clothes; now I poked them under the clothes; now I violently shot my legs straight out down to the bottom of the bed; now I convulsively coiled them up as near my chin as they would go; now I shook out my crumpled pillow, changed it to the cool side, patted it flat, and lay down quietly on my back; now I fiercely doubled it in two, set it up on end, thrust it against the board of the bed, and tried a sitting posture. Every effort was in vain; I groaned with vexation as I felt that I was in for a sleepless night.

What could I do? I had no book to read. And yet, unless I found out some method of diverting my mind, I felt certain that I was in the condition to imagine all sorts of horrors; to rack my brain with forebodings of every possible and impossible danger; in short, to pass the night in suffering all conceivable varieties of nervous terror.

I raised myself on my elbow, and looked about the room – which was brightened by a lovely moonlight pouring straight through the window – to see if it contained any pictures or ornaments that I could at all clearly distinguish. While my eyes wandered from wall to wall, a remembrance of Le Maistre's delightful little book, "Voyage autour de ma Chambre," occurred to me. I resolved to imitate the French author, and find occupation and amusement enough to relieve the tedium of my wakefulness, by making a mental inventory of every article of furniture I could see, and by following up to their sources the multitude of associations which even a chair, a table, or a wash-hand stand may be made to call forth.

In the nervous unsettled state of my mind at that moment, I found it much easier to make my inventory than to make my reflections, and thereupon soon gave up all hope of thinking in Le Maistre's fanciful track – or, indeed, of thinking at all. I looked about the room at the different articles of furniture, and did nothing more.

There was, first, the bed I was lying in; a four-post bed, of all things in the world to meet with in Paris – yes, a thorough clumsy British four-poster, with the regular top lined with chintz – the regular fringed valance all round – the regular stifling, unwholesome curtains, which I remembered having mechanically drawn back against the posts without particularly noticing the bed when I first got into the room. Then there was the marble-topped wash-hand stand, from which the water I had spilled, in my hurry to pour it out, was still dripping, slowly and more slowly, on to the brick floor. Then two small chairs, with my coat, waistcoat, and trousers flung on them. Then a large elbow-chair covered with dirty-white dimity, with my cravat and shirt collar thrown over the back. Then a chest of drawers with two of the brass handles off, and a tawdry, broken china inkstand placed on it by way of ornament for the top. Then the dressing-table, adorned by a very small looking-glass, and a very large pincushion. Then the window – an unusually large window. Then a dark old picture, which the feeble candle dimly showed me. It was a picture of a fellow in a high Spanish hat, crowned with a plume of towering feathers. A swarthy, sinister ruffian, looking upward, shading his eyes with his hand, and looking intently upward – it might be at some tall gallows at which he was going to be hanged. At any rate, he had the appearance of thoroughly deserving it.

This picture put a kind of constraint upon me to look upward too – at the top of the bed. It was a gloomy and not an interesting object, and I looked back at the picture. I counted the feathers in the man's hat – they stood out in relief – three white, two green. I observed the crown of his hat, which was of conical shape, according to the fashion supposed to have been favored by Guido Fawkes. I wondered what he was looking up at. It couldn't be at the stars; such a desperado was neither astrologer nor astronomer. It must be at the high gallows, and he was going to be hanged presently. Would the executioner come into possession of his conical crowned hat and plume of feathers? I counted the feathers again – three white, two green.

While I still lingered over this very improving and intellectual employment, my thoughts insensibly began to wander. The moonlight shining into the room reminded me of a certain moonlight night in England – the night after a picnic party in a Welsh valley. Every incident of the drive homeward, through lovely scenery, which the moonlight made lovelier than ever, came back to my remembrance, though I had never given the picnic a thought for years; though, if I had tried to recollect it, I could certainly have recalled little or nothing of that scene long past. Of all the wonderful faculties that help to tell us we are immortal, which speaks the sublime truth more eloquently than memory? Here was I, in a strange house of the most suspicious character, in a situation of uncertainty, and even of peril, which might seem to make the cool exercise of my recollection almost out of the question; nevertheless, remembering, quite involuntarily, places, people, conversations, minute circumstances of every kind, which I had thought forgotten forever; which I could not possibly have recalled at will, even under the most favorable auspices. And what cause had produced in a moment the whole of this strange, complicated, mysterious effect? Nothing but some rays of moonlight shining in at my bedroom window.

I was still thinking of the picnic – of our merriment on the drive home – of the sentimental young lady who would quote "Childe Harold" because it was moonlight. I was absorbed by these past scenes and past amusements, when, in an instant, the thread on which my memories hung snapped asunder; my attention immediately came back to present things more vividly than ever, and I found myself, I neither knew why nor wherefore, looking hard at the picture again.

Looking for what?

Good God! the man had pulled his hat down on his brows! No! the hat itself was gone! Where was the conical crown? Where the feathers – three white, two green? Not there! In place of the hat and feathers, what dusky object was it that now hid his forehead, his eyes, his shading hand?

Was the bed moving?

I turned on my back and looked up. Was I mad? drunk? dreaming? giddy again? or was the top of the bed really moving down – sinking slowly, regularly, silently, horribly, right down throughout the whole of its length and breadth – right down upon me, as I lay underneath?

My blood seemed to stand still. A deadly paralysing coldness stole all over me as I turned my head round on the pillow and determined to test whether the bed-top was really moving or not, by keeping my eye on the man in the picture.

The next look in that direction was enough. The dull, black, frowzy outline of the valance above me was within an inch of being parallel with his waist. I still looked breathlessly. And steadily and slowly – very slowly – I saw the figure, and the line of frame below the figure, vanish, as the valance moved down before it.

I am, constitutionally, anything but timid. I have been on more than one occasion in peril of my life, and have not lost my self-possession for an instant; but when the conviction first settled on my mind that the bed-top was really moving, was steadily and continuously sinking down upon me, I looked up shuddering, helpless, panic-stricken, beneath the hideous machinery for murder, which was advancing closer and closer to suffocate me where I lay.

I looked up, motionless, speechless, breathless. The candle, fully spent, went out; but the moonlight still brightened the room. Down and down, without pausing and without sounding, came the bed-top, and still my panic-terror seemed to bind me faster and faster to the mattress on which I lay – down and down it sank, till the dusty odor from the lining of the canopy came stealing into my nostrils.

At that final moment the instinct of self-preservation startled me out of my trance, and I moved at last. There was just room for me to roll myself sidewise off the bed. As I dropped noiselessly to the floor, the edge of the murderous canopy touched me on the shoulder.

Without stopping to draw my breath, without wiping the cold sweat from my face, I rose instantly on my knees to watch the bed-top. I was literally spellbound by it. If I had heard footsteps behind me, I could not have turned round; if a means of escape had been miraculously provided for me, I could not have moved to take advantage of it. The whole life in me was, at that moment, concentrated in my eyes.

It descended – the whole canopy, with the fringe round it, came down – down – close down; so close that there was not room now to squeeze my finger between the bed-top and the bed. I felt at the sides, and discovered that what had appeared to me from beneath to be the ordinary light canopy of a four-post bed was in reality a thick, broad mattress, the substance of which was concealed by the valance and its fringe. I looked up and saw the four posts rising hideously bare. In the middle of the bed-top was a huge wooden screw that had evidently worked it down through a hole in the ceiling, just as ordinary presses are worked down on the substance selected for compression. The frightful apparatus moved without making the faintest noise. There had been no creaking as it came down; there was now not the faintest sound from the room above. Amid a dead and awful silence I beheld before me – in the nineteenth century, and in the civilized capital of France – such a machine for secret murder by suffocation as might have existed in the worst days of the Inquisition, in the lonely inns among the Hartz Mountains, in the mysterious tribunals of Westphalia! Still, as I looked on it, I could not move, I could hardly breathe, but I began to recover the power of thinking, and in a moment I discovered the murderous conspiracy framed against me in all its horror.

My cup of coffee had been drugged, and drugged too strongly. I had been saved from being smothered by having taken an overdose of some narcotic. How I had chafed and fretted at the fever fit which had preserved my life by keeping me awake! How recklessly I had confided myself to the two wretches who had led me into this room, determined, for the sake of my winnings, to kill me in my sleep by the surest and most horrible contrivance for secretly accomplishing my destruction! How many men, winners like me, had slept, as I had proposed to sleep, in that bed, and had never been seen or heard of more! I shuddered at the bare idea of it.

But, ere long, all thought was again suspended by the sight of the murderous canopy moving once more. After it had remained on the bed – as nearly as I could guess – about ten minutes, it began to move up again. The villains who worked it from above evidently believed that their purpose was now accomplished. Slowly and silently, as it had descended, that horrible bed-top rose towards its former place. When it reached the upper extremities of the four posts, it reached the ceiling, too. Neither hole nor screw could be seen; the bed became in appearance an ordinary bed again – the canopy an ordinary canopy – even to the most suspicious eyes.

Now, for the first time, I was able to move – to rise from my knees – to dress myself in my upper clothing – and to consider of how I should escape. If I betrayed by the smallest noise that the attempt to suffocate me had failed, I was certain to be murdered. Had I made any noise already? I listened intently, looking towards the door.

No! no footsteps in the passage outside – no sound of a tread, light or heavy, in the room above – absolute silence everywhere. Besides locking and bolting my door, I had moved an old wooden chest against it, which I had found under the bed. To remove this chest (my blood ran cold as I thought of what its contents might be!) without making some disturbance was impossible; and, moreover, to think of escaping through the house, now barred up for the night, was sheer insanity. Only one chance was left me – the window. I stole to it on tiptoe.

My bedroom was on the first floor, above an entresol, and looked into a back street, which you have sketched in your view. I raised my hand to open the window, knowing that on that action hung, by the merest hair-breadth, my chance of safety. They keep vigilant watch in a House of Murder. If any part of the frame cracked, if the hinge creaked, I was a lost man! It must have occupied me at least five minutes, reckoning by time – five hours, reckoning by suspense – to open that window. I succeeded in doing it silently – in doing it with all the dexterity of a house-breaker – and then looked down into the street. To leap the distance beneath me would be almost certain destruction! Next, I looked round at the sides of the house. Down the left side ran a thick water-pipe which you have drawn – it passed close by the outer edge of the window. The moment I saw the pipe I knew I was saved. My breath came and went freely for the first time since I had seen the canopy of the bed moving down upon me!

To some men the means of escape which I had discovered might have seemed difficult and dangerous enough – to me the prospect of slipping down the pipe into the street did not suggest even a thought of peril. I had always been accustomed, by the practice of gymnastics, to keep up my school-boy powers as a daring and expert climber; and knew that my head, hands, and feet would serve me faithfully in any hazards of ascent or descent. I had already got one leg over the window-sill, when I remembered the handkerchief filled with money under my pillow. I could well have afforded to leave it behind me, but I was revengefully determined that the miscreants of the gambling-house should miss their plunder as well as their victim. So I went back to the bed and tied the heavy handkerchief at my back by my cravat.

Just as I had made it tight and fixed it in a comfortable place, I thought I heard a sound of breathing outside the door. The chill feeling of horror ran through me again as I listened. No! dead silence still in the passage – I had only heard the night air blowing softly into the room. The next moment I was on the window-sill – and the next I had a firm grip on the water-pipe with my hands and knees.

I slid down into the street easily and quietly, as I thought I should, and immediately set off at the top of my speed to a branch "Prefecture" of Police, which I knew was situated in the immediate neighborhood. A "Sub-prefect," and several picked men among his subordinates, happened to be up, maturing, I believe, some scheme for discovering the perpetrator of a mysterious murder which all Paris was talking of just then. When I began my story, in a breathless hurry and in very bad French, I could see that the Sub-prefect suspected me of being a drunken Englishman who had robbed somebody; but he soon altered his opinion as I went on, and before I had anything like concluded, he shoved all the papers before him into a drawer, put on his hat, supplied me with another (for I was bareheaded), ordered a file of soldiers, desired his expert followers to get ready all sorts of tools for breaking open doors and ripping up brick flooring, and took my arm, in the most friendly and familiar manner possible, to lead me with him out of the house. I will venture to say that when the Sub-prefect was a little boy, and was taken for the first time to the play, he was not half as much pleased as he was now at the job in prospect for him at the gambling-house!

Away we went through the streets, the Sub-prefect cross-examining and congratulating me in the same breath as we marched at the head of our formidable posse comitatus. Sentinels were placed at the back and front of the house the moment we got to it; a tremendous battery of knocks was directed against the door; a light appeared at a window; I was told to conceal myself behind the police – then came more knocks and a cry of "Open in the name of the law!" At that terrible summons bolts and locks gave way before an invisible hand, and the moment after the Sub-prefect was in the passage, confronting a waiter half-dressed and ghastly pale. This was the short dialogue which immediately took place:

"We want to see the Englishman who is sleeping in this house?"

"He went away hours ago."

"He did no such thing. His friend went away; he remained. Show us to his bedroom!"

"I swear to you, Monsieur le Sous-prefect, he is not here! he—"

"I swear to you, Monsieur le Garcon, he is. He slept here – he didn't find your bed comfortable – he came to us to complain of it – here he is among my men – and here am I ready to look for a flea or two in his bedstead. Renaudin! (calling to one of the subordinates, and pointing to the waiter) collar that man and tie his hands behind him. Now, then, gentlemen, let us walk upstairs!"

Every man and woman in the house was secured – the "Old Soldier" the first. Then I identified the bed in which I had slept, and then we went into the room above.

No object that was at all extraordinary appeared in any part of it. The Sub-prefect looked round the place, commanded everybody to be silent, stamped twice on the floor, called for a candle, looked attentively at the spot he had stamped on, and ordered the flooring there to be carefully taken up. This was done in no time. Lights were produced, and we saw a deep raftered cavity between the floor of this room and the ceiling of the room beneath. Through this cavity there ran perpendicularly a sort of case of iron thickly greased; and inside the case appeared the screw, which communicated with the bed-top below. Extra lengths of screw, freshly oiled; levers covered with felt; all the complete upper works of a heavy press – constructed with infernal ingenuity so as to join the fixtures below, and when taken to pieces again, to go into the smallest possible compass – were next discovered and pulled out on the floor. After some little difficulty the Sub-prefect succeeded in putting the machinery together, and, leaving his men to work it, descended with me to the bedroom. The smothering canopy was then lowered, but not so noiselessly as I had seen it lowered. When I mentioned this to the Sub-prefect, his answer, simple as it was, had a terrible significance. "My men," said he, "are working down the bed-top for the first time – the men whose money you won were in better practice."

We left the house in the sole possession of two police agents – every one of the inmates being removed to prison on the spot. The Sub-prefect, after taking down my "proces verbal" in his office, returned with me to my hotel to get my passport. "Do you think," I asked, as I gave it to him, "that any men have really been smothered in that bed, as they tried to smother me?"

"I have seen dozens of drowned men laid out at the Morgue," answered the Sub-prefect, "in whose pocket-books were found letters stating that they had committed suicide in the Seine, because they had lost everything at the gaming table. Do I know how many of those men entered the same gambling-house that you entered? won as you won? took that bed as you took it? slept in it? were smothered in it? and were privately thrown into the river, with a letter of explanation written by the murderers and placed in their pocket-books? No man can say how many or how few have suffered the fate from which you have escaped. The people of the gambling-house kept their bedstead machinery a secret from us – even from the police! The dead kept the rest of the secret for them. Good-night, or rather good-morning, Monsieur Faulkner! Be at my office again at nine o'clock – in the meantime, au revoir!"

The rest of my story is soon told. I was examined and re-examined; the gambling-house was strictly searched all through from top to bottom; the prisoners were separately interrogated; and two of the less guilty among them made a confession. I discovered that the Old Soldier was the master of the gambling-house – justice discovered that he had been drummed out of the army as a vagabond years ago; that he had been guilty of all sorts of villainies since; that he was in possession of stolen property, which the owners identified; and that he, the croupier, another accomplice, and the woman who had made my cup of coffee, were all in the secret of the bedstead. There appeared some reason to doubt whether the inferior persons attached to the house knew anything of the suffocating machinery; and they received the benefit of that doubt, by being treated simply as thieves and vagabonds. As for the Old Soldier and his two head myrmidons, they went to the galleys; the woman who had drugged my coffee was imprisoned for I forget how many years; the regular attendants at the gambling-house were considered "suspicious" and placed under "surveillance"; and I became, for one whole week (which is a long time) the head "lion" in Parisian society. My adventure was dramatized by three illustrious play-makers, but never saw theatrical daylight; for the censorship forbade the introduction on the stage of a correct copy of the gambling-house bedstead.

One good result was produced by my adventure, which any censorship must have approved: it cured me of ever again trying "Rouge et Noir" as an amusement. The sight of a green cloth, with packs of cards and heaps of money on it, will henceforth be forever associated in my mind with the sight of a bed canopy descending to suffocate me in the silence and darkness of the night.

Just as Mr. Faulkner pronounced these words he started in his chair, and resumed his stiff, dignified position in a great hurry. "Bless my soul!" cried he, with a comic look of astonishment and vexation, "while I have been telling you what is the real secret of my interest in the sketch you have so kindly given to me, I have altogether forgotten that I came here to sit for my portrait. For the last hour or more I must have been the worst model you ever had to draw from!"

"On the contrary, you have been the best," said I. "I have been trying to catch your likeness; and, while telling your story, you have unconsciously shown me the natural expression I wanted to insure my success."

NOTE BY MRS. KERBY.

I cannot let this story end without mentioning what the chance saying was which caused it to be told at the farmhouse the other night. Our friend the young sailor, among his other quaint objections to sleeping on shore, declared that he particularly hated four-post beds, because he never slept in one without doubting whether the top might not come down in the night and suffocate him. I thought this chance reference to the distinguishing feature of William's narrative curious enough, and my husband agreed with me. But he says it is scarcely worth while to mention such a trifle in anything so important as a book. I cannot venture, after this, to do more than slip these lines in modestly at the end of the story. If the printer should notice my few last words, perhaps he may not mind the trouble of putting them into some out-of-the-way corner.

L. K.

Crime and Punishment
Part I

Fyodor Dostoevsky

Chapter I

ON AN EXCEPTIONALLY HOT evening early in July a young man came out of the garret in which he lodged in S. Place and walked slowly, as though in hesitation, towards K. bridge.

He had successfully avoided meeting his landlady on the staircase. His garret was under the roof of a high, five-storied house and was more like a cupboard than a room. The landlady who provided him with garret, dinners, and attendance, lived on the floor below, and every time he went out he was obliged to pass her kitchen, the door of which invariably stood open. And each time he passed, the young man had a sick, frightened feeling, which made him scowl and feel ashamed. He was hopelessly in debt to his landlady, and was afraid of meeting her.

This was not because he was cowardly and abject, quite the contrary; but for some time past he had been in an overstrained irritable condition, verging on hypochondria. He had become so completely absorbed in himself, and isolated from his fellows that he dreaded meeting, not only his landlady, but anyone at all. He was crushed by poverty, but the anxieties of his position had of late ceased to weigh upon him. He had given up attending to matters of practical importance; he had lost all desire to do so. Nothing that any landlady could do had a real terror for him. But to be stopped on the stairs, to be forced to listen to her trivial, irrelevant gossip, to pestering demands for payment, threats and complaints, and to rack his brains for excuses, to prevaricate, to lie – no, rather than that, he would creep down the stairs like a cat and slip out unseen.

This evening, however, on coming out into the street, he became acutely aware of his fears.

"I want to attempt a thing like that and am frightened by these trifles," he thought, with an odd smile. "Hm... yes, all is in a man's hands and he lets it all slip from cowardice, that's an axiom. It would be interesting to know what it is men are most afraid of. Taking a new step, uttering a new word is what they fear most.... But I am talking too much. It's because I chatter that I do nothing. Or perhaps it is that I chatter because I do nothing. I've learned to chatter this last month, lying for days together in my den thinking... of Jack the Giant-killer. Why am I going there now? Am I capable of that? Is that serious? It is not serious at all. It's simply a fantasy to amuse myself; a plaything! Yes, maybe it is a plaything."

The heat in the street was terrible: and the airlessness, the bustle and the plaster, scaffolding, bricks, and dust all about him, and that special Petersburg stench, so familiar to all who are unable to get out of town in summer – all worked painfully upon the young man's already overwrought nerves. The insufferable stench from the pot-houses, which are particularly numerous in that part of the town, and the drunken men whom he met continually, although it was a working day, completed the revolting misery of the picture. An expression of the profoundest disgust gleamed for a moment in the young man's refined face. He was, by the way, exceptionally handsome, above the average in height, slim, well-built, with beautiful dark eyes and dark brown hair. Soon he sank into deep thought, or more accurately speaking into a complete blankness of mind; he walked along not observing what was about him and not caring to observe it. From time to time, he would mutter something, from the habit of talking to himself, to which he had just confessed. At these moments he would become conscious that his ideas were sometimes in a tangle and that he was very weak; for two days he had scarcely tasted food.

He was so badly dressed that even a man accustomed to shabbiness would have been ashamed to be seen in the street in such rags. In that quarter of the town, however, scarcely any shortcoming in dress would have created surprise. Owing to the proximity of the Hay Market, the number of establishments of bad character, the preponderance of the trading and working class population crowded in these streets and alleys in the heart of Petersburg, types so various were to be seen in the streets that no figure, however queer, would have caused surprise. But there was such accumulated bitterness and contempt in the young man's heart, that, in spite of all the fastidiousness of youth, he minded his rags least of all in the street. It was a different matter when he met with acquaintances or with former fellow students, whom, indeed, he disliked meeting at any time. And yet when a drunken man who, for some unknown reason, was being taken somewhere in a huge waggon dragged by a heavy dray horse, suddenly shouted at him as he drove past: "Hey there, German hatter" bawling at the top of his voice and pointing at him – the young man stopped suddenly and clutched tremulously at his hat. It was a tall round hat from Zimmerman's, but completely worn out, rusty with age, all torn and bespattered, brimless and bent on one side in a most unseemly fashion. Not shame, however, but quite another feeling akin to terror had overtaken him.

"I knew it," he muttered in confusion, "I thought so! That's the worst of all! Why, a stupid thing like this, the most trivial detail might spoil the whole plan. Yes, my hat is too noticeable.... It looks absurd and that makes it noticeable.... With my rags I ought to wear a cap, any sort of old pancake, but not this grotesque thing. Nobody wears such a hat, it would be noticed a mile off, it would be remembered.... What matters is that people would remember it, and that would give them a clue. For this business one should be as little conspicuous as possible.... Trifles, trifles are what matter! Why, it's just such trifles that always ruin everything...."

He had not far to go; he knew indeed how many steps it was from the gate of his lodging house: exactly seven hundred and thirty. He had counted them once when he had been lost in dreams. At the time he had put no faith in those dreams and was only tantalising himself by their hideous but daring recklessness. Now, a month later, he had begun to look upon them differently, and, in spite of the monologues in which he jeered at his own impotence and indecision, he had involuntarily come to regard this "hideous" dream as an exploit to be attempted, although he still did not realise this himself. He was positively going now for a "rehearsal" of his project, and at every step his excitement grew more and more violent.

With a sinking heart and a nervous tremor, he went up to a huge house which on one side looked on to the canal, and on the other into the street. This house was let out in tiny tenements and was inhabited by working people of all kinds – tailors, locksmiths, cooks, Germans of sorts, girls picking up a living as best they could, petty clerks, etc. There was a continual coming and going through the two gates and in the two courtyards of the house. Three or four door-keepers were employed on the building. The young man was very glad to meet none of them, and at once slipped unnoticed through the door on the right, and up the staircase. It was a back staircase, dark and narrow, but he was familiar with it already, and knew his way, and he liked all these surroundings: in such darkness even the most inquisitive eyes were not to be dreaded.

"If I am so scared now, what would it be if it somehow came to pass that I were really going to do it?" he could not help asking himself as he reached the fourth storey. There his progress was barred by some porters who were engaged in moving furniture out of a flat. He knew that the flat had been occupied by a German clerk in the civil service, and his family. This German was moving out then, and so the fourth floor on this staircase would be untenanted except by the old woman. "That's a good thing anyway," he thought to himself, as he rang the bell of the old woman's flat. The bell gave a faint tinkle as though it were made of tin and not of copper. The little flats in such houses always have bells that ring like that. He had forgotten the note of that bell, and now its peculiar tinkle seemed to remind him of something and to bring it clearly before him.... He started, his nerves were terribly overstrained by now. In a little while, the door was opened a tiny crack: the old woman eyed her visitor with evident distrust through the crack, and nothing could be seen but her little eyes, glittering in the darkness. But, seeing a number of people on the landing, she grew bolder, and opened the door wide. The young man stepped into the dark entry, which was partitioned off from the tiny kitchen. The old woman stood facing him in silence and looking inquiringly at him. She was a diminutive, withered up old woman of sixty, with sharp malignant eyes and a sharp little nose. Her colourless, somewhat grizzled hair was thickly smeared with oil, and she wore no kerchief over it. Round her thin long neck, which looked like a hen's leg, was knotted some sort of flannel rag, and, in spite of the heat, there hung flapping on her shoulders, a mangy fur cape, yellow with age. The old woman coughed and groaned at every instant. The young man must have looked at her with a rather peculiar expression, for a gleam of mistrust came into her eyes again.

"Raskolnikov, a student, I came here a month ago," the young man made haste to mutter, with a half bow, remembering that he ought to be more polite.

"I remember, my good sir, I remember quite well your coming here," the old woman said distinctly, still keeping her inquiring eyes on his face.

"And here... I am again on the same errand," Raskolnikov continued, a little disconcerted and surprised at the old woman's mistrust. "Perhaps she is always like that though, only I did not notice it the other time," he thought with an uneasy feeling.

The old woman paused, as though hesitating; then stepped on one side, and pointing to the door of the room, she said, letting her visitor pass in front of her:

"Step in, my good sir."

The little room into which the young man walked, with yellow paper on the walls, geraniums and muslin curtains in the windows, was brightly lighted up at that moment by the setting sun.

"So the sun will shine like this then too!" flashed as it were by chance through Raskolnikov's mind, and with a rapid glance he scanned everything in the room, trying as far as possible to notice and remember its arrangement. But there was nothing special in the room. The furniture, all very old and of yellow wood, consisted of a sofa with a huge bent wooden back, an oval table in front of the sofa, a dressing-table with a looking-glass fixed on it between the windows, chairs along the walls and two or three half-penny prints in yellow frames, representing German damsels with birds in their hands – that was all. In the corner a light was burning before a small ikon. Everything was very clean; the floor and the furniture were brightly polished; everything shone.

"Lizaveta's work," thought the young man. There was not a speck of dust to be seen in the whole flat.

"It's in the houses of spiteful old widows that one finds such cleanliness," Raskolnikov thought again, and he stole a curious glance at the cotton curtain over the door leading into another tiny room, in which stood the old woman's bed and chest of drawers and into which he had never looked before. These two rooms made up the whole flat.

"What do you want?" the old woman said severely, coming into the room and, as before, standing in front of him so as to look him straight in the face.

"I've brought something to pawn here," and he drew out of his pocket an old-fashioned flat silver watch, on the back of which was engraved a globe; the chain was of steel.

"But the time is up for your last pledge. The month was up the day before yesterday."

"I will bring you the interest for another month; wait a little."

"But that's for me to do as I please, my good sir, to wait or to sell your pledge at once."

"How much will you give me for the watch, Alyona Ivanovna?"

"You come with such trifles, my good sir, it's scarcely worth anything. I gave you two roubles last time for your ring and one could buy it quite new at a jeweler's for a rouble and a half."

"Give me four roubles for it, I shall redeem it, it was my father's. I shall be getting some money soon."

"A rouble and a half, and interest in advance, if you like!"

"A rouble and a half!" cried the young man.

"Please yourself" – and the old woman handed him back the watch. The young man took it, and was so angry that he was on the point of going away; but checked himself at once, remembering that there was nowhere else he could go, and that he had had another object also in coming.

"Hand it over," he said roughly.

The old woman fumbled in her pocket for her keys, and disappeared behind the curtain into the other room. The young man, left standing alone in the middle of the room, listened inquisitively, thinking. He could hear her unlocking the chest of drawers.

"It must be the top drawer," he reflected. "So she carries the keys in a pocket on the right. All in one bunch on a steel ring.... And there's one key there, three times as big as all the others, with deep notches; that can't be the key of the chest of drawers... then there must be some other chest or strong-box... that's worth knowing. Strong-boxes always have keys like that... but how degrading it all is."

The old woman came back.

"Here, sir: as we say ten copecks the rouble a month, so I must take fifteen copecks from a rouble and a half for the month in advance. But for the two roubles I lent you before, you owe me now twenty copecks on the same reckoning in advance. That makes thirty-five copecks altogether. So I must give you a rouble and fifteen copecks for the watch. Here it is."

"What! only a rouble and fifteen copecks now!"

"Just so."

The young man did not dispute it and took the money. He looked at the old woman, and was in no hurry to get away, as though there was still something he wanted to say or to do, but he did not himself quite know what.

"I may be bringing you something else in a day or two, Alyona Ivanovna – a valuable thing – silver – a cigarette-box, as soon as I get it back from a friend…" he broke off in confusion.

"Well, we will talk about it then, sir."

"Good-bye – are you always at home alone, your sister is not here with you?" He asked her as casually as possible as he went out into the passage.

"What business is she of yours, my good sir?"

"Oh, nothing particular, I simply asked. You are too quick…. Good-day, Alyona Ivanovna."

Raskolnikov went out in complete confusion. This confusion became more and more intense. As he went down the stairs, he even stopped short, two or three times, as though suddenly struck by some thought. When he was in the street he cried out, "Oh, God, how loathsome it all is! and can I, can I possibly…. No, it's nonsense, it's rubbish!" he added resolutely. "And how could such an atrocious thing come into my head? What filthy things my heart is capable of. Yes, filthy above all, disgusting, loathsome, loathsome! – and for a whole month I've been…." But no words, no exclamations, could express his agitation. The feeling of intense repulsion, which had begun to oppress and torture his heart while he was on his way to the old woman, had by now reached such a pitch and had taken such a definite form that he did not know what to do with himself to escape from his wretchedness. He walked along the pavement like a drunken man, regardless of the passers-by, and jostling against them, and only came to his senses when he was in the next street. Looking round, he noticed that he was standing close to a tavern which was entered by steps leading from the pavement to the basement. At that instant two drunken men came out at the door, and abusing and supporting one another, they mounted the steps. Without stopping to think, Raskolnikov went down the steps at once. Till that moment he had never been into a tavern, but now he felt giddy and was tormented by a burning thirst. He longed for a drink of cold beer, and attributed his sudden weakness to the want of food. He sat down at a sticky little table in a dark and dirty corner; ordered some beer, and eagerly drank off the first glassful. At once he felt easier; and his thoughts became clear.

"All that's nonsense," he said hopefully, "and there is nothing in it all to worry about! It's simply physical derangement. Just a glass of beer, a piece of dry bread – and in one moment the brain is stronger, the mind is clearer and the will is firm! Phew, how utterly petty it all is!"

But in spite of this scornful reflection, he was by now looking cheerful as though he were suddenly set free from a terrible burden: and he gazed round in a friendly way at the people in the room. But even at that moment he had a dim foreboding that this happier frame of mind was also not normal.

There were few people at the time in the tavern. Besides the two drunken men he had met on the steps, a group consisting of about five men and a girl with a concertina had gone out at the same time. Their departure left the room quiet and rather empty. The persons still in the tavern were a man who appeared to be an artisan, drunk, but not extremely so, sitting before a pot of beer, and his companion, a huge, stout man with a grey beard, in a short full-skirted coat. He was very drunk: and had dropped asleep on the bench; every now and then, he began as though in his sleep, cracking his fingers, with his arms wide apart and the upper part of his body bounding about on the bench, while he hummed some meaningless refrain, trying to recall some such lines as these:

> *"His wife a year he fondly loved*
> *His wife a – a year he – fondly loved."*
> *Or suddenly waking up again:*
> *"Walking along the crowded row*
> *He met the one he used to know."*

But no one shared his enjoyment: his silent companion looked with positive hostility and mistrust at all these manifestations. There was another man in the room who looked somewhat like a retired government clerk. He was sitting apart, now and then sipping from his pot and looking round at the company. He, too, appeared to be in some agitation.

Chapter II

RASKOLNIKOV was not used to crowds, and, as we said before, he avoided society of every sort, more especially of late. But now all at once he felt a desire to be with other people. Something new seemed to be taking place within him, and with it he felt a sort of thirst for company. He was so weary after a whole month of concentrated wretchedness and gloomy excitement that he longed to rest, if only for a moment, in some other world, whatever it might be; and, in spite of the filthiness of the surroundings, he was glad now to stay in the tavern.

The master of the establishment was in another room, but he frequently came down some steps into the main room, his jaunty, tarred boots with red turn-over tops coming into view each time before the rest of his person. He wore a full coat and a horribly greasy black satin waistcoat, with no cravat, and his whole face seemed smeared with oil like an iron lock. At the counter stood a boy of about fourteen, and there was another boy somewhat younger who handed whatever was wanted. On the counter lay some sliced cucumber, some pieces of dried black bread, and some fish, chopped up small, all smelling very bad. It was insufferably close, and so heavy with the fumes of spirits that five minutes in such an atmosphere might well make a man drunk.

There are chance meetings with strangers that interest us from the first moment, before a word is spoken. Such was the impression made on Raskolnikov by the person sitting a little distance from him, who looked like a retired clerk. The young man often recalled this impression afterwards, and even ascribed it to presentiment. He looked repeatedly at the clerk, partly no doubt because the latter was staring persistently at him, obviously anxious to enter into conversation. At the other persons in the room, including the tavern-keeper, the clerk looked as though he were used to their company, and weary of it, showing a shade of condescending contempt for them as persons of station and culture inferior to his own, with whom it would be useless for him to converse. He was a man over fifty, bald and grizzled, of medium height, and stoutly built. His face, bloated from continual drinking, was of a yellow, even greenish, tinge, with swollen eyelids out of which keen reddish eyes gleamed like little chinks. But there was something very strange in him; there was a light in his eyes as though of intense feeling – perhaps there were even thought and intelligence, but at the same time there was a gleam of something like madness. He was wearing an old and hopelessly ragged black dress coat, with all its buttons missing except one, and that one he had buttoned, evidently clinging to this last trace of respectability. A crumpled shirt front, covered with spots and stains, protruded from his canvas waistcoat. Like a clerk, he wore no beard, nor moustache, but had been so long unshaven that his chin looked like a stiff greyish brush. And there was something respectable and like an official about his manner too. But he was restless; he ruffled up his hair and from time to time let his head drop into his hands dejectedly resting his ragged elbows on the stained and sticky table. At last he looked straight at Raskolnikov, and said loudly and resolutely:

"May I venture, honoured sir, to engage you in polite conversation? Forasmuch as, though your exterior would not command respect, my experience admonishes me that you are a man of education and not accustomed to drinking. I have always respected education when in conjunction with genuine sentiments, and I am besides a titular counsellor in rank. Marmeladov – such is my name; titular counsellor. I make bold to inquire – have you been in the service?"

"No, I am studying," answered the young man, somewhat surprised at the grandiloquent style of the speaker and also at being so directly addressed. In spite of the momentary desire he had just been feeling for company of any sort, on being actually spoken to he felt immediately his habitual irritable and uneasy aversion for any stranger who approached or attempted to approach him.

"A student then, or formerly a student," cried the clerk. "Just what I thought! I'm a man of experience, immense experience, sir," and he tapped his forehead with his fingers in self-approval. "You've been a student or have attended some learned institution!... But allow me...." He got up, staggered, took up his jug and glass, and sat down beside the young man, facing him a little sideways. He was drunk, but spoke fluently and boldly, only occasionally losing the thread of his sentences and drawling his words. He pounced upon Raskolnikov as greedily as though he too had not spoken to a soul for a month.

"Honoured sir," he began almost with solemnity, "poverty is not a vice, that's a true saying. Yet I know too that drunkenness is not a virtue, and that that's even truer. But beggary, honoured sir, beggary is a vice. In poverty you may still retain your innate nobility of soul, but in beggary – never – no one. For beggary a man is not chased out of human society with a stick, he is swept out with a broom, so as to make it as humiliating as possible; and quite right, too, forasmuch as in beggary I am ready to be the first to humiliate myself. Hence the pot-house! Honoured sir, a month ago Mr. Lebeziatnikov gave my wife a beating, and my wife is a very different matter from me! Do you understand? Allow me to ask you another question out of simple curiosity: have you ever spent a night on a hay barge, on the Neva?"

"No, I have not happened to," answered Raskolnikov. "What do you mean?"

"Well, I've just come from one and it's the fifth night I've slept so...." He filled his glass, emptied it and paused. Bits of hay were in fact clinging to his clothes and sticking to his hair. It seemed quite probable that he had not undressed or washed for the last five days. His hands, particularly, were filthy. They were fat and red, with black nails.

His conversation seemed to excite a general though languid interest. The boys at the counter fell to sniggering. The innkeeper came down from the upper room, apparently on purpose to listen to the "funny fellow" and sat down at a little distance, yawning lazily, but with dignity. Evidently Marmeladov was a familiar figure here, and he had most likely acquired his weakness for high-flown speeches from the habit of frequently entering into conversation with strangers of all sorts in the tavern. This habit develops into a necessity in some drunkards, and especially in those who are looked after sharply and kept in order at home. Hence in the company of other drinkers they try to justify themselves and even if possible obtain consideration.

"Funny fellow!" pronounced the innkeeper. "And why don't you work, why aren't you at your duty, if you are in the service?"

"Why am I not at my duty, honoured sir," Marmeladov went on, addressing himself exclusively to Raskolnikov, as though it had been he who put that question to him. "Why am I not at my duty? Does not my heart ache to think what a useless worm I am? A month ago when Mr. Lebeziatnikov beat my wife with his own hands, and I lay drunk, didn't I suffer? Excuse me, young man, has it ever happened to you... hm... well, to petition hopelessly for a loan?"

"Yes, it has. But what do you mean by hopelessly?"

"Hopelessly in the fullest sense, when you know beforehand that you will get nothing by it. You know, for instance, beforehand with positive certainty that this man, this most reputable and exemplary citizen, will on no consideration give you money; and indeed I ask you why should he? For he knows of course that I shan't pay it back. From compassion? But Mr. Lebeziatnikov who keeps up with modern ideas explained the other day that compassion is forbidden nowadays by science itself, and that that's what is done now in England, where there is political economy. Why, I ask you, should he give it to me? And yet though I know beforehand that he won't, I set off to him and..."

"Why do you go?" put in Raskolnikov.

"Well, when one has no one, nowhere else one can go! For every man must have somewhere to go. Since there are times when one absolutely must go somewhere! When my own daughter first went out with a yellow ticket, then I had to go... (for my daughter has a yellow passport)," he added in parenthesis, looking with a certain uneasiness at the young man. "No matter, sir, no matter!" he went on hurriedly and with apparent composure when both the boys at the counter guffawed and even the innkeeper smiled – "No matter, I am not confounded by the wagging of their heads; for everyone knows everything about it already, and all that is secret is made open. And I accept it all, not with contempt, but with humility. So be it! So be it! 'Behold the man!' Excuse me, young man, can you.... No, to put it more strongly and more distinctly; not *can* you but *dare* you, looking upon me, assert that I am not a pig?"

The young man did not answer a word.

"Well," the orator began again stolidly and with even increased dignity, after waiting for the laughter in the room to subside. "Well, so be it, I am a pig, but she is a lady! I have the semblance of a beast, but Katerina Ivanovna, my spouse, is a person of education and an officer's daughter. Granted, granted, I am a scoundrel, but she is a woman of a noble heart, full of sentiments, refined by education. And yet... oh, if only she felt for me! Honoured sir, honoured sir, you know every man ought to have at least one place where people feel for him! But Katerina Ivanovna, though she is magnanimous, she is unjust.... And yet, although I realise that when she pulls my hair she only does it out of pity – for I repeat without being ashamed, she pulls my hair, young man," he declared with redoubled dignity, hearing the sniggering again – "but, my God, if she would but once.... But no, no! It's all in vain and it's no use talking! No use talking! For more than once, my wish did come true and more than once she has felt for me but... such is my fate and I am a beast by nature!"

"Rather!" assented the innkeeper yawning. Marmeladov struck his fist resolutely on the table.

"Such is my fate! Do you know, sir, do you know, I have sold her very stockings for drink? Not her shoes – that would be more or less in the order of things, but her stockings, her stockings I have sold for drink! Her mohair shawl I sold for drink, a present to her long ago, her own property, not mine; and we live in a cold room and she caught cold this winter and has begun coughing and spitting blood too. We have three little children and Katerina Ivanovna is at work from morning till night; she is scrubbing and cleaning and washing the children, for she's been used to cleanliness from a child. But her chest is weak and she has a tendency to consumption and I feel it! Do you suppose I don't feel it? And the more I drink the more I feel it. That's why I drink too. I try to find sympathy and feeling in drink.... I drink so that I may suffer twice as much!" And as though in despair he laid his head down on the table.

"Young man," he went on, raising his head again, "in your face I seem to read some trouble of mind. When you came in I read it, and that was why I addressed you at once. For in unfolding to you the story of my life, I do not wish to make myself a laughing-stock before these idle listeners, who indeed know all about it already, but I am looking for a man of feeling and education. Know then that my wife was educated in a high-class school for the daughters of noblemen, and on leaving she danced the shawl dance before the governor and other personages for which she was presented with a gold medal and a certificate of merit. The medal... well, the medal of course was sold – long ago, hm... but the certificate of merit is in her trunk still and not long ago she showed it to our landlady. And although she is most continually on bad terms with the landlady, yet she wanted to tell someone or other of her past honours and of the happy days that are gone. I don't condemn her for it, I don't blame her, for the one thing left her is recollection of the past, and all the rest is dust and ashes. Yes, yes, she is a lady of spirit, proud and determined. She scrubs the floors herself and has nothing but black bread to eat, but won't allow herself to be treated with disrespect. That's why she would not overlook Mr. Lebeziatnikov's rudeness to her, and so when he gave her a beating for it, she took to her bed more from the hurt to her feelings than from the blows. She was a widow when I married her, with three children, one smaller than the other. She married her first husband, an infantry officer, for love, and ran away with him from her father's house. She was exceedingly fond of her husband; but he gave way to cards, got into trouble and with that he died. He used to beat her at the end: and although she paid him back, of which I have authentic documentary evidence, to this day she speaks of him with tears and she throws him up to me; and I am glad, I am glad that, though only in imagination, she should think of herself as having once been happy.... And she was left at his death with three children in a wild and remote district where I happened to be at the time; and she was left in such hopeless poverty that, although I have seen many ups and downs of all sort, I don't feel equal to describing it even. Her relations had all thrown her off. And she was proud, too, excessively proud.... And then, honoured sir, and then, I, being at the time a widower, with a daughter of fourteen left me by my first wife, offered her my hand, for I could not bear the sight of such suffering. You can judge the extremity of her calamities, that she, a woman of education and culture and distinguished family, should have consented to be my wife. But she did! Weeping and sobbing and wringing her hands, she married me! For she had nowhere to turn! Do you understand, sir, do you understand what it means when you have absolutely nowhere to turn? No, that you don't understand yet.... And for a whole year, I performed my duties conscientiously and faithfully, and did not touch this" (he tapped the jug with his finger), "for I have feelings. But even so, I could not please her; and then I lost my place too, and that through no fault of mine but through changes in the office; and then I did touch it!… It will be a year and a half ago soon since we found ourselves at last after many wanderings and numerous calamities in this magnificent capital, adorned with innumerable monuments. Here I obtained a situation…. I obtained it and I lost it again. Do you understand? This time it was through my own fault I lost it: for my weakness had come out…. We have now part of a room at Amalia Fyodorovna Lippevechsel's; and what we live upon and what we pay our rent with, I could not say. There are a lot of people living there besides ourselves. Dirt and disorder, a perfect Bedlam… hm… yes… And meanwhile my daughter by my first wife has grown up; and what my daughter has had to put up with from her step-mother whilst she was growing up, I won't speak of. For, though Katerina Ivanovna is full of generous feelings, she is a spirited lady, irritable and short-tempered…. Yes. But it's no use going over that! Sonia, as you may well fancy, has had no education. I did make an effort four years ago to give her a course of geography and universal history, but as I was not very well up in those subjects myself and we had no suitable books, and what books we had… hm, anyway we have not even those now, so all our instruction came to an end. We stopped at Cyrus of Persia. Since she has attained years of maturity, she has read other books of romantic tendency and of late she had read with great interest a book she got through Mr. Lebeziatnikov, Lewes' Physiology – do you know it? – and even recounted extracts from it to us: and that's the whole of her education. And now may I venture to address you, honoured sir, on my own account with a private question. Do you suppose that a respectable poor girl can earn much by honest work? Not fifteen farthings a day can she earn, if she is respectable and has no special talent and that without putting her work down for an instant! And what's more, Ivan Ivanitch Klopstock the civil counsellor – have you heard of him? – has not to this day paid her for the half-dozen linen shirts she made him and drove her roughly away, stamping and reviling her, on the pretext that the shirt collars were not made like the pattern and were put in askew. And there are the little ones hungry…. And Katerina Ivanovna walking up and down and wringing her hands, her cheeks flushed red, as they always are in that disease: 'Here you live with us,' says she, 'you eat and drink and are kept warm and you do nothing to help.' And much she gets to eat and drink when there is not a crust for the little ones for three days! I was lying at the time… well, what of it! I was lying drunk and I heard my Sonia speaking (she is a gentle creature with a soft little voice… fair hair and such a pale, thin little face). She said: 'Katerina Ivanovna, am I really to do a thing like that?' And Darya Frantsovna, a woman of evil character and very well known to the police, had two or three times tried to get at her through the landlady. 'And why not?' said Katerina Ivanovna with a jeer, 'you are something mighty precious to be so careful of!' But don't blame her, don't blame her, honoured sir, don't blame her! She was not herself when she spoke, but driven to distraction by her illness and the crying of the hungry children; and it was said more to wound her than anything else…. For that's Katerina Ivanovna's character, and when children cry, even from hunger, she falls to beating them at once. At six o'clock I saw Sonia get up, put on her kerchief and her cape, and go out of the room and about nine o'clock she came back. She walked straight up to Katerina Ivanovna and she laid thirty roubles on the table before her in silence. She did not utter a word, she did not even look at her, she simply picked up our big green *drap de dames* shawl (we have a shawl, made of *drap de dames*), put it over her head and face and lay down on the bed with her face to the wall; only her little shoulders and her body kept shuddering…. And I went on lying there, just as before…. And then I saw, young man, I saw Katerina Ivanovna, in the same silence go up to Sonia's little bed; she was on her knees all the evening kissing Sonia's feet, and would not get up, and then they both fell asleep in each other's arms... together, together... yes... and I... lay drunk."

Marmeladov stopped short, as though his voice had failed him. Then he hurriedly filled his glass, drank, and cleared his throat.

"Since then, sir," he went on after a brief pause – "Since then, owing to an unfortunate occurrence and through information given by evil-intentioned persons – in all which Darya Frantsovna took a leading part on the pretext that she had been treated with want of respect – since then my daughter Sofya Semyonovna has been forced to take a yellow ticket, and owing to that she is unable to go on living with us. For our landlady, Amalia Fyodorovna would not hear of it (though she had backed up Darya Frantsovna before) and Mr. Lebeziatnikov too... hm.... All the trouble between him and Katerina Ivanovna was on Sonia's account. At first he was for making up to Sonia himself and then all of a sudden he stood on his dignity: 'how,' said he, 'can a highly educated man like me live in the same rooms with a girl like that?' And Katerina Ivanovna would not let it pass, she stood up for her... and so that's how it happened. And Sonia comes to us now, mostly after dark; she comforts Katerina Ivanovna and gives her all she can.... She has a room at the Kapernaumovs' the tailors, she lodges with them; Kapernaumov is a lame man with a cleft palate and all of his numerous family have cleft palates too. And his wife, too, has a cleft palate. They all live in one room, but Sonia has her own, partitioned off.... Hm... yes... very poor people and all with cleft palates... yes. Then I got up in the morning, and put on my rags, lifted up my hands to heaven and set off to his excellency Ivan Afanasyvitch. His excellency Ivan Afanasyvitch, do you know him? No? Well, then, it's a man of God you don't know. He is wax... wax before the face of the Lord; even as wax melteth!... His eyes were dim when he heard my story. 'Marmeladov, once already you have deceived my expectations... I'll take you once more on my own responsibility' – that's what he said, 'remember,' he said, 'and now you can go.' I kissed the dust at his feet – in thought only, for in reality he would not have allowed me to do it, being a statesman and a man of modern political and enlightened ideas. I returned home, and when I announced that I'd been taken back into the service and should receive a salary, heavens, what a to-do there was!..."

Marmeladov stopped again in violent excitement. At that moment a whole party of revellers already drunk came in from the street, and the sounds of a hired concertina and the cracked piping voice of a child of seven singing "The Hamlet" were heard in the entry. The room was filled with noise. The tavern-keeper and the boys were busy with the new-comers. Marmeladov paying no attention to the new arrivals continued his story. He appeared by now to be extremely weak, but as he became more and more drunk, he became more and more talkative. The recollection of his recent success in getting the situation seemed to revive him, and was positively reflected in a sort of radiance on his face. Raskolnikov listened attentively.

"That was five weeks ago, sir. Yes.... As soon as Katerina Ivanovna and Sonia heard of it, mercy on us, it was as though I stepped into the kingdom of Heaven. It used to be: you can lie like a beast, nothing but abuse. Now they were walking on tiptoe, hushing the children. 'Semyon Zaharovitch is tired with his work at the office, he is resting, shh!' They made me coffee before I went to work and boiled cream for me! They began to get real cream for me, do you hear that? And how they managed to get together the money for a decent outfit – eleven roubles, fifty copecks, I can't guess. Boots, cotton shirt-fronts – most magnificent, a uniform, they got up all in splendid style, for eleven roubles and a half. The first morning I came back from the office I found Katerina Ivanovna had cooked two courses for dinner

– soup and salt meat with horse radish – which we had never dreamed of till then. She had not any dresses... none at all, but she got herself up as though she were going on a visit; and not that she'd anything to do it with, she smartened herself up with nothing at all, she'd done her hair nicely, put on a clean collar of some sort, cuffs, and there she was, quite a different person, she was younger and better looking. Sonia, my little darling, had only helped with money 'for the time,' she said, 'it won't do for me to come and see you too often. After dark maybe when no one can see.' Do you hear, do you hear? I lay down for a nap after dinner and what do you think: though Katerina Ivanovna had quarrelled to the last degree with our landlady Amalia Fyodorovna only a week before, she could not resist then asking her in to coffee. For two hours they were sitting, whispering together. 'Semyon Zaharovitch is in the service again, now, and receiving a salary,' says she, 'and he went himself to his excellency and his excellency himself came out to him, made all the others wait and led Semyon Zaharovitch by the hand before everybody into his study.' Do you hear, do you hear? 'To be sure,' says he, 'Semyon Zaharovitch, remembering your past services,' says he, 'and in spite of your propensity to that foolish weakness, since you promise now and since moreover we've got on badly without you,' (do you hear, do you hear;) 'and so,' says he, 'I rely now on your word as a gentleman.' And all that, let me tell you, she has simply made up for herself, and not simply out of wantonness, for the sake of bragging; no, she believes it all herself, she amuses herself with her own fancies, upon my word she does! And I don't blame her for it, no, I don't blame her!... Six days ago when I brought her my first earnings in full – twenty-three roubles forty copecks altogether – she called me her poppet: 'poppet,' said she, 'my little poppet.' And when we were by ourselves, you understand? You would not think me a beauty, you would not think much of me as a husband, would you?... Well, she pinched my cheek, 'my little poppet,' said she."

Marmeladov broke off, tried to smile, but suddenly his chin began to twitch. He controlled himself however. The tavern, the degraded appearance of the man, the five nights in the hay barge, and the pot of spirits, and yet this poignant love for his wife and children bewildered his listener. Raskolnikov listened intently but with a sick sensation. He felt vexed that he had come here.

"Honoured sir, honoured sir," cried Marmeladov recovering himself – "Oh, sir, perhaps all this seems a laughing matter to you, as it does to others, and perhaps I am only worrying you with the stupidity of all the trivial details of my home life, but it is not a laughing matter to me. For I can feel it all.... And the whole of that heavenly day of my life and the whole of that evening I passed in fleeting dreams of how I would arrange it all, and how I would dress all the children, and how I should give her rest, and how I should rescue my own daughter from dishonour and restore her to the bosom of her family.... And a great deal more.... Quite excusable, sir. Well, then, sir" (Marmeladov suddenly gave a sort of start, raised his head and gazed intently at his listener) "well, on the very next day after all those dreams, that is to say, exactly five days ago, in the evening, by a cunning trick, like a thief in the night, I stole from Katerina Ivanovna the key of her box, took out what was left of my earnings, how much it was I have forgotten, and now look at me, all of you! It's the fifth day since I left home, and they are looking for me there and it's the end of my employment, and my uniform is lying in a tavern on the Egyptian bridge. I exchanged it for the garments I have on... and it's the end of everything!"

Marmeladov struck his forehead with his fist, clenched his teeth, closed his eyes and leaned heavily with his elbow on the table. But a minute later his face suddenly changed and with a certain assumed slyness and affectation of bravado, he glanced at Raskolnikov, laughed and said:

"This morning I went to see Sonia, I went to ask her for a pick-me-up! He-he-he!"

"You don't say she gave it to you?" cried one of the new-comers; he shouted the words and went off into a guffaw.

"This very quart was bought with her money," Marmeladov declared, addressing himself exclusively to Raskolnikov. "Thirty copecks she gave me with her own hands, her last, all she had, as I saw.... She said nothing, she only looked at me without a word.... Not on earth, but up yonder... they grieve over men, they weep, but they don't blame them, they don't blame them! But it hurts more, it hurts more when they don't blame! Thirty copecks yes! And maybe she needs them now, eh? What do you think, my dear sir? For now she's got to keep up her appearance. It costs money, that smartness, that special smartness, you know? Do you understand? And there's pomatum, too, you see, she must have things; petticoats, starched ones, shoes, too, real jaunty ones to show off her foot when she has to step over a puddle. Do you understand, sir, do you understand what all that smartness means? And here I, her own father, here I took thirty copecks of that money for a drink! And I am drinking it! And I have already drunk it! Come, who will have pity on a man like me, eh? Are you sorry for me, sir, or not? Tell me, sir, are you sorry or not? He-he-he!"

He would have filled his glass, but there was no drink left. The pot was empty.

"What are you to be pitied for?" shouted the tavern-keeper who was again near them.

Shouts of laughter and even oaths followed. The laughter and the oaths came from those who were listening and also from those who had heard nothing but were simply looking at the figure of the discharged government clerk.

"To be pitied! Why am I to be pitied?" Marmeladov suddenly declaimed, standing up with his arm outstretched, as though he had been only waiting for that question.

"Why am I to be pitied, you say? Yes! there's nothing to pity me for! I ought to be crucified, crucified on a cross, not pitied! Crucify me, oh judge, crucify me but pity me! And then I will go of myself to be crucified, for it's not merry-making I seek but tears and tribulation!... Do you suppose, you that sell, that this pint of yours has been sweet to me? It was tribulation I sought at the bottom of it, tears and tribulation, and have found it, and I have tasted it; but He will pity us Who has had pity on all men, Who has understood all men and all things, He is the One, He too is the judge. He will come in that day and He will ask: 'Where is the daughter who gave herself for her cross, consumptive step-mother and for the little children of another? Where is the daughter who had pity upon the filthy drunkard, her earthly father, undismayed by his beastliness?' And He will say, 'Come to me! I have already forgiven thee once.... I have forgiven thee once.... Thy sins which are many are forgiven thee for thou hast loved much....' And he will forgive my Sonia, He will forgive, I know it... I felt it in my heart when I was with her just now! And He will judge and will forgive all, the good and the evil, the wise and the meek.... And when He has done with all of them, then He will summon us. 'You too come forth,' He will say, 'Come forth ye drunkards, come forth, ye weak ones, come forth, ye children of shame!' And we shall all come forth, without shame and shall stand before him. And He will say unto us, 'Ye are swine, made in the Image of the Beast and with his mark; but come ye also!' And the wise ones and those of understanding will say, 'Oh Lord, why dost Thou receive these men?' And He will say, 'This is why I receive them, oh ye wise, this is why I receive them, oh ye of understanding, that not one of them believed himself to be worthy of this.' And He will hold out His hands to us and we shall fall down before him... and we shall weep... and we shall understand all things! Then we shall understand all!... and all will understand, Katerina Ivanovna even... she will understand.... Lord, Thy kingdom come!" And he sank down on the bench exhausted, and helpless, looking at no one, apparently oblivious of his surroundings and plunged in deep thought. His words had created a certain impression; there was a moment of silence; but soon laughter and oaths were heard again.

"That's his notion!"

"Talked himself silly!"

"A fine clerk he is!"

And so on, and so on.

"Let us go, sir," said Marmeladov all at once, raising his head and addressing Raskolnikov – "come along with me... Kozel's house, looking into the yard. I'm going to Katerina Ivanovna – time I did."

Raskolnikov had for some time been wanting to go and he had meant to help him. Marmeladov was much unsteadier on his legs than in his speech and leaned heavily on the young man. They had two or three hundred paces to go. The drunken man was more and more overcome by dismay and confusion as they drew nearer the house.

"It's not Katerina Ivanovna I am afraid of now," he muttered in agitation – "and that she will begin pulling my hair. What does my hair matter! Bother my hair! That's what I say! Indeed it will be better if she does begin pulling it, that's not what I am afraid of... it's her eyes I am afraid of... yes, her eyes... the red on her cheeks, too, frightens me... and her breathing too.... Have you noticed how people in that disease breathe... when they are excited? I am frightened of the children's crying, too.... For if Sonia has not taken them food... I don't know what's happened! I don't know! But blows I am not afraid of.... Know, sir, that such blows are not a pain to me, but even an enjoyment. In fact I can't get on without it.... It's better so. Let her strike me, it relieves her heart... it's better so... There is the house. The house of Kozel, the cabinet-maker... a German, well-to-do. Lead the way!"

They went in from the yard and up to the fourth storey. The staircase got darker and darker as they went up. It was nearly eleven o'clock and although in summer in Petersburg there is no real night, yet it was quite dark at the top of the stairs.

A grimy little door at the very top of the stairs stood ajar. A very poor-looking room about ten paces long was lighted up by a candle-end; the whole of it was visible from the entrance. It was all in disorder, littered up with rags of all sorts, especially children's garments. Across the furthest corner was stretched a ragged sheet. Behind it probably was the bed. There was nothing in the room except two chairs and a sofa covered with American leather, full of holes, before which stood an old deal kitchen-table, unpainted and uncovered. At the edge of the table stood a smoldering tallow-candle in an iron candlestick. It appeared that the family had a room to themselves, not part of a room, but their room was practically a passage. The door leading to the other rooms, or rather cupboards, into which Amalia Lippevechsel's flat was divided stood half open, and there was shouting, uproar and laughter within. People seemed to be playing cards and drinking tea there. Words of the most unceremonious kind flew out from time to time.

Raskolnikov recognised Katerina Ivanovna at once. She was a rather tall, slim and graceful woman, terribly emaciated, with magnificent dark brown hair and with a hectic flush in her cheeks. She was pacing up and down in her little room, pressing her hands against her chest; her lips were parched and her breathing came in nervous broken gasps.

Her eyes glittered as in fever and looked about with a harsh immovable stare. And that consumptive and excited face with the last flickering light of the candle-end playing upon it made a sickening impression. She seemed to Raskolnikov about thirty years old and was certainly a strange wife for Marmeladov.... She had not heard them and did not notice them coming in. She seemed to be lost in thought, hearing and seeing nothing. The room was close, but she had not opened the window; a stench rose from the staircase, but the door on to the stairs was not closed. From the inner rooms clouds of tobacco smoke floated in, she kept coughing, but did not close the door. The youngest child, a girl of six, was asleep, sitting curled up on the floor with her head on the sofa. A boy a year older stood crying and shaking in the corner, probably he had just had a beating. Beside him stood a girl of nine years old, tall and thin, wearing a thin and ragged chemise with an ancient cashmere pelisse flung over her bare shoulders, long outgrown and barely reaching her knees. Her arm, as thin as a stick, was round her brother's neck. She was trying to comfort him, whispering something to him, and doing all she could to keep him from whimpering again. At the same time her large dark eyes, which looked larger still from the thinness of her frightened face, were watching her mother with alarm. Marmeladov did not enter the door, but dropped on his knees in the very doorway, pushing Raskolnikov in front of him. The woman seeing a stranger stopped indifferently facing him, coming to herself for a moment and apparently wondering what he had come for. But evidently she decided that he was going into the next room, as he had to pass through hers to get there. Taking no further notice of him, she walked towards the outer door to close it and uttered a sudden scream on seeing her husband on his knees in the doorway.

"Ah!" she cried out in a frenzy, "he has come back! The criminal! the monster!... And where is the money? What's in your pocket, show me! And your clothes are all different! Where are your clothes? Where is the money! Speak!"

And she fell to searching him. Marmeladov submissively and obediently held up both arms to facilitate the search. Not a farthing was there.

"Where is the money?" she cried – "Mercy on us, can he have drunk it all? There were twelve silver roubles left in the chest!" and in a fury she seized him by the hair and dragged him into the room. Marmeladov seconded her efforts by meekly crawling along on his knees.

"And this is a consolation to me! This does not hurt me, but is a positive con-so-la-tion, ho-nou-red sir," he called out, shaken to and fro by his hair and even once striking the ground with his forehead. The child asleep on the floor woke up, and began to cry. The boy in the corner losing all control began trembling and screaming and rushed to his sister in violent terror, almost in a fit. The eldest girl was shaking like a leaf.

"He's drunk it! he's drunk it all," the poor woman screamed in despair – "and his clothes are gone! And they are hungry, hungry!" – and wringing her hands she pointed to the children. "Oh, accursed life! And you, are you not ashamed?" – she pounced all at once upon Raskolnikov – "from the tavern! Have you been drinking with him? You have been drinking with him, too! Go away!"

The young man was hastening away without uttering a word. The inner door was thrown wide open and inquisitive faces were peering in at it. Coarse laughing faces with pipes and cigarettes and heads wearing caps thrust themselves in at the doorway. Further in could be seen figures in dressing gowns flung open, in costumes of unseemly scantiness, some of them with cards in their hands. They were particularly diverted, when Marmeladov, dragged about by his hair, shouted that it was a consolation to him. They even began to come into the room; at last a sinister shrill outcry was heard: this came from Amalia

Lippevechsel herself pushing her way amongst them and trying to restore order after her own fashion and for the hundredth time to frighten the poor woman by ordering her with coarse abuse to clear out of the room next day. As he went out, Raskolnikov had time to put his hand into his pocket, to snatch up the coppers he had received in exchange for his rouble in the tavern and to lay them unnoticed on the window. Afterwards on the stairs, he changed his mind and would have gone back.

"What a stupid thing I've done," he thought to himself, "they have Sonia and I want it myself." But reflecting that it would be impossible to take it back now and that in any case he would not have taken it, he dismissed it with a wave of his hand and went back to his lodging. "Sonia wants pomatum too," he said as he walked along the street, and he laughed malignantly – "such smartness costs money.... Hm! And maybe Sonia herself will be bankrupt today, for there is always a risk, hunting big game... digging for gold... then they would all be without a crust tomorrow except for my money. Hurrah for Sonia! What a mine they've dug there! And they're making the most of it! Yes, they are making the most of it! They've wept over it and grown used to it. Man grows used to everything, the scoundrel!"

He sank into thought.

"And what if I am wrong," he cried suddenly after a moment's thought. "What if man is not really a scoundrel, man in general, I mean, the whole race of mankind – then all the rest is prejudice, simply artificial terrors and there are no barriers and it's all as it should be."

Chapter III

HE WAKED up late next day after a broken sleep. But his sleep had not refreshed him; he waked up bilious, irritable, ill-tempered, and looked with hatred at his room. It was a tiny cupboard of a room about six paces in length. It had a poverty-stricken appearance with its dusty yellow paper peeling off the walls, and it was so low-pitched that a man of more than average height was ill at ease in it and felt every moment that he would knock his head against the ceiling. The furniture was in keeping with the room: there were three old chairs, rather rickety; a painted table in the corner on which lay a few manuscripts and books; the dust that lay thick upon them showed that they had been long untouched. A big clumsy sofa occupied almost the whole of one wall and half the floor space of the room; it was once covered with chintz, but was now in rags and served Raskolnikov as a bed. Often he went to sleep on it, as he was, without undressing, without sheets, wrapped in his old student's overcoat, with his head on one little pillow, under which he heaped up all the linen he had, clean and dirty, by way of a bolster. A little table stood in front of the sofa.

It would have been difficult to sink to a lower ebb of disorder, but to Raskolnikov in his present state of mind this was positively agreeable. He had got completely away from everyone, like a tortoise in its shell, and even the sight of a servant girl who had to wait upon him and looked sometimes into his room made him writhe with nervous irritation. He was in the condition that overtakes some monomaniacs entirely concentrated upon one thing. His landlady had for the last fortnight given up sending him in meals, and he had not yet thought of expostulating with her, though he went without his dinner. Nastasya, the cook and only servant, was rather pleased at the lodger's mood and had entirely given up sweeping and doing his room, only once a week or so she would stray into his room with a broom. She waked him up that day.

"Get up, why are you asleep?" she called to him. "It's past nine, I have brought you some tea; will you have a cup? I should think you're fairly starving?"

Raskolnikov opened his eyes, started and recognised Nastasya.

"From the landlady, eh?" he asked, slowly and with a sickly face sitting up on the sofa.

"From the landlady, indeed!"

She set before him her own cracked teapot full of weak and stale tea and laid two yellow lumps of sugar by the side of it.

"Here, Nastasya, take it please," he said, fumbling in his pocket (for he had slept in his clothes) and taking out a handful of coppers – "run and buy me a loaf. And get me a little sausage, the cheapest, at the pork-butcher's."

"The loaf I'll fetch you this very minute, but wouldn't you rather have some cabbage soup instead of sausage? It's capital soup, yesterday's. I saved it for you yesterday, but you came in late. It's fine soup."

When the soup had been brought, and he had begun upon it, Nastasya sat down beside him on the sofa and began chatting. She was a country peasant-woman and a very talkative one.

"Praskovya Pavlovna means to complain to the police about you," she said.

He scowled.

"To the police? What does she want?"

"You don't pay her money and you won't turn out of the room. That's what she wants, to be sure."

"The devil, that's the last straw," he muttered, grinding his teeth, "no, that would not suit me... just now. She is a fool," he added aloud. "I'll go and talk to her today."

"Fool she is and no mistake, just as I am. But why, if you are so clever, do you lie here like a sack and have nothing to show for it? One time you used to go out, you say, to teach children. But why is it you do nothing now?"

"I am doing..." Raskolnikov began sullenly and reluctantly.

"What are you doing?"

"Work..."

"What sort of work?"

"I am thinking," he answered seriously after a pause.

Nastasya was overcome with a fit of laughter. She was given to laughter and when anything amused her, she laughed inaudibly, quivering and shaking all over till she felt ill.

"And have you made much money by your thinking?" she managed to articulate at last.

"One can't go out to give lessons without boots. And I'm sick of it."

"Don't quarrel with your bread and butter."

"They pay so little for lessons. What's the use of a few coppers?" he answered, reluctantly, as though replying to his own thought.

"And you want to get a fortune all at once?"

He looked at her strangely.

"Yes, I want a fortune," he answered firmly, after a brief pause.

"Don't be in such a hurry, you quite frighten me! Shall I get you the loaf or not?"

"As you please."

"Ah, I forgot! A letter came for you yesterday when you were out."

"A letter? for me! from whom?"

"I can't say. I gave three copecks of my own to the postman for it. Will you pay me back?"

"Then bring it to me, for God's sake, bring it," cried Raskolnikov greatly excited – "good God!"

A minute later the letter was brought him. That was it: from his mother, from the province of R—. He turned pale when he took it. It was a long while since he had received a letter, but another feeling also suddenly stabbed his heart.

"Nastasya, leave me alone, for goodness' sake; here are your three copecks, but for goodness' sake, make haste and go!"

The letter was quivering in his hand; he did not want to open it in her presence; he wanted to be left alone with this letter. When Nastasya had gone out, he lifted it quickly to his lips and kissed it; then he gazed intently at the address, the small, sloping handwriting, so dear and familiar, of the mother who had once taught him to read and write. He delayed; he seemed almost afraid of something. At last he opened it; it was a thick heavy letter, weighing over two ounces, two large sheets of note paper were covered with very small handwriting.

"My dear Rodya," wrote his mother – "it's two months since I last had a talk with you by letter which has distressed me and even kept me awake at night, thinking. But I am sure you will not blame me for my inevitable silence. You know how I love you; you are all we have to look to, Dounia and I, you are our all, our one hope, our one stay. What a grief it was to me when I heard that you had given up the university some months ago, for want of means to keep yourself and that you had lost your lessons and your other work! How could I help you out of my hundred and twenty roubles a year pension? The fifteen roubles I sent you four months ago I borrowed, as you know, on security of my pension, from Vassily Ivanovitch Vahrushin a merchant of this town. He is a kind-hearted man and was a friend of your father's too. But having given him the right to receive the pension, I had to wait till the debt was paid off and that is only just done, so that I've been unable to send you anything all this time. But now, thank God, I believe I shall be able to send you something more and in fact we may congratulate ourselves on our good fortune now, of which I hasten to inform you. In the first place, would you have guessed, dear Rodya, that your sister has been living with me for the last six weeks and we shall not be separated in the future. Thank God, her sufferings are over, but I will tell you everything in order, so that you may know just how everything has happened and all that we have hitherto concealed from you. When you wrote to me two months ago that you had heard that Dounia had a great deal to put up with in the Svidrigailovs' house, when you wrote that and asked me to tell you all about it – what could I write in answer to you? If I had written the whole truth to you, I dare say you would have thrown up everything and have come to us, even if you had to walk all the way, for I know your character and your feelings, and you would not let your sister be insulted. I was in despair myself, but what could I do? And, besides, I did not know the whole truth myself then. What made it all so difficult was that Dounia received a hundred roubles in advance when she took the place as governess in their family, on condition of part of her salary being deducted every month, and so it was impossible to throw up the situation without repaying the debt.

This sum (now I can explain it all to you, my precious Rodya) she took chiefly in order to send you sixty roubles, which you needed so terribly then and which you received from us last year. We deceived you then, writing that this money came from Dounia's savings, but that was not so, and now I tell you all about it, because, thank God, things have suddenly changed for the better, and that you may know how Dounia loves you and what a heart she has. At first indeed Mr. Svidrigailov treated her very rudely and used to make disrespectful and jeering remarks at table…. But I don't want to go into all those painful details, so as not to worry you for nothing when it is now all over. In short, in spite of the kind and generous behaviour of Marfa Petrovna, Mr. Svidrigailov's wife, and all the rest of the household, Dounia had a very hard time, especially when Mr. Svidrigailov, relapsing into his old regimental habits, was under the influence of Bacchus. And how do you think it was all explained later on? Would you believe that the crazy fellow had conceived a passion for Dounia from the beginning, but had concealed it under a show of rudeness and contempt. Possibly he was ashamed and horrified himself at his own flighty hopes, considering his years and his being the father of a family; and that made him angry with Dounia. And possibly, too, he hoped by his rude and sneering behaviour to hide the truth from others. But at last he lost all control and had the face to make Dounia an open and shameful proposal, promising her all sorts of inducements and offering, besides, to throw up everything and take her to another estate of his, or even abroad. You can imagine all she went through! To leave her situation at once was impossible not only on account of the money debt, but also to spare the feelings of Marfa Petrovna, whose suspicions would have been aroused: and then Dounia would have been the cause of a rupture in the family. And it would have meant a terrible scandal for Dounia too; that would have been inevitable. There were various other reasons owing to which Dounia could not hope to escape from that awful house for another six weeks. You know Dounia, of course; you know how clever she is and what a strong will she has. Dounia can endure a great deal and even in the most difficult cases she has the fortitude to maintain her firmness. She did not even write to me about everything for fear of upsetting me, although we were constantly in communication. It all ended very unexpectedly. Marfa Petrovna accidentally overheard her husband imploring Dounia in the garden, and, putting quite a wrong interpretation on the position, threw the blame upon her, believing her to be the cause of it all. An awful scene took place between them on the spot in the garden; Marfa Petrovna went so far as to strike Dounia, refused to hear anything and was shouting at her for a whole hour and then gave orders that Dounia should be packed off at once to me in a plain peasant's cart, into which they flung all her things, her linen and her clothes, all pell-mell, without folding it up and packing it. And a heavy shower of rain came on, too, and Dounia, insulted and put to shame, had to drive with a peasant in an open cart all the seventeen versts into town. Only think now what answer could I have sent to the letter I received from you two months ago and what could I have written? I was in despair; I dared not write to you the truth because you would have been very unhappy, mortified and indignant, and yet what could you do? You could only perhaps ruin yourself, and, besides, Dounia would not allow it; and fill up my letter with trifles when my heart was so full of sorrow, I could not. For a whole month the town was full of gossip about this scandal, and it came to such a pass that Dounia and I dared not even go to church on account of the contemptuous looks, whispers, and even remarks made aloud about us. All our acquaintances avoided us, nobody even bowed to us in the street, and I learnt that some shopmen and clerks were intending to insult us in a shameful way, smearing the gates of our house with pitch, so that the landlord began to tell us we must leave. All this was set going by Marfa Petrovna who managed to slander Dounia and throw dirt at her in every family. She knows everyone in the neighbourhood, and that month she was continually coming into the town, and as she is rather talkative and fond of gossiping about her family affairs and particularly of complaining to all and each of her husband – which is not at all right – so in a short time she had spread her story not only in the town, but over the whole surrounding district. It made me ill, but Dounia bore it better than I did, and if only you could have seen how she endured it all and tried to comfort me and cheer me up! She is an angel! But by God's mercy, our sufferings were cut short: Mr. Svidrigailov returned to his senses and repented and, probably feeling sorry for Dounia, he laid before Marfa Petrovna a complete and unmistakable proof of Dounia's innocence, in the form of a letter Dounia had been forced to write and give to him, before Marfa Petrovna came upon them in the garden. This letter, which remained in Mr. Svidrigailov's hands after her departure, she had written to refuse personal explanations and secret interviews, for which he was entreating her. In that letter she reproached him with great heat and indignation for the baseness of his behaviour in regard to Marfa Petrovna, reminding him that he was the father and head of a family and telling him how infamous it was of him to torment and make unhappy a defenceless girl, unhappy enough already. Indeed, dear Rodya, the letter was so nobly and touchingly written that I sobbed when I read it and to this day I cannot read it without tears. Moreover, the evidence of the servants, too, cleared Dounia's reputation; they had seen and known a great deal more than Mr. Svidrigailov had himself supposed – as indeed is always the case with servants. Marfa Petrovna was completely taken aback, and 'again crushed' as she said herself to us, but she was completely convinced of Dounia's innocence. The very next day, being Sunday, she went straight to the Cathedral, knelt down and prayed with tears to Our Lady to give her strength to bear this new trial and to do her duty. Then she came straight from the Cathedral to us, told us the whole story, wept bitterly and, fully penitent, she embraced Dounia and besought her to forgive her. The same morning without any delay, she went round to all the houses in the town and everywhere, shedding tears, she asserted in the most flattering terms Dounia's innocence and the nobility of her feelings and her behavior. What was more, she showed and read to everyone the letter in Dounia's own handwriting to Mr. Svidrigailov and even allowed them to take copies of it – which I must say I think was superfluous. In this way she was busy for several days in driving about the whole town, because some people had taken offence through precedence having been given to others. And therefore they had to take turns, so that in every house she was expected before she arrived, and everyone knew that on such and such a day Marfa Petrovna would be reading the letter in such and such a place and people assembled for every reading of it, even many who had heard it several times already both in their own houses and in other people's. In my opinion a great deal, a very great deal of all this was unnecessary; but that's Marfa Petrovna's character. Anyway she succeeded in completely re-establishing

Dounia's reputation and the whole ignominy of this affair rested as an indelible disgrace upon her husband, as the only person to blame, so that I really began to feel sorry for him; it was really treating the crazy fellow too harshly. Dounia was at once asked to give lessons in several families, but she refused. All of a sudden everyone began to treat her with marked respect and all this did much to bring about the event by which, one may say, our whole fortunes are now transformed. You must know, dear Rodya, that Dounia has a suitor and that she has already consented to marry him. I hasten to tell you all about the matter, and though it has been arranged without asking your consent, I think you will not be aggrieved with me or with your sister on that account, for you will see that we could not wait and put off our decision till we heard from you. And you could not have judged all the facts without being on the spot. This was how it happened. He is already of the rank of a counsellor, Pyotr Petrovitch Luzhin, and is distantly related to Marfa Petrovna, who has been very active in bringing the match about. It began with his expressing through her his desire to make our acquaintance. He was properly received, drank coffee with us and the very next day he sent us a letter in which he very courteously made an offer and begged for a speedy and decided answer. He is a very busy man and is in a great hurry to get to Petersburg, so that every moment is precious to him. At first, of course, we were greatly surprised, as it had all happened so quickly and unexpectedly. We thought and talked it over the whole day. He is a well-to-do man, to be depended upon, he has two posts in the government and has already made his fortune. It is true that he is forty-five years old, but he is of a fairly prepossessing appearance and might still be thought attractive by women, and he is altogether a very respectable and presentable man, only he seems a little morose and somewhat conceited. But possibly that may only be the impression he makes at first sight. And beware, dear Rodya, when he comes to Petersburg, as he shortly will do, beware of judging him too hastily and severely, as your way is, if there is anything you do not like in him at first sight. I give you this warning, although I feel sure that he will make a favourable impression upon you. Moreover, in order to understand any man one must be deliberate and careful to avoid forming prejudices and mistaken ideas, which are very difficult to correct and get over afterwards. And Pyotr Petrovitch, judging by many indications, is a thoroughly estimable man. At his first visit, indeed, he told us that he was a practical man, but still he shares, as he expressed it, many of the convictions 'of our most rising generation' and he is an opponent of all prejudices. He said a good deal more, for he seems a little conceited and likes to be listened to, but this is scarcely a vice. I, of course, understood very little of it, but Dounia explained to me that, though he is not a man of great education, he is clever and seems to be good-natured. You know your sister's character, Rodya. She is a resolute, sensible, patient and generous girl, but she has a passionate heart, as I know very well. Of course, there is no great love either on his side, or on hers, but Dounia is a clever girl and has the heart of an angel, and will make it her duty to make her husband happy who on his side will make her happiness his care. Of that we have no good reason to doubt, though it must be admitted the matter has been arranged in great haste. Besides he is a man of great prudence and he will see, to be sure, of himself, that his own happiness will be the more secure, the happier Dounia is with him. And as for some defects of character, for some habits and even certain differences of opinion – which indeed are inevitable even in the happiest marriages – Dounia has said that, as regards all that, she relies on herself, that there is nothing to be uneasy about, and that she is ready to put up with a great deal, if only their future relationship can be an honourable and straightforward one. He struck me, for instance, at first, as rather abrupt, but that may well come from his being an outspoken man, and that is no doubt how it is. For instance, at his second visit, after he had received Dounia's consent, in the course of conversation, he declared that before making Dounia's acquaintance, he had made up his mind to marry a girl of good reputation, without dowry and, above all, one who had experienced poverty, because, as he explained, a man ought not to be indebted to his wife, but that it is better for a wife to look upon her husband as her benefactor. I must add that he expressed it more nicely and politely than I have done, for I have forgotten his actual phrases and only remember the meaning. And, besides, it was obviously not said of design, but slipped out in the heat of conversation, so that he tried afterwards to correct himself and smooth it over, but all the same it did strike me as somewhat rude, and I said so afterwards to Dounia. But Dounia was vexed, and answered that 'words are not deeds,' and that, of course, is perfectly true. Dounia did not sleep all night before she made up her mind, and, thinking that I was asleep, she got out of bed and was walking up and down the room all night; at last she knelt down before the ikon and prayed long and fervently and in the morning she told me that she had decided.

"I have mentioned already that Pyotr Petrovitch is just setting off for Petersburg, where he has a great deal of business, and he wants to open a legal bureau. He has been occupied for many years in conducting civil and commercial litigation, and only the other day he won an important case. He has to be in Petersburg because he has an important case before the Senate. So, Rodya dear, he may be of the greatest use to you, in every way indeed, and Dounia and I have agreed that from this very day you could definitely enter upon your career and might consider that your future is marked out and assured for you. Oh, if only this comes to pass! This would be such a benefit that we could only look upon it as a providential blessing. Dounia is dreaming of nothing else. We have even ventured already to drop a few words on the subject to Pyotr Petrovitch. He was cautious in his answer, and said that, of course, as he could not get on without a secretary, it would be better to be paying a salary to a relation than to a stranger, if only the former were fitted for the duties (as though there could be doubt of your being fitted!) but then he expressed doubts whether your studies at the university would leave you time for work at his office. The matter dropped for the time, but Dounia is thinking of nothing else now. She has been in a sort of fever for the last few days, and has already made a regular plan for your becoming in the end an associate and even a partner in Pyotr Petrovitch's business, which might well be, seeing that you are a student of law. I am in complete agreement with her, Rodya, and share all her plans and hopes, and think there is every probability of realising them. And in spite of Pyotr Petrovitch's evasiveness, very natural at present (since he does not know you), Dounia is firmly persuaded that she will gain everything by her good influence over her future husband; this she is reckoning upon. Of course we are careful not to talk of any of these more remote plans to Pyotr Petrovitch, especially of your becoming his partner. He is a practical man and might take this very coldly, it might all seem to him simply a day-dream. Nor has either Dounia or I breathed a word to him of the great hopes

we have of his helping us to pay for your university studies; we have not spoken of it in the first place, because it will come to pass of itself, later on, and he will no doubt without wasting words offer to do it of himself, (as though he could refuse Dounia that) the more readily since you may by your own efforts become his right hand in the office, and receive this assistance not as a charity, but as a salary earned by your own work. Dounia wants to arrange it all like this and I quite agree with her. And we have not spoken of our plans for another reason, that is, because I particularly wanted you to feel on an equal footing when you first meet him. When Dounia spoke to him with enthusiasm about you, he answered that one could never judge of a man without seeing him close, for oneself, and that he looked forward to forming his own opinion when he makes your acquaintance. Do you know, my precious Rodya, I think that perhaps for some reasons (nothing to do with Pyotr Petrovitch though, simply for my own personal, perhaps old-womanish, fancies) I should do better to go on living by myself, apart, than with them, after the wedding. I am convinced that he will be generous and delicate enough to invite me and to urge me to remain with my daughter for the future, and if he has said nothing about it hitherto, it is simply because it has been taken for granted; but I shall refuse. I have noticed more than once in my life that husbands don't quite get on with their mothers-in-law, and I don't want to be the least bit in anyone's way, and for my own sake, too, would rather be quite independent, so long as I have a crust of bread of my own, and such children as you and Dounia. If possible, I would settle somewhere near you, for the most joyful piece of news, dear Rodya, I have kept for the end of my letter: know then, my dear boy, that we may, perhaps, be all together in a very short time and may embrace one another again after a separation of almost three years! It is settled for certain that Dounia and I are to set off for Petersburg, exactly when I don't know, but very, very soon, possibly in a week. It all depends on Pyotr Petrovitch who will let us know when he has had time to look round him in Petersburg. To suit his own arrangements he is anxious to have the ceremony as soon as possible, even before the fast of Our Lady, if it could be managed, or if that is too soon to be ready, immediately after. Oh, with what happiness I shall press you to my heart! Dounia is all excitement at the joyful thought of seeing you, she said one day in joke that she would be ready to marry Pyotr Petrovitch for that alone. She is an angel! She is not writing anything to you now, and has only told me to write that she has so much, so much to tell you that she is not going to take up her pen now, for a few lines would tell you nothing, and it would only mean upsetting herself; she bids me send you her love and innumerable kisses. But although we shall be meeting so soon, perhaps I shall send you as much money as I can in a day or two. Now that everyone has heard that Dounia is to marry Pyotr Petrovitch, my credit has suddenly improved and I know that Afanasy Ivanovitch will trust me now even to seventy-five roubles on the security of my pension, so that perhaps I shall be able to send you twenty-five or even thirty roubles. I would send you more, but I am uneasy about our travelling expenses; for though Pyotr Petrovitch has been so kind as to undertake part of the expenses of the journey, that is to say, he has taken upon himself the conveyance of our bags and big trunk (which will be conveyed through some acquaintances of his), we must reckon upon some expense on our arrival in Petersburg, where we can't be left without a halfpenny, at least for the first few days. But we have calculated it all, Dounia and I, to the last penny, and we see that the *journey will not cost very much. It is only ninety versts from us to the railway and we have come to an agreement with a driver we know, so as to be in readiness; and from there Dounia and I can travel quite comfortably third class. So that I may very likely be able to send to you not twenty-five, but thirty roubles. But enough; I have covered two sheets already and there is no space left for more; our whole history, but so many events have happened! And now, my precious Rodya, I embrace you and send you a mother's blessing till we meet. Love Dounia your sister, Rodya; love her as she loves you and understand that she loves you beyond everything, more than herself. She is an angel and you, Rodya, you are everything to us – our one hope, our one consolation. If only you are happy, we shall be happy. Do you still say your prayers, Rodya, and believe in the mercy of our Creator and our Redeemer? I am afraid in my heart that you may have been visited by the new spirit of infidelity that is abroad today; If it is so, I pray for you. Remember, dear boy, how in your childhood, when your father was living, you used to lisp your prayers at my knee, and how happy we all were in those days. Good-bye, till we meet then – I embrace you warmly, warmly, with many kisses.*

"Yours till death,
"PULCHERIA RASKOLNIKOV."

Almost from the first, while he read the letter, Raskolnikov's face was wet with tears; but when he finished it, his face was pale and distorted and a bitter, wrathful and malignant smile was on his lips. He laid his head down on his threadbare dirty pillow and pondered, pondered a long time. His heart was beating violently, and his brain was in a turmoil. At last he felt cramped and stifled in the little yellow room that was like a cupboard or a box. His eyes and his mind craved for space. He took up his hat and went out, this time without dread of meeting anyone; he had forgotten his dread. He turned in the direction of the Vassilyevsky Ostrov, walking along Vassilyevsky Prospect, as though hastening on some business, but he walked, as his habit was, without noticing his way, muttering and even speaking aloud to himself, to the astonishment of the passers-by. Many of them took him to be drunk.

Chapter IV

HIS MOTHER'S LETTER had been a torture to him, but as regards the chief fact in it, he had felt not one moment's hesitation, even whilst he was reading the letter. The essential question was settled, and irrevocably settled, in his mind: "Never such a marriage while I am alive and Mr. Luzhin be damned!" "The thing is perfectly clear," he muttered to himself, with a malignant smile anticipating the triumph of his decision. "No, mother, no, Dounia, you won't deceive me! and then they apologise for not asking my advice and for taking the decision without me! I dare say! They imagine it is arranged now and can't be broken off; but we will see whether it can or not! A magnificent excuse: 'Pyotr Petrovitch is such a busy man that even his wedding has to be in post-haste, almost by express.' No, Dounia, I see it all and I know what you want to say to me; and I know too what you were thinking about, when you walked up and down all night, and what your prayers were like before the Holy Mother of Kazan who stands in mother's bedroom. Bitter is the ascent to Golgotha.... Hm... so it is finally settled; you have determined to marry a sensible business man, Avdotya Romanovna, one who has a fortune (has *already* made his fortune, that is so much more solid and impressive), a man who holds two government posts and who shares the ideas of our most rising generation, as mother writes, and who *seems* to be kind, as Dounia herself observes. That *seems* beats everything! And that very Dounia for that very '*seems*' is marrying him! Splendid! splendid!

"... But I should like to know why mother has written to me about 'our most rising generation'? Simply as a descriptive touch, or with the idea of prepossessing me in favour of Mr. Luzhin? Oh, the cunning of them! I should like to know one thing more: how far they were open with one another that day and night and all this time since? Was it all put into *words*, or did both understand that they had the same thing at heart and in their minds, so that there was no need to speak of it aloud, and better not to speak of it. Most likely it was partly like that, from mother's letter it's evident: he struck her as rude *a little*, and mother in her simplicity took her observations to Dounia. And she was sure to be vexed and 'answered her angrily.' I should think so! Who would not be angered when it was quite clear without any naĀ̄ve questions and when it was understood that it was useless to discuss it. And why does she write to me, 'love Dounia, Rodya, and she loves you more than herself'? Has she a secret conscience-prick at sacrificing her daughter to her son? 'You are our one comfort, you are everything to us.' Oh, mother!"

His bitterness grew more and more intense, and if he had happened to meet Mr. Luzhin at the moment, he might have murdered him.

"Hm... yes, that's true," he continued, pursuing the whirling ideas that chased each other in his brain, "it is true that 'it needs time and care to get to know a man,' but there is no mistake about Mr. Luzhin. The chief thing is he is 'a man of business and *seems* kind,' that was something, wasn't it, to send the bags and big box for them! A kind man, no doubt after that! But his *bride* and her mother are to drive in a peasant's cart covered with sacking (I know, I have been driven in it). No matter! It is only ninety versts and then they can 'travel very comfortably, third class,' for a thousand versts! Quite right, too. One must cut one's coat according to one's cloth, but what about you, Mr. Luzhin? She is your bride.... And you must be aware that her mother has to raise money on her pension for the journey. To be sure it's a matter of business, a partnership for mutual benefit, with equal shares and expenses; – food and drink provided, but pay for your tobacco. The business man has got the better of them, too. The luggage will cost less than their fares and very likely go for nothing. How is it that they don't both see all that, or is it that they don't want to see? And they are pleased, pleased! And to think that this is only the first blossoming, and that the real fruits are to come! But what really matters is not the stinginess, is not the meanness, but the *tone* of the whole thing. For that will be the tone after marriage, it's a foretaste of it. And mother too, why should she be so lavish? What will she have by the time she gets to Petersburg? Three silver roubles or two 'paper ones' as *she* says.... that old woman... hm. What does she expect to live upon in Petersburg afterwards? She has her reasons already for guessing that she *could not* live with Dounia after the marriage, even for the first few months. The good man has no doubt let slip something on that subject also, though mother would deny it: 'I shall refuse,' says she. On whom is she reckoning then? Is she counting on what is left of her hundred and twenty roubles of pension when Afanasy Ivanovitch's debt is paid? She knits woollen shawls and embroiders cuffs, ruining her old eyes. And all her shawls don't add more than twenty roubles a year to her hundred and twenty, I know that. So she is building all her hopes all the time on Mr. Luzhin's generosity; 'he will offer it of himself, he will press it on me.' You may wait a long time for that! That's how it always is with these Schilleresque noble hearts; till the last moment every goose is a swan with them, till the last moment, they hope for the best and will see nothing wrong, and although they have an inkling of the other side of the picture, yet they won't face the truth till they are forced to; the very thought of it makes them shiver; they thrust the truth away with both hands, until the man they deck out in false colours puts a fool's cap on them with his own hands. I should like to know whether Mr. Luzhin has any orders of merit; I bet he has the Anna in his buttonhole and that he puts it on when he goes to dine with contractors or merchants. He will be sure to have it for his wedding, too! Enough of him, confound him!

"Well,… mother I don't wonder at, it's like her, God bless her, but how could Dounia? Dounia darling, as though I did not know you! You were nearly twenty when I saw you last: I understood you then. Mother writes that 'Dounia can put up with a great deal.' I know that very well. I knew that two years and a half ago, and for the last two and a half years I have been thinking about it, thinking of just that, that 'Dounia can put up with a great deal.' If she could put up with Mr. Svidrigailov and all the rest of it, she certainly can put up with a great deal. And now mother and she have taken it into their heads that she can put up with Mr. Luzhin, who propounds the theory of the superiority of wives raised from destitution and owing everything to their husband's bounty – who propounds it, too, almost at the first interview. Granted that he 'let it slip,' though he is a sensible man, (yet maybe it was not a slip at all, but he meant to make himself clear as soon as possible) but Dounia, Dounia? She understands the man, of course, but she will have to live with the man. Why! she'd live on black bread and water, she would not sell her soul, she would not barter her moral freedom for comfort; she would not barter it for all Schleswig-Holstein, much less Mr. Luzhin's money. No, Dounia was not that sort when I knew her and… she is still the same, of course! Yes, there's no denying, the Svidrigailovs are a bitter pill! It's a bitter thing to spend one's life a governess in the provinces for two hundred roubles, but I know she would rather be a nigger on a plantation or a Lett with a German master than degrade her soul, and her moral dignity, by binding herself for ever to a man whom she does not respect and with whom she has nothing in common – for her own advantage. And if Mr. Luzhin had been of unalloyed gold, or one huge diamond, she would never have consented to become his legal concubine. Why is she consenting then? What's the point of it? What's the answer? It's clear enough: for herself, for her comfort, to save her life she would not sell herself, but for someone else she is doing it! For one she loves, for one she adores, she will sell herself! That's what it all amounts to; for her brother, for her mother, she will sell herself! She will sell everything! In such cases, 'we overcome our moral feeling if necessary,' freedom, peace, conscience even, all, all are brought into the market. Let my life go, if only my dear ones may be happy! More than that, we become casuists, we learn to be Jesuitical and for a time maybe we can soothe ourselves, we can persuade ourselves that it is one's duty for a good object. That's just like us, it's as clear as daylight. It's clear that Rodion Romanovitch Raskolnikov is the central figure in the business, and no one else. Oh, yes, she can ensure his happiness, keep him in the university, make him a partner in the office, make his whole future secure; perhaps he may even be a rich man later on, prosperous, respected, and may even end his life a famous man! But my mother? It's all Rodya, precious Rodya, her first born! For such a son who would not sacrifice such a daughter! Oh, loving, over-partial hearts! Why, for his sake we would not shrink even from Sonia's fate. Sonia, Sonia Marmeladov, the eternal victim so long as the world lasts. Have you taken the measure of your sacrifice, both of you? Is it right? Can you bear it? Is it any use? Is there sense in it? And let me tell you, Dounia, Sonia's life is no worse than life with Mr. Luzhin. 'There can be no question of love,' mother writes. And what if there can be no respect either, if on the contrary there is aversion, contempt, repulsion, what then?

So you will have to 'keep up your appearance,' too. Is not that so? Do you understand what that smartness means? Do you understand that the Luzhin smartness is just the same thing as Sonia's and may be worse, viler, baser, because in your case, Dounia, it's a bargain for luxuries, after all, but with Sonia it's simply a question of starvation. It has to be paid for, it has to be paid for, Dounia, this smartness. And what if it's more than you can bear afterwards, if you regret it? The bitterness, the misery, the curses, the tears hidden from all the world, for you are not a Marfa Petrovna. And how will your mother feel then? Even now she is uneasy, she is worried, but then, when she sees it all clearly? And I? Yes, indeed, what have you taken me for? I won't have your sacrifice, Dounia, I won't have it, mother! It shall not be, so long as I am alive, it shall not, it shall not! I won't accept it!"

He suddenly paused in his reflection and stood still.

"It shall not be? But what are you going to do to prevent it? You'll forbid it? And what right have you? What can you promise them on your side to give you such a right? Your whole life, your whole future, you will devote to them *when you have finished your studies and obtained a post*? Yes, we have heard all that before, and that's all *words*, but now? Now something must be done, now, do you understand that? And what are you doing now? You are living upon them. They borrow on their hundred roubles pension. They borrow from the Svidrigailovs. How are you going to save them from Svidrigailovs, from Afanasy Ivanovitch Vahrushin, oh, future millionaire Zeus who would arrange their lives for them? In another ten years? In another ten years, mother will be blind with knitting shawls, maybe with weeping too. She will be worn to a shadow with fasting; and my sister? Imagine for a moment what may have become of your sister in ten years? What may happen to her during those ten years? Can you fancy?"

So he tortured himself, fretting himself with such questions, and finding a kind of enjoyment in it. And yet all these questions were not new ones suddenly confronting him, they were old familiar aches. It was long since they had first begun to grip and rend his heart. Long, long ago his present anguish had its first beginnings; it had waxed and gathered strength, it had matured and concentrated, until it had taken the form of a fearful, frenzied and fantastic question, which tortured his heart and mind, clamouring insistently for an answer. Now his mother's letter had burst on him like a thunderclap. It was clear that he must not now suffer passively, worrying himself over unsolved questions, but that he must do something, do it at once, and do it quickly. Anyway he must decide on something, or else...

"Or throw up life altogether!" he cried suddenly, in a frenzy – "accept one's lot humbly as it is, once for all and stifle everything in oneself, giving up all claim to activity, life and love!"

"Do you understand, sir, do you understand what it means when you have absolutely nowhere to turn?" Marmeladov's question came suddenly into his mind, "for every man must have somewhere to turn...."

He gave a sudden start; another thought, that he had had yesterday, slipped back into his mind. But he did not start at the thought recurring to him, for he knew, he had *felt beforehand*, that it must come back, he was expecting it; besides it was not only yesterday's thought. The difference was that a month ago, yesterday even, the thought was a mere dream: but now... now it appeared not a dream at all, it had taken a new menacing and quite unfamiliar shape, and he suddenly became aware of this himself.... He felt a hammering in his head, and there was a darkness before his eyes.

He looked round hurriedly, he was searching for something. He wanted to sit down and was looking for a seat; he was walking along the K— Boulevard. There was a seat about a hundred paces in front of him. He walked towards it as fast he could; but on the way he met with a little adventure which absorbed all his attention. Looking for the seat, he had noticed a woman walking some twenty paces in front of him, but at first he took no more notice of her than of other objects that crossed his path. It had happened to him many times going home not to notice the road by which he was going, and he was accustomed to walk like that. But there was at first sight something so strange about the woman in front of him, that gradually his attention was riveted upon her, at first reluctantly and, as it were, resentfully, and then more and more intently. He felt a sudden desire to find out what it was that was so strange about the woman. In the first place, she appeared to be a girl quite young, and she was walking in the great heat bareheaded and with no parasol or gloves, waving her arms about in an absurd way. She had on a dress of some light silky material, but put on strangely awry, not properly hooked up, and torn open at the top of the skirt, close to the waist: a great piece was rent and hanging loose. A little kerchief was flung about her bare throat, but lay slanting on one side. The girl was walking unsteadily, too, stumbling and staggering from side to side. She drew Raskolnikov's whole attention at last. He overtook the girl at the seat, but, on reaching it, she dropped down on it, in the corner; she let her head sink on the back of the seat and closed her eyes, apparently in extreme exhaustion. Looking at her closely, he saw at once that she was completely drunk. It was a strange and shocking sight. He could hardly believe that he was not mistaken. He saw before him the face of a quite young, fair-haired girl – sixteen, perhaps not more than fifteen, years old, pretty little face, but flushed and heavy looking and, as it were, swollen. The girl seemed hardly to know what she was doing; she crossed one leg over the other, lifting it indecorously, and showed every sign of being unconscious that she was in the street.

Raskolnikov did not sit down, but he felt unwilling to leave her, and stood facing her in perplexity. This boulevard was never much frequented; and now, at two o'clock, in the stifling heat, it was quite deserted. And yet on the further side of the boulevard, about fifteen paces away, a gentleman was standing on the edge of the pavement. He, too, would apparently have liked to approach the girl with some object of his own. He, too, had probably seen her in the distance and had followed her, but found Raskolnikov in his way. He looked angrily at him, though he tried to escape his notice, and stood impatiently biding his time, till the unwelcome man in rags should have moved away. His intentions were unmistakable. The gentleman was a plump, thickly-set man, about thirty, fashionably dressed, with a high colour, red lips and moustaches. Raskolnikov felt furious; he had a sudden longing to insult this fat dandy in some way. He left the girl for a moment and walked towards the gentleman.

"Hey! You Svidrigailov! What do you want here?" he shouted, clenching his fists and laughing, spluttering with rage.

"What do you mean?" the gentleman asked sternly, scowling in haughty astonishment.

"Get away, that's what I mean."

"How dare you, you low fellow!"

He raised his cane. Raskolnikov rushed at him with his fists, without reflecting that the stout gentleman was a match for two men like himself. But at that instant someone seized him from behind, and a police constable stood between them.

"That's enough, gentlemen, no fighting, please, in a public place. What do you want? Who are you?" he asked Raskolnikov sternly, noticing his rags.

Raskolnikov looked at him intently. He had a straight-forward, sensible, soldierly face, with grey moustaches and whiskers.

"You are just the man I want," Raskolnikov cried, catching at his arm. "I am a student, Raskolnikov.... You may as well know that too," he added, addressing the gentleman, "come along, I have something to show you."

And taking the policeman by the hand he drew him towards the seat.

"Look here, hopelessly drunk, and she has just come down the boulevard. There is no telling who and what she is, she does not look like a professional. It's more likely she has been given drink and deceived somewhere... for the first time... you understand? and they've put her out into the street like that. Look at the way her dress is torn, and the way it has been put on: she has been dressed by somebody, she has not dressed herself, and dressed by unpractised hands, by a man's hands; that's evident. And now look there: I don't know that dandy with whom I was going to fight, I see him for the first time, but he, too, has seen her on the road, just now, drunk, not knowing what she is doing, and now he is very eager to get hold of her, to get her away somewhere while she is in this state... that's certain, believe me, I am not wrong. I saw him myself watching her and following her, but I prevented him, and he is just waiting for me to go away. Now he has walked away a little, and is standing still, pretending to make a cigarette.... Think how can we keep her out of his hands, and how are we to get her home?"

The policeman saw it all in a flash. The stout gentleman was easy to understand, he turned to consider the girl. The policeman bent over to examine her more closely, and his face worked with genuine compassion.

"Ah, what a pity!" he said, shaking his head – "why, she is quite a child! She has been deceived, you can see that at once. Listen, lady," he began addressing her, "where do you live?" The girl opened her weary and sleepy-looking eyes, gazed blankly at the speaker and waved her hand.

"Here," said Raskolnikov feeling in his pocket and finding twenty copecks, "here, call a cab and tell him to drive her to her address. The only thing is to find out her address!"

"Missy, missy!" the policeman began again, taking the money. "I'll fetch you a cab and take you home myself. Where shall I take you, eh? Where do you live?"

"Go away! They won't let me alone," the girl muttered, and once more waved her hand.

"Ach, ach, how shocking! It's shameful, missy, it's a shame!" He shook his head again, shocked, sympathetic and indignant.

"It's a difficult job," the policeman said to Raskolnikov, and as he did so, he looked him up and down in a rapid glance. He, too, must have seemed a strange figure to him: dressed in rags and handing him money!

"Did you meet her far from here?" he asked him.

"I tell you she was walking in front of me, staggering, just here, in the boulevard. She only just reached the seat and sank down on it."

"Ah, the shameful things that are done in the world nowadays, God have mercy on us! An innocent creature like that, drunk already! She has been deceived, that's a sure thing. See how her dress has been torn too.... Ah, the vice one sees nowadays! And as likely as not she belongs to gentlefolk too, poor ones maybe.... There are many like that nowadays. She looks refined, too, as though she were a lady," and he bent over her once more.

Perhaps he had daughters growing up like that, "looking like ladies and refined" with pretensions to gentility and smartness....

"The chief thing is," Raskolnikov persisted, "to keep her out of this scoundrel's hands! Why should he outrage her! It's as clear as day what he is after; ah, the brute, he is not moving off!"

Raskolnikov spoke aloud and pointed to him. The gentleman heard him, and seemed about to fly into a rage again, but thought better of it, and confined himself to a contemptuous look. He then walked slowly another ten paces away and again halted.

"Keep her out of his hands we can," said the constable thoughtfully, "if only she'd tell us where to take her, but as it is.... Missy, hey, missy!" he bent over her once more.

She opened her eyes fully all of a sudden, looked at him intently, as though realising something, got up from the seat and walked away in the direction from which she had come. "Oh shameful wretches, they won't let me alone!" she said, waving her hand again. She walked quickly, though staggering as before. The dandy followed her, but along another avenue, keeping his eye on her.

"Don't be anxious, I won't let him have her," the policeman said resolutely, and he set off after them.

"Ah, the vice one sees nowadays!" he repeated aloud, sighing.

At that moment something seemed to sting Raskolnikov; in an instant a complete revulsion of feeling came over him.

"Hey, here!" he shouted after the policeman.

The latter turned round.

"Let them be! What is it to do with you? Let her go! Let him amuse himself." He pointed at the dandy, "What is it to do with you?"

The policeman was bewildered, and stared at him open-eyed. Raskolnikov laughed.

"Well!" ejaculated the policeman, with a gesture of contempt, and he walked after the dandy and the girl, probably taking Raskolnikov for a madman or something even worse.

"He has carried off my twenty copecks," Raskolnikov murmured angrily when he was left alone. "Well, let him take as much from the other fellow to allow him to have the girl and so let it end. And why did I want to interfere? Is it for me to help? Have I any right to help? Let them devour each other alive – what is to me? How did I dare to give him twenty copecks? Were they mine?"

In spite of those strange words he felt very wretched. He sat down on the deserted seat. His thoughts strayed aimlessly.... He found it hard to fix his mind on anything at that moment. He longed to forget himself altogether, to forget everything, and then to wake up and begin life anew....

"Poor girl!" he said, looking at the empty corner where she had sat – "She will come to herself and weep, and then her mother will find out.... She will give her a beating, a horrible, shameful beating and then maybe, turn her out of doors.... And even if she does not, the Darya Frantsovnas will get wind of it, and the girl will soon be slipping out on the sly here and there. Then there will be the hospital directly (that's always the luck of those girls with respectable mothers, who go wrong on the sly) and then... again the hospital... drink... the taverns... and more hospital, in two or three years – a wreck, and her life over at eighteen or nineteen.... Have not I seen cases like that? And how have they been brought to it? Why, they've all come to it like that. Ugh! But what does it matter? That's as it should be, they tell us. A certain percentage, they tell us, must every year go... that way... to the devil, I suppose, so that the rest may remain chaste, and not be interfered with. A percentage! What splendid words they have; they are so scientific, so consolatory.... Once you've said 'percentage' there's nothing more to worry about. If we had any other word... maybe we might feel more uneasy.... But what if Dounia were one of the percentage! Of another one if not that one?

"But where am I going?" he thought suddenly. "Strange, I came out for something. As soon as I had read the letter I came out.... I was going to Vassilyevsky Ostrov, to Razumihin. That's what it was... now I remember. What for, though? And what put the idea of going to Razumihin into my head just now? That's curious."

He wondered at himself. Razumihin was one of his old comrades at the university. It was remarkable that Raskolnikov had hardly any friends at the university; he kept aloof from everyone, went to see no one, and did not welcome anyone who came to see him, and indeed everyone soon gave him up. He took no part in the students' gatherings, amusements or conversations. He worked with great intensity without sparing himself, and he was respected for this, but no one liked him. He was very poor, and there was a sort of haughty pride and reserve about him, as though he were keeping something to himself. He seemed to some of his comrades to look down upon them all as children, as though he were superior in development, knowledge and convictions, as though their beliefs and interests were beneath him.

With Razumihin he had got on, or, at least, he was more unreserved and communicative with him. Indeed it was impossible to be on any other terms with Razumihin. He was an exceptionally good-humoured and candid youth, good-natured to the point of simplicity, though both depth and dignity lay concealed under that simplicity. The better of his comrades understood this, and all were fond of him. He was extremely intelligent, though he was certainly rather a simpleton at times. He was of striking appearance – tall, thin, blackhaired and always badly shaved. He was sometimes uproarious and was reputed to be of great physical strength. One night, when out in a festive company, he had with one blow laid a gigantic policeman on his back. There was no limit to his drinking powers, but he could abstain from drink altogether; he sometimes went too far in his pranks; but he could do without pranks altogether. Another thing striking about Razumihin, no failure distressed him, and it seemed as though no unfavourable circumstances could crush him. He could lodge anywhere, and bear the extremes of cold and hunger. He was very poor, and kept himself entirely on what he could earn by work of one sort or another. He knew of no end of resources by which to earn money. He spent one whole winter without lighting his stove, and used to declare that he liked it better, because one slept more soundly in the cold. For the present he, too, had been obliged to give up the university, but it was only for a time, and he was working with all his might to save enough to return to his studies again. Raskolnikov had not been to see him for the last four months, and Razumihin did not even know his address. About two months before, they had met in the street, but Raskolnikov had turned away and even crossed to the other side that he might not be observed. And though Razumihin noticed him, he passed him by, as he did not want to annoy him.

Chapter V

"OF COURSE, I've been meaning lately to go to Razumihin's to ask for work, to ask him to get me lessons or something..." Raskolnikov thought, "but what help can he be to me now? Suppose he gets me lessons, suppose he shares his last farthing with me, if he has any farthings, so that I could get some boots and make myself tidy enough to give lessons... hm... Well and what then? What shall I do with the few coppers I earn? That's not what I want now. It's really absurd for me to go to Razumihin...."

The question why he was now going to Razumihin agitated him even more than he was himself aware; he kept uneasily seeking for some sinister significance in this apparently ordinary action.

"Could I have expected to set it all straight and to find a way out by means of Razumihin alone?" he asked himself in perplexity.

He pondered and rubbed his forehead, and, strange to say, after long musing, suddenly, as if it were spontaneously and by chance, a fantastic thought came into his head.

"Hm... to Razumihin's," he said all at once, calmly, as though he had reached a final determination. "I shall go to Razumihin's of course, but... not now. I shall go to him... on the next day after It, when It will be over and everything will begin afresh...."

And suddenly he realised what he was thinking.

"After It," he shouted, jumping up from the seat, "but is It really going to happen? Is it possible it really will happen?" He left the seat, and went off almost at a run; he meant to turn back, homewards, but the thought of going home suddenly filled him with intense loathing; in that hole, in that awful little cupboard of his, all *this* had for a month past been growing up in him; and he walked on at random.

His nervous shudder had passed into a fever that made him feel shivering; in spite of the heat he felt cold. With a kind of effort he began almost unconsciously, from some inner craving, to stare at all the objects before him, as though looking for something to distract his attention; but he did not succeed, and kept dropping every moment into brooding. When with a start he lifted his head again and looked round, he forgot at once what he had just been thinking about and even where he was going. In this way he walked right across Vassilyevsky Ostrov, came out on to the Lesser Neva, crossed the bridge and turned towards the islands. The greenness and freshness were at first restful to his weary eyes after the dust of the town and the huge houses that hemmed him in and weighed upon him. Here there were no taverns, no stifling closeness, no stench. But soon these new pleasant sensations passed into morbid irritability. Sometimes he stood still before a brightly painted summer villa standing among green foliage, he gazed through the fence, he saw in the distance smartly dressed women on the verandahs and balconies, and children running in the gardens. The flowers especially caught his attention; he gazed at them longer than at anything. He was met, too, by luxurious carriages and by men and women on horseback; he watched them with curious eyes and forgot about them before they had vanished from his sight. Once he stood still and counted his money; he found he had thirty copecks. "Twenty to the policeman, three to Nastasya for the letter, so I must have given forty-seven or fifty to the Marmeladovs yesterday," he thought, reckoning it up for some unknown reason, but he soon forgot with what object he had taken the money out of his pocket. He recalled it on passing an eating-house or tavern, and felt that he was hungry.... Going into the tavern he drank a glass of vodka and ate a pie of some sort. He finished eating it as he walked away. It was a long while since he had taken vodka and it had an effect upon him at once, though he only drank a wineglassful. His legs felt suddenly heavy and a great drowsiness came upon him. He turned homewards, but reaching Petrovsky Ostrov he stopped completely exhausted, turned off the road into the bushes, sank down upon the grass and instantly fell asleep.

In a morbid condition of the brain, dreams often have a singular actuality, vividness, and extraordinary semblance of reality. At times monstrous images are created, but the setting and the whole picture are so truth-like and filled with details so delicate, so unexpectedly, but so artistically consistent, that the dreamer, were he an artist like Pushkin or Turgenev even, could never have invented them in the waking state. Such sick dreams always remain long in the memory and make a powerful impression on the overwrought and deranged nervous system.

Raskolnikov had a fearful dream. He dreamt he was back in his childhood in the little town of his birth. He was a child about seven years old, walking into the country with his father on the evening of a holiday. It was a grey and heavy day, the country was exactly as he remembered it; indeed he recalled it far more vividly in his dream than he had done in memory. The little town stood on a level flat as bare as the hand, not even a willow near it; only in the far distance, a copse lay, a dark blur on the very edge of the horizon. A few paces beyond the last market garden stood a tavern, a big tavern, which had always aroused in him a feeling of aversion, even of fear, when he walked by it with his father. There was always a crowd there, always shouting, laughter and abuse, hideous hoarse singing and often fighting. Drunken and horrible-looking figures were hanging about the tavern. He used to cling close to his father, trembling all over when he met them. Near the tavern the road became a dusty track, the dust of which was always black. It was a winding road, and about a hundred paces further on, it turned to the right to the graveyard. In the middle of the graveyard stood a stone church with a green cupola where he used to go to mass two or three times a year with his father and mother, when a service was held in memory of his grandmother, who had long been dead, and whom he had never seen. On these occasions they used to take on a white dish tied up in a table napkin a special sort of rice pudding with raisins stuck in it in the shape of a cross. He loved that church, the old-fashioned, unadorned ikons and the old priest with the shaking head. Near his grandmother's grave, which was marked by a stone, was the little grave of his younger brother who had died at six months old. He did not remember him at all, but he had been told about his little brother, and whenever he visited the graveyard he used religiously and reverently to cross himself and to bow down and kiss the little grave. And now he dreamt that he was walking with his father past the tavern on the way to the graveyard; he was holding his father's hand and looking with dread at the tavern. A peculiar circumstance attracted his attention: there seemed to be some kind of festivity going on, there were crowds of gaily dressed townspeople, peasant women, their husbands, and riff-raff of all sorts, all singing and all more or less drunk. Near the entrance of the tavern stood a cart, but a strange cart. It was one of those big carts usually drawn by heavy cart-horses and laden with casks of wine or other heavy goods. He always liked looking at those great cart-horses, with their long manes, thick legs, and slow even pace, drawing along a perfect mountain with no appearance of effort, as though it were easier going with a load than without it. But now, strange to say, in the shafts of such a cart he saw a thin little sorrel beast, one of those peasants' nags which he had often seen straining their utmost under a heavy load of wood or hay, especially when the wheels were stuck in the mud or in a rut. And the peasants would beat them so cruelly, sometimes even about the nose and eyes, and he felt so sorry, so sorry for them that he almost cried, and his mother always used to take him away from the window. All of a sudden there was a great uproar of shouting, singing and the balalaĀˉka, and from the tavern a number of big and very drunken peasants came out, wearing red and blue shirts and coats thrown over their shoulders.

"Get in, get in!" shouted one of them, a young thick-necked peasant with a fleshy face red as a carrot. "I'll take you all, get in!"

But at once there was an outbreak of laughter and exclamations in the crowd.

"Take us all with a beast like that!"

"Why, Mikolka, are you crazy to put a nag like that in such a cart?"

"And this mare is twenty if she is a day, mates!"

"Get in, I'll take you all," Mikolka shouted again, leaping first into the cart, seizing the reins and standing straight up in front. "The bay has gone with Matvey," he shouted from the cart – "and this brute, mates, is just breaking my heart, I feel as if I could kill her. She's just eating her head off. Get in, I tell you! I'll make her gallop! She'll gallop!" and he picked up the whip, preparing himself with relish to flog the little mare.

"Get in! Come along!" The crowd laughed. "D'you hear, she'll gallop!"

"Gallop indeed! She has not had a gallop in her for the last ten years!"

"She'll jog along!"

"Don't you mind her, mates, bring a whip each of you, get ready!"

"All right! Give it to her!"

They all clambered into Mikolka's cart, laughing and making jokes. Six men got in and there was still room for more. They hauled in a fat, rosy-cheeked woman. She was dressed in red cotton, in a pointed, beaded headdress and thick leather shoes; she was cracking nuts and laughing. The crowd round them was laughing too and indeed, how could they help laughing? That wretched nag was to drag all the cartload of them at a gallop! Two young fellows in the cart were just getting whips ready to help Mikolka. With the cry of "now," the mare tugged with all her might, but far from galloping, could scarcely move forward; she struggled with her legs, gasping and shrinking from the blows of the three whips which were showered upon her like hail. The laughter in the cart and in the crowd was redoubled, but Mikolka flew into a rage and furiously thrashed the mare, as though he supposed she really could gallop.

"Let me get in, too, mates," shouted a young man in the crowd whose appetite was aroused.

"Get in, all get in," cried Mikolka, "she will draw you all. I'll beat her to death!" And he thrashed and thrashed at the mare, beside himself with fury.

"Father, father," he cried, "father, what are they doing? Father, they are beating the poor horse!"

"Come along, come along!" said his father. "They are drunken and foolish, they are in fun; come away, don't look!" and he tried to draw him away, but he tore himself away from his hand, and, beside himself with horror, ran to the horse. The poor beast was in a bad way. She was gasping, standing still, then tugging again and almost falling.

"Beat her to death," cried Mikolka, "it's come to that. I'll do for her!"

"What are you about, are you a Christian, you devil?" shouted an old man in the crowd.

"Did anyone ever see the like? A wretched nag like that pulling such a cartload," said another.

"You'll kill her," shouted the third.

"Don't meddle! It's my property, I'll do what I choose. Get in, more of you! Get in, all of you! I will have her go at a gallop!..."

All at once laughter broke into a roar and covered everything: the mare, roused by the shower of blows, began feebly kicking. Even the old man could not help smiling. To think of a wretched little beast like that trying to kick!

Two lads in the crowd snatched up whips and ran to the mare to beat her about the ribs. One ran each side.

"Hit her in the face, in the eyes, in the eyes," cried Mikolka.

"Give us a song, mates," shouted someone in the cart and everyone in the cart joined in a riotous song, jingling a tambourine and whistling. The woman went on cracking nuts and laughing.

... He ran beside the mare, ran in front of her, saw her being whipped across the eyes, right in the eyes! He was crying, he felt choking, his tears were streaming. One of the men gave him a cut with the whip across the face, he did not feel it. Wringing his hands and screaming, he rushed up to the grey-headed old man with the grey beard, who was shaking his head in disapproval. One woman seized him by the hand and would have taken him away, but he tore himself from her and ran back to the mare. She was almost at the last gasp, but began kicking once more.

"I'll teach you to kick," Mikolka shouted ferociously. He threw down the whip, bent forward and picked up from the bottom of the cart a long, thick shaft, he took hold of one end with both hands and with an effort brandished it over the mare.

"He'll crush her," was shouted round him. "He'll kill her!"

"It's my property," shouted Mikolka and brought the shaft down with a swinging blow. There was a sound of a heavy thud.

"Thrash her, thrash her! Why have you stopped?" shouted voices in the crowd.

And Mikolka swung the shaft a second time and it fell a second time on the spine of the luckless mare. She sank back on her haunches, but lurched forward and tugged forward with all her force, tugged first on one side and then on the other, trying to move the cart. But the six whips were attacking her in all directions, and the shaft was raised again and fell upon her a third time, then a fourth, with heavy measured blows. Mikolka was in a fury that he could not kill her at one blow.

"She's a tough one," was shouted in the crowd.

"She'll fall in a minute, mates, there will soon be an end of her," said an admiring spectator in the crowd.

"Fetch an axe to her! Finish her off," shouted a third.

"I'll show you! Stand off," Mikolka screamed frantically; he threw down the shaft, stooped down in the cart and picked up an iron crowbar. "Look out," he shouted, and with all his might he dealt a stunning blow at the poor mare. The blow fell; the mare staggered, sank back, tried to pull, but the bar fell again with a swinging blow on her back and she fell on the ground like a log.

"Finish her off," shouted Mikolka and he leapt beside himself, out of the cart. Several young men, also flushed with drink, seized anything they could come across – whips, sticks, poles, and ran to the dying mare. Mikolka stood on one side and began dealing random blows with the crowbar. The mare stretched out her head, drew a long breath and died.

"You butchered her," someone shouted in the crowd.

"Why wouldn't she gallop then?"

"My property!" shouted Mikolka, with bloodshot eyes, brandishing the bar in his hands. He stood as though regretting that he had nothing more to beat.

"No mistake about it, you are not a Christian," many voices were shouting in the crowd.

But the poor boy, beside himself, made his way, screaming, through the crowd to the sorrel nag, put his arms round her bleeding dead head and kissed it, kissed the eyes and kissed the lips…. Then he jumped up and flew in a frenzy with his little fists out at Mikolka. At that instant his father, who had been running after him, snatched him up and carried him out of the crowd.

"Come along, come! Let us go home," he said to him.

"Father! Why did they… kill… the poor horse!" he sobbed, but his voice broke and the words came in shrieks from his panting chest.

"They are drunk…. They are brutal… it's not our business!" said his father. He put his arms round his father but he felt choked, choked. He tried to draw a breath, to cry out – and woke up.

He waked up, gasping for breath, his hair soaked with perspiration, and stood up in terror.

"Thank God, that was only a dream," he said, sitting down under a tree and drawing deep breaths. "But what is it? Is it some fever coming on? Such a hideous dream!"

He felt utterly broken: darkness and confusion were in his soul. He rested his elbows on his knees and leaned his head on his hands.

"Good God!" he cried, "can it be, can it be, that I shall really take an axe, that I shall strike her on the head, split her skull open… that I shall tread in the sticky warm blood, break the lock, steal and tremble; hide, all spattered in the blood… with the axe…. Good God, can it be?"

He was shaking like a leaf as he said this.

"But why am I going on like this?" he continued, sitting up again, as it were in profound amazement. "I knew that I could never bring myself to it, so what have I been torturing myself for till now? Yesterday, yesterday, when I went to make that… *experiment*, yesterday I realised completely that I could never bear to do it…. Why am I going over it again, then? Why am I hesitating? As I came down the stairs yesterday, I said myself that it was base, loathsome, vile, vile… the very thought of it made me feel sick and filled me with horror.

"No, I couldn't do it, I couldn't do it! Granted, granted that there is no flaw in all that reasoning, that all that I have concluded this last month is clear as day, true as arithmetic…. My God! Anyway I couldn't bring myself to it! I couldn't do it, I couldn't do it! Why, why then am I still…?"

He rose to his feet, looked round in wonder as though surprised at finding himself in this place, and went towards the bridge. He was pale, his eyes glowed, he was exhausted in every limb, but he seemed suddenly to breathe more easily. He felt he had cast off that fearful burden that had so long been weighing upon him, and all at once there was a sense of relief and peace in his soul. "Lord," he prayed, "show me my path – I renounce that accursed… dream of mine."

Crossing the bridge, he gazed quietly and calmly at the Neva, at the glowing red sun setting in the glowing sky. In spite of his weakness he was not conscious of fatigue. It was as though an abscess that had been forming for a month past in his heart had suddenly broken. Freedom, freedom! He was free from that spell, that sorcery, that obsession!

Later on, when he recalled that time and all that happened to him during those days, minute by minute, point by point, he was superstitiously impressed by one circumstance, which, though in itself not very exceptional, always seemed to him afterwards the predestined turning-point of his fate. He could never understand and explain to himself why, when he was tired and worn out, when it would have been more convenient for him to go home by the shortest and most direct way, he had returned by the Hay Market where he had no need to go. It was obviously and quite unnecessarily out of his way, though not much so. It is true that it happened to him dozens of times to return home without noticing what streets he passed through. But why, he was always asking himself, why had such an important, such a decisive and at the same time such an absolutely chance meeting happened in the Hay Market (where he had moreover no reason to go) at the very hour, the very minute of his life when he was just in the very mood and in the very circumstances in which that meeting was able to exert the gravest and most decisive influence on his whole destiny? As though it had been lying in wait for him on purpose!

It was about nine o'clock when he crossed the Hay Market. At the tables and the barrows, at the booths and the shops, all the market people were closing their establishments or clearing away and packing up their wares and, like their customers, were going home. Rag pickers and costermongers of all kinds were crowding round the taverns in the dirty and stinking courtyards of the Hay Market. Raskolnikov particularly liked this place and the neighbouring alleys, when he wandered aimlessly in the streets. Here his rags did not attract contemptuous attention, and one could walk about in any attire without scandalising people. At the corner of an alley a huckster and his wife had two tables set out with tapes, thread, cotton handkerchiefs, etc. They, too, had got up to go home, but were lingering in conversation with a friend, who had just come up to them. This friend was Lizaveta Ivanovna, or, as everyone called her, Lizaveta, the younger sister of the old pawnbroker, Alyona Ivanovna, whom Raskolnikov had visited the previous day to pawn his watch and make his *experiment*.... He already knew all about Lizaveta and she knew him a little too. She was a single woman of about thirty-five, tall, clumsy, timid, submissive and almost idiotic. She was a complete slave and went in fear and trembling of her sister, who made her work day and night, and even beat her. She was standing with a bundle before the huckster and his wife, listening earnestly and doubtfully. They were talking of something with special warmth. The moment Raskolnikov caught sight of her, he was overcome by a strange sensation as it were of intense astonishment, though there was nothing astonishing about this meeting.

"You could make up your mind for yourself, Lizaveta Ivanovna," the huckster was saying aloud. "Come round tomorrow about seven. They will be here too."

"Tomorrow?" said Lizaveta slowly and thoughtfully, as though unable to make up her mind.

"Upon my word, what a fright you are in of Alyona Ivanovna," gabbled the huckster's wife, a lively little woman. "I look at you, you are like some little babe. And she is not your own sister either – nothing but a step-sister and what a hand she keeps over you!"

"But this time don't say a word to Alyona Ivanovna," her husband interrupted; "that's my advice, but come round to us without asking. It will be worth your while. Later on your sister herself may have a notion."

"Am I to come?"

"About seven o'clock tomorrow. And they will be here. You will be able to decide for yourself."

"And we'll have a cup of tea," added his wife.

"All right, I'll come," said Lizaveta, still pondering, and she began slowly moving away.

Raskolnikov had just passed and heard no more. He passed softly, unnoticed, trying not to miss a word. His first amazement was followed by a thrill of horror, like a shiver running down his spine. He had learnt, he had suddenly quite unexpectedly learnt, that the next day at seven o'clock Lizaveta, the old woman's sister and only companion, would be away from home and that therefore at seven o'clock precisely the old woman *would be left alone*.

He was only a few steps from his lodging. He went in like a man condemned to death. He thought of nothing and was incapable of thinking; but he felt suddenly in his whole being that he had no more freedom of thought, no will, and that everything was suddenly and irrevocably decided.

Certainly, if he had to wait whole years for a suitable opportunity, he could not reckon on a more certain step towards the success of the plan than that which had just presented itself. In any case, it would have been difficult to find out beforehand and with certainty, with greater exactness and less risk, and without dangerous inquiries and investigations, that next day at a certain time an old woman, on whose life an attempt was contemplated, would be at home and entirely alone.

Chapter VI

LATER ON Raskolnikov happened to find out why the huckster and his wife had invited Lizaveta. It was a very ordinary matter and there was nothing exceptional about it. A family who had come to the town and been reduced to poverty were selling their household goods and clothes, all women's things. As the things would have fetched little in the market, they were looking for a dealer. This was Lizaveta's business. She undertook such jobs and was frequently employed, as she was very honest and always fixed a fair price and stuck to it. She spoke as a rule little and, as we have said already, she was very submissive and timid.

But Raskolnikov had become superstitious of late. The traces of superstition remained in him long after, and were almost ineradicable. And in all this he was always afterwards disposed to see something strange and mysterious, as it were, the presence of some peculiar influences and coincidences. In the previous winter a student he knew called Pokorev, who had left for Harkov, had chanced in conversation to give him the address of Alyona Ivanovna, the old pawnbroker, in case he might want to pawn anything. For a long while he did not go to her, for he had lessons and managed to get along somehow. Six weeks ago he had remembered the address; he had two articles that could be pawned: his father's old silver watch and a little gold ring with three red stones, a present from his sister at parting. He decided to take the ring. When he found the old woman he had felt an insurmountable repulsion for her at the first glance, though he knew nothing special about her. He got two roubles from her and went into a miserable little tavern on his way home. He asked for tea, sat down and sank into deep thought. A strange idea was pecking at his brain like a chicken in the egg, and very, very much absorbed him.

Almost beside him at the next table there was sitting a student, whom he did not know and had never seen, and with him a young officer. They had played a game of billiards and began drinking tea. All at once he heard the student mention to the officer the pawnbroker Alyona Ivanovna and give him her address. This of itself seemed strange to Raskolnikov; he had just come from her and here at once he heard her name. Of course it was a chance, but he could not shake off a very extraordinary impression, and here someone seemed to be speaking expressly for him; the student began telling his friend various details about Alyona Ivanovna.

"She is first-rate," he said. "You can always get money from her. She is as rich as a Jew, she can give you five thousand roubles at a time and she is not above taking a pledge for a rouble. Lots of our fellows have had dealings with her. But she is an awful old harpy...."

And he began describing how spiteful and uncertain she was, how if you were only a day late with your interest the pledge was lost; how she gave a quarter of the value of an article and took five and even seven percent a month on it and so on. The student chattered on, saying that she had a sister Lizaveta, whom the wretched little creature was continually beating, and kept in complete bondage like a small child, though Lizaveta was at least six feet high.

"There's a phenomenon for you," cried the student and he laughed.

They began talking about Lizaveta. The student spoke about her with a peculiar relish and was continually laughing and the officer listened with great interest and asked him to send Lizaveta to do some mending for him. Raskolnikov did not miss a word and learned everything about her. Lizaveta was younger than the old woman and was her half-sister, being the child of a different mother. She was thirty-five. She worked day and night for her sister, and besides doing the cooking and the washing, she did sewing and worked as a charwoman and gave her sister all she earned. She did not dare to accept an order or job of any kind without her sister's permission. The old woman had already made her will, and Lizaveta knew of it, and by this will she would not get a farthing; nothing but the movables, chairs and so on; all the money was left to a monastery in the province of N—, that prayers might be said for her in perpetuity. Lizaveta was of lower rank than her sister, unmarried and awfully uncouth in appearance, remarkably tall with long feet that looked as if they were bent outwards. She always wore battered goatskin shoes, and was clean in her person. What the student expressed most surprise and amusement about was the fact that Lizaveta was continually with child.

"But you say she is hideous?" observed the officer.

"Yes, she is so dark-skinned and looks like a soldier dressed up, but you know she is not at all hideous. She has such a good-natured face and eyes. Strikingly so. And the proof of it is that lots of people are attracted by her. She is such a soft, gentle creature, ready to put up with anything, always willing, willing to do anything. And her smile is really very sweet."

"You seem to find her attractive yourself," laughed the officer.

"From her queerness. No, I'll tell you what. I could kill that damned old woman and make off with her money, I assure you, without the faintest conscience-prick," the student added with warmth. The officer laughed again while Raskolnikov shuddered. How strange it was!

"Listen, I want to ask you a serious question," the student said hotly. "I was joking of course, but look here; on one side we have a stupid, senseless, worthless, spiteful, ailing, horrid old woman, not simply useless but doing actual mischief, who has not an idea what she is living for herself, and who will die in a day or two in any case. You understand? You understand?"

"Yes, yes, I understand," answered the officer, watching his excited companion attentively.

"Well, listen then. On the other side, fresh young lives thrown away for want of help and by thousands, on every side! A hundred thousand good deeds could be done and helped, on that old woman's money which will be buried in a monastery! Hundreds, thousands perhaps, might be set on the right path; dozens of families saved from destitution, from ruin, from vice, from the Lock hospitals – and all with her money. Kill her, take her money and with the help of it devote oneself to the service of humanity and the good of all. What do you think, would not one tiny crime be wiped out by thousands of good deeds? For one life thousands would be saved from corruption and decay. One death, and a hundred lives in exchange – it's simple arithmetic! Besides, what value has the life of that sickly, stupid, ill-natured old woman in the balance of existence! No more than the life of a louse, of a black-beetle, less in fact because the old woman is doing harm. She is wearing out the lives of others; the other day she bit Lizaveta's finger out of spite; it almost had to be amputated."

"Of course she does not deserve to live," remarked the officer, "but there it is, it's nature."

"Oh, well, brother, but we have to correct and direct nature, and, but for that, we should drown in an ocean of prejudice. But for that, there would never have been a single great man. They talk of duty, conscience – I don't want to say anything against duty and conscience; – but the point is, what do we mean by them? Stay, I have another question to ask you. Listen!"

"No, you stay, I'll ask you a question. Listen!"

"Well?"

"You are talking and speechifying away, but tell me, would you kill the old woman *yourself*?"

"Of course not! I was only arguing the justice of it…. It's nothing to do with me…."

"But I think, if you would not do it yourself, there's no justice about it…. Let us have another game."

Raskolnikov was violently agitated. Of course, it was all ordinary youthful talk and thought, such as he had often heard before in different forms and on different themes. But why had he happened to hear such a discussion and such ideas at the very moment when his own brain was just conceiving… *the very same ideas*? And why, just at the moment when he had brought away the embryo of his idea from the old woman had he dropped at once upon a conversation about her? This coincidence always seemed strange to him. This trivial talk in a tavern had an immense influence on him in his later action; as though there had really been in it something preordained, some guiding hint….

* * *

On returning from the Hay Market he flung himself on the sofa and sat for a whole hour without stirring. Meanwhile it got dark; he had no candle and, indeed, it did not occur to him to light up. He could never recollect whether he had been thinking about anything at that time. At last he was conscious of his former fever and shivering, and he realised with relief that he could lie down on the sofa. Soon heavy, leaden sleep came over him, as it were crushing him.

He slept an extraordinarily long time and without dreaming. Nastasya, coming into his room at ten o'clock the next morning, had difficulty in rousing him. She brought him in tea and bread. The tea was again the second brew and again in her own tea-pot.

"My goodness, how he sleeps!" she cried indignantly. "And he is always asleep."

He got up with an effort. His head ached, he stood up, took a turn in his garret and sank back on the sofa again.

"Going to sleep again," cried Nastasya. "Are you ill, eh?"

He made no reply.

"Do you want some tea?"

"Afterwards," he said with an effort, closing his eyes again and turning to the wall.

Nastasya stood over him.

"Perhaps he really is ill," she said, turned and went out. She came in again at two o'clock with soup. He was lying as before. The tea stood untouched. Nastasya felt positively offended and began wrathfully rousing him.

"Why are you lying like a log?" she shouted, looking at him with repulsion.

He got up, and sat down again, but said nothing and stared at the floor.

"Are you ill or not?" asked Nastasya and again received no answer. "You'd better go out and get a breath of air," she said after a pause. "Will you eat it or not?"

"Afterwards," he said weakly. "You can go."

And he motioned her out.

She remained a little longer, looked at him with compassion and went out.

A few minutes afterwards, he raised his eyes and looked for a long while at the tea and the soup. Then he took the bread, took up a spoon and began to eat.

He ate a little, three or four spoonfuls, without appetite, as it were mechanically. His head ached less. After his meal he stretched himself on the sofa again, but now he could not sleep; he lay without stirring, with his face in the pillow. He was haunted by day-dreams and such strange day-dreams; in one, that kept recurring, he fancied that he was in Africa, in Egypt, in some sort of oasis. The caravan was resting, the camels were peacefully lying down; the palms stood all around in a complete circle; all the party were at dinner. But he was drinking water from a spring which flowed gurgling close by. And it was so cool, it was wonderful, wonderful, blue, cold water running among the parti-coloured stones and over the clean sand which glistened here and there like gold.... Suddenly he heard a clock strike. He started, roused himself, raised his head, looked out of the window, and seeing how late it was, suddenly jumped up wide awake as though someone had pulled him off the sofa. He crept on tiptoe to the door, stealthily opened it and began listening on the staircase. His heart beat terribly. But all was quiet on the stairs as if everyone was asleep.... It seemed to him strange and monstrous that he could have slept in such forgetfulness from the previous day and had done nothing, had prepared nothing yet.... And meanwhile perhaps it had struck six. And his drowsiness and stupefaction were followed by an extraordinary, feverish, as it were distracted haste. But the preparations to be made were few. He concentrated all his energies on thinking of everything and forgetting nothing; and his heart kept beating and thumping so that he could hardly breathe. First he had to make a noose and sew it into his overcoat – a work of a moment. He rummaged under his pillow and picked out amongst the linen stuffed away under it, a worn out, old unwashed shirt. From its rags he tore a long strip, a couple of inches wide and about sixteen inches long. He folded this strip in two, took off his wide, strong summer overcoat of some stout cotton material (his only outer garment) and began sewing the two ends of the rag on the inside, under the left armhole. His hands shook as he sewed, but he did it successfully so that nothing showed outside when he put the coat on again. The needle and thread he had got ready long before and they lay on his table in a piece of paper. As for the noose, it was a very ingenious device of his own; the noose was intended for the axe. It was impossible for him to carry the axe through the street in his hands. And if hidden under his coat he would still have had to support it with his hand, which would have been noticeable. Now he had only to put the head of the axe in the noose, and it would hang quietly under his arm on the inside. Putting his hand in his coat pocket, he could hold the end of the handle all the way, so that it did not swing; and as the coat was very full, a regular sack in fact, it could not be seen from outside that he was holding something with the hand that was in the pocket. This noose, too, he had designed a fortnight before.

When he had finished with this, he thrust his hand into a little opening between his sofa and the floor, fumbled in the left corner and drew out the *pledge*, which he had got ready long before and hidden there. This pledge was, however, only a smoothly planed piece of wood the size and thickness of a silver cigarette case. He picked up this piece of wood in one of his wanderings in a courtyard where there was some sort of a workshop. Afterwards he had added to the wood a thin smooth piece of iron, which he had also picked up at the same time in the street. Putting the iron which was a little the smaller on the piece of wood, he fastened them very firmly, crossing and re-crossing the thread round them; then wrapped them carefully and daintily in clean white paper and tied up the parcel so that it would be very difficult to untie it. This was in order to divert the attention of the old woman for a time, while she was trying to undo the knot, and so to gain a moment. The iron strip was added to give weight, so that the woman might not guess the first minute that the "thing" was made of wood. All this had been stored by him beforehand under the sofa. He had only just got the pledge out when he heard someone suddenly about in the yard.

"It struck six long ago."

"Long ago! My God!"

He rushed to the door, listened, caught up his hat and began to descend his thirteen steps cautiously, noiselessly, like a cat. He had still the most important thing to do – to steal the axe from the kitchen. That the deed must be done with an axe he had decided long ago. He had also a pocket pruning-knife, but he could not rely on the knife and still less on his own strength, and so resolved finally on the axe. We may note in passing, one peculiarity in regard to all the final resolutions taken by him in the matter; they had one strange characteristic: the more final they were, the more hideous and the more absurd they at once became in his eyes. In spite of all his agonising inward struggle, he never for a single instant all that time could believe in the carrying out of his plans.

And, indeed, if it had ever happened that everything to the least point could have been considered and finally settled, and no uncertainty of any kind had remained, he would, it seems, have renounced it all as something absurd, monstrous and impossible. But a whole mass of unsettled points and uncertainties remained. As for getting the axe, that trifling business cost him no anxiety, for nothing could be easier. Nastasya was continually out of the house, especially in the evenings; she would run in to the neighbours or to a shop, and always left the door ajar. It was the one thing the landlady was always scolding her about. And so, when the time came, he would only have to go quietly into the kitchen and to take the axe, and an hour later (when everything was over) go in and put it back again. But these were doubtful points. Supposing he returned an hour later to put it back, and Nastasya had come back and was on the spot. He would of course have to go by and wait till she went out again. But supposing she were in the meantime to miss the axe, look for it, make an outcry – that would mean suspicion or at least grounds for suspicion.

But those were all trifles which he had not even begun to consider, and indeed he had no time. He was thinking of the chief point, and put off trifling details, until *he could believe in it all*. But that seemed utterly unattainable. So it seemed to himself at least. He could not imagine, for instance, that he would sometime leave off thinking, get up and simply go there…. Even his late experiment (i.e. his visit with the object of a final survey of the place) was simply an attempt at an experiment, far from being the real thing, as though one should say "come, let us go and try it – why dream about it!" – and at once he had broken down and had run away cursing, in a frenzy with himself. Meanwhile it would seem, as regards the moral question, that his analysis was complete; his casuistry had become keen as a razor, and he could not find rational objections in himself. But in the last resort he simply ceased to believe in himself, and doggedly, slavishly sought arguments in all directions, fumbling for them, as though someone were forcing and drawing him to it.

At first – long before indeed – he had been much occupied with one question; why almost all crimes are so badly concealed and so easily detected, and why almost all criminals leave such obvious traces? He had come gradually to many different and curious conclusions, and in his opinion the chief reason lay not so much in the material impossibility of concealing the crime, as in the criminal himself. Almost every criminal is subject to a failure of will and reasoning power by a childish and phenomenal heedlessness, at the very instant when prudence and caution are most essential. It was his conviction that this eclipse of reason and failure of will power attacked a man like a disease, developed gradually and reached its highest point just before the perpetration of the crime, continued with equal violence at the moment of the crime and for longer or shorter time after, according to the individual case, and then passed off like any other disease. The question whether the disease gives rise to the crime, or whether the crime from its own peculiar nature is always accompanied by something of the nature of disease, he did not yet feel able to decide.

When he reached these conclusions, he decided that in his own case there could not be such a morbid reaction, that his reason and will would remain unimpaired at the time of carrying out his design, for the simple reason that his design was "not a crime...." We will omit all the process by means of which he arrived at this last conclusion; we have run too far ahead already.... We may add only that the practical, purely material difficulties of the affair occupied a secondary position in his mind. "One has but to keep all one's will-power and reason to deal with them, and they will all be overcome at the time when once one has familiarised oneself with the minutest details of the business...." But this preparation had never been begun. His final decisions were what he came to trust least, and when the hour struck, it all came to pass quite differently, as it were accidentally and unexpectedly.

One trifling circumstance upset his calculations, before he had even left the staircase. When he reached the landlady's kitchen, the door of which was open as usual, he glanced cautiously in to see whether, in Nastasya's absence, the landlady herself was there, or if not, whether the door to her own room was closed, so that she might not peep out when he went in for the axe. But what was his amazement when he suddenly saw that Nastasya was not only at home in the kitchen, but was occupied there, taking linen out of a basket and hanging it on a line. Seeing him, she left off hanging the clothes, turned to him and stared at him all the time he was passing. He turned away his eyes, and walked past as though he noticed nothing. But it was the end of everything; he had not the axe! He was overwhelmed.

"What made me think," he reflected, as he went under the gateway, "what made me think that she would be sure not to be at home at that moment! Why, why, why did I assume this so certainly?"

He was crushed and even humiliated. He could have laughed at himself in his anger.... A dull animal rage boiled within him.

He stood hesitating in the gateway. To go into the street, to go a walk for appearance' sake was revolting; to go back to his room, even more revolting. "And what a chance I have lost for ever!" he muttered, standing aimlessly in the gateway, just opposite the porter's little dark room, which was also open. Suddenly he started. From the porter's room, two paces away from him, something shining under the bench to the right caught his eye.... He looked about him – nobody. He approached the room on tiptoe, went down two steps into it and in a faint voice called the porter. "Yes, not at home! Somewhere near though, in the yard, for the door is wide open." He dashed to the axe (it was an axe) and pulled it out from under the bench, where it lay between two chunks of wood; at once, before going out, he made it fast in the noose, he thrust both hands into his pockets and went out of the room; no one had noticed him! "When reason fails, the devil helps!" he thought with a strange grin. This chance raised his spirits extraordinarily.

He walked along quietly and sedately, without hurry, to avoid awakening suspicion. He scarcely looked at the passers-by, tried to escape looking at their faces at all, and to be as little noticeable as possible. Suddenly he thought of his hat. "Good heavens! I had the money the day before yesterday and did not get a cap to wear instead!" A curse rose from the bottom of his soul.

Glancing out of the corner of his eye into a shop, he saw by a clock on the wall that it was ten minutes past seven. He had to make haste and at the same time to go someway round, so as to approach the house from the other side....

When he had happened to imagine all this beforehand, he had sometimes thought that he would be very much afraid. But he was not very much afraid now, was not afraid at all, indeed. His mind was even occupied by irrelevant matters, but by nothing for long. As he passed the Yusupov garden, he was deeply absorbed in considering the building of great fountains, and of their refreshing effect on the atmosphere in all the squares. By degrees he passed to the conviction that if the summer garden were extended to the field of Mars, and perhaps joined to the garden of the Mihailovsky Palace, it would be a splendid thing and a great benefit to the town. Then he was interested by the question why in all great towns men are not simply driven by necessity, but in some peculiar way inclined to live in those parts of the town where there are no gardens nor fountains; where there is most dirt and smell and all sorts of nastiness. Then his own walks through the Hay Market came back to his mind, and for a moment he waked up to reality. "What nonsense!" he thought, "better think of nothing at all!"

"So probably men led to execution clutch mentally at every object that meets them on the way," flashed through his mind, but simply flashed, like lightning; he made haste to dismiss this thought.... And by now he was near; here was the house, here was the gate. Suddenly a clock somewhere struck once. "What! can it be half-past seven? Impossible, it must be fast!"

Luckily for him, everything went well again at the gates. At that very moment, as though expressly for his benefit, a huge waggon of hay had just driven in at the gate, completely screening him as he passed under the gateway, and the waggon had scarcely had time to drive through into the yard, before he had slipped in a flash to the right. On the other side of the waggon he could hear shouting and quarrelling; but no one noticed him and no one met him. Many windows looking into that huge quadrangular yard were open at that moment, but he did not raise his head – he had not the strength to. The staircase leading to the old woman's room was close by, just on the right of the gateway. He was already on the stairs....

Drawing a breath, pressing his hand against his throbbing heart, and once more feeling for the axe and setting it straight, he began softly and cautiously ascending the stairs, listening every minute. But the stairs, too, were quite deserted; all the doors were shut; he met no one. One flat indeed on the first floor was wide open and painters were at work in it, but they did not glance at him. He stood still, thought a minute and went on. "Of course it would be better if they had not been here, but... it's two storeys above them."

And there was the fourth storey, here was the door, here was the flat opposite, the empty one. The flat underneath the old woman's was apparently empty also; the visiting card nailed on the door had been torn off – they had gone away!... He was out of breath. For one instant the thought floated through his mind "Shall I go back?" But he made no answer and began listening at the old woman's door, a dead silence. Then he listened again on the staircase, listened long and intently... then looked about him for the last time, pulled himself together, drew himself up, and once more tried the axe in the noose. "Am I very pale?" he wondered. "Am I not evidently agitated? She is mistrustful.... Had I better wait a little longer... till my heart leaves off thumping?"

But his heart did not leave off. On the contrary, as though to spite him, it throbbed more and more violently. He could stand it no longer, he slowly put out his hand to the bell and rang. Half a minute later he rang again, more loudly.

No answer. To go on ringing was useless and out of place. The old woman was, of course, at home, but she was suspicious and alone. He had some knowledge of her habits... and once more he put his ear to the door. Either his senses were peculiarly keen (which it is difficult to suppose), or the sound was really very distinct. Anyway, he suddenly heard something like the cautious touch of a hand on the lock and the rustle of a skirt at the very door. Someone was standing stealthily close to the lock and just as he was doing on the outside was secretly listening within, and seemed to have her ear to the door.... He moved a little on purpose and muttered something aloud that he might not have the appearance of hiding, then rang a third time, but quietly, soberly, and without impatience, Recalling it afterwards, that moment stood out in his mind vividly, distinctly, for ever; he could not make out how he had had such cunning, for his mind was as it were clouded at moments and he was almost unconscious of his body.... An instant later he heard the latch unfastened.

Chapter VII

THE DOOR was as before opened a tiny crack, and again two sharp and suspicious eyes stared at him out of the darkness. Then Raskolnikov lost his head and nearly made a great mistake.

Fearing the old woman would be frightened by their being alone, and not hoping that the sight of him would disarm her suspicions, he took hold of the door and drew it towards him to prevent the old woman from attempting to shut it again. Seeing this she did not pull the door back, but she did not let go the handle so that he almost dragged her out with it on to the stairs. Seeing that she was standing in the doorway not allowing him to pass, he advanced straight upon her. She stepped back in alarm, tried to say something, but seemed unable to speak and stared with open eyes at him.

"Good evening, Alyona Ivanovna," he began, trying to speak easily, but his voice would not obey him, it broke and shook. "I have come... I have brought something... but we'd better come in... to the light...."

And leaving her, he passed straight into the room uninvited. The old woman ran after him; her tongue was unloosed.

"Good heavens! What it is? Who is it? What do you want?"

"Why, Alyona Ivanovna, you know me... Raskolnikov... here, I brought you the pledge I promised the other day..." And he held out the pledge.

The old woman glanced for a moment at the pledge, but at once stared in the eyes of her uninvited visitor. She looked intently, maliciously and mistrustfully. A minute passed;

he even fancied something like a sneer in her eyes, as though she had already guessed everything. He felt that he was losing his head, that he was almost frightened, so frightened that if she were to look like that and not say a word for another half minute, he thought he would have run away from her.

"Why do you look at me as though you did not know me?" he said suddenly, also with malice. "Take it if you like, if not I'll go elsewhere, I am in a hurry."

He had not even thought of saying this, but it was suddenly said of itself. The old woman recovered herself, and her visitor's resolute tone evidently restored her confidence.

"But why, my good sir, all of a minute…. What is it?" she asked, looking at the pledge.

"The silver cigarette case; I spoke of it last time, you know."

She held out her hand.

"But how pale you are, to be sure… and your hands are trembling too? Have you been bathing, or what?"

"Fever," he answered abruptly. "You can't help getting pale… if you've nothing to eat," he added, with difficulty articulating the words.

His strength was failing him again. But his answer sounded like the truth; the old woman took the pledge.

"What is it?" she asked once more, scanning Raskolnikov intently, and weighing the pledge in her hand.

"A thing… cigarette case…. Silver…. Look at it."

"It does not seem somehow like silver…. How he has wrapped it up!"

Trying to untie the string and turning to the window, to the light (all her windows were shut, in spite of the stifling heat), she left him altogether for some seconds and stood with her back to him. He unbuttoned his coat and freed the axe from the noose, but did not yet take it out altogether, simply holding it in his right hand under the coat. His hands were fearfully weak, he felt them every moment growing more numb and more wooden. He was afraid he would let the axe slip and fall…. A sudden giddiness came over him.

"But what has he tied it up like this for?" the old woman cried with vexation and moved towards him.

He had not a minute more to lose. He pulled the axe quite out, swung it with both arms, scarcely conscious of himself, and almost without effort, almost mechanically, brought the blunt side down on her head. He seemed not to use his own strength in this. But as soon as he had once brought the axe down, his strength returned to him.

The old woman was as always bareheaded. Her thin, light hair, streaked with grey, thickly smeared with grease, was plaited in a rat's tail and fastened by a broken horn comb which stood out on the nape of her neck. As she was so short, the blow fell on the very top of her skull. She cried out, but very faintly, and suddenly sank all of a heap on the floor, raising her hands to her head. In one hand she still held "the pledge." Then he dealt her another and another blow with the blunt side and on the same spot. The blood gushed as from an overturned glass, the body fell back. He stepped back, let it fall, and at once bent over her face; she was dead. Her eyes seemed to be starting out of their sockets, the brow and the whole face were drawn and contorted convulsively.

He laid the axe on the ground near the dead body and felt at once in her pocket (trying to avoid the streaming body) – the same right-hand pocket from which she had taken the key on his last visit. He was in full possession of his faculties, free from confusion or giddiness, but his hands were still trembling. He remembered afterwards that he had been particularly collected and careful, trying all the time not to get smeared with blood….

He pulled out the keys at once, they were all, as before, in one bunch on a steel ring. He ran at once into the bedroom with them. It was a very small room with a whole shrine of holy images. Against the other wall stood a big bed, very clean and covered with a silk patchwork wadded quilt. Against a third wall was a chest of drawers. Strange to say, so soon as he began to fit the keys into the chest, so soon as he heard their jingling, a convulsive shudder passed over him. He suddenly felt tempted again to give it all up and go away. But that was only for an instant; it was too late to go back. He positively smiled at himself, when suddenly another terrifying idea occurred to his mind. He suddenly fancied that the old woman might be still alive and might recover her senses. Leaving the keys in the chest, he ran back to the body, snatched up the axe and lifted it once more over the old woman, but did not bring it down. There was no doubt that she was dead. Bending down and examining her again more closely, he saw clearly that the skull was broken and even battered in on one side. He was about to feel it with his finger, but drew back his hand and indeed it was evident without that. Meanwhile there was a perfect pool of blood. All at once he noticed a string on her neck; he tugged at it, but the string was strong and did not snap and besides, it was soaked with blood. He tried to pull it out from the front of the dress, but something held it and prevented its coming. In his impatience he raised the axe again to cut the string from above on the body, but did not dare, and with difficulty, smearing his hand and the axe in the blood, after two minutes' hurried effort, he cut the string and took it off without touching the body with the axe; he was not mistaken – it was a purse. On the string were two crosses, one of Cyprus wood and one of copper, and an image in silver filigree, and with them a small greasy chamois leather purse with a steel rim and ring. The purse was stuffed very full; Raskolnikov thrust it in his pocket without looking at it, flung the crosses on the old woman's body and rushed back into the bedroom, this time taking the axe with him.

He was in terrible haste, he snatched the keys, and began trying them again. But he was unsuccessful. They would not fit in the locks. It was not so much that his hands were shaking, but that he kept making mistakes; though he saw for instance that a key was not the right one and would not fit, still he tried to put it in. Suddenly he remembered and realised that the big key with the deep notches, which was hanging there with the small keys could not possibly belong to the chest of drawers (on his last visit this had struck him), but to some strong box, and that everything perhaps was hidden in that box. He left the chest of drawers, and at once felt under the bedstead, knowing that old women usually keep boxes under their beds. And so it was; there was a good-sized box under the bed, at least a yard in length, with an arched lid covered with red leather and studded with steel nails. The notched key fitted at once and unlocked it. At the top, under a white sheet, was a coat of red brocade lined with hareskin; under it was a silk dress, then a shawl and it seemed as though there was nothing below but clothes. The first thing he did was to wipe his blood-stained hands on the red brocade. "It's red, and on red blood will be less noticeable," the thought passed through his mind; then he suddenly came to himself. "Good God, am I going out of my senses?" he thought with terror.

But no sooner did he touch the clothes than a gold watch slipped from under the fur coat. He made haste to turn them all over. There turned out to be various articles made of gold among the clothes – probably all pledges, unredeemed or waiting to be redeemed – bracelets, chains, ear-rings, pins and such things. Some were in cases, others simply wrapped in newspaper, carefully and exactly folded, and tied round with tape. Without any delay, he began filling up the pockets of his trousers and overcoat without examining or undoing the parcels and cases; but he had not time to take many....

He suddenly heard steps in the room where the old woman lay. He stopped short and was still as death. But all was quiet, so it must have been his fancy. All at once he heard distinctly a faint cry, as though someone had uttered a low broken moan. Then again dead silence for a minute or two. He sat squatting on his heels by the box and waited holding his breath. Suddenly he jumped up, seized the axe and ran out of the bedroom.

In the middle of the room stood Lizaveta with a big bundle in her arms. She was gazing in stupefaction at her murdered sister, white as a sheet and seeming not to have the strength to cry out. Seeing him run out of the bedroom, she began faintly quivering all over, like a leaf, a shudder ran down her face; she lifted her hand, opened her mouth, but still did not scream. She began slowly backing away from him into the corner, staring intently, persistently at him, but still uttered no sound, as though she could not get breath to scream. He rushed at her with the axe; her mouth twitched piteously, as one sees babies' mouths, when they begin to be frightened, stare intently at what frightens them and are on the point of screaming. And this hapless Lizaveta was so simple and had been so thoroughly crushed and scared that she did not even raise a hand to guard her face, though that was the most necessary and natural action at the moment, for the axe was raised over her face. She only put up her empty left hand, but not to her face, slowly holding it out before her as though motioning him away. The axe fell with the sharp edge just on the skull and split at one blow all the top of the head. She fell heavily at once. Raskolnikov completely lost his head, snatching up her bundle, dropped it again and ran into the entry.

Fear gained more and more mastery over him, especially after this second, quite unexpected murder. He longed to run away from the place as fast as possible. And if at that moment he had been capable of seeing and reasoning more correctly, if he had been able to realise all the difficulties of his position, the hopelessness, the hideousness and the absurdity of it, if he could have understood how many obstacles and, perhaps, crimes he had still to overcome or to commit, to get out of that place and to make his way home, it is very possible that he would have flung up everything, and would have gone to give himself up, and not from fear, but from simple horror and loathing of what he had done. The feeling of loathing especially surged up within him and grew stronger every minute. He would not now have gone to the box or even into the room for anything in the world.

But a sort of blankness, even dreaminess, had begun by degrees to take possession of him; at moments he forgot himself, or rather, forgot what was of importance, and caught at trifles. Glancing, however, into the kitchen and seeing a bucket half full of water on a bench, he bethought him of washing his hands and the axe. His hands were sticky with blood. He dropped the axe with the blade in the water, snatched a piece of soap that lay in a broken saucer on the window, and began washing his hands in the bucket. When they were clean, he took out the axe, washed the blade and spent a long time, about three minutes, washing the wood where there were spots of blood rubbing them with soap. Then he wiped it all with some linen that was hanging to dry on a line in the kitchen and then he was a long while attentively examining the axe at the window. There was no trace left on it, only the wood was still damp. He carefully hung the axe in the noose under his coat. Then as far as was possible, in the dim light in the kitchen, he looked over his overcoat, his trousers and his boots. At the first glance there seemed to be nothing but stains on the boots. He wetted the rag and rubbed the boots. But he knew he was not looking thoroughly, that there might be something quite noticeable that he was overlooking. He stood in the middle of the room, lost in thought. Dark agonising ideas rose in his mind – the idea that he was mad and that at that moment he was incapable of reasoning, of protecting himself, that he ought perhaps to be doing something utterly different from what he was now doing. "Good God!" he muttered "I must fly, fly," and he rushed into the entry. But here a shock of terror awaited him such as he had never known before.

He stood and gazed and could not believe his eyes: the door, the outer door from the stairs, at which he had not long before waited and rung, was standing unfastened and at least six inches open. No lock, no bolt, all the time, all that time! The old woman had not shut it after him perhaps as a precaution. But, good God! Why, he had seen Lizaveta afterwards! And how could he, how could he have failed to reflect that she must have come in somehow! She could not have come through the wall!

He dashed to the door and fastened the latch.

"But no, the wrong thing again! I must get away, get away...."

He unfastened the latch, opened the door and began listening on the staircase.

He listened a long time. Somewhere far away, it might be in the gateway, two voices were loudly and shrilly shouting, quarrelling and scolding. "What are they about?" He waited patiently. At last all was still, as though suddenly cut off; they had separated. He was meaning to go out, but suddenly, on the floor below, a door was noisily opened and someone began going downstairs humming a tune. "How is it they all make such a noise?" flashed through his mind. Once more he closed the door and waited. At last all was still, not a soul stirring. He was just taking a step towards the stairs when he heard fresh footsteps.

The steps sounded very far off, at the very bottom of the stairs, but he remembered quite clearly and distinctly that from the first sound he began for some reason to suspect that this was someone coming *there*, to the fourth floor, to the old woman. Why? Were the sounds somehow peculiar, significant? The steps were heavy, even and unhurried. Now *he* had passed the first floor, now he was mounting higher, it was growing more and more distinct! He could hear his heavy breathing. And now the third storey had been reached. Coming here! And it seemed to him all at once that he was turned to stone, that it was like a dream in which one is being pursued, nearly caught and will be killed, and is rooted to the spot and cannot even move one's arms.

At last when the unknown was mounting to the fourth floor, he suddenly started, and succeeded in slipping neatly and quickly back into the flat and closing the door behind him. Then he took the hook and softly, noiselessly, fixed it in the catch. Instinct helped him. When he had done this, he crouched holding his breath, by the door. The unknown visitor was by now also at the door. They were now standing opposite one another, as he had just before been standing with the old woman, when the door divided them and he was listening.

The visitor panted several times. "He must be a big, fat man," thought Raskolnikov, squeezing the axe in his hand. It seemed like a dream indeed. The visitor took hold of the bell and rang it loudly.

As soon as the tin bell tinkled, Raskolnikov seemed to be aware of something moving in the room. For some seconds he listened quite seriously. The unknown rang again, waited and suddenly tugged violently and impatiently at the handle of the door. Raskolnikov gazed in horror at the hook shaking in its fastening, and in blank terror expected every minute that the fastening would be pulled out. It certainly did seem possible, so violently was he shaking it. He was tempted to hold the fastening, but *he* might be aware of it. A giddiness came over him again. "I shall fall down!" flashed through his mind, but the unknown began to speak and he recovered himself at once.

"What's up? Are they asleep or murdered? D-damn them!" he bawled in a thick voice, "Hey, Alyona Ivanovna, old witch! Lizaveta Ivanovna, hey, my beauty! open the door! Oh, damn them! Are they asleep or what?"

And again, enraged, he tugged with all his might a dozen times at the bell. He must certainly be a man of authority and an intimate acquaintance.

At this moment light hurried steps were heard not far off, on the stairs. Someone else was approaching. Raskolnikov had not heard them at first.

"You don't say there's no one at home," the new-comer cried in a cheerful, ringing voice, addressing the first visitor, who still went on pulling the bell. "Good evening, Koch."

"From his voice he must be quite young," thought Raskolnikov.

"Who the devil can tell? I've almost broken the lock," answered Koch. "But how do you come to know me?"

"Why! The day before yesterday I beat you three times running at billiards at Gambrinus'."

"Oh!"

"So they are not at home? That's queer. It's awfully stupid though. Where could the old woman have gone? I've come on business."

"Yes; and I have business with her, too."

"Well, what can we do? Go back, I suppose, Aie – aie! And I was hoping to get some money!" cried the young man.

"We must give it up, of course, but what did she fix this time for? The old witch fixed the time for me to come herself. It's out of my way. And where the devil she can have got to, I can't make out. She sits here from year's end to year's end, the old hag; her legs are bad and yet here all of a sudden she is out for a walk!"

"Hadn't we better ask the porter?"

"What?"

"Where she's gone and when she'll be back."

"Hm…. Damn it all!… We might ask…. But you know she never does go anywhere."

And he once more tugged at the door-handle.

"Damn it all. There's nothing to be done, we must go!"

"Stay!" cried the young man suddenly. "Do you see how the door shakes if you pull it?"

"Well?"

"That shows it's not locked, but fastened with the hook! Do you hear how the hook clanks?"

"Well?"

"Why, don't you see? That proves that one of them is at home. If they were all out, they would have locked the door from the outside with the key and not with the hook from inside. There, do you hear how the hook is clanking? To fasten the hook on the inside they must be at home, don't you see. So there they are sitting inside and don't open the door!"

"Well! And so they must be!" cried Koch, astonished. "What are they about in there?" And he began furiously shaking the door.

"Stay!" cried the young man again. "Don't pull at it! There must be something wrong…. Here, you've been ringing and pulling at the door and still they don't open! So either they've both fainted or…"

"What?"

"I tell you what. Let's go fetch the porter, let him wake them up."

"All right."

Both were going down.

"Stay. You stop here while I run down for the porter."

"What for?"

"Well, you'd better."

"All right."

"I'm studying the law you see! It's evident, e-vi-dent there's something wrong here!" the young man cried hotly, and he ran downstairs.

Koch remained. Once more he softly touched the bell which gave one tinkle, then gently, as though reflecting and looking about him, began touching the door-handle pulling it and letting it go to make sure once more that it was only fastened by the hook. Then puffing and panting he bent down and began looking at the keyhole: but the key was in the lock on the inside and so nothing could be seen.

Raskolnikov stood keeping tight hold of the axe. He was in a sort of delirium. He was even making ready to fight when they should come in. While they were knocking and talking together, the idea several times occurred to him to end it all at once and shout to them through the door. Now and then he was tempted to swear at them, to jeer at them, while they could not open the door! "Only make haste!" was the thought that flashed through his mind.

"But what the devil is he about?..." Time was passing, one minute, and another – no one came. Koch began to be restless.

"What the devil?" he cried suddenly and in impatience deserting his sentry duty, he, too, went down, hurrying and thumping with his heavy boots on the stairs. The steps died away.

"Good heavens! What am I to do?"

Raskolnikov unfastened the hook, opened the door – there was no sound. Abruptly, without any thought at all, he went out, closing the door as thoroughly as he could, and went downstairs.

He had gone down three flights when he suddenly heard a loud voice below – where could he go! There was nowhere to hide. He was just going back to the flat.

"Hey there! Catch the brute!"

Somebody dashed out of a flat below, shouting, and rather fell than ran down the stairs, bawling at the top of his voice.

"Mitka! Mitka! Mitka! Mitka! Mitka! Blast him!"

The shout ended in a shriek; the last sounds came from the yard; all was still. But at the same instant several men talking loud and fast began noisily mounting the stairs. There were three or four of them. He distinguished the ringing voice of the young man. "Hey!"

Filled with despair he went straight to meet them, feeling "come what must!" If they stopped him – all was lost; if they let him pass – all was lost too; they would remember him. They were approaching; they were only a flight from him – and suddenly deliverance! A few steps from him on the right, there was an empty flat with the door wide open, the flat on the second floor where the painters had been at work, and which, as though for his benefit, they had just left. It was they, no doubt, who had just run down, shouting. The floor had only just been painted, in the middle of the room stood a pail and a broken pot with paint and brushes. In one instant he had whisked in at the open door and hidden behind the wall and only in the nick of time; they had already reached the landing. Then they turned and went on up to the fourth floor, talking loudly. He waited, went out on tiptoe and ran down the stairs.

No one was on the stairs, nor in the gateway. He passed quickly through the gateway and turned to the left in the street.

He knew, he knew perfectly well that at that moment they were at the flat, that they were greatly astonished at finding it unlocked, as the door had just been fastened, that by now they were looking at the bodies, that before another minute had passed they would guess and completely realise that the murderer had just been there, and had succeeded in hiding somewhere, slipping by them and escaping. They would guess most likely that he had been in the empty flat, while they were going upstairs. And meanwhile he dared not quicken his pace much, though the next turning was still nearly a hundred yards away. "Should he slip through some gateway and wait somewhere in an unknown street? No, hopeless! Should he fling away the axe? Should he take a cab? Hopeless, hopeless!"

At last he reached the turning. He turned down it more dead than alive. Here he was half way to safety, and he understood it; it was less risky because there was a great crowd of people, and he was lost in it like a grain of sand. But all he had suffered had so weakened him that he could scarcely move. Perspiration ran down him in drops, his neck was all wet. "My word, he has been going it!" someone shouted at him when he came out on the canal bank.

He was only dimly conscious of himself now, and the farther he went the worse it was. He remembered however, that on coming out on to the canal bank, he was alarmed at finding few people there and so being more conspicuous, and he had thought of turning back. Though he was almost falling from fatigue, he went a long way round so as to get home from quite a different direction.

He was not fully conscious when he passed through the gateway of his house! He was already on the staircase before he recollected the axe. And yet he had a very grave problem before him, to put it back and to escape observation as far as possible in doing so. He was of course incapable of reflecting that it might perhaps be far better not to restore the axe at all, but to drop it later on in somebody's yard. But it all happened fortunately, the door of the porter's room was closed but not locked, so that it seemed most likely that the porter was at home. But he had so completely lost all power of reflection that he walked straight to the door and opened it. If the porter had asked him, "What do you want?" he would perhaps have simply handed him the axe. But again the porter was not at home, and he succeeded in putting the axe back under the bench, and even covering it with the chunk of wood as before. He met no one, not a soul, afterwards on the way to his room; the landlady's door was shut. When he was in his room, he flung himself on the sofa just as he was – he did not sleep, but sank into blank forgetfulness. If anyone had come into his room then, he would have jumped up at once and screamed. Scraps and shreds of thoughts were simply swarming in his brain, but he could not catch at one, he could not rest on one, in spite of all his efforts.... ·

The Adventure of Abbey Grange

Arthur Conan Doyle

IT WAS ON a bitterly cold and frosty morning, towards the end of the winter of '97, that I was awakened by a tugging at my shoulder. It was Holmes. The candle in his hand shone upon his eager, stooping face, and told me at a glance that something was amiss.

"Come, Watson, come!" he cried. "The game is afoot. Not a word! Into your clothes and come!"

Ten minutes later we were both in a cab, and rattling through the silent streets on our way to Charing Cross Station. The first faint winter's dawn was beginning to appear, and we could dimly see the occasional figure of an early workman as he passed us, blurred and indistinct in the opalescent London reek. Holmes nestled in silence into his heavy coat, and I was glad to do the same, for the air was most bitter, and neither of us had broken our fast.

It was not until we had consumed some hot tea at the station and taken our places in the Kentish train that we were sufficiently thawed, he to speak and I to listen. Holmes drew a note from his pocket, and read aloud:

> *Abbey Grange, Marsham, Kent, 3:30 a.m.*
> *MY DEAR MR. HOLMES:*
> *I should be very glad of your immediate assistance in what promises to be a most remarkable case. It is something quite in your line. Except for releasing the lady I will see that everything is kept exactly as I have found it, but I beg you not to lose an instant, as it is difficult to leave Sir Eustace there. Yours faithfully,*
> *STANLEY HOPKINS.*

"Hopkins has called me in seven times, and on each occasion his summons has been entirely justified," said Holmes. "I fancy that every one of his cases has found its way into your collection, and I must admit, Watson, that you have some power of selection, which atones for much which I deplore in your narratives. Your fatal habit of looking at everything from the point of view of a story instead of as a scientific exercise has ruined what might have been an instructive and even classical series of demonstrations. You slur over work of the utmost finesse and delicacy, in order to dwell upon sensational details which may excite, but cannot possibly instruct, the reader."

"Why do you not write them yourself?" I said, with some bitterness.

"I will, my dear Watson, I will. At present I am, as you know, fairly busy, but I propose to devote my declining years to the composition of a textbook, which shall focus the whole art of detection into one volume. Our present research appears to be a case of murder."

"You think this Sir Eustace is dead, then?"

"I should say so. Hopkins's writing shows considerable agitation, and he is not an emotional man. Yes, I gather there has been violence, and that the body is left for our inspection. A mere suicide would not have caused him to send for me. As to the release of the lady, it would appear that she has been locked in her room during the tragedy. We are moving in high life, Watson, crackling paper, 'E.B.' monogram, coat-of-arms, picturesque address. I think that friend Hopkins will live up to his reputation, and that we shall have an interesting morning. The crime was committed before twelve last night."

"How can you possibly tell?"

"By an inspection of the trains, and by reckoning the time. The local police had to be called in, they had to communicate with Scotland Yard, Hopkins had to go out, and he in turn had to send for me. All that makes a fair night's work. Well, here we are at Chiselhurst Station, and we shall soon set our doubts at rest."

A drive of a couple of miles through narrow country lanes brought us to a park gate, which was opened for us by an old lodge-keeper, whose haggard face bore the reflection of some great disaster. The avenue ran through a noble park, between lines of ancient elms, and ended in a low, widespread house, pillared in front after the fashion of Palladio. The central part was evidently of a great age and shrouded in ivy, but the large windows showed that modern changes had been carried out, and one wing of the house appeared to be entirely new. The youthful figure and alert, eager face of Inspector Stanley Hopkins confronted us in the open doorway.

"I'm very glad you have come, Mr. Holmes. And you, too, Dr. Watson. But, indeed, if I had my time over again, I should not have troubled you, for since the lady has come to herself, she has given so clear an account of the affair that there is not much left for us to do. You remember that Lewisham gang of burglars?"

"What, the three Randalls?"

"Exactly; the father and two sons. It's their work. I have not a doubt of it. They did a job at Sydenham a fortnight ago and were seen and described. Rather cool to do another so soon and so near, but it is they, beyond all doubt. It's a hanging matter this time."

"Sir Eustace is dead, then?"

"Yes, his head was knocked in with his own poker."

"Sir Eustace Brackenstall, the driver tells me."

"Exactly – one of the richest men in Kent – Lady Brackenstall is in the morning-room. Poor lady, she has had a most dreadful experience. She seemed half dead when I saw her first. I think you had best see her and hear her account of the facts. Then we will examine the dining-room together."

Lady Brackenstall was no ordinary person. Seldom have I seen so graceful a figure, so womanly a presence, and so beautiful a face. She was a blonde, golden-haired, blue-eyed, and would no doubt have had the perfect complexion which goes with such colouring, had not her recent experience left her drawn and haggard. Her sufferings were physical as well as mental, for over one eye rose a hideous, plum-coloured swelling, which her maid, a tall, austere woman, was bathing assiduously with vinegar and water. The lady lay back exhausted upon a couch, but her quick, observant gaze, as we entered the room, and the alert expression of her beautiful features, showed that neither her wits nor her courage had been shaken by her terrible experience. She was enveloped in a loose dressing-gown of blue and silver, but a black sequin-covered dinner-dress lay upon the couch beside her.

"I have told you all that happened, Mr. Hopkins," she said, wearily. "Could you not repeat it for me? Well, if you think it necessary, I will tell these gentlemen what occurred. Have they been in the dining-room yet?"

"I thought they had better hear your ladyship's story first."

"I shall be glad when you can arrange matters. It is horrible to me to think of him still lying there." She shuddered and buried her face in her hands. As she did so, the loose gown fell back from her forearms. Holmes uttered an exclamation.

"You have other injuries, madam! What is this?" Two vivid red spots stood out on one of the white, round limbs. She hastily covered it.

"It is nothing. It has no connection with this hideous business tonight. If you and your friend will sit down, I will tell you all I can.

"I am the wife of Sir Eustace Brackenstall. I have been married about a year. I suppose that it is no use my attempting to conceal that our marriage has not been a happy one. I fear that all our neighbours would tell you that, even if I were to attempt to deny it. Perhaps the fault may be partly mine. I was brought up in the freer, less conventional atmosphere of South Australia, and this English life, with its proprieties and its primness, is not congenial to me. But the main reason lies in the one fact, which is notorious to everyone, and that is that Sir Eustace was a confirmed drunkard. To be with such a man for an hour is unpleasant. Can you imagine what it means for a sensitive and high-spirited woman to be tied to him for day and night? It is a sacrilege, a crime, a villainy to hold that such a marriage is binding. I say that these monstrous laws of yours will bring a curse upon the land – God will not let such wickedness endure." For an instant she sat up, her cheeks flushed, and her eyes blazing from under the terrible mark upon her brow. Then the strong, soothing hand of the austere maid drew her head down on to the cushion, and the wild anger died away into passionate sobbing. At last she continued:

"I will tell you about last night. You are aware, perhaps, that in this house all the servants sleep in the modern wing. This central block is made up of the dwelling-rooms, with the kitchen behind and our bedroom above. My maid, Theresa, sleeps above my room. There is no one else, and no sound could alarm those who are in the farther wing. This must have been well known to the robbers, or they would not have acted as they did.

"Sir Eustace retired about half-past ten. The servants had already gone to their quarters. Only my maid was up, and she had remained in her room at the top of the house until I needed her services. I sat until after eleven in this room, absorbed in a book. Then I walked round to see that all was right before I went upstairs. It was my custom to do this myself, for, as I have explained, Sir Eustace was not always to be trusted. I went into the kitchen, the butler's pantry, the gun-room, the billiard-room, the drawing-room, and finally the dining-room. As I approached the window, which is covered with thick curtains, I suddenly felt the wind blow upon my face and realized that it was open. I flung the curtain aside and found myself face to face with a broad-shouldered elderly man, who had just stepped into the room. The window is a long French one, which really forms a door leading to the lawn. I held my bedroom candle lit in my hand, and, by its light, behind the first man I saw two others, who were in the act of entering. I stepped back, but the fellow was on me in an instant. He caught me first by the wrist and then by the throat. I opened my mouth to scream, but he struck me a savage blow with his fist over the eye, and felled me to the ground. I must have been unconscious for a few minutes, for when I came to myself, I found that they had torn down the bell-rope, and had secured me tightly to the oaken chair which stands at the head of the dining-table. I was so firmly bound that I could not move, and a handkerchief round my mouth prevented me from uttering a sound. It was at this instant that my unfortunate husband entered the room. He had evidently heard some suspicious sounds, and he came prepared for such a scene as he found. He was dressed in nightshirt and trousers, with his favourite blackthorn cudgel in his hand. He rushed at the burglars, but another – it was an elderly man – stooped, picked the poker out of the grate and struck him a horrible blow as he passed. He fell with a groan and never moved again. I fainted once more, but again it could only have been for a very few minutes during which I was insensible. When I opened my eyes I found that they had collected the silver from the sideboard, and they had drawn a bottle of wine which stood there. Each of them had a glass in his hand. I have already told you, have I not, that one was elderly, with a beard, and the others young, hairless lads. They might have been a father with his two sons. They talked together in whispers. Then they came over and made sure that I was securely bound. Finally they withdrew, closing the window after them. It was quite a quarter of an hour before I got my mouth free. When I did so, my screams brought the maid to my assistance. The other servants were soon alarmed, and we sent for the local police, who instantly communicated with London. That is really all that I can tell you, gentlemen, and I trust that it will not be necessary for me to go over so painful a story again."

"Any questions, Mr. Holmes?" asked Hopkins.

"I will not impose any further tax upon Lady Brackenstall's patience and time," said Holmes. "Before I go into the dining-room, I should like to hear your experience." He looked at the maid.

"I saw the men before ever they came into the house," said she. "As I sat by my bedroom window I saw three men in the moonlight down by the lodge gate yonder, but I thought nothing of it at the time. It was more than an hour after that I heard my mistress scream, and down I ran, to find her, poor lamb, just as she says, and him on the floor, with his blood and brains over the room. It was enough to drive a woman out of her wits, tied there, and her very dress spotted with him, but she never wanted courage, did Miss Mary Fraser of Adelaide and Lady Brackenstall of Abbey Grange hasn't learned new ways. You've questioned her long enough, you gentlemen, and now she is coming to her own room, just with her old Theresa, to get the rest that she badly needs."

With a motherly tenderness the gaunt woman put her arm round her mistress and led her from the room.

"She has been with her all her life," said Hopkins. "Nursed her as a baby, and came with her to England when they first left Australia, eighteen months ago. Theresa Wright is her name, and the kind of maid you don't pick up nowadays. This way, Mr. Holmes, if you please!"

The keen interest had passed out of Holmes's expressive face, and I knew that with the mystery all the charm of the case had departed. There still remained an arrest to be effected, but what were these commonplace rogues that he should soil his hands with them? An abstruse and learned specialist who finds that he has been called in for a case of measles would experience something of the annoyance which I read in my friend's eyes. Yet the scene in the dining-room of the Abbey Grange was sufficiently strange to arrest his attention and to recall his waning interest.

It was a very large and high chamber, with carved oak ceiling, oaken panelling, and a fine array of deer's heads and ancient weapons around the walls. At the further end from the door was the high French window of which we had heard. Three smaller windows on the right-hand side filled the apartment with cold winter sunshine. On the left was a large, deep fireplace, with a massive, overhanging oak mantelpiece. Beside the fireplace was a heavy oaken chair with arms and cross-bars at the bottom. In and out through the open woodwork was woven a crimson cord, which was secured at each side to the crosspiece below. In releasing the lady, the cord had been slipped off her, but the knots with which it had been secured still remained. These details only struck our attention afterwards, for our thoughts were entirely absorbed by the terrible object which lay upon the tigerskin hearthrug in front of the fire.

It was the body of a tall, well-made man, about forty years of age. He lay upon his back, his face upturned, with his white teeth grinning through his short, black beard. His two clenched hands were raised above his head, and a heavy, blackthorn stick lay across them. His dark, handsome, aquiline features were convulsed into a spasm of vindictive hatred, which had set his dead face in a terribly fiendish expression. He had evidently been in his bed when the alarm had broken out, for he wore a foppish, embroidered nightshirt, and his bare feet projected from his trousers. His head was horribly injured, and the whole room bore witness to the savage ferocity of the blow which had struck him down. Beside him lay the heavy poker, bent into a curve by the concussion. Holmes examined both it and the indescribable wreck which it had wrought.

"He must be a powerful man, this elder Randall," he remarked.

"Yes," said Hopkins. "I have some record of the fellow, and he is a rough customer."

"You should have no difficulty in getting him."

"Not the slightest. We have been on the look-out for him, and there was some idea that he had got away to America. Now that we know that the gang are here, I don't see how they can escape. We have the news at every seaport already, and a reward will be offered before evening. What beats me is how they could have done so mad a thing, knowing that the lady could describe them and that we could not fail to recognize the description."

"Exactly. One would have expected that they would silence Lady Brackenstall as well."

"They may not have realized," I suggested, "that she had recovered from her faint."

"That is likely enough. If she seemed to be senseless, they would not take her life. What about this poor fellow, Hopkins? I seem to have heard some queer stories about him."

"He was a good-hearted man when he was sober, but a perfect fiend when he was drunk, or rather when he was half drunk, for he seldom really went the whole way. The devil seemed to be in him at such times, and he was capable of anything. From what I hear, in spite of all his wealth and his title, he very nearly came our way once or twice. There was a scandal about his drenching a dog with petroleum and setting it on fire – her ladyship's dog, to make the matter worse – and that was only hushed up with difficulty. Then he threw a decanter at that maid, Theresa Wright – there was trouble about that. On the whole, and between ourselves, it will be a brighter house without him. What are you looking at now?"

Holmes was down on his knees, examining with great attention the knots upon the red cord with which the lady had been secured. Then he carefully scrutinized the broken and frayed end where it had snapped off when the burglar had dragged it down.

"When this was pulled down, the bell in the kitchen must have rung loudly," he remarked.

"No one could hear it. The kitchen stands right at the back of the house."

"How did the burglar know no one would hear it? How dared he pull at a bell-rope in that reckless fashion?"

"Exactly, Mr. Holmes, exactly. You put the very question which I have asked myself again and again. There can be no doubt that this fellow must have known the house and its habits. He must have perfectly understood that the servants would all be in bed at that comparatively early hour, and that no one could possibly hear a bell ring in the kitchen. Therefore, he must have been in close league with one of the servants. Surely that is evident. But there are eight servants, and all of good character."

"Other things being equal," said Holmes, "one would suspect the one at whose head the master threw a decanter. And yet that would involve treachery towards the mistress to whom this woman seems devoted. Well, well, the point is a minor one, and when you have Randall you will probably find no difficulty in securing his accomplice. The lady's story certainly seems to be corroborated, if it needed corroboration, by every detail which we see before us." He walked to the French window and threw it open. "There are no signs here, but the ground is iron hard, and one would not expect them. I see that these candles in the mantelpiece have been lighted."

"Yes, it was by their light and that of the lady's bedroom candle, that the burglars saw their way about."

"And what did they take?"

"Well, they did not take much – only half a dozen articles of plate off the sideboard. Lady Brackenstall thinks that they were themselves so disturbed by the death of Sir Eustace that they did not ransack the house, as they would otherwise have done."

"No doubt that is true, and yet they drank some wine, I understand."

"To steady their nerves."

"Exactly. These three glasses upon the sideboard have been untouched, I suppose?"

"Yes, and the bottle stands as they left it."

"Let us look at it. Halloa, halloa! What is this?"

The three glasses were grouped together, all of them tinged with wine, and one of them containing some dregs of beeswing. The bottle stood near them, two-thirds full, and beside it lay a long, deeply stained cork. Its appearance and the dust upon the bottle showed that it was no common vintage which the murderers had enjoyed.

A change had come over Holmes's manner. He had lost his listless expression, and again I saw an alert light of interest in his keen, deep-set eyes. He raised the cork and examined it minutely.

"How did they draw it?" he asked.

Hopkins pointed to a half-opened drawer. In it lay some table linen and a large corkscrew.

"Did Lady Brackenstall say that screw was used?"

"No, you remember that she was senseless at the moment when the bottle was opened."

"Quite so. As a matter of fact, that screw was *not* used. This bottle was opened by a pocket screw, probably contained in a knife, and not more than an inch and a half long. If you will examine the top of the cork, you will observe that the screw was driven in three times before the cork was extracted. It has never been transfixed. This long screw would have transfixed it and drawn it up with a single pull. When you catch this fellow, you will find that he has one of these multiplex knives in his possession."

"Excellent!" said Hopkins.

"But these glasses do puzzle me, I confess. Lady Brackenstall actually *saw* the three men drinking, did she not?"

"Yes; she was clear about that."

"Then there is an end of it. What more is to be said? And yet, you must admit, that the three glasses are very remarkable, Hopkins. What? You see nothing remarkable? Well, well, let it pass. Perhaps, when a man has special knowledge and special powers like my own, it rather encourages him to seek a complex explanation when a simpler one is at hand. Of course, it must be a mere chance about the glasses. Well, good-morning, Hopkins. I don't see that I can be of any use to you, and you appear to have your case very clear. You will let me know when Randall is arrested, and any further developments which may occur. I trust that I shall soon have to congratulate you upon a successful conclusion. Come, Watson, I fancy that we may employ ourselves more profitably at home."

During our return journey, I could see by Holmes's face that he was much puzzled by something which he had observed. Every now and then, by an effort, he would throw off the impression, and talk as if the matter were clear, but then his doubts would settle down upon him again, and his knitted brows and abstracted eyes would show that his thoughts had gone back once more to the great dining-room of the Abbey Grange, in which this midnight tragedy had been enacted. At last, by a sudden impulse, just as our train was crawling out of a suburban station, he sprang on to the platform and pulled me out after him.

"Excuse me, my dear fellow," said he, as we watched the rear carriages of our train disappearing round a curve, "I am sorry to make you the victim of what may seem a mere whim, but on my life, Watson, I simply *can't* leave that case in this condition. Every instinct that I possess cries out against it. It's wrong – it's all wrong – I'll swear that it's wrong. And yet the lady's story was complete, the maid's corroboration was sufficient, the detail was fairly exact. What have I to put up against that? Three wine-glasses, that is all. But if I had not taken things for granted, if I had examined everything with the care which I should have shown had we approached the case *de novo* and had no cut-and-dried story to warp my mind, should I not then have found something more definite to go upon? Of course I should. Sit down on this bench, Watson, until a train for Chiselhurst arrives, and allow me to lay the evidence before you, imploring you in the first instance to dismiss from your mind the idea that anything which the maid or her mistress may have said must necessarily be true. The lady's charming personality must not be permitted to warp our judgment.

"Surely there are details in her story which, if we looked at in cold blood, would excite our suspicion. These burglars made a considerable haul at Sydenham a fortnight ago. Some account of them and of their appearance was in the papers, and would naturally occur to anyone who wished to invent a story in which imaginary robbers should play a part. As a matter of fact, burglars who have done a good stroke of business are, as a rule, only too glad to enjoy the proceeds in peace and quiet without embarking on another perilous undertaking. Again, it is unusual for burglars to operate at so early an hour, it is unusual for burglars to strike a lady to prevent her screaming, since one would imagine that was the sure way to make her scream, it is unusual for them to commit murder when their numbers are sufficient to overpower one man, it is unusual for them to be content with a limited plunder when there was much more within their reach, and finally, I should say, that it was very unusual for such men to leave a bottle half empty. How do all these unusuals strike you, Watson?"

"Their cumulative effect is certainly considerable, and yet each of them is quite possible in itself. The most unusual thing of all, as it seems to me, is that the lady should be tied to the chair."

"Well, I am not so clear about that, Watson, for it is evident that they must either kill her or else secure her in such a way that she could not give immediate notice of their escape. But at any rate I have shown, have I not, that there is a certain element of improbability about the lady's story? And now, on the top of this, comes the incident of the wineglasses."

"What about the wineglasses?"

"Can you see them in your mind's eye?"

"I see them clearly."

"We are told that three men drank from them. Does that strike you as likely?"

"Why not? There was wine in each glass."

"Exactly, but there was beeswing only in one glass. You must have noticed that fact. What does that suggest to your mind?"

"The last glass filled would be most likely to contain beeswing."

"Not at all. The bottle was full of it, and it is inconceivable that the first two glasses were clear and the third heavily charged with it. There are two possible explanations, and only two. One is that after the second glass was filled the bottle was violently agitated, and so the third glass received the beeswing. That does not appear probable. No, no, I am sure that I am right."

"What, then, do you suppose?"

"That only two glasses were used, and that the dregs of both were poured into a third glass, so as to give the false impression that three people had been here. In that way all the beeswing would be in the last glass, would it not? Yes, I am convinced that this is so. But if I have hit upon the true explanation of this one small phenomenon, then in an instant the case rises from the commonplace to the exceedingly remarkable, for it can only mean that Lady Brackenstall and her maid have deliberately lied to us, that not one word of their story is to be believed, that they have some very strong reason for covering the real criminal, and that we must construct our case for ourselves without any help from them. That is the mission which now lies before us, and here, Watson, is the Sydenham train."

The household at the Abbey Grange were much surprised at our return, but Sherlock Holmes, finding that Stanley Hopkins had gone off to report to headquarters, took possession of the dining-room, locked the door upon the inside, and devoted himself for two hours to one of those minute and laborious investigations which form the solid basis on which his brilliant edifices of deduction were reared. Seated in a corner like an interested student who observes the demonstration of his professor, I followed every step of that remarkable research. The window, the curtains, the carpet, the chair, the rope – each in turn was minutely examined and duly pondered. The body of the unfortunate baronet had been removed, and all else remained as we had seen it in the morning. Finally, to my astonishment, Holmes climbed up on to the massive mantelpiece. Far above his head hung the few inches of red cord which were still attached to the wire. For a long time he gazed upward at it, and then in an attempt to get nearer to it he rested his knee upon a wooden bracket on the wall. This brought his hand within a few inches of the broken end of the rope, but it was not this so much as the bracket itself which seemed to engage his attention. Finally, he sprang down with an ejaculation of satisfaction.

"It's all right, Watson," said he. "We have got our case – one of the most remarkable in our collection. But, dear me, how slow-witted I have been, and how nearly I have committed the blunder of my lifetime! Now, I think that, with a few missing links, my chain is almost complete."

"You have got your men?"

"Man, Watson, man. Only one, but a very formidable person. Strong as a lion – witness the blow that bent that poker! Six foot three in height, active as a squirrel, dexterous with his fingers, finally, remarkably quick-witted, for this whole ingenious story is of his concoction. Yes, Watson, we have come upon the handiwork of a very remarkable individual. And yet, in that bell-rope, he has given us a clue which should not have left us a doubt."

"Where was the clue?"

"Well, if you were to pull down a bell-rope, Watson, where would you expect it to break? Surely at the spot where it is attached to the wire. Why should it break three inches from the top, as this one has done?"

"Because it is frayed there?"

"Exactly. This end, which we can examine, is frayed. He was cunning enough to do that with his knife. But the other end is not frayed. You could not observe that from here, but if you were on the mantelpiece you would see that it is cut clean off without any mark of fraying whatever. You can reconstruct what occurred. The man needed the rope. He would not tear it down for fear of giving the alarm by ringing the bell. What did he do? He sprang up on the mantelpiece, could not quite reach it, put his knee on the bracket – you will see the impression in the dust – and so got his knife to bear upon the cord. I could not reach the place by at least three inches – from which I infer that he is at least three inches a bigger man than I. Look at that mark upon the seat of the oaken chair! What is it?"

"Blood."

"Undoubtedly it is blood. This alone puts the lady's story out of court. If she were seated on the chair when the crime was done, how comes that mark? No, no, she was placed in the chair *after* the death of her husband. I'll wager that the black dress shows a corresponding mark to this. We have not yet met our Waterloo, Watson, but this is our Marengo, for it begins in defeat and ends in victory. I should like now to have a few words with the nurse, Theresa. We must be wary for a while, if we are to get the information which we want."

She was an interesting person, this stern Australian nurse – taciturn, suspicious, ungracious, it took some time before Holmes's pleasant manner and frank acceptance of all that she said thawed her into a corresponding amiability. She did not attempt to conceal her hatred for her late employer.

"Yes, sir, it is true that he threw the decanter at me. I heard him call my mistress a name, and I told him that he would not dare to speak so if her brother had been there. Then it was that he threw it at me. He might have thrown a dozen if he had but left my bonny bird alone. He was forever ill-treating her, and she too proud to complain. She will not even tell me all that he has done to her. She never told me of those marks on her arm that you saw this morning, but I know very well that they come from a stab with a hatpin. The sly devil – God forgive me that I should speak of him so, now that he is dead! But a devil he was, if ever one walked the earth. He was all honey when first we met him – only eighteen months ago, and we both feel as if it were eighteen years. She had only just arrived in London. Yes, it was her first voyage – she had never been from home before. He won her with his title and his money and his false London ways. If she made a mistake she has paid for it, if ever a woman did. What month did we meet him? Well, I tell you it was just after we arrived. We arrived in June, and it was July. They were married in January of last year. Yes, she is down in the morning-room again, and I have no doubt she will see you, but you must not ask too much of her, for she has gone through all that flesh and blood will stand."

Lady Brackenstall was reclining on the same couch, but looked brighter than before. The maid had entered with us, and began once more to foment the bruise upon her mistress's brow.

"I hope," said the lady, "that you have not come to cross-examine me again?"

"No," Holmes answered, in his gentlest voice, "I will not cause you any unnecessary trouble, Lady Brackenstall, and my whole desire is to make things easy for you, for I am convinced that you are a much-tried woman. If you will treat me as a friend and trust me, you may find that I will justify your trust."

"What do you want me to do?"

"To tell me the truth."

"Mr. Holmes!"

"No, no, Lady Brackenstall – it is no use. You may have heard of any little reputation which I possess. I will stake it all on the fact that your story is an absolute fabrication."

Mistress and maid were both staring at Holmes with pale faces and frightened eyes.

"You are an impudent fellow!" cried Theresa. "Do you mean to say that my mistress has told a lie?"

Holmes rose from his chair.

"Have you nothing to tell me?"

"I have told you everything."

"Think once more, Lady Brackenstall. Would it not be better to be frank?"

For an instant there was hesitation in her beautiful face. Then some new strong thought caused it to set like a mask.

"I have told you all I know."

Holmes took his hat and shrugged his shoulders. "I am sorry," he said, and without another word we left the room and the house. There was a pond in the park, and to this my friend led the way. It was frozen over, but a single hole was left for the convenience of a solitary swan. Holmes gazed at it, and then passed on to the lodge gate. There he scribbled a short note for Stanley Hopkins, and left it with the lodge-keeper.

"It may be a hit, or it may be a miss, but we are bound to do something for friend Hopkins, just to justify this second visit," said he. "I will not quite take him into my confidence yet. I think our next scene of operations must be the shipping office of the Adelaide-Southampton line, which stands at the end of Pall Mall, if I remember right. There is a second line of steamers which connect South Australia with England, but we will draw the larger cover first."

Holmes's card sent in to the manager ensured instant attention, and he was not long in acquiring all the information he needed. In June of '95, only one of their line had reached a home port. It was the *Rock of Gibraltar*, their largest and best boat. A reference to the passenger list showed that Miss Fraser, of Adelaide, with her maid had made the voyage in her. The boat was now somewhere south of the Suez Canal on her way to Australia. Her officers were the same as in '95, with one exception. The first officer, Mr. Jack Crocker, had been made a captain and was to take charge of their new ship, *The Bass Rock*, sailing in two days' time from Southampton. He lived at Sydenham, but he was likely to be in that morning for instructions, if we cared to wait for him.

No, Mr. Holmes had no desire to see him, but would be glad to know more about his record and character.

His record was magnificent. There was not an officer in the fleet to touch him. As to his character, he was reliable on duty, but a wild, desperate fellow off the deck of his ship – hot-headed, excitable, but loyal, honest, and kind-hearted. That was the pith of the information with which Holmes left the office of the Adelaide-Southampton company. Thence he drove to Scotland Yard, but, instead of entering, he sat in his cab with his brows drawn down, lost in profound thought. Finally he drove round to the Charing Cross telegraph office, sent off a message, and then, at last, we made for Baker Street once more.

"No, I couldn't do it, Watson," said he, as we reentered our room. "Once that warrant was made out, nothing on earth would save him. Once or twice in my career I feel that I have done more real harm by my discovery of the criminal than ever he had done by his crime.

I have learned caution now, and I had rather play tricks with the law of England than with my own conscience. Let us know a little more before we act."

Before evening, we had a visit from Inspector Stanley Hopkins. Things were not going very well with him.

"I believe that you are a wizard, Mr. Holmes. I really do sometimes think that you have powers that are not human. Now, how on earth could you know that the stolen silver was at the bottom of that pond?"

"I didn't know it."

"But you told me to examine it."

"You got it, then?"

"Yes, I got it."

"I am very glad if I have helped you."

"But you haven't helped me. You have made the affair far more difficult. What sort of burglars are they who steal silver and then throw it into the nearest pond?"

"It was certainly rather eccentric behaviour. I was merely going on the idea that if the silver had been taken by persons who did not want it – who merely took it for a blind, as it were – then they would naturally be anxious to get rid of it."

"But why should such an idea cross your mind?"

"Well, I thought it was possible. When they came out through the French window, there was the pond with one tempting little hole in the ice, right in front of their noses. Could there be a better hiding-place?"

"Ah, a hiding-place – that is better!" cried Stanley Hopkins. "Yes, yes, I see it all now! It was early, there were folk upon the roads, they were afraid of being seen with the silver, so they sank it in the pond, intending to return for it when the coast was clear. Excellent, Mr. Holmes – that is better than your idea of a blind."

"Quite so, you have got an admirable theory. I have no doubt that my own ideas were quite wild, but you must admit that they have ended in discovering the silver."

"Yes, sir – yes. It was all your doing. But I have had a bad setback."

"A setback?"

"Yes, Mr. Holmes. The Randall gang were arrested in New York this morning."

"Dear me, Hopkins! That is certainly rather against your theory that they committed a murder in Kent last night."

"It is fatal, Mr. Holmes – absolutely fatal. Still, there are other gangs of three besides the Randalls, or it may be some new gang of which the police have never heard."

"Quite so, it is perfectly possible. What, are you off?"

"Yes, Mr. Holmes, there is no rest for me until I have got to the bottom of the business. I suppose you have no hint to give me?"

"I have given you one."

"Which?"

"Well, I suggested a blind."

"But why, Mr. Holmes, why?"

"Ah, that's the question, of course. But I commend the idea to your mind. You might possibly find that there was something in it. You won't stop for dinner? Well, good-bye, and let us know how you get on."

Dinner was over, and the table cleared before Holmes alluded to the matter again. He had lit his pipe and held his slippered feet to the cheerful blaze of the fire. Suddenly he looked at his watch.

"I expect developments, Watson."

"When?"

"Now – within a few minutes. I dare say you thought I acted rather badly to Stanley Hopkins just now?"

"I trust your judgment."

"A very sensible reply, Watson. You must look at it this way: what I know is unofficial, what he knows is official. I have the right to private judgment, but he has none. He must disclose all, or he is a traitor to his service. In a doubtful case I would not put him in so painful a position, and so I reserve my information until my own mind is clear upon the matter."

"But when will that be?"

"The time has come. You will now be present at the last scene of a remarkable little drama."

There was a sound upon the stairs, and our door was opened to admit as fine a specimen of manhood as ever passed through it. He was a very tall young man, golden-moustached, blue-eyed, with a skin which had been burned by tropical suns, and a springy step, which showed that the huge frame was as active as it was strong. He closed the door behind him, and then he stood with clenched hands and heaving breast, choking down some overmastering emotion.

"Sit down, Captain Crocker. You got my telegram?"

Our visitor sank into an armchair and looked from one to the other of us with questioning eyes.

"I got your telegram, and I came at the hour you said. I heard that you had been down to the office. There was no getting away from you. Let's hear the worst. What are you going to do with me? Arrest me? Speak out, man! You can't sit there and play with me like a cat with a mouse."

"Give him a cigar," said Holmes. "Bite on that, Captain Crocker, and don't let your nerves run away with you. I should not sit here smoking with you if I thought that you were a common criminal, you may be sure of that. Be frank with me and we may do some good. Play tricks with me, and I'll crush you."

"What do you wish me to do?"

"To give me a true account of all that happened at the Abbey Grange last night – a *true* account, mind you, with nothing added and nothing taken off. I know so much already that if you go one inch off the straight, I'll blow this police whistle from my window and the affair goes out of my hands forever."

The sailor thought for a little. Then he struck his leg with his great sunburned hand.

"I'll chance it," he cried. "I believe you are a man of your word, and a white man, and I'll tell you the whole story. But one thing I will say first. So far as I am concerned, I regret nothing and I fear nothing, and I would do it all again and be proud of the job. Damn the beast, if he had as many lives as a cat, he would owe them all to me! But it's the lady, Mary – Mary Fraser – for never will I call her by that accursed name. When I think of getting her into trouble, I who would give my life just to bring one smile to her dear face, it's that that turns my soul into water. And yet – and yet – what less could I do? I'll tell you my story, gentlemen, and then I'll ask you, as man to man, what less could I do?

"I must go back a bit. You seem to know everything, so I expect that you know that I met her when she was a passenger and I was first officer of the *Rock of Gibraltar*. From the first day I met her, she was the only woman to me. Every day of that voyage I loved her more, and many a time since have I kneeled down in the darkness of the night watch and kissed the deck of that ship because I knew her dear feet had trod it. She was never engaged to me. She treated me as fairly as ever a woman treated a man. I have no complaint to make. It was all love on my side, and all good comradeship and friendship on hers. When we parted she was a free woman, but I could never again be a free man.

"Next time I came back from sea, I heard of her marriage. Well, why shouldn't she marry whom she liked? Title and money – who could carry them better than she? She was born for all that is beautiful and dainty. I didn't grieve over her marriage. I was not such a selfish hound as that. I just rejoiced that good luck had come her way, and that she had not thrown herself away on a penniless sailor. That's how I loved Mary Fraser.

"Well, I never thought to see her again, but last voyage I was promoted, and the new boat was not yet launched, so I had to wait for a couple of months with my people at Sydenham. One day out in a country lane I met Theresa Wright, her old maid. She told me all about her, about him, about everything. I tell you, gentlemen, it nearly drove me mad. This drunken hound, that he should dare to raise his hand to her, whose boots he was not worthy to lick! I met Theresa again. Then I met Mary herself – and met her again. Then she would meet me no more. But the other day I had a notice that I was to start on my voyage within a week, and I determined that I would see her once before I left. Theresa was always my friend, for she loved Mary and hated this villain almost as much as I did. From her I learned the ways of the house. Mary used to sit up reading in her own little room downstairs. I crept round there last night and scratched at the window. At first she would not open to me, but in her heart I know that now she loves me, and she could not leave me in the frosty night. She whispered to me to come round to the big front window, and I found it open before me, so as to let me into the dining-room. Again I heard from her own lips things that made my blood boil, and again I cursed this brute who mishandled the woman I loved. Well, gentlemen, I was standing with her just inside the window, in all innocence, as God is my judge, when he rushed like a madman into the room, called her the vilest name that a man could use to a woman, and welted her across the face with the stick he had in his hand. I had sprung for the poker, and it was a fair fight between us. See here, on my arm, where his first blow fell. Then it was my turn, and I went through him as if he had been a rotten pumpkin. Do you think I was sorry? Not I! It was his life or mine, but far more than that, it was his life or hers, for how could I leave her in the power of this madman? That was how I killed him. Was I wrong? Well, then, what would either of you gentlemen have done, if you had been in my position?"

"She had screamed when he struck her, and that brought old Theresa down from the room above. There was a bottle of wine on the sideboard, and I opened it and poured a little between Mary's lips, for she was half dead with shock. Then I took a drop myself. Theresa was as cool as ice, and it was her plot as much as mine. We must make it appear that burglars had done the thing. Theresa kept on repeating our story to her mistress, while I swarmed up and cut the rope of the bell. Then I lashed her in her chair, and frayed out the end of the rope to make it look natural, else they would wonder how in the world a burglar could have got up there to cut it. Then I gathered up a few plates and pots of silver, to carry out the idea of the robbery, and there I left them, with orders to give the alarm when I had a quarter of an hour's start. I dropped the silver into the pond, and made off for Sydenham, feeling that for once in my life I had done a real good night's work. And that's the truth and the whole truth, Mr. Holmes, if it costs me my neck."

Holmes smoked for some time in silence. Then he crossed the room, and shook our visitor by the hand.

"That's what I think," said he. "I know that every word is true, for you have hardly said a word which I did not know. No one but an acrobat or a sailor could have got up to that bell-rope from the bracket, and no one but a sailor could have made the knots with which the cord was fastened to the chair. Only once had this lady been brought into contact with sailors, and that was on her voyage, and it was someone of her own class of life, since she was trying hard to shield him, and so showing that she loved him. You see how easy it was for me to lay my hands upon you when once I had started upon the right trail."

"I thought the police never could have seen through our dodge."

"And the police haven't, nor will they, to the best of my belief. Now, look here, Captain Crocker, this is a very serious matter, though I am willing to admit that you acted under the most extreme provocation to which any man could be subjected. I am not sure that in defence of your own life your action will not be pronounced legitimate. However, that is for a British jury to decide. Meanwhile I have so much sympathy for you that, if you choose to disappear in the next twenty-four hours, I will promise you that no one will hinder you."

"And then it will all come out?"

"Certainly it will come out."

The sailor flushed with anger.

"What sort of proposal is that to make a man? I know enough of law to understand that Mary would be held as accomplice. Do you think I would leave her alone to face the music while I slunk away? No, sir, let them do their worst upon me, but for heaven's sake, Mr. Holmes, find some way of keeping my poor Mary out of the courts."

Holmes for a second time held out his hand to the sailor.

"I was only testing you, and you ring true every time. Well, it is a great responsibility that I take upon myself, but I have given Hopkins an excellent hint and if he can't avail himself of it I can do no more. See here, Captain Crocker, we'll do this in due form of law. You are the prisoner. Watson, you are a British jury, and I never met a man who was more eminently fitted to represent one. I am the judge. Now, gentleman of the jury, you have heard the evidence. Do you find the prisoner guilty or not guilty?"

"Not guilty, my lord," said I.

"*Vox populi, vox Dei*. You are acquitted, Captain Crocker. So long as the law does not find some other victim you are safe from me. Come back to this lady in a year, and may her future and yours justify us in the judgment which we have pronounced this night!"

The Adventure of the Red Circle

Arthur Conan Doyle

Chapter I

"WELL, MRS. WARREN, I cannot see that you have any particular cause for uneasiness, nor do I understand why I, whose time is of some value, should interfere in the matter. I really have other things to engage me." So spoke Sherlock Holmes and turned back to the great scrapbook in which he was arranging and indexing some of his recent material.

But the landlady had the pertinacity and also the cunning of her sex. She held her ground firmly.

"You arranged an affair for a lodger of mine last year," she said – "Mr. Fairdale Hobbs."

"Ah, yes – a simple matter."

"But he would never cease talking of it – your kindness, sir, and the way in which you brought light into the darkness. I remembered his words when I was in doubt and darkness myself. I know you could if you only would."

Holmes was accessible upon the side of flattery, and also, to do him justice, upon the side of kindliness. The two forces made him lay down his gum-brush with a sigh of resignation and push back his chair.

"Well, well, Mrs. Warren, let us hear about it, then. You don't object to tobacco, I take it? Thank you, Watson – the matches! You are uneasy, as I understand, because your new lodger remains in his rooms and you cannot see him. Why, bless you, Mrs. Warren, if I were your lodger you often would not see me for weeks on end."

"No doubt, sir; but this is different. It frightens me, Mr. Holmes. I can't sleep for fright. To hear his quick step moving here and moving there from early morning to late at night, and yet never to catch so much as a glimpse of him – it's more than I can stand. My husband is as nervous over it as I am, but he is out at his work all day, while I get no rest from it. What is he hiding for? What has he done? Except for the girl, I am all alone in the house with him, and it's more than my nerves can stand."

Holmes leaned forward and laid his long, thin fingers upon the woman's shoulder. He had an almost hypnotic power of soothing when he wished. The scared look faded from her eyes, and her agitated features smoothed into their usual commonplace. She sat down in the chair which he had indicated.

"If I take it up I must understand every detail," said he. "Take time to consider. The smallest point may be the most essential. You say that the man came ten days ago and paid you for a fortnight's board and lodging?"

"He asked my terms, sir. I said fifty shillings a week. There is a small sitting-room and bedroom, and all complete, at the top of the house."

"Well?"

"He said, 'I'll pay you five pounds a week if I can have it on my own terms.' I'm a poor woman, sir, and Mr. Warren earns little, and the money meant much to me. He took out a ten-pound note, and he held it out to me then and there. 'You can have the same every fortnight for a long time to come if you keep the terms,' he said. 'If not, I'll have no more to do with you.'

"What were the terms?"

"Well, sir, they were that he was to have a key of the house. That was all right. Lodgers often have them. Also, that he was to be left entirely to himself and never, upon any excuse, to be disturbed."

"Nothing wonderful in that, surely?"

"Not in reason, sir. But this is out of all reason. He has been there for ten days, and neither Mr. Warren, nor I, nor the girl has once set eyes upon him. We can hear that quick step of his pacing up and down, up and down, night, morning, and noon; but except on that first night he had never once gone out of the house."

"Oh, he went out the first night, did he?"

"Yes, sir, and returned very late – after we were all in bed. He told me after he had taken the rooms that he would do so and asked me not to bar the door. I heard him come up the stair after midnight."

"But his meals?"

"It was his particular direction that we should always, when he rang, leave his meal upon a chair, outside his door. Then he rings again when he has finished, and we take it down from the same chair. If he wants anything else he prints it on a slip of paper and leaves it."

"Prints it?"

"Yes, sir; prints it in pencil. Just the word, nothing more. Here's the one I brought to show you – soap. Here's another – match. This is one he left the first morning – daily gazette. I leave that paper with his breakfast every morning."

"Dear me, Watson," said Homes, staring with great curiosity at the slips of foolscap which the landlady had handed to him, "this is certainly a little unusual. Seclusion I can understand; but why print? Printing is a clumsy process. Why not write? What would it suggest, Watson?"

"That he desired to conceal his handwriting."

"But why? What can it matter to him that his landlady should have a word of his writing? Still, it may be as you say. Then, again, why such laconic messages?"

"I cannot imagine."

"It opens a pleasing field for intelligent speculation. The words are written with a broad-pointed, violet-tinted pencil of a not unusual pattern. You will observe that the paper is torn away at the side here after the printing was done, so that the 's' of 'soap' is partly gone. Suggestive, Watson, is it not?"

"Of caution?"

"Exactly. There was evidently some mark, some thumbprint, something which might give a clue to the person's identity. Now. Mrs. Warren, you say that the man was of middle size, dark, and bearded. What age would he be?"

"Youngish, sir – not over thirty."

"Well, can you give me no further indications?"

"He spoke good English, sir, and yet I thought he was a foreigner by his accent."

"And he was well dressed?"

"Very smartly dressed, sir – quite the gentleman. Dark clothes – nothing you would note."

"He gave no name?"

"No, sir."

"And has had no letters or callers?"

"None."

"But surely you or the girl enter his room of a morning?"

"No, sir; he looks after himself entirely."

"Dear me! that is certainly remarkable. What about his luggage?"

"He had one big brown bag with him – nothing else."

"Well, we don't seem to have much material to help us. Do you say nothing has come out of that room – absolutely nothing?"

The landlady drew an envelope from her bag; from it she shook out two burnt matches and a cigarette-end upon the table.

"They were on his tray this morning. I brought them because I had heard that you can read great things out of small ones."

Holmes shrugged his shoulders.

"There is nothing here," said he. "The matches have, of course, been used to light cigarettes. That is obvious from the shortness of the burnt end. Half the match is consumed in lighting a pipe or cigar. But, dear me! this cigarette stub is certainly remarkable. The gentleman was bearded and moustached, you say?"

"Yes, sir."

"I don't understand that. I should say that only a clean-shaven man could have smoked this. Why, Watson, even your modest moustache would have been singed."

"A holder?" I suggested.

"No, no; the end is matted. I suppose there could not be two people in your rooms, Mrs. Warren?"

"No, sir. He eats so little that I often wonder it can keep life in one."

"Well, I think we must wait for a little more material. After all, you have nothing to complain of. You have received your rent, and he is not a troublesome lodger, though he is certainly an unusual one. He pays you well, and if he chooses to lie concealed it is no direct business of yours. We have no excuse for an intrusion upon his privacy until we have some reason to think that there is a guilty reason for it. I've taken up the matter, and I won't lose sight of it. Report to me if anything fresh occurs, and rely upon my assistance if it should be needed.

"There are certainly some points of interest in this case, Watson," he remarked when the landlady had left us. "It may, of course, be trivial – individual eccentricity; or it may be very much deeper than appears on the surface. The first thing that strikes one is the obvious possibility that the person now in the rooms may be entirely different from the one who engaged them."

"Why should you think so?"

"Well, apart from this cigarette-end, was it not suggestive that the only time the lodger went out was immediately after his taking the rooms? He came back – or someone came back – when all witnesses were out of the way. We have no proof that the person who came back was the person who went out. Then, again, the man who took the rooms spoke English well. This other, however, prints 'match' when it should have been 'matches.' I can imagine that the word was taken out of a dictionary, which would give the noun but not the plural. The laconic style may be to conceal the absence of knowledge of English. Yes, Watson, there are good reasons to suspect that there has been a substitution of lodgers."

"But for what possible end?"

"Ah! there lies our problem. There is one rather obvious line of investigation." He took down the great book in which, day by day, he filed the agony columns of the various London journals. "Dear me!" said he, turning over the pages, "what a chorus of groans, cries, and bleatings! What a rag-bag of singular happenings! But surely the most valuable hunting-ground that ever was given to a student of the unusual! This person is alone and cannot be approached by letter without a breach of that absolute secrecy which is desired. How is any news or any message to reach him from without? Obviously by advertisement through a newspaper. There seems no other way, and fortunately we need concern ourselves with the one paper only. Here are the Daily Gazette extracts of the last fortnight. 'Lady with a black boa at Prince's Skating Club' – that we may pass. 'Surely Jimmy will not break his mother's heart' – that appears to be irrelevant. 'If the lady who fainted on Brixton bus' – she does not interest me. 'Every day my heart longs—' Bleat, Watson – unmitigated bleat! Ah, this is a little more possible. Listen to this: 'Be patient. Will find some sure means of communications. Meanwhile, this column. G.' That is two days after Mrs. Warren's lodger arrived. It sounds plausible, does it not? The mysterious one could understand English, even if he could not print it. Let us see if we can pick up the trace again. Yes, here we are – three days later. 'Am making successful arrangements. Patience and prudence. The clouds will pass. G.' Nothing for a week after that. Then comes something much more definite: 'The path is clearing. If I find chance signal message remember code agreed – One A, two B, and so on. You will hear soon. G.' That was in yesterday's paper, and there is nothing in today's. It's all very appropriate to Mrs. Warren's lodger. If we wait a little, Watson, I don't doubt that the affair will grow more intelligible."

So it proved; for in the morning I found my friend standing on the hearthrug with his back to the fire and a smile of complete satisfaction upon his face.

"How's this, Watson?" he cried, picking up the paper from the table. "'High red house with white stone facings. Third floor. Second window left. After dusk. G.' That is definite enough. I think after breakfast we must make a little reconnaissance of Mrs. Warren's neighbourhood. Ah, Mrs. Warren! what news do you bring us this morning?"

Our client had suddenly burst into the room with an explosive energy which told of some new and momentous development.

"It's a police matter, Mr. Holmes!" she cried. "I'll have no more of it! He shall pack out of there with his baggage. I would have gone straight up and told him so, only I thought it was but fair to you to take your opinion first. But I'm at the end of my patience, and when it comes to knocking my old man about—"

"Knocking Mr. Warren about?"

"Using him roughly, anyway."

"But who used him roughly?"

"Ah! that's what we want to know! It was this morning, sir. Mr. Warren is a timekeeper at Morton and Waylight's, in Tottenham Court Road. He has to be out of the house before seven. Well, this morning he had not gone ten paces down the road when two men came up behind him, threw a coat over his head, and bundled him into a cab that was beside the curb. They drove him an hour, and then opened the door and shot him out. He lay in the roadway so shaken in his wits that he never saw what became of the cab. When he picked himself up he found he was on Hampstead Heath; so he took a bus home, and there he lies now on his sofa, while I came straight round to tell you what had happened."

"Most interesting," said Holmes. "Did he observe the appearance of these men – did he hear them talk?"

"No; he is clean dazed. He just knows that he was lifted up as if by magic and dropped as if by magic. Two at least were in it, and maybe three."

"And you connect this attack with your lodger?"

"Well, we've lived there fifteen years and no such happenings ever came before. I've had enough of him. Money's not everything. I'll have him out of my house before the day is done."

"Wait a bit, Mrs. Warren. Do nothing rash. I begin to think that this affair may be very much more important than appeared at first sight. It is clear now that some danger is threatening your lodger. It is equally clear that his enemies, lying in wait for him near your door, mistook your husband for him in the foggy morning light. On discovering their mistake they released him. What they would have done had it not been a mistake, we can only conjecture."

"Well, what am I to do, Mr. Holmes?"

"I have a great fancy to see this lodger of yours, Mrs. Warren."

"I don't see how that is to be managed, unless you break in the door. I always hear him unlock it as I go down the stair after I leave the tray."

"He has to take the tray in. Surely we could conceal ourselves and see him do it."

The landlady thought for a moment.

"Well, sir, there's the box-room opposite. I could arrange a looking-glass, maybe, and if you were behind the door—"

"Excellent!" said Holmes. "When does he lunch?"

"About one, sir."

"Then Dr. Watson and I will come round in time. For the present, Mrs. Warren, good-bye."

At half-past twelve we found ourselves upon the steps of Mrs. Warren's house – a high, thin, yellow-brick edifice in Great Orme Street, a narrow thoroughfare at the northeast side of the British Museum. Standing as it does near the corner of the street, it commands a view down Howe Street, with its more pretentious houses. Holmes pointed with a chuckle to one of these, a row of residential flats, which projected so that they could not fail to catch the eye.

"See, Watson!" said he. "'High red house with stone facings.' There is the signal station all right. We know the place, and we know the code; so surely our task should be simple. There's a 'to let' card in that window. It is evidently an empty flat to which the confederate has access. Well, Mrs. Warren, what now?"

"I have it all ready for you. If you will both come up and leave your boots below on the landing, I'll put you there now."

It was an excellent hiding-place which she had arranged. The mirror was so placed that, seated in the dark, we could very plainly see the door opposite. We had hardly settled down in it, and Mrs. Warren left us, when a distant tinkle announced that our mysterious neighbour had rung. Presently the landlady appeared with the tray, laid it down upon a chair beside the closed door, and then, treading heavily, departed. Crouching together in the angle of the door, we kept our eyes fixed upon the mirror. Suddenly, as the landlady's footsteps died away, there was the creak of a turning key, the handle revolved, and two thin hands darted out and lifted the tray from the chair. An instant later it was hurriedly replaced, and I caught a glimpse of a dark, beautiful, horrified face glaring at the narrow opening of the box-room. Then the door crashed to, the key turned once more, and all was silence. Holmes twitched my sleeve, and together we stole down the stair.

"I will call again in the evening," said he to the expectant landlady. "I think, Watson, we can discuss this business better in our own quarters."

"My surmise, as you saw, proved to be correct," said he, speaking from the depths of his easy-chair. "There has been a substitution of lodgers. What I did not foresee is that we should find a woman, and no ordinary woman, Watson."

"She saw us."

"Well, she saw something to alarm her. That is certain. The general sequence of events is pretty clear, is it not? A couple seek refuge in London from a very terrible and instant danger. The measure of that danger is the rigour of their precautions. The man, who has some work which he must do, desires to leave the woman in absolute safety while he does it. It is not an easy problem, but he solved it in an original fashion, and so effectively that her presence was not even known to the landlady who supplies her with food. The printed messages, as is now evident, were to prevent her sex being discovered by her writing. The man cannot come near the woman, or he will guide their enemies to her. Since he cannot communicate with her direct, he has recourse to the agony column of a paper. So far all is clear."

"But what is at the root of it?"

"Ah, yes, Watson – severely practical, as usual! What is at the root of it all? Mrs. Warren's whimsical problem enlarges somewhat and assumes a more sinister aspect as we proceed. This much we can say: that it is no ordinary love escapade. You saw the woman's face at the sign of danger. We have heard, too, of the attack upon the landlord, which was undoubtedly meant for the lodger. These alarms, and the desperate need for secrecy, argue that the matter is one of life or death. The attack upon Mr. Warren further shows that the enemy, whoever they are, are themselves not aware of the substitution of the female lodger for the male. It is very curious and complex, Watson."

"Why should you go further in it? What have you to gain from it?"

"What, indeed? It is art for art's sake, Watson. I suppose when you doctored you found yourself studying cases without thought of a fee?"

"For my education, Holmes."

"Education never ends, Watson. It is a series of lessons with the greatest for the last. This is an instructive case. There is neither money nor credit in it, and yet one would wish to tidy it up. When dusk comes we should find ourselves one stage advanced in our investigation."

When we returned to Mrs. Warren's rooms, the gloom of a London winter evening had thickened into one gray curtain, a dead monotone of colour, broken only by the sharp yellow squares of the windows and the blurred haloes of the gas-lamps. As we peered from the darkened sitting-room of the lodging-house, one more dim light glimmered high up through the obscurity.

"Someone is moving in that room," said Holmes in a whisper, his gaunt and eager face thrust forward to the window-pane. "Yes, I can see his shadow. There he is again! He has a candle in his hand. Now he is peering across. He wants to be sure that she is on the lookout. Now he begins to flash. Take the message also, Watson, that we may check each other. A single flash – that is A, surely. Now, then. How many did you make it? Twenty. So did I. That should mean T. AT— that's intelligible enough. Another T. Surely this is the beginning of a second word. Now, then —TENTA. Dead stop. That can't be all, Watson? ATTENTA gives no sense. Nor is it any better as three words AT, TEN, TA, unless T.A. are a person's initials. There it goes again! What's that? ATTE— why, it is the same message over again. Curious, Watson, very curious. Now he is off once more! AT— why he is repeating it for the third time. ATTENTA three times! How often will he repeat it? No, that seems to be the finish. He has withdrawn from the window. What do you make of it, Watson?"

"A cipher message, Holmes."

My companion gave a sudden chuckle of comprehension. "And not a very obscure cipher, Watson," said he. "Why, of course, it is Italian! The A means that it is addressed to a woman. 'Beware! Beware! Beware!' How's that, Watson?"

"I believe you have hit it."

"Not a doubt of it. It is a very urgent message, thrice repeated to make it more so. But beware of what? Wait a bit, he is coming to the window once more."

Again we saw the dim silhouette of a crouching man and the whisk of the small flame across the window as the signals were renewed. They came more rapidly than before – so rapid that it was hard to follow them.

"PERICOLO – pericolo – eh, what's that, Watson? 'Danger,' isn't it? Yes, by Jove, it's a danger signal. There he goes again! PERI. Halloa, what on earth—"

The light had suddenly gone out, the glimmering square of window had disappeared, and the third floor formed a dark band round the lofty building, with its tiers of shining casements. That last warning cry had been suddenly cut short. How, and by whom? The same thought occurred on the instant to us both. Holmes sprang up from where he crouched by the window.

"This is serious, Watson," he cried. "There is some devilry going forward! Why should such a message stop in such a way? I should put Scotland Yard in touch with this business – and yet, it is too pressing for us to leave."

"Shall I go for the police?"

"We must define the situation a little more clearly. It may bear some more innocent interpretation. Come, Watson, let us go across ourselves and see what we can make of it."

Chapter II

AS WE WALKED rapidly down Howe Street I glanced back at the building which we had left. There, dimly outlined at the top window, I could see the shadow of a head, a woman's head, gazing tensely, rigidly, out into the night, waiting with breathless suspense for the renewal of that interrupted message. At the doorway of the Howe Street flats a man, muffled in a cravat and greatcoat, was leaning against the railing. He started as the hall-light fell upon our faces.

"Holmes!" he cried.

"Why, Gregson!" said my companion as he shook hands with the Scotland Yard detective. "Journeys end with lovers' meetings. What brings you here?"

"The same reasons that bring you, I expect," said Gregson. "How you got on to it I can't imagine."

"Different threads, but leading up to the same tangle. I've been taking the signals."

"Signals?"

"Yes, from that window. They broke off in the middle. We came over to see the reason. But since it is safe in your hands I see no object in continuing this business."

"Wait a bit!" cried Gregson eagerly. "I'll do you this justice, Mr. Holmes, that I was never in a case yet that I didn't feel stronger for having you on my side. There's only the one exit to these flats, so we have him safe."

"Who is he?"

"Well, well, we score over you for once, Mr. Holmes. You must give us best this time." He struck his stick sharply upon the ground, on which a cabman, his whip in his hand, sauntered over from a four-wheeler which stood on the far side of the street. "May I introduce you to Mr. Sherlock Holmes?" he said to the cabman. "This is Mr. Leverton, of Pinkerton's American Agency."

"The hero of the Long Island cave mystery?" said Holmes. "Sir, I am pleased to meet you."

The American, a quiet, businesslike young man, with a clean-shaven, hatchet face, flushed up at the words of commendation. "I am on the trail of my life now, Mr. Holmes," said he. "If I can get Gorgiano—"

"What! Gorgiano of the Red Circle?"

"Oh, he has a European fame, has he? Well, we've learned all about him in America. We KNOW he is at the bottom of fifty murders, and yet we have nothing positive we can take him on. I tracked him over from New York, and I've been close to him for a week in London, waiting some excuse to get my hand on his collar. Mr. Gregson and I ran him to ground in that big tenement house, and there's only one door, so he can't slip us. There's three folk come out since he went in, but I'll swear he wasn't one of them."

"Mr. Holmes talks of signals," said Gregson. "I expect, as usual, he knows a good deal that we don't."

In a few clear words Holmes explained the situation as it had appeared to us. The American struck his hands together with vexation.

"He's on to us!" he cried.

"Why do you think so?"

"Well, it figures out that way, does it not? Here he is, sending out messages to an accomplice – there are several of his gang in London. Then suddenly, just as by your own account he was telling them that there was danger, he broke short off. What could it mean except that from the window he had suddenly either caught sight of us in the street, or in some way come to understand how close the danger was, and that he must act right away if he was to avoid it? What do you suggest, Mr. Holmes?"

"That we go up at once and see for ourselves."

"But we have no warrant for his arrest."

"He is in unoccupied premises under suspicious circumstances," said Gregson. "That is good enough for the moment. When we have him by the heels we can see if New York can't help us to keep him. I'll take the responsibility of arresting him now."

Our official detectives may blunder in the matter of intelligence, but never in that of courage. Gregson climbed the stair to arrest this desperate murderer with the same absolutely quiet and businesslike bearing with which he would have ascended the official staircase of Scotland Yard. The Pinkerton man had tried to push past him, but Gregson had firmly elbowed him back. London dangers were the privilege of the London force.

The door of the left-hand flat upon the third landing was standing ajar. Gregson pushed it open. Within all was absolute silence and darkness. I struck a match and lit the detective's lantern. As I did so, and as the flicker steadied into a flame, we all gave a gasp of surprise. On the deal boards of the carpetless floor there was outlined a fresh track of blood. The red steps pointed towards us and led away from an inner room, the door of which was closed. Gregson flung it open and held his light full blaze in front of him, while we all peered eagerly over his shoulders.

In the middle of the floor of the empty room was huddled the figure of an enormous man, his clean-shaven, swarthy face grotesquely horrible in its contortion and his head encircled by a ghastly crimson halo of blood, lying in a broad wet circle upon the white woodwork. His knees were drawn up, his hands thrown out in agony, and from the centre of his broad, brown, upturned throat there projected the white haft of a knife driven blade-deep into his body. Giant as he was, the man must have gone down like a pole-axed ox before that terrific blow. Beside his right hand a most formidable horn-handled, two-edged dagger lay upon the floor, and near it a black kid glove.

"By George! it's Black Gorgiano himself!" cried the American detective. "Someone has got ahead of us this time."

"Here is the candle in the window, Mr. Holmes," said Gregson. "Why, whatever are you doing?"

Holmes had stepped across, had lit the candle, and was passing it backward and forward across the window-panes. Then he peered into the darkness, blew the candle out, and threw it on the floor.

"I rather think that will be helpful," said he. He came over and stood in deep thought while the two professionals were examining the body. "You say that three people came out from the flat while you were waiting downstairs," said he at last. "Did you observe them closely?"

"Yes, I did."

"Was there a fellow about thirty, black-bearded, dark, of middle size?"

"Yes; he was the last to pass me."

"That is your man, I fancy. I can give you his description, and we have a very excellent outline of his footmark. That should be enough for you."

"Not much, Mr. Holmes, among the millions of London."

"Perhaps not. That is why I thought it best to summon this lady to your aid."

We all turned round at the words. There, framed in the doorway, was a tall and beautiful woman – the mysterious lodger of Bloomsbury. Slowly she advanced, her face pale and drawn with a frightful apprehension, her eyes fixed and staring, her terrified gaze riveted upon the dark figure on the floor.

"You have killed him!" she muttered. "Oh, Dio mio, you have killed him!" Then I heard a sudden sharp intake of her breath, and she sprang into the air with a cry of joy. Round and round the room she danced, her hands clapping, her dark eyes gleaming with delighted wonder, and a thousand pretty Italian exclamations pouring from her lips. It was terrible and amazing to see such a woman so convulsed with joy at such a sight. Suddenly she stopped and gazed at us all with a questioning stare.

"But you! You are police, are you not? You have killed Giuseppe Gorgiano. Is it not so?"

"We are police, madam."

She looked round into the shadows of the room.

"But where, then, is Gennaro?" she asked. "He is my husband, Gennaro Lucca. I am Emilia Lucca, and we are both from New York. Where is Gennaro? He called me this moment from this window, and I ran with all my speed."

"It was I who called," said Holmes.

"You! How could you call?"

"Your cipher was not difficult, madam. Your presence here was desirable. I knew that I had only to flash 'Vieni' and you would surely come."

The beautiful Italian looked with awe at my companion.

"I do not understand how you know these things," she said. "Giuseppe Gorgiano – how did he—" She paused, and then suddenly her face lit up with pride and delight. "Now I see it! My Gennaro! My splendid, beautiful Gennaro, who has guarded me safe from all harm, he did it, with his own strong hand he killed the monster! Oh, Gennaro, how wonderful you are! What woman could ever be worthy of such a man?"

"Well, Mrs. Lucca," said the prosaic Gregson, laying his hand upon the lady's sleeve with as little sentiment as if she were a Notting Hill hooligan, "I am not very clear yet who you are or what you are; but you've said enough to make it very clear that we shall want you at the Yard."

"One moment, Gregson," said Holmes. "I rather fancy that this lady may be as anxious to give us information as we can be to get it. You understand, madam, that your husband will be arrested and tried for the death of the man who lies before us? What you say may be used in evidence. But if you think that he has acted from motives which are not criminal, and which he would wish to have known, then you cannot serve him better than by telling us the whole story."

"Now that Gorgiano is dead we fear nothing," said the lady. "He was a devil and a monster, and there can be no judge in the world who would punish my husband for having killed him."

"In that case," said Holmes, "my suggestion is that we lock this door, leave things as we found them, go with this lady to her room, and form our opinion after we have heard what it is that she has to say to us."

Half an hour later we were seated, all four, in the small sitting-room of Signora Lucca, listening to her remarkable narrative of those sinister events, the ending of which we had chanced to witness. She spoke in rapid and fluent but very unconventional English, which, for the sake of clearness, I will make grammatical.

"I was born in Posilippo, near Naples," said she, "and was the daughter of Augusto Barelli, who was the chief lawyer and once the deputy of that part. Gennaro was in my father's employment, and I came to love him, as any woman must. He had neither money nor position – nothing but his beauty and strength and energy – so my father forbade the match. We fled together, were married at Bari, and sold my jewels to gain the money which would take us to America. This was four years ago, and we have been in New York ever since.

"Fortune was very good to us at first. Gennaro was able to do a service to an Italian gentleman – he saved him from some ruffians in the place called the Bowery, and so made a powerful friend. His name was Tito Castalotte, and he was the senior partner of the great firm of Castalotte and Zamba, who are the chief fruit importers of New York. Signor Zamba is an invalid, and our new friend Castalotte has all power within the firm, which employs more than three hundred men. He took my husband into his employment, made him head of a department, and showed his good-will towards him in every way. Signor Castalotte was a bachelor, and I believe that he felt as if Gennaro was his son, and both my husband and I loved him as if he were our father. We had taken and furnished a little house in Brooklyn, and our whole future seemed assured when that black cloud appeared which was soon to overspread our sky.

"One night, when Gennaro returned from his work, he brought a fellow-countryman back with him. His name was Gorgiano, and he had come also from Posilippo. He was a huge man, as you can testify, for you have looked upon his corpse. Not only was his body that of a giant but everything about him was grotesque, gigantic, and terrifying. His voice was like thunder in our little house. There was scarce room for the whirl of his great arms as he talked. His thoughts, his emotions, his passions, all were exaggerated and monstrous.

He talked, or rather roared, with such energy that others could but sit and listen, cowed with the mighty stream of words. His eyes blazed at you and held you at his mercy. He was a terrible and wonderful man. I thank God that he is dead!

"He came again and again. Yet I was aware that Gennaro was no more happy than I was in his presence. My poor husband would sit pale and listless, listening to the endless raving upon politics and upon social questions which made up our visitor's conversation. Gennaro said nothing, but I, who knew him so well, could read in his face some emotion which I had never seen there before. At first I thought that it was dislike. And then, gradually, I understood that it was more than dislike. It was fear – a deep, secret, shrinking fear. That night – the night that I read his terror – I put my arms round him and I implored him by his love for me and by all that he held dear to hold nothing from me, and to tell me why this huge man overshadowed him so.

"He told me, and my own heart grew cold as ice as I listened. My poor Gennaro, in his wild and fiery days, when all the world seemed against him and his mind was driven half mad by the injustices of life, had joined a Neapolitan society, the Red Circle, which was allied to the old Carbonari. The oaths and secrets of this brotherhood were frightful, but once within its rule no escape was possible. When we had fled to America Gennaro thought that he had cast it all off forever. What was his horror one evening to meet in the streets the very man who had initiated him in Naples, the giant Gorgiano, a man who had earned the name of 'Death' in the south of Italy, for he was red to the elbow in murder! He had come to New York to avoid the Italian police, and he had already planted a branch of this dreadful society in his new home. All this Gennaro told me and showed me a summons which he had received that very day, a Red Circle drawn upon the head of it telling him that a lodge would be held upon a certain date, and that his presence at it was required and ordered.

"That was bad enough, but worse was to come. I had noticed for some time that when Gorgiano came to us, as he constantly did, in the evening, he spoke much to me; and even when his words were to my husband those terrible, glaring, wild-beast eyes of his were always turned upon me. One night his secret came out. I had awakened what he called 'love' within him – the love of a brute – a savage. Gennaro had not yet returned when he came. He pushed his way in, seized me in his mighty arms, hugged me in his bear's embrace, covered me with kisses, and implored me to come away with him. I was struggling and screaming when Gennaro entered and attacked him. He struck Gennaro senseless and fled from the house which he was never more to enter. It was a deadly enemy that we made that night.

"A few days later came the meeting. Gennaro returned from it with a face which told me that something dreadful had occurred. It was worse than we could have imagined possible. The funds of the society were raised by blackmailing rich Italians and threatening them with violence should they refuse the money. It seems that Castalotte, our dear friend and benefactor, had been approached. He had refused to yield to threats, and he had handed the notices to the police. It was resolved now that such an example should be made of them as would prevent any other victim from rebelling. At the meeting it was arranged that he and his house should be blown up with dynamite. There was a drawing of lots as to who should carry out the deed. Gennaro saw our enemy's cruel face smiling at him as he dipped his hand in the bag. No doubt it had been prearranged in some fashion, for it was the fatal disc with the Red Circle upon it, the mandate for murder, which lay upon his palm. He was to kill his best friend, or he was to expose himself and me to the vengeance of his comrades. It was part of their fiendish system to punish those whom they feared or hated by injuring not only their own persons but those whom they loved, and it was the knowledge of this which hung as a terror over my poor Gennaro's head and drove him nearly crazy with apprehension.

"All that night we sat together, our arms round each other, each strengthening each for the troubles that lay before us. The very next evening had been fixed for the attempt. By midday my husband and I were on our way to London, but not before he had given our benefactor full warning of this danger, and had also left such information for the police as would safeguard his life for the future.

"The rest, gentlemen, you know for yourselves. We were sure that our enemies would be behind us like our own shadows. Gorgiano had his private reasons for vengeance, but in any case we knew how ruthless, cunning, and untiring he could be. Both Italy and America are full of stories of his dreadful powers. If ever they were exerted it would be now. My darling made use of the few clear days which our start had given us in arranging for a refuge for me in such a fashion that no possible danger could reach me. For his own part, he wished to be free that he might communicate both with the American and with the Italian police. I do not myself know where he lived, or how. All that I learned was through the columns of a newspaper. But once as I looked through my window, I saw two Italians watching the house, and I understood that in some way Gorgiano had found our retreat. Finally Gennaro told me, through the paper, that he would signal to me from a certain window, but when the signals came they were nothing but warnings, which were suddenly interrupted. It is very clear to me now that he knew Gorgiano to be close upon him, and that, thank God! he was ready for him when he came. And now, gentleman, I would ask you whether we have anything to fear from the law, or whether any judge upon earth would condemn my Gennaro for what he has done?"

"Well, Mr. Gregson," said the American, looking across at the official, "I don't know what your British point of view may be, but I guess that in New York this lady's husband will receive a pretty general vote of thanks."

"She will have to come with me and see the chief," Gregson answered. "If what she says is corroborated, I do not think she or her husband has much to fear. But what I can't make head or tail of, Mr. Holmes, is how on earth YOU got yourself mixed up in the matter."

"Education, Gregson, education. Still seeking knowledge at the old university. Well, Watson, you have one more specimen of the tragic and grotesque to add to your collection. By the way, it is not eight o'clock, and a Wagner night at Covent Garden! If we hurry, we might be in time for the second act."

Ripping

Meg Elison

THE POOR THING was not nearly as far gone as she thought she was, Marla realized as she touched the girl's low belly. Maybe she was too young to know. Maybe it was her first time.

She looked up at the girl's round face, her quivering chin.

"It's nothing," she told her. "Nothing at all, when it's this early. You'll be back on your feet tomorrow, and back on your back in a week."

The girl nodded and Marla went to work. She was well-known in London, skilled and tight-lipped. She left very few dead girls in her wake. After she had been working in her craft for a few years, she had even been called out to houses in Kensington in the middle of the night to handle some delicate clientele who would pay for her silence more than her skill.

She knew those houses in daytime, their eaves sooty and their gardens neat. She came as a midwife then, with a clean apron and a bright smile. By night the houses were different, run by whispering servants and terrified women. By night she was different: direct and businesslike, with no time for hand-wringing nonsense or the kind of myths whispered by ladies without hearts.

She told the girl on Marlborough Street what she told those ladies in Kensington or Notting Hill. *This will hurt but you will be fine. This will be hard, but you can always have another child. This won't kill you, and don't let guilt do that, either.*

The round-faced girl closed her eyes and Marla saw tears clotting her lashes.

"Breathe, child."

Marla kicked the basin closer to the edge of the bed where she sat on her little stool between the girl's dimply knees.

With the frank privilege of the madam of the house, Florence opened the door without knocking and let herself in.

"Marla, I'm so glad you could come. I know you've been quite busy, and I've heard tell of some crackpot peddling himself on Portobello who's nothing more than a butcher."

"Good day to you, Florence. I'm glad to be here as well." She waited for the girl to relax a little before pushing her slim metal tool to the sticking place. There. There it was. She began to chivvy.

Florence rose up behind Marla as she worked, fragrant and warm. Marla knew her sachet of lavender and verbena, she found it oddly sweet and comforting for a woman in such a position as hers.

"Is there something I can do for you, Florence? Want to learn the craft?"

Florence gave a low chuckle and Marla looked up past her own shoulder.

The older woman's hair was dressed in long, glorious, shining curls. They contrasted with the sweaty red-haired child in the bed, who could use a bath when all this was over. Florence's purple gown was long and cut modestly, announcing itself in lurid color rather than available flesh.

"No, not the trade," she said in her low voice. "I have another problem that I'd like your help with."

"Another?" Marla gestured with her head to the girl, who was beginning to drip and then stream fresh blood that smelled like copper halfpennies that had been fetched out of a seawater drain.

"No, lord love you. Not another girl who can't count days on her fingers. Something else. Will you come to my parlor when you're finished?"

"Of course."

Florence was gone in a sweep of skirts and Marla gradually tuned back in, hearing the girl crying softly.

"What's wrong, child? Does it hurt that much?"

"A… a little. More is I'm just sad I've gone and killed a baby. I've fallen so far in my life." She sobbed quietly, her face turned away.

"Hush now. Hush. It doesn't bear thinking of."

Once the bleeding had really begun, the girl started to contract. She moaned and the low, grinding sound of it was welcome to Marla's ears. She had done this enough times to know.

"Sit up halfway," she told the girl. "Make your belly tight."

The girl whimpered but obeyed.

"Now, bear down like you're trying to have a mighty shit," Marla hissed.

The girl, incredibly, laughed in surprise. That was just as good. The push came and a palm-sized fleshy clot came tearing out, missing the basin entirely and stamping the floor in crimson.

The girl's eyes were wide as Marla picked the object up off the floor.

"There now," she crooned. "Does that look like a babe to you?"

The girl gone to bed with a ration of gin and the mess cleaned up, Marla washed her hands and put her soiled apron into her bag before seeing Florence. The madam was as fussy as an old cat and Marla knew better than to enter her luxurious parlor in such a state as that.

Florence lay decorously across a long chaise, a glass of wine in her hand.

"Would you fancy a glass?" She rose immediately to pour. "It's from Milan."

"Thank you, madam."

Florence handed the glass to Marla, turning on her heel as precisely as a dancer. She returned to her artistic pose.

"I have a problem," she began.

"So you said." Marla sipped.

"There's someone tearing up girls on the street. I'm sure you've seen the papers."

"Of course," Marla said, taking a larger mouthful of the excellent wine. "Who has not?"

Florence sipped, unhurried. "I have my fingers in every pie in London," she sighed. "I can get silk from China. I can dine in the finest places, drink wine the queen would drink. I can even put a whore's child into a fine boy's school. However, I do not know someone who can be quick and silent and fearless. A hunter. A proper dealer of death. This is no ordinary errand."

Marla said nothing. When her glass was empty, Florence gestured to her that she might replenish it herself. Marla did.

"I can have a body buried," she said, sighing again. "I can have any name I like written on the headstone. But when I mention the actual work of this hunt, tracking down a dangerous predator," she said, coming down hard on that last word, "these hard men freeze up. Tell me it's too dangerous. I am done with detectives and I'll have no constable in my business. They hardly see this monster as a criminal, anyway. I need someone who solves problems as they come, without any nonsense about conscience and souls. Someone like you."

Marla said nothing.

"You face up to danger just fine."

"What I do," Marla began cautiously, but Florence cut her off.

"Oh, I know. I know it isn't the same. But I thought you might be interested in a sideline."

Marla gulped the wine. "Sideline. This *is* my sideline. I deliver babies, mostly. It was only when I realized how desperate—"

"Desperate," Florence said. "Yes, that's just what I am. Myself and my fellows on this street and across town and everywhere in London. Desperate because we know that no one will stop him. We've always had to do for ourselves, you know that. That's why you're here. That's why I pay you every month, and no matter how often I see you."

Marla nodded. "You're a businesswoman, Madam Florence."

"Of course I am," the woman said, the rouge spots on her cheek very red. "That's why I know there's something that must be done here. It must be done by someone who knows how to get about without being seen. Someone who can look helpless as a dove and then strike like a viper. No man can do this job, Marla. He has no eye for men. Do you understand me?"

Marla stared. She did understand, but she was uncertain, and more than a little afraid. Beside the fear, a small thrill ran like a lightning bolt through a storm cloud. Could she?

Florence set her glass on the low table and leaned forward. "This would be much more than your monthly pay," she said low, conspiratorially. "This is a bounty. The other madams and I have pooled money, thinking we'd have to pay a man. But you're better than any man. One hundred pounds."

Marla's ears rang at the thought of so much money. She could not hope to see so much in a year. Enough to do what she wanted most: sail to India and leave the bloody stews of London behind.

Florence, born and bred to read the faces of customers when the deal was on the table, smiled. She said it again: "One. Hundred. Pounds."

"I can do it," Marla said.

"I knew you could." Florence raised her glass and inclined her head toward the abortionist.

* * *

The rich woman had heard a name whispered here and there, the name of someone who could help her. It was in desperation that she sent her woman out into the night to drag Marla back to her home in Kensington.

Marla arrived, shaking the rain from the hood of her cloak just inside the servant's entrance.

She was led by candlelight to the serving-woman's bedroom, for her lady could not receive Marla in her marital bedchamber.

Marla found the dark-haired lady sitting on the edge of the bed, her hands in her lap. Marla said nothing. She waited.

The lady looked up, finally. "I'm so sorry to do this," she began. Her face broke apart. "But I am afraid." She sobbed into her soft hands.

Marla approached, standing before the woman. "It's alright, missus. It's alright. Can you tell me when the tide was in last?" She had long noted her high-class clients preference for vague euphemisms for a woman's monthly bleed.

"Yes, some three months ago."

Marla nodded. "And you've been ill? Hungry? Sore?" She gestured to her own breasts at this last, watching the woman.

The lady sighed. "I've had four other children. I'm sure."

"I can fix you up," Marla began.

"I'll pay you," the lady assured her. "But you must…"

"I must tell no one. For a lady's misfortunes belong to no one but her."

The lady nodded again, tear-stricken but resolute.

Marla laid her down and brought out her tools. She was as gentle as she knew how to be. The lady cried, but quietly.

She broke the quiet only once. "If… if only…"

"If only what, madam?" Marla was concentrating on making sure the woman didn't bleed to death.

"If only I wasn't sure he had been among trollops. I cannot believe I've been reduced to worrying about going blind and mad. Giving birth to a monster. That blackguard…" She gave way to low moaning.

Marla pushed the basin closer with her feet. The business was the same, whether youthful whore or middle-aged duchess. Always the same, despite how many coins jingled in her purse as she walked away.

"It's… only that…" the lady trailed off.

"What?" Marla asked, distracted.

"It's only that my woman tells me his valet cleaned blood out of his shoes. What sort of woman receives company when she has the curse? Is that something gentlemen like, despite their protestations? Is that why he's so cold to me? So distant? Does he want me to debase myself thus?"

"You're bleeding now," Marla said sharply, seeing the sudden downpour. She had learned from her mentor that sometimes the bleeding would not stop. Sometimes the woman just died.

She watched the volume of it in the basin. She waited.

"If only," the lady said dreamily, slipping away. "If only…"

Marla had dosed the woman with her own opium. She told the maid to watch her, feed her, give her gin, and get her through the night. She didn't so much flee as seek the shadows. She didn't so much smile as know what she knew.

She watched the house for days to no effect, with no payoff more than what was already in her purse.

She missed the lord of the house when he left. He was too stealthy. By the time she realized what had happened, the fourth (fifth?) body was cold and missing its uterus.

Most men couldn't point to the womb if you put a dueling pistol to their head. They'd point to a woman's sex or her stomach, but they'd never be able to describe it, or excise it on a bet.

Marla first acquainted herself with the story that had been in the papers. Some of them had happened quite a few days ago; she had to read greasy copies in a chip shop twice to catch up. She read that the Queen herself speculated that the man was a butcher, based on the precision of his cuts.

Marla knew that wasn't true. She had known butchers in her time; they knew only the animals they saw every day. A beef butcher had to be trained separately for mutton, and many of them could not be trusted to cut wild game.

No, the monster was a doctor. Marla was sure. She heard a rumor in the street that one victim had an ovary delicately removed and placed upon a bedsheet like an obscene piece of fruit. The butchers she had known could spot a liver, kidney, or heart. But the rest was just 'guts' and went into a bucket for sausages. They wouldn't know an ovary from a lung. They loved to make lewd jokes with testicles, but the interior mysteries of female animals were simply overlooked. No, a surgeon. There was no question in her mind.

She watched the doctors who attended births with her, waiting for him to reveal himself. She believed that any man who could murder a woman in such a way, carrying her womb away in his pocket, would be obvious. He would betray himself. She would know him by sight, by feel and scent.

She did not.

She came to suspect every doctor she knew, every gentleman, every man on the street. She shied away from their handshakes, their casual contact. She looked at men in pubs, assuming they were all killers. It turned her in on herself.

I could have been a doctor, had I been a boy. Half of them have no sense.

Florence sent for Marla one night, to show her that his handiwork was as gruesome as ever. The madam pulled back a maroon-stained sheet, showing her what he had left behind.

"Does that look like a girl to you?"

It had looked like a butcher's window. Florence had paid someone to weigh it and sink it in the river. She wanted no one to associate her house with a mess like that.

"You should call a constable," Marla told her.

"I called *you*," Florence said, before sweeping back through her front door.

The constabulary was the place to begin, after all. Marla had hoped to avoid it. The last thing she needed was for her face to be known to any London policeman who might see her around Whitechapel, Kensington, or Covent Garden under the wrong circumstances. But the rumors that swirled around were useless to her. He was well-dressed and he was shabby. He was tall and he was broad and short like an ape. He was swarthy as a Turk and white as a sheltered prince.

She considered going to the office of the Metropolitan Police and stealing a look at the files, but she could think of no pretense to get into the building except as a maid. But Marla knew the ways of the women who clean up after the world; they know where everything is and they do not make mistakes. She would be lost and obvious among them.

Instead, she went to the pub nearest the police department and waited for a shift to end whilst nursing a beer so thick she could almost take bites from it. The sun sank through the greenish, stinking fog. She itched to be out hunting; it had become her savage pleasure and most compelling. The light that filtered through the dirty windows made the shadows of men long and eerie when they burst in through the door.

She knew them by their uniforms, but she didn't spring to their sides like a camp follower. They took off their flat caps and a few loosened their stiff collars. They called for drinks and drinks came. They settled and sprawled, but their tongues were not yet loose. She waited. She drank.

It was an hour before she realized it was their payday, and another hour before the case came up. She tried to follow their jibes and speculations about their Commissioner Warren, or the various detectives on the case: Abberline, Andrews and Moore.

They scarcely knew more than she did. They were just as susceptible to rumor. They offered her only a few things she had not previously known. First, that there had been a girl named Smith who had sworn she had been set upon by a group of men instead of one. The girl had died, ramrodded through her most delicate parts and poisoned by her own bowels leaking into her bloodstream. Marla found she could not swallow. Second, there had been a young boy who had fallen victim in the same way, whose legs had been cut off his body.

She hadn't needed to speak to any of them, or even show them her face. She had merely sat nearby and stewed in the runoff of their professional horror.

That same foggy night, she went out to work. The labyrinthine run of alleys and narrow streets along the Thames were as familiar to her as the track to the racehorse, but the slanting darkness and swirling mist made them forbidding and strange.

The river reeked. Hollow-eyed women worked their customary eaves and corners, but Marla could smell their fear, cutting through the night. It was the goatish smell of prey. It was time to become one of them.

The whore in the popular imagination, Marla thought, was much better-dressed than the ones she met in practice. They typically wore the same clothes any other woman might, but unlaced and left open, as inviting as a door left ajar. Marla had clean hair and good teeth. Her shoes were whole. She found a class of girls she blended in with; not the poorest, but not the prettiest either. London was like a quilt of wealth and poverty, each square touching four others and switching from pretty gardens to putrid middens in a single street. In the spectrum of whoredom, she appraised herself well.

Some of them knew her, but no one asked why she was suddenly plying their trade. Each of them knew that circumstances in a woman's life could always induce her to this work. She interfered with no one, and so was left alone.

She didn't know how to do it. She had never frisked, never made advances, never whispered filth as some of them did to get their point across. She watched, still as a beetle, hardly ever speaking. Yet still they came.

On her first night she learned she must carry condoms. That night was very instructive, teaching her also that each deed could be over in minutes and that each and every one of them was boring and tender and dangerous. Boring in their desires. Tender in their need. Dangerous if refused or if they had come to work something out that their life gave them no other way to do so.

The first time one of them tried to hurt her, she wasn't expecting it. He was a mousy thing; a clark or perhaps a secretary. He had been businesslike and she had let her mind wander, allowing him use her body and getting on with the thing as usual. Until his hands settled around her neck, she had no idea what he was about.

Her thoughts were like startled birds. *This must be him it is him it is this is the one.*

The moment did not permit her the reflection to realize he held no knife. She reacted as she had rehearsed over and over again in her mind. Her trade had taught her the use of a few specific tools that no one would call a knife, yet many were sharp. Up her sleeve and nearly as long as her forearm, she carried her scraping tool. It was good, straight steel, and slim. Its end was gently scapulated with a slight curve and honed like a razor. The cutting edge was so small; a quarter of a fingernail. Her hands were accustomed to using it with great care, scraping a tiny bit at a time, cutting a hole between the world that is and the world yet to come.

But if she put her whole shoulder behind it, driving with her hip, the sharp edge would sink through the soft, stubbled flesh beneath a man's chin. The length of it would drive through his head with speed, stopping only at the roof of his skull. Marla could see the shock in his eyes in the last moment, when he was already dead but the news was still reaching all parts distant.

Panic had come right after, stark and unstoppable. She couldn't see or hear properly. She thought of India, her dreamy escape with her savings. She thought of the butcher shop thing that had once been a girl.

Marla dragged the body to the Thames. Every corner seemed to be full of eyes, but no voice called out to her. No police whistle shrieked out her guilt. The body floated away, face-down and caught in a busy bit of current with dirty papers and evil-looking foam.

She washed her hands in the water, though she knew it was filth. It was better than showing everyone the blood she wore. When she could get her bearings, she saw that she was close to Madam Florence's house. The kitchen girls there helped her wash up, thinking her disarray the result of no more than her usual business. Marla saw her own reflection haunting the porcelain basin and found that she could stand the sight of herself. Sorrow and guilt were remote possibilities. She felt relief and a giddy sort of glee that she had not been caught. Her work was not murder, she was very clear on that. This errand, however was exactly that. Yet she remained untroubled about it.

Maybe, sometimes, we're allowed to make our own justice. Maybe god is too busy with the affairs of men.

The next time it happened, she was doubly ready. A man threatened her with his polished black stick, its silver head glinting in the gaslight. He looked into her eyes like a thing that lives on terror and found her steely conviction where its meal should have been. He quailed and ran, leaving her to grip her metal pick and fight the tremors of excitement in her muscles for the rest of the night.

She did not walk the street every night. She couldn't keep up her work and her deadly charade. She wasn't sleeping well. She dreamt of the killer, but the killer was every man she saw. Every face she passed in a crowd turned into a leering solicitation. Each solicitation turned into the man who tried to throttle her, or the monster with the knife.

You're going about this like a fool. You're not a harlot. Think like a doctor.

She went over her smudgy newspapers and bought a paper map of London. Painstakingly, she mapped every murder that was surely his, and the ones that might have been. Hysteria was rampant in the streets and every murder was attached to the story of the Ripper. She stared at these at night, trying to trace where he might be coming from; where he might head home to.

There was no pattern. If the police had any truly useful information, they were keeping it from the press. The Ripper did not haunt outside of Whitechapel, but he had no favorite locations within it.

Of course not. If I returned to the same place again and again, no whore in London would go near there.

If I'm the Ripper, what do I want?

What do any of them want? What did that cunt who put his hands on my neck want?

But she couldn't answer that question. The answer wasn't in her.

Be the Ripper. Try to see London through his eyes. Stalk. Kill. Live in the pleasure of it.

A queer nostalgia rose in her. It wasn't pleasure that rose in her when she dropped a man into the river. It wasn't pleasure when she helped a girl out and saw her hale and well the very next week. It was something else. Something life rarely granted in all its chaos.

It was power.

I'm a doctor. Power is life and death. Power is mine. People look at my like I'm bloody God Almighty. But that isn't enough anymore. I want even more. I'm cleaning my knife. I'm thinking of taking a walk. I'm planning, I'm always planning. I'm thinking that girl I saw in the alley back there has no mother, no husband to miss her. I can take her apart, little by little. I can make it last a long time. I can enjoy it. There will be none to stop me.

Maybe I will wash my hands in the Thames. Maybe they will never catch me, and I will do it forever and ever, power without end.

She went back to her flat one night and spent time scrubbing blood out of her clothes. Long inured to the body's humors, she knew just how to do it. The smell on her was like birth: blood and terror and the sea. But this wasn't that. Her power of life and death was different than his.

Piece by piece she stripped over the wash basin, scrubbing with lye soap that turned her fingers bright pink.

When she came to her shoes, she knew. She remembered her last appointment in Kensington.

Blood on his shoes. Among the trollops. And wasn't her husband a surgeon?

She couldn't sleep. She tried all night to come up with a pretense to visit the house again and could not. There was no reason to return. The lady of the house was well by now and would not want to be reminded of her sin.

Marla lingered in doorways and beneath the eaves to catch him. It thrilled her to think of herself hunting the hunter.

She caught a flash of his cloak as he entered his carriage, dressed as fine as though he went to the theater.

Does that look like a hunter to you?

She could not follow the carriage, but she marked it. She found it again outside the opera house. There was no way to follow him here. Rich London would not suffer her. Poor London would continue to suffer him.

After the opera, there was another bloody wreck of a girl. Marla took up an alley between that spot and the opera house. She killed once or twice again. She told them her name was India when they asked.

It was autumn when he finally appeared. She had been worried that she would have to hunt him again after the winter had passed, his trail gone as cold as that of a white wolf. He had approached her, staggering and pretending to be drunk. She knew him by his finery. She was ready, tool up her sleeve. She opened her arms and called him 'love.'

He had his knife out quick, in the hand he had shoved up under her skirt. He held it cold, balanced against his thumb, the point digging into the soft seam that led downward from her navel.

"I'll cut your womanhood out," he breathed hotly against her neck. "And then I'll cut your face off."

Fear deserted her in a moment and she almost laughed in his face. This was the terror of Whitechapel? He had no stealth and almost no craft. He announced what he was going to do like the mere mention of it would terrify her into immobility.

But that's what's always happened for him. He tells people he's going to cut them on the operating table and they quail before him. He tells his wife she has no right to question him and she keeps her silence. He tells his driver where to go and the carriage takes him there, without question or argument.

He's killed more than I have, but that isn't where his mastery lies. The kill is the ending. He's here for terror.

Don't give it to him.

She put her hand on top of his without pushing, just gentle pressure. Her voice was sweet and pleasant still, as if she hadn't heard him. "You don't have to threaten me, sir. I'm here to make a living is all."

His face pulled away with surprise. He recovered, towering over her, brow lowering. "This is the last night of your life, whore."

"Why don't we make it a night to remember, gov'ner?"

He pressed the knife hard against her belly, beginning to prick her skin.

"Remember me by this, you witless harlot. Though... not for long."

She did laugh then, she couldn't help it. She twisted her waist away from him, moving the tip of his knife and shocking him again.

She slowly pulled out her own weapon: the slim metal tool of her trade. Easily concealed, sharp as a needle, and nobody would call it a knife. This was the moment. This was the death that would buy her freedom. What had other deaths bought? What did it matter?

There was only life and the freedom to live it. There was only death and the knowledge that sometimes it was the right gift, the only gift she could give.

"Come here, love." She pulled his head close to her bosom, as if to invite him to kiss her neck.

"Strumpet," he said, his pleasure evident in the word as he growled it out. "I am death itself and your time has come." The hand holding the knife grew rigid. He pulled his face up, inches from hers, to look into her eyes. His breath came faster. His gaze was blue, assured, noble. He had never heard the word 'no' in his life.

"No," she said to him now, purring like a cat. She was interested in his terror now. What a rare bird it would be. But there wasn't time.

"No man can say for sure when his time has come," she breathed back lightly before bringing her hand up as if to wrap her arms around his neck. She sank her long, piercing instrument into the dark hole of his ear. Once she pushed it to the sticking place, she began to chivvy madly, bringing the rain of blood that would change the world that was into the world that was never to be.

The look on his face wasn't properly described as fear, but only surprise. It showed the absolute shock of one who glimpses a world they had never imagined to exist. It was only an instant before he vacated his blue eyes forever, but it was a good instant. She would never forget it.

She ripped her tool out and gore spattered the alley wall. The bleeding started and her job was done, just like always. He went rigid, then slack all over. His hands opened up and relinquished his power. His own knife she found between her feet. She dropped it into the river after him, blood still trickling from his ear as she rolled him off the dock.

The papers didn't believe he was dead. His story only grew after Marla's job was done, he became a ghost, or an idea. His real power had lain in fear. It had been no trick at all to do him in. He was no more than a man, and no more troublesome than something that would never be one. Marla had had enough of legend to last her a lifetime. It wasn't true that the women she helped were damned for eight or ten weeks' worth of mistake, but legend persisted. The Ripper had been a clumsy, arrogant man who preyed on the least of women, the ones with no one to miss them, but legend was already making him into more than most men before his body was cold.

Marla would never know what it was to be feared, she knew as she packed to leave the island nation that had always been her home. Instead, her power lay thus far in invisibility. In India, things might be different. She had the power to make things different.

A day after Marla had sailed, two constables strolling past a flotilla of garbage and sewer in the stinking river looked out across a grey London morning. In the trash, one of them spotted the glint of a gold watch chain.

Nine Points of the Law

E.W. Hornung

"WELL," said Raffles, "what do you make of it?"

I read the advertisement once more before replying. It was in the last column of the *Daily Telegraph*, and it ran:

> TWO THOUSAND POUNDS REWARD
> *The above sum may be earned by any one qualified to undertake delicate mission and prepared to run certain risk. – Apply by telegram, Security, London.*

"I think," said I, "it's the most extraordinary advertisement that ever got into print!"

Raffles smiled.

"Not quite all that, Bunny; still, extraordinary enough, I grant you."

"Look at the figure!"

"It is certainly large."

"And the mission – and the risk!"

"Yes; the combination is frank, to say the least of it. But the really original point is requiring applications by telegram to a telegraphic address! There's something in the fellow who thought of that, and something in his game; with one word he chokes off the million who answer an advertisement every day – when they can raise the stamp. My answer cost me five bob; but then I prepaid another."

"You don't mean to say that you've applied?"

"Rather," said Raffles. "I want two thousand pounds as much as any man."

"Put your own name?"

"Well – no, Bunny, I didn't. In point of fact I smell something interesting and illegal, and you know what a cautious chap I am. I signed myself Glasspool, care of Hickey, 38, Conduit Street; that's my tailor, and after sending the wire I went round and told him what to expect. He promised to send the reply along the moment it came. I shouldn't be surprised if that's it!"

And he was gone before a double-knock on the outer door had done ringing through the rooms, to return next minute with an open telegram and a face full of news.

"What do you think?" said he. "Security's that fellow Addenbrooke, the police-court lawyer, and he wants to see me INSTANTER!"

"Do you know him, then?"

"Merely by repute. I only hope he doesn't know me. He's the chap who got six weeks for sailing too close to the wind in the Sutton-Wilmer case; everybody wondered why he wasn't struck off the rolls. Instead of that he's got a first-rate practice on the seamy side, and every blackguard with half a case takes it straight to Bennett Addenbrooke. He's probably the one man who would have the cheek to put in an advertisement like that, and the one man who could do it without exciting suspicion. It's simply in his line; but you may be sure there's something shady at the bottom of it. The odd thing is that I have long made up my mind to go to Addenbrooke myself if accidents should happen."

"And you're going to him now?"

"This minute," said Raffles, brushing his hat; "and so are you."

"But I came in to drag you out to lunch."

"You shall lunch with me when we've seen this fellow. Come on, Bunny, and we'll choose your name on the way. Mine's Glasspool, and don't you forget it."

Mr. Bennett Addenbrooke occupied substantial offices in Wellington Street, Strand, and was out when we arrived; but he had only just gone "over the way to the court"; and five minutes sufficed to produce a brisk, fresh-colored, resolute-looking man, with a very confident, rather festive air, and black eyes that opened wide at the sight of Raffles.

"Mr. – Glasspool?" exclaimed the lawyer.

"My name," said Raffles, with dry effrontery.

"Not up at Lord's, however!" said the other, slyly. "My dear sir, I have seen you take far too many wickets to make any mistake!"

For a single moment Raffles looked venomous; then he shrugged and smiled, and the smile grew into a little cynical chuckle.

"So you have bowled me out in my turn?" said he. "Well, I don't think there's anything to explain. I am harder up than I wished to admit under my own name, that's all, and I want that thousand pounds reward."

"Two thousand," said the solicitor. "And the man who is not above an alias happens to be just the sort of man I want; so don't let that worry you, my dear sir. The matter, however, is of a strictly private and confidential character." And he looked very hard at me.

"Quite so," said Raffles. "But there was something about a risk?"

"A certain risk is involved."

"Then surely three heads will be better than two. I said I wanted that thousand pounds; my friend here wants the other. We are both cursedly hard up, and we go into this thing together or not at all. Must you have his name too? I should give him my real one, Bunny."

Mr. Addenbrooke raised his eyebrows over the card I found for him; then he drummed upon it with his finger-nail, and his embarrassment expressed itself in a puzzled smile.

"The fact is, I find myself in a difficulty," he confessed at last. "Yours is the first reply I have received; people who can afford to send long telegrams don't rush to the advertisements in the Daily Telegraph; but, on the other hand, I was not quite prepared to hear from men like yourselves. Candidly, and on consideration, I am not sure that you ARE the stamp of men for me – men who belong to good clubs! I rather intended to appeal to the – er – adventurous classes."

"We are adventurers," said Raffles gravely.

"But you respect the law?"

The black eyes gleamed shrewdly.

"We are not professional rogues, if that's what you mean," said Raffles, smiling. "But on our beam-ends we are; we would do a good deal for a thousand pounds apiece, eh, Bunny?"

"Anything," I murmured.

The solicitor rapped his desk.

"I'll tell you what I want you to do. You can but refuse. It's illegal, but it's illegality in a good cause; that's the risk, and my client is prepared to pay for it. He will pay for the attempt, in case of failure; the money is as good as yours once you consent to run the risk. My client is Sir Bernard Debenham, of Broom Hall, Esher."

"I know his son," I remarked.

Raffles knew him too, but said nothing, and his eye drooped disapproval in my direction. Bennett Addenbrooke turned to me.

"Then," said he, "you have the privilege of knowing one of the most complete young black-guards about town, and the fons et origo of the whole trouble. As you know the son, you may know the father too, at all events by reputation; and in that case I needn't tell you that he is a very peculiar man. He lives alone in a storehouse of treasures which no eyes but his ever behold. He is said to have the finest collection of pictures in the south of England, though nobody ever sees them to judge; pictures, fiddles and furniture are his hobby, and he is undoubtedly very eccentric. Nor can one deny that there has been considerable eccentricity in his treatment of his son. For years Sir Bernard paid his debts, and the other day, without the slightest warning, not only refused to do so any more, but absolutely stopped the lad's allowance. Well, I'll tell you what has happened; but first of all you must know, or you may remember, that I appeared for young Debenham in a little scrape he got into a year or two ago. I got him off all right, and Sir Bernard paid me handsomely on the nail. And no more did I hear or see of either of them until one day last week."

The lawyer drew his chair nearer ours, and leant forward with a hand on either knee.

"On Tuesday of last week I had a telegram from Sir Bernard; I was to go to him at once. I found him waiting for me in the drive; without a word he led me to the picture-gallery, which was locked and darkened, drew up a blind, and stood simply pointing to an empty picture-frame. It was a long time before I could get a word out of him. Then at last he told me that that frame had contained one of the rarest and most valuable pictures in England – in the world – an original Velasquez. I have checked this," said the lawyer, "and it seems literally true; the picture was a portrait of the Infanta Maria Teresa, said to be one of the artist's greatest works, second only to another portrait of one of the Popes in Rome – so they told me at the National Gallery, where they had its history by heart. They say there that the picture is practically priceless. And young Debenham has sold it for five thousand pounds!"

"The deuce he has," said Raffles.

I inquired who had bought it.

"A Queensland legislator of the name of Craggs – the Hon. John Montagu Craggs, M.L.C., to give him his full title. Not that we knew anything about him on Tuesday last; we didn't even know for certain that young Debenham had stolen the picture. But he had gone down for money on the Monday evening, had been refused, and it was plain enough that he had helped himself in this way; he had threatened revenge, and this was it. Indeed, when I hunted him up in town on the Tuesday night, he confessed as much in the most brazen manner imaginable. But he wouldn't tell me who was the purchaser, and finding out took the rest of the week; but I did find out, and a nice time I've had of it ever since! Backwards and forwards between Esher and the Metropole, where the Queenslander is staying, sometimes twice a day; threats, offers, prayers, entreaties, not one of them a bit of good!"

"But," said Raffles, "surely it's a clear case? The sale was illegal; you can pay him back his money and force him to give the picture up."

"Exactly; but not without an action and a public scandal, and that my client declines to face. He would rather lose even his picture than have the whole thing get into the papers; he has disowned his son, but he will not disgrace him; yet his picture he must have by hook or crook, and there's the rub! I am to get it back by fair means or foul. He gives me carte blanche in the matter, and, I verily believe, would throw in a blank check if asked. He offered one to the Queenslander, but Craggs simply tore it in two; the one old boy is as much a character as the other, and between the two of them I'm at my wits' end."

"So you put that advertisement in the paper?" said Raffles, in the dry tones he had adopted throughout the interview.

"As a last resort. I did."

"And you wish us to STEAL this picture?"

It was magnificently said; the lawyer flushed from his hair to his collar.

"I knew you were not the men!" he groaned. "I never thought of men of your stamp! But it's not stealing," he exclaimed heatedly; "it's recovering stolen property. Besides, Sir Bernard will pay him his five thousand as soon as he has the picture; and, you'll see, old Craggs will be just as loath to let it come out as Sir Bernard himself. No, no – it's an enterprise, an adventure, if you like – but not stealing."

"You yourself mentioned the law," murmured Raffles.

"And the risk," I added.

"We pay for that," he said once more.

"But not enough," said Raffles, shaking his head. "My good sir, consider what it means to us. You spoke of those clubs; we should not only get kicked out of them, but put in prison like common burglars! It's true we're hard up, but it simply isn't worth it at the price. Double your stakes, and I for one am your man."

Addenbrooke wavered.

"Do you think you could bring it off?"

"We could try."

"But you have no—"

"Experience? Well, hardly!"

"And you would really run the risk for four thousand pounds?"

Raffles looked at me. I nodded.

"We would," said he, "and blow the odds!"

"It's more than I can ask my client to pay," said Addenbrooke, growing firm.

"Then it's more than you can expect us to risk."

"You are in earnest?"

"God wot!"

"Say three thousand if you succeed!"

"Four is our figure, Mr. Addenbrooke."

"Then I think it should be nothing if you fail."

"Doubles or quits?" cried Raffles. "Well, that's sporting. Done!"

Addenbrooke opened his lips, half rose, then sat back in his chair, and looked long and shrewdly at Raffles – never once at me.

"I know your bowling," said he reflectively. "I go up to Lord's whenever I want an hour's real rest, and I've seen you bowl again and again – yes, and take the best wickets in England on a plumb pitch. I don't forget the last Gentleman and Players; I was there. You're up to every trick – every one … I'm inclined to think that if anybody could bowl out this old Australian … Damme, I believe you're my very man!"

The bargain was clinched at the Cafe Royal, where Bennett Addenbrooke insisted on playing host at an extravagant luncheon. I remember that he took his whack of champagne with the nervous freedom of a man at high pressure, and have no doubt I kept him in countenance by an equal indulgence; but Raffles, ever an exemplar in such matters, was more abstemious even than his wont, and very poor company to boot. I can see him now, his eyes in his plate – thinking – thinking. I can see the solicitor glancing from him to me in an apprehension of which I did my best to disabuse him by reassuring looks. At the close Raffles apologized for his preoccupation, called for an A.B.C. time-table, and announced his intention of catching the 3.2 to Esher.

"You must excuse me, Mr. Addenbrooke," said he, "but I have my own idea, and for the moment I should much prefer to keep it to myself. It may end in fizzle, so I would rather not speak about it to either of you just yet. But speak to Sir Bernard I must, so will you write me one line to him on your card? Of course, if you wish, you must come down with me and hear what I say; but I really don't see much point in it."

And as usual Raffles had his way, though Bennett Addenbrooke showed some temper when he was gone, and I myself shared his annoyance to no small extent. I could only tell him that it was in the nature of Raffles to be self-willed and secretive, but that no man of my acquaintance had half his audacity and determination; that I for my part would trust him through and through, and let him gang his own gait every time. More I dared not say, even to remove those chill misgivings with which I knew that the lawyer went his way.

That day I saw no more of Raffles, but a telegram reached me when I was dressing for dinner:

"Be in your rooms tomorrow from noon and keep rest of day clear, Raffles."

It had been sent off from Waterloo at 6.42.

So Raffles was back in town; at an earlier stage of our relations I should have hunted him up then and there, but now I knew better. His telegram meant that he had no desire for my society that night or the following forenoon; that when he wanted me I should see him soon enough.

And see him I did, towards one o'clock next day. I was watching for him from my window in Mount Street, when he drove up furiously in a hansom, and jumped out without a word to the man. I met him next minute at the lift gates, and he fairly pushed me back into my rooms.

"Five minutes, Bunny!" he cried. "Not a moment more."

And he tore off his coat before flinging himself into the nearest chair.

"I'm fairly on the rush," he panted; "having the very devil of a time! Not a word till I tell you all I've done. I settled my plan of campaign yesterday at lunch. The first thing was to get in with this man Craggs; you can't break into a place like the Metropole, it's got to be done from the inside. Problem one, how to get at the fellow. Only one sort of pretext would do – it must be something to do with this blessed picture, so that I might see where he'd got it and all that. Well, I couldn't go and ask to see it out of curiosity, and I couldn't go as a second representative of the other old chap, and it was thinking how I could go that made me such a bear at lunch. But I saw my way before we got up. If I could only lay hold of a copy of the picture I might ask leave to go and compare it with the original. So down I went to Esher to find out if there was a copy in existence, and was at Broom Hall for one hour and a half yesterday afternoon. There was no copy there, but they must exist, for Sir Bernard himself (there's 'copy' THERE!) has allowed a couple to be made since the picture has been in his possession. He hunted up the painters' addresses, and the rest of the evening I spent in hunting up the painters themselves; but their work had been done on commission; one copy had gone out of the country, and I'm still on the track of the other."

"Then you haven't seen Craggs yet?"

"Seen him and made friends with him, and if possible he's the funnier old cuss of the two; but you should study 'em both. I took the bull by the horns this morning, went in and lied like Ananias, and it was just as well I did – the old ruffian sails for Australia by tomorrow's boat. I told him a man wanted to sell me a copy of the celebrated Infanta Maria Teresa of Velasquez, that I'd been down to the supposed owner of the picture, only to find that he had just sold it to him. You should have seen his face when I told him that! He grinned all round his wicked old head. 'Did OLD Debenham admit the sale?' says he; and when I said he had he chuckled to himself for about five minutes. He was so pleased that he did just what I hoped he would do; he showed me the great picture – luckily it isn't by any means a large one – also the case he's got it in. It's an iron map-case in which he brought over the plans of his land in Brisbane; he wants to know who would suspect it of containing an Old Master, too? But he's had it fitted with a new Chubb's lock, and I managed to take an interest in the key while he was gloating over the canvas. I had the wax in the palm of my hand, and I shall make my duplicate this afternoon."

Raffles looked at his watch and jumped up saying he had given me a minute too much.

"By the way," he added, "you've got to dine with him at the Metropole tonight!"

"I?"

"Yes; don't look so scared. Both of us are invited – I swore you were dining with me. I accepted for us both; but I sha'n't be there."

His clear eye was upon me, bright with meaning and with mischief.

I implored him to tell me what his meaning was.

"You will dine in his private sitting-room," said Raffles; "it adjoins his bedroom. You must keep him sitting as long as possible, Bunny, and talking all the time!"

In a flash I saw his plan.

"You're going for the picture while we're at dinner?"

"I am."

"If he hears you?"

"He sha'n't."

"But if he does!"

And I fairly trembled at the thought.

"If he does," said Raffles, "there will be a collision, that's all. Revolver would be out of place in the Metropole, but I shall certainly take a life-preserver."

"But it's ghastly!" I cried. "To sit and talk to an utter stranger and to know that you're at work in the next room!"

"Two thousand apiece," said Raffles, quietly.

"Upon my soul I believe I shall give it away!"

"Not you, Bunny. I know you better than you know yourself."

He put on his coat and his hat.

"What time have I to be there?" I asked him, with a groan.

"Quarter to eight. There will be a telegram from me saying I can't turn up. He's a terror to talk, you'll have no difficulty in keeping the ball rolling; but head him off his picture for all you're worth. If he offers to show it to you, say you must go. He locked up the case elaborately this afternoon, and there's no earthly reason why he should unlock it again in this hemisphere."

"Where shall I find you when I get away?"

"I shall be down at Esher. I hope to catch the 9.55."

"But surely I can see you again this afternoon?" I cried in a ferment, for his hand was on the door. "I'm not half coached up yet! I know I shall make a mess of it!"

"Not you," he said again, "but *I* shall if I waste any more time. I've got a deuce of a lot of rushing about to do yet. You won't find me at my rooms. Why not come down to Esher yourself by the last train? That's it – down you come with the latest news! I'll tell old Debenham to expect you: he shall give us both a bed. By Jove! he won't be able to do us too well if he's got his picture."

"If!" I groaned as he nodded his adieu; and he left me limp with apprehension, sick with fear, in a perfectly pitiable condition of pure stage-fright.

For, after all, I had only to act my part; unless Raffles failed where he never did fail, unless Raffles the neat and noiseless was for once clumsy and inept, all I had to do was indeed to "smile and smile and be a villain." I practiced that smile half the afternoon. I rehearsed putative parts in hypothetical conversations. I got up stories. I dipped in a book on Queensland at the club. And at last it was 7.45, and I was making my bow to a somewhat elderly man with a small bald head and a retreating brow.

"So you're Mr. Raffles's friend?" said he, overhauling me rather rudely with his light small eyes. "Seen anything of him? Expected him early to show me something, but he's never come."

No more, evidently, had his telegram, and my troubles were beginning early. I said I had not seen Raffles since one o'clock, telling the truth with unction while I could; even as we spoke there came a knock at the door; it was the telegram at last, and, after reading it himself, the Queenslander handed it to me.

"Called out of town!" he grumbled. "Sudden illness of near relative! What near relatives has he got?"

I knew of none, and for an instant I quailed before the perils of invention; then I replied that I had never met any of his people, and again felt fortified by my veracity.

"Thought you were bosom pals?" said he, with (as I imagined) a gleam of suspicion in his crafty little eyes.

"Only in town," said I. "I've never been to his place."

"Well," he growled, "I suppose it can't be helped. Don't know why he couldn't come and have his dinner first. Like to see the death-bed I'D go to without MY dinner; it's a full-skin billet, if you ask me. Well, must just dine without him, and he'll have to buy his pig in a poke after all. Mind touching that bell? Suppose you know what he came to see me about? Sorry I sha'n't see him again, for his own sake. I liked Raffles – took to him amazingly. He's a cynic. Like cynics. One myself. Rank bad form of his mother or his aunt, and I hope she will go and kick the bucket."

I connect these specimens of his conversation, though they were doubtless detached at the time, and interspersed with remarks of mine here and there. They filled the interval until dinner was served, and they gave me an impression of the man which his every subsequent utterance confirmed. It was an impression which did away with all remorse for my treacherous presence at his table. He was that terrible type, the Silly Cynic, his aim a caustic commentary on all things and all men, his achievement mere vulgar irreverence and unintelligent scorn. Ill-bred and ill-informed, he had (on his own showing) fluked into fortune on a rise in land; yet cunning he possessed, as well as malice, and he chuckled till he choked over the misfortunes of less astute speculators in the same boom. Even now I cannot feel much compunction for my behavior by the Hon. J. M. Craggs, M.L.C.

But never shall I forget the private agonies of the situation, the listening to my host with one ear and for Raffles with the other! Once I heard him – though the rooms were not divided by the old-fashioned folding-doors, and though the door that did divide them was not only shut but richly curtained, I could have sworn I heard him once. I spilt my wine and laughed at the top of my voice at some coarse sally of my host's. And I heard nothing more, though my ears were on the strain. But later, to my horror, when the waiter had finally withdrawn, Craggs himself sprang up and rushed to his bedroom without a word. I sat like stone till he returned.

"Thought I heard a door go," he said. "Must have been mistaken … imagination … gave me quite a turn. Raffles tell you priceless treasure I got in there?"

It was the picture at last; up to this point I had kept him to Queensland and the making of his pile. I tried to get him back there now, but in vain. He was reminded of his great ill-gotten possession. I said that Raffles had just mentioned it, and that set him off. With the confidential garrulity of a man who has dined too well, he plunged into his darling topic, and I looked past him at the clock. It was only a quarter to ten.

In common decency I could not go yet. So there I sat (we were still at port) and learnt what had originally fired my host's ambition to possess what he was pleased to call a "real, genuine, twin-screw, double-funnelled, copper-bottomed Old Master"; it was to "go one better" than some rival legislator of pictorial proclivities. But even an epitome of his monologue would be so much weariness; suffice it that it ended inevitably in the invitation I had dreaded all the evening.

"But you must see it. Next room. This way."

"Isn't it packed up?" I inquired hastily.

"Lock and key. That's all."

"Pray don't trouble," I urged.

"Trouble be hanged!" said he. "Come along."

And all at once I saw that to resist him further would be to heap suspicion upon myself against the moment of impending discovery. I therefore followed him into his bedroom without further protest, and suffered him first to show me the iron map-case which stood in one corner; he took a crafty pride in this receptacle, and I thought he would never cease descanting on its innocent appearance and its Chubb's lock. It seemed an interminable age before the key was in the latter. Then the ward clicked, and my pulse stood still.

"By Jove!" I cried next instant.

The canvas was in its place among the maps!

"Thought it would knock you," said Craggs, drawing it out and unrolling it for my benefit. "Grand thing, ain't it? Wouldn't think it had been painted two hundred and thirty years? It has, though, MY word! Old Johnson's face will be a treat when he sees it; won't go bragging about HIS pictures much more. Why, this one's worth all the pictures in Colony o' Queensland put together. Worth fifty thousand pounds, my boy – and I got it for five!"

He dug me in the ribs, and seemed in the mood for further confidences. My appearance checked him, and he rubbed his hands.

"If you take it like that," he chuckled, "how will old Johnson take it? Go out and hang himself to his own picture-rods, I hope!"

Heaven knows what I contrived to say at last. Struck speechless first by my relief, I continued silent from a very different cause. A new tangle of emotions tied my tongue. Raffles had failed – Raffles had failed! Could I not succeed? Was it too late? Was there no way?

"So long," he said, taking a last look at the canvas before he rolled it up – "so long till we get to Brisbane."

The flutter I was in as he closed the case!

"For the last time," he went on, as his keys jingled back into his pocket. "It goes straight into the strong-room on board."

For the last time! If I could but send him out to Australia with only its legitimate contents in his precious map-case! If I could but succeed where Raffles had failed!

We returned to the other room. I have no notion how long he talked, or what about. Whiskey and soda-water became the order of the hour. I scarcely touched it, but he drank copiously, and before eleven I left him incoherent. And the last train for Esher was the 11.50 out of Waterloo.

I took a hansom to my rooms. I was back at the hotel in thirteen minutes. I walked upstairs. The corridor was empty; I stood an instant on the sitting-room threshold, heard a snore within, and admitted myself softly with my gentleman's own key, which it had been a very simple matter to take away with me.

Craggs never moved; he was stretched on the sofa fast asleep. But not fast enough for me. I saturated my handkerchief with the chloroform I had brought, and laid it gently over his mouth. Two or three stertorous breaths, and the man was a log.

I removed the handkerchief; I extracted the keys from his pocket.

In less than five minutes I put them back, after winding the picture about my body beneath my Inverness cape. I took some whiskey and soda-water before I went.

The train was easily caught – so easily that I trembled for ten minutes in my first-class smoking carriage – in terror of every footstep on the platform, in unreasonable terror till the end. Then at last I sat back and lit a cigarette, and the lights of Waterloo reeled out behind.

Some men were returning from the theatre. I can recall their conversation even now. They were disappointed with the piece they had seen. It was one of the later Savoy operas, and they spoke wistfully of the days of "Pinafore" and "Patience." One of them hummed a stave, and there was an argument as to whether the air was out of "Patience" or the "Mikado." They all got out at Surbiton, and I was alone with my triumph for a few intoxicating minutes. To think that I had succeeded where Raffles had failed!

Of all our adventures this was the first in which I had played a commanding part; and, of them all, this was infinitely the least discreditable. It left me without a conscientious qualm; I had but robbed a robber, when all was said. And I had done it myself, single-handed – ipse egomet!

I pictured Raffles, his surprise, his delight. He would think a little more of me in future. And that future, it should be different. We had two thousand pounds apiece – surely enough to start afresh as honest men – and all through me!

In a glow I sprang out at Esher, and took the one belated cab that was waiting under the bridge. In a perfect fever I beheld Broom Hall, with the lower story still lit up, and saw the front door open as I climbed the steps.

"Thought it was you," said Raffles cheerily. "It's all right. There's a bed for you. Sir Bernard's sitting up to shake your hand."

His good spirits disappointed me. But I knew the man: he was one of those who wear their brightest smile in the blackest hour. I knew him too well by this time to be deceived.

"I've got it!" I cried in his ear. "I've got it!"

"Got what?" he asked me, stepping back.

"The picture!"

"WHAT?"

"The picture. He showed it me. You had to go without it; I saw that. So I determined to have it. And here it is."

"Let's see," said Raffles grimly.

I threw off my cape and unwound the canvas from about my body. While I was doing so an untidy old gentleman made his appearance in the hall, and stood looking on with raised eyebrows.

"Looks pretty fresh for an Old Master, doesn't she?" said Raffles.

His tone was strange. I could only suppose that he was jealous of my success.

"So Craggs said. I hardly looked at it myself."

"Well, look now – look closely. By Jove, I must have faked her better than I thought!"

"It's a copy!" I cried.

"It's THE copy," he answered. "It's the copy I've been tearing all over the country to procure. It's the copy I faked back and front, so that, on your own showing, it imposed upon Craggs, and might have made him happy for life. And you go and rob him of that!"

I could not speak.

"How did you manage it?" inquired Sir Bernard Debenham.

"Have you killed him?" asked Raffles sardonically.

I did not look at him; I turned to Sir Bernard Debenham, and to him I told my story, hoarsely, excitedly, for it was all that I could do to keep from breaking down. But as I spoke I became calmer, and I finished in mere bitterness, with the remark that another time Raffles might tell me what he meant to do.

"Another time!" he cried instantly. "My dear Bunny, you speak as though we were going to turn burglars for a living!"

"I trust you won't," said Sir Bernard, smiling, "for you are certainly two very daring young men. Let us hope our friend from Queensland will do as he said, and not open his map-case till he gets back there. He will find my check awaiting him, and I shall be very much surprised if he troubles any of us again."

Raffles and I did not speak till I was in the room which had been prepared for me. Nor was I anxious to do so then. But he followed me and took my hand.

"Bunny," said he, "don't you be hard on a fellow! I was in the deuce of a hurry, and didn't know that I should ever get what I wanted in time, and that's a fact. But it serves me right that you should have gone and undone one of the best things I ever did. As for YOUR handiwork, old chap, you won't mind my saying that I didn't think you had it in you. In future—"

"Don't talk to me about the future!" I cried. "I hate the whole thing! I'm going to chuck it up!"

"So am I," said Raffles, "when I've made my pile."

The Raffles Relics

E.W. Hornung

IT WAS IN one of the magazines for December, 1899, that an article appeared which afforded our minds a brief respite from the then consuming excitement of the war in South Africa. These were the days when Raffles really had white hair, and when he and I were nearing the end of our surreptitious second innings, as professional cracksmen of the deadliest dye. Piccadilly and the Albany knew us no more. But we still operated, as the spirit tempted us, from our latest and most idyllic base, on the borders of Ham Common. Recreation was our greatest want; and though we had both descended to the humble bicycle, a lot of reading was forced upon us in the winter evenings. Thus the war came as a boon to us both. It not only provided us with an honest interest in life, but gave point and zest to innumerable spins across Richmond Park, to the nearest paper shop; and it was from such an expedition that I returned with inflammatory matter unconnected with the war. The magazine was one of those that are read (and sold) by the million; the article was rudely illustrated on every other page. Its subject was the so-called Black Museum at Scotland Yard; and from the catchpenny text we first learned that the gruesome show was now enriched by a special and elaborate exhibit known as the Raffles Relics.

"Bunny," said Raffles, "this is fame at last! It is no longer notoriety; it lifts one out of the ruck of robbers into the society of the big brass gods, whose little delinquencies are written in water by the finger of time. The Napoleon Relics we know, the Nelson Relics we've heard about, and here are mine!"

"Which I wish to goodness we could see," I added, longingly. Next moment I was sorry I had spoken. Raffles was looking at me across the magazine. There was a smile on his lips that I knew too well, a light in his eyes that I had kindled.

"What an excellent idea? he exclaimed, quite softly, as though working it out already in his brain.

"I didn't mean it for one," I answered, "and no more do you."

"Certainly I do," said Raffles. "I was never more serious in my life."

"You would march into Scotland Yard in broad daylight?"

"In broad lime-light," he answered, studying the magazine again, "to set eyes on my own once more. Why here they all are, Bunny – you never told me there was an illustration. That's the chest you took to your bank with me inside, and those must be my own rope-ladder and things on top. They produce so badly in the baser magazines that it's impossible to swear to them; there's nothing for it but a visit of inspection."

"Then you can pay it alone," said I grimly. "You may have altered, but they'd know me at a glance."

"By all means, Bunny, if you'll get me the pass."

"A pass?" I cried triumphantly. "Of course we should have to get one, and of course that puts an end to the whole idea. Who on earth would give a pass for this show, of all others, to an old prisoner like me?"

Raffles addressed himself to the reading of the magazine with a shrug that showed some temper.

"The fellow who wrote this article got one," said he shortly. "He got it from his editor, and you can get one from yours if you tried. But pray don't try, Bunny: it would be too terrible for you to risk a moment's embarrassment to gratify a mere whim of mine. And if I went instead of you and got spotted, which is so likely with this head of hair, and the general belief in my demise, the consequences to you would be too awful to contemplate! Don't contemplate them, my dear fellow. And do let me read my magazine."

Need I add that I set about the rash endeavor without further expostulation? I was used to such ebullitions from the altered Raffles of these later days, and I could well understand them. All the inconvenience of the new conditions fell on him. I had purged my known offences by imprisonment, whereas Raffles was merely supposed to have escaped punishment in death. The result was that I could rush in where Raffles feared to tread, and was his plenipotentiary in all honest dealings with the outer world. It could not but gall him to be so dependent upon me, and it was for me to minimize the humiliation by scrupulously avoiding the least semblance of an abuse of that power which I now had over him. Accordingly, though with much misgiving, I did his ticklish behest in Fleet Street, where, despite my past, I was already making a certain lowly footing for myself. Success followed as it will when one longs to fail; and one fine evening I returned to Ham Common with a card from the Convict Supervision Office, New Scotland Yard, which I treasure to this day. I am surprised to see that it was undated, and might still almost "Admit Bearer to see the Museum," to say nothing of the bearer's friends, since my editor's name "and party" is scrawled beneath the legend.

"But he doesn't want to come," as I explained to Raffles. "And it means that we can both go, if we both like."

Raffles looked at me with a wry smile; he was in good enough humor now.

"It would be rather dangerous, Bunny. If they spotted you, they might think of me."

"But you say they'll never know you now."

"I don't believe they will. I don't believe there's the slightest risk; but we shall soon see. I've set my heart on seeing, Bunny, but there's no earthly reason why I should drag you into it."

"You do that when you present this card," I pointed out. "I shall hear of it fast enough if anything happens."

"Then you may as well be there to see the fun?"

"It will make no difference if the worst comes to the worst."

"And the ticket is for a party, isn't it?"

"It is."

"It might even look peculiar if only one person made use of it?"

"It might."

"Then we're both going, Bunny! And I give you my word," cried Raffles, "that no real harm shall come of it. But you mustn't ask to see the Relics, and you mustn't take too much interest in them when you do see them. Leave the questioning to me: it really will be a chance of finding out whether they've any suspicion of one's resurrection at Scotland Yard. Still I think I can promise you a certain amount of fun, old fellow, as some little compensation for your pangs and fears?"

The early afternoon was mild and hazy, and unlike winter but for the prematurely low sun struggling through the haze, as Raffles and I emerged from the nether regions at

Westminster Bridge, and stood for one moment to admire the infirm silhouettes of Abbey and Houses in flat gray against a golden mist. Raffles murmured of Whistler and of Arthur Severn, and threw away a good Sullivan because the smoke would curl between him and the picture. It is perhaps the picture that I can now see clearest of all the set scenes of our lawless life. But at the time I was filled with gloomy speculation as to whether Raffles would keep his promise of providing an entirely harmless entertainment for my benefit at the Black Museum.

We entered the forbidding precincts; we looked relentless officers in the face, and they almost yawned in ours as they directed us through swing doors and up stone stairs. There was something even sinister in the casual character of our reception. We had an arctic landing to ourselves for several minutes, which Raffles spent in an instinctive survey of the premises, while I cooled my heels before the portrait of a late commissioner.

"Dear old gentleman!" exclaimed Raffles, joining me. "I have met him at dinner, and discussed my own case with him, in the old days. But we can't know too little about ourselves in the Black Museum, Bunny. I remember going to the old place in Whitehall, years ago, and being shown round by one of the tip-top 'tecs. And this may be another."

But even I could see at a glance that there was nothing of the detective and everything of the clerk about the very young man who had joined us at last upon the landing. His collar was the tallest I have ever seen, and his face was as pallid as his collar. He carried a loose key, with which he unlocked a door a little way along the passage, and so ushered us into that dreadful repository which perhaps has fewer visitors than any other of equal interest in the world. The place was cold as the inviolate vault; blinds had to be drawn up, and glass cases uncovered, before we could see a thing except the row of murderers' death-masks – the placid faces with the swollen necks – that stood out on their shelves to give us ghostly greeting.

"This fellow isn't formidable," whispered Raffles, as the blinds went up; "still, we can't be too careful. My little lot are round the corner, in the sort of recess; don't look till we come to them in their turn."

So we began at the beginning, with the glass case nearest the door; and in a moment I discovered that I knew far more about its contents than our pallid guide. He had some enthusiasm, but the most inaccurate smattering of his subject. He mixed up the first murderer with quite the wrong murder, and capped his mistake in the next breath with an intolerable libel on the very pearl of our particular tribe.

"This revawlver," he began, "belonged to the celebrated burgular, Chawles Peace. These are his spectacles, that's his jimmy, and this here knife's the one that Chawley killed the policeman with."

Now I like accuracy for its own sake, strive after it myself, and am sometimes guilty of forcing it upon others. So this was more than I could pass.

"That's not quite right," I put in mildly. "He never made use of the knife."

The young clerk twisted his head round in its vase of starch.

"Chawley Peace killed two policemen," said he.

"No, he didn't; only one of them was a policeman; and he never killed anybody with a knife."

The clerk took the correction like a lamb. I could not have refrained from making it, to save my skin. But Raffles rewarded me with as vicious a little kick as he could administer unobserved. "Who was Charles Peace?" he inquired, with the bland effrontery of any judge upon the bench.

The clerk's reply came pat and unexpected. "The greatest burgular we ever had," said he, "till good old Raffles knocked him out!"

"The greatest of the pre-Raffleites," the master murmured, as we passed on to the safer memorials of mere murder. There were misshapen bullets and stained knives that had taken human life; there were lithe, lean ropes which had retaliated after the live letter of the Mosaic law. There was one bristling broadside of revolvers under the longest shelf of closed eyes and swollen throats. There were festoons of rope-ladders – none so ingenious as ours – and then at last there was something that the clerk knew all about. It was a small tin cigarette-box, and the name upon the gaudy wrapper was not the name of Sullivan. Yet Raffles and I knew even more about this exhibit than the clerk.

"There, now," said our guide, "you'll never guess the history of that! I'll give you twenty guesses, and the twentieth will be no nearer than the first."

"I'm sure of it, my good fellow," rejoined Raffles, a discreet twinkle in his eye. "Tell us about it, to save time."

And he opened, as he spoke, his own old twenty-five tin of purely popular cigarettes; there were a few in it still, but between the cigarettes were jammed lumps of sugar wadded with cotton-wool. I saw Raffles weighing the lot in his hand with subtle satisfaction. But the clerk saw merely the mystification which he desired to create.

"I thought that'd beat you, sir," said he. "It was an American dodge. Two smart Yankees got a jeweller to take a lot of stuff to a private room at Keliner's, where they were dining, for them to choose from. When it came to paying, there was some bother about a remittance; but they soon made that all right, for they were far too clever to suggest taking away what they'd chosen but couldn't pay for. No, all they wanted was that what they'd chosen might be locked up in the safe and considered theirs until their money came for them to pay for it. All they asked was to seal the stuff up in something; the jeweller was to take it away and not meddle with it, nor yet break the seals, for a week or two. It seemed a fair enough thing, now, didn't it, sir?"

"Eminently fair," said Raffles sententiously.

"So the jeweller thought," crowed the clerk. "You see, it wasn't as if the Yanks had chosen out the half of what he'd brought on appro.; they'd gone slow on purpose, and they'd paid for all they could on the nail, just for a blind. Well, I suppose you can guess what happened in the end? The jeweller never heard of those Americans again; and these few cigarettes and lumps of sugar were all he found."

"Duplicate boxes?" I cried, perhaps a thought too promptly.

"Duplicate boxes!" murmured Raffles, as profoundly impressed as a second Mr. Pickwick.

"Duplicate boxes!" echoed the triumphant clerk. "Artful beggars, these Americans, sir! You've got to crawss the 'Erring Pond to learn a trick worth one o' that?"

"I suppose so," assented the grave gentleman wit the silver hair. "Unless," he added, as if suddenly inspired, "unless it was that man Raffles."

"It couldn't 've bin," jerked the clerk from his conning-tower of a collar. "He'd gone to Davy Jones long before."

"Are you sure?" asked Raffles. "Was his body ever found?"

"Found and buried," replied our imaginative friend. "Malter, I think it was; or it may have been Giberaltar. I forget which."

"Besides," I put in, rather annoyed at all this wilful work, yet not indisposed to make a late contribution – "besides, Raffles would never have smoked those cigarettes. There was only one brand for him. It was – let me see—"

"Sullivans?" cried the clerk, right for once. "It's all a matter of 'abit," he went on, as he replaced the twenty-five tin box with the vulgar wrapper. "I tried them once, and I didn't like 'em myself. It's all a question of taste. Now, if you want a good smoke, and cheaper, give me a Golden Gem at quarter of the price."

"What we really do want," remarked Raffles mildly, "is to see something else as clever as that last."

"Then come this way," said the clerk, and led us into a recess almost monopolized by the iron-clamped chest of thrilling memory, now a mere platform for the collection of mysterious objects under a dust-sheet on the lid. "These," he continued, unveiling them with an air, "are the Raffles Relics, taken from his rooms in the Albany after his death and burial, and the most complete set we've got. That's his centre-bit, and this is the bottle of rock-oil he's supposed to have kept dipping it in to prevent making a noise. Here's the revawlver he used when he shot at a gentleman on the roof down Horsham way; it was afterward taken from him on the P. & O. boat before he jumped overboard."

I could not help saying I understood that Raffles had never shot at anybody. I was standing with my back to the nearest window, my hat jammed over my brows and my overcoat collar up to my ears.

"That's the only time we know about," the clerk admitted; "and it couldn't be brought 'ome, or his precious pal would have got more than he did. This empty cawtridge is the one he 'id the Emperor's pearl in, on the Peninsular and Orient. These gimlets and wedges were what he used for fixin' doors. This is his rope-ladder, with the telescope walking-stick he used to hook it up with; he's said to have 'ad it with him the night he dined with the Earl of Thornaby, and robbed the house before dinner. That's his life-preserver; but no one can make out what this little thick velvet bag's for, with the two holes and the elawstic round each. Perhaps you can give a guess, sir?"

Raffles had taken up the bag that he had invented for the noiseless filing of keys. Now he handled it as though it were a tobacco-pouch, putting in finger and thumb, and shrugging over the puzzle with a delicious face; nevertheless, he showed me a few grains of steel filing as the result of his investigations, and murmured in my ear, "These sweet police! I, for my part, could not but examine the life-preserver with which I had once smitten Raffles himself to the ground: actually, there was his blood upon it still; and seeing my horror, the clerk plunged into a characteristically garbled version of that incident also. It happened to have come to light among others at the Old Bailey, and perhaps had its share in promoting the quality of mercy which had undoubtedly been exercised on my behalf. But the present recital was unduly trying, and Raffles created a noble diversion by calling attention to an early photograph of himself, which may still hang on the wall over the historic chest, but which I had carefully ignored. It shows him in flannels, after some great feat upon the tented field. I am afraid there is a Sullivan between his lips, a look of lazy insolence in the half-shut eyes. I have since possessed myself of a copy, and it is not Raffles at his best; but the features are clean-cut and regular; and I often wish that I had lent it to the artistic gentlemen who have battered the statue out of all likeness to the man.

"You wouldn't think it of him, would you?" quoth the clerk. "It makes you understand how no one ever did think it of him at the time."

The youth was looking full at Raffles, with the watery eyes of unsuspecting innocence. I itched to emulate the fine bravado of my friend.

"You said he had a pal," I observed, sinking deeper into the collar of my coat. "Haven't you got a photograph of him?"

The pale clerk gave such a sickly smile, I could have smacked some blood into his pasty face.

"You mean Bunny?" said the familiar fellow. "No, sir, he'd be out of place; we've only room for real criminals here. Bunny was neither one thing nor the other. He could follow Raffles, but that's all he could do. He was no good on his own. Even when he put up the low-down job of robbing his old 'ome, it's believed he hadn't the 'eart to take the stuff away, and Raffles had to break in a second time for it. No, sir, we don't bother our heads about Bunny; we shall never hear no more of 'im. He was a harmless sort of rotter, if you awsk me."

I had not asked him, and I was almost foaming under the respirator that I was making of my overcoat collar. I only hoped that Raffles would say something, and he did.

"The only case I remember anything about," he remarked, tapping the clamped chest with his umbrella, "was this; and that time, at all events, the man outside must have had quite as much to do as the one inside. May I ask what you keep in it?"

"Nothing, sir."

"I imagined more relics inside. Hadn't he some dodge of getting in and out without opening the lid?"

"Of putting his head out, you mean," returned the clerk, whose knowledge of Raffles and his Relics was really most comprehensive on the whole. He moved some of the minor memorials and with his penknife raised the trap-door in the lid.

"Only a skylight," remarked Raffles, deliciously unimpressed.

"Why, what else did you expect?" asked the clerk, letting the trap-door down again, and looking sorry that he had taken so much trouble.

"A backdoor, at least!" replied Raffles, with such a sly look at me that I had to turn aside to smile. It was the last time I smiled that day.

The door had opened as I turned, and an unmistakable detective had entered with two more sight-seers like ourselves. He wore the hard, round hat and the dark, thick overcoat which one knows at a glance as the uniform of his grade; and for one awful moment his steely eye was upon us in a flash of cold inquiry. Then the clerk emerged from the recess devoted to the Raffles Relics, and the alarming interloper conducted his party to the window opposite the door.

"Inspector Druce," the clerk informed us in impressive whispers, "who had the Chalk Farm case in hand. He'd be the man for Raffles, if Raffles was alive today!"

"I'm sure he would," was the grave reply. "I should be very sorry to have a man like that after me. But what a run there seems to be upon your Black Museum!"

"There isn't reelly, sir," whispered the clerk. "We sometimes go weeks on end without having regular visitors like you two gentlemen. I think those are friends of the Inspector's, come to see the Chalk Farm photographs, that helped to hang his man. We've a lot of interesting photographs, sir, if you like to have a look at them."

"If it won't take long," said Raffles, taking out his watch; and as the clerk left our side for an instant he gripped my arm. "This is a bit too hot," he whispered, "but we mustn't cut and run like rabbits. That might be fatal. Hide your face in the photographs, and leave everything to me. I'll have a train to catch as soon as ever I dare."

I obeyed without a word, and with the less uneasiness as I had time to consider the situation. It even struck me that Raffles was for once inclined to exaggerate the undeniable risk that we ran by remaining in the same room with an officer whom both he and I knew only too well by name and repute. Raffles, after all, had aged and altered out of knowledge;

but he had not lost the nerve that was equal to a far more direct encounter than was at all likely to be forced upon us. On the other hand, it was most improbable that a distinguished detective would know by sight an obscure delinquent like myself; besides, this one had come to the front since my day. Yet a risk it was, and I certainly did not smile as I bent over the album of horrors produced by our guide. I could still take an interest in the dreadful photographs of murderous and murdered men; they appealed to the morbid element in my nature; and it was doubtless with degenerate unction that I called Raffles's attention to a certain scene of notorious slaughter. There was no response. I looked round. There was no Raffles to respond. We had all three been examining the photographs at one of the windows; at another three newcomers were similarly engrossed; and without one word, or a single sound, Raffles had decamped behind all our backs.

Fortunately the clerk was himself very busy gloating over the horrors of the album; before he looked round I had hidden my astonishment, but not my wrath, of which I had the instinctive sense to make no secret.

"My friend's the most impatient man on earth!" I exclaimed. "He said he was going to catch a train, and now he's gone without a word!"

"I never heard him," said the clerk, looking puzzled.

"No more did I; but he did touch me on the shoulder," I lied, "and say something or other. I was too deep in this beastly book to pay much attention. He must have meant that he was off. Well, let him be off! I mean to see all that's to be seen."

And in my nervous anxiety to allay any suspicions aroused by my companion's extraordinary behavior, I outstayed even the eminent detective and his friends, saw them examine the Raffles Relics, heard them discuss me under my own nose, and at last was alone with the anemic clerk. I put my hand in my pocket, and measured him with a sidelong eye. The tipping system is nothing less than a minor bane of my existence. Not that one is a grudging giver, but simply because in so many cases it is so hard to know whom to tip and what to tip him. I know what it is to be the parting guest who has not parted freely enough, and that not from stinginess but the want of a fine instinct on the point. I made no mistake, however, in the case of the clerk, who accepted my pieces of silver without demur, and expressed a hope of seeing the article which I had assured him I was about to write. He has had some years to wait for it, but I flatter myself that these belated pages will occasion more interest than offense if they ever do meet those watery eyes.

Twilight was falling when I reached the street; the sky behind St. Stephen's had flushed and blackened like an angry face; the lamps were lit, and under every one I was unreasonable enough to look for Raffles. Then I made foolishly sure that I should find him hanging about the station, and hung thereabouts myself until one Richmond train had gone without me. In the end I walked over the bridge to Waterloo, and took the first train to Teddington instead. That made a shorter walk of it, but I had to grope my way through a white fog from the river to Ham Common, and it was the hour of our cosy dinner when I reached our place of retirement. There was only a flicker of firelight on the blinds: I was the first to return after all. It was nearly four hours since Raffles had stolen away from my side in the ominous precincts of Scotland Yard. Where could he be? Our landlady wrung her hands over him; she had cooked a dinner after her favorite's heart, and I let it spoil before making one of the most melancholy meals of my life.

Up to midnight there was no sign of him; but long before this time I had reassured our landlady with a voice and face that must have given my words the lie. I told her that Mr. Ralph (as she used to call him) had said something about going to the theatre; that I thought he had given up the idea, but I must have been mistaken, and should certainly sit up for him. The attentive soul brought in a plate of sandwiches before she retired; and I prepared to make a night of it in a chair by the sitting-room fire. Darkness and bed I could not face in my anxiety. In a way I felt as though duty and loyalty called me out into the winter's night; and yet whither should I turn to look for Raffles? I could think of but one place, and to seek him there would be to destroy myself without aiding him. It was my growing conviction that he had been recognized when leaving Scotland Yard, and either taken then and there, or else hunted into some new place of hiding. It would all be in the morning papers; and it was all his own fault. He had thrust his head into the lion's mouth, and the lion's jaws had snapped. Had he managed to withdraw his head in time?

There was a bottle at my elbow, and that night I say deliberately that it was not my enemy but my friend. It procured me at last some surcease from my suspense. I fell fast asleep in my chair before the fire. The lamp was still burning, and the fire red, when I awoke; but I sat very stiff in the iron clutch of a wintry morning. Suddenly I slued round in my chair. And there was Raffles in a chair behind me, with the door open behind him, quietly taking off his boots.

"Sorry to wake you, Bunny," said he. "I thought I was behaving like a mouse; but after a three hours' tramp one's feet are all heels."

I did not get up and fall upon his neck. I sat back in my chair and blinked with bitterness upon his selfish insensibility. He should not know what I had been through on his account.

"Walk out from town?" I inquired, as indifferently as though he were in the habit of doing so.

"From Scotland Yard," he answered, stretching himself before the fire in his stocking soles.

"Scotland Yard?" I echoed. "Then I was right; that's where you were all the time; and yet you managed to escape!"

I had risen excitedly in my turn.

"Of course I did," replied Raffles. "I never thought there would be much difficulty about that, but there was even less than I anticipated. I did once find myself on one side of a sort of counter, and an officer dozing at his desk at the other side. I thought it safest to wake him up and make inquiries about a mythical purse left in a phantom hansom outside the Carlton. And the way the fellow fired me out of that was another credit to the Metropolitan Police: it's only in the savage countries that they would have troubled to ask how one had got in."

"And how did you?" I asked. "And in the Lord's name, Raffles, when and why?"

Raffles looked down on me under raised eyebrows, as he stood with his coat tails to the dying fire.

"How and when, Bunny, you know as well as I do," said he, cryptically. "And at last you shall hear the honest why and wherefore. I had more reasons for going to Scotland Yard, my dear fellow, than I had the face to tell you at the time."

"I don't care why you went there!" I cried. "I want to know why you stayed, or went back, or whatever it was you may have done. I thought they had got you, and you had given them the slip!"

Raffles smiled as he shook his head.

"No, no, Bunny; I prolonged the visit, as I paid it, of my own accord. As for my reasons, they are far too many for me to tell you them all; they rather weighed upon me as I walked out; but you'll see them for yourself if you turn round."

I was standing with my back to the chair in which I had been asleep; behind the chair was the round lodging-house table; and there, reposing on the cloth with the whiskey and sandwiches, was the whole collection of Raffles Relics which had occupied the lid of the silver-chest in the Black Museum at Scotland Yard! The chest alone was missing. There was the revolver that I had only once heard fired, and there the blood-stained life-preserver, brace-and-bit, bottle of rock-oil, velvet bag, rope-ladder, walking-stick, gimlets, wedges, and even the empty cartridge-case which had once concealed the gift of a civilized monarch to a potentate of color.

"I was a real Father Christmas," said Raffles, "when I arrived. It's a pity you weren't awake to appreciate the scene. It was more edifying than the one I found. You never caught me asleep in my chair, Bunny!"

He thought I had merely fallen asleep in my chair! He could not see that I had been sitting up for him all night long! The hint of a temperance homily, on top of all I had borne, and from Raffles of all mortal men, tried my temper to its last limit – but a flash of late enlightenment enabled me just to keep it.

"Where did you hide?" I asked grimly.

"At the Yard itself."

"So I gather; but whereabouts at the Yard?"

"Can you ask, Bunny?"

"I am asking."

"It's where I once hid before."

"You don't mean in the chest?"

"I do."

Our eyes met for a minute.

"You may have ended up there," I conceded. "But where did you go first when you slipped out behind my back, and how the devil did you know where to go?"

"I never did slip out," said Raffles, "behind your back. I slipped in."

"Into the chest?"

"Exactly."

I burst out laughing in his face.

"My dear fellow, I saw all these things on the lid just afterward. Not one of them was moved. I watched that detective show them to his friends."

"And I heard him."

"But not from the inside of the chest?"

"From the inside of the chest, Bunny. Don't look like that – it's foolish. Try to recall a few words that went before, between the idiot in the collar and me. Don't you remember my asking him if there was anything in the chest?"

"Yes."

"One had to be sure it was empty, you see. Then I asked if there was a backdoor to the chest as well as a skylight."

"I remember."

"I suppose you thought all that meant nothing?"

"I didn't look for a meaning."

"You wouldn't; it would never occur to you that I might want to find out whether anybody at the Yard had found out that there was something precisely in the nature of a sidedoor – it isn't a backdoor – to that chest. Well, there is one; there was one soon after I took the chest back from your rooms to mine, in the good old days. You push one of the handles down – which no one ever does – and the whole of that end opens like the front of a doll's house. I saw that was what I ought to have done at first: it's so much simpler than the trap at the top; and one likes to get a thing perfect for its own sake. Besides, the trick had not been spotted at the bank, and I thought I might bring it off again some day; meanwhile, in one's bedroom, with lots of things on top, what a port in a sudden squall!"

I asked why I had never heard of the improvement before, not so much at the time it was made, but in these later days, when there were fewer secrets between us, and this one could avail him no more. But I did not put the question out of pique. I put it out of sheer obstinate incredulity. And Raffles looked at me without replying, until I read the explanation in his look.

"I see," I said. "You used to get into it to hide from me!"

"My dear Bunny, I am not always a very genial man," he answered; "but when you let me have a key of your rooms I could not very well refuse you one of mine, although I picked your pocket of it in the end. I will only say that when I had no wish to see you, Bunny, I must have been quite unfit for human society, and it was the act of a friend to deny you mine. I don't think it happened more than once or twice. You can afford to forgive a fellow after all these years?

"That, yes," I replied bitterly; "but not this, Raffles."

"Why not? I really hadn't made up my mind to do what I did. I had merely thought of it. It was that smart officer in the same room that made me do it without thinking twice."

"And we never even heard you!" I murmured, in a voice of involuntary admiration which vexed me with myself. "But we might just as well!" I was as quick to add in my former tone.

"Why, Bunny?"

"We shall be traced in no time through our ticket of admission."

"Did they collect it?"

"No; but you heard how very few are issued."

"Exactly. They sometimes go weeks on end without a regular visitor. It was I who extracted that piece of information, Bunny, and I did nothing rash until I had. Don't you see that with any luck it will be two or three weeks before they are likely to discover their loss?"

I was beginning to see.

"And then, pray, how are they going to bring it home to us? Why should they even suspect us, Bunny? I left early; that's all I did. You took my departure admirably; you couldn't have said more or less if I had coached you myself. I relied on you, Bunny, and you never more completely justified my confidence. The sad thing is that you have ceased to rely on me. Do you really think that I would leave the place in such a state that the first person who came in with a duster would see that there had been a robbery?"

I denied the thought with all energy, though it perished only as I spoke.

"Have you forgotten the duster that was over these things, Bunny? Have you forgotten all the other revolvers and life preservers that there were to choose from? I chose most carefully, and I replaced my relics with a mixed assortment of other people's which really look just as well. The rope-ladder that now supplants mine is, of course, no patch upon it, but coiled up on the chest it really looks much the same. To be sure, there was no second velvet bag; but I replaced my stick with another quite like it, and I even found an empty cartridge to understudy the setting of the Polynesian pearl. You see the sort of fellow they have to show people round: do you think he's the kind to see the difference next time, or to connect it with us if he does? One left much the same things, lying much as he left them, under a dust-sheet which is only taken off for the benefit of the curious, who often don't turn up for weeks on end."

I admitted that we might be safe for three or four weeks. Raffles held out his hand.

"Then let us be friends about it, Bunny, and smoke the cigarette of Sullivan and peace! A lot may happen in three or four weeks; and what should you say if this turned out to be the last as well as the least of all my crimes? I must own that it seems to me their natural and fitting end, though I might have stopped more characteristically than with a mere crime of sentiment. No, I make no promises, Bunny; now I have got these things, I may be unable to resist using them once more. But with this war one gets all the excitement one requires – and rather more than usual may happen in three or four weeks?"

Was he thinking even then of volunteering for the front? Had he already set his heart on the one chance of some atonement for his life – nay, on the very death he was to die? I never knew, and shall never know. Yet his words were strangely prophetic, even to the three or four weeks in which those events happened that imperilled the fabric of our empire, and rallied her sons from the four winds to fight beneath her banner on the veldt. It all seems very ancient history now. But I remember nothing better or more vividly than the last words of Raffles upon his last crime, unless it be the pressure of his hand as he said them, or the rather sad twinkle in his tired eyes.

The Mystery of a Hansom Cab
Chapters I–IX

Fergus Hume

Chapter I
What the Argus Said

THE FOLLOWING REPORT appeared in the Argus newspaper of Saturday, the 28th July, 18—

"Truth is said to be stranger than fiction, and certainly the extraordinary murder which took place in Melbourne on Thursday night, or rather Friday morning, goes a long way towards verifying this saying. A crime has been committed by an unknown assassin, within a short distance of the principal streets of this great city, and is surrounded by an inpenetrable mystery. Indeed, from the nature of the crime itself, the place where it was committed, and the fact that the assassin has escaped without leaving a trace behind him, it would seem as though the case itself had been taken bodily from one of Gaboreau's novels, and that his famous detective Lecoq alone would be able to unravel it. The facts of the case are simply these:

"On the twenty-seventh day of July, at the hour of twenty minutes to two o'clock in the morning, a hansom cab drove up to the police station in Grey Street, St. Kilda, and the driver made the startling statement that his cab contained the body of a man who he had reason to believe had been murdered. Being taken into the presence of the inspector, the cabman, who gave his name as Malcolm Royston, related the following strange story:

"At the hour of one o'clock in the morning, he was driving down Collins Street East, when, as he was passing the Burke and Wills' monument, he was hailed by a gentleman standing at the corner by the Scotch Church. He immediately drove up, and saw that the gentleman who hailed him was supporting the deceased, who appeared to be intoxicated. Both were in evening dress, but the deceased had on no overcoat, while the other wore a short covert coat of a light fawn colour, which was open. As Royston drove up, the gentleman in the light coat said, 'Look here, cabby, here's some fellow awfully tight, you'd better take him home!'

"Royston then asked him if the drunken man was his friend, but this the other denied, saying that he had just picked him up from the footpath, and did not know him from Adam. At this moment the deceased turned his face up to the light of the lamp under which both were standing, and the other seemed to recognise him, for he recoiled a pace, letting the drunken man fall in a heap on the pavement, and gasping out 'You?' he turned on his heel, and walked rapidly away down Russell Street in the direction of Bourke Street.

"*Royston was staring after him, and wondering at his strange conduct, when he was recalled to himself by the voice of the deceased, who had struggled to his feet, and was holding on to the lamp-post, swaying to and fro. 'I wan' g'ome,' he said in a thick voice, 'St. Kilda.' He then tried to get into the cab, but was too drunk to do so, and finally sat down again on the pavement. Seeing this, Royston got down, and lifting him up, helped him into the cab with some considerable difficulty. The deceased fell back into the cab, and seemed to drop off to sleep; so, after closing the door, Royston turned to remount his driving-seat, when he found the gentleman in the light coat whom he had seen holding up the deceased, close to his elbow. Royston said, 'Oh, you've come back,' and the other answered, 'Yes, I've changed my mind, and will see him home.' As he said this he opened the door of the cab, stepped in beside the deceased, and told Royston to drive down to St. Kilda. Royston, who was glad that the friend of the deceased had come to look after him, drove as he had been directed, but near the Church of England Grammar School, on the St. Kilda Road, the gentleman in the light coat called out to him to stop. He did so, and the gentleman got out of the cab, closing the door after him.*

"'*He won't let me take him home,' he said, 'so I'll just walk back to the city, and you can drive him to St. Kilda.'*

"'*What street, sir?' asked Royston.*

"'*Grey Street, I fancy,' said the other, 'but my friend will direct you when you get to the Junction.' "'Ain't he too much on, sir?' said Royston, dubiously.*

"'*Oh, no! I think he'll be able to tell you where he lives – it's Grey Street or Ackland Street, I fancy. I don't know which.'*

"*He then opened the door of the cab and looked in. 'Good night, old man,' he said – the other apparently did not answer, for the gentleman in the light coat, shrugging his shoulders, and muttering 'sulky brute,' closed the door again. He then gave Royston half-a-sovereign, lit a cigarette, and after making a few remarks about the beauty of the night, walked off quickly in the direction of Melbourne. Royston drove down to the Junction, and having stopped there, according to his instructions he asked his 'fare' several times where he was to drive him to. Receiving no response and thinking that the deceased was too drunk to answer, he got down from his seat, opened the door of the cab, and found the deceased lying back in the corner with a handkerchief across his mouth. He put out his hand with the intention of rousing him, thinking that he had gone to sleep. But on touching him the deceased fell forward, and on examination, to his horror, he found that he was quite dead. Alarmed at what had taken place, and suspecting the gentleman in the light coat, he drove to the police station at St. Kilda, and there made the above report. The body of the deceased was taken out of the cab and brought into the station, a doctor being sent for at once. On his arrival, however, he found that life was quite extinct, and also discovered that the handkerchief which was tied lightly over the mouth was saturated with chloroform. He had no hesitation in stating that from the way in which the handkerchief was placed, and the presence of chloroform, that a murder had been committed, and from all appearances the deceased died easily, and without a struggle. The deceased is a slender man, of medium height, with a dark complexion, and is dressed in evening dress, which will render identification difficult, as it is a costume which has no distinctive mark to render it noticeable. There were no papers or cards found on the deceased from which his name could be discovered, and the clothing was not marked in any way. The handkerchief, however, which was tied across his mouth, was of white silk, and marked in one of the corners with the letters 'O.W.' in red silk. The assassin, of course, may have used his own handkerchief to commit the crime, so that if the initials are those of his name they may ultimately lead to his detection. There will be an inquest held on the body of the deceased this morning, when, no doubt, some evidence may be elicited which may solve the mystery."*

In Monday morning's issue of the ARGUS the following article appeared with reference to the matter:

"The following additional evidence which has been obtained may throw some light on the mysterious murder in a hansom cab of which we gave a full description in Saturday's issue: 'Another hansom cabman called at the police office, and gave a clue which will, no doubt, prove of value to the detectives in their search for the murderer. He states that he was driving up the St. Kilda Road on Friday morning about half-past one o'clock, when he was hailed by a gentleman in a light coat, who stepped into the cab and told him to drive to Powlett Street, in East Melbourne. He did so, and, after paying him, the gentleman got out at the corner of Wellington Parade and Powlett Street and walked slowly up Powlett Street, while the cab drove back to town. Here all clue ends, but there can be no doubt in the minds of our readers as to the identity of the man in the light coat who got out of Royston's cab on the St. Kilda Road, with the one who entered the other cab and alighted therefrom at Powlett Street. There could have been no struggle, as had any taken place the cabman, Royston, surely would have heard the noise. The supposition is, therefore, that the deceased was too drunk to make any resistance, and that the other, watching his opportunity, placed the handkerchief saturated with chloroform over the mouth of his victim. Then after perhaps a few ineffectual struggles the latter would succumb to the effects of his inhalation. The man in the light coat, judging from his conduct before getting into the cab, appears to have known the deceased, though the circumstance of his walking away on recognition, and returning again, shows that his attitude towards the deceased was not altogether a friendly one.

"The difficulty is where to start from in the search after the author of what appears to be a deliberate murder, as the deceased seems to be unknown, and his presumed murderer has escaped. But it is impossible that the body can remain long without being identified by someone, as though Melbourne is a large city, yet it is neither Paris nor London, where a man can disappear in a crowd and never be heard of again. The first thing to be done is to establish the identity of the deceased, and then, no doubt, a clue will be obtained leading to the detection of the man in the light coat who appears to have been the perpetrator of the crime. It is of the utmost importance that the mystery in which the crime is shrouded should be cleared up, not only in the interests of justice, but also in those of the public – taking place as it did in a public conveyance, and in the public street. To think that the author of such a crime is at present at large, walking in our midst, and perhaps preparing for the committal of another, is enough to shake the strongest nerves. In one of Du Boisgobey's stories, entitled 'An Omnibus Mystery,' a murder closely resembling this tragedy takes place in an omnibus, but we question if even that author would have

been daring enough to write about a crime being committed in such an unlikely place as a hansom cab. Here is a great chance for some of our detectives to render themselves famous, and we feel sure that they will do their utmost to trace the author of this cowardly and dastardly murder."

Chapter II
The Evidence at the Inquest

AT THE INQUEST held on the body found in the hansom cab the following articles taken from the deceased were placed on the table:

1. Two pounds ten shillings in gold and silver.

2. The white silk handkerchief which was saturated with chloroform, and was found tied across the mouth of the deceased, marked with the letters O.W. in red silk.

3. A cigarette case of Russian leather, half filled with "Old Judge" cigarettes. 4. A left-hand white glove of kid – rather soiled – with black seams down the back. Samuel Gorby, of the detective office, was present in order to see if anything might be said by the witnesses likely to point to the cause or to the author of the crime.

The first witness called was Malcolm Royston, in whose cab the crime had been committed. He told the same story as had already appeared in the ARGUS, and the following facts were elicited by the Coroner:

Q. Can you give a description of the gentleman in the light coat, who was holding the deceased when you drove up?

A. I did not observe him very closely, as my attention was taken up by the deceased; and, besides, the gentleman in the light coat was in the shadow.

Q Describe him from what you saw of him.

A. He was fair, I think, because I could see his moustache, rather tall, and in evening dress, with a light coat over it. I could not see his face very plainly, as he wore a soft felt hat, which was pulled down over his eyes.

Q. What kind of hat was it he wore – a wide-awake?

A. Yes. The brim was turned down, and I could see only his mouth and moustache.

Q. What did he say when you asked him if he knew the deceased?

A. He said he didn't; that he had just picked him up.

Q. And afterwards he seemed to recognise him?

A. Yes. When the deceased looked up he said "You!" and let him fall on to the ground; then he walked away towards Bourke Street.

Q. Did he look back?

A. Not that I saw.

Q. How long were you looking after him?

A. About a minute.

Q. And when did you see him again?

A. After I put deceased into the cab I turned round and found him at my elbow.

Q. And what did he say?

A. I said, "Oh! you've come back," and he said, "Yes, I've changed my mind, and will see him home," and then he got into the cab, and told me to drive to St. Kilda.

Q. He spoke then as if he knew the deceased?

A. Yes; I thought that he recognised him only when he looked up, and perhaps having had a row with him walked away, but thought he'd come back.

Q. Did you see him coming back?

A. No; the first I saw of him was at my elbow when I turned.

Q. And when did he get out? A. Just as I was turning down by the Grammar School on the St. Kilda Road.

Q. Did you hear any sounds of fighting or struggling in the cab during the drive?

A. No; the road was rather rough, and the noise of the wheels going over the stones would have prevented my hearing anything.

Q. When the gentleman in the light coat got out did he appear disturbed?

A. No; he was perfectly calm.

Q. How could you tell that?

A. Because the moon had risen, and I could see plainly.

Q. Did you see his face then?

A. No; his hat was pulled down over it. I only saw as much as I did when he entered the cab in Collins Street.

Q. Were his clothes torn or disarranged in any way?

A. No; the only difference I remarked in him was that his coat was buttoned.

Q. And was it open when he got in?

A. No; but it was when he was holding up the deceased.

Q. Then he buttoned it before he came back and got into the cab?

A. Yes. I suppose so.

Q. What did he say when he got out of the cab on the St. Kilda Road?

A. He said that the deceased would not let him take him home, and that he would walk back to Melbourne.

Q. And you asked him where you were to drive the deceased to?

A. Yes; and he said that the deceased lived either in Grey Street or Ackland Street, St. Kilda, but that the deceased would direct me at the Junction.

Q. Did you not think that the deceased was too drunk to direct you?

A. Yes, I did; but his friend said that the sleep and the shaking of the cab would sober him a bit by the time I got to the Junction.

Q. The gentleman in the light coat apparently did not know where the deceased lived?

A. No; he said it was either in Ackland Street or Grey Street.

Q. Did you not think that curious?

A. No; I thought he might be a club friend of the deceased.

Q. For how long did the man in the light coat talk to you?

A. About five minutes.

Q. And during that time you heard no noise in the cab?

A. No; I thought the deceased had gone to sleep.

Q. And after the man in the light coat said "good-night" to the deceased, what happened?

A. He lit a cigarette, gave me a half-sovereign, and walked off towards Melbourne.

Q. Did you observe if the gentleman in the light coat had his handkerchief with him?

A. Oh, yes; because he dusted his boots with it. The road was very dusty.

Q. Did you notice any striking peculiarity about him?

A. Well, no; except that he wore a diamond ring.

Q. What was there peculiar about that?

A. He wore it on the forefinger of the right hand, and I never saw it that way before.

Q. When did you notice this?

A. When he was lighting his cigarette.

Q. How often did you call to the deceased when you got to the Junction?

A. Three or four times. I then got down, and found he was quite dead.

Q. How was he lying?

A. He was doubled up in the far corner of the cab, very much in the same position as I left him when I put him in. His head was hanging on one side, and there was a handkerchief across his mouth. When I touched him he fell into the other corner of the cab, and then I found out he was dead. I immediately drove to the St. Kilda police station and told the police.

At the conclusion of Royston's evidence, during which Gorby had been continually taking notes, Robert Chinston was called. He deposed:

I am a duly qualified medical practitioner, residing in Collins Street East. I made a POST-MORTEM examination of the body of the deceased on Friday.

Q. That was within a few hours of his death?

A. Yes, judging from the position of the handkerchief and the presence of chloroform that the deceased had died from the effects of ANAESTHESIA, and knowing how rapidly the poison evaporates I made the examination at once.

Coroner: Go on, sir.

Dr. Chinston: Externally, the body was healthy-looking and well nourished. There were no marks of violence. The staining apparent at the back of the legs and trunk was due to POST-MORTEM congestion. Internally, the brain was hyperaemic, and there was a considerable amount of congestion, especially apparent in the superficial vessels. There was no brain disease. The lungs were healthy, but slightly congested. On opening the thorax there was a faint spirituous odour discernible. The stomach contained about a pint of completely digested food. The heart was flaccid. The right-heart contained a considerable quantity of dark, fluid blood. There was a tendency to fatty degeneration of that organ.

I am of opinion that the deceased died from the inhalation of some such vapour as chloroform or methylene.

Q. You say there was a tendency to fatty degeneration of the heart? Would that have anything to do with the death of deceased?

A. Not of itself. But chloroform administered while the heart was in such a state would have a decided tendency to accelerate the fatal result. At the same time, I may mention that the POST-MORTEM signs of poisoning by chloroform are mostly negative.

Dr. Chinston was then permitted to retire, and Clement Rankin, another hansom cabman, was called. He deposed: I am a cabman, living in Collingwood, and usually drive a hansom cab. I remember Thursday last. I had driven a party down to St. Kilda, and was returning about half-past one o'clock. A short distance past the Grammar School I was hailed by a gentleman in a light coat; he was smoking a cigarette, and told me to drive him to Powlett Street, East Melbourne. I did so, and he got out at the corner of Wellington Parade and Powlett Street. He paid me half-a-sovereign for my fare, and then walked up Powlett Street, while I drove back to town.

Q. What time was it when you stopped at Powlett Street?

A. Two o'clock exactly.

Q. How do you know?

A. Because it was a still night, and I heard the Post Office clock strike two o'clock.

Q. Did you notice anything peculiar about the man in the light coat?

A. No! He looked just the same as anyone else. I thought he was some swell of the town out for a lark. His hat was pulled down over his eyes, and I could not see his face.

Q. Did you notice if he wore a ring?

A. Yes! I did. When he was handing me the half-sovereign, I saw he had a diamond ring on the forefinger of his right hand.

Q. He did not say why he was on the St. Kilda Road at such an hour?

A. No! He did not.

Clement Rankin was then ordered to stand down, and the Coroner then summed up in an address of half-an-hour's duration. There was, he pointed out, no doubt that the death of the deceased had resulted not from natural causes, but from the effects of poisoning. Only slight evidence had been obtained up to the present time regarding the circumstances of the case, but the only person who could be accused of committing the crime was the unknown man who entered the cab with the deceased on Friday morning at the corner of the Scotch Church, near the Burke and Wills' monument. It had been proved that the deceased, when he entered the cab, was, to all appearances, in good health, though in a state of intoxication, and the fact that he was found by the cabman, Royston, after the man in the light coat had left the cab, with a handkerchief, saturated with chloroform, tied over his mouth, would seem to show that he had died through the inhalation of chloroform, which had been deliberately administered. All the obtainable evidence in the case was circumstantial, but, nevertheless, showed conclusively that a crime had been committed. Therefore, as the circumstances of the case pointed to one conclusion, the jury could not do otherwise than frame a verdict in accordance with that conclusion.

The jury retired at four o'clock, and, after an absence of a quarter of an hour, returned with the following verdict:

"That the deceased, whose name there is no evidence to determine, died on the 27th day of July, from the effects of poison, namely, chloroform, feloniously administered by some person unknown; and the jury, on their oaths, say that the said unknown person feloniously, wilfully, and maliciously did murder the said deceased."

Chapter III
One Hundred Pounds Reward

V.R. MURDER. 100 POUNDS REWARD

Whereas, on Friday, the 27th day of July, the body of a man, name unknown, was found in a hansom cab. AND WHEREAS, at an inquest held at St. Kilda, on the 30th day of July, a verdict of wilful murder, against some person unknown, was brought in by the jury. The deceased is of medium height, with a dark complexion, dark hair, clean shaved, has a mole on the left temple, and was dressed in evening dress. Notice is hereby given that a reward of 100 pounds will be paid by the Government for such information as will lead to the conviction of the murderer, who is presumed to be a man who entered the hansom cab with the deceased at the corner of Collins and Russell Streets, on the morning of the 27th day of July.

Chapter IV
Mr. Gorby Makes A Start

"WELL," SAID MR. GORBY, addressing his reflection in the looking-glass, "I've been finding out things these last twenty years, but this is a puzzler, and no mistake."

Mr. Gorby was shaving, and, as was his usual custom, conversed with his reflection. Being a detective, and of an extremely reticent disposition, he never talked outside about his business, or made a confidant of anyone. When he did want to unbosom himself, he retired to his bedroom and talked to his reflection in the mirror. This method of procedure he found to work capitally, for it relieved his sometimes overburdened mind with absolute security to himself. Did not the barber of Midas when he found out what was under the royal crown of his master, fret and chafe over his secret, until one morning he stole to the reeds by the river, and whispered, "Midas, has ass's ears?" In the like manner Mr. Gorby felt a longing at times to give speech to his innermost secrets; and having no fancy for chattering to the air, he made his mirror his confidant. So far it had never betrayed him, while for the rest it joyed him to see his own jolly red face nodding gravely at him from out the shining surface, like a mandarin. This morning the detective was unusually animated in his confidences to his mirror. At times, too, a puzzled expression would pass over his face. The hansom cab murder had been placed in his hands for solution, and he was trying to think how he should make a beginning.

"Hang it," he said, thoughtfully stropping his razor, "a thing with an end must have a start, and if I don't get the start how am I to get the end?"

As the mirror did not answer this question, Mr. Gorby lathered his face, and started shaving in a somewhat mechanical fashion, for his thoughts were with the case, and ran on in this manner:

"Here's a man – well, say a gentleman – who gets drunk, and, therefore, don't know what he's up to. Another gent who is on the square comes up and sings out for a cab for him – first he says he don't know him, and then he shows plainly he does – he walks away in a temper, changes his mind, comes back and gets into the cab, after telling the cabby to drive down to St. Kilda. Then he polishes the drunk one off with chloroform, gets out of the cab, jumps into another, and after getting out at Powlett Street, vanishes – that's the riddle I've got to find out, and I don't think the Sphinx ever had a harder one. There are three things to be discovered – First, who is the dead man? Second, what was he killed for? And third, who did it?

"Once I get hold of the first the other two won't be very hard to find out, for one can tell pretty well from a man's life whether it's to anyone's interest that he should be got off the books. The man that murdered that chap must have had some strong motive, and I must find out what that motive was. Love? No, it wasn't that – men in love don't go to such lengths in real life – they do in novels and plays, but I've never seen it occurring in my experience. Robbery? No, there was plenty of money in his pocket. Revenge? Now, really it might be that – it's a kind of thing that carries most people further than they want to go. There was no violence used, for his clothes weren't torn, so he must have been taken sudden, and before he knew what the other chap was up to. By the way, I don't think I examined his clothes sufficiently, there might be something about them to give a clue; at any rate it's worth looking after, so I'll start with his clothes."

So Mr. Gorby, having dressed and breakfasted, walked quickly to the police station, where he asked for the clothes of the deceased to be shown to him. When he received them he retired into a corner, and commenced an exhaustive examination of them.

There was nothing remarkable about the coat. It was merely a well-cut and well-made dress coat; so with a grunt of dissatisfaction Mr. Gorby threw it aside, and picked up the waistcoat. Here he found something to interest him, in the shape of a pocket made on the left-hand side and on the inside, of the garment.

"Now, what the deuce is this for?" said Mr. Gorby, scratching his head; "it ain't usual for a dress waistcoat to have a pocket on its inside as I'm aware of; and," continued the detective, greatly excited, "this ain't tailor's work, he did it himself, and jolly badly he did it too. Now he must have taken the trouble to make this pocket himself, so that no one else would know anything about it, and it was made to carry something valuable – so valuable that he had to carry it with him even when he wore evening clothes. Ah! here's a tear on the side nearest the outside of the waistcoat; something has been pulled out roughly. I begin to see now. The dead man possessed something which the other man wanted, and which he knew the dead one carried about with him. He sees him drunk, gets into the cab with him, and tries to get what he wants. The dead man resists, upon which the other kills him by means of the chloroform which he had with him, and being afraid that the cab will stop, and he will be found out, snatches what he wants out of the pocket so quickly that he tears the waistcoat and then makes off. That's clear enough, but the question is, What was it he wanted? A case with jewels? No! It could not have been anything so bulky, or the dead man would never have carried it about inside his waistcoat. It was something flat, which could easily lie in the pocket – a paper – some valuable paper which the assassin wanted, and for which he killed the other."

"This is all very well," said Mr. Gorby, throwing down the waistcoat, and rising. "I have found number two before number one. The first question is: Who is the murdered man. He's a stranger in Melbourne, that's pretty clear, or else some one would have been sure to recognise him before now by the description given in the reward. Now, I wonder if he has any relations here? No, he can't, or else they would have made enquiries, before this. Well, there's one thing certain, he must have had a landlady or landlord, unless he slept in the open air. He can't have lived in an hotel, as the landlord of any hotel in Melbourne would have recognised him from the description, especially when the whole place is ringing with the murder. Private lodgings more like, and a landlady who doesn't read the papers and doesn't gossip, or she'd have known all about it by this time. Now, if he did live, as I think, in private lodgings, and suddenly disappeared, his landlady wouldn't keep quiet. It's a whole week since the murder, and as the lodger has not been seen or heard of, the landlady will naturally make enquiries. If, however, as I surmise, the lodger is a stranger, she will not know where to enquire; therefore, under these circumstances, the most natural thing for her to do would be to advertise for him, so I'll have a look at the newspapers."

Mr. Gorby got a file of the different newspapers, and looked carefully through those columns in which missing friends and people who will hear "something to their advantage" are generally advertised for.

"He was murdered," said Mr. Gorby to himself, "on a Friday morning, between one and two o'clock, so he might stay away till Monday without exciting any suspicion. On Monday, however, the landlady would begin to feel uneasy, and on Tuesday she would advertise for him. Therefore," said Mr. Gorby, running his fat finger down the column, "Wednesday it is."

It did not appear in Wednesday's paper, neither did it in Thursday's, but in Friday's issue, exactly one week after the murder, Mr. Gorby suddenly came upon the following advertisement:

"If Mr. Oliver Whyte does not return to Possum Villa, Grey Street, St. Kilda, before the end of the week, his rooms will be let again. Rubina Hableton."

"Oliver Whyte," repeated Mr. Gorby slowly, "and the initials on the pocket-handkerchief which was proved to have belonged to the deceased were 'O.W.' So his name is Oliver Whyte, is it? Now, I wonder if Rubina Hableton knows anything about this matter. At any rate," said Mr. Gorby, putting on his hat, "as I'm fond of sea breezes, I think I'll go down, and call at Possum Villa, Grey Street, St. Kilda."

Chapter V
Mrs. Hamilton Unbosoms Herself

Mrs. Hableton was a lady with a grievance, as anybody who happened to become acquainted with her, soon found out. It is Beaconsfield who says, in one of his novels, that no one is so interesting as when he is talking about himself; and, judging Mrs. Hableton by this statement, she was an extremely fascinating individual, as she never by any chance talked upon any other subject. What was the threat of a Russian invasion to her so long as she had her special grievance – once let that be removed, and she would have time to attend to such minor details as affected the colony.

Mrs. Hableton's particular grievance was want of money. Not by any means an uncommon one, you might remind her; but she snappishly would tell you that "she knowd that, but some people weren't like other people." In time one came to learn what she meant by this. She had come to the Colonies in the early days – days when the making of money in appreciable quantity was an easier matter than it is now. Owing to a bad husband, she had failed to save any. The late Mr. Hableton – for he had long since departed this life – had been addicted to alcohol, and at those times when he should have been earning, he was usually to be found in a drinking shanty spending his wife's earnings in "shouting" for himself and his friends. The constant drinking, and the hot Victorian climate, soon carried him off, and when Mrs. Hableton had seen him safely under the ground in the Melbourne Cemetery, she returned home to survey her position, and see how it could be bettered. She gathered together a little money from the wreck of her fortune, and land being cheap, purchased a small "section" at St. Kilda, and built a house on it. She supported herself by going out charing, taking in sewing, and acting as a sick nurse, So, among this multiplicity of occupations, she managed to exist fairly well.

And in truth it was somewhat hard upon Mrs. Hableton. For at the time when she should have been resting and reaping the fruit of her early industry, she was obliged to toil more assiduously than ever. It was little consolation to her that she was but a type of many women, who, hardworking and thrifty themselves, are married to men who are nothing but an incubus to their wives and to their families. Small wonder, then, that Mrs. Hableton should condense all her knowledge of the male sex into the one bitter aphorism, "Men is brutes."

Possum Villa was an unpretentious-looking place, with one bow-window and a narrow verandah in front. It was surrounded by a small garden in which were a few sparse flowers – the especial delight of Mrs. Hableton. It was her way to tie an old handkerchief round her head and to go out into the garden and dig and water her beloved flowers until, from sheer desperation at the overwhelming odds, they gave up all attempt to grow. She was engaged in this favourite occupation about a week after her lodger had gone. She wondered where he was.

"Lyin' drunk in a public-'ouse, I'll be bound," she said, viciously pulling up a weed, "a-spendin' 'is, rent and a-spilin' 'is inside with beer – ah, men is brutes, drat 'em!"

Just as she said this, a shadow fell across the garden, and on looking up, she saw a man leaning over the fence, staring at her.

"Git out," she said, sharply, rising from her knees and shaking her trowel at the intruder. "I don't want no apples today, an' I don't care how cheap you sells 'em."

Mrs. Hableton evidently laboured under the delusion that the man was a hawker, but seeing no hand-cart with him, she changed her mind.

"You're takin' a plan of the 'ouse to rob it, are you?" she said. "Well, you needn't, 'cause there ain't nothin' to rob, the silver spoons as belonged to my father's mother 'avin' gone down my 'usband's, throat long ago, an' I ain't 'ad money to buy more. I'm a lone pusson as is put on by brutes like you, an' I'll thank you to leave the fence I bought with my own 'ard earned money alone, and git out."

Mrs. Hableton stopped short for want of breath, and stood shaking her trowel, and gasping like a fish out of water.

"My dear lady," said the man at the fence, mildly, "are you—"

"No, I ain't," retorted Mrs. Hableton, fiercely, "I ain't neither a member of the 'Ouse, nor a school teacher, to answer your questions. I'm a woman as pays my rates an' taxes, and don't gossip nor read yer rubbishin' newspapers, nor care for the Russings, no how, so git out."

"Don't read the papers?" repeated the man, in a satisfied tone, "ah! that accounts for it."

Mrs. Hableton stared suspiciously at the intruder. He was a burly-looking man, with a jovial red face, clean shaven, and his sharp, shrewd-looking grey eyes twinkled like two stars. He was well-dressed in a suit of light clothes, and wore a stiffly-starched white waistcoat, with a massive gold chain stretched across it. Altogether he gave Mrs. Hableton finally the impression of being a well-to-do tradesman, and she mentally wondered what he wanted.

"What d'y want?" she asked, abruptly.

"Does Mr. Oliver Whyte live here?" asked the stranger.

"He do, an' he don't," answered Mrs. Hableton, epigrammatically. "I ain't seen 'im for over a week, so I s'pose 'e's gone on the drink, like the rest of 'em, but I've put sumthin' in the paper as 'ill pull him up pretty sharp, and let 'im know I ain't a carpet to be trod on, an' if you're a friend of 'im, you can tell 'im from me 'e's a brute, an' it's no more but what I expected of 'im, 'e bein' a male."

The stranger waited placidly during the outburst, and Mrs. Hableton, having stopped for want of breath, he interposed, quietly—

"Can I speak to you for a few moments?"

"An' who's a-stoppin' of you?" said Mrs. Hableton, defiantly. "Go on with you, not as I expects the truth from a male, but go on."

"Well, really," said the other, looking up at the cloudless blue sky, and wiping his face with a gaudy red silk pocket-handkerchief, "it is rather hot, you know, and—"

Mrs. Hableton did not give him time to finish, but walking to the gate, opened it with a jerk.

"Use your legs and walk in," she said, and the stranger having done so, she led the way into the house, and into a small neat sitting-room, which seemed to overflow with antimacassars, wool mats, and wax flowers. There were also a row of emu eggs on the mantelpiece, a cutlass on the wall, and a grimy line of hard-looking little books, set in a stiff row on a shelf, presumably for ornament, for their appearance in no way tempted one to read them.

The furniture was of horsehair, and everything was hard and shiny, so when the stranger sat down in the slippery-looking arm-chair that Mrs. Hableton pushed towards him; he could not help thinking it had been stuffed with stones, it felt so cold and hard. The lady herself sat opposite to him in another hard chair, and having taken the handkerchief off her head, folded it carefully, laid it on her lap, and then looked straight at her unexpected visitor.

"Now then," she said, letting her mouth fly open so rapidly that it gave one the impression that it was moved by strings like a marionette, "Who are you? what are you? and what do you want?"

The stranger put his red silk handkerchief into his hat, placed it on the table, and answered deliberately—

"My name is Gorby. I am a detective. I want Mr. Oliver Whyte."

"He ain't here," said Mrs. Hableton, thinking that Whyte had got into trouble, and was in danger of arrest.

"I know that," answered Mr. Gorby.

"Then where is 'e?"

Mr. Gorby answered abruptly, and watched the effect of his words.

"He is dead."

Mrs. Hableton grew pale, and pushed back her chair. "No," she cried, "he never killed 'im, did 'e?"

"Who never killed him?" queried Mr. Gorby, sharply.

Mrs. Hableton evidently knew more than she intended to say, for, recovering herself with a violent effort, she answered evasively—

"He never killed himself."

Mr. Gorby looked at her keenly, and she returned his gaze with a defiant stare.

"Clever," muttered the detective to himself; "knows something more than she chooses to tell, but I'll get it out of her." He paused a moment, and then went on smoothly:

"Oh, no! he did not commit suicide; what makes you think so?" Mrs. Hableton did not answer, but, rising from her seat, went over to a hard and shiny-looking sideboard, from whence she took a bottle of brandy and a small wine-glass. Half filling the glass, she drank it off, and returned to her seat.

"I don't take much of that stuff," she said, seeing the detective's eyes fixed curiously on her, "but you 'ave given me such a turn that I must take something to steady my nerves; what do you want me to do?"

"Tell me all you know," said Mr. Gorby, keeping his eyes fixed on her face.

"Where was Mr. Whyte killed?" she asked.

"He was murdered in a hansom cab on the St. Kilda Road."

"In the open street?" she asked in a startled tone.

"Yes, in the open street."

"Ah!" she drew a long breath, and closed her lips, firmly. Mr. Gorby said nothing. He saw that she was deliberating whether or not to speak, and a word from him might seal her lips, so, like a wise man, he kept silent. He obtained his reward sooner than he expected.

"Mr. Gorby," she said at length, "I 'ave 'ad a 'ard struggle all my life, which it came along of a bad husband, who was a brute and a drunkard, so, God knows, I ain't got much inducement to think well of the lot of you, but – murder," she shivered slightly, though the room was quite warm, "I didn't think of that."

"In connection with whom?"

"Mr. Whyte, of course," she answered, hurriedly.

"And who else?"

"I don't know."

"Then there is nobody else?"

"Well, I don't know – I'm not sure."

The detective was puzzled.

"What do you mean?" he asked.

"I will tell you all I know," said Mrs. Hableton, "an' if 'e's innocent, God will 'elp 'im."

"If who is innocent?"

"I'll tell you everythin' from the start," said Mrs. Hableton, "an' you can judge for yourself."

Mr. Gorby assented, and she began:

"It's only two months ago since I decided to take in lodgers; but charin's 'ard work, and sewin's tryin' for the eyes, so, bein' a lone woman, 'avin' bin badly treated by a brute, who is now dead, which I was allays a good wife to 'im, I thought lodgers 'ud 'elp me a little, so I put a notice in the paper, an' Mr. Oliver Whyte took the rooms two months ago."

"What was he like?"

"Not very tall, dark face, no whiskers nor moustache, an' quite the gentleman."

"Anything peculiar about him?"

Mrs. Hableton thought for a moment.

"Well," she said at length, "he 'ad a mole on his left temple, but it was covered with 'is 'air, an' few people 'ud 'ave seen it."

"The very man," said Gorby to himself, "I'm on the right path."

"Mr. Whyte said 'e 'ad just come from England," went on the woman.

"Which," thought Mr. Gorby, "accounts for the corpse not being recognised by friends."

"He took the rooms, an' said 'e'd stay with me for six months, an' paid a week's rent in advance, an' 'e allays paid up reg'ler like a respectable man, tho' I don't believe in 'em myself. He said 'e'd lots of friends, an' used to go out every night."

"Who were his friends?"

"That I can't tell you, for 'e were very close, an' when 'e went out of doors I never knowd where 'e went, which is jest like 'em; for they ses they're goin' to work, an' you finds 'em in the beershop. Mr. Whyte told me 'e was a-goin' to marry a heiress, 'e was."

"Ah!" interjected Mr. Gorby, sapiently.

"He 'ad only one friend as I ever saw – a Mr. Moreland – who comed 'ere with 'm, an' was allays with 'im – brother-like."

"What is this Mr. Moreland like?"

"Good-lookin' enough," said Mrs. Hableton sourly, "but 'is 'abits weren't as good as 'is face – 'andsom is as 'andsom does, is what I ses."

"I wonder if he knows anything about this affair," thought Gorby to himself "Where is Mr. Moreland to be found?" he asked.

"Not knowin', can't tell," retorted the landlady, "'e used to be 'ere reg'lar, but I ain't seen 'im for over a week."

"Strange! very!" said Gorby, shaking his head. "I should like to see this Mr. Moreland. I suppose it's probable he'll call again?"

"'Abit bein' second nature I s'pose he will," answered the woman, "'e might call at any time, mostly 'avin' called at night."

"Ah! then I'll come down this evening on chance of seeing him," replied the detective. "Coincidences happen in real life as well as in novels, and the gentleman in question may turn up in the nick of time. Now, what else about Mr. Whyte?"

"About two weeks ago, or three, I'm not cert'in which, a gentleman called to see Mr. Whyte; 'e was very tall, and wore a light coat."

"Ah! a morning coat?"

"No! 'e was in evenin' dress, and wore a light coat over it, an' a soft 'at."

"The very man," said the detective below his breath; "go on."

"He went into Mr. Whyte's room, an' shut the door. I don't know how long they were talkin' together; but I was sittin' in this very room and heard their voices git angry, and they were a-swearin' at one another, which is the way with men, the brutes. I got up and went into the passage in order to ask 'em not to make such a noise, when Mr. Whyte's door opens, an' the gentleman in the light coat comes out, and bangs along to the door. Mr. Whyte 'e comes to the door of 'is room, an' 'e 'ollers out. 'She is mine; you can't do anything; an' the other turns with 'is 'and on the door an' says, 'I can kill you, an' if you marry 'er I'll do it, even in the open street.'"

"Ah!" said Mr. Gorby, drawing a long breath, "and then?"

"Then he bangs the door to, which it's never shut easy since, an' I ain't got no money to get it put right, an' Mr. Whyte walks back to his room, laughing."

"Did he make any remark to you?"

"No; except he'd been worried by a loonatic."

"And what was the stranger's name?"

"That I can't tell you, as Mr. Whyte never told me. He was very tall, with a fair moustache, an' dressed as I told you."

Mr. Gorby was satisfied.

"That is the man," he said to himself, "who got into the hansom cab, and murdered Whyte; there's no doubt of it! Whyte and he were rivals for the heiress."

"What d'y think of it?" said Mrs. Hableton curiously.

"I think," said Mr. Gorby slowly, with his eyes fixed on her, "I think that there is a woman at the bottom of this crime."

Chapter VI
Mr. Gorby Makes Further Discoveries

When Mr. Gorby left Possum Villa no doubt remained in his mind as to who had committed the murder. The gentleman in the light coat had threatened to murder Whyte, even in the open street – these last words being especially significant – and there was no doubt that he had carried out his threat. The committal of the crime was merely the fulfilment of the words uttered in anger. What the detective had now to do was to find who the gentleman in the light coat was, where he lived, and, that done, to ascertain his doings on the night of the murder. Mrs. Hableton had described him, but was ignorant of his name, and her very vague description might apply to dozens of young men in Melbourne. There was only one person who, in Mr. Gorby's opinion, could tell the name of the gentleman in the light coat, and that was Moreland, the intimate friend of the dead man. They appeared, from the landlady's description, to have been so friendly that it was more than likely Whyte would have told Moreland all about his angry visitor. Besides, Moreland's knowledge of his dead friend's life and habits might be able to supply information on two points, namely, who was most likely to gain by Whyte's death, and who the heiress was that the deceased boasted he would marry. But the fact that Moreland should be ignorant of his friend's tragic death, notwithstanding that the papers were full of it, and that the reward gave an excellent description of his personal appearance, greatly puzzled Gorby.

The only way in which to account for Moreland's extraordinary silence was that he was out of town, and had neither seen the papers nor heard anyone talking about the murder. If this were the case he might either stay away for an indefinite time or return after a few days. At all events it was worth while going down to St. Kilda in the evening on the chance that Moreland might have returned to town, and would call to see his friend. So, after his tea, Mr. Gorby put on his hat, and went down to Possum Villa, on what he could not help acknowledging to himself was a very slender possibility.

Mrs. Hableton opened the door for him, and in silence led the way, not into her own sitting-room, but into a much more luxuriously furnished apartment, which Gorby guessed at once was that of Whyte's. He looked keenly round the room, and his estimate of the dead man's character was formed at once.

"Fast," he said to himself, "and a spendthrift. A man who would have his friends, and possibly his enemies, among a very shady lot of people."

What led Mr. Gorby to this belief was the evidence which surrounded him of Whyte's mode of life. The room was well furnished, the furniture being covered with dark-red velvet, while the curtains on the windows and the carpet were all of the same somewhat sombre hue.

"I did the thing properly," observed Mrs. Hableton, with a satisfactory smile on her hard face. "When you wants young men to stop with you, the rooms must be well furnished, an' Mr. Whyte paid well, tho' 'e was rather pertickler about 'is food, which I'm only a plain cook, an' can't make them French things which spile the stomach."

The globes of the gas lamps were of a pale pink colour, and Mrs. Hableton having lit the gas in expectation of Mr. Gorby's arrival, there was a soft roseate hue through the room. Mr. Gorby put his hands in his capacious pockets, and strolled leisurely through the room, examining everything with a curious eye. The walls were covered with pictures of celebrated horses and famous jockeys. Alternating with these were photographs of ladies of the stage, mostly London actresses, Nellie Farren, Kate Vaughan, and other burlesque stars, evidently being the objects of the late Mr. Whyte's adoration. Over the mantelpiece hung a rack of pipes, above which were two crossed foils, and under these a number of plush frames of all colours, with pretty faces smiling out of them; a remarkable fact being, that all the photographs were of ladies, and not a single male face was to be seen, either on the walls or in the plush frames.

"Fond of the ladies, I see," said Mr. Gorby, nodding his head towards the mantelpiece.

"A set of hussies," said Mrs. Hableton grimly, closing her lips tightly. "I feel that ashamed when I dusts 'em as never was – I don't believe in gals gettin' their picters taken with 'ardly any clothes on, as if they just got out of bed, but Mr. Whyte seems to like 'em."

"Most young men do," answered Mr. Gorby dryly, going over to the bookcase.

"Brutes," said the lady of the house. "I'd drown 'em in the Yarrer, I would, a settin' 'emselves and a callin' 'emselves lords of creation, as if women were made for nothin' but to earn money 'an see 'em drink it, as my 'usband did, which 'is inside never seemed to 'ave enough beer, an' me a poor lone woman with no family, thank God, or they'd 'ave taken arter their father in 'is drinkin' 'abits."

Mr. Gorby took no notice of this tirade against men, but stood looking at Mr. Whyte's library, which seemed to consist mostly of French novels and sporting newspapers.

"Zola," said Mr. Gorby, thoughtfully, taking down a flimsy yellow book rather tattered. "I've heard of him; if his novels are as bad as his reputation I shouldn't care to read them."

Here a knock came at the front door, loud and decisive. On hearing it Mrs. Hableton sprang hastily to her feet. "That may be Mr. Moreland," she said, as the detective quickly replaced "Zola" in the bookcase. "I never 'ave visitors in the evenin', bein' a lone widder, and if it is 'im I'll bring 'im in 'ere."

She went out, and presently Gorby, who was listening intently, heard a man's voice ask if Mr. Whyte was at home.

"No, sir, he ain't," answered the landlady; "but there's a gentleman in his room askin' after 'im. Won't you come in, sir?"

"For a rest, yes," returned the visitor, and immediately afterwards Mrs. Hableton appeared, ushering in the late Oliver Whyte's most intimate friend. He was a tall, slender man, with a pink and white complexion, curly fair hair, and a drooping straw-coloured moustache – altogether a strikingly aristocratic individual. He was well-dressed in a suit of check, and had a cool, nonchalant air about him.

"And where is Mr. Whyte tonight?" he asked, sinking into a chair, and taking no more notice of the detective than if he had been an article of furniture.

"Haven't you seen him lately?" asked the detective quickly. Mr. Moreland stared in an insolent manner at his questioner for a few moments, as if he were debating the advisability of answering or not. At last he apparently decided that he would, for slowly pulling off one glove he leaned back in his chair.

"No, I have not," he said with a yawn. "I have been up the country for a few days, and arrived back only this evening, so I have not seen him for over a week. Why do you ask?"

The detective did not answer, but stood looking at the young man before him in a thoughtful manner.

"I hope," said Mr. Moreland, nonchalantly, "I hope you will know me again, my friend, but I didn't know Whyte had started a lunatic asylum during my absence. Who are you?"

Mr. Gorby came forward and stood under the gas light.

"My name is Gorby, sir, and I am a detective," he said quietly.

"Ah! indeed," said Moreland, coolly looking him up and down. "What has Whyte been doing; running away with someone's wife, eh? I know he has little weaknesses of that sort."

Gorby shook his head.

"Do you know where Mr. Whyte is to be found?" he asked, cautiously.

Moreland laughed.

"Not I, my friend," said he, lightly. "I presume he is somewhere about here, as these are his head-quarters. What has he been doing? Nothing that can surprise me, I assure you – he was always an erratic individual, and—"

"He paid reg'ler," interrupted Mrs. Hableton, pursing up her lips.

"A most enviable reputation to possess," answered the other with a sneer, "and one I'm afraid I'll never enjoy. But why all this questioning about Whyte? What's the matter with him?"

"He's dead!" said Gorby, abruptly.

All Moreland's nonchalance vanished on hearing this, and he started up from his chair.

"Dead," he repeated mechanically. "What do you mean?"

"I mean that Mr. Oliver Whyte was murdered in a hansom cab." Moreland stared at the detective in a puzzled sort of way, and passed his hand across his forehead.

"Excuse me, my head is in a whirl," he said, as he sat down again. "Whyte murdered! He was all right when I left him nearly two weeks ago."

"Haven't you seen the papers?" asked Gorby.

"Not for the last two weeks," replied Moreland. "I have been up country, and it was only on arriving back in town tonight that I heard about the murder at all, as my landlady gave me a garbled account of it, but I never for a moment connected it with Whyte, and

I came down here to see him, as I had agreed to do when I left. Poor fellow! poor fellow! poor fellow!" and much overcome, he buried his face in his hands.

Mr. Gorby was touched by his evident distress, and even Mrs. Hableton permitted a small tear to roll down one hard cheek as a tribute of sorrow and sympathy. Presently Moreland raised his head, and spoke to Gorby in a husky tone.

"Tell me all about it," he said, leaning his cheek on his hand. "Everything you know."

He placed his elbows on the table, and buried his face in his hands again, while the detective sat down and related all that he knew about Whyte's murder. When it was done he lifted up his head, and looked sadly at the detective.

"If I had been in town," he said, "this would not have happened, for I was always beside Whyte."

"You knew him very well, sir?" said the detective, in a sympathetic tone.

"We were like brothers," replied Moreland, mournfully.

"I came out from England in the same steamer with him, and used to visit him constantly here."

Mrs. Hableton nodded her head to imply that such was the case.

"In fact," said Mr. Moreland, after a moment's thought, "I believe I was with him on the night he was murdered."

Mrs. Hableton gave a slight scream, and threw her apron over her face, but the detective sat unmoved, though Moreland's last remark had startled him considerably.

"What's the matter?" said Moreland, turning to Mrs. Hableton.

"Don't be afraid; I didn't kill him – no – but I met him last Thursday week, and I left for the country on Friday morning at half-past six."

"And what time did you meet Whyte on Thursday night?" asked Gorby.

"Let me see," said Moreland, crossing his legs and looking thoughtfully up to the ceiling, "it was about half-past nine o'clock. I was in the Orient Hotel, in Bourke Street. We had a drink together, and then went up the street to an hotel in Russell Street, where we had another. In fact," said Moreland, coolly, "we had several other drinks."

"Brutes!" muttered Mrs. Hableton, below her breath.

"Yes," said Gorby, placidly. "Go on."

"Well of – it's hardly the thing to confess it," said Moreland, looking from one to the other with a pleasant smile, "but in a case like this, I feel it my duty to throw all social scruples aside. We both became very drunk."

"Ah! Whyte was, as we know, drunk when he got into the cab – and you—?"

"I was not quite so bad as Whyte," answered the other. "I had my senses about me. I fancy he left the hotel some minutes before one o'clock on Friday morning."

"And what did you do?"

"I remained in the hotel. He left his overcoat behind him, and I picked it up and followed him shortly afterwards, to return it. I was too drunk to see in which direction he had gone, and stood leaning against the hotel door in Bourke Street with the coat in my hand. Then some one came up, and, snatching the coat from me, made off with it, and the last thing I remember was shouting out: 'Stop, thief!' Then I must have fallen down, for next morning I was in bed with all my clothes on, and they were very muddy. I got up and left town for the country by the six-thirty train, so I knew nothing about the matter until I came back to Melbourne tonight. That's all I know."

"And you had no impression that Whyte was watched that night?"

"No, I had not," answered Moreland, frankly. "He was in pretty good spirits, though he was put out at first."

"What was the cause of his being put out?"

Moreland arose, and going to a side table, brought Whyte's album, which he laid on the table and opened in silence. The contents were very much the same as the photographs in the room, burlesque actresses and ladies of the ballet predominating; but Mr. Moreland turned over the pages till nearly the end, when he stopped at a large cabinet photograph, and pushed the album towards Mr. Gorby.

"That was the cause," he said.

It was the portrait of a charmingly pretty girl, dressed in white, with a sailor hat on her fair hair, and holding a lawn-tennis racquet. She was bending half forward, with a winning smile, and in the background bloomed a mass of tropical plants. Mrs. Hableton uttered a cry of surprise at seeing this.

"Why, it's Miss Frettlby," she said. "How did he know her?"

"Knew her father – letter of introduction, and all that sort of thing," said Mr. Moreland, glibly.

"Ah! indeed," said Mr. Gorby, slowly. "So Mr. Whyte knew Mark Frettlby, the millionaire; but how did he obtain a photograph of the daughter?"

"She gave it to him," said Moreland. "The fact is, Whyte was very much in love with Miss Frettlby."

"And she—"

"Was in love with someone else," finished Moreland. "Exactly! Yes, she loved a Mr. Brian Fitzgerald, to whom she is now engaged. He was mad on her; and Whyte and he used to quarrel desperately over the young lady."

"Indeed!" said Mr. Gorby. "And do you know this Mr. Fitzgerald?"

"Oh, dear, no!" answered the other, coolly. "Whyte's friends were not mine. He was a rich young man who had good introductions. I am only a poor devil on the outskirts of society, trying to push my way in the world."

"You are acquainted with his personal appearance, of course?" observed Mr. Gorby.

"Oh, yes, I can describe that," said Moreland. "In fact, he's not at all unlike me, which I take to be rather a compliment, as he is said to be good-looking. He is tall, rather fair, talks in a bored sort of manner, and is altogether what one would call a heavy swell; but you must have seen him," he went on, turning to Mrs. Hableton, "he was here three or four weeks ago, Whyte told me."

"Oh, that was Mr. Fitzgerald, was it?" said Mrs. Hableton, in surprise. "Yes, he is rather like you; the lady they quarrelled over must have been Miss Frettlby."

"Very likely," said Moreland, rising. "Well, I'm off; here's my address," putting a card in Gorby's, hand. "I'm glad to be of any use to you in this matter, as Whyte was my dearest friend, and I'll do all in my power to help you to find out the murderer."

"I don't think that is a very difficult matter," said Mr. Gorby, slowly.

"Oh, you have your suspicions?" asked Moreland, looking at him.

"I have."

"Then who do you think murdered Whyte?"

Mr. Gorby paused a moment, and then said deliberately: "I have an idea – but I am not certain – when I am certain, I'll speak."

"You think Fitzgerald killed my friend," said Moreland. "I see it in your face."

Mr. Gorby smiled. "Perhaps," he said, ambiguously. "Wait till I'm certain."

Chapter VII
The Wool King

THE OLD GREEK LEGEND of Midas turning everything he touched into gold, is truer than most people imagine. Mediaeval superstition changed the human being who possessed such a power into the philosopher's stone – the stone which so many alchemists sought in the dark ages. But we of the nineteenth century have given back into human hands this power of transformation.

But we do not ascribe it either to Greek deity, or to superstition; we call it luck. And he who possesses luck should be happy notwithstanding the proverb which hints the contrary. Luck means more than riches – it means happiness in most of those things, which the fortunate possessor of it may choose to touch. Should he speculate, he is successful; if he marry, his wife will surely prove everything to be desired; should he aspire to a position, social or political, he not only attains it, but does so with comparative ease. Worldly wealth, domestic happiness, high position, and complete success – all these things belong to the man who has luck.

Mark Frettlby was one of these fortunate individuals, and his luck was proverbial throughout Australia. If there was any speculation for which Mark Frettlby went in, other men would surely follow, and in every case the result turned out as well, and in many cases even better than they expected. He had come out in the early days of the colony with comparatively little money, but his great perseverance and never-failing luck had soon changed his hundreds into thousands, and now at the age of fifty-five he did not himself know the extent of his income. He had large stations scattered all over the Colony of Victoria, which brought him in a splendid income; a charming country house, where at certain seasons of the year he dispensed hospitality to his friends; and a magnificent town house down in St. Kilda, which would have been not unworthy of Park Lane.

Nor were his domestic relations less happy – he had a charming wife, who was one of the best known and most popular ladies of Melbourne, and an equally charming daughter, who, being both pretty and an heiress, naturally attracted crowds of suitors. But Madge Frettlby was capricious, and refused innumerable offers. Being an extremely independent young person, with a mind of her own, she decided to remain single, as she had not yet seen anyone she could love, and with her mother continued to dispense the hospitality of the mansion at St. Kilda.

But the fairy prince comes at length to every woman, and in this instance he came at his appointed time, in the person of one Brian Fitzgerald, a tall, handsome, fair-haired young man hailing from Ireland.

He had left behind him in the old country a ruined castle and a few acres of barren land, inhabited by discontented tenants, who refused to pay the rent, and talked darkly about the Land League and other agreeable things. Under these circumstances, with no rent coming in, and no prospect of doing anything in the future, Brian had left the castle of his forefathers to the rats and the family Banshee, and had come out to Australia to make his fortune.

He brought letters of introduction to Mark Frettlby, and that gentleman, taking a fancy to him, assisted him by every means in his power. Under Frettlby's advice Brian bought a station, and, to his astonishment, in a few years he found himself growing rich. The Fitzgeralds had always been more famous for spending than for saving, and it was an agreeable surprise to their latest representative to find the money rolling in instead of out. He began to indulge in castles in the air concerning that other castle in Ireland, with the barren acres and discontented tenants. In his mind's-eye he saw the old place rise up in all its pristine splendour from out its ruins; he saw the barren acres well cultivated, and the tenants happy and content – he was rather doubtful on this latter point, but, with the rash confidence of eight and twenty, determined to do his best to perform even the impossible.

Having built and furnished his castle in the air, Brian naturally thought of giving it a mistress, and this time actual appearance took the place of vision. He fell in love with Madge Frettlby, and having decided in his own mind that she and none other was fitted to grace the visionary halls of his renovated castle, he watched his opportunity, and declared himself. She, woman-like, coquetted with him for some time, but at last, unable to withstand the impetuosity of her Irish lover, confessed in a low voice, with a pretty smile on her face, that she could not live without him. Whereupon – well – lovers being of a conservative turn of mind, and accustomed to observe the traditional forms of wooing, the result can easily be guessed. Brian hunted all over the jewellers' shops in Melbourne with lover-like assiduity, and having obtained a ring wherein were set turquoise stones as blue as his own eyes, he placed it on her slender finger, and at last felt that his engagement was an accomplished fact.

He next proceeded to interview the father, and had just screwed up his courage to the awful ordeal, when something occurred which postponed the interview indefinitely. Mrs. Frettlby was out driving, and the horses took fright and bolted. The coachman and groom both escaped unhurt, but Mrs. Frettlby was thrown out and killed instantly.

This was the first really great trouble which had fallen on Mark Frettlby, and he seemed stunned by it. Shutting himself up in his room he refused to see anyone, even his daughter, and appeared at the funeral with a white and haggard face, which shocked everyone. When everything was over, and the body of the late Mrs. Frettlby was consigned to the earth, with all the pomp and ceremony which money could give, the bereaved husband rode home, and resumed his old life. But he was never the same again. His face, which had always been so genial and so bright, became stern and sad. He seldom smiled, and when he did, it was a faint wintry smile, which seemed mechanical. His whole interest in life was centred in his daughter. She became the sole mistress of the St. Kilda mansion, and her father idolised her. She was apparently the one thing left to him which gave him a pleasure in existence. In truth, had it not been for her bright presence, Mark Frettlby would fain have been lying beside his dead wife in the quiet graveyard.

After a time Brian again resolved to ask Mr. Frettlby for the hand of his daughter. But for the second time fate interposed. A rival suitor made his appearance, and Brian's hot Irish temper rose in anger at him.

Mr. Oliver Whyte had come out from England a few months previously, bringing with him a letter of introduction to Mr. Frettlby, who received him hospitably, as was his custom. Taking advantage of this, Whyte lost no time in making himself perfectly at home in the St. Kilda mansion.

From the outset Brian took a dislike to the new-comer. He was a student of Lavater, and prided himself on his perspicuity in reading character. His opinion of Whyte was anything but flattering to that gentleman; while Madge shared his repulsion towards the new-comer.

On his part Mr. Whyte was nothing if not diplomatic. He affected not to notice the coldness of Madge's reception of him. On the contrary he began to pay her the most marked attentions, much to Brian's disgust. At length he asked her to be his wife, and notwithstanding her prompt refusal, spoke to her father on the subject. Much to the astonishment of his daughter, Mr. Frettlby not only consented to Whyte paying his addresses to Madge, but gave that young lady to understand that he wished her to consider his proposals favourably.

In spite of all Madge could say, he refused to alter his decision, and Whyte, feeling himself safe, began to treat Brian with an insolence which was highly galling to Fitzgerald's proud nature. He had called on Whyte at his lodgings, and after a violent quarrel he had left the house vowing to kill him, should he marry Madge Frettlby.

The same night Fitzgerald had an interview with Mr. Frettlby. He confessed that he loved Madge, and that his love was returned. So, when Madge added her entreaties to Brian's, Mr. Frettlby found himself unable to withstand the combined forces, and gave his consent to their engagement.

Whyte was absent in the country for the next few days after his stormy interview with Brian, and it was only on his return that he learnt that Madge was engaged to his rival. He saw Mr. Frettlby, and having learnt from his own lips that such was the case, he left the house at once, and swore that he would never enter it again. He little knew how prophetic were his words, for on that same night he met his death in the hansom cab. He had passed out of the life of both the lovers, and they, glad that he troubled them no more, never suspected for a moment that the body of the unknown man found in Royston's cab was that of Oliver Whyte.

About two weeks after Whyte's disappearance Mr. Frettlby gave a dinner party in honour of his daughter's birthday. It was a delightful evening, and the wide French windows which led on to the verandah were open, letting in a gentle breeze from the ocean. Outside there was a kind of screen of tropical plants, and through the tangle of the boughs the guests, seated at the table, could just see the waters of the bay glittering in the pale moonlight. Brian was seated opposite to Madge, and every now and then he caught a glimpse of her bright face from behind the fruit and flowers, which stood in the centre of the table. Mark Frettlby was at the head of the table, and appeared in very good spirits. His stern features were somewhat relaxed, and he drank more wine than usual.

The soup had just been removed when some one, who was late, entered with apologies and took his seat. Some one in this case was Mr. Felix Rolleston, one of the best known young men in Melbourne. He had an income of his own, scribbled a little for the papers, was to be seen at every house of any pretensions in Melbourne, and was always bright, happy, and full of news. For details of any scandal you were safe in applying to Felix Rolleston. He knew all that was going on, both at home and abroad. And his knowledge, if not very accurate, was at least extensive, while his conversation was piquant, and at times witty. Calton, one of the leading lawyers of the city, remarked that "Rolleston put him in mind of what Beaconsfield said of one of the personages in Lothair, 'He wasn't an intellectual Croesus, but his pockets were always full of sixpences.'" Be it said in his favour that Felix was free with his sixpences.

The conversation, which had shown signs of languishing before his arrival, now brightened up.

"So awfully sorry, don't you know," said Felix, as he slipped into a seat by Madge; "but a fellow like me has got to be careful of his time – so many calls on it."

"So many calls in it, you mean," retorted Madge, with a disbelieving smile. "Confess, now, you have been paying a round of visits."

"Well, yes," assented Mr. Rolleston; "that's the disadvantage of having a large circle of acquaintances. They give you weak tea and thin bread and butter, whereas—"

"You would rather have something else," finished Brian.

There was a laugh at this, but Mr. Rolleston disdained to notice the interruption.

"The only advantage of five o'clock tea," he went on, "is, that it brings people together, and one hears what's going on."

"Ah, yes, Rolleston," said Mr. Frettlby, who was looking at him with an amused smile. "What news have you?"

"Good news, bad news, and such news as you have never heard of," quoted Rolleston gravely. "Yes, I have a bit of news – haven't you heard it?"

Rolleston felt he held sensation in his hands. There was nothing he liked better.

"Well, do you know," he said, gravely fixing in his eye-glass, "they have found out the name of the fellow who was murdered in the hansom cab."

"Never!" cried every one eagerly.

"Yes," went on Rolleston, "and what's more, you all know him."

"It's never Whyte?" said Brian, in a horrified tone.

"Hang it, how did you know?" said Rolleston, rather annoyed at being forestalled. "Why, I just heard it at the St. Kilda station."

"Oh, easily enough," said Brian, rather confused. "I used to meet Whyte constantly, and as I have not seen him for the last two weeks, I thought he might be the victim."

"How did they find out?" asked Mr. Frettlby, idly toying with his wine-glass.

"Oh, one of those detective fellows, you know," answered Felix. "They know everything."

"I'm sorry to hear it," said Frettlby, referring to the fact that Whyte was murdered. "He had a letter of introduction to me, and seemed a clever, pushing young fellow."

"A confounded cad," muttered Felix, under his breath; and Brian, who overheard him, seemed inclined to assent. For the rest of the meal nothing was talked about but the murder, and the mystery in which it was shrouded. When the ladies retired they chatted about it in the drawingroom, but finally dropped it for more agreeable subjects. The men, however, when the cloth was removed, filled their glasses, and continued the discussion with unabated vigour. Brian alone did not take part in the conversation. He sat moodily staring at his untasted wine, wrapped in a brown study.

"What I can't make out," observed Rolleston, who was amusing himself with cracking nuts, "is why they did not find out who he was before."

"That is not hard to answer," said Frettlby, filling his – glass. "He was comparatively little known here, as he had been out from England such a short time, and I fancy that this was the only house at which he visited."

"And look here, Rolleston," said Calton, who was sitting near him, "if you were to find a man dead in a hansom cab, dressed in evening clothes – which nine men out of ten are in the habit of wearing in the evening – no cards in his pockets, and no name on his linen, I rather think you would find it hard to discover who he was. I consider it reflects great credit on the police for finding out so quickly."

"Puts one in mind of 'The Leavenworth Case,' and all that sort of thing," said Felix, whose reading was of the lightest description. "Awfully exciting, like putting a Chinese puzzle together. Gad, I wouldn't mind being a detective myself."

"I'm afraid if that were the case," said Mr. Frettlby, with an amused smile, "criminals would be pretty safe."

"Oh, I don't know so much about that," answered Felix, shrewdly; "some fellows are like trifle at a party, froth on top, but something better underneath."

"What a greedy simile," said Calton, sipping his wine; "but I'm afraid the police will have a more difficult task in discovering the man who committed the crime. In my opinion he's a deuced clever fellow."

"Then you don't think he will be discovered?" asked Brian, rousing himself out of his brown study.

"Well, I don't go as far as that," rejoined Calton; "but he has certainly left no trace behind him, and even the Red Indian, in whom instinct for tracking is so highly developed, needs some sort of a trail to enable him to find out his enemies. Depend upon it," went on Calton, warming to his subject, "the man who murdered Whyte is no ordinary criminal; the place he chose for the committal of the crime was such a safe one."

"Do you think so?" said Rolleston. "Why, I should think that a hansom cab in a public street would be very unsafe."

"It is that very fact that makes it safer," replied Mr. Calton, epigrammatically. "You read De Quincey's account of the Marr murders in London, and you will see that the more public the place the less risk there is of detection. There was nothing about the gentleman in the light coat who murdered Whyte to excite Royston's suspicions. He entered the cab with Whyte; no noise or anything likely to attract attention was heard, and then he alighted. Naturally enough, Royston drove to St. Kilda, and never suspected Whyte was dead till he looked inside and touched him. As to the man in the light coat, he doesn't live in Powlett Street – no – nor in East Melbourne either."

"Why not?" asked Frettlby.

"Because he wouldn't have been such a fool as to leave a trail to his own door; he did what the fox often does – he doubled. My opinion is that he went either right through East Melbourne to Fitzroy, or he walked back through the Fitzroy Gardens into town. There was no one about at that time of the morning, and he could return to his lodgings, hotel, or wherever he is staying, with impunity. Of course, this is a theory that may be wrong; but from what insight into human nature my profession has given me, I think that my idea is a correct one."

All present agreed with Mr. Calton's idea, as it really did seem the most natural thing that would be done by a man desirous of escaping detection.

"Tell you what," said Felix to Brian, as they were on their way to the drawing-room, "if the fellow that committed the crime, is found out, by gad, he ought to get Calton to defend him."

Chapter VIII
Brian Takes a Walk and a Drive

WHEN THE GENTLEMEN entered the drawing-room a young lady was engaged in playing one of those detestable pieces of the MORCEAU DE SALON order, in which an unoffending air is taken, and variations embroidered on it, till it becomes a perfect agony to distinguish the tune, amid the perpetual rattle of quavers and demi-semi-quavers. The melody in this case was "Over the Garden Wall," with variations by Signor Thumpanini, and the young lady who played it was a pupil of that celebrated Italian musician. When the male portion of the guests entered, the air was being played in the bass with a great deal of power (that is, the loud pedal was down), and with a perpetual rattle of treble notes, trying with all their shrill might to drown the tune.

"Gad! it's getting over the garden wall in a hailstorm," said Felix, as he strolled over to the piano, for he saw that the musician was Dora Featherweight, an heiress to whom he was then paying attention, in the hope that she might be induced to take the name of Rolleston. So, when the fair Dora had paralysed her audience with one final bang and rattle, as if the gentleman going over the garden wall had tumbled into the cucumber-frame, Felix was loud in his expressions of delight.

"Such power, you know, Miss Featherweight," he said, sinking into a chair, and mentally wondering if any of the piano strings had given way at that last crash. "You put your heart into it – and all your muscle, too, by gad," he added mentally.

"It's nothing but practice," answered Miss Featherweight, with a modest blush. "I am at the piano four hours every day."

"Good heavens!" thought Felix, "what a time the family must have of it." But he kept this remark to himself, and, screwing his eye-glass into his left organ of vision, merely ejaculated, "Lucky piano."

Miss Featherweight, not being able to think of any answer to this, looked down and blushed, while the ingenuous Felix looked up and sighed.

Madge and Brian were in a corner of the room talking over Whyte's death.

"I never liked him," she said, "but it is horrible to think of him dying like that."

"I don't know," answered Brian, gloomily; "from all I can hear dying by chloroform is a very easy death."

"Death can never be easy," replied Madge, "especially to a young man so full of health and spirits as Mr. Whyte was."

"I believe you are sorry he's dead," said Brian, jealously.

"Aren't you?" she asked in some surprise.

"De mortuis nil nisi bonum," quoted Fitzgerald. "But as I detested him when alive, you can't expect me to regret his end."

Madge did not answer him, but glanced quickly at his face, and for the first time it struck her that he looked ill.

"What is the matter with you, dear?" she asked, placing her hand on his arm. "You are not looking well."

"Nothing – nothing," he answered hurriedly. "I've been a little worried about business lately – but come," he said, rising, "let us go outside, for I see your father has got that girl with the steam-whistle voice to sing."

The girl with the steam-whistle voice was Julia Featherweight, the sister of Rolleston's inamorata, and Madge stifled a laugh as she went on to the verandah with Fitzgerald.

"What a shame of you," she said, bursting into a laugh when they were safely outside; "she's been taught by the best masters."

"How I pity them," retorted Brian, grimly, as Julia wailed out, "Meet me once again," with an ear-piercing shrillness.

"I'd much rather listen to our ancestral Banshee, and as to meeting her again, one interview would be more than enough." Madge did not answer, but leaning lightly over the high rail of the verandah looked out into the beautiful moonlit night. There were a number of people passing along the Esplanade, some of whom stopped and listened to Julia's shrill notes. One man in particular seemed to have a taste for music, for he persistently stared over the fence at the house. Brian and Madge talked of divers subjects, but every time Madge looked up she saw the man watching the house.

"What does that man want, Brian?" she asked.

"What man?" asked Brian, starting. "Oh," he went on indifferently, as the watcher moved away from the gate and crossed the road on to the footpath, "he's taken up with the music, I suppose; that's all."

Madge said nothing, but she could not help thinking there was more in it than the music. Presently Julia ceased, and she proposed to go in.

"Why?" asked Brian, who was lying back in a comfortable seat, smoking a cigarette. "It's nice enough here."

"I must attend to my guests," she answered, rising. "You stop here and finish your cigarette," and with a gay laugh she flitted into the house.

Brian sat and smoked, staring out into the moonlight the while. Yes, the man was certainly watching the house, for he sat on one of the seats, and kept his eyes fixed on the brilliantly-lighted windows. Brian threw away his cigarette and shivered slightly.

"Could anyone have seen me?" he muttered, rising uneasily.

"Pshaw! of course not; and the cabman would never recognise me again. Curse Whyte, I wish I'd never set eyes upon him."

He gave one glance at the dark figure on the seat, and then, with a shiver, passed into the warm, well-lighted room. He did not feel easy in his mind, and he would have felt still less so had he known that the man on the seat was one of the cleverest of the Melbourne detectives.

Mr. Gorby had been watching the Frettlby mansion the whole evening, and was getting rather annoyed. Moreland did not know where Fitzgerald lived, and as that was one of the primary facts the detective wished to ascertain, he determined to watch Brian's movements, and to trace him home.

"If he's the lover of that pretty girl, I'll wait till he leaves the house," argued Mr. Gorby to himself, as he took his seat on the Esplanade. "He won't long remain away from her, and once he leaves the house it will be no difficult matter to find out where he lives."

When Brian made his appearance early in the evening, on his way to Mark Frettlby's mansion, he wore evening dress, a light overcoat, and a soft hat.

"Well, I'm dashed!" ejaculated Mr. Gorby, when he saw Fitzgerald disappear; "if he isn't a fool I don't know who is, to go about in the very clothes he wore when he polished Whyte off, and think he won't be recognised. Melbourne ain't Paris or London, that he can afford to be so careless, and when I put the darbies on him he will be astonished. Ah, well," he went on, lighting his pipe and taking a seat on the Esplanade, "I suppose I'll have to wait here till he comes out."

Mr. Gorby's patience was pretty severely tried, for hour after hour passed, and no one appeared. He smoked several pipes, and watched the people strolling along in the soft silver moonlight. A bevy of girls passed by with their arms round one another's waists. Then a young man and woman, evidently lovers, came walking along. They sat down by Mr. Gorby and looked hard at him, to hint that he need not stay. But the detective took no heed of them, and kept his eyes steadily upon the great house opposite. Finally, the lovers took themselves off with a very bad grace.

Then Mr. Gorby saw Madge and Brian come out on to the verandah, and heard in the stillness of the night, a sound weird and unearthly. It was Miss Featherweight singing. He saw Madge go in, shortly followed by Brian. The latter turned and stared at him for a moment.

"Ah," said Gorby to himself as he re-lit his pipe; "your conscience is a-smiting you, is it? Wait a bit, my boy, till I have you in gaol."

Then the guests came out of the house, and their black figures disappeared one by one from the moonlight as they shook hands and said good-night.

Shortly after Brian came down the path with Frettlby at his side, and Madge hanging on her father's arm. Frettlby opened the gate and held out his hand.

"Good-night, Fitzgerald," he said, in a hearty voice; "come soon again."

"Good-night, Brian, dearest," said Madge, kissing him, "and don't forget tomorrow."

Then father and daughter closed the gate, leaving Brian outside, and walked back to the house.

"Ah!" said Mr. Gorby to himself, "if you only knew what I know, you wouldn't be so precious kind to him."

Brian strolled along the Esplanade, and crossing over, passed by Gorby and walked on till he was opposite the Esplanade Hotel. Then he leaned his arms on the fence, and, taking off his hat, enjoyed the calm beauty of the hour.

"What a good-looking fellow," murmured Mr. Gorby, in a regretful tone. "I can hardly believe it of him, but the proofs are too clear."

The night was perfectly still. Not a breath of wind stirred, for what breeze there had been had long since died away. But Brian could see the white wavelets breaking lightly on the sands. The long narrow pier ran out like a black thread into the sheet of gleaming silver, and away in the distance the line of the Williamstown lights sparkled like some fairy illumination.

Over all this placid scene of land and water was a sky such as Doré loved – a great heavy mass of rain-clouds heaped one on top of the other, as the rocks the Titans piled to reach Olympus. Then a break in the woof, and a bit of dark blue sky could be seen glittering with stars, in the midst of which sailed the serene moon, shedding down her light on the cloudland beneath, giving to it all, one silver lining.

Somewhat to the annoyance of Mr. Gorby, who had no eye for the picturesque, Brian gazed at the sky for several minutes, admiring the wonderful beauty of its broken masses of light and shade. At length he lit a cigarette and walked down the steps on to the pier.

"Oh, suicide, is it?" muttered Mr. Gorby. "Not if I can help it." And he lit his pipe and followed him.

He found Brian leaning over the parapet at the end of the pier, looking at the glittering waters beneath, which kept rising and falling in a dreamy rhythm, that soothed and charmed the ear. "Poor girl! poor girl!" the detective heard him mutter as he came up. "If she only knew all! If she—"

At this moment he heard the approaching step, and turned round sharply. The detective saw that his face was ghastly pale in the moonlight, and his brows wrinkled in anger.

"What the devil do you want?" he burst out, as Gorby paused.

"What do you mean by following me all over the place?"

"Saw me, watching the house," said Gorby to himself. "I'm not following you, sir," he said aloud. "I suppose the pier ain't private property. I only came down here for a breath of fresh air."

Fitzgerald did not answer, but turned sharply on his heel, and walked quickly up the pier, leaving Gorby staring after him.

"He's getting frightened," soliloquised the detective to himself, as he strolled easily along, keeping the black figure in front well in view. "I'll have to keep a sharp eye on him or he'll be clearing out of Victoria."

Brian walked rapidly up to the St. Kilda station, for on looking at his watch he found that he would just have time to catch the last train. He arrived a few minutes before it started, so, getting into the smoking carriage at the near end of the platform, he lit a cigarette, and, leaning back in his seat, watched the late comers hurrying into the station. Just as the last bell rang he saw a man rush along, to catch the train. It was the same man who had been watching him the whole evening, and Brian felt confident that he was being followed. He comforted himself, however, with the thought that this pertinacious follower might lose the train, and, being in the last carriage himself, he kept a look out along the platform, expecting to see his friend of the Esplanade standing disappointed on it. There was no appearance of him, so Brian, sinking back into his seat, lamented his ill-luck in not shaking off this man who kept him under such strict surveillance.

"Confound him!" he muttered softly. "I expect he will follow me to East Melbourne, and find out where I live, but he shan't if I can help it."

There was no one but himself in the carriage, and he felt relieved at this because he was in no humour to hear chatter.

"Murdered in a cab," he said, lighting a fresh cigarette, and blowing a cloud of smoke. "A romance in real life, which beats Miss Braddon hollow. There is one thing certain, he won't come between Madge and me again. Poor Madge!" with an impatient sigh. "If she only knew all, there would not be much chance of our marriage; but she can never find out, and I don't suppose anyone else will."

Here a thought suddenly struck him, and rising out of his seat, he walked to the other end of the carriage, and threw himself on the cushions, as if desirous to escape from himself.

"What grounds can that man have for suspecting me?" he said aloud. "No one knows I was with Whyte on that night, and the police can't possibly bring forward any evidence to show that I was. Pshaw!" he went on, impatiently buttoning up his coat. "I am like a child, afraid of my shadow – the fellow on the pier is only some one out for a breath of fresh air, as he said himself – I am quite safe."

At the same time, he felt by no means easy in his mind, and as he stepped out on to the platform at the Melbourne station he looked round apprehensively, as if he half expected to feel the detective's hand upon his shoulder. But he saw no one at all like the man he had met on the St. Kilda pier, and with a sigh of relief he left the station. Mr. Gorby, however, was not far away. He was following at a safe distance. Brian walked slowly along Flinders Street apparently deep in thought. He turned up Russell Street and did not stop until he found himself close to the Burke and Wills' monument – the exact spot where the cab had stopped on the night of Whyte's murder.

"Ah!" said the detective to himself, as he stood in the shadow on the opposite side of the street. "You're going to have a look at it, are you? – I wouldn't, if I were you – it's dangerous."

Fitzgerald stood for a few minutes at the corner, and then walked up Collins Street. When he got to the cab-stand, opposite the Melbourne Club, still suspecting he was followed, he hailed a hansom, and drove away in the direction of Spring Street. Gorby was rather perplexed at this sudden move, but without delay, he hailed another cab, and told the driver to follow the first till it stopped.

"Two can play at that game," he said, settling himself back in the cab, "and I'll get the better of you, clever as you are – and you are clever," he went on in a tone of admiration, as he looked round the luxurious hansom, "to choose such a convenient place for a murder; no disturbance and plenty of time for escape after you had finished; it's a pleasure going after a chap like you, instead of after men who tumble down like ripe fruit, and ain't got any brains to keep their crime quiet."

While the detective thus soliloquised, his cab, following on the trail of the other, had turned down Spring Street, and was being driven rapidly along the Wellington Parade, in the direction of East Melbourne. It then turned up Powlett Street, at which Mr. Gorby was glad.

"Ain't so clever as I thought," he said to himself. "Shows his nest right off, without any attempt to hide it."

The detective, however, had reckoned without his host, for the cab in front kept driving on, through an interminable maze of streets, until it seemed as though Brian were determined to drive the whole night.

"Look 'ere, sir!" cried Gorby's cabman, looking through his trap-door in the roof of the hansom, "'ow long's this 'ere game agoin' to larst? My 'oss is knocked up, 'e is, and 'is blessed old legs is agivin' way under 'im!"

"Go on! Go on!" answered the detective, impatiently; "I'll pay you well."

The cabman's spirits were raised by this, and by dint of coaxing and a liberal use of the whip, he managed to get his jaded horse up to a pretty good pace. They were in Fitzroy by this time, and both cabs turned out of Gertrude Street into Nicholson Street; thence passed on to Evelyn Street and along Spring Street, until Brian's cab stopped at the corner of Collins Street, and Gorby saw him alight and dismiss his cab-man. He then walked down the street and disappeared into the Treasury Gardens.

"Confound it," said the detective, as he got out and paid his fare, which was by no means a light one, but over which he had no time to argue, "we've come in a circle, and I do believe he lives in Powlett Street after all."

He went into the gardens, and saw Brian some distance ahead of him, walking rapidly. It was bright moonlight, and he could easily distinguish Fitzgerald by his light coat.

As he went along that noble avenue with its elms in their winter dress, the moon shining through their branches wrought a fantastic tracery, on the smooth asphalte. And on either side Gorby could see the dim white forms of the old Greek gods and goddesses – Venus Victrix, with the apple in her hand (which Mr. Gorby, in his happy ignorance of heathen mythology, took for Eve offering Adam the forbidden fruit); Diana, with the hound at her feet, and Bacchus and Ariadne (which the detective imagined were the Babes in the Wood). He knew that each of the statues had queer names, but thought they were merely allegorical. Passing over the bridge, with the water rippling quietly underneath, Brian went up the smooth yellow path to where the statue of Hebe, holding the cup, seems instinct with life; and turning down the path to the right, he left the gardens by the end gate, near which stands the statue of the Dancing Faun, with the great bush of scarlet geranium burning like an altar before it. Then he went along the Wellington Parade, and turned up Powlett Street, where he stopped at a house near Cairns' Memorial Church, much to Mr. Gorby's relief, who, being like Hamlet, "fat and scant of breath," found himself rather exhausted. He kept well in the shadow, however, and saw Fitzgerald give one final look round before he disappeared into the house. Then Mr. Gorby, like the Robber Captain in Ali Baba, took careful stock of the house, and fixed its locality and appearance well in his mind, as he intended to call at it on the morrow.

"What I'm going to do," he said, as he walked slowly back to Melbourne, "is to see his landlady when he's out, and find out what time he came in on the night of the murder. If it fits into the time he got out of Rankin's cab, I'll get out a warrant, and arrest him straight off."

Chapter IX
Mr. Gorby is Satisfied at Last

IN SPITE OF HIS LONG WALK, and still longer drive, Brian did not sleep well that night. He kept tossing and turning, or lying on his back, wide awake, looking into the darkness and thinking of Whyte. Towards dawn, when the first faint glimmer of morning came through the venetian blinds, he fell into a sort of uneasy doze, haunted by horrible dreams. He thought he was driving in a hansom, when suddenly he found Whyte by his side, clad in white cerements, grinning and gibbering at him with ghastly merriment. Then the cab went over a precipice, and he fell from a great height, down, down, with the mocking laughter still sounding in his ears, until he woke with a loud cry, and found it was broad daylight, and that drops of perspiration were standing on his brow. It was no use trying to sleep any longer, so, with a weary sigh, he arose and went to his tub, feeling jaded and worn out by worry and want of sleep. His bath did him some good. The cold water brightened him up and pulled him together. Still he could not help giving a start of surprise when he saw his face reflected in the mirror, old and haggard-looking, with dark circles round the eyes.

"A pleasant life I'll have of it if this sort of thing goes on," he said, bitterly, "I wish I had never seen, or heard of Whyte."

He dressed himself carefully. He was not a man to neglect his toilet, however worried and out of sorts he might happen to feel. Yet, notwithstanding all his efforts the change in his appearance did not escape the eye of his landlady. She was a small, dried-up little woman, with a wrinkled yellowish face. She seemed parched up and brittle. Whenever she moved she crackled, and one went in constant dread of seeing a wizen-looking limb break off short like the branch of some dead tree. When she spoke it was in a voice hard and shrill, not unlike the chirp of a cricket. When – as was frequently the case – she clothed her attenuated form in a faded brown silk gown, her resemblance to that lively insect was remarkable.

And, as on this morning she crackled into Brian's sitting-room with the ARGUS and his coffee, a look of dismay at his altered appearance, came over her stony little countenance.

"Dear me, sir," she chirped out in her shrill voice, as she placed her burden on the table, "are you took bad?"

Brian shook his head.

"Want of sleep, that's all, Mrs. Sampson," he answered, unfolding the ARGUS.

"Ah! that's because ye ain't got enough blood in yer 'ead," said Mrs. Sampson, wisely, for she had her own ideas on the subject of health. "If you ain't got blood you ain't got sleep."

Brian looked at her as she said this, for there seemed such an obvious want of blood in her veins that he wondered if she had ever slept in all her life.

"There was my father's brother, which, of course, makes 'im my uncle," went on the landlady, pouring out a cup of coffee for Brian, "an' the blood 'e 'ad was somethin' astoundin', which it made 'im sleep that long as they 'ad to draw pints from 'im afore 'e'd wake in the mornin'."

Brian had the ARGUS before his face, and under its friendly cover he laughed quietly to himself.

"His blood poured out like a river," went on the landlady, still drawing from the rich stores of her imagination, "and the doctor was struck dumb with astonishment at seein' the Nigagerer which burst from 'im – but I'm not so full-blooded myself."

Fitzgerald again stifled a laugh, and wondered that Mrs. Sampson was not afraid of being treated as were Ananias and Sapphira. However, he said nothing, but merely intimated that if she would leave the room he would take his breakfast.

"An' if you wants anythin' else, Mr. Fitzgerald," she said, going to the door, "you knows your way to the bell as easily as I do to the kitching," and, with a final chirrup, she crackled out of the room.

As soon as the door was closed, Brian put down his paper and roared, in spite of his worries. He had that extraordinary vivacious Irish temperament, which enables a man to put all trouble behind his back, and thoroughly enjoy the present. His landlady, with her Arabian Nightlike romances, was a source of great amusement to him, and he felt considerably cheered by the odd turn her humour had taken this morning. After a time, however, his laughter ceased, and his troubles came crowding on him again. He drank his coffee, but pushed away the food which was before him; and looked through the ARGUS, for the latest report about the murder case. What he read made his cheek turn a shade paler than before. He could feel his heart thumping wildly.

"They've found a clue, have they?" he muttered, rising and pacing restlessly up and down. "I wonder what it can be? I threw that man off the scent last night, but if he suspects me, there will be no difficulty in his finding out where I live. Bah! What nonsense I am talking. I am the victim of my own morbid imagination. There is nothing to connect me with the crime, so I need not be afraid of my shadow. I've a good mind to leave town for a time, but if I am suspected that would excite suspicion. Oh, Madge! my darling," he cried passionately, "if you only knew what I suffer, I know that you would pity me – but you must never know the truth – Never! Never!" and sinking into a chair by the window, he covered his face with his hands. After remaining in this position for some minutes, occupied with his own gloomy thoughts, he arose and rang the bell. A faint crackle in the distance announced that Mrs. Sampson had heard it, and she soon came into the room, looking more like a cricket than ever. Brian had gone into his bedroom, and called out to her from there—

"I am going down to St. Kilda, Mrs. Sampson," he said, "and probably I shall not be back all day."

"Which I 'opes it 'ull do you good," she answered, "for you've eaten nothin', an' the sea breezes is miraculous for makin' you take to your victuals. My mother's brother, bein' a sailor, an' wonderful for 'is stomach, which, when 'e 'ad done a meal, the table looked as if a low-cuss had gone over it."

"A what?" asked Fitzgerald, buttoning his gloves.

"A low-cuss!" replied the landlady, in surprise at his ignorance, "as I've read in 'Oly Writ, as 'ow John the Baptist was partial to 'em, not that I think they'd be very fillin', tho', to be sure, 'e 'ad a sweet tooth, and ate 'oney with 'em."

"Oh! you mean locusts," said Brian now enlightened.

"An' what else?" asked Mrs. Sampson, indignantly; "which, tho' not bein' a scholar'd, I speaks English, I 'opes, my mother's second cousin 'avin' 'ad first prize at a spellin' bee, tho' 'e died early through brain fever, 'avin' crowded 'is 'ead over much with the dictionary."

"Dear me!" answered Brian, mechanically. "How unfortunate!" He was not listening to Mrs. Sampson's remarks. He suddenly remembered an arrangement which Madge had made, and which up till now had slipped his memory.

"Mrs. Sampson," he said, turning round at the door, "I am going to bring Mr. Frettlby and his daughter to have a cup of afternoon tea here, so you might have some ready."

"You 'ave only to ask and to 'ave," answered Mrs. Sampson, hospitably, with a gratified crackle of all her joints. "I'll make the tea, sir, an' also some of my own perticler cakes, bein' a special kind I 'ave, which my mother showed me 'ow to make, 'avin' been taught by a lady as she nussed thro' the scarlet fever, tho' bein' of a weak constitootion, she died soon arter, bein' in the 'abit of contractin' any disease she might chance on."

Brian hurried off lest in her Poe-like appreciation of them, Mrs. Sampson should give vent to more charnel-house horrors.

At one period of her life, the little woman had been a nurse, and it was told of her that she had frightened one of her patients into convulsions during the night by narrating to her the history of all the corpses she had laid out. This ghoul-like tendency in the end proved fatal to her professional advancement.

As soon as Fitzgerald had gone, she went over to the window and watched him as he walked slowly down the street – a tall, handsome man, of whom any woman would be proud.

"What an awful thing it are to think 'e'll be a corpse some day," she chirped cheerily to herself, "tho' of course bein' a great swell in 'is own place, 'e'll 'ave a nice airy vault, which 'ud be far more comfortable than a close, stuffy grave, even tho' it 'as a tombstone an' vi'lets over it. Ah, now! Who are you, impertinence?" she broke off, as a stout man in a light suit of clothes crossed the road and rang the bell, "a-pullin' at the bell as if it were a pump 'andle."

As the gentleman at the door, who was none other than Mr. Gorby, did not hear her, he of course did not reply, so she hurried down the stairs, crackling with anger at the rough usage her bell had received.

Mr. Gorby had seen Brian go out, and deeming it a good opportunity for enquiry had lost no time in making a start.

"You nearly tored the bell down," said Mrs. Sampson, as she presented her thin body and wrinkled face to the view of the detective.

"I'm very sorry," answered Gorby, meekly. "I'll knock next time."

"Oh, no you won't," said the landlady, tossing her head, "me not 'avin' a knocker, an' your 'and a-scratchin' the paint off the door, which it ain't been done over six months by my sister-in-law's cousin, which 'e is a painter, with a shop in Fitzroy, an' a wonderful heye to colour."

"Does Mr. Fitzgerald live here?" asked Mr. Gorby, quietly.

"He do," replied Mrs. Sampson, "but 'e's gone out, an' won't be back till the arternoon, which any messige 'ull be delivered to 'im punctual on 'is arrival."

"I'm glad he's not in," said Mr. Gorby. "Would you allow me to have a few moments' conversation?"

"What is it?" asked the landlady, her curiosity being roused.

"I'll tell you when we get inside," answered Mr. Gorby.

She looked at him with her sharp little eyes, and seeing nothing disreputable about him, led the way upstairs, crackling loudly the whole time. This so astonished Mr. Gorby that he cast about in his own mind for an explanation of the phenomenon.

"Wants oiling about the jints," was his conclusion, "but I never heard anything like it, and she looks as if she'd snap in two, she's that brittle."

Mrs. Sampson took Gorby into Brian's sitting-room, and having closed the door, sat down and prepared to hear what he had to say for himself.

"I 'ope it ain't bills," she said. "Mr. Fitzgerald 'avin' money in the bank, and everythin' respectable like a gentleman as 'e is, tho', to be sure, your bill might come down on him unbeknown, 'e not 'avin' kept it in mind, which it ain't everybody as 'ave sich a good memory as my aunt on my mother's side, she 'avin' been famous for 'er dates like a 'istory, not to speak of 'er multiplication tables, and the numbers of people's 'ouses."

"It's not bills," answered Mr. Gorby, who, having vainly attempted to stem the shrill torrent of words, had given in, and waited mildly until she had finished; "I only want to know a few things about Mr. Fitzgerald's habits."

"And what for?" asked Mrs. Sampson, indignantly. "Are you a noospaper a-putin' in articles about people who don't want to see 'emselves in print, which I knows your 'abits, my late 'usband 'avin' bin a printer on a paper which bust up, not 'avin' the money to pay wages, thro' which, there was doo to him the sum of one pound seven and sixpence halfpenny, which I, bein' 'is widder, ought to 'ave, not that I expects to see it on this side of the grave – oh, dear, no!" and she gave a shrill, elfish laugh.

Mr. Gorby, seeing that unless he took the bull by the horns, he would never be able to get what he wanted, grew desperate, and plunged in MEDIAS RES.

"I am an insurance agent," he said, rapidly, so as to prevent any interruption, "and Mr. Fitzgerald desires to insure his life in our company. I, therefore, want to find out if he is a good life to insure; does he live temperately? keep early hours? and, in fact, all about him?"

"I shall be 'appy to answer any enquiries which may be of use to you, sir," replied Mrs. Sampson; "knowin' as I do, 'ow good a insurance is to a family, should the 'ead of it be taken off unexpected, leavin' a widder, which, as I know, Mr. Fitzgerald is a-goin' to be married soon, an' I 'opes 'e'll be 'appy, tho' thro' it I loses a lodger as 'as allays paid regler, an' be'aved like a gentleman."

"So he is a temperate man?" said Mr. Gorby, feeling his way cautiously.

"Not bein' a blue ribbing all the same," answered Mrs. Sampson; "and I never saw him the wuss for drink, 'e being allays able to use his latch-key, and take 'is boots off afore going to bed, which is no more than a woman ought to expect from a lodger, she 'avin' to do 'er own washin'."

"And he keeps good hours?"

"Allays in afore the clock strikes twelve," answered the landlady; "tho', to be sure, I uses it as a figger of speech, none of the clocks in the 'ouse strikin' but one, which is bein' mended, 'avin' broke through overwindin'."

"Is he always in before twelve?" asked Mr. Gorby, keenly disappointed at this answer.

Mrs. Sampson eyed him waggishly, and a smile crept over her wrinkled little face.

"Young men, not bein' old men," she replied, cautiously, "and sinners not bein' saints, it's not nattral as latch-keys should be made for ornament instead of use, and Mr. Fitzgerald bein' one of the 'andsomest men in Melbourne, it ain't to be expected as 'e should let 'is latch-key git rusty, tho' 'avin' a good moral character, 'e uses it with moderation."

"But I suppose you are seldom awake when he comes in really late," said the detective.

"Not as a rule," assented Mrs. Sampson; "bein' a 'eavy sleeper, and much disposed for bed, but I 'ave 'eard 'im come in arter twelve, the last time bein' Thursday week."

"Ah!" Mr. Gorby drew a long breath, for Thursday week was the night upon which the murder was committed.

"Bein' troubled with my 'ead," said Mrs. Sampson, "thro' 'avin' been out in the sun all day a-washin', I did not feel so partial to my bed that night as in general, so went down to the kitching with the intent of getting a linseed poultice to put at the back of my 'ead, it being calculated to remove pain, as was told to me, when a nuss, by a doctor in the horspital, 'e now bein' in business for hisself, at Geelong, with a large family, 'avin' married early. Just as I was leavin' the kitching I 'eard Mr. Fitzgerald a-comin' in, and, turnin' round, looked at the clock, that 'avin' been my custom when my late 'usband came in, in the early mornin', I bein' a-preparin' 'is meal."

"And the time was?" asked Mr. Gorby, breathlessly.

"Five minutes to two o'clock," replied Mrs. Sampson. Mr. Gorby thought for a moment.

"Cab was hailed at one o'clock – started for St. Kilda at about ten minutes past – reached Grammar School, say, at twenty-five minutes past – Fitzgerald talks five minutes to cabman, making it half-past – say, he waited ten minutes for other cab to turn up, makes it twenty minutes to two – it would take another twenty minutes to get to East Melbourne – and five minutes to walk up here – that makes it five minutes past two instead of before – confound it. 'Was your clock in the kitchen right?'" he asked, aloud.

"Well, I think so," answered Mrs. Sampson. "It does get a little slow sometimes, not 'avin' been cleaned for some time, which my nevy bein' a watchmaker I allays 'ands it over to 'im."

"Of course it was slow on that night," said Gorby, triumphantly.

"He must have come in at five minutes past two – which makes it right."

"Makes what right?" asked the landlady, sharply. "And 'ow do you know my clock was ten minutes wrong?"

"Oh, it was, was it?" asked Gorby, eagerly.

"I'm not denyin' of it," replied Mrs. Sampson; "clocks ain't allays to be relied on more than men an' women – but it won't be anythin' agin 'is insurance, will it, as in general 'e's in afore twelve?"

"Oh, all that will be quite safe," answered the detective, delighted with the information he had obtained. "Is this Mr. Fitzgerald's room?"

"Yes, it is," replied the landlady; "but 'e furnished it 'imself, bein' of a luxurus turn of mind, not but what 'is taste is good, tho' far be it from me to deny I 'elped 'im to select; but 'avin' another room of the same to let, any friends as you might 'ave in search of a 'ome 'ud be well looked arter, my references bein' very 'igh, an' my cookin' tasty – an' if—"

Here a ring at the front door bell called Mrs. Sampson away, so with a hurried word to Gorby she crackled downstairs. Left to himself, Mr. Gorby arose and looked round the room. It was excellently furnished, and the pictures were good. At one end of the room, by the window, there was a writing-table covered with papers.

"It's no good looking for the papers he took out of Whyte's pocket, I suppose," said the detective to himself, as he turned over some letters, "as I don't know what they are, and I couldn't tell them if I saw them; but I'd like to find that missing glove and the bottle that held the chloroform – unless he's done away with them. There doesn't seem any sign of them here, so I'll have a look in his bedroom."

There was no time to lose, as Mrs. Sampson might return at any moment, so Mr. Gorby walked quickly into the bedroom, which opened off the sitting-room. The first thing that caught the detective's eye was a large photograph, in a plush frame, of Madge Frettlby. It stood on the dressing-table, and was similar to that one which he had already seen in Whyte's album. He took it up with a laugh.

"You're a pretty girl," he said, apostrophising the picture, "but you give your photograph to two young men, both in love with you, and both hot-tempered. The result is that one is dead, and the other won't survive him long. That's what you've done."

He put it down again, and looking round the room, caught sight of a light covert coat hanging behind the door and also a soft hat.

"Ah," said the detective, going up to the door, "here is the very coat you wore when you killed that poor fellow. Wonder what you have in the pockets," and he plunged his hand into them in turn. There were an old theatre programme and a pair of brown gloves in one, but in the second pocket Mr. Gorby made a discovery – none other than that of the missing glove. There it was – a soiled white glove for the right hand, with black bands down the back; and the detective smiled in a gratified manner as he put it carefully in his pocket.

"My morning has not been wasted," he said to himself. "I've found out that he came in at a time which corresponds to all his movements after one o'clock on Thursday night, and this is the missing glove, which clearly belonged to Whyte. If I could only get hold of the chloroform bottle I'd be satisfied."

But the chloroform bottle was not to be found, though he searched most carefully for it. At last, hearing Mrs. Sampson coming upstairs again, he gave up the search, and came back to the sitting-room.

"Threw it away, I suspect," he said, as he sat down in his, old place; "but it doesn't matter. I think I can form a chain of evidence, from what I have discovered, which will be sufficient to convict him. Besides, I expect when he is arrested he will confess everything; he seems to feel remorse for what he has done."

The door opened, and Mrs. Sampson entered the room in a state of indignation.

"One of them Chinese 'awkers," she explained, "'e's bin a-tryin' to git the better of me over carrots – as if I didn't know what carrots was – and 'im a-talkin' about a shillin' in his gibberish, as if 'e 'adn't been brought up in a place where they don't know what a shillin' is. But I never could abide furreigners ever since a Frenchman, as taught me 'is language, made orf with my mother's silver tea-pot, unbeknown to 'er, it bein' set out on the sideboard for company."

Mr. Gorby interrupted these domestic reminiscences of Mrs. Sampson's by stating that, now she had given him all necessary information, he would take his departure.

"An' I 'opes," said Mrs. Sampson, as she opened the door for him, "as I'll 'ave the pleasure of seein' you again should any business on be'alf of Mr. Fitzgerald require it."

"Oh, I'll see you again," said Mr. Gorby, with heavy jocularity, "and in a way you won't like, as you'll be called as a witness," he added, mentally. "Did I understand you to say, Mrs. Sampson," he went on, "that Mr. Fitzgerald would be at home this afternoon?"

"Oh, yes, sir, 'e will," answered Mrs. Sampson, "a-drinkin' tea with his young lady, who is Miss Frettlby, and 'as got no end of money, not but what I mightn't 'ave 'ad the same 'ad I been born in a 'igher spear."

"You need not tell Mr. Fitzgerald I have been here," said Gorby, closing the gate; "I'll probably call and see him myself this afternoon."

"What a stout person 'e are," said Mrs. Sampson to herself, as the detective walked away, "just like my late father, who was allays fleshy, bein' a great eater, and fond of 'is glass, but I took arter my mother's family, they bein' thin-like, and proud of keeping 'emselves so, as the vinegar they drank could testify, not that I indulge in it myself."

She shut the door, and went upstairs to take away the breakfast things, while Gorby was being driven along at a good pace to the police office, to obtain a warrant for Brian's arrest, on a charge of wilful murder.

A Scattered Body

Rich Larson

TWENTY-FOUR HOUR gyms are where insomniacs go to die. Isolated treadmill junkies rocketing nowhere, watching their own blank faces bob in the windows. Obsessive iPod-cyborgs mouthing rap lyrics as the weights rattle and clank. A desperate dead-lifter whose steroids are slowly turning to fat.

All of this was illuminated with hospital-white florescents, stage lighting for any cars on the dark fresh-paved road outside, for any 12:33 a.m. drivers who might want to worship a pantheon of sweating gods. During the day, when it was full, the gym was like one big machine of flesh and metal. During the night, the cogs kept to their own devices.

Ty, for instance, alone at the chinning bar. His grip was wide, pronated, magazine-approved. He pumped up and down soundlessly, with back muscles skimming just under his skin like sharks. A tattoo of crossed keys was imploding and unfurling at the base of his neck. The rack was boxed in by mirrors, and each one showed a Michelangelo. One also showed Jonny come in wearing a rumpled suit and jumped up on speed. Ty watched him wander past the runners and sneer at the lifters.

"Look at you," Jonny said, taking position directly behind him. "Like a Greek god. You spend too much time here, you know that?" His New Zealand accent was thicker than usual.

"What's up?" Ty asked, still bobbing.

"Found us something to do, mate." Jonny slapped a tree-trunk thigh on its way up. "Some easy cash. Have a look at this." He had a tablet tucked up under his arm, and now he whizzed over it with his finger, grinning down at the screen. With a soft "Aha," Jonny shuffled around the side of the rack and held the tablet up waiter-style.

"Cute," Ty said. Jonny flicked through a few more photographs, all of a girl with fake-blonde hair making a typical webcam pout, Myspace poses.

"Isn't she?" Jonny rubbed a hand through the black hair that shot off his forehead in spikes. He grinned like a wolf. "That's the premier's son."

Ty stopped at the top of his pull.

"Yeah, the bloke with the fucking signs everywhere," Jonny continued. "Do you see where I'm leading you, Ty? Are you using those cancerous biceps to pick up what I'm laying down?"

"Details," Ty said, resuming. His book-case shoulders were straining now.

"Not here, mate." Jonny gave the gym a contemptuous scan. "Let's grab a bite to eat. You know, once you've finished."

"I'm done." Ty made another slow pull, then another. Gravity had found the brash offender and was focusing all its attention on him now, fighting him back to Earth. Ty quivered. Dropped. Mopped his face with a towel.

"Man, why do you come here?" Jonny asked. "Not a bird in sight. And those jokers by the punching bag, bet they've never broken knuckles in their life. I mean if they got in a scrap with a, a rowing machine or something, maybe they'd come out top-wise." He stared at the tanned bodies with disdain. Jonny was bones and tendon, built like a ferret.

Ty was stuffing two sacks of Jell-O into the sleeves of his thermal. "Self-improvement, Jonny. Maybe you'll go in for it some day."

"Oh, I'm fine," Jonny said, eyeing an ape doing butterfly presses. The man gave him a dead eye. "Oi. Some kind of gangbanger here in his mum's shirt, Ty."

"Don't start shit." Ty was staring at himself in the mirror, grimacing. Jonny hopped impatiently from foot to foot. Then Ty flipped off his reflection, as was custom, and started for the exit.

"Go get your chest waxed, you pussy," Jonny said to the back of the butterfly machine. The man pulled his earbud and swung around. By that time, Jonny was slouching down the stairs and all that was visible was the mountain range of Ty's back. The fight chemical got all crossed up with the flight one and the man did not get up. People usually didn't where Ty was concerned.

* * *

Neon and grease. They had moved the conversation to a fast-food joint staffed by bored Filipinos. It seemed like a natural progression. Sweat was sticking Ty to the Lego-colored seat. Across from him, Jonny was reassembling his cheeseburger.

"Blackmail," he said, dumping his fries onto the patty.

"The premier doesn't know? About, uh."

"About his son's little hobby? Don't know, man. Doesn't matter." The ketchup packet burst like a pillbug. Jonny licked his hand edgewise. "What matters is, nobody else knows. None of his voters. He's a bloody Conservative, man. Two words. Family. Values." He drizzled the ketchup. "Gay son, that doesn't look so great for him, you know?"

Ty dipped a brace of fries into mayo. "You don't know that he's gay, Jonny."

"The fuck? He's a fairy, no doubt about it." Jonny frowned. His eyes had circles under them. "Dressing up as a girl and putting little cocktease videos on the web? What else do you call that? Oi, you want the pickle?"

"I'm good. How do you know it's him?"

"Never forget a face, right?" Jonny slapped the top back onto his burger. "Saw one of those big advertisements, premier and his family sitting all nice and waspy. Middle America and all that shit. Very same night, I see this."

The tablet was skewed between them. Jonny didn't seem concerned with the ketchup smeared on it. Ty had another look at the photos while his friend attacked the cheeseburger.

"And you saw this video why?"

Jonny swallowed. His grin smelled like onions. "Ask me no questions, and I'll tell you no lies. Or whatever." He made a curt gesture under the table. "Any case, this stuff is golden. I put the screen caps through a little facial recognition comparison. It's him. He's been at it for a month or so. And his daddy is up for re-election. Bad, bad timing."

"You want to blackmail the premier."

"Fuck yeah, man. Easy cash. Easier than some other shit we've done."

Ty found the rest of his fries were cold. He pushed them across the gritty table and thought. "It'll ruin the kid's life, Jonny."

"Mate. The kid would've ended up doing odd things at a truckstop for fivers anyway." Jonny scarfed the last of the cheeseburger down. "How often's an opportunity like this going to drop right in your lap? One in a million here, Ty."

"But it's not. I mean. Anyone could find that website."

"Yeah, they can find it, yeah? But will they know who it is? Not bloody likely." Jonny tossed a balled-up napkin from hand to hand. "We give the premier the web address. He'll get the little fairy to pull it the videos down, delete the account, all that. Then he has it on our good faith that we get rid of the screen caps."

"Good faith."

"Well, he'll have to, won't he." Jonny grinned. "And if he's lucky, none of the old pervies with it saved to the spank bank are, eh, deeply invested in regional politics."

Ty studied his knuckles. "How much do you think we can take him for?"

"Oh, he's loaded. Got a swimming pool. Drove by the place." Jonny leaned back and tongued some beef out of his molars. "Fifty thousand fast cash. That's him getting off easy."

"Split down the middle." Ty said it so casually it almost slipped by.

Jonny slapped the table, making the cold fries jump. "Holy God, man, you aren't even doing anything!"

"I am." Ty folded his arms to a portcullis. "Or you wouldn't have told me."

"Eh." Jonny smiled ruefully and shook out his shirt cuffs. "The premier's a sizeable bloke. Former policeman, too, so I'm thinking he has a few guns to pick from. The gay apple fell far from the tree, as they say. So you come, maybe come packing, and it all goes down very peacably, right?" He fingered a spike of his hair.

"For half," Ty told him.

"For half, because you're my best mate." Jonny wrapped the second burger back into its greasy paper. "You know why these taste so fucking good? Chemical engineering. They engineer them to taste like this. Natural verus unnatural for you."

"You should go home." Ty shrugged his aching shoulders and stood up. "Get some sleep."

"Holy God, Ty," said Jonny. "You know I don't sleep."

* * *

They drove instead, Jonny surfing the wireless from stoplight to stoplight and trying to pack a bowl at the same time, Ty at the wheel with his foot tired on the gas pedal. The gray compact skimmed along the empty road, alternately purring and snorting. They looped onto the highway. Dotted white line ate away under Ty's window like a zipper sealing shut. Comets whizzed by on top of lamp posts.

"Password, password, everyone's got a fucking password now." Jonny put the tablet away as they sped out of range. "So, time to find ourselves a phone booth."

"Yeah."

"What's got up your arse, Ty?" Jonny found a lighter on the dashboard and pinned it down. "You're being more quiet than your quiet self."

"Pass me that," Ty said. He steered with his knees and lit up. The smoke went down smooth.

"I mean, yeah, it's illegal," Jonny said, taking it back. His thumb snapped once, twice on the lighter. The bowl flared in the dark. "But so's jay-walking. Or nicking a film off the internet. We just do a little cost-benefit analysis is all. And fifty grand, well…" He tried for a smoke ring. "Well."

"You want me to talk, right?"

"Accent's a fucking curse." Jonny put one loafer up on the glove compartment. "Except where the women are concerned, that is. I'll fake an Australian any day for pussy."

They merged back into the city main, snaking through residential areas. Wooden fences slid by, manicured lawns where the automated sprinklers chattered to each other. It took a long time to find a phone booth, and neither of them remembered how much change they needed. Ty was feeling the weed by the time he got out of the car. His head was light but sharp.

"Short and sweet, Ty." Jonny was punching the number in. He held the receiver out and Ty took it from him.

Two rings.

Three.

An irritated voice. "Hello?"

"How well you know your son, Mister Premier?"

"Who is this? Is this a prank or something?"

"I'm going to quote you a URL," Ty said. "What you see might be, uh. It'll be surprising. And if you don't want your voters to see it, you'd better cover your ass."

There was static on the line, then: "What's this got to do with my son?"

"Ha, say we kidnapped him." Jonny, stifling a giggle.

"Need to keep an eye on your kids' computer," Ty said. The words seemed to be coming out on their own, now. It was like he was in some gangster movie. It felt silly and smooth at the same time. Ty motioned at Jonny for the web address, then read it aloud into the phone.

"Got that?" Ty asked. The silence was a long one, and it stopped feeling like a movie. Ty's fingers slackened around the phone. His stomach was guilty.

When the voice came back, it was loaded with shock. "What do you want?"

"Fifty grand." Ty read it off Jonny's lips. "We'll get it at your house. Tomorrow night. That's it."

"This is fake."

"Ask the kid," Jonny broke in. "Please, don't tell me you never guessed at him being light in the loafers. Needs a fucking haircut, too—"

Ty shoved him away. He mouthed the haircut bit again.

"Not fake," Ty told the receiver. "Put it through, uh, facial recognition. If you want. Be there with the money tomorrow night."

Another long silence.

"And don't touch the kid," Ty added. The line went dead, so he hung up. They trooped out of the phone booth and back to the car. Sirens from an ambulance gave them both a jolt, then died away. Ty slumped back in the seat and started the ignition.

"Not bloody likely," Jonny laughed suddenly, slamming the door. "He's going to kick the shit out of him. Know I would."

"Yeah, well you'd be a piece of shit father," Ty said.

"Woah, let's not get serious." Jonny stabbed around in the bowl with his thumbnail. "We just earned ourselves insane money, Ty. Relax and enjoy the feeling."

* * *

They smoked enough that the headlights of distant cars and the glow of street-lamps became the same thing, an abstract yellow kind of symbol, some sort of machine code, and Ty's hands began burning and freezing on the steering wheel.

Jonny was laughing, head thrown back, about a story he'd remembered from the old days, and would tell, if he could stop fucking laughing. Lazy circuits through another neighborhood, a classier one. Jonny balancing the tablet on his knees. Ty thinking about the photographs, the girl, the angle of her chin and the dress she was wearing. Bought? Or stolen from mother's closet with shaky fingers?

And then they were parked slantwise in the middle of a deserted street, leaching wireless from an invisible hotel, looking at the site and reading the capslocked comments to each other. Something about hormone costs and early transitioning. Another bowl, but this was the last of it. Jonny said that, not Ty.

Then: looking at the screen caps again. Would you be fooled in a bar? How about on the street, though? Man, that's a minor. Jonny kept asking and pushing the tablet at him and Ty kept wincing at it and pushing it back. When Jonny dropped it Ty felt relieved and achy at the same time.

He cranked the seat back and buzzed somewhere between awake and asleep. "When you can't walk away from what you want, you have to run," he said.

"You're high as a kite, motherfucker," Jonny said back.

The bowl was pooched. Jonny said he could drop a hit of speed right now, get sharp again. Ty found a case of knock-off energy drinks under the backseat. They swirled lukewarm sugar in tingling mouths instead and they rambled about familiar things. Professional sports. They were paid too much, weren't they? But still, what a fucking life. Jonny complained about a lack of rugby. Then it was the autoshop where Ty worked. Any new beauties in there? And then girls they had fucked back in school. Ty invented names.

And then, eventually, the world turned dull and cold again. Ty drove Jonny home. When he arrived back at his own apartment, he stripped down and went into the bathroom. For the first time in a long time, he showered in the dark.

* * *

"Alright, let's do this." Jonny shouted it over a car stereo pushed to breaking point. "Hop in, man. Shit, you're looking big. Just from the gym again or what?"

Ty climbed in and dropped the volume. "Yeah."

"Holy God." Jonny drummed a tattoo on the wheel and they pulled away. Ty'd slept badly with plenty of old dreams. They were like a stain when he woke up. The gym had been the only solution for it. He was better now, and he'd figured out his gameplan. He felt ready to extort money from a local politican again.

They pulled in against the corner of the street. The premier's house was just visible, a big brick and smoked glass behemoth that screamed money. It was getting dark, but they'd agreed on eight o'clock as an arbitrary doorbell time. Five minutes to.

Jonny was nervous, and so he was talking. "Why do you hit the iron so much? I mean, really. Why? You have someone you need to shit-kick?"

Ty hadn't thought of it that way. "Sort of. Sort of do it to exorcise."

"Yeah, yeah." Jonny snorted. "Smart ass. I know." But he didn't.

Both of them watched the dashboard clock like a time bomb. When it hit eight, Jonny hissed through his teeth and keyed the ignition. They crept out and forward, down the street. The premier's house had a wide driveway. Pristine basketball hoop. Aquamarine glow from the back, where pool lights were just switching on. Ty looked up at the windows and wondered whose room was whose. Jonny shoved a wooly ski mask into his hands.

"Only tug it down at the door," he suggested.

"Alright."

"Just up and ring the doorbell," Jonny said. "Like Halloween. Trick-or-treat. That's a big thing over here, right? Dress up? You ever go as a burglar?"

"A cowboy," Ty said. "Every fucking year."

He pulled the ski mask onto his head and went to the door. Jonny kept the engine running. When he came back to the car with a grocery bag full of cash, they peeled away like bats out of hell.

* * *

Ty caught him on the way to the city bus stop. He was small and skinny for seventeen. Twitchy-looking, but nothing that made it easy to imagine him sitting with lip-gloss on in front of a laptop, or telling anonymous screen-names that he wanted out, at least to his mother, but wasn't ready.

"Hey, excuse me. Need to talk to you for a second."

The kid turned around. His bookbag migrated to the other shoulder, where it would be harder to snatch. Ty was used to that. The kid was wearing makeup, liberally applied, but the blue bruise showed through.

"You need money for hormone replacement, right?" Ty asked.

His eyes went wide. He smoothed a hand along his hair and cast around, like someone else might be listening with a clipboard. "What?"

"And to get out of the house. Your dad beat on you pretty hard. Don't take that shit."

The boy's fingers flew to his eye. "Who the hell are you?"

Ty gathered up his guts and pulled the wad of cash out of his jacket. "If this is what you really want, take some cash. You have someone to stay with? Like, safe?"

"Yeah," the kid muttered. He stared at the cash, hand on his hair again. "I've been, um, talking to my cousin. She's on the coast. Who the hell are you?"

"I gave up on solving that right about when I hit six feet and grew stubble."

Understanding flashed onto the boy's face. "You?" Surprise, and a needle of scorn that Ty wanted to slap out of his mouth.

"Yeah, me." Ty grabbed the bookbag and stuffed the money inside.

"But, you—" The boy stared into the bag. "Oh. I just, you know, I wouldn't have guessed."

A pause.

"Good luck," Ty said gruffly. He wanted to say more. It was a gamble, and maybe the kid was picking wrong. Maybe Ty'd picked right, and a few more lifts would make him perfect in another way, a better way, and he could forget everything else.

Ty didn't say more. He put his earbuds in and forgot that he had ever seen the kid in his life.

The Escape of Arsène Lupin

Maurice Leblanc

ARSÈNE LUPIN had just finished his repast and taken from his pocket an excellent cigar, with a gold band, which he was examining with unusual care, when the door of his cell was opened. He had barely time to throw the cigar into the drawer and move away from the table. The guard entered. It was the hour for exercise.

"I was waiting for you, my dear boy," exclaimed Lupin, in his accustomed good humor.

They went out together. As soon as they had disappeared at a turn in the corridor, two men entered the cell and commenced a minute examination of it. One was Inspector Dieuzy; the other was Inspector Folenfant. They wished to verify their suspicion that Arsène Lupin was in communication with his accomplices outside of the prison. On the preceding evening, the 'Grand Journal' had published these lines addressed to its court reporter:

> "*Monsieur:*
> "*In a recent article you referred to me in most unjustifiable terms. Some days before the opening of my trial I will call you to account. Arsène Lupin.*"

The handwriting was certainly that of Arsène Lupin. Consequently, he sent letters; and, no doubt, received letters. It was certain that he was preparing for that escape thus arrogantly announced by him.

The situation had become intolerable. Acting in conjunction with the examining judge, the chief of the Sûreté, Mon. Dudouis, had visited the prison and instructed the gaoler in regard to the precautions necessary to insure Lupin's safety. At the same time, he sent the two men to examine the prisoner's cell. They raised every stone, ransacked the bed, did everything customary in such a case, but they discovered nothing, and were about to abandon their investigation when the guard entered hastily and said:

"The drawer.... look in the table-drawer. When I entered just now he was closing it."

They opened the drawer, and Dieuzy exclaimed:

"Ah! we have him this time."

Folenfant stopped him.

"Wait a moment. The chief will want to make an inventory."

"This is a very choice cigar."

"Leave it there, and notify the chief."

Two minutes later Mon. Dudouis examined the contents of the drawer. First he discovered a bundle of newspaper clippings relating to Arsène Lupin taken from the 'Argus de la Presse,' then a tobacco-box, a pipe, some paper called "onion-peel," and two books. He read the titles of the books. One was an English edition of Carlyle's "Hero-worship"; the other was a charming elzevir, in modern binding, the "Manual of Epictetus," a German translation published at Leyden in 1634. On examining the books, he found that all the pages were underlined and annotated. Were they prepared as a code for correspondence, or did they simply express the studious character of the reader? Then he examined the tobacco-box and the pipe. Finally, he took up the famous cigar with its gold band.

"Fichtre!" he exclaimed. "Our friend smokes a good cigar. It's a Henry Clay."

With the mechanical action of an habitual smoker, he placed the cigar close to his ear and squeezed it to make it crack. Immediately he uttered a cry of surprise. The cigar had yielded under the pressure of his fingers. He examined it more closely, and quickly discovered something white between the leaves of tobacco. Delicately, with the aid of a pin, he withdrew a roll of very thin paper, scarcely larger than a toothpick. It was a letter. He unrolled it, and found these words, written in a feminine handwriting:

"The basket has taken the place of the others. Eight out of ten are ready. On pressing the outer foot the plate goes downward. From twelve to sixteen every day, H-P will wait. But where? Reply at once. Rest easy; your friend is watching over you."

Mon. Dudouis reflected a moment, then said:

"It is quite clear.... the basket.... the eight compartments.... From twelve to sixteen means from twelve to four o'clock."

"But this H-P, that will wait?"

"H-P must mean automobile. H-P, horsepower, is the way they indicate strength of the motor. A twenty-four H-P is an automobile of twenty-four horsepower."

Then he rose, and asked:

"Had the prisoner finished his breakfast?"

"Yes."

"And as he has not yet read the message, which is proved by the condition of the cigar, it is probable that he had just received it."

"How?"

"In his food. Concealed in his bread or in a potato, perhaps."

"Impossible. His food was allowed to be brought in simply to trap him, but we have never found anything in it."

"We will look for Lupin's reply this evening. Detain him outside for a few minutes. I shall take this to the examining judge, and, if he agrees with me, we will have the letter photographed at once, and in an hour you can replace the letter in the drawer in a cigar similar to this. The prisoner must have no cause for suspicion."

It was not without a certain curiosity that Mon. Dudouis returned to the prison in the evening, accompanied by Inspector Dieuzy. Three empty plates were sitting on the stove in the corner.

"He has eaten?"

"Yes," replied the guard.

"Dieuzy, please cut that macaroni into very small pieces, and open that bread-roll.... Nothing?"

"No, chief."

Mon. Dudouis examined the plates, the fork, the spoon, and the knife – an ordinary knife with a rounded blade. He turned the handle to the left; then to the right. It yielded and unscrewed. The knife was hollow, and served as a hiding-place for a sheet of paper.

"Peuh!" he said, "that is not very clever for a man like Arsène. But we mustn't lose any time. You, Dieuzy, go and search the restaurant."

Then he read the note:

"I trust to you, H-P will follow at a distance every day. I will go ahead. Au revoir, dear friend."

"At last," cried Mon. Dudouis, rubbing his hands gleefully, "I think we have the affair in our own hands. A little strategy on our part, and the escape will be a success in so far as the arrest of his confederates are concerned."

"But if Arsène Lupin slips through your fingers?" suggested the guard.

"We will have a sufficient number of men to prevent that. If, however, he displays too much cleverness, ma foi, so much the worse for him! As to his band of robbers, since the chief refuses to speak, the others must."

* * *

And, as a matter of fact, Arsène Lupin had very little to say. For several months, Mon. Jules Bouvier, the examining judge, had exerted himself in vain. The investigation had been reduced to a few uninteresting arguments between the judge and the advocate, Maître Danval, one of the leaders of the bar. From time to time, through courtesy, Arsène Lupin would speak. One day he said:

"Yes, monsieur, le judge, I quite agree with you: the robbery of the Crédit Lyonnais, the theft in the rue de Babylone, the issue of the counterfeit bank-notes, the burglaries at the various châteaux, Armesnil, Gouret, Imblevain, Groseillers, Malaquis, all my work, monsieur, I did it all."

"Then will you explain to me—"

"It is useless. I confess everything in a lump, everything and even ten times more than you know nothing about."

Wearied by his fruitless task, the judge had suspended his examinations, but he resumed them after the two intercepted messages were brought to his attention; and regularly, at mid-day, Arsène Lupin was taken from the prison to the Dépôt in the prison-van with a certain number of other prisoners. They returned about three or four o'clock.

Now, one afternoon, this return trip was made under unusual conditions. The other prisoners not having been examined, it was decided to take back Arsène Lupin first, thus he found himself alone in the vehicle.

These prison-vans, vulgarly called "panniers à salade" – or salad-baskets – are divided lengthwise by a central corridor from which open ten compartments, five on either side. Each compartment is so arranged that the occupant must assume and retain a sitting posture, and, consequently, the five prisoners are seated one upon the other, and yet separated one from the other by partitions. A municipal guard, standing at one end, watches over the corridor.

Arsène was placed in the third cell on the right, and the heavy vehicle started. He carefully calculated when they left the quai de l'Horloge, and when they passed the Palais de Justice. Then, about the centre of the bridge Saint Michel, with his outer foot, that is to say, his right foot, he pressed upon the metal plate that closed his cell. Immediately something clicked, and the metal plate moved. He was able to ascertain that he was located between the two wheels.

He waited, keeping a sharp look-out. The vehicle was proceeding slowly along the boulevard Saint Michel. At the corner of Saint Germain it stopped. A truck horse had fallen. The traffic having been interrupted, a vast throng of fiacres and omnibuses had gathered there. Arsène Lupin looked out. Another prison-van had stopped close to the one he occupied. He moved the plate still farther, put his foot on one of the spokes of the wheel and leaped to the ground. A coachman saw him, roared with laughter, then tried to raise an outcry, but his voice was lost in the noise of the traffic that had commenced to move again. Moreover, Arsène Lupin was already far away.

He had run for a few steps; but, once upon the sidewalk, he turned and looked around; he seemed to scent the wind like a person who is uncertain which direction to take. Then, having decided, he put his hands in his pockets, and, with the careless air of an idle stroller, he proceeded up the boulevard. It was a warm, bright autumn day, and the cafés were full. He took a seat on the terrace of one of them. He ordered a bock and a package of cigarettes. He emptied his glass slowly, smoked one cigarette and lighted a second. Then he asked the waiter to send the proprietor to him. When the proprietor came, Arsène spoke to him in a voice loud enough to be heard by everyone:

"I regret to say, monsieur, I have forgotten my pocketbook. Perhaps, on the strength of my name, you will be pleased to give me credit for a few days. I am Arsène Lupin."

The proprietor looked at him, thinking he was joking. But Arsène repeated:

"Lupin, prisoner at the Santé, but now a fugitive. I venture to assume that the name inspires you with perfect confidence in me."

And he walked away, amidst shouts of laughter, whilst the proprietor stood amazed.

Lupin strolled along the rue Soufflot, and turned into the rue Saint Jacques. He pursued his way slowly, smoking his cigarettes and looking into the shop-windows. At the Boulevard de Port Royal he took his bearings, discovered where he was, and then walked in the direction of the rue de la Santé. The high forbidding walls of the prison were now before him. He pulled his hat forward to shade his face; then, approaching the sentinel, he asked:

"Is this the prison de la Santé?"

"Yes."

"I wish to regain my cell. The van left me on the way, and I would not abuse—"

"Now, young man, move along – quick!" growled the sentinel.

"Pardon me, but I must pass through that gate. And if you prevent Arsène Lupin from entering the prison it will cost you dear, my friend."

"Arsène Lupin! What are you talking about!"

"I am sorry I haven't a card with me," said Arsène, fumbling in his pockets.

The sentinel eyed him from head to foot, in astonishment. Then, without a word, he rang a bell. The iron gate was partly opened, and Arsène stepped inside. Almost immediately he encountered the keeper of the prison, gesticulating and feigning a violent anger. Arsène smiled and said:

"Come, monsieur, don't play that game with me. What! they take the precaution to carry me alone in the van, prepare a nice little obstruction, and imagine I am going to take to my heels and rejoin my friends. Well, and what about the twenty agents of the Sûreté who accompanied us on foot, in fiacres and on bicycles? No, the arrangement did not please me. I should not have got away alive. Tell me, monsieur, did they count on that?"

He shrugged his shoulders, and added:

"I beg of you, monsieur, not to worry about me. When I wish to escape I shall not require any assistance."

On the second day thereafter, the 'Echo de France,' which had apparently become the official reporter of the exploits of Arsène Lupin, – it was said that he was one of its principal shareholders – published a most complete account of this attempted escape. The exact wording of the messages exchanged between the prisoner and his mysterious friend, the means by which correspondence was constructed, the complicity of the police, the promenade on the Boulevard Saint Michel, the incident at the café Soufflot, everything was disclosed. It was known that the search of the restaurant and its waiters by Inspector Dieuzy had been fruitless. And the public also learned an extraordinary thing which demonstrated the infinite variety of resources that Lupin possessed: the prison-van, in which he was being carried, was prepared for the occasion and substituted by his accomplices for one of the six vans which did service at the prison.

The next escape of Arsène Lupin was not doubted by anyone. He announced it himself, in categorical terms, in a reply to Mon. Bouvier on the day following his attempted escape. The judge having made a jest about the affair, Arsène was annoyed, and, firmly eyeing the judge, he said, emphatically:

"Listen to me, monsieur! I give you my word of honor that this attempted flight was simply preliminary to my general plan of escape."

"I do not understand," said the judge.

"It is not necessary that you should understand."

And when the judge, in the course of that examination which was reported at length in the columns of the 'Echo de France,' when the judge sought to resume his investigation, Arsène Lupin exclaimed, with an assumed air of lassitude:

"Mon Dieu, Mon Dieu, what's the use! All these questions are of no importance!"

"What! No importance?" cried the judge.

"No; because I shall not be present at the trial."

"You will not be present?"

"No; I have fully decided on that, and nothing will change my mind."

Such assurance combined with the inexplicable indiscretions that Arsène committed every day served to annoy and mystify the officers of the law. There were secrets known only to Arsène Lupin; secrets that he alone could divulge. But for what purpose did he reveal them? And how?

Arsène Lupin was changed to another cell. The judge closed his preliminary investigation. No further proceedings were taken in his case for a period of two months, during which time Arsène was seen almost constantly lying on his bed with his face turned toward the wall. The changing of his cell seemed to discourage him. He refused to see his advocate. He exchanged only a few necessary words with his keepers.

During the fortnight preceding his trial, he resumed his vigorous life. He complained of want of air. Consequently, early every morning he was allowed to exercise in the courtyard, guarded by two men.

Public curiosity had not died out; every day it expected to be regaled with news of his escape; and, it is true, he had gained a considerable amount of public sympathy by reason of his verve, his gayety, his diversity, his inventive genius and the mystery of his life. Arsène Lupin must escape. It was his inevitable fate. The public expected it, and was surprised that the event had been delayed so long. Every morning the Préfect of Police asked his secretary:

"Well, has he escaped yet?"

"No, Monsieur le Préfect."

"Tomorrow, probably."

And, on the day before the trial, a gentleman called at the office of the 'Grand Journal,' asked to see the court reporter, threw his card in the reporter's face, and walked rapidly away. These words were written on the card: "Arsène Lupin always keeps his promises."

* * *

It was under these conditions that the trial commenced. An enormous crowd gathered at the court. Everybody wished to see the famous Arsène Lupin. They had a gleeful anticipation that the prisoner would play some audacious pranks upon the judge. Advocates and magistrates, reporters and men of the world, actresses and society women were crowded together on the benches provided for the public.

It was a dark, sombre day, with a steady downpour of rain. Only a dim light pervaded the courtroom, and the spectators caught a very indistinct view of the prisoner when the guards brought him in. But his heavy, shambling walk, the manner in which he dropped into his seat, and his passive, stupid appearance were not at all prepossessing. Several times his advocate – one of Mon. Danval's assistants – spoke to him, but he simply shook his head and said nothing.

The clerk read the indictment, then the judge spoke:

"Prisoner at the bar, stand up. Your name, age, and occupation?"

Not receiving any reply, the judge repeated:

"Your name? I ask you your name?"

A thick, slow voice muttered:

"Baudru, Désiré."

A murmur of surprise pervaded the courtroom. But the judge proceeded:

"Baudru, Désiré? Ah! a new alias! Well, as you have already assumed a dozen different names and this one is, no doubt, as imaginary as the others, we will adhere to the name of Arsène Lupin, by which you are more generally known."

The judge referred to his notes, and continued:

"For, despite the most diligent search, your past history remains unknown. Your case is unique in the annals of crime. We know not whom you are, whence you came, your birth and breeding – all is a mystery to us. Three years ago you appeared in our midst as Arsène Lupin, presenting to us a strange combination of intelligence and perversion, immorality and generosity. Our knowledge of your life prior to that date is vague and problematical. It may be that the man called Rostat who, eight years ago, worked with Dickson, the prestidigitator, was none other than Arsène Lupin. It is probable that the Russian student who, six years ago, attended the laboratory of Doctor Altier at the Saint Louis Hospital, and who often astonished the doctor by the ingenuity of his hypotheses on subjects of bacteriology and the boldness of his experiments in diseases of the skin, was none other than Arsène Lupin. It is probable, also, that Arsène Lupin was the professor who introduced the Japanese art of jiu-jitsu to the Parisian public. We have some reason to believe that Arsène Lupin was the bicyclist who won the Grand Prix de l'Exposition, received his ten thousand francs, and was never heard of again. Arsène Lupin may have been, also, the person who saved so many lives through the little dormer-window at the Charity Bazaar; and, at the same time, picked their pockets."

The judge paused for a moment, then continued:

"Such is that epoch which seems to have been utilized by you in a thorough preparation for the warfare you have since waged against society; a methodical apprenticeship in which you developed your strength, energy and skill to the highest point possible. Do you acknowledge the accuracy of these facts?"

During this discourse the prisoner had stood balancing himself, first on one foot, then on the other, with shoulders stooped and arms inert. Under the strongest light one could observe his extreme thinness, his hollow cheeks, his projecting cheek-bones, his earthen-colored face dotted with small red spots and framed in a rough, straggling beard. Prison life had caused him to age and wither. He had lost the youthful face and elegant figure we had seen portrayed so often in the newspapers.

It appeared as if he had not heard the question propounded by the judge. Twice it was repeated to him. Then he raised his eyes, seemed to reflect, then, making a desperate effort, he murmured:

"Baudru, Désiré."

The judge smiled, as he said:

"I do not understand the theory of your defense, Arsène Lupin. If you are seeking to avoid responsibility for your crimes on the ground of imbecility, such a line of defense is open to you. But I shall proceed with the trial and pay no heed to your vagaries."

He then narrated at length the various thefts, swindles and forgeries charged against Lupin. Sometimes he questioned the prisoner, but the latter simply grunted or remained silent. The examination of witnesses commenced. Some of the evidence given was immaterial; other portions of it seemed more important, but through all of it there ran a vein of contradictions and inconsistencies. A wearisome obscurity enveloped the proceedings, until Detective Ganimard was called as a witness; then interest was revived.

From the beginning the actions of the veteran detective appeared strange and unaccountable. He was nervous and ill at ease. Several times he looked at the prisoner, with obvious doubt and anxiety. Then, with his hands resting on the rail in front of him, he recounted the events in which he had participated, including his pursuit of the prisoner across Europe and his arrival in America. He was listened to with great avidity, as his capture of Arsène Lupin was well known to everyone through the medium of the press. Toward the close of his testimony, after referring to his conversations with Arsène Lupin, he stopped, twice, embarrassed and undecided. It was apparent that he was possessed of some thought which he feared to utter. The judge said to him, sympathetically:

"If you are ill, you may retire for the present."

"No, no, but—"

He stopped, looked sharply at the prisoner, and said:

"I ask permission to scrutinize the prisoner at closer range. There is some mystery about him that I must solve."

He approached the accused man, examined him attentively for several minutes, then returned to the witness-stand, and, in an almost solemn voice, he said:

"I declare, on oath, that the prisoner now before me is not Arsène Lupin."

A profound silence followed the statement. The judge, nonplused for a moment, exclaimed:

"Ah! What do you mean? That is absurd!"

The detective continued:

"At first sight there is a certain resemblance, but if you carefully consider the nose, the mouth, the hair, the color of skin, you will see that it is not Arsène Lupin. And the eyes! Did he ever have those alcoholic eyes!"

"Come, come, witness! What do you mean? Do you pretend to say that we are trying the wrong man?"

"In my opinion, yes. Arsène Lupin has, in some manner, contrived to put this poor devil in his place, unless this man is a willing accomplice."

This dramatic dénouement caused much laughter and excitement amongst the spectators. The judge adjourned the trial, and sent for Mon. Bouvier, the gaoler, and guards employed in the prison.

When the trial was resumed, Mon. Bouvier and the gaoler examined the accused and declared that there was only a very slight resemblance between the prisoner and Arsène Lupin.

"Well, then!" exclaimed the judge, "who is this man? Where does he come from? What is he in prison for?"

Two of the prison-guards were called and both of them declared that the prisoner was Arsène Lupin. The judged breathed once more.

But one of the guards then said:

"Yes, yes, I think it is he."

"What!" cried the judge, impatiently, "you *think* it is he! What do you mean by that?"

"Well, I saw very little of the prisoner. He was placed in my charge in the evening and, for two months, he seldom stirred, but laid on his bed with his face to the wall."

"What about the time prior to those two months?"

"Before that he occupied a cell in another part of the prison. He was not in cell 24."

Here the head gaoler interrupted, and said:

"We changed him to another cell after his attempted escape."

"But you, monsieur, you have seen him during those two months?"

"I had no occasion to see him. He was always quiet and orderly."

"And this prisoner is not Arsène Lupin?"

"No."

"Then who is he?" demanded the judge.

"I do not know."

"Then we have before us a man who was substituted for Arsène Lupin, two months ago. How do you explain that?"

"I cannot."

In absolute despair, the judge turned to the accused and addressed him in a conciliatory tone:

"Prisoner, can you tell me how, and since when, you became an inmate of the Prison de la Santé?"

The engaging manner of the judge was calculated to disarm the mistrust and awaken the understanding of the accused man. He tried to reply. Finally, under clever and gentle questioning, he succeeded in framing a few phrases from which the following story was gleaned: Two months ago he had been taken to the Dépôt, examined and released. As he was leaving the building, a free man, he was seized by two guards and placed in the prison-van. Since then he had occupied cell 24. He was contented there, plenty to eat, and he slept well – so he did not complain.

All that seemed probable; and, amidst the mirth and excitement of the spectators, the judge adjourned the trial until the story could be investigated and verified.

* * *

The following facts were at once established by an examination of the prison records: Eight weeks before a man named Baudru Désiré had slept at the Dépôt. He was released the next day, and left the Dépôt at two o'clock in the afternoon. On the same day at two o'clock, having been examined for the last time, Arsène Lupin left the Dépôt in a prison-van.

Had the guards made a mistake? Had they been deceived by the resemblance and carelessly substituted this man for their prisoner?

Another question suggested itself: Had the substitution been arranged in advance? In that event Baudru must have been an accomplice and must have caused his own arrest for the express purpose of taking Lupin's place. But then, by what miracle had such a plan, based on a series of improbable chances, been carried to success?

Baudru Désiré was turned over to the anthropological service; they had never seen anything like him. However, they easily traced his past history. He was known at Courbevois, at Asnières and at Levallois. He lived on alms and slept in one of those rag-picker's huts near the barrier de Ternes. He had disappeared from there a year ago.

Had he been enticed away by Arsène Lupin? There was no evidence to that effect. And even if that was so, it did not explain the flight of the prisoner. That still remained a mystery. Amongst twenty theories which sought to explain it, not one was satisfactory. Of the escape itself, there was no doubt; an escape that was incomprehensible, sensational, in which the public, as well as the officers of the law, could detect a carefully prepared plan, a combination of circumstances marvelously dove-tailed, whereof the dénouement fully justified the confident prediction of Arsène Lupin: "I shall not be present at my trial."

After a month of patient investigation, the problem remained unsolved. The poor devil of a Baudru could not be kept in prison indefinitely, and to place him on trial would be ridiculous. There was no charge against him. Consequently, he was released; but the chief of the Sûreté resolved to keep him under surveillance. This idea originated with Ganimard. From his point of view there was neither complicity nor chance. Baudru was an instrument upon which Arsène Lupin had played with his extraordinary skill. Baudru, when set at liberty, would lead them to Arsène Lupin or, at least, to some of his accomplices. The two inspectors, Folenfant and Dieuzy, were assigned to assist Ganimard.

One foggy morning in January the prison gates opened and Baudru Désiré stepped forth – a free man. At first he appeared to be quite embarrassed, and walked like a person who has no precise idea whither he is going. He followed the rue de la Santé and the rue Saint Jacques. He stopped in front of an old-clothes shop, removed his jacket and his vest, sold his vest on which he realized a few sous; then, replacing his jacket, he proceeded on his way. He crossed the Seine. At the Châtelet an omnibus passed him. He wished to enter it, but there was no place. The controller advised him to secure a number, so he entered the waiting-room.

Ganimard called to his two assistants, and, without removing his eyes from the waiting room, he said to them:

"Stop a carriage.... no, two. That will be better. I will go with one of you, and we will follow him."

The men obeyed. Yet Baudru did not appear. Ganimard entered the waiting-room. It was empty.

"Idiot that I am!" he muttered, "I forgot there was another exit."

There was an interior corridor extending from the waiting-room to the rue Saint Martin. Ganimard rushed through it and arrived just in time to observe Baudru upon the top of the Batignolles-Jardin de Plates omnibus as it was turning the corner of the rue de Rivoli. He ran and caught the omnibus. But he had lost his two assistants. He must continue the pursuit alone. In his anger he was inclined to seize the man by the collar without ceremony. Was it not with premeditation and by means of an ingenious ruse that his pretended imbecile had separated him from his assistants?

He looked at Baudru. The latter was asleep on the bench, his head rolling from side to side, his mouth half-opened, and an incredible expression of stupidity on his blotched face.

No, such an adversary was incapable of deceiving old Ganimard. It was a stroke of luck – nothing more.

At the Galleries-Lafayette, the man leaped from the omnibus and took the La Muette tramway, following the boulevard Haussmann and the avenue Victor Hugo. Baudru alighted at La Muette station; and, with a nonchalant air, strolled into the Bois de Boulogne.

He wandered through one path after another, and sometimes retraced his steps. What was he seeking? Had he any definite object? At the end of an hour, he appeared to be faint from fatigue, and, noticing a bench, he sat down. The spot, not far from Auteuil, on the edge of a pond hidden amongst the trees, was absolutely deserted. After the lapse of another half-hour, Ganimard became impatient and resolved to speak to the man. He approached and took a seat beside Baudru, lighted a cigarette, traced some figures in the sand with the end of his cane, and said:

"It's a pleasant day."

No response. But, suddenly the man burst into laughter, a happy, mirthful laugh, spontaneous and irresistible. Ganimard felt his hair stand on end in horror and surprise. It was that laugh, that infernal laugh he knew so well!

With a sudden movement, he seized the man by the collar and looked at him with a keen, penetrating gaze; and found that he no longer saw the man Baudru. To be sure, he saw Baudru; but, at the same time, he saw the other, the real man, Lupin. He discovered the intense life in the eyes, he filled up the shrunken features, he perceived the real flesh beneath the flabby skin, the real mouth through the grimaces that deformed it. Those were the eyes and mouth of the other, and especially his keen, alert, mocking expression, so clear and youthful!

"Arsène Lupin, Arsène Lupin," he stammered.

Then, in a sudden fit of rage, he seized Lupin by the throat and tried to hold him down. In spite of his fifty years, he still possessed unusual strength, whilst his adversary was apparently in a weak condition. But the struggle was a brief one. Arsène Lupin made only a slight movement, and, as suddenly as he had made the attack, Ganimard released his hold. His right arm fell inert, useless.

"If you had taken lessons in jiu-jitsu at the quai des Orfèvres," said Lupin, "you would know that that blow is called udi-shi-ghi in Japanese. A second more, and I would have broken your arm and that would have been just what you deserve. I am surprised that you, an old friend whom I respect and before whom I voluntarily expose my incognito, should abuse my confidence in that violent manner. It is unworthy – Ah! What's the matter?"

Ganimard did not reply. That escape for which he deemed himself responsible – was it not he, Ganimard, who, by his sensational evidence, had led the court into serious error? That escape appeared to him like a dark cloud on his professional career. A tear rolled down his cheek to his gray moustache.

"Oh! mon Dieu, Ganimard, don't take it to heart. If you had not spoken, I would have arranged for some one else to do it. I couldn't allow poor Baudru Désiré to be convicted."

"Then," murmured Ganimard, "it was you that was there? And now you are here?"

"It is I, always I, only I."

"Can it be possible?"

"Oh, it is not the work of a sorcerer. Simply, as the judge remarked at the trial, the apprenticeship of a dozen years that equips a man to cope successfully with all the obstacles in life."

"But your face? Your eyes?"

"You can understand that if I worked eighteen months with Doctor Altier at the Saint-Louis hospital, it was not out of love for the work. I considered that he, who would one day have the honor of calling himself Arsène Lupin, ought to be exempt from the ordinary laws governing appearance and identity. Appearance? That can be modified at will. For instance, a hypodermic injection of paraffine will puff up the skin at the desired spot. Pyrogallic acid will change your skin to that of an Indian. The juice of the greater celandine will adorn you with the most beautiful eruptions and tumors. Another chemical affects the growth of your beard and hair; another changes the tone of your voice. Add to that two months of dieting in cell 24; exercises repeated a thousand times to enable me to hold my features in a certain grimace, to carry my head at a certain inclination, and adapt my back and shoulders to a stooping posture. Then five drops of atropine in the eyes to make them haggard and wild, and the trick is done."

"I do not understand how you deceived the guards."

"The change was progressive. The evolution was so gradual that they failed to notice it."

"But Baudru Désiré?"

"Baudru exists. He is a poor, harmless fellow whom I met last year; and, really, he bears a certain resemblance to me. Considering my arrest as a possible event, I took charge of Baudru and studied the points wherein we differed in appearance with a view to correct them in my own person. My friends caused him to remain at the Dépôt overnight, and to leave there next day about the same hour as I did – a coincidence easily arranged. Of course, it was necessary to have a record of his detention at the Dépôt in order to establish the fact that such a person was a reality; otherwise, the police would have sought elsewhere to find out my identity. But, in offering to them this excellent Baudru, it was inevitable, you understand, inevitable that they would seize upon him, and, despite the insurmountable difficulties of a substitution, they would prefer to believe in a substitution than confess their ignorance."

"Yes, yes, of course," said Ganimard.

"And then," exclaimed Arsène Lupin, "I held in my hands a trump-card: an anxious public watching and waiting for my escape. And that is the fatal error into which you fell, you and the others, in the course of that fascinating game pending between me and the officers of the law wherein the stake was my liberty. And you supposed that I was playing to the gallery; that I was intoxicated with my success. I, Arsène Lupin, guilty of such weakness! Oh, no! And, no longer ago than the Cahorn affair, you said: "When Arsène Lupin cries from the housetops that he will escape, he has some object in view." But, sapristi, you must understand that in order to escape I must create, in advance, a public belief in that escape, a belief amounting to an article of faith, an absolute conviction, a reality as glittering as the sun. And I did create that belief that Arsène Lupin would escape, that Arsène Lupin would not be present at his trial. And when you gave your evidence and said: "That man is not Arsène Lupin," everybody was prepared to believe you. Had one person doubted it, had any one uttered this simple restriction: Suppose it is Arsène Lupin? – from that moment, I was lost. If anyone had scrutinized my face, not imbued with the idea that I was not Arsène Lupin, as you and the others did at my trial, but with the idea that I might be Arsène Lupin; then, despite all my precautions, I should have been recognized. But I had no fear. Logically, psychologically, no once could entertain the idea that I was Arsène Lupin."

He grasped Ganimard's hand.

"Come, Ganimard, confess that on the Wednesday after our conversation in the prison de la Santé, you expected me at your house at four o'clock, exactly as I said I would go."

"And your prison-van?" said Ganimard, evading the question.

"A bluff! Some of my friends secured that old unused van and wished to make the attempt. But I considered it impractical without the concurrence of a number of unusual circumstances. However, I found it useful to carry out that attempted escape and give it the widest publicity. An audaciously planned escape, though not completed, gave to the succeeding one the character of reality simply by anticipation."

"So that the cigar...."

"Hollowed by myself, as well as the knife."

"And the letters?"

"Written by me."

"And the mysterious correspondent?"

"Did not exist."

Ganimard reflected a moment, then said:

"When the anthropological service had Baudru's case under consideration, why did they not perceive that his measurements coincided with those of Arsène Lupin?"

"My measurements are not in existence."

"Indeed!"

"At least, they are false. I have given considerable attention to that question. In the first place, the Bertillon system of records the visible marks of identification – and you have seen that they are not infallible – and, after that, the measurements of the head, the fingers, the ears, etc. Of course, such measurements are more or less infallible."

"Absolutely."

"No; but it costs money to get around them. Before we left America, one of the employees of the service there accepted so much money to insert false figures in my measurements. Consequently, Baudru's measurements should not agree with those of Arsène Lupin."

After a short silence, Ganimard asked:

"What are you going to do now?"

"Now," replied Lupin, "I am going to take a rest, enjoy the best of food and drink and gradually recover my former healthy condition. It is all very well to become Baudru or some other person, on occasion, and to change your personality as you do your shirt, but you soon grow weary of the change. I feel exactly as I imagine the man who lost his shadow must have felt, and I shall be glad to be Arsène Lupin once more."

He walked to and fro for a few minutes, then, stopping in front of Ganimard, he said:

"You have nothing more to say, I suppose?"

"Yes. I should like to know if you intend to reveal the true state of facts connected with your escape. The mistake that I made—"

"Oh! no one will ever know that it was Arsène Lupin who was discharged. It is to my own interest to surround myself with mystery, and therefore I shall permit my escape to retain its almost miraculous character. So, have no fear on that score, my dear friend. I shall say nothing. And now, good-bye. I am going out to dinner this evening, and have only sufficient time to dress."

"I though you wanted a rest."

"Ah! there are duties to society that one cannot avoid. Tomorrow, I shall rest."

"Where do you dine tonight?"

"With the British Ambassador!"

When the World Was Young

Jack London

Chapter I

HE WAS A VERY QUIET, self-possessed sort of man, sitting a moment on top of the wall to sound the damp darkness for warnings of the dangers it might conceal. But the plummet of his hearing brought nothing to him save the moaning of wind through invisible trees and the rustling of leaves on swaying branches. A heavy fog drifted and drove before the wind, and though he could not see this fog, the wet of it blew upon his face, and the wall on which he sat was wet.

Without noise he had climbed to the top of the wall from the outside, and without noise he dropped to the ground on the inside. From his pocket he drew an electric night-stick, but he did not use it. Dark as the way was, he was not anxious for light. Carrying the night-stick in his hand, his finger on the button, he advanced through the darkness. The ground was velvety and springy to his feet, being carpeted with dead pine-needles and leaves and mold which evidently had been undisturbed for years. Leaves and branches brushed against his body, but so dark was it that he could not avoid them. Soon he walked with his hand stretched out gropingly before him, and more than once the hand fetched up against the solid trunks of massive trees. All about him he knew were these trees; he sensed the loom of them everywhere; and he experienced a strange feeling of microscopic smallness in the midst of great bulks leaning toward him to crush him. Beyond, he knew, was the house, and he expected to find some trail or winding path that would lead easily to it.

Once, he found himself trapped. On every side he groped against trees and branches, or blundered into thickets of underbrush, until there seemed no way out. Then he turned on his light, circumspectly, directing its rays to the ground at his feet. Slowly and carefully he moved it about him, the white brightness showing in sharp detail all the obstacles to his progress. He saw, an opening between huge-trunked trees, and advanced through it, putting out the light and treading on dry footing as yet protected from the drip of the fog by the dense foliage overhead. His sense of direction was good, and he knew he was going toward the house.

And then the thing happened – the thing unthinkable and unexpected. His descending foot came down upon something that was soft and alive, and that arose with a snort under the weight of his body. He sprang clear, and crouched for another spring, anywhere, tense and expectant, keyed for the onslaught of the unknown. He waited a moment, wondering what manner of animal it was that had arisen from under his foot and that now made no sound nor movement and that must be crouching and waiting just as tensely and expectantly as he. The strain became unbearable. Holding the night-stick before him, he pressed the button, saw, and screamed aloud in terror. He was prepared for anything, from a frightened calf or fawn to a belligerent lion, but he was not prepared for what he saw. In that instant his tiny searchlight, sharp and white, had shown him what a thousand years would not enable him to forget – a man, huge and blond, yellow-haired and yellow-bearded, naked except for soft-tanned moccasins and what seemed a goat-skin about his middle. Arms and legs were bare, as were his shoulders and most of his chest. The skin was smooth and hairless, but browned by sun and wind, while under it heavy muscles were knotted like fat snakes. Still, this alone, unexpected as it well was, was not what had made the man scream out. What had caused his terror was the unspeakable ferocity of the face, the wild-animal glare of the blue eyes scarcely dazzled by the light, the pine-needles matted and clinging in the beard and hair, and the whole formidable body crouched and in the act of springing at him. Practically in the instant he saw all this, and while his scream still rang, the thing leaped, he flung his night-stick full at it, and threw himself to the ground. He felt its feet and shins strike against his ribs, and he bounded up and away while the thing itself hurled onward in a heavy crashing fall into the underbrush.

As the noise of the fall ceased, the man stopped and on hands and knees waited. He could hear the thing moving about, searching for him, and he was afraid to advertise his location by attempting further flight. He knew that inevitably he would crackle the underbrush and be pursued. Once he drew out his revolver, then changed his mind. He had recovered his composure and hoped to get away without noise. Several times he heard the thing beating up the thickets for him, and there were moments when it, too, remained still and listened. This gave an idea to the man. One of his hands was resting on a chunk of dead wood. Carefully, first feeling about him in the darkness to know that the full swing of his arm was clear, he raised the chunk of wood and threw it. It was not a large piece, and it went far, landing noisily in a bush. He heard the thing bound into the bush, and at the same time himself crawled steadily away. And on hands and knees, slowly and cautiously, he crawled on, till his knees were wet on the soggy mold, When he listened he heard naught but the moaning wind and the drip-drip of the fog from the branches. Never abating his caution, he stood erect and went on to the stone wall, over which he climbed and dropped down to the road outside.

Feeling his way in a clump of bushes, he drew out a bicycle and prepared to mount. He was in the act of driving the gear around with his foot for the purpose of getting the opposite pedal in position, when he heard the thud of a heavy body that landed lightly and evidently on its feet. He did not wait for more, but ran, with hands on the handles of his bicycle, until he was able to vault astride the saddle, catch the pedals, and start a spurt. Behind he could hear the quick thud-thud of feet on the dust of the road, but he drew away from it and lost it. Unfortunately, he had started away from the direction of town and was heading higher up into the hills. He knew that on this particular road there were no cross roads. The only way back was past that terror, and he could not steel himself to face it. At the end of half an hour, finding himself on an ever increasing grade, he dismounted. For still greater safety, leaving the wheel by the roadside, he climbed through a fence into what he decided was a hillside pasture, spread a newspaper on the ground, and sat down.

"Gosh!" he said aloud, mopping the sweat and fog from his face.

And "Gosh!" he said once again, while rolling a cigarette and as he pondered the problem of getting back.

But he made no attempt to go back. He was resolved not to face that road in the dark, and with head bowed on knees, he dozed, waiting for daylight.

How long afterward he did not know, he was awakened by the yapping bark of a young coyote. As he looked about and located it on the brow of the hill behind him, he noted the change that had come over the face of the night. The fog was gone; the stars and moon were out; even the wind had died down. It had transformed into a balmy California summer night. He tried to doze again, but the yap of the coyote disturbed him. Half asleep, he heard a wild and eery chant. Looking about him, he noticed that the coyote had ceased its noise and was running away along the crest of the hill, and behind it, in full pursuit, no longer chanting, ran the naked creature he had encountered in the garden. It was a young coyote, and it was being overtaken when the chase passed from view. The man trembled as with a chill as he started to his feet, clambered over the fence, and mounted his wheel. But it was his chance and he knew it. The terror was no longer between him and Mill Valley.

He sped at a breakneck rate down the hill, but in the turn at the bottom, in the deep shadows, he encountered a chuck-hole and pitched headlong over the handle bar.

"It's sure not my night," he muttered, as he examined the broken fork of the machine.

Shouldering the useless wheel, he trudged on. In time he came to the stone wall, and, half disbelieving his experience, he sought in the road for tracks, and found them – moccasin tracks, large ones, deep-bitten into the dust at the toes. It was while bending over them, examining, that again he heard the eery chant. He had seen the thing pursue the coyote, and he knew he had no chance on a straight run. He did not attempt it, contenting himself with hiding in the shadows on the off side of the road.

And again he saw the thing that was like a naked man, running swiftly and lightly and singing as it ran. Opposite him it paused, and his heart stood still. But instead of coming toward his hiding-place, it leaped into the air, caught the branch of a roadside tree, and swung swiftly upward, from limb to limb, like an ape. It swung across the wall, and a dozen feet above the top, into the branches of another tree, and dropped out of sight to the ground. The man waited a few wondering minutes, then started on.

Chapter II

DAVE SLOTTER leaned belligerently against the desk that barred the way to the private office of James Ward, senior partner of the firm of Ward, Knowles & Co. Dave was angry. Every one in the outer office had looked him over suspiciously, and the man who faced him was excessively suspicious.

"You just tell Mr. Ward it's important," he urged.

"I tell you he is dictating and cannot be disturbed," was the answer. "Come tomorrow."

"Tomorrow will be too late. You just trot along and tell Mr. Ward it's a matter of life and death."

The secretary hesitated and Dave seized the advantage.

"You just tell him I was across the bay in Mill Valley last night, and that I want to put him wise to something."

"What name?" was the query.

"Never mind the name. He don't know me."

When Dave was shown into the private office, he was still in the belligerent frame of mind, but when he saw a large fair man whirl in a revolving chair from dictating to a stenographer to face him, Dave's demeanor abruptly changed. He did not know why it changed, and he was secretly angry with himself.

"You are Mr. Ward?" Dave asked with a fatuousness that still further irritated him. He had never intended it at all.

"Yes," came the answer.

"And who are you?"

"Harry Bancroft," Dave lied. "You don't know me, and my name don't matter."

"You sent in word that you were in Mill Valley last night?"

"You live there, don't you?" Dave countered, looking suspiciously at the stenographer.

"Yes. What do you mean to see me about? I am very busy."

"I'd like to see you alone, sir."

Mr. Ward gave him a quick, penetrating look, hesitated, then made up his mind.

"That will do for a few minutes, Miss Potter."

The girl arose, gathered her notes together, and passed out. Dave looked at Mr. James Ward wonderingly, until that gentleman broke his train of inchoate thought.

"Well?"

"I was over in Mill Valley last night," Dave began confusedly.

"I've heard that before. What do you want?"

And Dave proceeded in the face of a growing conviction that was unbelievable. "I was at your house, or in the grounds, I mean."

"What were you doing there?"

"I came to break in," Dave answered in all frankness.

"I heard you lived all alone with a Chinaman for cook, and it looked good to me. Only I didn't break in. Something happened that prevented. That's why I'm here. I come to warn you. I found a wild man loose in your grounds – a regular devil. He could pull a guy like me to pieces. He gave me the run of my life. He don't wear any clothes to speak of, he climbs trees like a monkey, and he runs like a deer. I saw him chasing a coyote, and the last I saw of it, by God, he was gaining on it."

Dave paused and looked for the effect that would follow his words. But no effect came. James Ward was quietly curious, and that was all.

"Very remarkable, very remarkable," he murmured. "A wild man, you say. Why have you come to tell me?"

"To warn you of your danger. I'm something of a hard proposition myself, but I don't believe in killing people… that is, unnecessarily. I realized that you was in danger. I thought I'd warn you. Honest, that's the game. Of course, if you wanted to give me anything for my trouble, I'd take it. That was in my mind, too. But I don't care whether you give me anything or not. I've warned you any way, and done my duty."

Mr. Ward meditated and drummed on the surface of his desk. Dave noticed they were large, powerful hands, withal well-cared for despite their dark sunburn. Also, he noted what had already caught his eye before – a tiny strip of flesh-colored courtplaster on the forehead over one eye. And still the thought that forced itself into his mind was unbelievable.

Mr. Ward took a wallet from his inside coat pocket, drew out a greenback, and passed it to Dave, who noted as he pocketed it that it was for twenty dollars.

"Thank you," said Mr. Ward, indicating that the interview was at an end.

"I shall have the matter investigated. A wild man running loose IS dangerous."

But so quiet a man was Mr. Ward, that Dave's courage returned. Besides, a new theory had suggested itself. The wild man was evidently Mr. Ward's brother, a lunatic privately confined. Dave had heard of such things. Perhaps Mr. Ward wanted it kept quiet. That was why he had given him the twenty dollars.

"Say," Dave began, "now I come to think of it that wild man looked a lot like you—"

That was as far as Dave got, for at that moment he witnessed a transformation and found himself gazing into the same unspeakably ferocious blue eyes of the night before, at the same clutching talon-like hands, and at the same formidable bulk in the act of springing upon him. But this time Dave had no night-stick to throw, and he was caught by the biceps of both arms in a grip so terrific that it made him groan with pain. He saw the large white teeth exposed, for all the world as a dog's about to bite. Mr. Ward's beard brushed his face as the teeth went in for the grip on his throat. But the bite was not given. Instead, Dave felt the other's body stiffen as with an iron restraint, and then he was flung aside, without effort but with such force that only the wall stopped his momentum and dropped him gasping to the floor.

"What do you mean by coming here and trying to blackmail me?" Mr. Ward was snarling at him. "Here, give me back that money."

Dave passed the bill back without a word.

"I thought you came here with good intentions. I know you now. Let me see and hear no more of you, or I'll put you in prison where you belong. Do you understand?"

"Yes, sir," Dave gasped.

"Then go."

And Dave went, without further word, both his biceps aching intolerably from the bruise of that tremendous grip. As his hand rested on the door knob, he was stopped.

"You were lucky," Mr. Ward was saying, and Dave noted that his face and eyes were cruel and gloating and proud.

"You were lucky. Had I wanted, I could have torn your muscles out of your arms and thrown them in the waste basket there."

"Yes, sir," said Dave; and absolute conviction vibrated in his voice.

He opened the door and passed out. The secretary looked at him interrogatively.

"Gosh!" was all Dave vouchsafed, and with this utterance passed out of the offices and the story.

Chapter III

JAMES G. WARD was forty years of age, a successful business man, and very unhappy. For forty years he had vainly tried to solve a problem that was really himself and that with increasing years became more and more a woeful affliction. In himself he was two men, and, chronologically speaking, these men were several thousand years or so apart. He had studied the question of dual personality probably more profoundly than any half dozen of the leading specialists in that intricate and mysterious psychological field. In himself he was a different case from any that had been recorded. Even the most fanciful flights of the fiction-writers had not quite hit upon him. He was not a Dr. Jekyll and Mr. Hyde, nor was he like the unfortunate young man in Kipling's "Greatest Story in the World." His two personalities were so mixed that they were practically aware of themselves and of each other all the time.

His other self he had located as a savage and a barbarian living under the primitive conditions of several thousand years before. But which self was he, and which was the other, he could never tell. For he was both selves, and both selves all the time. Very rarely indeed did it happen that one self did not know what the other was doing. Another thing was that he had no visions nor memories of the past in which that early self had lived. That early self lived in the present; but while it lived in the present, it was under the compulsion to live the way of life that must have been in that distant past.

In his childhood he had been a problem to his father and mother, and to the family doctors, though never had they come within a thousand miles of hitting upon the clue to his erratic, conduct. Thus, they could not understand his excessive somnolence in the forenoon, nor his excessive activity at night. When they found him wandering along the hallways at night, or climbing over giddy roofs, or running in the hills, they decided he was a somnambulist. In reality he was wide-eyed awake and merely under the nightroaming compulsion of his early self. Questioned by an obtuse medico, he once told the truth and suffered the ignominy of having the revelation contemptuously labeled and dismissed as "dreams."

The point was, that as twilight and evening came on he became wakeful. The four walls of a room were an irk and a restraint. He heard a thousand voices whispering to him through the darkness. The night called to him, for he was, for that period of the twenty-four hours, essentially a night-prowler. But nobody understood, and never again did he attempt to explain. They classified him as a sleep-walker and took precautions accordingly – precautions that very often were futile. As his childhood advanced, he grew more cunning, so that the major portion of all his nights were spent in the open at realizing his other self. As a result, he slept in the forenoons. Morning studies and schools were impossible, and it was discovered that only in the afternoons, under private teachers, could he be taught anything. Thus was his modern self educated and developed.

But a problem, as a child, he ever remained. He was known as a little demon, of insensate cruelty and viciousness. The family medicos privately adjudged him a mental monstrosity and degenerate. Such few boy companions as he had, hailed him as a wonder, though they were all afraid of him. He could outclimb, outswim, outrun, outdevil any of them; while none dared fight with him. He was too terribly strong, madly furious.

When nine years of age he ran away to the hills, where he flourished, night-prowling, for seven weeks before he was discovered and brought home. The marvel was how he had managed to subsist and keep in condition during that time. They did not know, and he never told them, of the rabbits he had killed, of the quail, young and old, he had captured and devoured, of the farmers' chicken-roosts he had raided, nor of the cave-lair he had made and carpeted with dry leaves and grasses and in which he had slept in warmth and comfort through the forenoons of many days.

At college he was notorious for his sleepiness and stupidity during the morning lectures and for his brilliance in the afternoon. By collateral reading and by borrowing the notebook of his fellow students he managed to scrape through the detestable morning courses, while his afternoon courses were triumphs. In football he proved a giant and a terror, and, in almost every form of track athletics, save for strange Berserker rages that were sometimes displayed, he could be depended upon to win. But his fellows were afraid to box with him, and he signalized his last wrestling bout by sinking his teeth into the shoulder of his opponent.

After college, his father, in despair, sent him among the cow-punchers of a Wyoming ranch. Three months later the doughty cowmen confessed he was too much for them and telegraphed his father to come and take the wild man away. Also, when the father arrived to take him away, the cowmen allowed that they would vastly prefer chumming with howling cannibals, gibbering lunatics, cavorting gorillas, grizzly bears, and man-eating tigers than with this particular Young college product with hair parted in the middle.

There was one exception to the lack of memory of the life of his early self, and that was language. By some quirk of atavism, a certain portion of that early self's language had come down to him as a racial memory. In moments of happiness, exaltation, or battle, he was prone to burst out in wild barbaric songs or chants. It was by this means that he located in time and space that strayed half of him who should have been dead and dust for thousands of years. He sang, once, and deliberately, several of the ancient chants in the presence of Professor Wertz, who gave courses in old Saxon and who was a philogist of repute and passion. At the first one, the professor pricked up his ears and demanded to know what mongrel tongue or hog-German it was. When the second chant was rendered, the professor was highly excited. James Ward then concluded the performance by giving a song that always irresistibly rushed to his lips when he was engaged in fierce struggling or fighting. Then it was that Professor Wertz proclaimed it no hog-German, but early German, or early Teuton, of a date that must far precede anything that had ever been discovered and handed down by the scholars. So early was it that it was beyond him; yet it was filled with haunting reminiscences of word-forms he knew and which his trained intuition told him were true and real. He demanded the source of the songs, and asked to borrow the precious book that contained them. Also, he demanded to know why young Ward had always posed as being profoundly ignorant of the German language. And Ward could neither explain his ignorance nor lend the book. Whereupon, after pleadings and entreaties that extended through weeks, Professor Wert took a dislike to the young man, believed him a liar, and classified him as a man of monstrous selfishness for not giving him a glimpse of this wonderful screed that was older than the oldest any philologist had ever known or dreamed.

But little good did it do this much-mixed young man to know that half of him was late American and the other half early Teuton. Nevertheless, the late American in him was no weakling, and he (if he were a he and had a shred of existence outside of these two) compelled an adjustment or compromise between his one self that was a nightprowling savage that kept his other self sleepy of mornings, and that other self that was cultured and refined and that wanted to be normal and live and love and prosecute business like other people. The afternoons and early evenings he gave to the one, the nights to the other; the forenoons and parts of the nights were devoted to sleep for the twain. But in the mornings he slept in bed like a civilized man. In the night time he slept like a wild animal, as he had slept Dave Slotter stepped on him in the woods.

Persuading his father to advance the capital, he went into business and keen and successful business he made of it, devoting his afternoons whole-souled to it, while his partner devoted the mornings. The early evenings he spent socially, but, as the hour grew to nine or ten, an irresistible restlessness overcame him and he disappeared from the haunts of men until the next afternoon. Friends and acquaintances thought that he spent much of his time in sport. And they were right, though they never would have dreamed of the nature of the sport, even if they had seen him running coyotes in night-chases over the hills of Mill Valley. Neither were the schooner captains believed when they reported seeing, on cold winter mornings, a man swimming in the tide-rips of Raccoon Straits or in the swift currents between Goat island and Angel Island miles from shore.

In the bungalow at Mill Valley he lived alone, save for Lee Sing, the Chinese cook and factotum, who knew much about the strangeness of his master, who was paid well for saying nothing, and who never did say anything. After the satisfaction of his nights, a morning's sleep, and a breakfast of Lee Sing's, James Ward crossed the bay to San Francisco on a midday ferryboat and went to the club and on to his office, as normal and conventional a man of business as could be found in the city. But as the evening lengthened, the night called to him. There came a quickening of all his perceptions and a restlessness. His hearing was suddenly acute; the myriad night-noises told him a luring and familiar story; and, if alone, he would begin to pace up and down the narrow room like any caged animal from the wild.

Once, he ventured to fall in love. He never permitted himself that diversion again. He was afraid. And for many a day the young lady, scared at least out of a portion of her young ladyhood, bore on her arms and shoulders and wrists divers black-and-blue bruises – tokens of caresses which he had bestowed in all fond gentleness but too late at night. There was the mistake. Had he ventured love-making in the afternoon, all would have been well, for it would have been as the quiet gentleman that he would have made love – but at night it was the uncouth, wife-stealing savage of the dark German forests. Out of his wisdom, he decided that afternoon love-making could be prosecuted successfully; but out of the same wisdom he was convinced that marriage as would prove a ghastly failure. He found it appalling to imagine being married and encountering his wife after dark.

So he had eschewed all love-making, regulated his dual life, cleaned up a million in business, fought shy of match-making mamas and bright-eyed and eager young ladies of various ages, met Lilian Gersdale and made it a rigid observance never to see her later than eight o'clock in the evening, run of nights after his coyotes, and slept in forest lairs – and through it all had kept his secret safe save Lee Sing… and now, Dave Slotter. It was the latter's discovery of both his selves that frightened him. In spite of the counter fright he had given the burglar, the latter might talk. And even if he did not, sooner or later he would be found out by some one else.

Thus it was that James Ward made a fresh and heroic effort to control the Teutonic barbarian that was half of him. So well did he make it a point to see Lilian in the afternoons, that the time came when she accepted him for better or worse, and when he prayed privily and fervently that it was not for worse. During this period no prize-fighter ever trained more harshly and faithfully for a contest than he trained to subdue the wild savage in him. Among other things, he strove to exhaust himself during the day, so that sleep would render him deaf to the call of the night. He took a vacation from the office and went on long hunting trips, following the deer through the most inaccessible and rugged country he could find – and always in the daytime. Night found him indoors and tired. At home he installed a score of exercise machines, and where other men might go through a particular movement ten times, he went hundreds. Also, as a compromise, he built a sleeping porch on the second story. Here he at least breathed the blessed night air. Double screens prevented him from escaping into the woods, and each night Lee Sing locked him in and each morning let him out.

The time came, in the month of August, when he engaged additional servants to assist Lee Sing and dared a house party in his Mill Valley bungalow. Lilian, her mother and brother, and half a dozen mutual friends, were the guests. For two days and nights all went well. And on the third night, playing bridge till eleven o'clock, he had reason to be proud of himself. His restlessness fully hid, but as luck would have it, Lilian Gersdale was his opponent on his right. She was a frail delicate flower of a woman, and in his night-mood her very frailty incensed him. Not that he loved her less, but that he felt almost irresistibly impelled to reach out and paw and maul her. Especially was this true when she was engaged in playing a winning hand against him.

He had one of the deer-hounds brought in and, when it seemed he must fly to pieces with the tension, a caressing hand laid on the animal brought him relief. These contacts with the hairy coat gave him instant easement and enabled him to play out the evening.

Nor did anyone guess the while terrible struggle their host was making, the while he laughed so carelessly and played so keenly and deliberately.

When they separated for the night, he saw to it that he parted from Lilian in the presence or the others. Once on his sleeping porch and safely locked in, he doubled and tripled and even quadrupled his exercises until, exhausted, he lay down on the couch to woo sleep and to ponder two problems that especially troubled him. One was this matter of exercise. It was a paradox. The more he exercised in this excessive fashion, the stronger he became. While it was true that he thus quite tired out his night-running Teutonic self, it seemed that he was merely setting back the fatal day when his strength would be too much for him and overpower him, and then it would be a strength more terrible than he had yet known. The other problem was that of his marriage and of the stratagems he must employ in order to avoid his wife after dark. And thus, fruitlessly pondering, he fell asleep.

Now, where the huge grizzly bear came from that night was long a mystery, while the people of the Springs Brothers' Circus, showing at Sausalito, searched long and vainly for "Big Ben, the Biggest Grizzly in Captivity." But Big Ben escaped, and, out of the mazes of half a thousand bungalows and country estates, selected the grounds of James J. Ward for visitation. The self first Mr. Ward knew was when he found him on his feet, quivering and tense, a surge of battle in his breast and on his lips the old war-chant. From without came a wild baying and bellowing of the hounds. And sharp as a knife-thrust through the pandemonium came the agony of a stricken dog – his dog, he knew.

Not stopping for slippers, pajama-clad, he burst through the door Lee Sing had so carefully locked, and sped down the stairs and out into the night. As his naked feet struck the graveled driveway, he stopped abruptly, reached under the steps to a hiding-place he knew well, and pulled forth a huge knotty club – his old companion on many a mad night adventure on the hills. The frantic hullabaloo of the dogs was coming nearer, and, swinging the club, he sprang straight into the thickets to meet it.

The aroused household assembled on the wide veranda. Somebody turned on the electric lights, but they could see nothing but one another's frightened faces. Beyond the brightly illuminated driveway the trees formed a wall of impenetrable blackness. Yet somewhere in that blackness a terrible struggle was going on. There was an infernal outcry of animals, a great snarling and growling, the sound of blows being struck and a smashing and crashing of underbrush by heavy bodies.

The tide of battle swept out from among the trees and upon the driveway just beneath the onlookers. Then they saw. Mrs. Gersdale cried out and clung fainting to her son. Lilian, clutching the railing so spasmodically that a bruising hurt was left in her finger-ends for days, gazed horror-stricken at a yellow-haired, wild-eyed giant whom she recognized as the man who was to be her husband. He was swinging a great club, and fighting furiously and calmly with a shaggy monster that was bigger than any bear she had ever seen. One rip of the beast's claws had dragged away Ward's pajama-coat and streaked his flesh with blood.

While most of Lilian Gersdale's fright was for the man beloved, there was a large portion of it due to the man himself. Never had she dreamed so formidable and magnificent a savage lurked under the starched shirt and conventional garb of her betrothed. And never had she had any conception of how a man battled. Such a battle was certainly not modern; nor was she there beholding a modern man, though she did not know it. For this was not Mr. James J. Ward, the San Francisco business man, but one, unnamed and unknown, a crude, rude savage creature who, by some freak of chance, lived again after thrice a thousand years.

The hounds, ever maintaining their mad uproar, circled about the fight, or dashed in and out, distracting the bear. When the animal turned to meet such flanking assaults, the man leaped in and the club came down. Angered afresh by every such blow, the bear would rush, and the man, leaping and skipping, avoiding the dogs, went backwards or circled to one side or the other. Whereupon the dogs, taking advantage of the opening, would again spring in and draw the animal's wrath to them.

The end came suddenly. Whirling, the grizzly caught a hound with a wide sweeping cuff that sent the brute, its ribs caved in and its back broken, hurtling twenty feet. Then the human brute went mad. A foaming rage flecked the lips that parted with a wild inarticulate cry, as it sprang in, swung the club mightily in both hands, and brought it down full on the head of the uprearing grizzly. Not even the skull of a grizzly could withstand the crushing force of such a blow, and the animal went down to meet the worrying of the hounds. And through their scurrying leaped the man, squarely upon the body, where, in the white electric light, resting on his club, he chanted a triumph in an unknown tongue – a song so ancient that Professor Wertz would have given ten years of his life for it.

His guests rushed to possess him and acclaim him, but James Ward, suddenly looking out of the eyes of the early Teuton, saw the fair frail Twentieth Century girl he loved, and felt something snap in his brain. He staggered weakly toward her, dropped the club, and nearly fell. Something had gone wrong with him. Inside his brain was an intolerable agony. It seemed as if the soul of him were flying asunder. Following the excited gaze of the others, he glanced back and saw the carcass of the bear. The sight filled him with fear. He uttered a cry and would have fled, had they not restrained him and led him into the bungalow.

* * *

James J. Ward is still at the head of the firm of Ward, Knowles & Co. But he no longer lives in the country; nor does he run of nights after the coyotes under the moon. The early Teuton in him died the night of the Mill Valley fight with the bear. James J. Ward is now wholly James J. Ward, and he shares no part of his being with any vagabond anachronism from the younger world. And so wholly is James J. Ward modern, that he knows in all its bitter fullness the curse of civilized fear. He is now afraid of the dark, and night in the forest is to him a thing of abysmal terror. His city house is of the spick and span order, and he evinces a great interest in burglarproof devices. His home is a tangle of electric wires, and after bed-time a guest can scarcely breathe without setting off an alarm. Also, he had invented a combination keyless door-lock that travelers may carry in their vest pockets and apply immediately and successfully under all circumstances. But his wife does not deem him a coward. She knows better. And, like any hero, he is content to rest on his laurels. His bravery is never questioned by those friends who are aware of the Mill Valley episode.

Winged Blackmail

Jack London

PETER WINN lay back comfortably in a library chair, with closed eyes, deep in the cogitation of a scheme of campaign destined in the near future to make a certain coterie of hostile financiers sit up. The central idea had come to him the night before, and he was now reveling in the planning of the remoter, minor details. By obtaining control of a certain up-country bank, two general stores, and several logging camps, he could come into control of a certain dinky jerkwater line which shall here be nameless, but which, in his hands, would prove the key to a vastly larger situation involving more mainline mileage almost than there were spikes in the aforesaid dinky jerkwater. It was so simple that he had almost laughed aloud when it came to him. No wonder those astute and ancient enemies of his had passed it by.

The library door opened, and a slender, middle-aged man, weak-eyed and eye glassed, entered. In his hands was an envelope and an open letter. As Peter Winn's secretary it was his task to weed out, sort, and classify his employer's mail.

"This came in the morning post," he ventured apologetically and with the hint of a titter. "Of course it doesn't amount to anything, but I thought you would like to see it."

"Read it," Peter Winn commanded, without opening his eyes.

The secretary cleared his throat.

"It is dated July seventeenth, but is without address. Postmark San Francisco. It is also quite illiterate. The spelling is atrocious. Here it is:

"Mr. Peter Winn, SIR: I send you respectfully by express a pigeon worth good money. She's a loo-loo—"

"What is a loo-loo?" Peter Winn interrupted.

The secretary tittered.

"I'm sure I don't know, except that it must be a superlative of some sort. The letter continues:

"Please freight it with a couple of thousand-dollar bills and let it go. If you do I wont never annoy you no more. If you dont you will be sorry.

"That is all. It is unsigned. I thought it would amuse you."

"Has the pigeon come?" Peter Winn demanded.

"I'm sure I never thought to enquire."

"Then do so."

In five minutes the secretary was back.

"Yes, sir. It came this morning."

"Then bring it in."

The secretary was inclined to take the affair as a practical joke, but Peter Winn, after an examination of the pigeon, thought otherwise.

"Look at it," he said, stroking and handling it. "See the length of the body and that elongated neck. A proper carrier. I doubt if I've ever seen a finer specimen. Powerfully winged and muscled. As our unknown correspondent remarked, she is a loo-loo. It's a temptation to keep her."

The secretary tittered.

"Why not? Surely you will not let it go back to the writer of that letter."

Peter Winn shook his head.

"I'll answer. No man can threaten me, even anonymously or in foolery."

On a slip of paper he wrote the succinct message, "Go to hell," signed it, and placed it in the carrying apparatus with which the bird had been thoughtfully supplied.

"Now we'll let her loose. Where's my son? I'd like him to see the flight."

"He's down in the workshop. He slept there last night, and had his breakfast sent down this morning."

"He'll break his neck yet," Peter Winn remarked, half-fiercely, half-proudly, as he led the way to the veranda.

Standing at the head of the broad steps, he tossed the pretty creature outward and upward. She caught herself with a quick beat of wings, fluttered about undecidedly for a space, then rose in the air.

Again, high up, there seemed indecision; then, apparently getting her bearings, she headed east, over the oak-trees that dotted the park-like grounds.

"Beautiful, beautiful," Peter Winn murmured. "I almost wish I had her back."

But Peter Winn was a very busy man, with such large plans in his head and with so many reins in his hands that he quickly forgot the incident. Three nights later the left wing of his country house was blown up. It was not a heavy explosion, and nobody was hurt, though the wing itself was ruined. Most of the windows of the rest of the house were broken, and there was a deal of general damage. By the first ferry boat of the morning half a dozen San Francisco detectives arrived, and several hours later the secretary, in high excitement, erupted on Peter Winn.

"It's come!" the secretary gasped, the sweat beading his forehead and his eyes bulging behind their glasses.

"What has come?" Peter demanded. "It – the – the loo-loo bird."

Then the financier understood.

"Have you gone over the mail yet?"

"I was just going over it, sir."

"Then continue, and see if you can find another letter from our mysterious friend, the pigeon fancier."

The letter came to light. It read:

Mr. Peter Winn, HONORABLE SIR: Now dont be a fool. If youd came through, your shack would not have blew up – I beg to inform you respectfully, am sending same pigeon. Take good care of same, thank you. Put five one thousand dollar bills on her and let her go. Dont feed her. Dont try to follow bird. She is wise to the way now and makes better time. If you dont come through, watch out.

Peter Winn was genuinely angry. This time he indited no message for the pigeon to carry. Instead, he called in the detectives, and, under their advice, weighted the pigeon heavily with shot. Her previous flight having been eastward toward the bay, the fastest motor-boat in Tiburon was commissioned to take up the chase if it led out over the water.

But too much shot had been put on the carrier, and she was exhausted before the shore was reached. Then the mistake was made of putting too little shot on her, and she rose high in the air, got her bearings and started eastward across San Francisco Bay. She flew straight over Angel Island, and here the motor-boat lost her, for it had to go around the island.

That night, armed guards patrolled the grounds. But there was no explosion. Yet, in the early morning Peter Winn learned by telephone that his sister's home in Alameda had been burned to the ground.

Two days later the pigeon was back again, coming this time by freight in what had seemed a barrel of potatoes. Also came another letter:

Mr. Peter Winn, RESPECTABLE SIR: It was me that fixed yr sisters house. You have raised hell, aint you. Send ten thousand now. Going up all the time. Dont put any more handicap weights on that bird. You sure cant follow her, and its cruelty to animals.

Peter Winn was ready to acknowledge himself beaten. The detectives were powerless, and Peter did not know where next the man would strike – perhaps at the lives of those near and dear to him. He even telephoned to San Francisco for ten thousand dollars in bills of large denomination. But Peter had a son, Peter Winn, Junior, with the same firm-set jaw as his fathers, and the same knitted, brooding determination in his eyes. He was only twenty-six, but he was all man, a secret terror and delight to the financier, who alternated between pride in his son's aeroplane feats and fear for an untimely and terrible end.

"Hold on, father, don't send that money," said Peter Winn, Junior. "Number Eight is ready, and I know I've at last got that reefing down fine. It will work, and it will revolutionize flying. Speed – that's what's needed, and so are the large sustaining surfaces for getting started and for altitude. I've got them both. Once I'm up I reef down. There it is. The smaller the sustaining surface, the higher the speed. That was the law discovered by Langley. And I've applied it. I can rise when the air is calm and full of holes, and I can rise when its boiling, and by my control of my plane areas I can come pretty close to making any speed I want. Especially with that new Sangster-Endholm engine."

"You'll come pretty close to breaking your neck one of these days," was his father's encouraging remark.

"Dad, I'll tell you what I'll come pretty close to-ninety miles an hour – Yes, and a hundred. Now listen! I was going to make a trial tomorrow. But it won't take two hours to start today. I'll tackle it this afternoon. Keep that money. Give me the pigeon and I'll follow her to her loft where ever it is. Hold on, let me talk to the mechanics."

He called up the workshop, and in crisp, terse sentences gave his orders in a way that went to the older man's heart. Truly, his one son was a chip off the old block, and Peter Winn had no meek notions concerning the intrinsic value of said old block.

Timed to the minute, the young man, two hours later, was ready for the start. In a holster at his hip, for instant use, cocked and with the safety on, was a large-caliber automatic pistol. With a final inspection and overhauling he took his seat in the aeroplane. He started the engine, and with a wild burr of gas explosions the beautiful fabric darted down the launching ways and lifted into the air. Circling, as he rose, to the west, he wheeled about and jockeyed and maneuvered for the real start of the race.

This start depended on the pigeon. Peter Winn held it. Nor was it weighted with shot this time. Instead, half a yard of bright ribbon was firmly attached to its leg – this the more easily to enable its flight being followed. Peter Winn released it, and it arose easily enough despite the slight drag of the ribbon. There was no uncertainty about its movements. This was the third time it had made particular homing passage, and it knew the course.

At an altitude of several hundred feet it straightened out and went due east. The aeroplane swerved into a straight course from its last curve and followed. The race was on.

Peter Winn, looking up, saw that the pigeon was outdistancing the machine. Then he saw something else. The aeroplane suddenly and instantly became smaller. It had reefed. Its high-speed plane-design was now revealed. Instead of the generous spread of surface with which it had taken the air, it was now a lean and hawklike monoplane balanced on long and exceedingly narrow wings.

* * *

When young Winn reefed down so suddenly, he received a surprise. It was his first trial of the new device, and while he was prepared for increased speed he was not prepared for such an astonishing increase. It was better than he dreamed, and, before he knew it, he was hard upon the pigeon. That little creature, frightened by this, the most monstrous hawk it had ever seen, immediately darted upward, after the manner of pigeons that strive always to rise above a hawk.

In great curves the monoplane followed upward, higher and higher into the blue. It was difficult, from underneath to see the pigeon, and young Winn dared not lose it from his sight. He even shook out his reefs in order to rise more quickly. Up, up they went, until the pigeon, true to its instinct, dropped and struck at what it thought to be the back of its pursuing enemy. Once was enough, for, evidently finding no life in the smooth cloth surface of the machine, it ceased soaring and straightened out on its eastward course.

A carrier pigeon on a passage can achieve a high rate of speed, and Winn reefed again. And again, to his satisfaction, he found that he was beating the pigeon. But this time he quickly shook out a portion of his reefed sustaining surface and slowed down in time. From then on he knew he had the chase safely in hand, and from then on a chant rose to his lips which he continued to sing at intervals, and unconsciously, for the rest of the passage. It was: "Going some; going some; what did I tell you! – going some."

Even so, it was not all plain sailing. The air is an unstable medium at best, and quite without warning, at an acute angle, he entered an aerial tide which he recognized as the gulf stream of wind that poured through the drafty-mouthed Golden Gate. His right wing caught it first – a sudden, sharp puff that lifted and tilted the monoplane and threatened to capsize it. But he rode with a sensitive "loose curb," and quickly, but not too quickly, he shifted the angles of his wing-tips, depressed the front horizontal rudder, and swung over the rear vertical rudder to meet the tilting thrust of the wind. As the machine came back to an even keel, and he knew that he was now wholly in the invisible stream, he readjusted the wing-tips, rapidly away from him during the several moments of his discomfiture.

The pigeon drove straight on for the Alameda County shore, and it was near this shore that Winn had another experience. He fell into an air-hole. He had fallen into air-holes before, in previous flights, but this was a far larger one than he had ever encountered. With his eyes strained on the ribbon attached to the pigeon, by that fluttering bit of color he marked his fall. Down he went, at the pit of his stomach that old sink sensation which he had known as a boy he first negotiated quick-starting elevators. But Winn, among other secrets of aviation, had learned that to go up it was sometimes necessary first to go down. The air had refused to hold him. Instead of struggling futilely and perilously against this lack of sustension, he yielded to it. With steady head and hand, he depressed the forward horizontal rudder – just recklessly enough and not a fraction more – and the monoplane dived head foremost and sharply down the void. It was falling with the keenness of a knife-blade. Every instant the speed accelerated frightfully. Thus he accumulated the momentum that would save him. But few instants were required, when, abruptly shifting the double horizontal rudders forward and astern, he shot upward on the tense and straining plane and out of the pit.

At an altitude of five hundred feet, the pigeon drove on over the town of Berkeley and lifted its flight to the Contra Costa hills. Young Winn noted the campus and buildings of the University of California – his university – as he rose after the pigeon.

Once more, on these Contra Costa hills, he early came to grief. The pigeon was now flying low, and where a grove of eucalyptus presented a solid front to the wind, the bird was suddenly sent fluttering wildly upward for a distance of a hundred feet. Winn knew what it meant. It had been caught in an air-surf that beat upward hundreds of feet where the fresh west wind smote the upstanding wall of the grove. He reefed hastily to the uttermost, and at the same time depressed the angle of his flight to meet that upward surge. Nevertheless, the monoplane was tossed fully three hundred feet before the danger was left astern.

Two or more ranges of hills the pigeon crossed, and then Winn saw it dropping down to a landing where a small cabin stood in a hillside clearing. He blessed that clearing. Not only was it good for alighting, but, on account of the steepness of the slope, it was just the thing for rising again into the air.

A man, reading a newspaper, had just started up at the sight of the returning pigeon, when he heard the burr of Winn's engine and saw the huge monoplane, with all surfaces set, drop down upon him, stop suddenly on an air-cushion manufactured on the spur of the moment by a shift of the horizontal rudders, glide a few yards, strike ground, and come to rest not a score of feet away from him. But when he saw a young man, calmly sitting in the machine and leveling a pistol at him, the man turned to run. Before he could make the corner of the cabin, a bullet through the leg brought him down in a sprawling fall.

"What do you want!" he demanded sullenly, as the other stood over him.

"I want to take you for a ride in my new machine," Winn answered. "Believe me, she is a loo-loo."

The man did not argue long, for this strange visitor had most convincing ways. Under Winn's instructions, covered all the time by the pistol, the man improvised a tourniquet and applied it to his wounded leg. Winn helped him to a seat in the machine, then went to the pigeon-loft and took possession of the bird with the ribbon still fast to its leg.

A very tractable prisoner, the man proved. Once up in the air, he sat close, in an ecstasy of fear. An adept at winged blackmail, he had no aptitude for wings himself, and when he gazed down at the flying land and water far beneath him, he did not feel moved to attack his captor, now defenseless, both hands occupied with flight.

Instead, the only way the man felt moved was to sit closer.

* * *

Peter Winn, Senior, scanning the heavens with powerful glasses, saw the monoplane leap into view and grow large over the rugged backbone of Angel Island. Several minutes later he cried out to the waiting detectives that the machine carried a passenger. Dropping swiftly and piling up an abrupt air-cushion, the monoplane landed.

"That reefing device is a winner!" young Winn cried, as he climbed out. "Did you see me at the start? I almost ran over the pigeon. Going some, dad! Going some! What did I tell you? Going some!"

"But who is that with you?" his father demanded.

The young man looked back at his prisoner and remembered.

"Why, that's the pigeon-fancier," he said. "I guess the officers can take care of him."

Peter Winn gripped his son's hand in grim silence, and fondled the pigeon which his son had passed to him. Again he fondled the pretty creature. Then he spoke.

"Exhibit A, for the People," he said.

Wet Work

C.L. McDaniel

RAIN CASCADED from above, relentless, sluicing over trees and ground. Lamp posts cringed and hugged the street, the moisture-infused air scattering their feeble beams in a million directions, everywhere and nowhere, rendering it useless.

Hauptkommissarin Gunther pulled off the road and drove up the broad walkway that angled toward the canal. She stopped fifty meters short of the crime scene. Had to preserve the evidence, though God knew what remained.

Why couldn't the victim have gotten herself killed earlier in the week? The weather had been clear, unseasonably warm for late winter in Berlin. Perfect for conducting an afterhours investigation, but that was murder for you. Inconvenient under the best of circumstances.

During Gunther's quick dash to the site, water engulfed her. It trickled off the graying hair she'd tucked into a bun, then slithered down her collar. She shivered but said a prayer of thanks for the efficiency of her people. They had erected a large tarp-tent above the body. The patter of liquid on plastic was deafening, but at least the damp remained at bay. Small consolation. The damage had been done.

The victim seemed small, shrunken. She lay on her left side, glassy eyeballs pointed toward the canal, which rippled and sloshed a mere two meters away. Her coat, a cheap but serviceable Lycra blend, was open at the collar, and her denim-covered legs angled away from each other in a broken 'V.'

Perched on a portable table next to the body were a wallet, a personal ID card, and a rolling suitcase, the kind that fits snuggly in an airplane's overhead bin. Its canvas sides drooped from saturation.

Gunther's assistant stood close by, tapping on an electronic pad. Long blonde hair hid her shoulders while her legs, in contrast to the victim's, were sheathed in sparkly tights and inserted into very impractical high heels. Called away from a club, no doubt. How the younger generation found the time or the stamina, the *Hauptkommissarin* hadn't a clue.

"Schiller." Gunther's voice came out gruff, hoarse. "What have you got for me?"

"A mess." Schiller grinned, her face aglow. Regardless of how she dressed, the girl lived for the chase, the thrill of running bad guys to ground, and heaven help any date who got in her way.

Gunther popped a stick of gum in her mouth. Chewing helped her think.

"Tell me about the victim," she demanded.

"Veronika Stahl. Twenty-seven. Has a record, but mostly small stuff: shoplifting, drug possession, one collar for theft. A friend accused her of lifting seventy-five Euros, but she gave the money back, claimed it was a misunderstanding. The friend wouldn't testify, so they let her go, no indictment."

"Anything recent?"

"Only one incident in the past two years. According to her parole counselor, she got clean, had a job in a shop, seemed to be pulling her life together – until she lost the baby. She filed on her live-in, but the charges didn't stick. Want to see them?"

Gunther took the pad and scrolled through the sketchy report. When Veronika was twenty-three weeks pregnant, an ambulance had transported her to St. Elisabeth's hospital. Her breathing was shallow, her pulse weak, and her pupils had shrunk to the size of pinheads.

While the emergency nurses began a standard overdose protocol, Veronika mumbled over and over that her boyfriend did this to her, that he stuck a needle in her while she slept, to get her high and force a miscarriage.

If the accusation was true, Klaus Finkel, the boyfriend in question, got his wish. The doctors saved Veronika's life but not the baby's. Premature and partially formed, it had been stillborn on arrival.

Patrol officers followed up, but Finkel denied everything, claiming Veronika had succumbed to the needle again with no help from him. Since it was 'he said/she said' with questionable evidence, the prosecutor declined to press charges either way. One of those lose-lose situations the legal system faces daily.

"Do we have a current address?" Gunther asked.

"Same as in the report. The apartment's in her name. And here's an interesting tidbit. After she got out of the hospital, she amended her *Anmeldung*, deleted the boyfriend's name from her registration. Looks like she found a backbone and threw the bum out."

"Where's he living?"

"Never reregistered, so there's no telling. Flopping with friends, most likely."

"Could she have taken him back?"

"Would you?"

Gunther blew air out her nose and handed the pad back to Schiller. "Witnesses?"

"Two. A couple. They'd been out dancing and were running for the *S-bahn*."

The *Hauptkommissarin*'s head swiveled back and forth. "Where are they?"

"I sent them home."

"Without me speaking to them first?" Gunther's lips tightened into a thin slash.

"They were soaked to the skin, boss, and they didn't have much to say. I couldn't let them freeze."

"Were they sober, at least?"

"Sober enough. Do you want to see their statements?"

Schiller's fingers danced over the pad and a woman sprang into view. Twenty-ish, wisps of green-blue hair plastered across her forehead. She trembled as she recounted how she and her girlfriend had cut through the park. They heard a cry, then a scream. She called the police while her partner shined her phone light ahead. They found the victim lying on the ground, a large pool of blood next to her. She wasn't breathing, and her eyes were fixed, not moving. No one else was around, but they were worried the killer might come back, so they retreated to the *Bahnhof* and stayed there until the police arrived.

Inspector Schiller paused the recording.

"You interviewed the partner separately?" Gunther asked.

"Of course."

"And she corroborated this story."

"She did, but with more detail. Listen to this."

Schiller dragged a finger across the screen and a second woman started speaking. Her dark hair bristled, short and spikey, and her expression was smoother than her partner's, calmer.

"Then we heard the woman call out," she said.

Schiller's voice filtered in from off camera. "What exactly did the woman say?"

"'Leave me alone! No, don't!' Then she screamed."

"A long scream? Short?"

"In the middle."

"Did it trail off? Gurgle?"

"It just…ended."

"Did you see the killer? Hear which way he ran?"

"No. We waited a minute on the path before we went ahead, just in case. Nobody came by us and we couldn't hear anything else, the rain was so loud."

"That I believe," the Chief Inspector muttered. She frowned and tapped the side of the pad with her forefinger. "What do you make of all this?"

"A passion killing." Schiller pointed at the portable table. "In addition to her ID card, Frau Stahl had sixty-seven Euros and the wallet was sitting in her coat pocket, easy pickings, so robbery is out. The way I see it, the victim noticed the perp stalking her and panicked. Instead of heading straight for the *Bahnhof*, she cut through the park and got caught by the canal. The killer struck and bolted. And he picked the perfect night for it."

"Didn't he, though?"

The arrival of the medical examiner cut their musings short. Dr. Kramer waddled up to the body. "Evening, ladies." He bobbed his balding head. "Hellish weather, eh? It'll take more than a nightcap to wash this chill away."

A whiff of brandy tickled Gunther's nostrils. The doctor had already consumed several nightcaps to fortify himself, no doubt. Not that it would make a difference. Kramer was a rock, whatever the circumstances.

Strong, thick hands eased the body onto its back. He loosened the dead woman's clothes and ran his nylon-sheathed palms over her skin, like a potter checking a new dish for defects.

Arms, torso, pelvis. Kramer slid the woman's frayed gloves off, humming as he worked, something from Mozart. At last he straightened and signaled for his orderly to bring the body bag.

"Well?" Gunther raised an eyebrow.

Kramer sighed and pulled his coat tight. "Died here, on this spot. Cause of death was a single puncture to the right carotid artery. Clean wound, no jagged edges. Just in and out with the blade facing forward toward the chin. You should take some soil samples to the right of the body, have them tested for blood. You'll find it."

"Was the victim under the influence?"

"I'll run a tox screen, but I doubt it. The pupils are normal, plus no fresh needle marks, just old scars. And there's something else."

He paused for dramatic effect. Gunther withered him with a stare and he deflated like a balloon on a cold day.

"I think she was raped," the doctor said.

The Chief Inspector rolled the gum between her teeth. "Why?"

"There's seminal fluid in the vagina and bruises on the upper thighs. I'll know more when I get her back to the lab and run samples. But that's not all." He lifted the victim's left hand. "Can you see it?"

"The bandage around her middle finger?"

"No. The redness under her fingernails. It's tissue. She fought her attacker."

"Could it have been rough sex?"

"Possible, but the victim's kinks are your concern. My preliminary observation is she appears to be a sexual assault victim. The bruises and fluids are fresh and consistent with her being forced."

Kramer bagged both the victim's hands. Then he and his orderly lifted the corpse and set it in a body bag on a rolling trauma cart. The doctor zipped the bag closed and released the brakes. "I'll move this case to the front of my list. You'll have my report tomorrow."

He and the orderly wheeled the remains out from under the sheltering tarp and into the downpour. The pummeling rain drowned out the squeak of the cart wheels.

"What next, boss?" Schiller shifted her weight from one foot to the other.

"Tell me what's in the suitcase."

"I don't know."

"You haven't examined the contents?"

"I thought you'd want to do the honors."

Gunther's smile was grim. "You thought correctly."

The inside of the case was as forlorn as its outside. A few blouses, two pairs of underwear, jeans, assorted toiletry items, all jumbled together as if they'd been gathered in haste and crammed in. Water had soaked every item through and through. Every item except one.

In the bottom lay a small blanket, meticulously folded and sealed in a plastic zip bag. The piece had been hand-sewn from fluffy cloth with a teddy bear print. Imperfections in the seams indicated careful work by an amateur. Likewise the initials embroidered in the corner. LS, with a tiny dent in the top of the 'L' and an extra crinkle in the 'S.'

Gunther studied the blanket. Veronika must have made it for her unborn child, a labor of love. So sad. So...futile.

"Any relatives we need to notify?" she asked Schiller.

"No one I could find. An only child, parents are dead. Veronika Stahl was completely on her own."

"And you have her keys?"

"Right here." Schiller produced an evidence bag.

Gunther rubbed the back of her neck. "I know it's late. Or early, depending how you look at it. I.... Her apartment is close. I want you to take one of the patrol officers and swing by there, lock it down, make sure it's secure." She stuck her hands in her coat pockets and rocked back and forth on her heels. "I have a bad feeling."

Without hesitation, Schiller packed up her pad and gathered her things. Her boss's intuition was legendary, one of the reasons she'd risen to such a high rank at a time when women on the force were both scarce and downtrodden. No, you didn't question one of Gunther's 'feelings.' Not ever.

"You don't mind?" Gunther tilted her head to the side.

"Of course not. Just let me text Raphael and tell him to stay."

"Stay where?"

"My place."

"You gave someone named 'Raphael' a key to your place?"

"Don't be silly. He was already there when the call came in." Her thumb flitted across her phone in a blur. "He's part Italian and Italians are always willing to wait, so long as they get 'fed' in the end."

Oh, to be so young. "What if he rips you off while you're out?"

"He wouldn't dare." Her cheeks dimpled. "He knows I carry a gun."

Schiller grabbed Officer Dürer, the hunky one with the half-sideburns, and dragged him into the darkness. Gunther instructed the remaining personnel to collect soil samples.

While the officers dug up chunks of grass and dirt, the Chief Inspector removed her gum, covered it with the old wrapper, and stuck it in her pocket. This case was a bad one. To make it through she'd need fresh flavor, two new sticks, at a minimum. Her jaw clenched and loosened as she worked the mass, smoothed it out, pulped it until it was soft enough for a consistent chewing rhythm. Then she began bagging the rest of the evidence.

She had just packed Veronika's limp suitcase into a sealed plastic container when her phone beeped, the ringtone demanding a face-to-face.

"Boss!" Schiller's eyes danced as she stared up from the screen of Gunther's phone. "I'm at the apartment. We've got another body."

The Chief Inspector rubbed her forehead. "Do we know whose?"

"Take a look." Shiller's pad swung around to show a dead male lying on a bed. The deceased was naked. His chest was furrowed with gouges.

"It's Klaus Finkel." The young woman's voice had risen a quarter of an octave.

"How do you know it's him?"

"The body matches his file photo and the skull tattoo is an identifying mark."

"Any indication as to what killed him?"

"Looks like he overdosed."

"Accident?"

"Suicide."

Gunther chomped her gum once, twice, a third time. "Show me the note he left."

"There isn't one. But his clothes are piled at the foot of the bed. They're soaked, and you can still see traces of blood on the coat cuffs and on his pants and shoes. Testing will show it's the victim's and that the skin under her nails and the semen inside her are his, too, I'll bet you anything."

"So you're sticking with your 'crime of passion' theory?"

"You bet. It's classic. He shoots up, barges in and rapes her. No entry problems, he still had his keys from when they were together. They were in his jeans. Once he's done his business, he settles down for a post-ejaculation nap and she sees a chance to escape. She throws some clothes in a bag and runs, planning not to come back. But Finkel's not as out of it as she thinks. He snaps to when the front door slams and he gets furious. He stops in the kitchen to pick up a knife. There's one missing from the knife block, a small one, just the right size to inflict the wound she had. He stumbles after her, catches her at the canal and it's lights out, game over."

Schiller's lips scrunched into a smug, little bow. "At that point he realizes what he's done, and the guilt overwhelms him, not to mention the thought of how much hard time he'll have to do. So he staggers back to the apartment, strips off the wet clothes, and fixes himself a lethal shot—"

"I thought he already had one fix."

"He did. Look at this." The pad cam zoomed in on the dead man's arm. Two fresh needle marks pooched up from the skin, side-by-side. "That's not an accident, boss. Every junkie knows you don't double dose."

"You have a point." Gunther's jaw pistoned up and down, mangling the gum. "What about the murder weapon?"

"Not in the apartment. It could be anywhere between here and the crime scene. The canal, a dumpster, buried under a tree. We'll have to search, but even if we don't find it, Dr. Kramer can match a duplicate to the wound. I already called him, by the way."

"And he's overjoyed at having to come back out."

"Finkel better be glad he's dead. The good doctor has a bag of scalpels, and he's grumpy as a starving bear. To tell the truth, I wouldn't mind removing a few Finkel parts myself."

Something in her tone sent a shudder down Gunther's back.

"What's wrong?" the *Hauptkommissarin* asked.

"Check this out." The camera panned over to a dingy nightstand littered with Finkel's drug paraphernalia: needle, lighter, blackened spoon. In the midst of the debris stood a framed photo. No, not a photo. An ultrasound, neatly matted with 'Louisa' printed in bold across the bottom.

"The bastard," Schiller hissed. "First her baby, then her. It's too bad he took the coward's way out. Nailing him would've been such a pleasure."

"It would." Gunther's chewing slowed. "Look, I have ten, maybe fifteen more minutes here. Let me finish, and I'll join you."

"No need, boss. I got this. You go home, get some rest." The picture vibrated from Schiller holding her pad too tight. "I can handle it. I promise."

Gunther let the lull in the conversation lengthen, the rain pounding a tattoo in the background. Maybe it was time to loosen the chain, let her little bird fly solo. Besides, she was tired, marrow-draining tired. Her protégé could steer the investigation into safe harbor, which was just as well. Gunther didn't have the strength.

"*Kommissarin* Schiller." Gunther used her official voice. "You are in charge of the crime scene. Secure the remaining evidence, write up the report, and submit it to the prosecutor by the end of business tomorrow. I'm sure he'll agree with your findings."

"Thanks." Schiller's smile could've given her superior a sun tan. "I won't let you down."

Gunther's phone went dark and she stuck it in her coat pocket. It was wrong, all of it: the crime scene layout, the body, the second corpse. Especially the second corpse.

Junkie ex-boyfriends didn't do in their former lovers, then conveniently off themselves. No, they lied, they ran, they hid, anything to escape the consequences of their actions because, in the end, it was all about them...

Hold a moment. Consequences...

The Chief Inspector hoisted up the plastic bag containing the baby blanket and pulled the seal open, heavy air rushing inside with a whoosh. Her right glove came off and her hand grew damp, but not from the moisture all about her.

Weary eyes flicked over to where the body had lain. The wound to Veronika's neck had been clean and precise, a perfect puncture. According to Schiller's theory, the victim's drugged-up, out-of-control ex had chased her across wet grass and landed a seamless strike with no tearing at all. In the dark.

Luck? An unhappy coincidence?

Gunther gnawed on her gum and regarded the open bag with a wariness reserved for crouching vermin or poisonous snakes. She had an inkling of what had, in fact, transpired, but to be absolutely certain she would have to 'become' the killer.

This gift, her special ability, her curse, was something Schiller and the rest of the Chief Inspector's colleagues had no knowledge of, didn't even suspect. Whether it was some supernatural power or the supreme insight of a woman well-steeped in the human sewage of her city, Gunther couldn't tell. In either case, by focusing her thoughts and letting her senses and memories guide her, she found she could slip into the criminal's skin, witness the world from the villain's perspective, commit the crime in her mind's eye with the same deliberation and forethought its progenitor had employed.

The *Hauptkommissarin* sucked in a breath and plunged her hand into the bag. Her fingers slid over the cloth, caressing each uneven stitch, every slight imperfection. She bent down and inhaled, taking in the mingled scents of soap, synthetic fibers, and cheap perfume. She paused and reoriented her inner vision until she saw what Veronika Stahl had seen, felt what Veronika Stahl had felt.

The ultrasound sat on the bedside table. Her Louisa. Fingernails dug into her palms. She never had the chance to touch the little dear, run a finger across her lips, say goodbye. Instead, her darling had been disposed of, tossed away with the hospital garbage.

A vein throbbed in her throat. Louisa's murderer still walked the Berlin streets, unfettered, living free. Bit by bit, the shards of a plan gathered under her skin, coalesced, urged her to action.

First, she needed heroin, high grade, enough for a double shot. No problem. The neighbor dealer was available 24/7, ready to welcome a lost customer back into the fold.

Once she had the bait, she tempted her prey. A quick phone call, a few clichés. "Babe, I've missed you so much, I need you so bad." Men were easy, full of themselves, believing you had nothing better to do than dream about their bodies every minute of every day.

When Finkel arrived, she could barely keep herself from vomiting on his shoes. His hair was matted, and his body reeked as if he hadn't showered in days. She avoided inhaling and bit the inside of her cheek while he forced his slobbering lips over hers, pressed her into the bed with his bulk, shoved himself inside her body.

In spite of her revulsion, she feigned passion, cooing and crying out, raking her fingernails down his chest. And when he was done, she scooted out from under and prepared him a shot, a 'special treat.' His mouth twisted into the smile of the sexually sated, and he extended his arm to accept her tribute to his prowess.

While the dose took effect, she prepared a second, for herself, she said. Finkel's eyes closed, then flew open when the needle again jabbed into his arm. He tried to speak but could only mumble and drool.

As his breathing slowed, she dressed herself, gathered up his clothes and thrust them out the window into the deluge. She dropped the sodden heap at the foot of the bed.

Her victim's final rattling breaths, when they came, sounded like church bells to her ears, a benediction.

Time to finish the job. Her extra set of keys went into the pocket of his jeans. Her own fist bruised her inner thighs, disgust adding force to every blow. The knife from the kitchen sliced her finger and she sprinkled her blood over her dead lover's garments. After carefully applying the bandage, leaving the fingernail exposed, she pulled her pre-packed bag from under the bed and stalked into the night, to the spot where she would cry out to strangers, plunge the blade into her throat, then hurl it into the canal. There, lying in a pool of her blood, she would serve as the final piece of evidence, one that would give a killer the label he so richly deserved…

The wind hurled raindrops under the tarp and into Gunther's cheek. The frigid barbs pricked her skin and yanked her back into her body.

Close by, the canal bulged and roiled. If she sent divers to sift its murky bottom, they might find a knife matching the wound in Veronika's neck, but what would that prove? How would it matter?

Two murderers were dead. Better to let the universe sort out their guilt and avoid terrestrial hassles.

Gunther had her remaining officers stow the evidence bags in their vehicle. She stood to the side while they collapsed the tarp. Her face lifted toward the sky, and she breathed in the damp. It reminded her she was alive. She gloried in it.

The tarp tilted downward, torrents spilling onto the ground, filling the holes her people had dug. Rain buffeted the earth, but soon enough the storm would slacken, dwindle, then cease altogether. A few weeks later, spring would arrive. The sun would shine, the days would grow warm and wildflowers would shroud the blood-soaked ground, concealing it beneath a carpet of color.

Sirens

Dan Micklethwaite

EVEN WITHOUT looking, without being able to see, Kellie knows exactly what the knife has just done. It's split the third line of the lyrics tattooed on her side; the chorus from a song that she's never liked, but which Zara had loved and so declared to be theirs. If it scars, Kellie thinks, then it will be like a redaction. The tease of a secret. A memory blanked.

Blood gushes out through the tear in her coat, and she presses hard with both hands in an effort to staunch it. The cracked rib shapes the wound into a model volcano; a science fair back at school, Second Prize in her year.

She used to be smart in that way. She used to be sensible. Too sensible to ever end up like this, to ever get involved with someone like Zara; to ever go exploring in the middle of a blackout; to ever decide to get a tattoo.

She'd had it done seven months ago, after a few drinks too many. She hadn't really planned on it, but Zara had persuaded her. When Zara was in a good mood, when she was fun, it felt like the only way to live well was to follow her lead – anything else was a dereliction of duty.

"Growing up is giving up," Zara had said, and how she said it made you hate the quitters, made you hate yourself for being one. Or nearly being. And every time you got close to the edge of all that, there Zara would be, to lead you out through the door.

And straight on 'til morning.

Their song had been playing that night in the last club they'd gone to, and guys had kept approaching them, and Zara had kept on pushing them away, and pulling Kellie closer, whispering things that she hadn't been able to hear – that she wishes she had heard, could hear again now – and then kissed her, and stuck a finger up at the guys who were filming with their phones.

Afterwards, they'd stumbled out past the bouncers into the four a.m. moonscape, up the road to a falafel van, and from there to a tattoo parlour that Zara knew well. Kellie only went that one time, but she remembers it clearly – she hadn't been *that* drunk – though she remembers mostly just staring at the designs on the wall.

Zara had ignored that selection and explained to the artist what she wanted instead. They would each get half of the chorus on their right-hand-side ribs; every line shared between them, so it would only join up and make sense when they spooned.

It wasn't until the following evening, when they'd finally woken up, that they realised it should have been inked upside down, so they could read it, recite from it, without any fuss.

A stupid thing to fight over. As if they didn't already know the lyrics by heart.

As if Kellie still doesn't, whether she likes them or not. They tumble out of her, ragged, and she tries to find a position where it doesn't hurt as they leave. She stops to pant, almost choking, after every other word. She presses harder on the wound, but the blood isn't slowing. She used to know all about biology and all about chemistry and quite a bit about physics, but she can't remember which organ is underneath where she's cut. She can't think of anything apart from the song. Apart from what people must think of her singing.

A group of six lights – or is it just three? – are drifting along on the far side of the street, but as the people holding them notice her, they stutter and pause. Kellie wants to try and ask them for help, but she can't find any words besides these lyrics in her head. She can't think of any way to tell them what's wrong.

The lights begin moving again, in the other direction; the passers-by must have pegged her as a pitiful drunk. Or maybe they're scared. Perhaps they were already out somewhere else when the power went down, and they're nothing like Zara, they just want to get home.

Kellie can't blame them.

But she can't stop herself singing. No matter how difficult, how much it hurts.

There are sirens in the night, a block or two distant, and they seem like a backing track, a real-time trance electronica remix. If she still had her own phone, she could call the police, and serenade them down the line until they came to investigate.

And then she could explain.

Try to, at least.

That this wasn't supposed to happen. That she knew it had been risky to hit the streets in a blackout, but Zara had wanted to know how the city adapted. How it felt and behaved. She'd heard stories about previous times it had happened, they both had – but Zara didn't believe in second-hand stories. She believed only in what she could see and smell and taste and touch.

"I believe in you, Kellie," she'd said. "But my faith's a little shaky. Why don't you come over here and remind me?"

Zara was the sole arbiter of what was real and what was not. And she could certainly be fickle when determining between the two. Her arms were a palimpsest of other lyrics and quotes linked to previous lovers, and there were a couple more on her back, and even one near the top of her inside-right thigh; but she hadn't been able to afford the removal, and so simply pretended they were no longer there.

"And what if you ever leave me, or I ever leave you?" Kellie had asked her, with their ink still in cellophane. Zara had been cooking something, a lentil curry, in a lull between fights.

Kellie didn't like lentils.

The lull didn't last long.

"Are you planning to leave me?" Zara had spun round, and the tendons in her neck had been warped with the strain.

The way she could flip, just like that, like a cat with its claws out, like a gold carriage at midnight, that was one of the reasons the answer should have been *Yes.* Was *yes,* though of course Kellie didn't say that. She couldn't say it, because she never knew what Zara would actually do; especially in the kitchen, with so many sharp objects lying around.

Instead, Kellie had told her not to be stupid, and moved in for a kiss, because it had always been best when Zara was angry. They'd half-stripped and gone at it right there on the floor. The curry boiled over and burnt to the hob.

She is running a fever. Or is she just very cold? It's difficult to tell. Why is it so difficult? She shivers, keeps shivering, and it tugs at the wound. The blood seems to be slowing, but the breath rips in her throat. Is she still singing? Is it just in her head?

More lights floating by on the far side of the street. Only one, or is it two? It seems to come closer, and she stops singing, swallows, tries once again to form the word, "Help."

The words, "Save me. My friend. Hospital." But when she shuts up she vanishes, and the half-hearted Samaritan vanishes too.

It's like echolocation. Bio-sonar. In this blackout, and with the cloud cover as heavy as it is, it's like being underwater. It's like those deep-sea documentaries that she loves, but that she could only watch if she promised to do something for Zara, to reward her for sitting still and not complaining throughout.

Sometimes, she would ask Zara questions, to test whether or not she'd been paying attention. How far down can a blue whale swim? What is the name of the deepest point in the ocean? Which fish are famous for using a flashing blue lure?

Anglerfish, is the answer.

These phones – the few that pass – are beginning to look a lot like them. Bioluminescent. Kellie wants to swim over, to take the bait – no, better yet, she wants to *be* one of them, to have her own bait, to draw them towards *her*. But she doesn't. She can't.

Her phone has been stolen.

And now she thinks that maybe she doesn't actually want to be noticed – what if the wrong person finds her, another deep-sea monstrosity?

Can you name a shark species that dives down to eight thousand feet?

Zara can't answer, and neither can Kellie, not with the blood oozing out through her side.

Her pulse throbs in her head. She can still hear their song but it's much quieter now, as if she's singing it whispered, she's struggling to breathe. Perhaps it still carries to the rare passers-by, and probably if it does then they still think she's a drunk. The wrong kind of siren, trying to captivate sailors and smash them up on the rocks. They remain at a distance, bound to their masts.

But Kellie isn't drunk and she doesn't care what they think, about her, about this song, and she doesn't even care at this point that she hates it, that the lyrics are crap and the beat is derivative. She whispers it anyway, because it's a dirge. Because Zara had claimed it was theirs, and so it might as well be.

Zara had other songs on her body, from other relationships, but she would turn off the radio at their opening notes, and never put them in playlists, and always dragged Kellie to the toilets if they came on in a club. She was merciless when she stopped believing in something. She pulled it right out of existence and did her best to deny that it had ever even been. They had never, not once, run into any of her exes, and Kellie had often wondered if they'd all been made-up.

The few times she'd let Zara get her high, or if it was too hot in the night and sleep was impossible, she'd started to wonder the same of herself. Or if instead Zara just hijacked readymade hosts, moved into their headspace and used them for storage. And then when she left them they'd reverted to type, become their old selves again, conformist and vague. Easy to walk past without recognition.

At three in the morning, covered in sweat, that had felt slightly more plausible – that her soul had a squatter, someone else at the wheel. After all, she had always been sensible, smart, before she met Zara. She'd been totally different. She would have never got wasted, nor got tattooed.

She certainly wouldn't have come out tonight.

She hadn't really wanted to, as soon as she'd seen the street, the dimness, but Zara had stood firm and told her not to be a wuss. Said they'd only go as far as the nearby park. Ten minutes' walk, at the most. There were bound to be people there lighting campfires, she'd said, and setting paper lanterns adrift on the river. And Zara didn't want to miss that. She never wanted to miss anything.

They held their phones out in front of them, the only glimmers on the street, and bins and piles of garbage bags looked ghostly where the torchlight caught them.

"Like ectoplasmic blobs," Kellie said.

"Who ya gonna call?" said Zara, and strutted ahead, screeching out the famous tune. She thrust her arms in the air with the phone-torch still glowing, and it skewered up like a Bat-signal, or a searchlight for drones.

But there was far too much cloud cover to spot anything much; the sky seemed as empty as the street spread around them.

No birds, even. Quiet.

The shadow sprang out of nowhere, from a doorway, from a side alley. Zara spun at the sound, and the blade flickered blue in the glow from her phone, and so did half of her face, and then she just fell. Then the attacker was on Kellie, and her phone went, her hand grabbing thin air, then hair, and then a fist hit her chin, and then came the knife.

Bluntnose sixgill shark, is the answer.

Eight thousand feet down until it rises to feed.

A sharp savage impact and then it was done.

It hurts less, in a way, than when she got the tattoo, even though she was hammered for that and is stone sober right now. She's beginning to lose feeling. The shivering has stopped. She isn't even sure if her eyes are still open, or whether or not she's still singing, or if it's all in her head. The backing track sirens are still playing, somewhere, but they must be fixing a problem for somebody else.

Kellie's problem is about twelve feet away, she guesses, up the street to her left. Kellie's problem is in and around the right side of her torso. It's a terrible chorus; it's the same old song. You heard plenty of stories about this kind of thing, and people had said to watch out for this neighbourhood, because the statistics about muggings and violent crime were not good. But Zara had never believed in second-hand stories. She'd only believed in what she could see and smell and taste and touch.

Kellie's hands are still pressed against the hole in her coat, but the blood seems to be clotting, to have halted its flow. Though her mouth when she swallows is bitter with iron, she decides to risk moving, to rise up on her knees.

Straight away, she drops forwards, but still begins to crawl hesitantly across the cold, pitch-black ground. She is no longer singing, not even whispering, because the forward momentum requires too much breath. Too much strength. She's only just about able to grope ahead blindly. She wishes that Zara could glow like an anglerfish. She feels like a bottom-feeder. She feels like the drowned.

Then she hits something. A bump in the road. A lump in the throat. She wants to be sick, but her insides are so drained and so sore that she can't. There is nothing left. Only this shoe, this ankle, this calf, this knee. This right thigh, which bears somebody else's lost hymn at the top of it, and then in between, and towards the left hip. Then the thin, taut belly, the breasts, and the collar bone, and the throat, where the hurt is, and the face the mouth the nose the eyes. She gathers the body in her arms to reposition it, and as she does this there are lights, right on cue, and she can see what she's doing; she can unzip the jacket, and then her own coat, and she can curl like an atmosphere around this cold little star. She tries to wipe the blood clear from her half of the chorus, tries to match it together so she can read upside down, even though she knows the all the words off by heart. And the lights have gone blue now and red now and blue, and the sirens are louder, and another voice says something, but she doesn't hear clearly because she's singing again. And she kisses the back of that beautiful neck, where it is still whole and normal, and decorated only by another tattoo, of a butterfly emerging from a chrysalis skull – the first Zara got, when she was fifteen years-old – and it really does look good, great, brilliant, perfect, and Kellie thinks she might go and get one just like it, to remind her, and she doesn't listen to anything the other voice says, even though it's closer now, really close, right next to her, booming. Even though it comes with a baton slamming into her back.

Even though hands wrap around and try and tear her away.

Even though the full weight of the water is pressing above her.

She doesn't really feel it.

She doesn't feel smart and she doesn't feel sensible.

She just carries on singing, and tightens her grip.

Breaking News

Trixie Nisbet

I GLANCE DOWN at the monitor concealed beneath the smoked glass top of the news desk. It shows exactly what the viewers can see from the camera directly in front of me. I am relieved to see that I look composed. Not a hair out of place. *I have nothing to fear*, I tell myself, *no one will suspect*.

As a TV news presenter, I realise that I have to cope with more than my fair share of crime in the city. Fortunately, mine is the *local* news bulletin, so at least I can ignore the global catastrophes and tedious political wrangling. But that leaves the smaller disasters, and in places closer to home. These are more important; they are more personal. And none more personal to me than the story I have to report next.

"Ready, Richard?" The floor manager is speaking in my ear – a countdown as the feature on a random stabbing outside a night club comes to an end. Four. Three. Two. One...

A green light appears on the camera. There hasn't been time for a rehearsal. *Stay detached.* All I have to do is focus on the autocue that scrolls up in front of the lens.

"In a traffic accident this afternoon," I read, "a woman was hit by a coach on the busy one-way system in Kentish Town. The woman, who has not been named, was taken to the nearby Royal Free Hospital, but died later of her injuries."

Dead! She's dead. I know I must *not* react. *Don't think about it.* The autocue pauses for a second, waiting for me to carry on reading.

"Police have been appealing for witnesses to the incident; they are particularly keen to speak to a man, believed to be in his thirties, who, it appears, had been arguing with the woman moments before the accident took place." A phone number caption appears on the screen as if hovering next to my right shoulder. "Anyone with information is asked to call the police incident desk on this number."

The phone number disappears, and I am thankful that it was shown for only a few seconds. It is replaced by a stylised sunshine graphic. I take a quick breath. My voice is steady – hasn't given me away, and the autocue prompts me to announce the link into the weather report.

The floor manager is counting down the cut to the weather presenter, then signals that I may leave the news desk. He crosses over to me, his eyes wide and excitable. "Have you heard, Richard?" he asks. "I didn't want to mention it before the bulletin, but that woman – the one in the road accident – not confirmed yet, but rumours are that it was Stephanie, Stephanie Stokes that used to work here as an admin assistant."

I give a creditable show of surprise. "But she moved away, years ago," I say. "Somewhere on the south coast, wasn't it?"

The floor manager shrugs. "Evidently, she was back in town. I thought I'd better mention it to you. I knew you'd remember her."

* * *

Yeah, there was no way I could ever forget Stephanie. She was about five years younger than me, slim, funny, attractive. Always watching me. You get used to that in this profession, being recognised sometimes on the street. But that wasn't the way Stephanie looked at me. It sounds conceited, but I'm not bad looking; you can't look like a baboon's backside if you're on the telly. And, on the day she left, four years ago, Stephanie confessed that she had what amounted to a girlish crush on me. She was moving south, somewhere near Brighton, to look after her elderly mother. A bit late to say that she fancied me! I told her that I'd miss her.

"I doubt that," she said, and there was a knowing look in her mascaraed eyes. "You may think you've kept it secret, Richard, but everyone knows you're sleeping with Carla from the accounts department."

Now that *had* surprised me. Yeah, some people were bound to find out, but I hadn't realised that Carla and I were studio floor gossip.

"You can see it in her face, whenever she passes you in the corridors." Stephanie's eyes were fixed on mine. "You know that she's married," she said, "with two young children?"

Of course, I knew. But the way Stephanie mentioned it sounded like a warning. She didn't approve. Or perhaps she didn't like to think of me seeing someone else.

I told her that I was single, and it was no business of hers who I slept with.

She just smiled and walked away. That was years ago, and the last I had seen of her – until this morning.

* * *

Stephanie left the news team, I remember, on a Friday. The following day, in fact *every* Saturday, was when I met Carla. Her husband ran a couple of market stalls in Camden Town and Carla, *supposedly*, did the weekly shop while a friend looked after the kids. It's surprising, sometimes, how long a weekly shop can take.

Carla had come to my flat that day, and was about to leave for the supermarket, when I told her about Stephanie's departure and the warning she had dared to give me.

I laughed it off, but Carla's eyes were serious. I knew her well. She's frankly not the brightest of women, and I could see her mind working, as if she was choosing her words, deciding what to tell me.

"I know Stephanie too," she said eventually. "Only slightly. I help with the accounts for the admin department. She knows about us." Carla gestured to the crumpled bed with, I thought, a tinge of uncharacteristic guilt. "Then, this morning – well, she phoned me."

I didn't like the sound of this. "Go on," I said.

Carla took a breath. I could see that she had decided what to say. "She threatened to tell Simon about us."

Simon was Carla's husband. I ran a hand through my hair and sat heavily on the bed. "Blackmail?" I hadn't seen that coming; Stephanie didn't seem the type. But I'd never seen Carla look so worried. She seemed suddenly terrified, as if she wished she could take back her words. Then the story poured out of her. Stephanie hadn't only threatened to tell Simon, apparently the newspapers would want to know of our affair – I *was* a minor celebrity after all.

I cut through Carla's spiel. "What does she want?" I asked.

"Money." Carla was almost sobbing now. But I don't have any, what with the children, there's nothing to spare."

"How much?"

Carla told me the amount, to be sent to Stephanie's new address on the Sussex coast every six months.

"The scheming cow!" I was making calculations in my head, pacing back and forth. "Only yesterday she said she fancied me – now this." *She's jealous*, I thought, *this is her way of getting back at me.*

"But what should I do, Richard?" Carla wrung her hands. "If she tells Simon… And I can't afford to pay her."

I was in a less volatile situation. I was single. But Carla looked so wretched. I guess it boiled down to how much I valued our secret liaisons. "Don't snivel," I said. I could see Carla trying to pull herself together. She has kept her figure well, you wouldn't believe that she'd had two kids. "OK, here's what we do. I'll pay," I said. "I'll give you the money; you send it to Stephanie to keep her quiet. And we – well, carry on as we are."

Carla shook her head, scared of what she'd told me, but I knew she would agree. What choice did she have?

So, that's what we did. The arrangement continued for the next four years or so. I could afford the money – just. Though when I handed over the first payment, Carla stared at the pile of notes. I could see in her eyes that she thought it was a fortune. "She's evil, that Stephanie, that's what she is." Carla asked me to seal the subsequent payments in a package, ready to be posted. That way she didn't have to see or handle the money. She told me she found that easier.

Things carried on that way for years. The payments irritated me, of course, every six months, but it soon became routine.

I was promoted over those intervening years, to presenting the more prestigious late evening news. And I made other close friendships. Some lasted longer than others; the more emotional the attachment, the shorter it seemed to last. But I kept up my uncomplicated physical arrangement with Carla. Her husband is a particularly stupid man, as far as I could tell he didn't suspect a thing; the affair became something I paid for – like any other hobby. Until the day, quite by chance, that I bumped into Stephanie.

It was in London. Not somewhere I'd have expected to see her, so it took me a moment to identify the woman I thought I recognised. We were walking towards each other near the news studio in Kentish Town, the busy one-way system droning with cars streaming past us. She had changed very little, her hair was shorter, but she was still trim and attractive. She would have recognised me, of course, from TV.

"Richard?" Her brow furrowed; she fiddled absently with a pendant around her neck. Perhaps she had been unsure of my identity. Or perhaps she knew perfectly well who I was.

"It's Stephanie, isn't it?"

Then she forced a smile. "I'm surprised you remember me," she said. "It's been how long – four years?"

I mentally calculated how much money this bitch had cost me in that time. "I thought you'd moved away. Somewhere near Brighton to look after your mother."

"You *do* have a good memory," she said, and her face dropped. "Mum *was* seriously ill. She died only a few months after I moved down to care for her."

"I'm sorry to hear that," I said. It was a polite reply. I was feeling my way. How much did she think I knew – if anything. She was blackmailing Carla; would she assume that I knew this? Or did she assume that Carla wouldn't tell me? It was impossible to tell; her manner was pleasant but with a distance; it told me nothing.

"So," I asked, "are you *still* living on the coast?"

"Oh no. It sounds crazy, but I missed the London bustle." She waved around at the busy crowds on the street and the traffic hurtling past. "I guess I'm a city girl at heart. No, I moved back as soon as I could. I'm still in admin, for a firm of solicitors, been there nearly three years now."

This, of course, didn't tally with what I knew. Carla still sent the payments to an address in Sussex. Stephanie was deliberately lying to me, and suddenly I saw in her eyes the scheming jealous blackmailer I knew her to be.

"Liar." My voice had turned to stone.

"Sorry?" Her fingers slipped back to her pendant: a St. Christopher, I noticed.

"Don't you care that you made Carla sick with worry?"

"Carla?" Her brow creased again. "Wasn't she..."

"Don't pretend." I squared up to her, close, face to face. "Surely you remember the woman you've been blackmailing."

There: now *she* knew that *I* knew, and I could see a confusion in her eyes as she tried to process what I'd said. There was no more pretence now; I prodded her sharply with a finger. "You think yourself so smug," I snarled. "So clever."

She backed away. "You're crazy!"

"Yeah. Crazy to have ever sent you a penny!"

She was on the edge of the curb now. She looked frightened, and that just spurred me on. The gold St. Christopher glinted in the sun. "How much did this cost me?" I demanded, reaching out.

She flinched. And stumbled from the curb. I had seen the coach in the corner of my eye, travelling fast. Stephanie didn't have a chance.

The thud was sickening. Then a scream of brakes and a horrifying silence that, for a lingering instant, froze the busy street. I scrambled round to the front of the coach. Other people were already there, crowding around her. She was twisted, smeared beneath the front bumper. She didn't move. Her eyes were closed.

"She's alive!" someone shouted.

A couple of people were already calling 999. I kept to the edge of the growing circle. "I'll get help," I murmured to nobody in particular, and walked swiftly away. I turned a corner, then another, and kept walking. *What have I done?* Eventually I heard the undulating wail of a police car or ambulance approaching.

I had to get to the studio for the evening bulletin. I used roads parallel to my usual route, avoiding the site of the accident. It *was* an accident. I hadn't pushed her. I'd barely touched her. I couldn't get her twisted body out of my mind. Had I been seen? Had I been recognised?

A thought shuddered through me. Stephanie was alive, would she tell the police about me? She was blackmailing my lover. I had the perfect motive for attempted murder. No one would ever believe it was an accident.

The news team's department is *always* a clamour of phone calls. I dreaded each one as we sifted through the day's stories. I was half expecting the police to call – or would they just turn up to take me away?

Then reports came in about the incident. Vague, then with more detail, and the editor wanted it featured, especially as the police were keen to trace a man who may have useful information.

There was no time to review the story. No rehearsal. That's often the case with breaking news.

"It's on autocue, Richard," the floor manager told me.

I glanced down at the monitor concealed beneath the smoked glass top of the news desk. I was relieved that I looked composed. *I have nothing to fear*, I told myself. *No one will suspect.*

* * *

And no one has suspected. It's Saturday now, three days since Stephanie died. I am still dreading that phone call, or that knock at the door. No one can see my heart pounding. I can bluff this out; I'm clever. The strange thing is that I don't feel any guilt. I feel as if justice has been done; Stephanie deserved what happened – *she* was blackmailing *me*.

I realise that the police won't see it that way though. To me, my connections to Stephanie seem glaringly obvious. Perhaps the authorities aren't treating her death as suspicious. There is so much I can only guess at. Perhaps they haven't checked into her bank records yet. Perhaps she spent the blackmail money as untraceable cash, otherwise the payments into her account will match the withdrawals from mine, and there's no way I can blag myself out of that.

It's heartless, I know, but, taking a detached view, I feel glad that she died. She wasn't able to name me as being there, and obviously nobody had recognised me in the scrum of people around her body. I feel sure I'd have been taken for questioning by now.

The useful thing about working in the news is the information we get. Any follow-up on a story is sent to us. And I am using this to my advantage, making sure that I'm kept informed. There have been no leads on the man seen arguing at the roadside. In fact, apart from repeating the report on the late evening bulletin, there have been no newsworthy developments.

I had pulled myself together by the later report. It was the same wording on the autocue, and this time I stressed the word *'accident'*. The public are fickle. They crave sensation, if not murder. Hopefully half the viewers would have lost interest and zoned out at that point.

I am beginning to feel safe. *And it's Saturday*. Carla and I never contact each other during the week, not that I think her husband is clever enough to check her phone, but silence is safer.

These last few days have been such a turmoil: watching my back, checking for news, that it's strange for me to think that Carla knows nothing about it. She may have heard of the accident, but there's no reason for her to suspect that the woman was Stephanie.

Very occasionally Carla and I will see each other in the news building. We try not to be conspicuous about knowing each other. It is perhaps just as well that I haven't seen her these last few days. I would probably have warned her, told her the whole story, and I don't trust Carla to keep her head as well as I have done. Her thoughts tend to show themselves in her face.

Then I realise, perhaps I'm not safe after all.

I had given Carla the latest parcel of cash for Stephanie the previous Saturday. If she hadn't already posted it, I had to stop her. Somebody would eventually open Stephanie's mail, and a bundle of fifties could start an investigation leading straight to my door.

The doorbell rings.

My breath snags somewhere in my throat. Then I check the time and realise it will be Carla. I rush to the door and let her in. She smiles and wanders through to the lounge as normal. Her face is obliviously relaxed and open.

"That last parcel of money," I need to know straight away, "have you posted it yet?"

Carla turns to look suspiciously at me; she's never been good at hiding her feelings. "Why do you ask?" she says.

She isn't usually evasive; I'd expected a simple yes or no. She takes off her coat. "I haven't had time to post it yet," she says. "It's hidden at home. Don't worry, Simon will never find it."

There is something furtive in the way she avoids my eye. "What's wrong?" I ask. "There's something you're not telling me."

She doesn't answer but reaches out to stroke the side of my face, pushing her body against mine. She's wearing a smart new outfit I notice. She likes to dress-up when we meet. I reach up to hold her hand against my cheek. I want to be distracted from my worries. Then, what Stephanie had said about moving back to London, pops into my mind. "You still send the packages to Sussex, don't you," I say. "Somewhere near Brighton?"

She turns away with a shrug. "Yes, of course. Nothing's changed."

And there it is, *the lie*, written huge across her face. I can't take it in for a moment, can't think who to believe. "I met Stephanie, earlier this week," I say.

And Carla crumbles.

There are tears. And a babble of excuses. New school uniforms for the kids. The market stalls aren't doing so well recently.

"Stephanie's dead," I say. And that cuts through her wailing.

Everything is suddenly turned on its head. I'd come to terms with Stephanie's death because I'd thought she was a blackmailer. I'd managed to reason with myself that I was some instrument of justice. But Carla, unsophisticated stupid Carla, has managed to make a fool out of me. Stephanie had been innocent all along. The *real* blackmailer is standing right here.

I am furious, and snap at her. "We need to talk." It's not just the money she's had out of me. "You've no idea what you've caused."

Carla pulls away from me. "I'm sorry." She is wiping at her eyes, heading for the sofa.

"Not here," I say, picking up her coat. "Somewhere quiet. We'll walk along the canal, so I can think."

* * *

"Ready, Richard?" The floor manager counts down and a green light appears on the camera. *Stay detached*. All I have to do is focus on the autocue that scrolls up in front of the lens.

"The body, discovered today floating in the Regent's Canal near Camden Lock, has been identified as mother-of-two Mrs Carla Susan Williams. High healed shoes were found in the water and it is believed that Mrs Williams stumbled on the uneven tow path, hitting her head as she fell into the water. Her husband, Mr Simon Williams, a stallholder at the nearby market, is being treated for shock. His wife, he says, was a wonderful woman and the perfect mother. He had assumed his wife was shopping and can offer no reason for her being in the canal area."

I glance down at the monitor concealed beneath the smoked glass top of the news desk. It shows my face as the viewers will see it. I look composed. *I have nothing to fear*, I tell myself, *no one will suspect*.

From Hell to Eternity

Thana Niveau

THE DAY AFTER THE MURDER everyone was talking about Jack the Ripper. The manner of death and the victim's profession made the comparison unavoidable.

The body was discovered by two nurses coming off the graveyard shift at the Royal London Hospital. On reaching the staff car park they noticed a sprawled figure which they took for an unconscious drunk. As they drew closer they saw the pool of blood and the extent of the injuries. The throat had been cut and the body disembowelled. Entrails lay like a nest of giant worms over and around the victim's limbs and torso. The face was hacked into mince. One ear was missing.

Naturally, the tabloids capitalised on the brutality of the crime and the location of the body, turning every doctor at the hospital into a suspect. But any able-bodied person was capable of spilling blood and viscera with no knowledge whatsoever of anatomy.

BLOODY MURDER! cried more than one paper, adopting the lurid style of a Victorian broadsheet. WHITECHAPEL HORROR! RENT BOY RIPPER!

The victim, Ben Garman, had only been on the game a few months. The previous evening he'd left a nightclub after responding to a text message. He wasn't seen again until the nurses found his body at dawn, his pretty features savagely mutilated.

"There were steam comin' off his body, like," said the younger of the two nurses. "So it must 'ave 'appened just as we were leaving 'ospital. Poor lad."

It was only the beginning. Three nights later a security guard found Aidan Courtley lying in a stairwell near Tower Hill Tube station, his throat slit so wide he was nearly decapitated. Some of his organs had been removed, though not with any apparent skill.

"Frenzied," was the coroner's dry observation. "Like a bloody shark."

Inspector Ralph Miles stared at the dead boy while the police photographer captured the grisly scene from every angle. The press was already turning the events into a circus.

Letters poured in to Scotland Yard, their writers either confessing to the killings or condemning their neighbours. Even the most outlandish claims had to be investigated. It was a frustrating waste of manpower, chasing down false leads and reinforcing the attention seekers.

It didn't help matters that Courtley was a porn star. Apparently films weren't enough to fund his taste for white powder and so he hired himself out to discriminating gentlemen on the side. This time the Ripper wasn't content with straightforward murder and mutilation. Courtley had been stabbed over two hundred times, many of the cuts shallow and superficial. His death had been slow. Protracted. The only mercy was the fact that he was dead by the time the killer emasculated him.

* * *

The boy's eyes widened when he saw the knife. The blade pressed against his throat and he whimpered softly. A question, a demand. He couldn't remember, couldn't think straight. Whatever it was, he didn't know the answer. All he knew was that there had been something in that drink. His legs felt like rubber and he thought he would faint.

"Look, I don't—"

The blade jabbed him and he let out a yelp. Warm blood seeped down the side of his neck and into his shirt.

"OK, OK, I see him maybe two – three time. He like – how you say? – pretty boys, pretty like girls. Now I tell you everything, please, you let me go!"

But it wasn't that simple. Without warning, a hammer blow struck him in the chest, hard, slamming him back against the brick wall. For a moment he stood, wavering dizzily. Then he crumpled to the ground. He felt a crazy sense of relief that his assailant hadn't hit him in the face. He couldn't work if his face was ruined. Then he saw the blood, leaping from his chest in rapid spurts.

The blade flashed again and he knew with cold certainty that he was about to die. Although he screamed, he felt no pain. Not even when the point of the knife claimed each deep brown eye. In fact, he imagined he could see more clearly than ever before. The world was suddenly alive with colour and beauty. He was in the presence of an angel.

* * *

Steve Chalmers saw the headline on a discarded copy of the *Daily Mail* as he joined the queue at Starbucks. MURDER FOR RENT: THIRD VICTIM IN SHOCKING RIPPER BLOODBATH! Beneath the screaming capitals was a photograph of a beautiful Chinese boy with jet black hair and eyes as fathomless as the ocean.

Steve's stomach lurched and his hand contracted around the paper, his fingernails gouging the image. It was Danny.

All at once he tasted bile. He stuffed the paper into his briefcase and ran to the toilet. He just managed to slam the door and lock it before falling to his knees and clutching the sides of the bowl as violent spasms overtook him. He retched painfully until there was nothing left in his stomach.

At last, shaky and sweating, he clambered to his feet and splashed his face with cold water. His eyes filled with tears, but he blinked them away. He couldn't fall apart here. But he couldn't go home either; Gina was there. He stared down his pale reflection in the mirror, willing himself to calm down, regain control. A few deep breaths slowed his pounding heart and he unbolted the door, dreading the crowd.

A girl in a green Starbucks apron was waiting for him, looking anxious. "You OK, sir?"

Steve forced his lips apart in an approximation of a smile. "Yeah. Sorry about that. Touch of swine flu."

She leapt back as though she'd been electrocuted, murmuring apologies and get-well wishes.

"Think I'll skip the coffee this morning," he said, "maybe phone in sick too."

"Good idea," said the girl, retreating to safety behind the counter.

The other customers cleared a path for him as he made his way back out onto the street. He stopped when he reached the corner and scrolled through the messages on his phone.

see u TMRW! xx danny

He knew he should delete it, knew how incriminating it was. But the thought of erasing all he had left of Danny made him feel ill again. He'd warned the boy, begged him to be careful. There was a maniac stalking the streets of Whitechapel, butchering pretty boys. First Ben and then that gay-for-pay porn star, Aidan.

Steve had erased their numbers from his phone after the first two murders but he couldn't bring himself to purge Danny from the list. He was the most exquisite creature Steve had ever seen. It didn't matter that he was half Steve's age; it felt like love to him. As real as he had once felt for Gina. It hurt; it obsessed; it demanded expression.

He snapped the phone shut and shoved it into his coat pocket. His chest ached with a loss he knew he must hide at all costs. Hastily he devised a plan. He would go to the bank and lock himself in his office. There he would open the paper and read the terrible story of what had been done to Daniel Cheng. After that he would put on his work face and get through the rest of the day, one moment at a time, before going home and trying to hide his grief from his wife.

* * *

"Hey Miles, take a look at this."

PC Cuthbert held a Nokia phone in one gloved hand. Cheng's. Miles read the text on the screen.

7 PM Beaumont Hotel. Bring something kinky. I've got some E.

It wasn't signed, but the number was listed in the phone contacts as 'Steve'.

"Probably not his real name," Cuthbert said.

But Miles shook his head. "You'd be surprised. Let's see who answers, shall we?"

He scribbled the number on the back of his hand and called it from his own mobile, although a mischievous part of him was tempted to ring from the victim's phone, startling the killer with a call from beyond the grave.

After several rings a recorded voice began speaking. "Hi. You've reached Steve Chalmers. I can't take your call right now but…"

Miles disconnected and grinned at Cuthbert. "Steve Chalmers," he said. "Find him."

* * *

"Mr. Chalmers?"

Steve wiped his nose and looked up at Susan. His flu excuse had seemed to satisfy everyone's concern over his red eyes and runny nose.

"What?" he snapped.

She flinched like a kicked puppy. "I'm really sorry to disturb you, but there's two gentlemen here to see you."

"Tell them I'm busy!"

"They're from Scotland Yard."

All the blood drained from Steve's face. His throat suddenly felt full of sand but he managed to pretend nonchalance. "Oh? Well, in that case you'd better send them in."

Susan nodded and vanished into the outer office. Steve sank into his chair, his heart rate increasing by the second, so rapid it became painful. How had they found him? What did they know?

He arranged his features into a welcoming but curious and concerned expression. The face of innocence.

* * *

Miles took in the bank manager's pallor at once. His tremulous, sweaty handshake. Oh yes, he was hiding something.

"Good afternoon, gentlemen," the suspect said pleasantly. "I hope no one's tried to rob the bank."

Miles cleared his throat. "Sir, I'll come straight to the point. Your number was found in the mobile phone of a murder victim. I see you've already read about it." He nodded towards the copy of the *Daily Mail* lying crumpled on the desk.

Steve suddenly looked even paler. "Good lord," he exclaimed with an unconvincing laugh. "I don't read that rubbish!"

Both policemen maintained inscrutable expressions.

"I just… picked it up by mistake. At Starbucks. I wasn't feeling well and I—"

Miles held up a hand. "Mr. Chalmers, we saw the text you sent to Daniel Cheng yesterday. It's the last message he received. The last before he was killed."

"What are you implying?" Steve spluttered.

"Sir, I have to ask your whereabouts last night, around midnight."

For a moment Steve appeared outraged, as though he were about to deny knowing there'd even *been* a murder. Then he seemed to think better of it and he sat staring forlornly at his hands. "My wife doesn't have any idea about me," he said softly.

Miles let his eyes flick to Cuthbert, a silent warning not to interrupt. Steve looked about to crack and it was best to let him talk.

"I was on the verge of telling her all about me, about the boys. But I just couldn't do it, couldn't face it. I tried to stop, really I did. But they were just so beautiful, so innocent…" His voice caught as he looked at the torn front page article. His hand twitched, as though resisting an urge to touch the photo of the boy. "I couldn't stop. Not after I found Danny. He was in the country illegally and I helped him out a little. And in return…"

He seemed to come to his senses then and he stopped himself.

Miles didn't need to hear the sordid details; he knew the score. A pretty young thing playing up his vulnerability to the gullible older man. The street hustler with no one else to turn to. This uptight little bank manager was a perfect mark.

"Gina doesn't understand me. She says I'm cold. But she doesn't know what I'm like with them. How it was with Danny." His voice sounded pleading now and he swallowed a little sob as he swiped the tissue across his eyes.

"Mr. Chalmers," Miles said gently, "were you with Danny last night?"

Steve stared at the paper, tears spilling over his cheeks. "No."

Miles waited, but Steve didn't offer more. "The text mentioned a meeting at the Beaumont Hotel, 7 pm," he prompted. "Did you go there?"

Steve nodded miserably. "We were supposed to meet in the bar but Danny never showed. I rang him but only got his voicemail."

"Did you leave a message?"

"No, I hung up."

Miles nodded like a priest hearing a confession. He didn't dare resume cop mode while the man was unburdening himself so freely. "What did you do after that?"

Steve hung his head. "Just stayed in the bar and drank. I don't even know how long I was there. The bartender called me a cab. I must have passed out when I got home."

"Did you give Danny drugs last night?"

"I told you, I didn't *see* him!"

"Did you also know Ben Garman and Aidan Courtley?"

Steve's face crumpled like a child's. "Yes," he sobbed. "But I didn't kill them either. I wouldn't. I couldn't!"

Miles had heard enough. It was time to play Bad Cop before the suspect turned to stone or demanded a lawyer. "Mr. Chalmers, I'm afraid I'm going to have to inform you of your rights."

"I'm not a murderer!" he cried. Then he wept quietly while Miles cuffed him and led him out of the bank and into the waiting police car.

Steve spent two nights in jail before his wife bailed him out, assuring Inspector Miles that he'd been home with her when the murders took place.

* * *

"Want a drink?" Gina called.

"Yes, please," Steve said, desperate to obliterate his senses.

Gina returned from the kitchen with a bottle of J&B and a pint glass. She poured him a generous measure.

Steve took two hefty swallows, enjoying the burn as it slithered down his throat like a living thing, clawing furrows along the way. He imagined it was searing away the horror of the past few days.

He drank fast and greedily, eager to be drunk, and Gina topped up his glass as soon as it was empty. There was something bothering him about the whole situation. Of course, *he'd* known he hadn't killed those boys, but he didn't have an alibi. Why had Gina lied for him?

As he finished the second glass he caught her watching him. An unsettling smile played at the corners of her mouth.

"I knew about the boys, Steve," she said coolly. "Did you know that one of them actually rang the house once looking for you?"

No, Steve hadn't known that. He set the empty glass down with a thump, watching as tracers of light seemed to follow the wake of his hand, like a tiny comet.

"The first one was so easy," she continued. "Surprisingly easy. I mean, once I screwed up the nerve to do it, to make the first cut. Was it like that for you too? Screwing up your courage for the first time, I mean?"

Steve looked at her blankly, as though she were speaking a language he only vaguely understood. He seemed to comprehend on some rudimentary level what she was telling him but at the same time he was weirdly detached from his emotions. Fear was there somewhere, fluttering at the back of his mind.

"I couldn't believe how easy it was. It was like I'd been born to it. The second one was awkward, though. I told him I wanted to hire him for a custom porn shoot but the little prima donna kept raising the price on me. Tried to screw me over too. So I made him suffer. Made it last as long as I could. And it felt *good,* Steve! You've no idea how good it felt! Oh,

I've really got a taste for it now." She laughed, a girlish giggle that was even more disturbing than the confession.

Steve was dazzled by the colours her words produced in his head. His eyes drifted to the empty glass as the fog lifted for a moment. Then it blanketed him with darkness.

When he opened his eyes she was still talking. He was praying. No, he was on his knees, but he certainly wasn't praying. He didn't know how he'd got there.

"That last one, the Chinese boy, he didn't fight at all. He went like a willing sacrifice."

Sacrifice. Steve managed to turn his head enough to see his predicament. He was kneeling on the floor, bending forward with his elbows resting on the seat of a chair. He couldn't move.

"Duct tape, in case you're wondering," Gina said icily. "I suspect you're not the willing victim type."

His mind was still cloudy but he strained against his bonds. Gina didn't seem to notice.

"I'm not surprised they never caught Jack the Ripper," she said. "He was good. He knew what he was doing, going after East End whores. No one cares what happens to them. He was ridding the city of an undesirable element. Just like I am. But there's one last thing I want to do. I want to be remembered like he was."

With sudden lucidity Steve realised that she was holding a knife. He made muffled sounds of protest through the strip of tape across his mouth, but his murmurings were cut short by a sudden searing pain in his right side, just underneath his rib cage. He screamed behind the gag, struggling impotently against the tape. It felt like being turned inside-out. Then, to his further horror, he felt Gina plunge her hands into the wound, felt her shoving his insides out of the way as she reached up underneath his ribs. Blood fountained from the wound.

Lights flashed behind Steve's eyes and his entire being became a single scream of agony.

"There!" Gina said. She displayed her trophy to him – a ripe kidney, sitting in her hand like a fistful of blood. In delirium, he watched as she placed it on the table and neatly sliced it in two.

"Seems a pity to waste half of it on the police," she said, "but if you're going to pay tribute…" She dropped one piece into a box, where it landed with a wet thud. "This half, however, is mine."

She disappeared into the kitchen and before Steve finally lost consciousness, he heard the clatter of pans on the stove and smelled something cooking.

The Regent's Park Murder

Baroness Orczy

BY THIS TIME Miss Polly Burton had become quite accustomed to her extraordinary vis-á-vis in the corner.

He was always there, when she arrived, in the selfsame corner, dressed in one of his remarkable check tweed suits; he seldom said good morning, and invariably when she appeared he began to fidget with increased nervousness, with some tattered and knotty piece of string.

"Were you ever interested in the Regent's Park murder?" he asked her one day.

Polly replied that she had forgotten most of the particulars connected with that curious murder, but that she fully remembered the stir and flutter it had caused in a certain section of London Society.

"The racing and gambling set, particularly, you mean," he said. "All the persons implicated in the murder, directly or indirectly, were of the type commonly called 'Society men,' or 'men about town,' whilst the Harewood Club in Hanover Square, round which centred all the scandal in connection with the murder, was one of the smartest clubs in London.

"Probably the doings of the Harewood Club, which was essentially a gambling club, would for ever have remained 'officially' absent from the knowledge of the police authorities but for the murder in the Regent's Park and the revelations which came to light in connection with it.

"I dare say you know the quiet square which lies between Portland Place and the Regent's Park and is called Park Crescent at its south end, and subsequently Park Square East and West. The Marylebone Road, with all its heavy traffic, cuts straight across the large square and its pretty gardens, but the latter are connected together by a tunnel under the road; and of course you must remember that the new tube station in the south portion of the Square had not yet been planned.

"February 6th, 1907, was a very foggy night, nevertheless Mr. Aaron Cohen, of 30, Park Square West, at two o'clock in the morning, having finally pocketed the heavy winnings which he had just swept off the green table of the Harewood Club, started to walk home alone. An hour later most of the inhabitants of Park Square West were aroused from their peaceful slumbers by the sounds of a violent altercation in the road. A man's angry voice was heard shouting violently for a minute or two, and was followed immediately by frantic screams of 'Police' and 'Murder.' Then there was the double sharp report of firearms, and nothing more.

"The fog was very dense, and, as you no doubt have experienced yourself, it is very difficult to locate sound in a fog. Nevertheless, not more than a minute or two had elapsed before Constable F 18, the point policeman at the corner of Marylebone Road, arrived on the scene, and, having first of all whistled for any of his comrades on the beat, began to grope his way about in the fog, more confused than effectually assisted by contradictory directions from the inhabitants of the houses close by, who were nearly falling out of the upper windows as they shouted out to the constable.

"'By the railings, policeman.'

"'Higher up the road.'

"'No, lower down.'

"'It was on this side of the pavement I am sure.'

"'No, the other.'

"At last it was another policeman, F 22, who, turning into Park Square West from the north side, almost stumbled upon the body of a man lying on the pavement with his head against the railings of the Square. By this time quite a little crowd of people from the different houses in the road had come down, curious to know what had actually happened.

"The policeman turned the strong light of his bull's-eye lantern on the unfortunate man's face.

"'It looks as if he had been strangled, don't it?' he murmured to his comrade.

"And he pointed to the swollen tongue, the eyes half out of their sockets, bloodshot and congested, the purple, almost black, hue of the face.

"At this point one of the spectators, more callous to horrors, peered curiously into the dead man's face. He uttered an exclamation of astonishment.

"'Why, surely, it's Mr. Cohen from No. 30!'

"The mention of a name familiar down the length of the street had caused two or three other men to come forward and to look more closely into the horribly distorted mask of the murdered man.

"'Our next-door neighbour, undoubtedly,' asserted Mr. Ellison, a young barrister, residing at No. 31.

"'What in the world was he doing this foggy night all alone, and on foot?' asked somebody else.

"'He usually came home very late. I fancy he belonged to some gambling club in town. I dare say he couldn't get a cab to bring him out here. Mind you, I don't know much about him. We only knew him to nod to.'

"'Poor beggar! it looks almost like an old-fashioned case of garroting.'

"'Anyway, the blackguardly murderer, whoever he was, wanted to make sure he had killed his man!' added Constable F 18, as he picked up an object from the pavement. 'Here's the revolver, with two cartridges missing. You gentlemen heard the report just now?'

"'He don't seem to have hit him though. The poor bloke was strangled, no doubt.'

"'And tried to shoot at his assailant, obviously,' asserted the young barrister with authority.

"'If he succeeded in hitting the brute, there might be a chance of tracing the way he went.'

"'But not in the fog.'

"Soon, however, the appearance of the inspector, detective, and medical officer, who had quickly been informed of the tragedy, put an end to further discussion.

"The bell at No. 30 was rung, and the servants – all four of them women – were asked to look at the body.

"Amidst tears of horror and screams of fright, they all recognized in the murdered man their master, Mr. Aaron Cohen. He was therefore conveyed to his own room pending the coroner's inquest.

"The police had a pretty difficult task, you will admit; there were so very few indications to go by, and at first literally no clue.

"The inquest revealed practically nothing. Very little was known in the neighbourhood about Mr. Aaron Cohen and his affairs. His female servants did not even know the name or whereabouts of the various clubs he frequented.

"He had an office in Throgmorton Street and went to business every day. He dined at home, and sometimes had friends to dinner. When he was alone he invariably went to the club, where he stayed until the small hours of the morning.

"The night of the murder he had gone out at about nine o'clock. That was the last his servants had seen of him. With regard to the revolver, all four servants swore positively that they had never seen it before, and that, unless Mr. Cohen had bought it that very day, it did not belong to their master.

"Beyond that, no trace whatever of the murderer had been found, but on the morning after the crime a couple of keys linked together by a short metal chain were found close to a gate at the opposite end of the Square, that which immediately faced Portland Place. These were proved to be, firstly, Mr. Cohen's latch-key, and, secondly, his gate-key of the Square.

"It was therefore presumed that the murderer, having accomplished his fell design and ransacked his victim's pockets, had found the keys and made good his escape by slipping into the Square, cutting under the tunnel, and out again by the further gate. He then took the precaution not to carry the keys with him any further, but threw them away and disappeared in the fog.

"The jury returned a verdict of wilful murder against some person or persons unknown, and the police were put on their mettle to discover the unknown and daring murderer. The result of their investigations, conducted with marvellous skill by Mr. William Fisher, led, about a week after the crime, to the sensational arrest of one of London's smartest young bucks.

"The case Mr. Fisher had got up against the accused briefly amounted to this:

"On the night of February 6th, soon after midnight, play began to run very high at the Harewood Club, in Hanover Square. Mr. Aaron Cohen held the bank at roulette against some twenty or thirty of his friends, mostly young fellows with no wits and plenty of money. 'The Bank' was winning heavily, and it appears that this was the third consecutive night on which Mr. Aaron Cohen had gone home richer by several hundreds than he had been at the start of play.

"Young John Ashley, who is the son of a very worthy county gentleman who is M.F.H. somewhere in the Midlands, was losing heavily, and in his case also it appears that it was the third consecutive night that Fortune had turned her face against him.

"Remember," continued the man in the corner, "that when I tell you all these details and facts, I am giving you the combined evidence of several witnesses, which it took many days to collect and to classify.

"It appears that young Mr. Ashley, though very popular in society, was generally believed to be in what is vulgarly termed 'low water'; up to his eyes in debt, and mortally afraid of his dad, whose younger son he was, and who had on one occasion threatened to ship him off to Australia with a £5 note in his pocket if he made any further extravagant calls upon his paternal indulgence.

"It was also evident to all John Ashley's many companions that the worthy M.F.H. held the purse-strings in a very tight grip. The young man, bitten with the desire to cut a smart figure in the circles in which he moved, had often recourse to the varying fortunes which now and again smiled upon him across the green tables in the Harewood Club.

"Be that as it may, the general consensus of opinion at the Club was that young Ashley had changed his last 'pony' before he sat down to a turn of roulette with Aaron Cohen on that particular night of February 6th.

"It appears that all his friends, conspicuous among whom was Mr. Walter Hatherell, tried their very best to dissuade him from pitting his luck against that of Cohen, who had been having a most unprecedented run of good fortune. But young Ashley, heated with wine, exasperated at his own bad luck, would listen to no one; he tossed one £5 note after another on the board, he borrowed from those who would lend, then played on parole for a while. Finally, at half-past one in the morning, after a run of nineteen on the red, the young man found himself without a penny in his pockets, and owing a debt – gambling debt – a debt of honour of £1500 to Mr. Aaron Cohen.

"Now we must render this much maligned gentleman that justice which was persistently denied to him by press and public alike; it was positively asserted by all those present that Mr. Cohen himself repeatedly tried to induce young Mr. Ashley to give up playing. He himself was in a delicate position in the matter, as he was the winner, and once or twice the taunt had risen to the young man's lips, accusing the holder of the bank of the wish to retire on a competence before the break in his luck.

"Mr. Aaron Cohen, smoking the best of Havanas, had finally shrugged his shoulders and said: 'As you please!'

"But at half-past one he had had enough of the player, who always lost and never paid – never could pay, so Mr. Cohen probably believed. He therefore at that hour refused to accept Mr. John Ashley's 'promissory' stakes any longer. A very few heated words ensued, quickly checked by the management, who are ever on the alert to avoid the least suspicion of scandal.

"In the meanwhile Mr. Hatherell, with great good sense, persuaded young Ashley to leave the Club and all its temptations and go home; if possible to bed.

"The friendship of the two young men, which was very well known in society, consisted chiefly, it appears, in Walter Hatherell being the willing companion and helpmeet of John Ashley in his mad and extravagant pranks. But tonight the latter, apparently tardily sobered by his terrible and heavy losses, allowed himself to be led away by his friend from the scene of his disasters. It was then about twenty minutes to two.

"Here the situation becomes interesting," continued the man in the corner in his nervous way. "No wonder that the police interrogated at least a dozen witnesses before they were quite satisfied that every statement was conclusively proved.

"Walter Hatherell, after about ten minutes' absence, that is to say at ten minutes to two, returned to the club room. In reply to several inquiries, he said that he had parted with his friend at the corner of New Bond Street, since he seemed anxious to be alone, and that Ashley said he would take a turn down Piccadilly before going home – he thought a walk would do him good.

"At two o'clock or thereabouts Mr. Aaron Cohen, satisfied with his evening's work, gave up his position at the bank and, pocketing his heavy winnings, started on his homeward walk, while Mr. Walter Hatherell left the club half an hour later.

"At three o'clock precisely the cries of 'Murder' and the report of fire-arms were heard in Park Square West, and Mr. Aaron Cohen was found strangled outside the garden railings."

The Dilmun Exchange

Josh Pachter

THE MUEZZIN'S CALL to dawn prayer echoed sadly down Bab-al-Bahrain Avenue. It was four a.m., and the long narrow street – the main artery of Manama's old shopping district, the *suq* – was almost deserted. A beggar woman squatted, motionless, beside the doorway of Dilmun Exchange Services and Wholesale Jewelers, completely covered by her black silk *abba*, even her face and her extended palm swathed in black and invisible. Except for her, the road was empty. It would be hours yet before the merchants began to arrive, to raise the heavy metal shutters which protected their shop windows, to unlock their glass doors and switch on their electric cash registers, to look over their merchandise and drink one quiet cup of strong coffee before the madness began.

It was October 1, the first day of the autumn sales. For the next two weeks, by official decree of the Emir himself, every shop in the tiny island-nation of Bahrain would slash twenty per cent or more from its prices on all items but food. At eight a.m., the sales would begin, and thousands of Arabs and expatriates would pour into the *suq* from all over the country, showering tens of thousands of dinars on the merchants and artisans, driving home to dinner with the backs of their cars filled with a mind-boggling array of television sets, video recorders, stereo systems, cameras, typewriters, pocket calculators, digital watches, electronic games, refrigerators, air conditioners, washing machines, microwave ovens, furniture, hand-woven carpets, antique pearl chests, bracelets and necklaces of gold and silver, shirts and skirts and shoes and suits and dresses.

But the beginning of the madness was still hours away, and when Mahboob Chaudri turned off Government Road and walked under the tall white arches of the *bab*, the narrow street which stretched out before him was lonely and still, except for the solitary beggar and the dying echoes of the *muezzin*'s call.

Chaudri crossed the small plaza just inside the *bab* and paused to look up at the blue-and-white sign above the doorway of the squat off-white building on the corner. STATE OF BAHRAIN, the sign announced in English and Arabic, MINISTER OF THE INTERIOR, PUBLIC SECURITY, MANAMA POLICE STATION.

Why only English and Arabic? he wondered, as he wondered every morning. *Why not Baluchi and Punjabi and Urdu, since almost two-thirds of us on the police force are Pakistani?*

Then, as always, he shrugged his shoulders, pushed the thought aside, and walked up the three stone steps into the station house.

A small group of *mahsools*, all of them Bahraini, lounged in the hallway, smoking imported cigarettes and talking idly. Chaudri greeted them with deference – he was always careful to be courteous to his superior officers – and walked on back to the locker room.

He was early this morning and no one else was there yet. He unbuttoned his sports shirt and hung it away in his locker, took off his blue jeans and folded them onto a second hanger, and placed his tennis shoes neatly beneath them. Many of the other men came to work in *jutti* and the traditional Pakistani *punjab* – knee-length cotton shirt and baggy trousers, both in the same pale shade of orange or brown or blue – but Chaudri liked the look of Western clothes and wore them whenever he was off duty.

He pulled on his drab-green uniform shirt and pants, adjusted his shoulder braid, knotted his olive-green tie, tucking the bottom half of it away between the second and third buttons of his shirt, and stepped into his sturdy black shoes. Then he faced the mirror inside the door of his locker and positioned his dark-green beret on his head, turning this way and that to make sure it was sitting well.

Satisfied at last, he stepped back from the mirror so he could see more of himself. He liked what he saw: Mahboob Ahmed Chaudri, twenty-eight years of age and not bad-looking, with his deep-brown skin, his regular features, and his immaculate, imposing uniform.

Mahboob Ahmed Chaudri, eighteen months a *natoor* on the Bahraini police force and ready any day now for his first promotion. He would be sorry to give up that lovely green beret, but glad to trade it in for the peaked cap of a *mahsool*.

The room was beginning to fill up now, and Chaudri closed the door of his locker and joined one of the half dozen conversations going on around him. It was 4:20 a.m., and he still had ten minutes of his own time left before roll call.

* * *

By the time his half hour break began, at 9 a.m., the sales were well under way. Bab-al-Bahrain Avenue and the labyrinth of side streets and alleyways branching off from it were inundated with honking cars and bustling shoppers. The air was hot and still, and heavy with the smells of cooking oil and automobile exhaust and sweat, the sounds of humanity and machinery joined together in grating cacophony.

But Mahboob Chaudri walked along with a smile on his face, patiently allowing the throngs to surge around him and jostle against him – small knots of Arab women in long black *abbas*, their faces hidden behind thin veils or the birdlike leather masks called *berga'a*; businessmen in ankle-length *thobes* with red-and-white checkered *ghutras* arranged carefully on their heads; bankers of forty countries in expensive three-piece suits; expat wives in modest skirts and blouses; Dutch construction workers and Korean longshoremen and British oil riggers in grease-stained jeans; Indian nannies in flowing saris, their midriffs bare or swathed in filmy gauze; children of every color and nationality and description.

Chaudri's monthly pay envelope was in his pocket, he had half an hour free, and he was on his way to the Dilmun Exchange to buy rupees to send home to his wife and children in Karachi.

Outside the money-changing office, the lone beggar woman still sat. Or was this a different one? Shrouded in black, not an inch of skin visible, unmoving, there was no way to tell. Chaudri pulled a 100-*fils* piece from his pocket and laid it gently on her covered, outstretched palm. "*El lo, majee*," he mumbled in his native Punjabi.

"Take this, mother."

The woman did not answer him, not even with a nod.

Under that *abba*, she could be fast asleep, thought Chaudri. She could even be dead.

He went into the exchange office. It was a plain room. Behind a wooden counter running along the far wall, a gray-bearded Bahraini in *thobe* and *ghutra* sat working a pocket calculator. Above his head hung a large black board with the day's exchange rates – buying and selling prices for American and Canadian and Australian dollars, French and Swiss francs, Danish, Swedish and Norwegian kronor, British pounds, German marks, Dutch guilders, Italian lira, Saudia Arabian riyals, Japanese yen, and a dozen other currencies. There were a few faded travel posters taped to the walls, an ashtray standing in front of the counter for the use of the clientele, an oversized air conditioner humming morosely, and that was all.

Five men and a woman were waiting to be helped, as the Bahraini made his computations and counted out stacks of ten- and twenty-dinar notes.

Chaudri took his place at the end of the line and looked up at the rate board. Almost thirty rupees to the dinar, he read happily. A good rate. Shazia and the children would have a comfortable month.

The first man in line scooped up his wad of bills from the counter, muttered a low-pitched "*Shukran*," and left the office. Chaudri and the other clients shuffled a place forward.

And then the door behind them banged open, and Chaudri whirled around at the noise.

A tall man with dark-brown hair and burning eyes stood just inside the doorway. It was impossible to tell whether he was a native or an expat. A woman's leather *berga'a* hid most of his face, and he did not speak. There was a gun in his hand, a dull-black revolver, and he held it firmly, not trembling.

He stood for a moment, allowing the realization of danger to reach through layers of shock into the minds of his victims, then he reached behind him and flipped the sign hanging inside the glass door to read CLOSED, turned the key in the deadbolt, and pulled down the shade. Only then did he wave his gun at them, motioning them to the side wall of the office.

"Turn around," he told them, "faces to the wall. Hands high above your heads, feet spread wide." His voice was cold and hard; he spoke accented but precise Arabic.

A Yemeni? thought Chaudri automatically, his eyes fixed on a flyspeck on the wall two inches before him. *A Kuwaiti?*

Over the irritated hum of the air-conditioner, he could hear the thief unfold a plastic grocery bag and begin to stuff it with stacks of crisp banknotes. *He'll take the dinars, the American dollars and the riyals*, Chaudri guessed, *and leave the rest of it be—*

"Now listen carefully," the voice interrupted his thoughts, "especially you, *natoor*. Do exactly what I tell you and by Allah's grace no one will get hurt."

"By Allah's grace!" the grey-haired clerk burst out furiously. "How *dare* you talk about—"

There was a blur of sound as the thief dashed across the room and clubbed the old Bahraini fiercely with the butt end of his revolver.

Chaudri stole a look to the side in time to see the clerk crumple limply to the ground and the masked figure back away.

"Do what he says," Chaudri instructed the rest of them. "Don't speak, don't move, and don't worry. It will be all right."

"Thank you for your assistance, *natoor*," the bandit said crisply. Chaudri could hear no sarcasm in it, which surprised him. *This man is truly calm*, he thought. *He knows just what he is doing.*

"If you follow the advice which the *natoor* has so intelligently given you," the voice resumed, "no one else will have to be hurt. And as you have seen, if you do *not* heed that advice, I will show you no mercy. No mercy at all."

Chaudri listened intently. *If I can't memorize his face*, he thought, *at least I can memorize that heartless voice.*

"In a few moments I will be leaving you," the thief went on. "Before I go, I will say to you the word 'Begin.' When I say that word, you will begin to count aloud, in unison, from one to one hundred. You will keep your faces to the wall and your hands high and go on counting, no matter what happens. When you reach one hundred, you may put your hands down and turn around and go about your business. If any of you should decide to take a chance and come after me before you have finished counting – well, that is a chance I would recommend you avoid. I have a confederate in the street, who is armed and will shoot to kill. Your families will be saddened to hear of your senseless death."

That was a lie, Chaudri was certain. There was no confederate in the street. *This man works alone and will share his loot with no one, I can feel it. But can I afford to gamble my life on that feeling?*

No, he decided. *No.*

"Thank you all for your cooperation," the voice concluded. "And now, you may begin."

"*Oahed,*" Mahboob Chaudri said tightly, and the others spoke with him. "*Th'neen, t'lasse, arba'a, hamseh....*"

As they counted, he heard the door bolt being thrown and the door swing smoothly open and then, after soft footsteps passed through it, shut. The temptation to give chase, or at least to raise the alarm, was very strong, but the thief's words rang loudly in Chaudri's ears: *Your family will be saddened to hear of your senseless death.*

"*Thamnta'ash,*" he counted grimly, "*tsata'ash, ashreen, oahed ashreen....*"

Suddenly there was the sound of a shot, and glass shattering, and an overwhelming clamor from the startled mobs of shoppers outside.

Chaudri stiffened. *Allah give me strength,* he prayed silently, as he continued to count the Arabic numbers out in the charged atmosphere of the exchange office. Forty, he reached as the bedlam outside swelled riotously, and sixty as it crested, then seventy as it began a slow descent back toward the everyday pandemonium of the October sales, and eighty-five as the strident cries of a dozen police officers became audible above the din, shouting questions and issuing commands to the crowd...

"*Sa'ba'ah watis'een,*" Chaudri counted diligently, his palms itching with a feverish ache to be out in the street, "*thamania watis'een, tis'ah watis'een, ma'ah!*"

Before the dull echo of the final number had faded, Chaudri was on the sidewalk outside the Dilmun Exchange, his eyes drinking in the scene before him greedily: a tight half circle of police and passersby across the street gathered in front of the smashed display window of the Akhundawazi Trading Company. Up and down Bab-al-Bahrain Avenue as far as he could see in either direction the shoppers ebbed and flowed, laden with bags and boxes and gaily wrapped packages, an endless tide of bargain-hunting humanity.

"Did you see him?" Chaudri demanded of the black-draped beggar, who had not moved from her perch beside the door. Unlike the first time he had addressed her, he spoke now in flawless Arabic. "The last man to leave this office, mother – did you see which way he went?"

The woman nodded her head stiffly and moved a hand underneath her *abba* to point south.

Chaudri was off at once. "Thank you, mother," he threw back over his shoulder as he ran, his feet pounding against the concrete paving stones, his clenched teeth jarring with every stride.

But it was hopeless, he realized, before he had gone a hundred yards. Completely hopeless. By now the thief could have bolted down any one of a dozen side streets, could have strolled casually into any of a thousand shops, could be trying on a pair of trousers or pricing gold bangles or sipping sweet tea from a gently steaming glass.

What chance did he, Mahboob Chaudri, have of being lucky enough to stumble across a single man with a bag of money, a woman's face mask and a gun, intent on losing himself in the tangled, teeming maze of the old *suq*?

Hopeless, he thought as he ran, disgusted with his caution back at the exchange office, with the cumbersome uniform and clumsy shoes which slowed him down, with the infuriating crowds.

What could he do? What, if it came to that, could the entire 6,000-man Public Security Force do? *One hundred friends are not enough*, as the old Bedouin saying had it, *but a single enemy is too many.*

Yes, they could close off the airport and watch the fishing *dhows* and almost certainly prevent the criminal from leaving the country.

But if the man chose to stay, if he went to ground, say, out in A'ali or Bani Jamra or one of the other villages, if he actually had a confederate, after all, who was willing to hide him, then there was no way they would ever find him. He could disappear into the desert sands of Bahrain, and the country would swallow him up so completely that it would be as if he had never existed.

Chaudri stopped running, leaned weakly against a stretch of wooden scaffolding, and lowered his head, gasping hoarsely and filling his exhausted lungs with air.

Was it but a single enemy he was faced with? What if he'd been wrong, if there *had* been a confederate out in the street? The thief could have passed him that incriminating plastic bag, gotten rid of the money and mask and gun, and melted invisibly away into the crowd.

But that made no sense. Giving the bag to a confederate would leave the thief in the clear, yes, but then what about the confederate? If *he* were found with the bag in his possession, then—

And what was the point of the gunshot? Was it intended simply to draw the crowd's attention away from the thief's escape? If so, then why had he bothered? The shoppers hadn't known that the Dilmun Exchange was being robbed.

Chaudri pulled himself upright and began to retrace his steps. He arranged and rearranged the pieces in his head, manipulating them like the misshapen interlocking loops of the silver puzzle ring he had bought for his daughter Peveen's last birthday, trying to fit them together into an organized, sensible whole.

The Dilmun Exchange. A tall, controlled thief, his identity hidden behind a leather mask. The violent attack on the harmless old Bahraini clerk. "Count to one hundred"…"Your families will be saddened"…a gunshot…the crowds…the clamor…the Dilmun Exchange….

And then suddenly the pieces dropped softly into place.

"Merea rabba!" Chaudri exclaimed aloud, reverting unconsciously to Punjabi. "Oh, dearie me, of course!"

He was sure of it, he was positive, but before he could prove it there was one question he would have to ask – if only he was not too late! He broke into a jog, weaving carefully from side to side to avoid the scores of shoppers milling in his path.

As he neared the Dilmun Exchange, he saw that the old beggar woman was still there, rocking rhythmically back and forth, her upturned palm – still covered by the black fabric of her *abba* – a silent plea for charity.

He walked up to her, stood over her, looked down at her – and asked her his question. "Tell me, mother, what is your name?"

The black shape that was her head turned up to him, but the woman did not speak.

"Your name, mother," Chaudri repeated. "Tell me your name."

She put a hand to her lips and shook her head.

"Oh, no, mother," said Chaudri, "you are not mute. It is only that you do not wish to speak. And why is that, I find myself wondering?"

Her other hand began to rise, but the *natoor* gripped the wrist firmly and pointed it towards the sky.

"No, mother," he said. "Your friend has already fired one shot this morning, and one shot was more than enough for today."

* * *

"I was certain the thief had lied when he told us about his confederate in the street," Chaudri admitted to the eager ring of *shurtis* who surrounded him, "but I was wrong. There *was* a confederate, strategically situated right outside the door of the Dilmun Exchange while the robbery took place."

"The beggar woman," supplied Sikander Malek.

"Of course." Chaudri leaned back in his chair and sipped slowly at his tea. He was enjoying himself immensely. "She was out in front of the Exchange very early this morning," he told his listeners. "I saw her there when I reported to work at dawn. And when I went to the exchange office at nine to buy a bank draft to send home to my wife, she was still there. I even gave her a hundred *fils*, laid the coin on her palm and blessed her, and scolded myself for not giving more. She never said a word of thanks, but I thought nothing of it at the time. It was not until later, after the robbery, that I realized the importance of her silence – realized that her silence had been necessary in order to preserve the illusion."

"The illusion?" one of the *shurtis* prompted.

"The illusion that the figure underneath that all-concealing black *abba* was an innocent beggar, an innocent beggar *woman*, no less – when in fact it was a man, our thief's accomplice and brother."

"But how could you have known they were brothers?"

"I didn't know. But when I pulled the *abba* away from him, revealing the bag of money and the mask and the gun, proving his complicity in the crime, he confessed the entire scheme to me and led me straight to the small apartment in Umm al Hassam where they lived together – where his brother, unarmed, was awaiting him."

"And their scheme?"

"A simple plan, devised by simple men, but a clever one nonetheless. As soon as he stepped out of the exchange office, the thief fired a shot across the street, above the heads of the crowd, shattering the window of the Akhundawazi Trading Company. Then he stuffed his gun and mask into the plastic bag which already held his loot, set the bag down next to the black-draped form of his brother, and melted away into the crowd. With a quick readjustment of his *abba*, the beggar woman brother covered over the bag, and that was that. Transferring the incriminating evidence from brother to brother took no more than a few swift seconds and easily went unnoticed in the excitement and confusion that followed the gunshot. Then, when I finally reached the street and asked the beggar which way the thief had gone, 'she' had only to point in the wrong direction – and I, suspecting nothing, chased futilely after a thief who had in truth gone exactly the other way."

"But why did the brother sit there and wait for your return? Why didn't he make good his own escape as soon as you'd gone? No one would have seen the bag beneath the folds of his *abba*."

"A good question, my friend," said Chaudri. "But before I answer it, let me raise another, equally interesting. Why did the thief's brother take up his position in front of the Dilmun Exchange before four o'clock this morning, when his presence there would not be required until after nine? The answer to your question and to mine will seem obvious once you recognize it: the thief's brother arrived at the scene much earlier than he needed to be there, and stayed on well after his role in the commission of the crime was finished, *because he could not risk being seen walking either to or from the Dilmun Exchange.* And why not? Because if he had been seen, it would have shattered the illusion he had created so carefully – shattered it as finally as his brother's bullet shattered the plate-glass window of the Akhundawazi store. They were brothers, you see, similar in appearance and – this is the critical point – almost equal in height. And have you ever seen a beggar woman as tall as our unhappy prisoners? No, he had to get there early, before anyone else was about, and he had to sit there until the streets were again deserted before he could try to escape. Otherwise his height would surely have been noticed."

"One more question," said Sikander Malek. "How did you figure it all out?"

"Ah, now *that* is a question I would much prefer to leave unanswered. Because, you see, I'm not really sure that I *did* figure it out at all. I was thinking over the features of the robbery when the explanation suddenly came to me from nowhere – or perhaps I should say 'by Allah's grace.' The Dilmun *Exchange*: that was not only the scene of the crime, it was the solution to the crime as well. For there *had* been several exchanges, you see: first when the bag of money changed hands

and, more importantly, when the thief's brother exchanged his own identity for that of an old beggar woman. I had been running away from the Dilmun Exchange, but the answer was there, back where I had started, all the time."

An appreciative murmur rose from Chaudri's audience.

"When I was a boy in Punjab," he went on, "my grandfather once said to me, 'If you are on the road to knowledge, my child, then you are journeying in the wrong direction. For knowledge is not a place you can get to by traveling. It is a place you come *from*, by standing still and listening to your heart.'"

Mahboob Ahmed Chaudri, *natoor*, smiled broadly and drank the last of his tea.

"Stand still," he repeated contentedly, thinking of the promotion which this day's work was certain to bring him, of the raise in salary that would go along with a higher rank, and of the bungalow back home in Jhang-Maghiana that he was saving to build for Shazia and the children. "Stand still and trust in your heart."

The Gauntlet

Michael Penncavage

YOU LINE UP the cue ball. The five ball is going to be a tough sink but with a little English it's still possible. The cue glides across the felt, taps the five, which strikes the bumper briefly before disappearing into the corner pocket.

Your opponent folds his arms in annoyance. "Nice shot."

"Thanks." Without looking up, you ask, "You from town?"

"Yeah."

"What part?"

"Silverton."

You glance up at the man. He's studying the table, trying to strategize his moves if you ever allow him the opportunity to get back into the game. But not tonight. You toss the pool stick onto the table. It knocks into several of the balls before coming to a rest.

"What the hell are you doing?"

"I forfeit. You win." You remove a twenty from your wallet and drop it onto the felt.

The man looks down at the bill as if it's wired to explode. "What's the matter with you?"

"I don't shoot pool with idiots who think Silverton is part of Hillcrest."

"But it is."

You stare at him for a moment annoyed. "It's time for you to leave."

The man sees the look in your eyes. He grabs the twenty and leaves. "Asshole."

From behind the bar, Bob slowly wags his head. "You owe me eighty dollars for that stunt."

"How do you figure that?"

"He had a good two hours left of drinking in him. With tips that puts me at a sixty-dollar loss."

"Where do you get the other twenty from?"

"That's my inconvenience fee."

"Sounds like extortion."

Bob sticks a thumb towards the exit. "Feel free to leave the moment you don't like playing by my rules." He shakes his head. "Kicking the guy out because he's from Silverton. I should ban you from here just on principle, Wade."

"Yeah? Who's going to listen to your British naval war stories then?"

Bob places the mug onto the counter. "You're an annoying shit. Has anyone ever told you that?"

"I love you too." You glance down at your watch. It's late. Real late. "I think you got your wish, my friend. I got to get out of here." You toss four twenties onto the bar.

Bob picks them up and hands them back. "Keep your damn money. I would hate for you to be poor until the next paycheck."

"Put it against my tab. Goodnight, Bob," you answer. "See you soon."

"Yeah? Don't do me any favors."

* * *

The night air is hot as you walk out of the pool hall. Three hours' worth of cigarette soot has settled onto your clothes and you smell like shit. You try to shake it off but it's a futile effort. Parking sucks in this part of town and you begin the long trek back to your vehicle that is several blocks away. Each time you visit Bob's bar you say a prayer that you won't find your Dodge Dakota up on blocks. Bob insists that once upon a time this was actually in a decent part of town. And though gentrification has begun to reclaim parts of West Hillcrest from the gangs progress has been like a game of whack-a-mole. There are still parts like Ghost town that people avoid like the plague. Someone once told you that Jack London lived around here while penning *The Call of the Wild* but you think they were full of shit.

A slight wind picks up. Discarded plastic bags wrap themselves into the wire barbs of a security gate.

Leaves rustle from a massive oak tree that's larger than any other in the area. You're baffled as to how it's managed to survive as long as it has. Years of dog urinations… and things much more vile than that. You look at the tree again. It's probably going to outlive you.

The Dakota comes into view down the side street. Amazingly, it's still in one piece.

A cat darts in front of you. It's a little white and black spotted one. *Definitely not the best place to be a stray.*

As you walk towards the truck you point the car keys to disarm the alarm system. Instead of the familiar *chirp, chirp* of the alarm, it's replaced by a scream. You stop in mid-step, thinking you just imagined the sound. But a moment later you hear it again. The same scream. A woman's scream. And it's not a *someone just dropped a spider down my shirt* scream. This one has pain to it.

The street is full of row houses. Half of them are vacant or burnt out. The other half are barely livable. You turn to where the scream came from and frown. If there was an award for the shittiest house on the block this one would have won it. Plywood covers the first floor windows. Tall weeds sprout from the cracks in the concrete sidewalk as if mother-nature is trying to swallow up the blight and reclaim her land inch by inch. But surprisingly, it looks inhabited.

You pull out your cellphone. The battery is dead. Again. One of the fifty apps you've downloaded is sucking the life from the phone faster than a vampire drinks blood.

The car keys dangle in your hand. You stand at the front of the truck, drumming your fingers on the hood, staring at the house. You contemplate walking back to Bob's. But that will take time. Getting someone on 911 will take time. The closest Patrol Division is a distance away. For units to get over here is going to take time. It all adds up to lots and lots of *time*. And the woman who owned that scream didn't sound like she had much time to spare.

You remove your off-duty pistol and spare clips from the glove box. You're suddenly glad all you've been drinking has been tonic and lime.

The house is immense and completely foreboding. Once it was probably a sight to behold. *Hell, the whole neighborhood probably was.* The walkway is pitted and cracked. The porch looks like it is going to implode at any moment from the termites.

In complete contrast is the front door. It's made of steel and looks like it can withstand an artillery shell. You walk up and reach for the handle when you notice that the door has a punch code lock.

Rhythmic thumping permeates from inside. Someone's playing bad music with far too much base.

The scream sounds again. It's louder and clearer and without a doubt comes from inside.

Right about when you are just about to start scaling the drainpipe to the open second floor window, you hear a faint *click, click* from behind. You turn and find yourself staring down the barrel of a Glock. The weapon is shaking slightly as its user is standing on unsteady ground.

It's been years since someone has gotten the jump on you. *Sloppy, sloppy, sloppy.* You feel like a rookie.

"What are you doing here?" The man's voice is raspy and jagged, as if he has just sprinted from the other side of town. You can't make out his eyes in the dim light but you're certain he's strung out on something. "You're not trying to break into this house, are you?"

"You live here?" Your hand slowly makes its way to your beltline. It's going to be a long, slow journey to reach your gun. You hope you can diffuse the situation before then. "I couldn't find the doorbell and was trying to get someone in the house's attention."

"What do you want with Maurice this time of night? Man's probably sleeping. End up waking him... you won't like the consequences."

There's a shout from somewhere inside the house and the man's attention is drawn upwards to where it came from. His eyes go off you for a moment but it's just long enough for you to draw your gun.

"I'm going to have to ask you to lower that weapon."

You only get heavy breathing in reply as the man stares at you.

"What's your name?" you ask.

The synapses in the man's brain begin to fire. "Winston."

"All right, Winston. This can either go down one of two ways. Happy or tragic. To prevent it from not going tragic I really need you to put that gun down right *now*."

Winston continues to stare at you. The poor lighting makes it impossible to get a good read on the man. But then slowly, *excruciatingly* slowly, Winston begins lowering the gun. He places it onto the porch.

"That's great, Winston. Now I need you to take ten steps backwards. Can you do that for me?"

The man complies. You reach down and pick up the weapon.

"You a cop? You sound like a cop."

"You're a smart man, Winston."

"You gonna give me my gun back?"

"I'm going to do something even better. You punch in that door code for me, I promise not to arrest you."

"I don't know the code."

"Oh, I think you do, Winston." You gesture over to the Dakota with your gun. "We can always take a spin to the Patrol Division to help jog your memory."

He considers that for a moment. "1-3-7-4-5."

"That's going to get me in?"

"Yeah."

"No other security? Nothing else I need to worry about?"

"No. That's it." The man shuffles his feet nervously. "Can I go now?"

You look at the house again. It's even more foreboding than before. "How many people are inside?"

It takes Winston a moment to reply. "Maurice usually runs with three or four. This time of night… I don't know."

"I heard a woman's scream before. You wouldn't happen to know anything about *that* would you, Winston?"

"No."

You motion to the door with the gun. "Punch the code in."

He walks over and does it. The door opens with a dull *clack*. You listen for a moment. No one seems to be on the other side.

"Where's your cellphone?"

"I don't have one."

You look at him skeptically.

"Search my damn pockets if you don't believe me."

You wave your gun at Winston. "Go."

Winston steps off the porch and disappears into the night.

You glance into the house again. It's quiet. You contemplate your options. It's the point of no return if you cross the doorway.

Muttering a string of expletives, you go in.

It's unbelievably hot inside as if someone has turned the thermostat all the way up. Sweat beads on your forehead. A long, dimly lit hallway extends out in front of you, illuminated solely by a light bulb dangling from the ceiling. Peeling wallpaper lines the walls. At the end is a room that you suppose is the kitchen.

Along with the sweltering heat, self-doubt begins to wash over you. But just when you think your nerves might be called into question the woman screams out again. It comes from upstairs.

The music goes on again and the ceiling begins to vibrate. It's a good thing and a bad thing. They're not going to be able to hear *you* but at the same time you're not going to be able to hear *them*.

A man passes by the kitchen doorway. He doesn't notice you and quickly disappears from sight. A moment later you hear the refrigerator door open.

You creep down the hallway, staying clear of the center floorboards which will be the squeakiest.

The man is making a sandwich. From what he is slathering on the bread, it looks completely uneatable. He is dressed in underwear and a stained tee shirt. He reminds you of Larry from the Three Stooges. But then you notice the 12 Gauge nestled between the gallon of milk and the jar of mayonnaise. Larry never walked around with one of those on the show.

Sweat dribbles down your brow, stinging your eyes. The heat is unbearable. You're confident you can get to the shotgun before Larry can get his wits together. The man starts to walk back to the refrigerator, widening the gap between him and the weapon. You stride into the kitchen to make your move.

At that moment all hell breaks loose.

The front door opens with a *boom*. "Yo, Maurice! You upstairs? We got a Five-O lurking around!"

Shit.

Larry turns to his gun. Or at least where his 12 Gauge should have been. You strike him across the brow with the butt. With a faint gasp, Larry goes down in a heap, just missing the kitchen table in the process.

You glance around the room but the only thing resembling an exit is the pantry door.

Footsteps pound overhead. It's impossible to tell how many are up there. It sounds like an entire heard of buffalo. They're going to be heading back downstairs any moment.

You grab the 12 Gauge and ram a shell into the chamber. The buffalo begin pounding down the stairs.

"You better not be talking bullshit again, Monroe."

"No way. Just ran into Winston. Told me he was mixing it up with a Five-O out on the street. Told me to be on the lookout."

The booted feet pound across the floorboards and then out the front door. You breathe a sigh of relief. Winston's pride prevents him from telling the whole truth and has bought you some time. They don't realize you are in the house.

A bottle of gin is on the counter. You pour a good amount onto Larry and let the rest spill out across the cracked linoleum floor to make it look like he'd been drinking and passed out.

Upstairs sounds eerily quiet. Even the shit music has been shut off. You decide to risk the staircase. It's the only way up. Hopefully, they're all outside.

You manage to get to the top of the stairs without having to confront anyone. Doors line the hallway. Most of them are ajar. For a moment you listen for any sounds of distress but silence is the only reply. The woman is somewhere up here. She has to be. You choose the first door on the right.

A feeble lamp does a poor job at lighting the room. A king bed that sags in the middle takes up most of the room. A coffee table fills out the remainder. On top of the table is enough cocaine to light up the whole neighborhood.

A muffled grunt comes from the other side of a closed door in the room. Shotgun in hand, you open it. A woman is lying face down in the closet, gagged and hog tied. She catches a glimpse of you and starts squirming on the floor. You motion for her to be quiet but it only serves to rile her up even more. You pin her down and whisper *Police* a dozen times before the words begin to resonate. She calms down a little and you use the moment to remove a pocketknife. The blade is small but it's sharp enough to get through the bindings. You work quickly and remove the gag last, hoping she has settled down enough not to start screaming.

"I need you to be calm." You stare directly into her eyes. "Can you be calm for me?"

She swallows and nods.

"What's your name?"

"Sharon."

"Can you walk, Sharon?"

"She nods again.

"Good. We need to leave and we need to leave *now*."

You help her to her feet. She's an absolute mess. Her clothes are torn and soiled. Her left eye is swollen. Dried blood covers her shirt. There are a thousand and one questions you want to ask her but there isn't any time.

Her legs wobble but she manages to keep on her feet. "What about Denise?"

"Denise?"

"My girlfriend. She's in one of the other bedrooms."

A baseball settles down in the pit of your stomach. "When was the last time you saw her?"

"Yesterday. Maybe the day before that. I'm not too sure."

"Okay," you grip your gun. "Let's go find your friend."

You make your way from the room and into the hallway. No one is around.

"Which room did you see her last?"

She points to a door across the hallway. "In there. That's where they take us to…" She doesn't say anything more.

You raise the 12 Gauge. "Okay. Stay close."

The bedroom door is shut. You decide to risk it by charging in shotgun raised. There's just not enough time to be careful.

A dirty lamp casts just enough light to make out a woman passed out on the couch. A mattress is off to the side on the floor. Another coffee table is in front of Denise, yielding a shitload of drugs. You press two fingers against Denise's neck for a pulse. It's there but it's weak. You only fathom what she is strung out on. You glance at Sharon. "I'm going to need your help."

A door leading into the bathroom swings open. A man walks into the bedroom wiping his face with a towel. He sees you, drops the towel, and goes straight for the gun tucked in his belt. Towel Man is quick. Surprisingly quick.

But you're quicker.

The shotgun blast is deafening. It's as if a 747 has just landed in the bedroom. Towel Man lands on his back and doesn't move.

"Close the bedroom door and lock it," you say.

Sharon does so and you slide the couch, with Denise still in it, across the floor and against the door.

"What are you doing?"

"We just ran out of time."

"What do you mean?"

You stride over to Towel Man's body. "They're going to come for us. I need you to get your friend into the bathtub."

"The bathtub?"

"That will give her some protection from the bullets." You pat Towel Man down praying for a little luck. *Bingo*. A cellphone is in his pocket. You punch in 911. The dispatcher comes on after two rings. You give your name, ID, address, and a quick rundown.

"Squad cars en route."

You breathe a sigh of relief. But it's fleetingly brief as a voice sounds on the other side of the door.

"That you in there, Five-O? We can smell you out here in the hallway."

Towel Man's gun is still clutched in his hand. You pry it loose and add it to your growing collection. Sharon walks out of the bathroom and you motion for her. "We're going to lean the mattress up caddie-corner in the room," you whisper.

"I know you're in there," the voice yells.

You position the mattress and place Sharon behind it. "You wouldn't happen to know how to use a gun, would you?"

Sharon grabs the 12 Gauge confidently. "I had three older brothers who loved to go buck hunting."

"That's good to know."

"Hector in there with you?" the voice calls out again.

"Yeah. He's with me." You pull the cord on the lamp. With the exception of the bathroom light, the room is dark.

"Those bitches in there with you, too?"

"That's right." You make your way behind the mattress. "We're all thinking of lighting up some of these fine drugs and having ourselves a real good time."

"You send Hector out, maybe we can talk about things."

"Is that right?"

"Yeah. Maybe we'll let you live."

"You know, that's a tempting offer but I think I'll have to pass."

The bedroom door takes a long burst from an automatic weapon. Wood chips fly through the air. The opposite wall takes a pounding from the bullets. Fortunately, none of the bullets come close to you.

"You still alive?"

"I'm still here, Scumbag." You spot a shadow pass in front of the bullet holes in the door. You quickly aim and send a single shot back at them. Someone bellows out in pain for a moment until it's replaced by silence.

"You still out there, Scumbag?"

"I'm here. I want you to know that you're not leaving that room alive. You hear me?"

"That's fine. The couch in here looks comfy. I think I might take a nap."

"Yeah. You go do that."

"You got me outnumbered?"

"Unless you got a mini-army in one of your pockets."

"I guess we're at a standoff then, aren't we?"

"If you say so."

You look around. There are two ways out of the room. Through the door or through the window. Neither are much of an option.

Sharon is against the mattress holding the shotgun. She looks exhausted. She cracks a smile and nods her head. "Thank you."

"Excuse me?"

"For coming to get us."

You check Towel Man's gun. Full clip. "How did you two end up here?"

"Denise and I were at a club just off of Interstate 71. Some sleaze-bags approached us. We told them to get lost. I think they somehow managed to get a drug into our drinks. Next thing I know we're here."

"Well, don't thank me just yet. We've still got a long way to go before we are out of this." You sigh and glance around. Something is wrong. Scumbag is stalling. He has to assume you have a phone and that you've used it. He has to know backup is on its way.

The window is open and you hear hushed voices outside. They're from Scumbag's crew.

Your eyes widen. "Help me cover the window with this mattress."

"Why?"

You never get to answer as a Molotov Cocktail sails through the opening. It crashes onto the floor and instantly the room is engulfed in flames. And then in rapid succession three more are lobbed into the room.

"That will keep you nice and warm, Five-O!" shouts Scumbag from outside on the street. You hear engines rev and tires squeal.

You rush into the bathroom to get Denise. She's still completely out of it. You crank on the shower and the cold water jars Denise from her slumber. You hoist her over your shoulder. Thankfully, she's a petite woman.

Sharon peers into the hallway through one of the bullet holes. "There doesn't seem to be anyone out there."

"Try the door."

She shoves the couch away and tugs at the handle. "The door won't budge. It's jammed."

"You sure you're good with that thing?"

"What do you mean?"

"Take out the hinges."

Smoke begins to fill as she aims at the door hinges. She squeezes off two rounds. The shots are perfect but the door still holds. You throw your weight into it as you slam your boot against the door. Two strikes and it crashes outwards.

You make your way down the hallway. The flames are spreading rapidly. The heat is strong against your back. You glance up warily. The old house is one large tinderbox.

You reach the top of the staircase. Denise is only semi-conscious. It's going to be an effort reaching the bottom without tumbling. But there's no time left to be careful. You take the chance and somehow manage to get down to the bottom without getting riddled with bullets.

The hallway looms ahead. The front door is at the other end and it feels like a mile away. All seems clears until a fleeting shadow passes across the floor down the hallway from an adjoining room. Scumbag has left some of his crew behind.

You place Denise onto the floor and remove the Glock from under your belt. "You got that 12 Gauge ready?"

Sharon looks at you concerned. "Yes. Why?"

"There's someone up ahead." You motion to a nearby room. "I want you to go into that room and unload some rounds into the wall that's facing the front of the house."

"Do you think I'll be able to hit them?"

"That depends."

"On what?"

"If you're as good with that thing as you claim to be."

She looks at you annoyed.

"Just a joke. Now go. We're running out of time. This whole damn house is going to come crashing down on us at any moment."

"When do you want me to start shooting?"

"Count to thirty. And then pretend like you're going after one of those big bucks."

She nods and goes.

You slowly make your way down the hallway. You keep a mental count of when Sharon might start shooting. You look down at the floor but don't see the shadow anymore. Whoever's there has gotten into position and they're going to have a bead on you the moment you step into view. You're going to have one try at this. If you don't time this just right you're going to have a chest full of lead.

Ten seconds left. The doorway leading into the room where the man is is only a few steps away.

Five seconds. The gun's grip digs into your palm. You wish you were back at the bar shooting pool with the asshole from Silverton.

Three seconds. You mentally picture where the man might be. If there's more than one you're screwed.

Two seconds.

One.

Showtime.

You go into motion just as the first shotgun blast erupts. The second blast goes off as you step into the doorway.

One of Scumbag's men is there by himself. A TEC-9 is clutched in his hands. He's in a good enough position to have turned you into Swiss cheese.

While none of the 12 Gauge's shots penetrated through the sheetrock, it's made enough noise to cause the man to spin around and be caught off guard.

You capitalize on the moment of confusion. The moment you step through the doorway you drain the guns into the room. Most of the bullets miss their mark but one strikes the man in the stomach and another in his throat.

But the man is still able to get a burst off with the automatic. The bullets come at you low, ripping up the floorboards. But a lucky stray plants itself right into your thigh.

You clench your jaw and stumble backwards as your legs buckle, sending you straight to the floor.

The man stares with wide, vacant eyes up at the ceiling as a rapidly growing pool of blood spreads out across the floor. Still, you keep your gun trained on him as if you expect him to rise up as a zombie. But the man remains still.

You glance around but he seems to have been alone.

Your leg is throbbing. A puddle of your own blood is forming. You remove your belt and quickly wrap it tightly around your leg in an effort to stem the flow. You glance up. A black haze is collecting at the ceiling.

"You got him!" Sharon is standing at the doorway, clutching the 12 Gauge in one hand and holding Denise up with the other, who looks more conscious than before.

You pull yourself up on your feet.

Sharon notices the wounds. "Jesus. You've been shot."

Something crashes loudly above you. "That was the roof," you say. "Time to go."

You make your way to the front door. *Where the hell is the backup? It's been an eternity since you dialed 911.* You look to Sharon. "You ready? There might be more of them outside."

She nods. You open the door. Outside, people have gathered but they look more bystander-ish than drug dealer-ish. They all are glowing with a reddish hue and it isn't until you see the burning embers raining down onto the street that you realize just how engulfed the house has become. The faint wail of a siren can finally be heard in the distance.

You all stagger outside, not stopping until you reach the street curb on the opposite side of the street. Sharon and Denise collapse down alongside you and stare at the inferno in stunned silence, watching as the building is consumed by the flames.

A new puddle of blood begins to form by your leg. A chill passes between your shoulder blades as you wonder if the bullet has struck an artery.

You look over at Sharon. "The ambulances should be here soon. I need you to make sure I stay conscious until they do."

You glance over at the oak tree you passed before. It's far enough away that it will be spared from the fire. The leaves don't even look wilted. It's as if it's welcoming what is taking place.

You glance up at the night sky. Whatever stars that have ventured out that night have been obscured by plumes of smoke and soot.

Scumbag is still out there. But as you watch the roof of the house collapse upon itself into a red inferno, taking with it all of its ills, you realize he can wait until tomorrow.

The End of the Road

Melville Davisson Post

THE MAN laughed.

It was a faint cynical murmur of a laugh. Its expression hardly disturbed the composition of his features.

"I fear, Lady Muriel," he said, "that your profession is ruined. Our friend – 'over the water' – is no longer concerned about the affairs of England."

The woman fingered at her gloves, turning them back about the wrists. Her face was anxious and drawn.

"I am rather desperately in need of money," she said.

The cynicism deepened in the man's face.

"Unfortunately," he replied, "a supply of money cannot be influenced by the intensity of one's necessity for it."

He was a man indefinite in age. His oily black hair was brushed carefully back. His clothes were excellent, with a precise detail. Everything about him was conspicuously correct in the English fashion. But the man was not English. One could not say from what race he came. Among the races of Southern Europe he could hardly have been distinguished. There was a chameleon quality strongly dominant in the creature.

The woman looked up quickly, as in a strong aversion.

"What shall you do?" she said.

"I?"

The man glanced about the room. There was a certain display within the sweep of his vision. Some rugs of great value, vases and bronzes; genuine and of extreme age. He made a careless gesture with his hands.

"I shall explore some ruins in Syria, and perhaps the aqueduct which the French think carried a water supply to the Carthage of Hanno. It will be convenient to be beyond British inquiry for some years to come; and after all, I am an antiquarian, like Prosper Merimee."

Lady Muriel continued to finger her gloves. They had been cleaned and the cryptic marks of the shopkeeper were visible along the inner side of the wrist hem. This was, to the woman, the first subterfuge of decaying smartness. When a woman began to send her gloves to the laundry she was on her way down. Other evidences were not entirely lacking in the woman's dress, but they were not patent to the casual eye. Lady Muriel was still, to the observer, of the gay top current in the London world.

The woman followed the man's glance about the room.

"You must be rich, Hecklemeir," she said. "Lend me a hundred pounds."

The man laughed again in his queer chuckle.

"Ah, no, my Lady," he replied, "I do not lend." Then he added.

"If you have anything of value, bring it to me…. not information from the ministry, and not war plans; the trade in such commodities is ended."

It was the woman's turn to laugh.

"The shopkeepers in Oxford Street have been before you, Baron…I've nothing to sell."

Hecklemeir smiled, kneading his pudgy hands.

"It will be hard to borrow," he said. "Money is very dear to the Britisher just now – right against his heart…. Still…perhaps one's family could be thumb screwed…. An elderly relative with no children would be the most favorable, I think. Have you got such a relative concealed somewhere in a nook of London? Think about it. If you could recall one, he would be like a buried nut."

The man paused; then he added, with the offensive chuckling laugh:

"Go to such an one, Lady Muriel. Who shall turn aside from virtue in distress? Perhaps, in the whole of London, I alone have the brutality – shall we call it – to resist that spectacle."

The woman rose. Her face was now flushed and angry.

"I do not know of any form of brutality in which you do not excel, Hecklemeir," she said. "I have a notion to, go to Scotland Yard with the whole story of your secret traffic."

The man continued to smile.

"Alas, my Lady," he replied, "we are coupled together. Scotland Yard would hardly separate us…you could scarcely manage to drown me and, keep afloat yourself. Dismiss the notion; it is from the pit."

There was no virtue in her threat as the woman knew. Already her mind was on the way that Hecklemeir had ironically suggested – an elderly relative, with no children, from whom one might borrow, – she valued the ramifications of her family, running out to the remote, withered branches of that noble tree. She appraised the individuals and rejected them.

Finally her searching paused.

There was her father's brother who had gone in for science – deciding against the army and the church – Professor Bramwell Winton, the biologist. He lived somewhere toward Covent Garden.

She had not thought of him for years. Occasionally his name appeared in some note issued by the museum, or a college at Oxford.

For almost four years she had been relieved of this thought about one's family. The one "over the water" for whom Hecklemeir had stolen the Scottish toast to designate, had paid lavishly for what she could find out.

She had been richly, for these four years, in funds.

The habit was established of dipping her hand into the dish. And now to find the dish empty appalled her. She could not believe that it was empty. She had come again, and again to this apartment above the shops in Regent Street, selected for its safety of ingress; a modiste and a hairdresser on either side of a narrow flight of steps.

A carriage could stop here; one could be seen here.

Even on the right, above, at the landing of the flight of steps Nance Coleen altered evening gowns with the skill of one altering the plumage of the angels. It must have cost the one "over the water" a pretty penny to keep this whole establishment running through four years of war.

She spoke finally.

"Have you a directory of London, Hecklemeir?"

The man had been watching her closely.

"If it is Scotland Yard, my Lady," he said, "you will not require a direction. I can give you the address. It is on the Embankment, near…"

"Don't be a fool, Hecklemeir," she interrupted, and taking the book from his hands, she whipped through the pages, got the address she sought, and went out onto the narrow landing and down the steps into Regent Street:

She took a hansom.

With some concern she examined the contents of her purse. There was a guinea, a half crown and some shillings in it – the dust of the bin. And her profession, as Hecklemeir had said, was ended.

She leaned over, like a man, resting her arms on the closed doors.

The future looked troublous. Money was the blood current in the life she knew. It was the vital element. It must be got.

And thus far she had been lucky.

Even in this necessity Bramwell Winton had emerged, when she could not think of any one. He would not have much. These scientific creatures never accumulated money, but he would have a hundred pounds. He had no wife or children to scatter the shillings of his income.

True these creatures spent a good deal on the absurd rubbish of their hobbies. But they got money sometimes, not by thrift but by a sort of chance. Had not one of them, Sir Isaac Martin, found the lost mines from which the ancient civilization of Syria drew its supply of copper. And Hector Bartlett, little more than a mummy in the Museum, had gone one fine day into Asia and dug up the gold plates that had roofed a temple of the Sun.

He had been shown in the drawing rooms, on his return, and she had stopped a moment to look him over – he was a sort of mummy. She was not hoping to find Bramwell Winton one of these elect. But he was a hive that had not been plundered.

She reflected, sitting bent forward in the hansom, her face determined and unchanging. She did not undertake to go forward beyond the hundred pounds. Something would turn up. She was lucky…others had gone to the tower; gone before the firing squad for lesser activities in what Hecklemeir called her profession, but she had floated through…carrying what she gleaned to the paymaster. Was it skill, or was she a child of Fortune?

And like every gambler, like every adventurer in a life of hazard, she determined for the favorite of some immense Fatality.

It was an old house she came to, built in the prehistoric age of London, with thick, heavy walls, one of a row, deadly in its monotony. The row was only partly tenanted.

She dismissed the hansom and got out.

It was a moment before she found the number. The houses adjoining on either side were empty, the windows were shuttered. One might have considered the middle house with the two, for its step was unscrubbed, and it presented unwashed windows.

It was a heavy, deep-walled structure like a monument. Even the street in the vicinity was empty. If the biologist had been seeking an undisturbed quarter of London, he had, beyond doubt, found it here.

There was a bridged-over court before the house. Lady Muriel crossed. She paused before the door. There had been a bell pull in the wall, but the brass handle was broken and only the wire remained.

She was uncertain whether one was supposed to pull this wire, and in the hesitation she took hold of the door latch. To her surprise the door yielded, and following the impulse of her extended hand, she went in.

The hall was empty. There was no servant to be seen. And immediately the domestic arrangement of the biologist were clear to her. They would be that of one who had a cleaning woman in on certain days, and so lived alone. She was not encouraged by this economy, and yet such a custom in a man like Bramwell Winton might be habit.

The scientist, in the popular conception, was not concerned with the luxury of life – they were a rum lot.

But the house was not empty. A smart hat and stick were in the rack and from what should be a drawing room, above, there descended faintly the sound of voices.

It seemed ridiculous to Lady Muriel to go out and struggle with the broken bell wire. She would go up, now that she had entered, and announce herself, since, in any event, it must come to that.

The heavy oak door closed without a sound, as it had opened. Lady Muriel went up the stairway. She had nothing to put down. The only thing she carried was a purse, and lest it should appear suggestive – as of one coming with his empty wallet in his hand – she tucked the gold mesh into the bosom of her jacket.

The door to the drawing room was partly open, and as Lady Muriel approached the top of the stair she heard the voices of two men in an eager colloquy; a smart English accent from the world that she was so desperately endeavoring to remain in, and a voice that paused and was unhurried. But they were both eager, as I have written, as though commonly impulsed by an unusual concern.

And now that she was near, Lady Muriel realized that the conversation was not low or under uttered. The smart voice was, in fact, loud and incisive. It was the heavy house that reduced the sounds. In fact, the conversation was keyed up. The two men were excited about something.

A sentence arrested the woman's advancing feet.

"My word! Bramwell, if some one should go there and bring the things out, he would make a fortune, and would be famous. Nobody ever believed these stories."

"There was Le Petit, Sir Godfrey," replied the deliberate voice. "He declared over his signature that he had seen them."

"But who believed Le Petit," continued the other. "The world took him to be a French imaginist like Chateaubriand...who the devil, Bramwell, supposed there was any truth in this old story? But by gad, sir, it's true! The water color shows it, and if you turn it over you will see that the map on the back of it gives the exact location of the spot. It's all exact work, even the fine lines of the map have the bearings indicated. The man who made that water color, and the drawing on the back of it, had been on the spot.

"Of course, we don't know conclusively who made it. Tony had gone in from the West coast after big game, and he found the thing put up as a sort of fetish in a devil house. It was one of the tribes near the Karamajo range. As I told you, we have only Tony's diary for it. I found the thing among his effects after he was killed in Flanders. It's pretty certain Tony did not understand the water color. There was only this single entry in the diary about how he found it, and a query in pencil.

"My word! if he had understood the water color, he would have beaten over every foot of Africa to Lake Leopold. And it would have been the biggest find of his time. Gad! what a splash he'd have made! But he never had any luck, the beggar...stopped a German bullet in the first week out.

"Now, how the devil, Bramwell, do you suppose that water color got into a native medicine house?"

The reflective voice replied slowly.

"I've thought about the thing, Sir Godfrey. It must have been the work of the Holland explorer, Maartin. He was all about in Africa, and he died in there somewhere, at least he never came out…that was ten years ago. I've looked him up, and I find that he could do a water color – in fact there's a collection of his water colors in, the Dutch museum. They're very fine work, like this one; exquisite, I'd say. The fellow was born an artist.

"How it got into the hands of a native devil doctor is not difficult to imagine. The sleeping sickness may have wiped Maartin out, or the natives may have rushed his camp some morning, or he may have been mauled by a beast. Any article of a white man is medicine stuff you know. When you first showed me the thing I was puzzled. I knew what it was because I had read Le Petit's pretension…I can't call it a pretension now; the things are there whether he saw them or not.

"I think he did not see them. But it is certain from this water color that some one did; and Maartin is the only explorer that could have done such a color. As soon as I thought of Maartin I knew the thing could have been done by no other."

Lady Muriel had remained motionless on the stair. The door to the drawing room, before her, was partly open. She stepped in to the angle of the wall and drew the door slowly back until it covered this angle in which she stood.

She was rich in such experiences, for her success had depended, not a little, on overhearing what was being said. Through the crack of the door the whole interior of the room was visible.

Sir Godfrey Halleck, a little dapper man, was sitting across the table from Bramwell Winton. His elbows were on the table, and he was looking eagerly at the biologist. Bramwell Winton had in his hands the thing under discussion.

It seemed to be a piece of cardboard or heavy paper about six inches in length by, perhaps, four in width. Lady Muriel could not see what was drawn or painted on this paper. But the heart in her bosom quickened. She had chanced on the spoor of something worth while.

The little dapper man flung his head up.

"Oh, it's certain, Bramwell; it's beyond any question now. My word! If Tony were only alive, or I twenty years younger! It's no great undertaking, to go in to the Karamajo Mountains. One could start from the West Coast, unship any place and pick up a bunch of natives. The map on the back of the water color is accurate. The man who made that knew how to travel in an unknown country. He must have had a theodolite and the very best equipment. Anybody could follow that map."

There was a battered old dispatch box on the table beside Sir Godfrey's arm – one that had seen rough service.

"Of course," he went on, "we don't know when Tony picked up this drawing. It was in this box here with his diary, an automatic pistol and some quinine. The date of the diary entry is the only clue. That would indicate that he was near the Karamajo range at the time, not far from the spot."

He snapped his fingers.

"What damned luck!"

He clinched his hands and brought them down on the table.

"I'm nearly seventy, Bramwell, but you're ten years under that. You could go in. No one need know the object of your expedition. Hector Bartlett didn't tell the whole of England when he went out to Syria for the gold plates. A scientist can go anywhere. No one wonders what he is about. It wouldn't take three months. And the climate isn't poisonous. I think it's mostly high ground. Tony didn't complain about it."

The biologist answered without looking up.

"I haven't got the money, Sir Godfrey."

The dapper little man jerked his head as over a triviality.

"I'll stake you. It wouldn't cost above five hundred pounds."

The biologist sat back in his chair, at the words, and looked over the table at his guest.

"That's awfully decent of you, Godfrey," he said, "and I'd go if I saw a way to get your money to you if anything happened."

"Damn the money!" cried the other.

The biologist smiled.

"Well," he said, "let me think about it. I could probably fix up some sort of insurance. Lloyd's will bet nearly any sane man that he won't die for three months. And besides I should wish to look things up a little."

Sir Godfrey rose.

"Oh, to be sure," he said, "you want to make certain about the thing. We might be wrong. I hadn't an idea what it was until I brought it to you, and of course Tony hadn't an idea. Make certain of it by all means."

The biologist extended his long legs under the table. He indicated the water color in his hand.

"This thing's certain," he said. "I know what this thing is."

He rapped the water color with the fingers of his free hand.

"This thing was painted on the spot. Maartin was looking at this thing when he painted it. You can see the big shadows underneath. No living creature could have imagined this or painted it from hearsay. He had to see it. And he did see it. I wasn't thinking about this, Godfrey. I was thinking the Dutch government might help a bit in the hope of finding some trace of Maartin and I should wish to examine any information they might have about him."

"Damn the Dutch government!" cried the little man. "And damn Lloyd's. We will go it on our own hook."

The biologist smiled.

"Let me think about it, a little," he said.

The dapper man flipped a big watch out of his waistcoat pocket.

"Surely!" he cried, "I must get the next train up. Have you got a place to lock the stuff? I had to cut this lid open with a chisel."

He indicated the tin dispatch box.

"Better keep it all. You'll want to run through the diary, I imagine. Tony's got down the things explorer chaps are always keen about; temperature, water supply, food and all that..... Now, I'm off. See you Thursday afternoon at the United Service Club. Better lunch with me."

Then he pushed the dispatch box across the table. The biologist rose and turned back the lid of the box. The contents remained as Sir Godfrey's dead son had left them; a limp leather diary, an automatic pistol of some American make, a few glass tubes of quinine, packed in cotton wool.

He put the water color on the bottom of the box and replaced them.

Then he took the dispatch box over to an old iron safe at the farther end of the room, opened it, set the box within, locked the door, and, returning, thrust the key under a pile of journals on the corner of the table. Then he went out, and down the stairway with his guest to the door.

They passed within a finger touch of Lady Muriel.

The woman was quick to act. There would be no borrowing from Bramwell Winton. He would now, with this expedition on the way, have no penny for another. But here before her, as though arranged by favor of Fatality, was something evidently of enormous value that she could cash in to Hecklemeir.

There was fame and fortune on the bottom of that dispatch box.

Something that would have been the greatest find of the age to Tony Halleck...something that the biologist, clearly from his words and manner, valued beyond the gold plates of Sir Hector Bartlett.

It was a thing that Hecklemeir would buy with money...the very thing which he would be at this opportune moment interested to purchase. She saw it in the very first comprehensive glance.

Her luck was holding Fortune was more than favorable, merely. It exercised itself actively, with evident concern, in her behalf.

Lady Muriel went swiftly into the room. She slipped the key from under the pile of journals and crossed to the safe sitting against the wall.

It was an old safe of some antediluvian manufacture and the lock was worn. The stem of the key was smooth and it slipped in her gloved hands. She could not hold it firm enough to turn the lock. Finally with her bare fingers and with one hand to aid the other she was able to move the lock and so open the safe.

She heard the door to the street close below, and the faint sound of Bramwell Winton's footsteps as though he went along the hall into the service portion of the house. She was nervous and hurried, but this reassured her.

The battered dispatch box sat within on the empty bottom of the a safe.

She lifted the lid; an automatic pistol lay on a limp leather-backed journal, stained, discolored and worn. Lady Muriel slipped her hand under these articles and lifted out the thing she sought.

Even in the pressing haste of her adventure, the woman could not forbear to look at the thing upon which these two men set so great a value. She stopped then a moment on her knees beside the safe, the prized article in her hands.

A map, evidently drawn with extreme care, was before her. She glanced at it hastily and turned the thing quickly over. What she saw amazed and puzzled her. Even in this moment of tense emotions she was astonished: She saw a pool of water, – not a pool of water in the ordinary sense – but a segment of water, as one would take a certain limited area of the surface of the sea or a lake or river. It was amber-colored and as smooth as glass, and on the surface of this water, as though they floated, were what appeared to be three, reddish-purple colored flowers, and beneath them on the bottom of the water were huge indistinct shadows.

The water was not clear to make out the shadows. But the appearing flowers were delicately painted. They stood out conspicuously on the glassy surface of the water as though they were raised above it.

Amazement held the woman longer than she thought, over this extraordinary thing. Then she thrust it into the bosom of her jacket, fastening the button securely over it.

The act kept her head down. When she lifted it Bramwell Winton was standing in the door.

In terror her hand caught up the automatic pistol out of the tin box. She acted with no clear, no determined intent. It was a gesture of fear and of indecision; escape through menace was perhaps the subconscious motive; the most primitive, the most common motive of all creatures in the corner. It extends downward from the human mind through all life.

To spring up, to drag the veil over her face with her free hand, and to thrust the weapon at the figure in the doorway was all simultaneous and instinctive acts in the expression of this primordial impulse of escape through menace.

Then a thing happened.

There was a sharp report and the figure standing in the doorway swayed a moment and fell forward into the room. The unconscious gripping of the woman's fingers had fired the pistol.

For a moment Lady Muriel stood unmoving, arrested in every muscle by this accident. But her steady wits – skilled in her profession – did not wholly desert her. She saw that the man was dead. There was peril in that – immense, uncalculated peril, but the prior and immediate peril, the peril of discovery in the very accomplishment of theft, was by this act averted.

She stooped over, her eyes fixed on the sprawling body and with her free hand closed the door of the safe. Then she crossed the room, put the pistol down on the floor near the dead man's hand and went out.

She went swiftly down the stairway and paused a moment at the door to look out. The street was empty. She hurried away.

She met no one. A cab in the distance was appearing. She hailed it as from a cross street and returned to Regent. It was characteristic of the woman that her mind dwelt upon the spoil she carried rather than upon the act she had done.

She puzzled at the water color. How could these things be flowers?

Bramwell Winton was a biologist; he would not be concerned with flowers. And Sir Godfrey Halleck and his son Tony, the big game hunter, were not men to bother themselves with blossoms. Sir Godfrey, as she now remembered vaguely, had, like his dead son, been a keen sportsman in his youth; his country house was full of trophies.

She carried buttoned in the bosom of her jacket something that these men valued. But, what was it? Well, at any rate it was something that would mean fame and fortune to the one who should bring it out of Africa. That one would now be Hecklemeir, and she should have her share of the spoil.

Lady Muriel found the drawing-room of her former employer in some confusion; rugs were rolled up, bronzes were being packed. But in the disorder of it the proprietor was imperturbable. He merely elevated his eyebrows at her reappearance. She went instantly to the point.

"Hecklemeir," she said, "how would you like to have a definite objective in your explorations?"

The man looked at her keenly.

"What do you mean precisely?" he replied.

"I mean," she continued, "something that would bring one fame and fortune if one found it." And she added, as a bit of lure, "You remember the gold plates Hector Bartlett dug up in Syria?"

He came over closer to her; his little eyes narrowed.

"What have you got?" he said.

His facetious manner – that vulgar persons imagine to be distinguished – was gone out of him. He was direct and simple.

She replied with no attempt at subterfuge.

"I've got a map of a route to some sort of treasure – I don't know what – it's in the Karamajo Mountains in the French Congo; a map to it and a water color of the thing."

Hecklemeir did not ask how Lady Muriel came by the thing she claimed; his profession always avoided such detail. But he knew that she had gone to Bramwell Winton; and what she had must have come from some scientific source. The mention of Hector Bartlett was not without its virtue.

Lady Muriel marked the man's changed manner, and pushed her trade.

"I want a check for a hundred pounds and a third of the thing when you bring it out."

Hecklemeir stood for a moment with the tips of his fingers pressed against his lips; then replied.

"If you have anything like the thing you describe, I'll give you a hundred pounds…let me see it."

She took the water color out of the bosom of her jacket and gave it to him.

He carried it over to the window and studied it a moment. Then he turned with a sneering oath.

"The devil take your treasure," he said, "these things are water-elephants. I don't care a farthing if they stand on the bottom of every lake in Africa!"

And he flung the water color toward her. Mechanically the stunned woman picked it up and smoothed it out in her fingers.

With the key to the picture she saw it clearly, the shadowy bodies of the beasts and the tips of their trunks distended on the surface like a purple flower. And vaguely, as though it were a memory from a distant life, she recalled hearing the French Ambassador and Baron Rudd discussing the report of an explorer who pretended to have seen these supposed fabulous elephants come out of an African forest and go down under the waters of Lake Leopold.

She stood there a moment, breaking the thing into pieces with her bare hands. Then she went out. At the door on the landing she very nearly stepped against a little cockney.

"My Lidy," he whined, "I was bringing your gloves; you dropped them on your way up."

She took them mechanically and began to draw them on…the cryptic sign of the cleaner on the wrist hem was now to her indicatory of her submerged estate. The little cockney hung about a moment as for a gratuity delayed, then he disappeared down the stair before her.

She went slowly down, fitting the gloves to her fingers.

Midway of the flight she paused. The voice of the little cockney, but without the accent, speaking to a Bobby standing beside the entrance reached her.

"It was Sir Henry Marquis who set the Yard to register all laundry marks in London. Great C.I.D. Chief, Sir Henry!"

And Lady Muriel remembered that she had removed these gloves in order to turn the slipping key in Bramwell Winton's safe lock.

A Father's Child

Jennifer Quail

ANDERS KJELSEN knew his city and that included knowing its underside. Copenhagen was not a violent place even compared to the rest of Scandinavia, and his unit was not nearly as busy as it would have been in Stockholm or Oslo, to say nothing of megalopolises like New York and London. But any city had major crimes. Homicide most of all.

In the summer, the girls who worked the night shift in the old red-light district Vesterbro had only a few hours of true darkness to walk the streets before dawn came. Then the 'industry' shifted to the native-born women who hadn't yet moved their operation to a less gentrified part of the city. Anders had walked the neighborhood at all times of day and night while working kidnaps and murders. He sometimes made a pass through on his way home or on his way to work, carrying a victim's photograph and hoping this time someone had seen her and one more cold case could be laid to rest.

Today he saw one of the daytime regulars standing in front of a porn shop, watching the police vehicles and no doubt totaling up the lost business from the disruption. Her gaze wandered his way, and her painted lips quirked in a professional smirk as she recognized him.

"Looking for company, Inspector?" She crooked a finger, the iridescent blue nail varnish sparkling in the lights from the cruisers.

"Not that kind, Bibiana." And even if he were, she was not the sort Anders would have chosen. She had been attractive at some point in her life, but there was a hard edge to her face that mirrored something hard inside her. Whenever he showed around pictures of missing girls, Bibiana barely glanced at them before saying no. "I'm here on business."

"So am I." She took a drag on a cigarette that was nearly burnt down, and examined it before apparently thinking better of throwing it on the ground in front of a cop. Instead she gestured with it toward the alley. "Nothing down that way but the clap. Only the Nigerian girls are desperate enough to do it back there."

"Did you see who was working there last night?" He'd have to ask her later anyway.

Bibiana shrugged. "Just the usual – new girls off the boat. Is it one of them?"

"Is what one of them?" She didn't even bother answering, only looked disdainfully at the coroner's van. Anders shrugged in return. "Did you see something?"

"Only new girls. Tourists looking to buy young. You know." She tossed the cigarette on the pavement and ground it with the toe of her boot. "You look like you'd prefer experienced. I might even do a special price."

"Some other lifetime. Don't go too far, though. I may have questions." He turned off Istegade into the narrow side street, ducking under the police tape and nodding to the constable keeping watch over the crime scene. The body was still on the ground, marked off by more tape, and Sandsgård, one of the sergeants from his department, was already crouching beside it, using a flashlight to illuminate the remains. He barely glanced up as Anders joined him. "Photographer's on the way," he said, shifting the light a fraction of an inch down the girl's torso. He wasn't taking notes, but Anders knew he'd have a list of details he wanted recorded when the photographer did arrive.

Anders took his first, establishing look at the victim. The girl was African, probably Nigerian. Most of the foreign girls in Vesterbro were these days. He tried not to think of just how young she looked – seventeen or eighteen, probably. Her clothes – short-cropped jeans, an inexpensive but tight-fitting shirt, boots with the heels not yet worn down by walking the pavement – looked new enough and generic enough she had probably bought them or been given them in Denmark. Either she had made some cash quickly, or more likely whatever pimp had paid to bring her in had given her the clothes.

Anders grimaced and looked away. "Does she have any identification?" It was a long shot, and if she did it was probably a forgery, but there was a chance the name was right. It was also possible the quality of the forgery would be helpful in identifying the forger and the purchaser.

"A residence card." Sandsgård had already bagged it, of course. It was either real or a better-than-average fake, identifying their victim as Adanna Obialom. She was indeed from Nigeria, seventeen (barely), and if the card was accurate she'd been in Denmark for a little over three months. "No other cards on her, no cash."

"Either she hadn't had any business yet, or whoever killed her robbed her, too." It was also possible she had a phone to take payments, or that her pimp had controlled the money. Finding him, and it was almost always a 'him' with the girls trafficked from Africa, would be difficult, as profiting off prostitution was illegal even if the sale or purchase of sex was not. Even if the pimp was not her killer, he would have no desire to admit the relationship to police. "Nothing else?"

"No phone, no keys, no transit cards." Sandsgård stood up, stretching his back wearily. "They do have a client, though. He called it in. A foreigner," and Anders knew by that he meant English-speaking, probably American or Canadian, and either a boy looking for free-for-all sex tourism that suggested he'd confused the Dutch and the Danes, or a business traveler who knew exactly what he was looking for and was counting on a quick departure to cover it. "The constables are holding him. I thought you'd want to talk to him yourself."

"Hm. In a minute." Anders looked at the body again, crouching down beside her. Adanna, if that was her real name, had been a pretty girl under the makeup. Seventeen was far too young to be lying dead anywhere. He wondered if her family thought she had gone to make a better life, whether she had a family at all, and if someone would wonder what had happened to her.

Chances were he'd never know. Crimes like this robbed him of one of the only truly satisfying moments in working a homicide: giving a victim's family and friends some sort of closure. Even when the punishment never quite fit the crime, even when nothing could fill the void in their lives, certainty brought a particular kind of comfort. Usually it was all he could give.

He studied Adanna's face, glad her eyes were closed, and saw no bruises. Her head was tilted to one side, but not at the extreme angle of someone who'd taken a hard blow or fall and broken their neck. But there was something about her throat that drew his eye. "Get the light on her neck here," he said, and Sandsgård obliged. "Did you notice these contusions?"

"Finger marks, I think." They were deep, the bruising harder to see against the girl's dark skin, but under close inspection they looked distinctly like hands. Tiny crescent marks were pressed into her skin. Fingernails. "John who got rough?"

"Maybe." Anders had far too much experience with the variety of ways transactions in the sex trade could go wrong. Half his caseload wouldn't exist without them. But he also had been a policeman long enough to know not to jump to conclusions. "No other witnesses?"

"None so far." Sandsgård shrugged. "But it's still early. Not many people out here who aren't in the trade themselves. Even if they saw something you know it'll be like pulling teeth. Anyway, chances are we've already got him. If we're lucky they can lift fingerprints from her neck in the post-mortem and keep it quick."

Anders didn't reply. Instead he tugged out the pair of disposable vinyl gloves he kept in his coat pocket and pulled them on. When he gently pried back one of her eyelids, besides the usual dullness of death, he saw the telltale red of burst blood vessels in the sclera. She'd put up a fight, however futile. "Someone wanted her dead. That kind of pressure isn't an accident." He straightened up, feeling all his thirty-two years in this business in his knees and back and soul. "I'll talk to the john. Probably he's our man, worse luck. I'd rather get the pimp."

"It's something. Might convince the sex tourists to stick with Amsterdam." Sandsgård pointed down the alley opposite the way Anders had come in. "Down there."

The john was the former type: a boy more than a man, university age or just past it, and he was American. Anders switched to English after asking the constables to take a step back. "I'm Detective Inspector Kjelsen, Copenhagen Police. I'm handling this case. You called the police?"

"I—yeah, I called you." Anders couldn't tell American accents apart, so he didn't venture a guess what this one was. California? The boy was blond enough to blend in here, reasonably fit for someone from the US, and dressed in student sloppy-casual rather than tour-group sloppy casual. From the dark circles and bloodshot eyes, this was the end of his night, not the start of his day, or so he'd planned. "That girl – is she dead? I know I should have done CPR or checked her pulse or something but the hook – the girl I was with started screaming, and she ran, and I ran after her, but I couldn't find her."

Anders kept his expression professionally blank, hoping it wasn't obvious how many mental contortions he needed to follow the rapid-fire English. It was a painfully convoluted to his ear. "What's your name?"

"Mike – Michael Weeks, I've got my passport here somewhere," he said, fumbling in his pockets until Anders waved him off. He'd probably given it to the constables and forgotten. "I'm just visiting, I'm going on to Stockholm tomorrow, or I was, and I thought...there was an article about Vesterbro, and the kind of...shops and things there are—"

"Yes, I've read some of these articles." He could happily have lived without them. "You were going into the alley with a girl? A prostitute, you mean?"

Now he saw the kind of anger he expected with foreigners. "Yeah, okay, she was a hooker – a prostitute. A prostitureret? It's legal, isn't it? I just wanted..."

"Et prostituer," Anders corrected. "And English is fine." Vastly preferable to Google Translate Danish, in fact, but it would have been rude to say so. "Yes, buying sex is legal. That doesn't mean killing prostitutes is overlooked."

"I didn't – you don't think I killed her?" Anger, and unless he was mistaken, real fear. But not, Anders thought, the sort of fear when someone saw punishment coming. The disbelieving sort. "I never even saw her!"

"You just said you saw her in the alley. That's why you called the police."

"No! I mean, I saw her dead. The girl I was with saw her first, then she ran out in the street, and I didn't know what to do so I ran after her. But she disappeared, and I called the police. I swear, the girl in the alley was dead before we found her!"

"I thought you said you didn't check." It was pro forma, and Anders almost skipped the challenge entirely. It was a pat story, but it had the benefit of sounding true. Some instinct, three decades' experience, was telling Anders this boy might be rude and probably not the most respectful client to the working girls on his European tour, but a killer? It felt wrong.

"I didn't! But she looked dead, and hooker I was going to – she screamed like she was next!" The look was definitely fear, and desperation. Disbelief, maybe? He'd probably anticipated a very different visit to the red-light district. "I figured if she was running I better run. But there was no one there, and I waited – I was here when your cops arrived, you can ask them!"

"I believe you," at least about the last. "I don't suppose you know the name of the girl you'd hired? Or how to find her?" Small chance of that. Girls working the late night or early morning in the alleys here were not the sort who took clients by advertisement.

Of course, the boy was shaking his head. "No. I met her on the street. She said her name was Annika, but I didn't ask for a business card! And I didn't see anyone in the alley – besides, well, the dead girl." That look of slow-dawning horror was certainly convincing.

"No one on Istegade – the main street there?" Anders pointed back through the alley.

He looked blank. "No, I don't think so. Well, there was that other woman. She was standing on the other side of the street, smoking, but she just ignored me when I called for help. I think she was pissed," and Anders remembered to Americans that meant angry, not drunk like it did to Brits. "She'd said something to me when I came down the street before but I passed. Not my type, you know?" He paused, with the look of someone remembering details they hadn't expected to. "She lit another cigarette instead. I don't know if she didn't understand I needed help, or she just didn't care."

Anders frowned. "Could you describe her?"

He shrugged, shaking his head. "Old. Maybe forty. Blond hair, kind of…not curly, sort of ratty, you know? Lots of makeup – dark nail polish, really red lips. Boots, short shorts, okay…you know…for her age?" He made a vague gesture in the direction of his chest, and a very half-hearted attempt at a male-camaraderie grin.

Anders kept his expression studiously neutral, mostly at the notion forty was old. Instead, he considered the description and found it familiar. "She was standing across from the alley. Are you certain?" The boy nodded too eagerly. "Could you recognize her again?" Another nod. "All right. I would appreciate you giving your information to the constables – your hotel, your mobile number, address at home. And that you do not leave Copenhagen until given permission to do so. Your assistance may be required."

The boy looked absurdly relieved, and Anders left the constables to deal with him. Obnoxious, the kind of tourist he wished would stick to Amsterdam or better yet America, but a murderer? He hadn't been completely useless, though. Not quite a witness, but he had noticed more than could be expected.

Back in the alley, the photographer had arrived, and the coroner's assistants were waiting with the stretcher while he photographed Adanna where she'd been found. As soon as the documenting was done she'd be bagged and taken away for the post-mortem examination. After that…if they found her family, her body would be returned to them. If not, cremation, most probably, after the hold period ended and no one claimed her. Anders had attended more than a few committals for victims who had no one but the police and the undertaker to stand for them at the end. He looked at her face again, noticing the slackness of death and the graying, even of darker skin, starting to set in.

Then he paused. "Give me the flashlight again." Sandsgård looked puzzled, but complied. Anders crouched down, waving the photographer back, and shone the light on her neck, looking at the finger marks and specifically at the tiny glitter that had caught his eye in one of them. "I need tweezers and a small evidence bag. And photograph this, I want to make sure we document."

He worked the point of the tweezers into the nail mark, knowing how the medical examiner would complain, but he needed to know now if his hunch was correct. Sandsgård held open the bag for the tiny flake that Anders had seen glittering in the light of the photographer's flash, sparkling against Adanna's skin where the force of the strangling grip had dug it in. Anders held it up to the light, studying the paint-like chip of blue nail varnish before depositing it delicately into the evidence bag.

This time when he stood there was no pain, from his back or otherwise, only a strange lightness he always felt when he knew he was going to close a case. "Tell the medical examiner to make sure to examine the neck wounds for more of this. And I want any fingerprints they lift sent over as soon as they're lifted. Sandsgård, go tell the constables I'm going to need them on the Istegade end of the alley." He started walking before he heard the acknowledgment.

Bibiana was still standing by the door of the porn shop, smoking her third cigarette judging by the number of butts discarded on the pavement. She watched him coming, that same smirk on her lips. "Looking for company after all, Inspector?" She flicked the ash from her cigarette, the chipped blue nail varnish glittering in the light from the street lamp.

Anders didn't smile, only looked back to make sure the constables were coming from the alley. "Not that kind, Bibiana," he said, and her smirk started to fade. "Not that kind."

Lovely Young Losers

Zandra Renwick

A LIGHT GUST of wind was enough to drive cold Vancouver rain under Maggie's hoody, individual droplets stabbing her numbed cheeks like icy needles. The light changed green and she stepped carefully off the curb only to be doused with spray from a passing taxi. She was already drenched so it shouldn't have made such a difference, one more wide muddy spatter on her jeans, reaching halfway to her knees. But it did.

Disgusted, she squinted through the eternal grey gloom at the low flat windows of rundown shops along this forsaken stretch of Main. Further south had been hipster-gentrified, all artisanal coffee shops and local handmade clothes where you could buy stuff that looked like your dead grandma knitted it for your birthday, though it cost more than Maggie made in a month. Here, it was all grimy key shops that looked like the doors hadn't been unlocked in years. A military surplus store. Used restaurant supply, the window crammed with a tangled jumble of crusted chrome baker's racks.

At last she spotted it, just like Lorraine had described in her email: a metal side-alley door, covered in street graffiti and peeling plastered handbills, no sign marking the entry to the basement dive bar but a wooden bench and a patch of gravel turned cigarette-filter soup in the rain. A joint called The Narrow.

Maggie fought the urge to hold her breath descending the steep graffitied well into darkness, though there'd been no whiff of urine, or vomit, or worse. It simply reminded her too much of their punk rock days back when they were kids, scoring drugs in some weedy lot off Hastings. Shooting up behind dumpsters, wandering Chinatown like it was a theme park, scruffing up their suburban mall-punk clothes to panhandle Gastown tourists straying off the main drag. But that was all before Maggie's dad had split back to Toronto, before she got clean. Before Lorraine's overdose and the permanent neurological damage that had brought an end to their habit and their friendship. No more theme park then.

Lorraine was easy to spot, even in the dim, red-lit bar. Something about the flocked wallpaper, the dead animal heads mounted on the walls, the tightness of the space gave it the feel of a speakeasy or an old-fashioned movie-western whorehouse. Even Lorraine, her heavy black eyeliner a remnant of their punk days, her bombshell-blonde hair glimmering pink under the darkroom-red lights. Her cane stood hooked over the table edge like it was at attention, a trained pet begging for treats.

Catching sight of her, Lorraine lifted a lipstick-stained glass and nudged another, full and with a rim that at least looked clean in what little light there was, toward Maggie.

Maggie slid the glass away. "Three years sober," she said, easing onto the empty stool.

"But you came anyway."

"I always did."

Lorraine gave one of those tiny smiles that used to twist Maggie's guts all ways to Sunday. Still did. "Richard said to meet him under Cambie Bridge. He'll give back Rex when I give him the money."

When Maggie had got Lorraine's email out of the blue, she'd been surprised by three things: that Lorraine's ancient dog Rex was still alive; that Lorraine's junkie ex-boyfriend Richard was still alive; and that hearing from her old friend was enough to send Maggie's stomach into familiar flutters. Lorraine may have cleaned up, rehabbed after her overdose, learned to walk again, to talk again, to brush her teeth. May have married rich, then divorced the guy for his money. May look more beautiful than ever – more beautiful even than when they were just teenagers, a couple lovely young losers slumming downtown on weekends, Maggie playing Sid Vicious to Lorraine's Nancy despite her boyfriend Richard looking more the part...

But Lorraine still needed her.

Maggie slid off her stool and lifted Lorraine's cane from the table edge, handed it to her, and said, "Let's go."

Typical Vancouver, the rain had disappeared by the time they made it back up the narrow stairwell to the street, Lorraine first, taking each step in a twisting lurch, crimson nails clawing the rusty spray-painted wall for balance, cane gripped tight in her other hand. Maggie went behind, knowing better than to offer help without being asked. It'd been years since they'd seen each other last, but some things never changed. Lorraine wanted her only when she wanted her; Maggie wasn't allowed to choose when or how or where. It had always been that way.

They crossed on First Street and dropped down Ontario to the seawalk. Hard to picture this area as an outmoded industrial sprawl without its post-Olympic improvements, without the half empty glassy-eyed condos and the meticulous stone paths and public art and landscaping. Hard to remember that just a fifteen-minute walk north was one of the most impoverished urban postal codes in the country, people shooting up in plain view, passing out on the sidewalk, living on the sidewalk, dying on the sidewalk. Hard to imagine that one of them had almost been Lorraine.

The rain started up again as they reached the bridge. The water ebbed at low tide, exposing green striations high up the concrete pylons, leaving the air briny and crisp. High overhead, evening traffic on the bridge drummed its shushing sameness, wet tires on wet road, echo and thrum reverberating downward through metal and cement.

Richard stepped from between two piles of enormous concrete blocks, stacked taller than three Maggies one on top of the other and still not reaching the bottom of the bridge: something stored there by the city, or maybe leftovers from abandoned Olympic building projects.

"I should've known," he said when he saw Maggie. And to Lorraine: "You still leading her on? Figures."

"Hi, Richard," said Maggie. "You look like shit."

He did. His clothes were dry, but stained and ragged. He smelled even from a distance. Where his loose jacket sleeves flapped open, scabs riddled his arms, between his fingers, running in branching linear patterns like ink dots stabbed onto dirty paper.

"It's temporary," he said. "Lorraine's going to lend me some cash, help me get back on my feet. Enough to get a place to stay a while, get clean. Maybe start a little dog-walking business for all those fancy chicks over in Kitsilano. Right, Lorraine? That's what you said. If I took good care of Rex, walk him good, you'd hook me up."

Maggie frowned. "Lorraine's email said you kidnapped her dog."

Richard's blank look of surprise was too quick to be faked. "Kidnapped? Naw, I just took him for a walk like she asked. See?"

Maggie stepped past Richard in the direction he pointed. Smelled like something had died in Richard's pants, but she tried not to gag. If things had gone different, it might be her living under a bridge. Just a slightly higher dose, a slightly bigger shot, a slightly different admixture of impurities and Lorraine might not be living at all. Might never have woken from the coma, even with her muscle damage, her photosensitivity, her limp.

Plywood had been wedged between two of the huge concrete blocks. Shredded blue tarp kept out enough gusting rain to leave a dry spot, a bed of flattened cardboard boxes several layers thick. The bottom layers had been reduced to sopping pulp, but on top was a nest of mostly-dry packing blankets, and in the nest was Rex.

"Hey, boy," Maggie crooned, crawling in. "Remember me?"

The old dog's tail thumped a few times. As she untied his leash from a forked stick driven into the damp ground, he licked her fingers. She ducked back out of the makeshift hovel, leading Rex by his leash. Richard watched in his ripped clothes and muddy boots and crooked smile, Lorraine beside him. If not for Lorraine's shiny designer raincoat and the cane it could've been like the old days, the three of them headed to East Pender to score a hit, Richard and Lorraine standing together and Maggie slightly apart, always apart. Maggie was about to say Rex seemed fine when, with the hand not gripping her cane, Lorraine drew a syringe from her coat pocket and plunged it into Richard's neck.

Maggie dropped the leash and lunged to catch Richard as he staggered forward, his hands batting at his throat. Rex ambled, stiff-hipped, to Lorraine, wagging his tail as Maggie eased Richard onto the packing-blanket nest, where he was trying to crawl.

"Richard!" Maggie yanked the syringe out and tossed it into the weeds. She couldn't see an entry wound on his neck, it was so creased with grime. Not even a drop of blood.

His eyelids fluttered shut and a smile blossomed on his face. "That was one thing we had in common, huh Mags?" he said. "She always knew how to play us."

Maggie dug in her pocket for her phone. "What did you give him? What was in that thing?" Her voice echoed up under the bridge between the tinny patter of rain and the constant slushy rumble of tires overhead.

Lorraine stood, one hand fondling Rex's ears. If her cane had been an umbrella she might've been any Kitsilano divorcee walking the seawall with her dog. "He's the one who used to score for us, remember? Scored for us that day. I'm just returning the favour. Plus a couple clicks'-worth of internet research, a few almost-common household ingredients added for good measure. He always did like a bit of a kick."

As Maggie dialed 911, Richard went into convulsions. One moment the ambulance wasn't there and the next moment it was, and medics were brushing Maggie aside, opening Richard's shirt. Maggie joined Lorraine on a park bench facing the water, her knees shaking, a sour taste in her throat. Didn't matter that the bench was soaked, that Maggie's jeans clung wetly to her legs, that her elbows and knees were stained with mud, that there was vomit in her hair and on her hands.

Three police cars drew up near the ambulance. Officers would walk over in a moment to talk to them, take Lorraine away. Maggie studied Lorraine's profile against the slanting slivered rain. Her black painted lashes hadn't smeared or run. Her lips curved in a perfect vermillion bow.

"Why did you play me, Lorraine?"

Her salon-perfect eyebrows rose. "Oh, Mags. If I'd played you, I would've left you here holding a dead body, with your fingerprints on that syringe and Richard's vomit on your jacket, and your handprints all over his squat."

Maggie glanced over her shoulder at the medics pumping Richard's chest. Two cops were walking toward them, one male, one female. "Richard's not dead," she said.

"He will be." Lorraine bent to fondle Rex's ears. The dog sat, patient, beneath the caress. With a last kiss to Rex's head she handed the leash to Maggie, some expensive leather accessory with brass buckles and hardware, heavy and impractical. "Take care of him, okay? That's why I emailed you. You're the only one I could trust with my dog. The only one I could ever trust with anything."

Maggie took the leash as, leaning on her cane, Lorraine stood to greet the officers.

Someone's Out There

K.W. Roberts

I HAD NEVER seen anyone look as stressed as Tom did skulking into the warehouse that day. He looked like a rat in a corner staring at a great big cat and nowhere to run. I was hauling a pallet down for the guys on the dock and couldn't help my surprise. I had never seen Tom scared. It gave me a kick. But mostly I was mad at him for showing up here where everyone could see us together when he knew damned well I had gone straight. I hustled him out back and we stood watching snow drip off the roof. I tried to make him leave but he wouldn't. He just kept staring around the parking lot almost like a crazy man.

"Glad to see me?" He sounded like a crazy man too. He kept grabbing my collar the way he used to when he bossed me around, and then letting go because, after all, he was the one asking a favor. "Put me up a few nights, pal? I need a place to crash – bad."

When I said no he shoved me against the dumpster so hard I slammed my head.

"Okay, okay!" I gave in on the spot. You can't change the mind of a lug like Tom once it's set. "Thing is, don't hang around here. That can only get me in trouble and I won't go back to the pen for anyone. What are you so scared of anyway?"

All he said was, "Somebody's following me." Which wasn't much of an answer.

"Who?" I asked.

"I dunno. Some man. A crook, a cop, a devil maybe. I dunno." And all of a sudden that fear was back on his face.

His ugly face. Yeah, Tom had the ugliest mug I've ever seen. But I'm prejudiced. Chicks thought it was cute, usually, and especially with that corduroy cap he always wore. His hair would spill out from underneath all curly. It was a face a chick could love. Even if his hands didn't know the meaning of the word gentle. I never met a girlfriend of his that didn't have at least one black eye. Chicks, they're tough to figure.

"Aw, you're seeing things," I told him.

"I'm telling you there's someone following me around. Some man in a huge, heavy coat. I've seen him a dozen places."

"Take it easy," I said. "Nobody's here but us. You can see that." He peered around with eyes that almost popped from his head. Winter isn't Chicago's choice season. Some cars, dead weeds, and snow melting, that was all there was. "There's a bar down the street. Why don't you wait there till I get off?"

He didn't like the idea but didn't see much choice. He made me give him money. Took all I had except some change. Same old Tom, such a polite guy. I was glad nobody at the plant had noticed us together. The last thing I needed was to get my nose dirty. I didn't need anyone wrecking my freedom. Which was why I didn't stay at the bar, just picked him up and split.

We were just leaving the parking lot, the sun fading rapidly, when all of a sudden Tom started screaming and pointing. "That's him! That's the guy!"

"What guy?" I was playing dumb, see.

"The guy that's been following me, you idiot! Two cars behind. Driving that red Ferrari with that same big coat on."

I had to admit I saw the guy, although he looked pretty ordinary. Zillionaires from Barrington commuted here all the time. There was nothing shady about him except maybe his sunglasses. But what the hell, what kind of a spy would be lacking those? Tom didn't like the way I joked. He kept prattling on about how weird it was, because every time he saw the guy he was doing something different like buying a paper from a vending box, or walking out of a store, or driving a different car. He'd just pop out of nowhere, then vanish just as quickly. He looked like Dirty Harry out to make his day, and Tom couldn't seem more scared if he'd been a zombie. Like zombies made a habit of driving red Ferraris. After awhile Tom got pissed at my wisecracking.

"You think I'm nuts, don't you, you bastard! You think I'm psycho or something."

"I didn't say that." He started begging me to lose the guy, to keep him from learning where we were going. But swerve as I might backstreets stayed confusing, so I tried to keep him distracted with small talk. Could be coincidence. Or blather. But their alternative kept him craning to peer out the back. "Why don't you just talk to him?" I asked. "Catch him off guard and ask him why he's following you?"

Tom's voice shook. "I've tried. One really cold night I slept at the shelter and he took a bed on the other side of the room like some destitute bum. Played cards till late. There was always someone around and I wanted our talk to be private. Besides, I wasn't sure at the time he really was dogging me. So I waited till a few hours after lights-out and went over to his bed. It was empty."

"Must've known you were onto him," I said.

"Yeah. There were other times too," Tom went on. "I saw him once at a crosswalk. He was a little ahead and by the time I recognized him he was already halfway across the street and there was too much traffic to chase him. He even got onto a bus with me once and flashed the smuggest glare walking past. I bailed a mile from Ma's and walking home I saw him drive by in a Jaguar. Now it's a Ferrari. Always something flashy. If he finds where we're going I'm sunk. Lose him, for Christ's sake!"

"What do you think I'm trying to do?" I answered.

All of a sudden Tom lunged for the wheel and we squealed into a one-way street going the wrong way. I fought him off. The trick hadn't worked and the Ferrari's headlights stabbed the mirror right into my eyes. I had to slam my brakes or crash. I veered at the next street, expecting those lights to follow but they had fixed their slip and swung back. When Tom saw he heaved a sigh of relief.

"We've lost him," I said. "Satisfied?"

Tom seemed edgy. "No. Too easy. Whenever he disappears like that he always turns up again later."

"Well, you want to head to my place or not?" I asked. "I can't cruise around much longer. I'm almost out of gas."

So we wound up at my place. My dumpy apartment. Tom looked around the parking lot, and looked and looked. When a cat jumped off a windowsill I thought he'd shit bricks. The first thing he wanted when we went in was a drink. I might have known. That dude was always pouring something down his craw. His favorite drink was rum and I happened to have a brand-new bottle.

"Almost like you knew I was coming," Tom raved, holding it up to admire. "Oh, man, even my brand!"

I handed him a glass, ice, and Coke from the fridge, and grabbed myself a brew. I don't go for the hard stuff much, nothing like Tom. Then I tossed some leftovers into the oven.

"Well, I figured you were out of the slammer," I admitted. "That bank holdup's been making big news. Sounded like you. And that crashed getaway car and the corpse they found inside had your signature all over it. Yeah, I figured you were back to your old tricks. Said to myself, 'I bet old Tom Parker's out. Nobody but Tom could screw up that bad.'"

I was only joking, trying to have some fun. But Tom got mad and came at me with that mean look on his face. It had been so long I'd forgotten he had no sense of humor – nor the humility to deny my charges. He started shoving me around and calling me names like he'd done in the old days and reminding me he hadn't told the cops on me after our last job, the one that sent him to prison.

"I could still send you up the river, buddy," he warned me, polishing off his drink and wiping his mouth with a disgusting grunt. "Yep, I'll bet the cops would love to know who pulled the trigger on that poor, defenseless clerk. Poor guy was only about thirty, had a house and family and a station wagon with a dog in back, the whole bit. Now he'll spend the rest of his life in a wheelchair all because Y-O-U got trigger-happy. That's one hell of a rap for me to take, pal!"

"Now wait a minute." I stopped. It's no use trying to reason with Tom when he starts making up stuff, especially when he's drinking. That rum never stood a chance. Luckily I'd got it on sale. Truth is Tom preferred to pull jobs alone, and if he dragged anyone else along it was just to drive the car. Or ride in it. Half the time he'd decide to rob a joint on the spur of the moment. He'd just stroll in like any customer and get back in the car calm as a cucumber and you wouldn't find out he'd robbed the place till twenty miles down the road. He took it pretty casual. There's a rumor that he robbed a gas station on the way to church with his mother but I don't know if it's true. I don't doubt it.

"You pulled the trigger, baby!" Tom wagged a finger. "You owe me! If I told the goddamn cops you wouldn't see daylight for the next eight years at least. Just like I didn't."

One thing about Tom. He could talk himself into believing anything. He had imagined people shadowing him before and right then I'm sure he could have passed any lie detector test, even though he knows I've never shot a gun in my life, let alone paralyzed anyone. I'm a tame dude except when riled but even then I keep my cool. When I'm mad I react logically even if things take longer.

"Too bad you don't like cards," said Tom.

I plucked a deck from a drawer and started shuffling them in the fancy way I had seen Tom do. About the only thing I know Tom was good at was shuffling cards. He was a master. But I could tell by his frown that he was surprised to see me shuffling as good as I did.

"You used to say cards were boring," he marveled.

"People change." Sometimes.

Pretty soon we were into a serious poker game, not even stopping for dinner but just stuffing the reheated pizza slices into our mouths while we played. Even though we were just playing for cigarettes I could tell Tom was sorry he'd brought up the idea and I didn't bother to explain I'd developed a professional knack. I scrounged some stale Winstons, having stopped smoking the damned things years ago. No point mentioning the loot I'd stashed from my Vegas wins. I had plans for that. Like a baby, Tom snatched half the cigarettes from my pile.

"You steal more cigs than that damn Debbie!" he whined.

"Doesn't killing a girl bother you?" I asked.

"No. That was an accident."

I followed an idea. "You know, Tom, maybe that guy who's following you is trying to take revenge for her death. I mean, sure she was a loser to hang around you but nobody is completely alone in the world. Maybe it's her father. Maybe some boyfriend or husband from years ago. A close friend? A co-worker at her job?"

"Naw!" Tom laughed. "She was useless."

"Maybe some cheater's mistress?"

"I'm no suspect. I wore gloves the whole time, and the cops say no fingerprints were found. Bad crash, but I barely got scratched."

"Do you have a better explanation?"

"Look here!" Tom jumped up. "It ain't Sunday. I don't need no sermon."

"No, *you lo*ok." Ordinarily I wouldn't have badmouthed him so bad but he was too drunk to throw a straight punch and I was furious. "I'm gonna tell the truth. I don't like you, and I never did. Now just because you've killed your girlfriend and your mom threw you out, don't think you can bully me into letting you stay here. You can't. But here's a tip. There's a building near here that the city's gonna tear down in the spring with a joke for a fence where nobody's living but some vagabonds. It's a roof at least."

"You want me to squat in some rat hole?"

"Perfect place." I couldn't get much blunter.

I didn't blow up when Tom stuffed my winnings into his coat, threw cards all over the room, then tipped the table with a crash that probably got my neighbors steamed. But it was the last straw. If any doubt stuck in my mind what to do it disappeared now. I locked my bedroom door, unable to even force a healthy hatred. The guy was a pathetic nuisance like a cockroach. He had no redeeming qualities at all.

In the morning he wasn't any happier about my kicking him out but he'd started to like the idea of having a whole building largely to himself. He'd stopped arguing. When pests like Tom see they can't push you around they slink off. After he left I grabbed my phone.

"He'll be camping at those condemned apartments," I said.

And that clinched it. The reason that the dude dogging Tom owned a lot of fancy cars was that he whacked people for dough. He's worth the outlay. Never slips nor leaves a trail. Taunts his prey for tips but gets frustrated if they're never alone, so when he saw us together he probably guessed I would arrange things. When Debbie told me she had gotten mixed up with Tom I had warned her she was headed for trouble. Sure hadn't taken long to prove me right. I feel better now. Tom never felt remorse for any of the people he hurt. But when he killed Deb slamming his stolen car into a tree running from the cops he should have guessed she might be somebody's sister.

Mr. Sleepy

Leo X. Robertson

I STOOD at Clapham Junction station, waiting in the rain for FratBoy88.

Beyond the many people milling about – engaged in their typical loud London conversations as they headed out to clubs, or went home late with the shopping – residential tower blocks glowed in the night sky. I watched shadows move in their many living rooms and got lost in comforting thoughts of heading back home before my companion's arrival. So I didn't notice, at first, when someone hugged me.

"Fancy running into you here, darling." It was Gareth. He twirled his umbrella and flicked his self-bleached quiff. "What's up? Everything okay?"

I touched my face. Oh, I was crying. I had, after all, spent the bulk of my evening chasing my now-ex's social media with gin.

"I can't talk right now," I said. "I'm, uh, waiting to meet someone."

"Oh! I've been there." He patted my arm and turned away. "Say no more! I'll get out of your— wait." He shuffled closer to me and held the umbrella low, covering our heads. "The guy in the pink tracksuit is staring at you."

I looked over Gareth's shoulder and poked the umbrella's fabric out the way. There was my date for the evening.

Gareth's mouth fell open. "Is *that* who you're here to meet?"

Okay, FratBoy was older, and no looker. And sure, his dress sense was questionable – not that I'd planned on either of us wearing anything for long. But he did have a few things going for him. On his Grindr profile, he hadn't requested 'chemsex', nor did he use pejoratives like 'no fats no fems' or 'no spice no rice.' Plus, he'd provided real photos.

"This is important," Gareth said. "I'm not judging."

I smiled. "Then why did you announce it for no reason?"

He rolled his eyes. "Either way, we gotta go. Come with me."

He hooked his arm in mine and walked me away, into the evening's throng of bustling Londoners.

When I tried to look behind me, Gareth elbowed me in the ribs.

"Ow!" I said. "Where are you taking me anyway?"

"To my flat."

"Why?"

He gripped my arm tighter. "I'll explain when we get there."

* * *

Gareth's building was in a gated complex. He entered different codes in three separate keypads before we reached his flat's front door.

When we went inside, he guided me into the kitchen.

There were brushed steel appliances all around. A marble breakfast area separated the kitchen from the living room, where there was a long gray couch and large TV. On the walls, in black frames, were favorite quotes over images of beaches at sunset.

Mummy and Daddy – or *someone's* daddy – were surely involved. Well, good for Gareth: his place was way better than my own mouse-ridden, fruit fly-infested hovel.

"Your flat is lovely," I said. "I didn't know you lived nearby."

"I invited you to the flat warming." He was making us espressos using a fancy machine. "Myself and the whole Yellow Lamppost crew gave a performance, followed by cocktails on the terrace. The café girls said we were geniuses."

Waitresses at The Breakfast Specialists, that is, where Gareth and I were baristas. Every time Gareth's improv troupe performed, at least one of 'the girls' attended. I'd planned on catching a Yellow Lamppost production eventually – but it was the 'cocktail on the terrace' aspect that bothered me. I'd been afraid Gareth would cry at me and confess how, shock horror, he constantly entertained because of a fear that no one would stick around for the real him. Not that I was special, just that it was my turn. I assumed he'd done it already with most others. Everyone looked at him like they shared a secret.

My phone buzzed, messages popping up on its screen.

YOU STOOD ME UP CAN'T BELIEVE IT
LOST YOUR CHANCE WITH ME NOW IM OUT WITHOUT YOU MUCH BETTER

Gareth held out my espresso. In his other hand was a wet paper towel and a small plastic travel canister filled with an expensive-smelling cream.

"L'Occitane serum." He pointed lazily at my face. "Because, y'know." He shook the tension out his shoulders. "So. The guy in the pink trackie."

I tutted. "Yeah yeah." He'd dragged me away from my evening plans to get the gossip for the café girls, under the pretense of caring.

"He's Mr. Sleepy." His eyes widened like I should've known who that was.

"He's a kid's entertainer or something? That's kinda neat." I sipped the espresso carefully. The drunken numbness made it easy to burn my mouth.

He held his hands up as if to pre-emptively brace me for what came next. "He's in his forties, has *My Little Pony* figurines hanging on his bedroom wall, cartoon stickers on his wardrobe and those plastic glow in the dark stars on the ceiling."

Weird, but not necessarily a deal breaker. And I'd guessed he was more FratBoy78 than '88 from his photos. They were too ropey to be fake. He had strange scars on his chest and malformed abs that looked like a bag of beaten chicken breasts.

Gareth turned away and picked up his espresso. "Guess that's not enough for you. Well, you won't like this next part." He turned and walked slowly toward me. "He drugs his victims with GHB. You know, the club drug. They may only be unconscious while he rapes them, but the overdose kills them eventually. When he's done, he disposes of their bodies in Barnes Cemetery. Dumps them there for anyone to find. Beside them, he leaves falsified suicide notes, written in badly spelled, child-like handwriting."

The shock, and the caffeine, sobered me up. My initial reaction was distaste, as if Gareth saying this about FratBoy had made it true.

He must've seen it in my expression. "Ask me how I know," he said. "The name Barry McCafferty mean anything to you? My ex. And Sleepy's first victim."

His big deer-like brown eyes shimmered with incipient tears. When he wiped them away on his sleeve, disguising his sobs with a cough, I knew he'd told me the truth. He hated real emotions but braved them for me – because I'd been in real danger.

All I could think to say was, "That's why they call him Mr. Sleepy? It seems offensive somehow."

He scraped a fingernail on his bottom teeth in thought. "True. They should've thought of something else."

The implications of what I'd done hit me. I burst into tears.

Gareth placed a hand on my arm while looking away.

That I'd thought so poorly of him, without evidence, made me cry even harder.

He guided me over to the couch and sat me down.

"We call the police, then," I said.

He scoffed at me. "You don't think others tried? What would you say anyway?" He leaned in. "They don't give a shit about us, darling. They claim ignorance or lack of diversity in their ranks. It's all newspeak for homophobia. To them, us gays all hook up, take too many drugs and die in cemeteries. Serves us right!" At that point, if he'd had one, he would've flicked a fan open.

"Wow."

He gave me a sympathetic smile. "I know I'm not good at this stuff, but – don't beat yourself up. Could happen to anyone, really." He grit his teeth as if to stifle what came next. "I actually moved here because of a regrettable Tinder date. When I was living in the east end, I met this guy who couldn't accept that we didn't have chemistry. He knocked on my bedroom window, after climbing four stories up a drainpipe, to let me know." He looked me in the eye. "And no, I hadn't told him my address." He got up and stretched his legs. "It's not cheap to live here. I caught you on the way home after a shift at Kensington and Maple, the bar on Northcote Road? My new second job. The security here is worth it, though."

My phone buzzed again.

FratBoy88 – Mr. Sleepy, rather – sent me bad high-angle photos of himself in a dark room, overexposed flash masking the faces of those in the background.

I AM IN A CLUB NOW THESE GUYS MUCH HOTTER THAN YOU HAVING THE BEST TIME

More selfies appeared. A steamy hallway, angry half-naked men behind him, holding hands over their faces – though most hadn't noticed that he'd taken a photo.

THIS IS A BATHHOUSE MANY MEN WITH MUCH SEX HERE

Given how quickly they'd arrived in succession, he must've saved the photos from previous ventures. It was a pro forma response.

Gareth sat beside me again and pushed me on the shoulder. "You know what? Let's make sure he never harms anyone in our community again. Text him back, tell him we'll meet him at his place."

What?

HERE I AM IN BED WITH SOMEONE ELSE YOU WISH YOU WERE HERE

In the attached picture was a skinny pale kid who looked terrified. That was somebody's son. That was – me, on an alternate timeline.

Still I hesitated.

Gareth snatched my phone and ran back to the kitchen. He used the marble countertop as a shield as he texted. When I chased him one way, he dodged the other.

He read what he'd written out loud. "Sorry about earlier. Got scared. Meet back at your place? Tell me address. Will even bring a friend." He turned the screen to face me. "Look, he texted back already!"

I leapt across the counter and grabbed the phone from him.

SOUNDS GREAT BABES VERY INTERESTING SORRY FOR MY REACTION U JUST SO HOTTIE AND I MAD YOU STAND ME UP

I AM GOOD GUY I PROMISE BRING YOUR FRIEND AND SEE SOUNDS LIKE HOT NITE

He wrote all that back, that quickly?

He was unhinged. And this was a terrible idea.

I said this to Gareth.

"It would be worse to let this chance go by and pass him onto the next unsuspecting kid." He reached across the counter, splaying his fingers at me. "I'll be right there with you. I'm not going to let him hurt you. He's not physically dangerous, I promise! Just don't accept any food or drink from him and we'll be fine." He met my silence with a grin, his lips curling with prurient pleasure. "I'm going whether you are or not."

I clasped my hands behind my head. "You stopped me from going to his place alone. I guess I have to do the same for you."

Gareth clapped with glee.

* * *

The dread in my heart ramped up with every footstep on our way to Sleepy's place. Was there really nothing else we could do?

Before long, we stood by the door of Sleepy's haggard-looking building, on its patio of old, stained bricks. The sky was dark now, filled with marauding clouds.

Gareth wrapped his arms around himself. It set off a strange dread in me. I realized it was the longest he'd ever been silent in my presence.

"In case you were having second thoughts," he said, "this is where they found my ex. Sleepy called the police himself and claimed to have found him out here. The police searched Sleepy's flat and didn't find anything. If we just leave, it'll happen to someone else."

"Gareth, I get what you're trying to do, but if the cops already came here and—"

He hissed at me through gritted teeth. "Don't mention my real – hey!"

Mr. Sleepy had arrived.

Streetlight cast shadows over his long nose, heavy brow, his pockmarks and colorless moles.

No, he couldn't have been to all those places in his photos since we'd seen him at the station – but he had been somewhere. He'd changed out of his trackies into a leather trench coat, a black mesh tank top and long baggy jeans with straps and chains hanging off them.

The gear was probably cool to a certain niche group of people, back when he was the appropriate age to have worn it.

He lowered his head, revealing the shiny gauze of his toupee where he'd messily glued it to his scalp. He hunched his shoulders and held out his hand to Gareth and then to me.

He looked between us. "You'll do. You'll really do!"

He unlocked the building's front door and walked in without holding it open. We walked briskly, following him to his flat.

Again, he opened the door and left it swinging. We entered behind and went to the living room.

The place was, if not scary, depressing. A worn, faux-leather couch flaked in the room's center. The carpet was gritty beneath our feet, unwashed and covered in food bits. The windows' frames were painted shut, which accounted for the air's stuffiness.

Sleepy turned on the light and it buzzed at low power. The plastic dome covering the bulb looked like a rage punch had shattered it.

He tore off the trench coat and threw it on the couch. "I'll get us some wine."

"No need, babe," Gareth said. "I don't drink."

Before I could jump in, Sleepy looked at me and said, "I know this one does. He smells like gin."

He walked through to the adjoining kitchen and bashed some glasses about. As he did, Gareth walked back out the living room.

I turned in a panic to see where he went. Had he bailed without me?

Sleepy returned. He held two glasses of wine in one fist. The glasses were different styles – one large and simple, one smaller and with a gold stem – but both had greasy fingerprints on them. The larger glass was fuller.

I reached for the less full one.

Sleepy pulled his hand back and gave me the other glass. "I ran out, so you can have the one with more wine." That didn't make much sense.

I accepted the glass. My wine was paler than his, and it felt lukewarm.

"Don't just look at it. You weren't too good to drink earlier tonight." His dehydrated breath went up my nose.

What would he do if I refused? How did Gareth know he wouldn't get physical?

I looked away and raised the glass to my lips. His gaze burned into me.

Gareth returned.

My whole body had been tense. Now it released again.

Gareth cocked his head at Sleepy. "Hey, you ever do chems?"

What was he playing at?

Sleepy's shoulders slumped. "A couple times." A deep crevice sliced up half his forehead as he frowned. "But I don't wanna do any now."

He slammed his glass down on the coffee table. As he walked back to the kitchen, the chains on his jeans scraped off the table's glass, but he didn't react.

More smashing.

I looked to Gareth.

"Quick, take this!" He held out an open sandwich bag. Inside was a clear plastic canister of liquid.

"What is it?"

He shook the bag at me. "He's coming back soon. Hurry!"

I reached in and took the canister. "Wait, is this—"

"There are loads of them in the bathroom. He must've put this in your drink."

"Well what do you want me to do with—" I dropped it. "Just put it back!"

He picked it up from the floor with the bag. Through the sleeve of his jacket, he unscrewed the top, then poured the contents into Sleepy's glass.

"Gareth!"

Sleepy returned from the kitchen. He stared at the carpet. "I didn't have a reason to go in there. You are both so pretty and it made me nervous. I've never had two guys back here at once and I don't know what to do. Maybe you should just go."

"Sure," I said. "Another night."

"Or," Gareth said, "we're all here, so we could do it now?" He clasped his hands together and looked between us for a reaction.

I wanted to run but froze instead.

"Okay then." Sleepy downed his wine. He winced, shivered, then stormed out the living room and into the hall. Toward the bedroom, I supposed.

I took my glass through to the kitchen.

There were oily smudges all over the window. Green streaks of washing-up liquid ran down the cabinets. A magnet pinned what looked like a slice of dried-out ham to the fridge. I accidentally kicked a plastic bowl on the floor and wet cat food scattered across the linoleum. Where was the cat?

I flicked the tap on with my elbow, emptied my wine and cleaned the glass.

Gareth followed. "What are you doing?"

"Removing my fingerprints then getting out of here."

"Why?"

"I didn't come here for this!"

Gareth looked concerned. "For what?"

He left the kitchen, and soon I heard him screaming. "Come here, quick!"

I went through to the hall.

Gareth stood by the bedroom's entrance. Sleepy was naked, face down, hanging off the edge of the bare broken mattress on his floor.

"What do we do now?" I asked.

"What do you mean?" Gareth got on his knees and flipped Sleepy over, guiding his body to the floor.

He checked for a pulse, for breathing. "I think he's dying! What did you do?"

"You're the one that—"

That's when I heard the sirens wailing, just outside.

Gareth stood up again and gestured in my face. "Don't lie to me! You slipped something in his drink, didn't you? What was it, some sort of poison? A drug?" He clicked his fingers. "It was GHB!"

In his signature travel canister, which he'd held out for me to touch.

His tears were so convincing. "You're that killer, aren't you?"

I jumped at the sound of loud knocks on the door.

"This is the police!"

The door broke down with a slam.

I looked in the bedroom. There were no toys on the wall, no stickers on the wardrobe, no glow-in-the-dark stars on the ceiling. Sleepy was just FratBoy88. A weirdo for sure, but nothing more.

"Why?" I said to Gareth. "Because I never saw you do improv?"

He grinned. "You sure about that?"

An officer shouted behind me. "Get down on the ground, hands behind your back!"

I did as he said, my face rubbing in the carpet's dust.

As they cuffed me, I heard Gareth talking to them. "I'm so glad you're here. I was worried that my call didn't make sense. I had to make it quickly. I-In the bathroom. So I didn't raise suspicion. A-Anyway, that's him. He killed my friend!"

Two officers carted me up and walked me back out the flat.

"It's not me, it's him!" I shouted. "He's Mr. Sleepy!"

The officers chuckled to themselves and one said: "Who the hell is that?"

Step Light

David Tallerman

LIEUTENANT FEIST was forced to brake hard as he turned onto the street. Already a throng of gawkers had set up, maybe thirty bodies clustered in the middle of the road, craning their necks toward the rooftops. He allowed the siren a couple of shrill whoops and they swelled back, enough that he could tuck his own car behind the two black-and-whites already pulled up on the sidewalk.

He deliberately shuffled over to get out the passenger side, forcing a middle-aged man in grubby vest and slacks to take two sharp steps back. The man turned to glare, then his expression changed to one of recognition and he looked away abruptly, mumbling something apologetic. At that, half a dozen faces turned Feist's way, and he saw recognition there too.

Well, any audience was better than none. But were there any press? Yes, he could make out a news crew just setting up on the far side of the crowd. This wasn't a front page story in anyone's book, but his presence might easily turn that around.

Of course, he thought, *if I screw up, it'll be all over the front page, quick as dying and twice as ugly.*

Feist spared one brief glance upward. He considered the building first – new, no more than five years old, a dozen storeys of glossy mock-Georgian architecture – and then let his eyes drift to the figure perched halfway up its height. She was very still, arms and palms pressed against the brick behind, feet slightly splayed, her head hung forward and a little to one side, so that thick coils of black hair draped her face. There was something statuesque about her posture, as though up there on the ledge she'd finally found her calling.

Feist couldn't tell anything useful, though, except that nothing suggested to him that she was seconds away from taking her final plunge. Yet as his eyes dipped back to street level, he was struck by a sense of familiarity, so abrupt and strong that it ran like a shock through him. As soon as he considered it, he knew he hadn't seen this building before, or the ones to either side. Yet that didn't make the feeling go away.

So instead, Feist pushed it aside and began walking. Just as he was despairing that the hack they'd sent would ever look round and see him, he heard a shout of, "Lieutenant Feist! Kevin Paige, Evening Standard. Got a few words for us?"

"Not the time, son," Feist growled. "Don't you see a woman's life's in danger?"

"Are you here in a police capacity," called the reporter, "or just trying to get the lady's vote?"

A ripple of laughter ran through the crowd. Feist fought back a surge of anger, kept his voice steady. "Always police first, Mr Paige. Now if you'll excuse me…"

Before the reporter could come back at him, Feist was through the doors, held open by one ruffled patrolman, and looking inquiringly at a second across a plush entrance lobby.

Reading his expression correctly, the second patrolman responded, "Sixth floor, sir. There's a solicitors' office there. Up in the lift and turn left, you'll see the door's open."

Feist nodded. "One of you go out and give that cocksucker a statement," he said. "Keep it simple. Don't tell him more than he needs to know."

"Sir," said the second patrolman, and marched past and through the doors.

Inside the lift, Feist wondered again at the familiarity he'd felt outside. He'd never been in this building before, he knew that much. He'd been working this town for nigh on twenty years, there probably wasn't a street he'd been down less than a dozen times, so that this one had caught in his memory surely meant something. More than that, when he probed the recollection, the wash of emotion that followed was none too pleasant. Only, there wasn't a damn thing he could grasp.

The lift pinged, the doors slid open. Feist put aside his introspection with long-honed ease and stepped into a wide hallway. Though it was clear that some of the building was given over to apartments, this floor was split between half a dozen smallish business premises. There was a physiatrist's off to the left, a door marked Holier Technical Design at the far end, and to his right, the open entrance of the solicitors' firm.

He marched on through into a plain reception room, with a second door off to the left beside a large wooden desk. A high sash window stood open in the back wall, and a third patrolman leaned against the sill. His partner loomed over a young girl with high-piled blonde hair and a tearful expression that Feist figured to be mostly for the benefit of the fourth patrolman. As he entered, the two young cops came clumsily to attention, and the receptionist snuffled and rubbed a sleeve across her eyes.

The patrolman by the window said, "Good morning, sir. They radioed us that you'd be handling this one yourself." He lowered his voice, tilting his head toward the figure invisible on the far side of the wall. "She won't say one whit to us, anyway. Figure maybe she's only out there hoping you might show up and get her in the evening edition."

Feist nodded. Twelve months ago he'd put the word out that certain types of cases, the ones with headline potential, were to be pushed his way. Mostly that meant getting his name attached to occasional high profile arrests, but he'd also kept a regular sideline of exploits like this. For a year now, where there was a child threatened or a woman in danger, there too had been Feist.

In a city he could never have got away with it, but White Glade was no city, and he knew exactly how far he could push, exactly how much weight his edict carried. The local papers had made a show of seeing through his act, of turning it into a joke, but none of that mattered. He knew he'd earned himself the mocking nickname 'Saint Feist' – and that was fine too. If it meant everyone knew him, they could call him any damn thing they liked.

"We got a minute?" he asked the patrolman by the window. "You confident she won't do anything we'll regret out there?"

"As I can be. If I didn't know better, I'd say she was just taking the morning air."

Feist gave the patrolman a hard look that said, *Not in front of the witness.* Yet by the time his gaze had reached said witness, his expression was all compassion, with just enough grit behind it to show he meant business. "What's your name, miss?"

"It's Betty." She was snivelling again now, perhaps in advance of difficult questions.

"Don't you worry," he said, "you've done nothing wrong here. Just tell me as quick as you can what happened."

"What can I say? She came in demanding to see Mr Rosen. I asked if she had an appointment and she said, no, but if I just described her face then she was sure he'd see her. I thought about arguing, but I knew Mr Rosen was quiet and she looked like she might be the type to make a fuss. So I put my head round the door to ask him. Then I heard a noise. By the time I looked back, she was half out the window. It was open already, it gets awful warm in here. I ran straight over, but I didn't want to try and grab her in case … you know, in case I ended up pushing her by accident."

Feist wondered what she'd have come back with if he'd asked for the long version. "You sure you didn't recognise her?"

"Not one bit. Mr Rosen took a look out and he doesn't either." Her voice dropping to a conspiratorial hush, she added, "I think she's just some crazy, Lieutenant Feist, and we got the short straw."

Well, at least she recognised him, that was something. "Okay then," he said, "I'm going to step out and say my hellos."

Feist paced toward the window. Before the patrolman who'd been hovering there moved aside, he leaned closer and whispered, "Chief, you're sure you don't want us to call the fire rescue guys?"

"What," hissed Feist back, "you don't think I'm up to this?"

"Just a back-up," muttered the patrolman, abruptly nervous.

"If you're so worried," said Feist, "why don't you and your partner get down there with a sheet or something."

While the patrolman was trying to figure out whether he was meant to take that seriously, Feist turned his back, hoisted a foot to the windowsill – and steeled himself.

This was his eighth prospective jumper in barely as many months. He'd learned long ago that he had an aptitude for such things, and had asked for them particularly. To Feist's mind, people who wanted to die didn't make a song and dance. They locked themselves in a room with a handgun or a car running its exhaust flat out. Anyone who chose an audience didn't want death, they wanted attention. And what they *really* wanted was someone to take the choice out of their hands. Once you understood that, it wasn't so difficult. That persona, kindly but firm, was precisely what he'd been cultivating in his burgeoning political career these last few months, and it came so easily by now that he almost believed in it himself.

For all that, though, Feist was no fan of heights. Six storeys didn't sound like much, but it made an impression when you were staring down it. Were it a man up here, he might have made do with a bullhorn from the street, and he'd have certainly let the fire brigade in on the act. A young, pretty woman though? That required a little chivalry. He could see the photograph of him escorting her out, one arm slung around her shoulder, in his mind's eye.

It looked good, enough to help him overcome a spot of vertigo. Feist clambered up and ducked out onto the ledge, steadying himself with one hand against the window frame. He was becoming a connoisseur of ledges, and this one was wide as these things went, a touch over a foot except where support columns cut into its depth. Like the wall behind him, it was made from blocks of stark grey stone.

Feist turned his focus to the reason he was out here risking his life. She was to his left, at the farthest point of the ledge, where it finished to make way for the next building. There was another window halfway between them, presumably the solicitor's office. Feist cursed himself for not starting there instead, cursed her for making this as difficult as she could. Well, it was good drama, that was for sure.

As far as he could tell, she hadn't twitched a finger since he'd first seen her from the street. His first assessment had been right, though; she was certainly pretty. Even with that dark hair mostly covering her face, her features were striking, a mite sharp overall maybe but softened by her wide and full-lipped mouth. She was wearing a long dress, cream with patterns of blue flowers, and flat-soled shoes of the same cornflower shade. He wondered how she was faring with the cold wind on those tanned calves – and whether the sensible shoes were a sign that she'd dressed that morning with the intention of spending it stood on the outside of a building.

With his back pressed to the wall, Feist took a hesitant sidestep toward her and said, "Young lady, my name is Lieutenant Feist. I'm here to get you safe."

She didn't respond, not even to glance his way.

He took another short step, another. "I'm sure you've got all sorts of troubles, to be out here like this. Probably you think you can't go on another minute. But I'm here to tell you, you can and you will. You just need help … and we're going to make certain you get that."

No answer. No look his way.

Feist took another step. He was passing by the second window now. He imagined the solicitor watching from behind his desk, as though this were all some show laid on to break up his day – but he didn't bother to check. "And when I say we, I mean me. You have my word that I personally will get you the help you need."

He was starting to think that this conversation would be one-sided all the way, so that he started when she said, "It's all gone wrong."

Feist took a deep breath, bracing himself. "I don't doubt it seems that way."

"It's been wrong for the longest time."

"Perhaps so," he said, with a force of calm he didn't quite feel, "but there's nothing in this life that can't be put right. Only, this isn't the way. So why don't we traipse on back inside before we talk anymore?"

"The longest time," she echoed – and it was as if he hadn't spoken. She was talking very softly, as though to herself. "I can look back and see every stage of it, like watching dominoes fall. Only there's nothing I can do to change it. If I could just make it right somehow, even a little, then maybe I could start over."

"Then that's what we'll help you do."

She looked at him then, finally. The motion brushed the hair back from her face, and he was surprised to see no fear there, not even anxiety – really, no expression at all. "Do you mean that, Lieutenant?"

So she knew who he was. And she was a talker. In Feist's experience, the world boiled down to talkers and doers, and it was the doers you had to watch out for. She was a talker, and probably she liked the idea that she'd got a celebrity to tell her tale to. All he needed to do was listen, make the right noises, and sooner or later she'd get bored with this routine.

Except, there'd been something in her tone that he didn't altogether like. It was enough to make him hesitate before taking another step. "Course I mean it. So what say we—"

"I can't go back in. Not just yet. Not until you understand."

Feist suppressed a sigh. A talker, all right. Didn't she realise they were playing to a crowd? If they were out here all damn day, the news crew might get sick of waiting for their headline. At the thought, he glanced down – something he'd sworn not to do – and immediately his stomach bobbed like an apple in a water barrel, his vision tilted and swam. He pressed back hard against the wall, trying not to let on how near to panic he'd found himself.

It wasn't only the height. The building he'd parked in front of, a decrepit laundry – he'd seen it before. Not only that, he'd seen it before from *this* angle. That didn't make any sense, yet there it was. Feist forced himself to look again, this time tilting his gaze by degrees. Yes, he recognised the building opposite, all right. Not the stores to left and right, both of which boasted new facades, but he'd seen that laundry before, and he'd seen it from above. What he couldn't tell was when – or why the fact scared him so severely.

Don't lose it, he told himself. *Just do what you came to do. Talk to her, damn you. Get this over with.*

"All right," he said, successfully keeping the fear down to the barest tremor, "why don't we start by you telling me your name?"

"It's Mary," she said. "Mary Tucker. But that's not the name I was born with."

A strange thing to say – and he felt sure this time, there was something in her tone, an edge he couldn't figure. "So you're married, Mary? Not happily, I'm guessing?"

"He's not a bad man. The badness came from me more than him. When you've seen too much hurt, it gets inside you. It builds in your head, so you think if you don't let it out it'll kill you."

"So the problem was your parents?" Feist hazarded, taking another short sidestep as he spoke. "They fought? Sure, I've seen what that can do."

"They fought," she agreed. "But they loved each other, they did. Even in the end, they still loved each other. Only, after what happened – it got into them, like a sickness. There just wasn't any cure."

Feist took another shallow step. Now the distance between them was less than half a dozen feet. Something else was starting to nag at him. Common sense told him she was pouring her heart out here, yet there was no hint of passion in her voice. But it was more than that.

She's dancing around something.

Yes. That was it. She was *leading* him. "Mary," he said, "what is it you're not telling me?"

She was looking at him fully now. He found himself imagining the scene as it must appear from the street: he in his charcoal suit, her in her blue-patterned dress, both standing straight-backed with their necks twisted to watch each other, like old folks talking at a bus stop, as the wind whipped their hair into odd, quick sculptures.

"My father was black," she said, "and my mother was white. So maybe they never stood a chance."

So that was it – a part, at any rate. He reappraised her face in this new light and knew she was telling the truth. "Folks didn't have much tolerance for that in those days." *Hell, they still don't.*

"I took after my mother. My older brother got his father's colour. It was hard for us – harder for him than me. He started to go wrong fast. Fighting at first, then worse. He wasn't bad, but he was doing bad things. I guess sooner or later the police were bound to come knocking."

A cold, creeping sensation, like an insect crawling with feet of ice, ran the length of Feist's spine.

She was, what, pushing thirty? Say what she was talking about had happened twenty years ago. Twenty years. About when Feist had joined the force.

It hadn't been an auspicious start. His career had almost been derailed altogether in that first year. He wondered what hope there was of grabbing her, of forcing her inside. He was strong as any man in his early forties, but the attempt would be awfully risky – and that press crew were still watching.

"Leroy wasn't in when the policeman came to the door," she said. "But he came home at exactly the wrong time. They figured each other straight away. If Leroy had run down the stairs, into the street, he might have got away. But he didn't, Lieutenant Feist. I guess Leroy just panicked … because he went up those stairs instead."

Yes. The kid had been scared, all right. And Feist's blood had been boiling. Nothing had gone right in days, and here he was, chasing down some dumb kid who'd been lifting from liquor stores. It was too damn much.

So he'd run like a man possessed, he'd bellowed at the top of his lungs. The kid got more scared, ran harder. That only made Feist madder. Up the stairs they went, on to the roof. The place had been a decrepit tenement, nothing but garbage and a couple of old sun loungers up there, the wall around the edge too low to serve much purpose.

It had been here ... just here. A different age, a different building. Where a rooftop had been was now the ledge outside a solicitor's office, but this was still that selfsame spot.

"It was an accident," he said. "He kept on running. He got to the edge. I tried to grab him."

"He was thirteen years old. Would you have run down a white boy in a good neighbourhood like a dog?"

Feist ignored the question. They both knew the answer – even as he knew in his heart that it hadn't been entirely and truly an accident. Oh, he'd reached for the kid, all right, but inside his head, something had been grinning all the while.

That incident had almost ended his career. These days it would have. It had taught him a lot, too, before he'd made himself forget.

"What do you want?" he asked harshly. "Your brother's dying was an accident, and one that happened a hell of a long time ago."

"I want to put the past to rest," she said.

"Then you ought to. It's nothing to do with me."

"You know, I tried to tell myself that."

Feist took a step back, felt his back foot scud on the lip of the ledge. He drew a deep, shuddering breath that didn't calm him one iota. What was he so scared of? This chit of a girl?

Yes.

She'd watched him. She'd planned. She'd seen her opportunity, and now here they were and she was so damn *calm*.

Feist hissed through clenched teeth. "You won't get away with this."

"What's to get away with?" she asked, almost sweetly.

"You crazy bitch," he said. "They're all watching." He tried for another step, but his ankles were like jelly.

"Anyone can panic, Lieutenant," she whispered, the words hardly reaching him over the incessant wind. "*Anyone* can slip."

"Like hell!" Feist flailed with his left hand, hoping to touch the window of the solicitor's office, maybe to draw the man's attention. But all his fingers found was raw stone, rasping across his knuckles. He staggered then, as though he were performing a small dance on the spot, as though he didn't have the moves down right yet. He could feel the void beside him, feel its tug. The wall, the ledge, seemed to be wavering.

Suddenly, quicker than his eyes could follow, her hand shot out toward him. Instinct, unmodified by judgement, jerked his whole body back. By the time he realised that maybe she was merely trying to grab him – at least, that was how it would look – he'd already lost his footing. The world tilted, tipped.

Feist's last thought, as the wall sheered away before him, was that her scream was damned convincing.

Even more real-sounding than his own.

My Jack

Salinda Tyson

August 1888, London

GILLY PULLED her shawl about her shoulders, heading for the bakery, whose ovens, fired at two in the morning, kept the brick wall warm as toast. A raindrop hit her shoulder as she drew closer, splattering the sleeve of the second-hand silk. She cursed, hoping rain would not drench her. The worse she looked, the worse her clothes looked, the worse the customers looked, the worse they paid. And behaved. Mother Meg, who stripped the dead, sold clothes cheap to working girls, but not that cheap. Clothes had to last. Aye, through the pulling and pawing and pinching and slapping and tumbling about.

She pressed against the bricks so that, despite the bustle, she could stand against the wall. Ah. Blessed heat. Closing her eyes, she dreamed of standing there forever, warm.

"Eh, Gilly, got yourself a sweet bloke?" A hand touched her shoulder.

She started, her eyes flying wide open. Her younger sister, her fellow lodger, hat and veil wet with rain, grinned at her. "Mary, you frightful tease." She made room against the wall.

"No business with rain and fog. Sends the customers in to drink or watch dogfights or gamble, or home to their wives." She made a pleased noise, easing her rump and her hands against the wall.

"Better than many a man, this old wall," Gilly said. "Always warm and friendly. No nonsense."

They laughed.

Rain drizzled down, but the building's eaves offered a half-foot of sanctuary. Beyond that the wet cobbles glistened black, hard, treacherous walking in thin, worn shoes. Both girls had learned to wear men's boots like the other women. Boots were much better in a fight.

"Come with me," Gilly said. "We can get pastries and loaves from the oven. We'll have bread for two days."

Mary snorted. "At what price?"

Gilly touched her sister's hand, as cold as her own. "It's heavenly warm inside. The bakers will just want their bit of fun, no more. Come on. My mouth's watering for fresh bread."

* * *

The sisters shared a room on Dorset Street in Whitechapel. They were young to the streets, their faces not puffed out by gin, their front teeth still in their mouths. Neither touched gin. Both knew that was the beginning of the end. Their mother had died in Lambeth workhouse a year ago and both chose to risk life on the streets rather than return to the place. The sisters had picked oakum there until their fingers bled. The workhouse had hawked Gilly's tatting and embroidery to rich patrons without giving her a farthing. Gilly had embroidered gloves to protect her sister's hands and started a pair for herself. Her needle earned money, but tricks paid more. By day, she worked for a dressmaker and bargained hard for wages. Nights, the sisters walked the streets together. Rich men liked sisters, licked their chops and stared, their eyes glassy with that familiar look.

Lately, Gilly's favorite lad was Jack. John Clarey. During a performance of street tumblers, he'd tapped Gilly's arm as if he knew her. "Give me a kiss," he'd said, but blushed when she turned, because she wasn't the girl he expected.

"A kiss?" she retorted. "That's a shilling, sir."

"Pardon, miss." He blushed furiously.

As if she was the kind of girl one needed to say, 'Pardon, miss' to. She grinned at him. In truth he looked decent, a big man with curly black hair and sharp, intelligent eyes, and no extra flesh on his long bones. No smell of gin or tobacco or opium hung about him.

"Is your kiss worth a shilling?" he asked.

Gilly gestured with her chin down an alleyway. "Come see."

"So your fellow can clout me on the head and rob me, eh?"

She laughed. He'd be a hard one. Might claim she had robbed him and call a constable. Sometimes she wished she had a man to protect her and Mary.

"If you don't want a kiss, I won't take your shilling. I bid you good day, sir."

"No." They were face to face, Gilly against the wall. Suddenly, he stroked three fingers along her chin, a gesture so tender, so unlike the usual, that she held her breath. *Wondering: Will he strike me, curse me, call me whore, knock me down, or slit my throat? There is that moment with men when you can never tell.* He kissed her. The kiss was at first as tentative as his touch, but turned fierce. He focused only on the kiss, caressing her waist with his hands, doing nothing else, until she kissed him back, unsure at first then so keenly that she felt dizzy and drunken, full of sensation, her ears ringing. How long that kiss lasted she could never reckon. She had not kissed a man like that, ever.

"Umm," he said and at last drew away from her. His eyes were dark and unfocused. He smiled. "No false advertising with you." He brushed a finger across her lips. "That kiss was well worth a shilling." He shifted to stand with his back to the mouth of the alleyway, sheltering her from view of passers by. Reaching into his pocket, he withdrew a bright new shilling, which he pressed into her hand.

Taking no chances, she tucked it inside the pocket sewn into the front of her bodice.

"What's your name? Where d'ye live?"

"I'm Gillian – Gilly. I live in this neighborhood."

"You lodge near here?"

She nodded, unwilling to say more.

"John Clarey. I work in Spitalfields market. Might I walk you to your lodging?"

He took her arm as if she was not what she was. When they left the alley, the bells of Saint Botolph's were ringing the hour. She let him walk her to within two blocks of the room the sisters shared.

He came back faithfully, two or three times a week, and never cheated her of money. The ploy of pressing a girl's knees together or crossing her thighs tightly and letting a man think he had penetrated her, outwitted most of the hasty, gin-soaked clients fumbling at a working girl's skirts. The ruse kept Mary and Gilly from pregnancy and pox. Of course, mean drunks who caught on grew meaner indeed and used their fists on women's faces.

With John Clarey the trick was useless. He was never drunk. So she let him inside her, a risky thing Gilly had avoided since the abortion for which the midwife had charged a month's rent. She knew she had done a foolish thing – gone soft.

He always bought her food and ale. With a perfectly straight face one day, while other clients clustered around a butcher's stall at the market, he handed her a packet of chops, murmuring "I'll put it on the bill," as if she were a proper maid or cook's helper fetching home the meat for dinner. He took her to music hall plays. Like the bakers, he knew the streets' rough life, and did not despise her and Mary.

Mary teased her about marrying him. "Every week, is it now? He's as faithful as a husband. Maybe he'll take you away from this place. Teach you his trade so you can help him in his shop."

"Tradesmen marry tradesmen's daughters. He's a butcher's helper. Don't devil me with hopes."

* * *

Gilly's eyes burned and her thumb felt stiff. The embroidery curled and snaked over the fabric like an endless dream. She smiled, pleased with the delicate patterns and fine stitches of her work. She pulled the lamp closer, but misjudged with the thimble. The needle stabbed her fingertip. Shifting the precious work so it would not stain, she sucked the bead of blood, thinking of the beds she and her Jack had shared. It was inevitable she would get with child, and his eyes grow cold, his voice grow hard. She imagined him at the market stand, refusing to recognize her, as if she were boiled down soup bones to be cast to the street's rag-and-bone pickers. Potteries bought bones to grind for making bone china. She imagined her bones ground and mixed into the porcelain clay that made up the fancy cups which the dressmaker who bought Gilly's work used to serve tea to fancy ladies. Shuddering, she foresaw another visit to the abortionist, with those gleaming knitting needles and bitter potions. Heart broken, how soon before she would swill gin to fortify herself for the night instead of watered ale or cider? How soon before she used more laudanum or took to the opium dens, or raised a sloshing, gin-filled glass just like one of the battered trollops who sat in the Ten Bells pub on Commercial Street? Her heart trusted no man, yet she longed to trust.

* * *

The first girl the constables found set tongues clacking. Mary and Gilly learned of it from the newsboys' placards, and the lurid details the patterers reeled off to hawk papers. Butchered, one said. Throat slit, belly slashed. Gilly snatched cast-off newspaper pages from the gutter, drawn by the horror written on every passing face. Big inky black headlines smeared the sisters' fingers as they sounded out the letters and read, word by word, sentence by sentence, pausing to study the woodcut pictures in the Penny Illustrated Paper. A Mary, a 'soiled dove'. Left dead on her back in her own blood. In Bucks Row, an area of rooming houses where a girl might do business in privacy, a spot the sisters often passed walking home. Throat and stomach slashed and her womb cut out, the news sellers cried. Bobbies took pictures with cameras, gossips said, and carted her body to the police morgue.

Butchered. And left like dog meat.

* * *

One day Gilly spied on John at work in the market. Your Jack, Mary called him. Blood crusted his fingernails and knuckles. He wore a massive white apron smudged with bloody streaks, and a leather apron over that. Seeing his quick hands steady beef ribs and whack the cleaver down, severing bone and flesh, made her suddenly queasy. He was the butcher, not the helper! He had not told her that. The odor of blood, the flies that buzzed round the stalls had never bothered Gilly before. The streets near the Aldgate slaughterhouses ran with blood and urine from the droves of cattle herded there.

It bothered her when he acknowledged her with only a curt nod, not enough to give away their acquaintance to the gaggle of respectable maids and cooks and tradesmen's wives. Just a jerked chin. He could have pretended he didn't see her, simply ignored her. When he held out a packet of paper-wrapped meat, with blood dripping from the paper's torn edge, for a maid to place in her basket, Gilly saw only his large, strong hands, smeared with blood, fingernails crusted with the dirt of a day's work.

All the things those hands had done to her. Turning away, she wondered if they had done those terrible things to the dead woman.

* * *

A second horror came eight days later. Saturday morning, another woman's body was found behind a lodging house. Rumors blazed through the streets. Throat and belly slashed, guts slung on her shoulders like ropes of sausages. Her womb hacked out and carried off by the fiend. Her pockets were also slit and rings, pennies and farthings laid out at her feet. Her name was Annie.

Mary and Gilly stared at each other as they read the stories, wiping smeared ink from their fingers.

"Why would a man do that to a woman?" Mary asked.

"A pimp might cut her to scare her," Gilly said. "He'd get no use nor money from her dead. But to leave money laying there – what sense is that?" Three pence bought a night in a common doss house. Had the bastard refused to pay her even a penny more, which would have been the price of a night's lodging?

* * *

Jack rented a hotel room near the Fenchurch railway station, signed them in as Mr. and Mrs. Clarey. Veiled, arm-in-arm with him, she passed for respectable even to the clerk in his starched collar. Play-acting thrilled her despite the many rooms to which she had climbed. Winking, Jack turned the key, pushed open the door. Inside she glanced out at rooftops, St. Botolph's spire, and the railroad viaduct to Fenchurch Street Station, bouncing to determine the firmness of the bed, whose sheets smelled clean enough when she pressed her face into them. Sitting demurely on the bed she frowned at him. He looked strange.

"Mrs. Clarey, is it?" she said.

Suddenly his face twisted; he roared and punched the bed so hard she nearly slid off. "Damn the coppers, they questioned me!" His mouth twisted. He yanked her veil aside. His mouth was suddenly on her throat.

"Mrs. Clarey for a night," he said, an edge to his voice. "Undress while I wash my hands."

He was touchy about that, scrubbing over the ewer and basin on the washstand to clean the blood from under his nails, from the creases and lines in his callused palms and on each finger. Uneasy, she stripped down to corset and stockings and unpinned her hair while he bathed his hands. She could understand about his hands, for her own were hard and ugly from the needle pricks of her other trade. After he had spent himself in her the first time, as they lay on those rented sheets, he said more about the peelers, or constables, Sir Robert Peele's men.

"They questioned all us lads at the market. Especially the Germans and the Irishman. Wanted to see our knives and cleavers." He turned to her, tracing lazy patterns across her belly. "Did you know her, Gilly?"

"No, nor did Mary. Likely her pimp got drunk and accused her of holding her money." She spoke without thinking. Pimps often blacked girls' eyes or stabbed their bellies. But money had been left by the dead woman's body. Money. *Who could leave money laying about like that?*

His finger stopped its travels across Gilly's belly. "You must take care out there."

"I do. And you take care of me."

"So I try to." He slid a hand along her arm, pulling her atop him.

* * *

Jack saw her home near dawn, but Gilly lay late in her hard, narrow bed, staring at the ceiling. Jack's hand had smeared her veil with blood, and she recalled his flash of temper. She was drunk with memory of his kisses and caresses. But would he begin beating her? Wives, with only one man to deal with, were lucky. Yet she kept seeing Jack's slow, careful washing of his hands in the hotel room and the red tinge left in the washing water. *We need a way to protect ourselves,* Gilly thought, *not just stout boots.* Mary had gone to haggle with the used clothes dealers and she needed more laudanum-laced Kendal Black Drops to help her sleep. Gilly had embroidery to deliver and errands to run, food to fetch. Would she ever wear the fancy tatting or beadwork she made? She must finish the gloves to hide her damaged fingertips. Two steps outside her door, just as she pocketed the key and flexed and rubbed her sore hands, a newsboy's high-pitched voice cut through the street clatter. Coppers with glue pots and brushes were slapping handbills on lodging house doors. POLICE NOTICE, TO THE OCCUPIER. Anyone who had seen a suspicious person was asked to "communicate at once with the nearest Police Station."

Knots of people filled the streets, trading rumors and bloody details. The Butcher of Whitechapel, they called the killer. Jack's flash of temper twisted through her mind. Doomsayers, flapping ink-smeared copies of the illustrated newspaper, appeared on street corners and drew crowds as grand as for a dog fight or rat baiting. Peelers stalked the neighborhood, making things difficult for pickpockets and working girls. Toffs and ladies got off the new streetcar to stroll Whitechapel, to see the crime scenes and to see how the poor lived. Gilly sneered at them and spat behind their backs.

The milliner in Threadneedle Street faulted Gilly's work and tried to pay less than the agreed-on price of ten pence a child's smock, but Gilly snapped, "Pay fair, madam, or find another embroiderer." The milliner narrowed her eyes but paid up and set Gilly a tablecloth for two pounds. "And extra money for the silken floss," Gilly added. All along her way home, the yellowing notices flapped on lodging house doors, begging people to sing to the peelers. Until light faded, she plied her needle, then ate when Mary returned home. Together, the sisters walked to Saint Botolph's Church, called the Prostitute's Church. Streetwalkers used it as cabdrivers used stands, lining up at a starting point before the church, so that the first man traveling this main road into London went to the first girl in line.

Girls spoke of little else but the latest killing. Rumors said it was a German butcher, an Irish butcher, a Jewish butcher. A medical student. A madman escaped direct from Hell, come to Whitechapel on the new streetcar that was carrying curious Londoners to see where the horrible things illustrated in the papers had taken place.

One old whore, a notorious drunk who eyed the sisters and told them they'd hit the gin someday soon, hiked up her skirts and showed a big knife tucked into her stout boot. "Bugger tries to slit my throat, ha! I may surprise him." She wagged a finger at the pair. "Pretty birds, you should keep a friend like this."

Mary and Gilly drew closer. Fighting off drunks they knew. Maudlin drunks were easy to lead, easy to sidestep, easy to fool, easy to rob. Mean drunks were different, although a stout kick to the shins with their men's boots did wonders. Drink twisted men into many kinds of rage, but neither had ever carried a knife.

Another woman in line cursed. "Take your place like the rest of us, no cheating. What d'ye think we're all waiting for? The Prince o' Wales to call?"

The hag laughed and muttered.

They moved a couple steps forward as the woman at the head of the line walked off arm in arm with a fat, rich-looking gent with door-knocker whiskers.

* * *

Two weeks later, a double killing. Gilly's heart went cold. Someone who knew the area and its working girls must be the killer. Someone who could let the price of a night's lodging lay in the street. Headlines screamed about the coroner's inquests and the coppers' hunt for the killer. On the Sunday, a woman's still warm body was found outside a working men's club after midnight, throat slashed. A bobby making rounds found another body in Miter Square near a church. The coppers found a torn bit of her apron, perhaps used to wipe the bloody murder knife, near a chalked message about Jews.

Mary knew her sister's agony over Jack.

"Police questioned him, after the first one," Gilly told her. "The night in the hotel, he couldn't have done the second one, unless straightaway after we parted.... He said he was going to the market."

Mary stared at her. "The papers say the second one was killed about dawn. They say a butcher or slaughterhouse man is likely the killer. The notices ask folks to sing about a man called Leather Apron."

Her Jack. She pictured again the swift skilled hands as he sawed bones and unhinged joints, and wiped his knives on his leather apron. All the things those hands of his had done to her.... What else had they done?

* * *

Jack came to her, his eyes haunted, fever bright. Was he drunk? But no. He begged her not to go out at night. "It's too dangerous for you and Mary."

Should she love him or fear him? Her heart pounded. Did he try to shield her because he cared for her or because he knew his fiendish urges would turn on her and Mary? She feared him suddenly.

"Don't you see?" He grabbed her hands. "Coppers won't protect you or any street-walker. The papers say the killings happen in places with people about, but the women don't cry out."

Because they think their killer's buying their time? Gilly nodded, thinking of chloroform, but recalling the midwife-abortionist's trick, pressing the place on the neck that made hysterical women faint. But she remained silent.

"Mary and I will stick together," she said to calm him.

* * *

Mary's face was ashen. "Gilly," she said. "Jane the flower market girl said she saw your Jack talking and laughing with Annie, the second one who was killed. I asked was she sure? She swore it was him. I've never known her to lie about anything."

Gilly felt sick as she looked into her sister's eyes. She felt a dreadful sureness that he would go for Mary first, that he would take what she loved most.

"We must carry knives in our boots, like that old hag."

"Go talk to the peelers," Mary urged. "Maybe they can help us."

"They haven't protected any of us girls. We're together, we stick together. We're sisters."

* * *

Coming home one night, they spotted Jack following. Under a gaslight, Mary and Gilly exchanged a glance.

"John Clarey," Gilly called, forcing him to come face them under the streetlight. "Are ye spying on us?"

His eyes and his mouth tightened. "Protecting you. D'ye think – d'ye think the peelers will protect you? Four women murdered and they've no idea who did it. You think they care a fig about East End whores?"

"I know what I am but you usually don't call me that so bluntly, Jack."

"Must I beg your pardon? Consider my manners slipshod, then? You stubborn girls will get yourselves killed." He drew a breath. She had never seen him so fierce. "I followed after to protect you, to keep you safe. No bastard will get you if I can help it. You dare question why?"

Mary touched Gilly's arm and smiled at Jack.

"Could you walk us home to keep us safe, Mr. Clarey?" Gilly asked him as sweetly as her drumming heart would allow.

* * *

"Do you trust him?" Mary asked one night as they walked the edges of the Spitalfields fruit and flower market, seeking customers. "He follows us everywhere."

"To protect us."

"Truly? Or do you think he's waiting to kill us, some night when that other urge comes on him?"

"Stop it. Shut up. Isn't it bad enough, with all this other—" Gilly gestured at the marketplace, broad Commercial Street, the pub opposite, where their sisters in the life sat inside, trolling for drinks from customers – the whole grimy, hard circle of their lives, closing like shackles.

Mary would not let the matter rest. "Has he asked you to move into his house? Or promised to marry you?"

Gilly shook her head in annoyance. "No. I dunno if he has a house. But—"

"Do you trust him, or love him?" Mary took Gilly by both arms, forcing her sister to look her in the eye.

"Let me go. We've business to attend to."

"He could be the man," Mary said.

"So could any butcher or slaughterhouse man in Aldgate!" Gilly huffed. She would have preferred to work alone that night, but Mary stuck to her. Both now carried knives in their boots, wore leather aprons Gilly had stolen under their skirts to protect their bellies, and broad leather collars around their necks.

They soon netted a portly gentleman who offered absinthe and food. He wanted nothing queer and paid without protest. Mary tapped Gilly's arm as they walked off. "I'm giddy from drinking that stuff." She jerked her chin to indicate a man standing in shadow across the street, and chuckled. "See, your Jack's ever faithful."

Gilly stared but the shape seemed off. She blinked. "Best go home straightaway."

Their sturdy boots rang on the cobblestones; they had more than a mile to march. They coughed in the sulfurous air. A thick fog muffled sound and veiled and distorted the glowing orbs of the few gaslights. The yellow-green liquor had muddled Gilly's head. A bittersweet taste hung in her mouth. Her ears pricked up. Boots thudded on the cobbles behind them. A hansom cab passed, its wheels thundering on the road, the horses' breath pluming fantastically about their silhouetted heads like embroidery patterns. Light from the coach lanterns cut the gloom and blinded them for a moment. Had the footsteps behind halted? Joined by one thought, the sisters quickened their pace. Gilly's ears strained for the sound of footsteps. Had Jack stopped to speak with someone, or decided they were safe and need not be followed home? Or had he circled, knowing their probable route, to catch them up and attack them somewhere farther along?

They ducked down a side street to hurry home. A voice came drifting through the gloom. A man's voice, off-key, singing "for love of Barbara Allen," then humming. A drunk stumbling home with an old song in his head? From the soupy fog beside Mary came a harsh scrape, a sudden flicker of light, the stink of a sulfurous lucifer match. Someone wrenched her arm viciously backward. "Gilly!" Mary screamed. Two faces appeared in the light of the dying match: Mary's was terrified, and a smiling man held a knife at her throat. The match died; the world became shadow. "Mary," Gilly yelled, grabbing her sister's arm to yank Mary away from the man, shifting her skirts with the other for the knife in her boot. She drew the knife. "Jack!" she screamed.

The man laughed, the deepest nastiest sound this side of hell. "That's my name, tart."

So her Jack was not the fiend. She kicked, praying to hit this devil's shin, as Mary struggled and thrashed. Her boot connected. Bone cracked. A hard slap exploded as Mary cracked the man's face, knocked off his hat, and spun away. He came up, knife in hand, growling. She and Gilly faced him, knives drawn. Another shadow moved in the end of the street. Christ, did he have friends? It was no peeler, they would blow their whistles, swing their bulls-eye lanterns, and yell.

"Whores that fight, what a novelty." The man lunged. Mary countered and Gilly kicked for his knife hand, hitting his forearm hard. He cried out. His knife slid from his hand just as the shadow blocking the end of the street resolved into her Jack, who sprang forward and clubbed the man on the head. That dropped him.

Mary was holding her wrist. "He nicked me." She held a spot to her mouth.

Gilly's Jack tied the man's hands, with the cord butchers use to hoist hams from rafters. As he rolled the man over, a slim leather case fell from his coat. Inside was a long, thin-bladed knife, and scalpels, likely what he'd used on the others.

Three pairs of eyes met over the man face-down on the cobbles. A constable's whistle cut the quiet.

"Christ Jesus," her Jack said. "Do we give him to them?"

"Would they believe us?" Gilly asked. "He sounded well-born, posh."

"We'd be arrested for assaulting a toff. And hanged or transported." Jack knelt over the man

"I've an idea," Gilly said. "We walk him along as if he's drunk."

John bashed him on the head again for good measure, then hauled him up, bracing under his arms as he would to see a tipsy friend home. "Gilly, get his other side. Mary, you walk the other side of me, as if I'm sotted, too. Get his other knife, his hat."

"Where to?" Mary took her place beside Jack.

"We put him to bed in the river. Let him sleep forever."

That walk was the strangest of their lives, play-acting drunken roisterers and dragging a dying man through twisted streets and alleyways to the Thames. They evaded drunks and coppers, street sweepers and coaches and music hall crowds and slipped him in, his feet weighted with a sack of bricks found along the way.

* * *

They were home in their beds that day, Lord Mayor's Day, November 9. As the parade wound into Ludgate Hill before St. Paul's Cathedral, newsboys dashed into the crowds with placards reading MURDER – HORRIBLE MURDER. The latest discovery broke up the parade.

A young woman's body was found in a rented room in Millers Court. Throat slashed so the head was near severed. Belly ripped open. Skin and flesh hacked off her legs like he was fixing a soup bone, hissed the voices in the street. Breasts and kidney left on the bedside table, whispered the voices of the little people, the poor people who knew they did not matter to the great ones. And she was a Mary – a Mary Kelly.

Had the killer finished just before they met him?

* * *

Jack took both sisters to his house, which he shared with his brother, a cooper, and married Gilly properly. "I must marry you," he said slyly. "A wife's cheaper to keep than a mistress."

New Year's Eve the body of a Mr. Druitt surfaced in the river, a suspect and an apparent suicide. Jack and Gilly lay in bed holding each other, poring over the description in the newspapers, wondering. Was this Mr. Druitt the one put to bed in the Thames? Or just another bad one?

Who they did put there they never knew. There were no papers on his body and little money, no watch, just those knives in that posh leather case, which they slid into the river weighted with stones.

Jack taught Gilly and Mary his trade and Gilly continued embroidering and beading, creating flourishes and tendrils, patterns of light and shadow that fetched decent prices. The three kept their secret, being folk who knew how to keep their mouths shut. The murders remained unsolved; the newspapers mocked the police. Gilly could not have children because of the abortion in her dark, younger days. She poured her passion into her needlework, her husband, and her sister. Three years later they hired a cook and Gilly, Mary, and the dressmaker, after hard negotiations, kept shop together. But Gilly could not see Saint Botolph's church or hear its bells without recalling her shadowed past life, which had brought them all together. When the church bells pealed, in her heart and brain rang another toll, sounded in the voices of children and those who fancy themselves East End wits, repeating a deadpan sing-song rhyme:

> *I'm not a butcher,*
> *I'm not a Yid,*
> *Or yet a foreign skipper.*
> *I'm just your old light-hearted friend,*
> *Yours truly,*
> *Jack the Ripper.*

When the Gangs Came to London

Edgar Wallace

Chapter I

ALL THIS BEGAN on the day in 1929 when 'Kerky' Smith met his backer in the Beach View Cafe and put up a proposition. This was at the time when Big Bill was lording it in Chicago, and everything was wide open and the safe- deposit boxes were bursting with grands. But to cut into the history of these remarkable happenings the historian would probably choose the adventures of a lady in search of a job.

The girl who walked up the two steps of 147 Berkeley Square and rang the bell with such assurance and decision was difficult to place. She was straight of back, so well proportioned that one did not notice how much taller she was than the average. She was at that stage of development when, if you looked to find a woman, you discovered a child or, if prepared for a child, found a woman.

You saw and admired her shape, yet were conscious of no part of it: there was a harmony here not usually found in the attractive. Her feet were small, her hands delicately made, her head finely poised. Her face had an arresting quality which was not beauty in its hackneyed sense. Grey eyes, rather tired-looking; red mouth, larger than perfect. Behind the eyes, a hint of a mind outside the ordinary.

The door opened and a footman looked at her inquiringly, yet his manner was faintly deferential, for she might just as easily have been a duchess as one of the many girls who had called that day in answer to Mr. Decadon's advertisement.

"Is it about the position, miss?" he dared to ask.

"About the advertisement, yes."

The footman looked dubious. "There have been a lot of young ladies here today."

"The situation is filled, then?"

"Oh no, miss," he said hastily. It was a dreadful thought that he should take such a responsibility. "Will you come in?"

She was ushered into a large, cold room, rather like the waiting-room of a Harley Street doctor. The footman came back after five minutes and opened the door.

"Will you come this way, miss?"

She was shown into a library which was something more than an honorary title for a smoke-room, for the walls were lined with books, and one table was completely covered by new volumes still in their dust jackets. The gaunt old man behind the big writing-table looked up over his glasses.

"Sit down," he said. "What's your name?"

"Leslie Ranger."

"The daughter of a retired Indian colonel or something equally aristocratic?" He snapped the inquiry.

"The daughter of a clerk who worked himself to death to support his wife and child decently," she answered, and saw a gleam in the old man's eye.

"You left your last employment because the hours were too long?" He scowled at her.

"I left my last employment because the manager made love to me, and he was the last man in the world I wanted to be made love to by."

"Splendid," he said sarcastically. "You write shorthand at an incredible speed, and your typing has been approved by Chambers of Commerce. There's a typewriter." He pointed a skinny forefinger. "Sit down there and type at my dictation. You'll find paper on the table. You needn't be frightened of me."

"I'm not frightened of you."

"And you needn't be nervous," he boomed angrily.

"I'm not even nervous," she smiled.

She fitted the paper into the machine, turned the platen and waited. He began to dictate with extraordinary rapidity, and the keys rattled under her fingers.

"You're going too fast for me," she said at last.

"Of course I am. All right; come back here." He pointed dictatorially to the chair on the other side of the desk, "What salary do you require?"

"Five pounds a week," she said.

"I've never paid anybody more than three: I'll pay you four."

She got up and gathered her bag. "I'm sorry—"

"Four ten," he said. "All right, five. How many modern languages do you speak?"

"I speak French and I can read German," she said, "but I'm not a linguist."

He pouted his long lips, and looked even more repulsive than ever.

"Five pounds is a lot of money," he said.

"French and German are a lot of languages," said Leslie.

"Is there anything you want to know?" She shook her head. "Nothing about the conditions of service?"

"No. I take it that I'm not resident?"

"You don't want to know what the hours are – no? You disappoint me. If you had asked me what the hours were I should have told you to go to the devil! As it is, you're engaged. Here's your office."

He got up, walked to the end of the big room and opened a recessed door. There was a small apartment here, very comfortably furnished, with a large walnut writing-desk and, by its side, a typing desk. In the angle of two walls was a big safe.

"You'll start tomorrow morning at ten. Your job is not to allow any person to get through to me on the telephone, not to bother me with silly questions, to post letters promptly, and to tell my nephew none of my business."

He waved his hand to the door.

She went, walking on air, had turned the handle and was half-way into the hall when he shouted for her to come back. "Have you got a young man – engaged, or anything?"

She shook her head. "Is it necessary?"

"Most unnecessary," he said emphatically.

In this way Fate brought Leslie Ranger into a circle which was to have vast influence on her own life, bring her to the very verge of hideous death, and satisfy all the unformed desires of her heart.

The next morning she was to meet Edwin Tanner, the nephew against whom Mr. Decadon had warned her. He was a singularly inoffensive, indeed very pleasant person. He was thirty-five, with a broad forehead, pleasant, clean- shaven face and very easily smiling eyes that were usually hidden by his glasses.

He came into her room with a broad beam soon after her arrival.

"I've got to introduce myself, Miss Ranger. I'm Mr. Decadon's nephew."

She was a little surprised that he spoke with an American accent, and apparently he was prepared for this.

"I'm an American. My mother was Mr. Decadon's sister. I suppose he's warned you not to give me any information about his affairs? He always does that, but as there's no information which isn't everybody's property, you needn't take that very seriously. I don't suppose you'll want me, but if you do my house phone number is six. I have a little suite on the top floor, and it will be part of your duty to collect every Saturday morning the rent my uncle charges for the use of his beautiful home – he's no philanthropist, but there's a lot about him that's very likeable."

So Leslie was to discover in the course of the next few months.

Decadon very rarely mentioned his nephew. Only once had she seen them together. She often wondered why Tanner lived in the house at all. He was obviously a man with some private income of his own, and could have afforded a suite in a good London hotel.

Decadon expressed the wonder himself, but his innate frugality prevented his getting rid of a man for whom he had no very deep affection. He was suspicious of Edwin Tanner, who apparently visited England once every year and invariably lived with his uncle.

"Only relation I've got in the world," growled old Decadon one day. "If he had any sense he'd keep away from me!"

"He seems very inoffensive," said the girl.

"How can he be inoffensive when he offends me?" snapped the old man.

He liked her, had liked her from the first. Edwin Tanner neither liked nor disliked her: he gave her the impression of a picture painted by a man who had no imagination. His personality did not live. He was invariably pleasant, but there was something about him that she could not reduce to a formula. Old Decadon once referred to him as a gambler, but explained the term at no length. It was strange that he should employ that term, for he himself was a gambler, had built his fortune on speculations which had, when they were made, the appearance of being hazardous.

It was a strange household, unreal, a little inhuman. Leslie never ceased to be thankful that she lived away from the house, and in comfort, as it happened, for most unexpectedly Mr. Decadon doubled her salary the second week of her service. She had some odd experiences. Decadon had a trick of losing things – valuable books, important leases. And when he lost things he sent for the police; and invariably before the police arrived they were found. This alarming eccentricity of his was unknown to the girl. The first time it happened she was genuinely terrified. A rare manuscript was missing. It was worth £2,000. Mr. Decadon rang up Scotland Yard while the girl searched frantically. There arrived a very young and good-looking chief inspector whose name was Terry Weston – the manuscript was found in the big safe in Leslie's room before he arrived.

"Really, Mr. Decadon," said Terry gently, "this little habit of yours is costing the public quite a lot of money."

"What are the police for?" demanded the old man.

"Not," said Terry, "to run around looking for things you've left in your other suit."

Decadon snorted and went up to his room, where he sulked for the rest of the day. "You're new to this, aren't you?"

"Yes, Mr…"

"Chief Inspector Weston – Terry Weston, I won't ask you to call me Terry."

She did not smile readily, but she smiled now. There was an air of gaiety about him which she had never associated with the police.

For his part he found a quality in her which was very rare in women. If she had told him that she was Mr. Decadon's granddaughter he would not have been surprised. Curiously enough, her undoubted loveliness did not strike him at first. It was later that this haunting characteristic brought him unease.

He met her again. She lunched at a restaurant off Bond Street, He came there one day and sat with her. It was not an accidental meeting as far as he was concerned. No accident was more laboriously designed. Once he met her when she was on her way home. But he never asked her to go out with him, or gave her the impression that he wished to know more of her. If he had, he might not have seen her at all, and he knew this.

"Why do you work for that old grump?" he asked her once.

"He's not really a grump," she defended her employer a little half- heartedly – it was the end of a trying day.

"Is Eddie Tanner a grump?"

She shot a swift look at him. "You mustn't cross-examine me."

"Was I? I'm sorry. You get that way in my job. I'm not really interested." Nor was he – then.

Leslie had little to do: a few letters to write, a few books to read and references to examine. The old man was a great lover of books and spent most of his time reading.

The second unusual incident that occurred in that household took place when she had been there about four months. She had been out to register some letters, and was going up the steps to the house, when a man she had noticed as she passed called her. He was a little man with a large, grotesque bowler hat. His collar was turned up to his chin – it was raining, so there was an excuse for that – and when he spoke it was with a distinctly American accent.

"Say, missie, will you give this to Ed?"

He jerked a letter out of his pocket.

"To Mr. Tanner?"

"Ed Tanner," nodded the man. "Tell him it's from the Big Boy."

She smiled at this odd description, but when she went up in the little elevator to the top floor where Edwin Tanner had his suite, and gave it to him, he neither smiled nor displayed any emotion.

"The Big Boy, eh?" he said thoughtfully. "Who gave it to you – a little man, about so high?"

He seemed particularly anxious to have a description of the messenger. Then she remembered the extraordinary hat he wore, and described it.

"Is that so?" said Mr. Tanner thoughtfully. "Thank you very much, Miss Ranger."

He was always polite to her; never invited her into his suite, was scrupulously careful never to earn the least rebuff.

Events were moving rather rapidly to a climax, but there was no indication of this. When it came with dramatic suddenness, Leslie was to think that the world had gone mad, and she was not to be alone in that view.

* * *

"There are two supreme and dominating factors in life: the first is the love of women, and the second the fear of death – get that?"

Captain Jiggs Allerman, of the Chicago Detective Bureau, sat back in his chair and sent a ring of cigarette smoke whirling upward to the ceiling. He was tall and spare. His face was almost as brown as an Indian's from his native Nevada.

Terry Western grinned: Jiggs was a joy to him.

"You're a chief inspector or sump'n'," Jiggs went on. "Maybe they're takin' children for chief inspectors nowadays. First time I saw you I said to meself, 'Gee, that's a kid for a detective,' and when they told me you were chief inspector I just thought Scotland Yard had gone plumb crazy. How old are you now, Terry?"

"Thirty-five."

Jiggs' nose concertina'd. "That's a lie! If you're more'n twenty-three I don't know anything."

Terry chuckled. "Every year you come to Scotland Yard you pull that crack and it isn't even getting stale. You were telling me about the dominating factors of life."

"Sure – women and death." Jiggs nodded violently. The first have been a racket for years, but up to now only doctors an' funeral parlours have exploited the second. But that racket's on the jig, Terry – I'm tellin' you!"

"I'd hate to believe it," said Terry Weston, "and I'll be interested to know just why you say that."

Jiggs shifted his lank form into a more comfortable position.

"I've got nothing to go on: it's just instinct," he said. "The only thing I can tell you is that rackets are profitable. They're easy money. In the United States of America, my dear native land, umpteen billions a year are spent by the citizens for protection. What's a good racket in the United States must be a good racket in England, or in France. Germany – anywhere you like."

Terry Weston shook his head. "I don't know how to put it to you…" he began.

"Fire away, if you have anything to say about law enforcement."

"I was thinking of prohibition for the moment," said Terry.

Jiggs sniffed. "Bit tough that we can't enforce prohibition, ain't it? I suppose it couldn't happen in this country – that there'd be a law that the police couldn't enforce?"

"I don't think it's possible," said Terry, and Jiggs Allerman laughed silently. "Ever heard of the Street Betting Act?" Terry winced. "There's a law, isn't there? Maybe it's not called that, but it's against the law to bet on the streets, and if a fellow's pinched he's fined and maybe goes to prison. And a thousand million dollars changes hands every year – on the streets. And when you're talking about prohibition, turn your brilliant intellect in that direction, will you? No, Terry, where human nature is human nature, the thing that goes for one goes for all. I can tell you, they've been prospecting in England, some of the big boys in Chicago and New York, and when those guys get busy they go in with both feet. Your little crooks think in tenners, your big men think in thousands and don't often get at 'em. But the crowd I've been dealing with work to eight figures in dollars. Last year they opened a new territory and spent two million dollars seeding it down. No crops came up, so they sold the farm – I'm speaking metaphorically. I mean they cut their losses. That makes you stare. And here's London, England. They could take out a hundred million dollars every year and you'd hardly know they were gone."

It was Jiggs Allerman's favourite argument. He had used it before, and Terry had combated it glibly.

He went out to lunch with his visitor, and a lunch with Jiggs Allerman was an additional stripe to his education.

It was in the Ritz Grill that he saw Elijah Decadon and pointed him out.

"That's the meanest millionaire in the world."

"I could match him," said Jiggs. "Who's the dark fellow with him? He seems kind of familiar to me—"

"That's his nephew. You might know him; he lived in Chicago. Not on the records by any chance?" he asked sarcastically.

Jiggs shook his head. "No, sir. None of the best crooks are. That surprises you, that the big fellers behind the rackets have never seen the inside of a police station? I've got him! Tanner – that's his name, Ed Tanner, playboy, and a regular fellow."

"Does that mean he's good or bad?"

"It means he's just what he is," said Jiggs. "I often wondered where he got his money. His uncle's a millionaire, eh?"

"He didn't get it from him," said Terry grimly. Jiggs shook his head. "You never know."

Mr. Decadon, that severe old man, sat bolt upright in his chair, his frugal lunch before him, his eyes fixed malignantly upon his sister's son. Elijah Decadon was an unusually tall man, powerfully built and, for his age, remarkably well preserved. His straight, ugly mouth, his big, powerful nose, his shaggy grey eyebrows, were familiar to every London restaurateur. The sixpence he left behind for the waiter was as much a part of him as his inevitable dispute over the bill. The bill was not bothering him now.

"You understand, Mr. Edwin Tanner, that the money I have I keep. I want none of your wildcat American schemes for making quick money."

"There's no reason why you should go in for it. Uncle Elijah," said the other good-humouredly, "but I had private advice about this oil-field, and it looks to be good to me. It doesn't benefit me a penny whether you go in or whether you stay out. I thought you were a gambler."

"I'm not your kind of gambler," growled Elijah Decadon. The two men sitting at the other side of the room saw him leave, and thought there had been a quarrel.

"I wonder what those two guys had to talk about. No, I don't know Decadon – I know Ed. He's the biggest psychologist in the United States, believe me, and...Suffering snakes! Here's the Big Boy himself!"

A man had come into the dining-room. He was very thin, of middle height, and perfectly tailored in a large-pattern grey check. His hair was close- cropped; his long, emaciated face, seamed and lined from eye to jaw, was not pleasant to look upon, and the two scars that ran diagonally down the left side of his face did not add to his attractiveness.

Jiggs whistled. He was sitting bolt upright, his eyes bright and eager. "The Big Boy himself! Now what in hell..."

"Who is he?" asked Terry.

"You ought to know him. He'll be over here in a minute."

"He didn't see you..." began Terry.

"I was the first man in the room he saw, believe me! That guy sees all the pins on the floor. Never heard of him? Kerky Smith – or Albuquerque Smith – or Alfred J. Smith, just according to whether you know him or read about him."

Kerky Smith strolled aimlessly along the room and suddenly, with an exaggerated lift of his eyebrows, caught Tanner's eye. Ed Tanner was smiling.

"Lo, Kerky," he said. "When did you get in? Well, who'd have expected to see you?" He held out his hand. Kerky shook it limply, "Will you sit down?"

"Staying long?" asked Kerky, ignoring the invitation.

"I come over here every two years. My uncle lives here."

"Is that so?" Kerky Smith's voice was almost sympathetic. "Left Chicago in a hurry, didn't you, Ed?"

"Not so," said the other coolly.

Kerky was leaning on the table, looking down at Tanner. On his thin lips was a peculiarly knowing smile. "Heard you were in the bread line. Caught in the market for two million, someone told me. Staying long?"

Ed leaned back in his chair. He was chewing a toothpick. "Just about as long as I darn well please," he said pleasantly. "Jiggs is having an eyeful."

Kerky Smith nodded. "Yeah. I seen him – damn rat! Who's he talking to?"

"A Scotland Yard man."

Kerky Smith drew himself up and laid his long, slim paw on Ed's shoulder. "You're going to be a good boy, ain't you – stand in or get out. You'll want a lot of money for this racket, Ed – more money than you've got, boy." A friendly pat, and he was strolling over to where Allerman sat. "Why, Jiggs!"

He hastened forward, his face beaming. Jiggs Allerman kicked out a chair.

"Sit down, you yellow thief," he said calmly. "What are you doing in London? The British Government issue visas pretty carelessly, I guess."

Kerky smiled. He had a beautiful set of teeth, many of which were gold- plated. "Wouldn't you say a thing like that! You might introduce me to your friend."

"He knows all about you. Meet Chief Inspector Terry Weston. If you stay long enough he'll know you by your; finger-prints. What's the racket, Kerky?"

Kerky shrugged his thin shoulders. "Listen, chief, would I be here on a racket? This is my vacation, and I'm just over looking around for likely propositions. I've been bearing the market, and how! I make my money that way. I'm not like you Chicago coppers – taking a cut from the racketeer and pretending you're chasing him."

Into Jiggs Allerman's eye came a look that was half stone and half fire. "Some day I'll be grilling you, big boy, up at police headquarters, and I'll remember what you say."

Kerky Smith flashed a golden smile. "Listen, chief, you take me all wrong. Can't you stand a joke! I'm all for law and order. Why, I saved your life once. Some of them North Side hoodlums was going to give you the works, and I got in touch with a pal who stopped it."

He had a trick of dropping his hand casually on shoulders, He did so now as he rose. "You don't know your best friend, kid."

"My best friend is a forty-five," said Jiggs with suppressed malignity, "and the day he puts you on the slab I'm going to put diamonds all round his muzzle."

Kerky laughed. "Ain't you the boy!" he said, and strolled off with a cheerful wave of his hand.

Jiggs watched him sit down at a table, where he was joined by a very pretty blonde girl.

"That's the kind you don't know in England – killers without mercy, without pity, without anything human to 'em! And never had a conviction, Terry. He's always been in Michigan when something happened in Illinois, or floatin' around Indiana when there was a killing in Brooklyn. You don't know the cold-bloodedness of 'em – I hope you never will. Hear him talking about saving my life? I'll tell you sump'n'. Four of his guns have made four different attempts to get me. One of his aides, Dago Pete, followed me two thousand miles and missed me by that." He snapped his fingers. "Got him? Of course I got him! He was eight days dying, and every day was a Fourth of July to me."

Terry was hardened, but he shivered at the brutality of it; and yet he realised that only Jiggs and his kind knew just what they were up against. "Thank the Lord we haven't got that type here…" he began.

"Wait," said Jiggs ominously.

Terry had hardly got to his office the next morning, when the Assistant Commissioner phoned through to him. "Go down to Berkeley Square and see old Decadon," he said.

"What's he lost, sir?" asked Terry, almost offensively

"It isn't a loss, it's a much bigger thing…the girl phoned through, and she asked whether you would go."

Terry drove to Berkeley Square; Leslie must have been watching for him, for she opened the door herself. "Lost something?" he asked.

"No, it's something rather serious, or else it's a very bad joke. It's a letter he received this morning. He's upstairs in his room, and he asked me to tell you all about it. As a matter of fact I can tell you as much as he can."

She led the way into her own little office, unlocked a drawer, and took out a printed blank on which certain words had been inserted in handwriting. Terry took it and read.

"MUTUAL PROTECTION

"These are dangerous days for folks with property and money, and they need protection. The Citizens' Welfare Society offers this to Mr.…."

Here the name of Elijah Decadon was filled in in ink.

"They undertake to protect his life and his property, to prevent any illegal interference with his liberty, and they demand in return the sum of £50,000. If Mr.…."

Again the name of Elijah Decadon was filled in in ink.

"Will agree, he will put an announcement in The Times of Wednesday the letters 'WJS.' and the word 'Agree.' followed by the initials of the person advertising."

Here followed in heavy black type this announcement

"If you do not comply with our request within thirty days, or if you call in the police, or consult them, directly or indirectly, you will be killed."

There was no signature printed or otherwise.

Terry read it again until he had memorised it, then he folded it and put it in his pocket. "Have you the envelope in which this came?"

She had this. The address was typewritten; the type was new; the postmark was E.C.1; the envelope itself was of an ordinary commercial type. Leslie was looking at him anxiously.

"Is it a joke?" she asked.

"I don't know." Terry was doubtful. "It came by the early morning post. Does anybody else know about this being received? Mr. Eddie Tanner, for example, does he know anything about it?"

"Nobody except Mr. Decadon and myself," said the girl. "Mr. Decadon is terribly upset. What had we better do, Mr. Weston?"

"You can call me Terry, unless you feel very bad about it. Of course, no money will be sent, and you did the right thing when you sent for the police."

She shook her head. "I'm not so sure about that," she said, to his surprise. "I'm willing to confess that I tried to persuade Mr. Decadon not to phone you."

"That's not like a law-abiding citizen," he smiled. "No, you did the right thing. It's probably a bluff, and anyway we'll see that no harm comes to Elijah Decadon. I'd better have a talk with him."

He went upstairs, and after considerable delay Decadon unlocked the door of his bedroom and admitted him. The old man was more than perturbed, he was in a state of panic. Terry telephoned to Scotland Yard, and three officers were detailed to guard the premises.

"I've asked Mr. Decadon not to go out, but if he does, the two men on duty in the front of the house are not to let him out of their sight."

He put through a second call to Jiggs Allerman's hotel, asking the American to meet him at Scotland Yard. When he got to headquarters Jiggs had already found the most comfortable chair in the room.

"Here's something for your big brain to work on," said Terry.

He handed the printed letter to the visitor. Jiggs read it, his brows knit. "When did this come?"

"This morning," said Terry. "Now what is it? Something serious or a little joke?"

Jiggs shook his head. "No, sir, that's no joke. That's the pay-and-live racket. It's been worked before, and it's been pretty successful. So that's the game!"

"Do you think there's any real danger to Decadon?"

"Yes, sir." Jiggs Allerman was emphatic. "And I'll tell you why. This racket doesn't really start working till somebody's killed. You've got to have a couple of dead people to prove you mean business. Maybe a lot of others have had this notification, and they'll be coming in all day, but it's just as likely that only one has been sent out and Decadon is the bad example." He took the paper again, held it up to the light, but found no watermark. "I've never seen it done this way before – a printed blank – but it's got its reason. Anyway, it's an intimation to everybody that these birds mean business."

Terry got an interview with the Commissioner and took Jiggs along with him. The Chief was interested but rather sceptical. "We don't expect this sort of thing to happen in our country, Captain Allerman," he said.

"Why shouldn't it?" demanded Jiggs. "Say, Commissioner, get this idea out of your head about England being a little country surrounded by water, and that it's difficult for people to leave once they're known. This isn't an ordinary felony. When the shooting starts it'll start good and plenty, and all the theories about this sort of thing not being done in England – will go sky- ways!"

Usually Leslie left about five o'clock in the afternoon. Decadon had been very nervous and morose all the afternoon, and she was so sorry for him that, when he suggested she might stay late, she readily agreed. She had plenty of work to do. Ed Tanner saw her coming back from her tea and was surprised.

"Why, what's keeping you so late tonight. Miss Ranger? Is the old gentleman busy?"

She made some explanation, which did not seem convincing even to herself.

Tanner had not been told; the old man had been very insistent about this.

At about seven o'clock that evening she heard Tanner's voice in the library, and she wondered whether Mr. Decadon had told him. They were talking for quite a long time. After a while she heard the squeak of the elevator as it went up to Eddie Tanner's suite. A little later the bell rang, and she went into the library.

The old man was writing rapidly. He always used sheets of foolscap, and wrote in a very neat and legible hand for one so old. He had half covered the sheet when she came in.

"Get Danes," he said, naming one of his footmen. "Ring for him, my girl," he went on impatiently. "Ring for him!" She pressed the bell and Danes came in. "Put your name, your occupation, and your address here, Danes."

He pointed to the bottom of the paper, and Danes signed. "You know what you're signing, you fool, don't you? You're witnessing my signature, and you haven't seen my signature," stormed the irritable old gentleman. "Watch this. Miss What's-your-name."

He invariably addressed Leslie by this strange title, for he could not remember names.

He took up a pen and signed it with a flourish, and Danes obediently put his name, address and occupation by the side of the signature. "That will do, Danes."

The man was going, when Leslie said quietly: "If this is a will I think you will find that both signatures must be attested together and in the presence of one another."

He glared at her. "How do you know it's a will?" he demanded, He had covered the writing over with one big hand.

"I'm guessing it's a will," she smiled. "I can't imagine any other kind of document…"

"That will do – don't talk about it," he grumbled. "Sign here." He watched her as she wrote. "'Ranger' – that's it," he muttered. "Never can remember it. Thank you."

He blotted the sheet, dismissed the footman with a wave of his hand and thrust the document into a drawer of his desk.

Presently he frowned at her. "I've left you a thousand pounds," he said, and she laughed. "What the devil are you laughing at?"

"I'm laughing because I shan't get the thousand pounds. The fact that I've witnessed your will invalidates the bequest."

He blinked at her, "I hate people who know so much about the law," he complained.

After Leslie was dismissed he rang the bell himself, had Danes up again and the cook, and procured a new witness. She did not know this till afterwards. At half-past eight she was tidying up her desk when she heard a faint click, and looked up. It seemed to be in the room. She heard the click again, and this time she heard the sound of the old man's voice, raised in anger. He was expostulating with somebody. She could not hear who it was.

And then she heard a piercing cry of fear, and two shots fired in rapid succession. For a moment she stood paralysed, then she ran to the door which led to the library and tried to open it. It was locked. She ran to the passage door; that was locked too. She flew to the wall, pressed the bell, heard a running of feet, and Danes hammered on the door. "What is it, miss?"

"The door's locked. The key's on the outside," she cried. In another second it turned.

"Go into the library and see what's happened." Danes and the second footman ran along, and returned with the report that the library door was locked and that the key was missing.

It was an eccentricity of Mr. Decadon that he kept keys in all locks, usually on the outside of doors. With trembling hands she took that which had opened her own door and, kneeling down, looked through the keyhole into the library. Carefully she thrust in her own key and pushed. That which was on the inside of the door had by chance been left so that the thrust pushed it out. As it dropped on the floor she unlocked the door with a heart that was quaking and ran into the room. She took three paces and stopped. Old Elijah Decadon lay across the desk in a pool of blood, and she knew before she touched him that he was dead.

Chapter II

TERRY HAD ARRANGED to go that night with Jiggs to see a musical comedy, and he was just leaving the house when the urgent call came through. Fortunately Jiggs, who was collecting him, drove up at that moment, and the two men went straight to Berkeley Square.

There was already a crowd outside the house. Somehow the news had got around. Terry pushed his way to the steps and was instantly admitted.

The two plain-clothes officers who had been on duty outside the house were in the passage, and their report was a simple one. Nobody had entered or left within half an hour of the shooting.

Terry went in and saw the body. The old man had been shot at close quarters by a heavy-calibre revolver, which lay on the floor within a few feet of the desk. It had not been moved.

He sent for a pair of sugar-tongs and, after marking the position of the revolver with a piece of chalk, he lifted the weapon on to a small table and turned on a powerful reading-lamp. It was a heavy, rather old-fashioned Colt revolver. As far as he could see, there were still four unused cartridges. What was more important, there were distinct fingerprints on the shiny steel plate between the butt and the chambers.

There was something more than this – a set of fingerprints on a sheet of foolscap paper. They were visible even before they were dusted. There was a third set on the polished mahogany edge of the desk, as though somebody had been resting their fingers on it.

Terry went into the girl's room and interviewed her. She was as pale as death, but very calm, and told him all she knew.

"Has Tanner been told?"

She nodded.

"Yes, he came down and saw…poor Mr. Decadon, and then went up to his room again. He said nothing had to be touched, but by this time of course the police were in the house. Mr. Tanner didn't know that they'd been outside watching."

He sent one of the servants for him. Ed Tanner came down, a very grave man. He went without hesitation into the library.

"It's dreadful…simply shocking," he said. "I can't believe it."

"Have you seen this revolver before?" Terry pointed to the gun on the table. To his amazement, Tanner nodded.

"Yes," he said quietly, "that's my revolver. I'm pretty certain of it. I didn't touch it when I came into the room, but I could almost swear to it. A month ago a suitcase of mine was stolen at the railway station, and it contained this revolver. I notified the police of my loss and gave them the number of the missing weapon."

Terry remembered the incident because the theft of firearms came within his department, and he had a distinct recollection of the loss being reported.

"You haven't seen the pistol since?"

"No, sir."

"Mr. Tanner," said Terry quietly, "on that revolver and on the desk there are certain fingerprints. In a few moments the fingerprint department will be here with their apparatus. Have you any objections to giving the police a set of your fingerprints in order that they may be compared with those found on the revolver?"

Eddie Tanner shook his head with a smile.

"I haven't the least objection. Inspector," he said.

Almost as he said the words the fingerprint men came in, carrying their mystery box and Terry, taking the sergeant in charge aside, explained what he wanted. In a few minutes Tanner's fingerprints were on a plain sheet of paper, and the sergeant set to work with his camera men making the record of the other prints which had been found. The easiest to do were those on the sheet of foolscap. A dusting with powder brought them out clearly. The sergeant examined them, and Terry saw a look of wonder in his face.

"Why, these are the same as that gentleman's."

"What?" said Terry. He took up the revolver, made a dusting, and again examined it. "These also."

Terry looked at the imperturbable Mr. Tanner, He was smiling slightly.

"I was in this room at seven o'clock, but I didn't touch the paper or the desk or any article in the room," he said. "I hope you'll realise, Mr. Weston" – he turned to Terry – "that the fact that I was here at seven o'clock could be offered as a very simple explanation of those fingerprints – apart, of course, from those on the revolver. But I couldn't possibly have made them, because I was wearing gloves. In fact, I intended going out, and changed my mind after interviewing my uncle."

"What was the interview about?" asked Terry.

There was a pause. "It concerned his will. He called me down to tell me that he intended making a will for the first time in his life."

"Did he tell you how he was disposing of his property?"

Tanner shook his head. "No."

Terry went out in search of the girl, and learned to his surprise that the will had been made and witnessed. She had not seen its contents, and knew nothing about it except that it was a document which she had witnessed, and in which she had been left a thousand pounds.

"I told him the fact I had witnessed the will invalidated it, as I was a beneficiary," she said.

"Have you any idea where he put it?"

She could answer this readily. "In the top left-hand drawer of his desk."

Terry went back to the chamber of death. The divisional surgeon had arrived and was examining the body. "Do you know how your uncle was leaving his money in the will?"

"No, I don't," repeated Tanner. "He told me nothing."

Terry went round the desk and pulled open the top left-hand drawer. It was empty! He went back to Tanner. "You realise how serious this is, Mr. Tanner? If what you say is true, and your uncle never made a will, you, as his only relative, are the sole legatee. If, on the other hand, your uncle made a will, as he undoubtedly did, it is quite possible that you were disinherited, and the destruction of the will, as well as the killing of your uncle, are circumstances which suggest a very important motive."

Tanner nodded. "Does that mean…"

"It merely means that I shall ask you to go with an officer to Scotland Yard, and to wait there until I come. It doesn't mean you're under arrest."

Tanner thought for a moment. "Can I see my attorney?"

Terry shook his head. "That is not customary in this country. When any definite charge is made you may have a lawyer, but it's by no means certain that any charge will be made. The circumstances are suspicious. You agree that the revolver is yours, and the sergeant says that the finger-prints resemble yours; though of course that will be subject to a more careful scrutiny, and I am afraid there is no other course than that which I am now taking."

"That I understand," said Tanner, and went off with one of the officers.

Jiggs Allerman had been a silent witness to the proceedings, so silent that Terry had forgotten his presence. Now he went across to where the American was standing watching the photographing of the body.

"Is this a gang killing or just plain interested murder? I can't decide."

Jiggs shook his head. "The only thing that strikes me as odd are those finger-prints on the foolscap paper. Do you notice how coarse they are?"

The finger-print sergeant looked round. "That struck me too, Mr. Weston. The lines are curiously blurred; you'd think the impressions had been purposely made, and that whoever put them there laid his hand down deliberately, intending to make them."

"That's just what I was going to say," said Jiggs. "And the gun on the floor – whoever heard of a gangster leaving his gun behind? He'd as soon think of leaving his visiting-card."

Terry's own sergeant had come on the scene, and to him he delegated the task of making a careful search of the house.

"I particularly want Tanner's room gone through with a fine tooth-comb," he said. "Look for cartridges or any evidence that may connect him with the crime. I'm particularly anxious to find a will made by Decadon this evening, so you'll make a search of fireplaces or any other place where such a will might have been destroyed."

After the body had been removed and the grosser traces of the crime had been obliterated he called in Leslie. She was feeling the reaction: her face was white, her lips were inclined to tremble.

"You go home, young lady. I'll send an officer with you – and God knows I envy him! – and be here tomorrow morning at your usual hour. There'll be a whole lot of questions asked you, but you'll have to endure that."

"Poor Mr. Decadon!" Her voice quivered.

"I know, I know," he said soothingly, and dared put his arm about her shoulder.

She did not resent this, and his familiarity gave him the one happy moment of his day.

"You've got to forget all about it tonight; and tomorrow we'll look facts more squarely in the face. The only thing I want to know is, did you hear Tanner talking in the library, and at what time?"

She could place this exactly, and it corresponded with the story Tanner had told.

"And you heard voices just before the shooting?"

"Mr. Decadon's," she said, "not the other's."

"You heard the click as the key was turned, both on the library door and on your own?"

She nodded.

"The first click was on your own door?" he went on. "That is to say, the corridor door. The last click was the door into the library. So we may suppose that somebody walked along the corridor, locked your door first, went into the library, and then, either known or unknown to Mr. Decadon, locked the communicating door between library and office?"

She nodded again. "I suppose so," she said wearily.

He took her by the arm.

"That's enough for tonight," he said. "You go home, go to bed and dream of anybody you like, preferably me."

She tried to smile, but it was a miserable failure. When she had gone: "What do you make of that, Jiggs?"

"Very much what you make of it, old pal," said Jiggs. "The murderer came from the back of the house…"

"It might have been Tanner," suggested Terry, and Jiggs nodded.

"Sure. It might also have been one of the servants. Let's take a look at these premises."

They went along the corridor to the far end. The elevator was here on the left. On the right was a flight of stairs leading down to the kitchen. Under the stairs was a large locker, containing overcoats, waterproofs, umbrellas and rubber over-shoes. Jiggs opened the door of the elevator, switched on the light, and the two men got in. Closing the door, he pressed the button and the lift shot up to the top floor, where it stopped.

Apparently there were no intermediate stations, and no other floor was served by this conveyance.

They got out on a small landing. On the left was a half-glass door marked 'Fire.' Terry tried this and it opened readily. As far as he could see, a narrow flight of iron stairs zig-zagged to a small courtyard. Terry came in, closed the door and went on to Tanner's apartment, which was being searched by the sergeant and an assistant.

"Nothing here that I can find, sir," reported the officer, "except these, and I can't make them out."

He pointed to a chair on which were placed a pair of muddy and broken shoes. They were the most dilapidated examples of footwear that Terry remembered seeing.

"No, they weren't on the chair when I found them: they were under it. I put them up to examine them more closely."

They were in Tanner's bedroom, and the sergeant drew attention to the fact that a small secretaire was open and that a number of papers were on the floor. Several pigeon-holes must have been emptied in some haste.

"It looks as if the room has been carefully searched, or else that Tanner has been in a hurry to find something."

Terry looked at the shoes again and shook his head.

"Did you find any burnt paper in the grate?"

"No, sir," said the sergeant. "No smell of burnt paper either."

"Listen, Terry," said Jiggs suddenly. "You've had a couple of coppers outside since when?"

"Since about half-past ten this morning."

"Any at the back of the premises?"

"One," said Terry.

"It's easier to get past one than two," said Jiggs. "Let's go down the fire escape and see if anybody could have got in that way. You notice all the windows are open in this room? It's a bit chilly, too."

Terry had noticed that fact.

"I don't think the idea of the fire-escape is a bad one," he said, and the two men went out to investigate.

Terry left his companion outside the elevator door while he went down to borrow a torch from one of the policemen. When he came back the fire-escape door was open and Jiggs had disappeared. He flashed his lamp down and saw the American on the second landing below. "That's better than matches," he said. "Look at this, Terry."

Terry ran down the stairs to where his companion was standing. Jiggs had something in his hand – a rubber overshoe.

In the light of the torch Terry made a quick examination. The shoe was an old one, and subsequently proved to be one of the unfortunate Decadon's.

"What's it doing here?" asked Jiggs.

They went down the next two flights, but found nothing. At the bottom the stairs turned abruptly into the courtyard. Jiggs was walking ahead, Terry behind with a light showing him the way.

"There's a door in that wall. Where does it lead to-a mews?" asked Jiggs. "That's what you call it…"

Suddenly he stopped.. "For God's sake!" he said softly. "Look at that!"

Almost at their feet was a huddled heap. It was a man, ill-clad, his trousers almost in rags. On one foot was a rubber overshoe, on the other a slipper. His hat had fallen some distance from him.

Terry moved the light; he saw the back of the head and the crimson pool that lay beyond.

"Here's our second dead man," said Terry. "Who is he?"

Jiggs leaped over the body and reached for the lamp. His examination was a careful one. "If he isn't a tramp he looks like one. Shot at close range through the back of the head. A small-calibre pistol…dead half an hour. Can you beat that?"

Terry found a door which opened into the kitchen and sent one of the horrified servants in search of the police surgeon, whom he had left writing his report at Leslie's desk. While he awaited his coming he scrutinised the dead man's feet.

He wore soft leather slippers, which were a little too small for him, and over these had evidently drawn the overshoes.

A detective came running out, and Terry sent him back to bring the fingerprint outfit. He then began a careful search of the dead man's clothes. In the left-hand pocket of the shabby overcoat he found a small metal box, rather like a child's money-box. It was black-japanned and fastened with a small lock. Terry tried to open it, but failed. "It wouldn't have been much use as an indicator of flnger-prints," he said. "It's been in his pocket. Did you find anything else, Jiggs?"

Allerman had taken up the search where Terry left off. The inspector heard the jingle of coins, and Jiggs held out his hand.

"That's an unusual phenomenon in England," he said, and Terry gasped.

There were about ten or twelve English sovereigns. "In the waistcoat pocket, wrapped up in a piece of paper, "and this man is a hobo or nothing."

They left the body to the care of the surgeon and drove back to Scotland Yard in a squad car. Tanner was waiting in Terry's room. He was smoking a cigarette and reading a newspaper, which he put down as they entered.

"Did you find the will?" he asked.

"No, but we found one or two other things," said Terry. "When were you in your bedroom last?"

Tanner's eyebrows rose. "Do you mean in Berkeley Square? I haven't been there since morning."

Terry eyed him keenly. "Are you sure?" The man nodded. "Have you been to your desk for anything?"

"Desk? Oh, you mean the little secretaire. No."

"Was there anything valuable there?"

Eddie Tanner considered. "Yes, there were twelve pounds in gold. It's been amusing me to collect English sovereigns since your people came off the gold standard. As for me going into my bedroom, I've just remembered that when I tried to get into the room this afternoon it was locked. I thought the housekeeper had locked it, but I didn't bother to send for her. She does lock up sometimes. Mr. Decadon had a servant who stole things a few months ago – I wasn't in the house at the time, but I've heard about it – and apparently there was quite an epidemic of caution. Has the money gone?"

"I have it in my pocket, as a matter of fact," said Terry grimly, "but I can't give it to you yet."

He took from his pocket the little tin box, went to his desk, took out a collection of keys and tried them on the lock. Presently he found one that fitted, and the box opened. One side fell down; behind it was a small linen pad. When he pushed back the lid he saw the contents.

"A rubber stamp outfit!" he said in surprise.

Jiggs, looking over his shoulder, picked out one of the three wooden- backed stamps and examined it in amazement.

"Well, I'll go to...!"

They were the rubber impressions of fingerprints, and their surface still bore a thin film of moisture.

"That's where the fingerprints came from," said Terry slowly. "The man who killed Decadon stopped to fix the blame on somebody." He looked at Eddie Tanner. "You must have some pretty powerful enemies, Mr, Tanner."

Tanner smiled. "I've got one," he said softly, "and he's got a whole lot of friends."

He looked up, caught Jiggs' questioning eye, and smiled again.

At three o'clock in the morning there was a conference of all heads of Scotland Yard, and it was a delicate compliment to Jiggs Allerman's prescience and popularity that he was admitted.

The fingerprint officer on duty brought one or two interesting facts.

"The tramp has been identified," he said. "His name is William Board, alias William Crane, alias Walter Cork. He has seven convictions for vagrancy and five for petty larceny."

"He's a tramp, then?" said Terry.

"That's all we know about him," said the fingerprint man.

Jiggs shook his head vigorously.

"He committed no murder," he said. "I never met a hobo who was quick enough for that kind of crime. He may have put the prints on. How did he get into the yard?"

The Assistant Commissioner, wise in the ways of criminals, had a logical explanation to give.

"The man who killed Mr. Decadon also killed Board. He was used as a tool and destroyed because he would have made a dangerous witness. He was shot with a powerful air-pistol at close range, according to the doctor. You've released Tanner?"

Terry nodded. "Yes, we couldn't very well keep him after we found the stamps. The only tenable theory is that Board broke into the house earlier in the day, before the police came on the scene, and concealed himself in Tanner's bedroom. He was wearing Tanner's slippers and a pair of overshoes which were admittedly in the bedroom. What I can't understand is why he should take that risk. Tanner was in and out of the suite all day."

"Suppose Tanner had him there?" said Jiggs. They looked at him.

"Why should Tanner have him there?" asked Terry scornfully. "To manufacture evidence against himself?"

"That sounds illogical, doesn't it?" said Jiggs with strange gentleness. "Maybe at this late hour I've got a little tired and foolish. One thing is certain, gentlemen: the first shot in the campaign has been fired. Tomorrow morning's newspapers are going to carry the story of the demand for fifty thousand pounds – old man Decadon is the awful example that will start the ball rolling. The point is, will it start both balls rolling? I rather think it will."

The Assistant Commissioner laughed. "You're being mysterious, Jiggs."

"Ain't I just!" said Jiggs.

Terry went back to his office, and sat down in the quietude of that hour and worked out the puzzle of the day. It was not going to be an easy one to solve, and he had a depressed feeling that Jiggs' pessimistic prophecy might be fulfilled.

He was sitting with his head on his hands, near to being asleep, when the telephone rang and jerked him awake. The Scotland Yard operator spoke to him. "There's a woman on the phone who wishes to speak to you, sir. I think she's talking from a call box."

"Who is she?" asked Terry.

"Mrs. Smith. But I don't think you know her. Shall I put you through?"

Terry heard a click, and then an anxious voice hailed him.

"Is that Mr. Terry, of Scotland Yard, the detective?"

It was rather a common voice.

"Yes, I'm Mr. Terry Weston."

"Excuse me for bothering you, sir, but is Miss Ranger coming home soon? I'm getting a little anxious."

"Miss Ranger?" Terry sat up. "What do you mean – is she coming home soon? She went home a long time ago."

"Yes, sir, but she was called out again by a Scotland Yard gentleman – an American gentleman. They told her you wanted to see her."

"What time was this?" asked Terry, a little breathlessly.

She thought it was about ten, but was vague on the subject. "She'd only just got in, and was having a bite of supper, which I made her have…"

"How long after she came in did she go out?"

The woman thought it was a quarter of an hour.

"Where do you live?"

She told him. It was a little street in Bloomsbury.

"I'll be there in five minutes," said Terry. "Just wait for me, will you?"

He rang for a car, and went down the stairs two at a time. In less than five minutes he was in the neat parlour of the landlady. She could only tell him substantially the story she had already told.

There had been a knock at the door and she had answered it. A man was standing there, and by the kerb was a car and another man. He said he was from Scotland Yard and spoke distinctly with an American accent. He said Mr. Terry Weston wished the young lady to go to the Yard immediately. She remembered definitely that he said "Weston."

"Would you recognise him again?" asked Terry, his heart sinking.

She did not think so. It was a very dark night and she had not taken much notice of him. The girl had gone almost at once. She had been particularly impressed by the fact that the two men had raised their hats to her as she came out of the house. She thought it was so nice to see detectives being polite to a lady.

"They drove off towards Bloomsbury Square," she said.

She had stood at the door and watched the car go. Then, to Terry's astonishment: "The car was numbered XYD7000."

"You noticed the number?" he asked quickly. The landlady had a weakness for counting up numbers on number-plates. She had, she said, a faith – and a very complete faith – that if the numbers added up to four and she saw two fours in succession, she was going to have a lucky day. She betted on races, she added unnecessarily.

Terry went round to the call box from which she had telephoned, got through to the Yard and handed in the number. "Find out who owns this, and ask the Flying Squad to supply me with a unit."

By the time he reached the Yard the information was available. The car was owned by the Bloomsbury and Holborn Car Hire Company, but it was impossible to discover from their garage to whom it was hired at the moment. All inquiries in this direction were suddenly blocked when a report came up that a car bearing this number, and genuinely hired to a doctor, had been stolen that night in Bloomsbury Park.

"That's that!" groaned Terry. "Warn all stations to look for it and arrest the driver and its occupants."

Then began a feverish search which was almost without parallel in the annals of the Flying Squad. Crew after crew were brought in on urgent summons, and shot off east, west, north and south.

In the morning, as day was breaking, a motorcyclist patrol saw a car abandoned in a field by the side of the Colnbrook by-pass. He went forward to investigate, and instantly recognised the number for which the whole of the Metropolitan police had been searching. He jumped off his machine and ran forward. The blinds were drawn. He pulled open the door and saw a girl lying in one corner of the car. She was fast asleep. It was Leslie Ranger.

* * *

Leslie had had no idea that anything was wrong till the speed of the car increased and one of the two 'detectives' who were sitting with her leaned forward and began to pull down the blinds.

"Don't do that," she said.

"You just sit quiet, missie, and don't talk," said the man, "and if you just sit quiet and don't talk you ain't going to be hurt – see?"

She nearly fainted when she realised that she had been the victim of a trick.

"Where are we going?" she asked, but they did not answer. In fact, neither of the men spoke.

They must have travelled for the better part of an hour, when the car swerved suddenly round a sharp corner, followed a bumpy road, turned again to the left and stopped. One of the men took a scarf from his pocket and blindfolded her, and she submitted meekly. She was assisted from the car, walked along a paved pathway and into a house.

It must have been a small house, because the two men had to walk behind her, one of them guiding her by her elbows. She turned sharp left again, and guessed that she was in a room where there were several men. She could smell the pungent odour of cigar smoke.

"Tell her to sit down," said somebody in a whisper, and, when she had obeyed: "Now, miss, perhaps you'll tell us what happened at old man Decadon's house. You'll tell us the truth and you'll answer any questions that are put to you, and nothing's going to happen to you."

The man who said all this spoke in a sort of harsh, high whisper. He was obviously disguising his voice.

She was terribly frightened, but felt that there was nothing to be gained by refusing to speak or by suppressing anything she knew; so she told them very frankly and freely, and answered their questions without hesitation.

They seemed most interested and insistent in their inquiries about Eddie Tanner. Where had he been? Was she sure they were his fingerprints? When she told about the revolver on the floor somebody laughed, and the questioner snarled an angry admonition, after which there was silence. This inquisition lasted two hours. They brought her hot coffee, for which she was grateful, and eventually she said:

"All right, kid. You can tell the police all about this – there's no reason why you shouldn't. But don't tell more'n the truth, or ever try to line me up by my voice."

They had taken her back to the car and made her comfortable, and that was all she remembered, except that another car was following them all the time. She fell asleep while the vehicle was still in motion, and knew nothing until the policeman woke her up.

Terry expected something big in the morning Press, but he was hardly prepared for the importance which the newspapers gave to the two murders. "Is this the beginning of a new era of lawlessness?" asked the Megaphone blackly.

Fleet Street seemed to recognise instantly the significance of the two crimes which shocked London that morning. 'The Beginning of the Rackets' was a headline in one journal. Fleet Street, living on print, was impressed by print. That notice, which had been sent to Elijah Decadon, neatly printed in blue ink, spelt organisation on a large scale.

And yet Scotland Yard received no intimation that any other rich or prominent man had had a similar warning. From one end of England to the other the newspapers were shocked and wrathful, and their leading articles revealed an energy to combat the new peril which impressed even Jiggs Allerman.

The tramp's antecedents had been quickly traced. He had been living in a lodging-house, but had not been to his room for two nights prior to the murder. He was a fairly reticent man, and had not discussed his business with anybody.

During the night the Assistant Commissioner had been on the telephone to Chicago, and had secured permission to attach Jiggs Allerman to the Scotland Yard staff as a temporary measure. Jiggs, with his new authority, had spent all the morning at the house in Berkeley Square. He came back to the Yard to find Terry reading the newspapers. "Did you find anything?" asked Terry.

"Yeah." Jiggs nodded. "The old man had fitted up a kitchenette for Tanner. There's a gas-stove there."

He took out of his pocket an envelope, opened it carefully and picked out a strand of thin wire six inches in length.

"Found this wound around one of the burners, and outside the top landing of the fire-escape there's a hook fixed into the wall, and fixed recently."

"What do you make of that?" asked Terry.

Jiggs scratched his chin. "Why, I make a lot of that," he said. "What was the direction of the wind last night?"

Terry took up a newspaper and turned the pages till he came to the weather report. "Moderate north-west."

"Grand. What's been puzzling me more than anything else has been the disappearance of the air-pistol. That had to be got rid of pretty quick, and the tramp Board wasn't the kind of man to think quick and, anyway, he didn't get rid of it! But he helped."

Terry frowned at him. "You're being a little mysterious, Jiggs."

"I know I am," admitted Jiggs. "That's my speciality." He leaned down over the table and spoke emphatically. "There was only one possible way that gun could be got rid of, and I knew just how it had happened when one of the maids in the next house said somebody had smashed the window of her bedroom a few minutes after the murder was committed – I'm talking about the murder of the tramp, and the time we've got to guess at." He took a pencil from his pocket and made a rough plan. "There's the courtyard. One side of it's made up of the back premises of the next-door house. The maid slept on the fourth floor; she'd gone to bed early because she had to be up at six.

"She was just going off to sleep, when her window was smashed in by somebody on the outside. When I say 'somebody' I mean 'something.' Now the fourth floor of that house is one floor higher – roughly fifteen feet – than the top floor in Decadon's house, and when I heard about that window being smashed and found the wire on the gas burner and the hook on the wall, I got your people to phone every balloon-maker in London and find out who made a toy balloon that could lift a couple of pounds when it was filled with coal- gas."

Terry stared at him. "I've heard of that being done once."

"Now you've heard of it being done twice," Jiggs finished for him. "The balloon was filled in the kitchenette; the end of it was tied round the burner – the gas pressure is pretty high in that neighbourhood. Just before the murder the mouth was tied, the balloon was taken out on to the fire-escape and fastened with a string or wire to the hook. The hook was upside down; that is to say, the point of it was downward. After Board was killed the murderer tied the gun to the balloon and let it go. The wind must have been fresh then, and as it went upwards the pistol smashed against the window of the housemaid's room. You know my methods, Weston," he added sardonically.

Terry figured this out for a few minutes. Then

"But if your theory is correct, the murderer must have come up the fire- escape after he'd killed Board."

Jiggs nodded slowly. "You've said it, kid."

"Do you still believe that Tanner was the murderer?"

Jiggs smiled. "It's no question of believing, it's knowing. Sure he was the murderer!"

"And that he deliberately left evidence to incriminate himself?"

"Well, he's free, isn't he?" demanded Jiggs. "And clear of suspicion. You haven't a case to go to the Grand Jury, have you? Those stamps with his fingerprints on let him out. You couldn't get a conviction. And in a way you've taken all suspicion from him, made him a victim instead of a murderer. He's free – that's the answer. I've told you, he's the greatest psychologist I've met. Suppose you hadn't found fingerprints or a gun, where would suspicion have pointed – at Ed! There's the will gone, and Ed's the old man's legatee at law. What he did was to bring suspicion on himself at once, and destroy it at once. How far is the sea from here?"

"About fifty miles," said Terry.

Jiggs whistled softly to himself. "Ed never made a mistake. The gasbag he used would stay up two hours, so you'll never see that pistol again. It'll drop in the sea somewhere."

"We've had no further complaints from people about these demands," said Terry.

"You'll get 'em," said the other, with a grim smile. "Give 'em time to let it soak in." He looked at his watch. "I'm going along to the American bar at the Cecilia," he said. "I've got quite an idea I'll hear a lot of interesting news."

The Cecilia bar is the rendezvous of most Americans visiting London. The gorgeous Egyptian room, dedicated to the cocktail, was filled by the time Jiggs got there. He found a little table and a chair that was vacant, and sat down patiently for the arrival of his man. It was nearing noon when Kerky Smith came leisurely into the bar, the bony chin lifted, the thin, set smile on his face. He looked round, apparently did not see Jiggs, and strolled to the door. Jiggs finished his drink deliberately, beckoned the waiter and put his hand in his pocket. He had no intention of leaving, but it would require such a gesture as this to bring the Big Boy to him.

"Why, Jiggs!"

Kerky Smith came forward with a flashing smile, his ring-laden hands extended. He took Jiggs' hand in both of his and pressed it affectionately.

"Not going, are you? Say, I wanted to talk to you." He looked round, found a chair and dragged it to the table. "Isn't it too bad about that old guy? I'll bet Ed is just prostrated with grief!"

"Where did you get that international expression from – 'prostrated with grief'?"

"Saw it in a book somewhere," said Kerky shamelessly. "Funny how you can get all kinds of swell expressions if you keep your eyes open. Left him all his money, ain't he? Well, he needed it. He was short of a million to carry out all the big ideas he has."

"It will be months before he can touch a cent," said Jiggs.

The thin eyebrows of Kerky Smith rose. "Is that so? I guess you can borrow money on wills, can't you? Ed was down at a moneylender's this morning."

Jiggs was politely interested. "What kind of a racket was he in when he was running round Chi?" he asked.

Kerky shook his head slowly. There was in his face a hint of disapproval. "I hardly know the man," he said. "And what's all this about rackets? I read about 'em in the newspapers, but I don't know any of these birds." He said this with a perfectly straight face. Jiggs would have been surprised if he had not. "Seems to be some kind of racket starting here," he went on. "Has anybody asked Ed to pay? He's a rich guy now."

"What was his racket in Chicago?" repeated Jiggs, without any hope of being satisfied, for gangland does not talk scandal even of its worst enemies.

"He was just a playboy, I guess. I used to see him around Arlington, and he lived at the Blackstone, That's the kind of bird he was."

Jiggs leaned across the table and lowered his voice. "Kerky, you remember the shooting of Big Sam Polini? The choppers got him as he came out of mass one morning – a friend of yours, wasn't he?"

There was a hard look in Kerky's eyes, but he was still smiling.

"I knew the man," he said simply.

"One of your crowd, wasn't he? Who got him?"

Kerky's smile broadened. "Why, if I knew I'd tell the police," he said. "Joe Polini was a swell fellow. Too bad he was shot up."

"Did Ed know anything about it?"

Kerky wagged his head wearily. "Now what's the use of asking fool questions like that, Jiggs? I've told you before I don't know anything about him, He seems a nice feller to me, and I wouldn't say a word against him. Especially now, when he's in mourning."

Jiggs saw the sly, quick, sidelong glance that the other shot at him, and supplied his own interpretation.

"I'm going off to Paris one day this week," said Kerky. "If they start any racket here I want to be out of it. London's the last place you'd expect gunplay. Say, you're at Scotland Yard now, ain't you?"

"Who told you that?"

Kerky shrugged his thin shoulders. "Sort of story going round that you've been loaned." He bent over and laid his hand on Jiggs' shoulder. "I kinda like you, Jiggs. You're a swell guy. I wouldn't stay around here if I were you – no, sir! Of course, you could stay and make it pay.

A friend of mine wants some detective work done, and he'd pay a hundred thousand dollars to the right kind of guy. All he'd have to do would be just to sit around and be dumb when anything was happening. You might be very useful to my friend."

"Is your friend seeking a divorce or just salvation from the gallows?" asked Jiggs bluntly.

Kerky got up from the table. "You make me tired, Jiggs," he said. "Some of you fellers are swell, but you can't think with your heads."

"I can think better with my head than with my pocket, Kerky. Tell your friends there's nothing doing and, if they try another way of making me drunk, that I'm packing two guns, and they've got to do their shooting pretty quick."

Kerky shook his head and sighed. "You're talking like one of them gang pictures which are so popular in Hollywood," he said.

He called the waiter to him and paid him, beamed on his guest and, with a wave of his hand, sauntered across the room to the bar.

Jiggs went out, all his senses alert. There was a little dark-faced man, elaborately dressed, sitting in the vestibule of the hotel, gazing vacantly at the wall opposite. He wore a gold and diamond ring on the little finger of his left hand. Jiggs watched him as he passed; he so manoeuvred himself that his back was never towards the idler, who apparently was taking no notice of him, and did not even turn his head.

By the door leading out to the courtyard of the hotel was another little man, blue-chinned, dark-eyed, quite unconscious, apparently, of Jiggs' presence. Captain Allerman avoided him, but he did not take his eyes off him until there were half a dozen people between them.

There would be quite an exciting time in London before the end of the week, he decided, as a cab took him back to his hotel, and he wondered if the English people in general, and the English police in particular, quite knew what was going to happen. Prohibition was something they read about in the newspaper and the resulting gang warfare a disaster which happened only in the States.

When he went in to lunch he met some men he knew. They were talking about the Decadon murder. None of them apparently saw anything in the threatening note that in any way menaced their own security.

He was called from lunch by a telephone message from Terry.

"I'll come along and join you," said Terry. "There's been a development. Can we go up to your room?"

"Sure," said Jiggs.

He was waiting for the inspector when he arrived, and they went up in the lift together to Jiggs' suite.

"Here's a new one."

Terry took from his pocket a leather case and extracted a folded note. It was exactly the same size as the warning which old Decadon had received, but it was printed in green ink and differently worded.

"Dear Friend (it began)

"We are out to ensure your comfort and security. We are a band of men who will offer you protection against your enemies and even against your friends. You need not worry about burglars or hold-up men if you trust us. If you agree to employ us, put a lighted candle in the window of your dining-room between 8 and 8.30 tonight. We are offering you, for the sum of £1000, payable within the next three days, the protection that only our organisation can give you. If you decline our services you will, we fear, be killed. If you take this note to the police or consult them in any way, nothing can save you. Have a thousand pounds in American or French currency in an envelope, and after you have put the candle in your window you will receive a telephone message explaining how this money is to be paid."

It was signed "Safety and Welfare Corporation."

"Printed in green ink, eh? Well, we've got 'em both working now, the green and the blue. Who had this?"

"A very rich young man called Salaman. He lives in Brook Street, and had it this morning by the first post. We've got no evidence that anybody else has had the warning. Salaman sent it to us at once, and we've put a guard on his house."

"He didn't come to Scotland Yard?"

"No, we avoided that. He telephoned first and sent the letter by special messenger."

Jiggs pursed his lips. "They'll know all about it. What have you advised him to do?"

"To put a candle in his window, and we'll get a man into the house tonight who'll take the message."

Jiggs was not impressed. "I'm telling you that they know he's been to the police. What sort of man is he?"

Terry hesitated. "Not the highest type of citizen. Plenty of money and a few odd tastes. He's a bachelor, a member of the smartest set – which doesn't necessarily mean the best set. I've got an idea that he's rather on the decadent side."

Jiggs nodded. "He'll be very lucky if he's not on the dead side," he said ominously.

Chapter III

LESLIE WENT TO HER WORK rather late that morning, and with a sense of growing desolation. The tragedy of old Elijah Decadon's death was sufficiently depressing, and she had not yet recovered from the terrifying experience of the previous night.

The situation, so far as she was concerned, was reducible to bread-and- butter dimensions. She had lost her job, or would lose it when she had finished the week. For a second or two she thought of Terry Weston and the possibility of his using his influence to find her another situation, but this was hardly thought of before the idea was dismissed.

The police were still in occupation of the house. They had made a methodical search of the study, and the contents of the desk had been gone over by two men practised in this kind of search. There was plenty of work for her to do: arranging, sorting and extracting papers. For two hours she was with the police sergeant who was in charge of the work, explaining the importance of various documents.

Danes brought her some tea. He had had an exciting morning.

"About that will, miss, that we signed. The police have been trying to get me to say what was in it."

"Well, you didn't know, Danes," she smiled, "so you couldn't very well tell them."

Danes was doubtful whether he might not have offered more information than he had. "It's a funny thing, miss, that Mr. Decadon locked the drawer when he put the will away – you remember? He sent for us again because he'd left you some money in it and it wasn't legal. Well, we got the cook to come up and witness his signature. He didn't exactly sign, but he ran a pen over his name and said that legally that was the same thing. He locked the drawer and put the key in his pocket, yet when that detective started searching the drawer was unlocked. That's a mystery to me."

"It isn't much of a mystery, Danes," she said good-humouredly. "Poor Mr. Decadon may have taken the will out of the drawer and put it somewhere else."

"That's what I told Mr. Tanner, miss," said Danes. "He's been asking me a lot of questions too – he just telephoned down to ask if you were in, and…"

The door opened at that moment: it was Eddie Tanner. He greeted the girl with his quiet smile and waited till the footman had left.

"You had a very unpleasant experience last night, they tell me," he said. "I'm sorry. I wonder if you'd mind telling me what happened?"

She told her story, which seemed less exciting to her than it had sounded when Terry Weston was her audience.

"Well, nothing happened to you – that's good," he said.

She thought he was not particularly enthusiastic about her own safety.

"About this will. Miss Ranger – the one you signed. I suppose you didn't see anything that was in it…or to whom the money was left?"

She shook her head.. "It may have been left to you."

"I shouldn't think that was very likely. My uncle really didn't like me – and I didn't really like my uncle. Have you seen Captain Allerman?"

The name seemed familiar, but she; could not recall ever having met that officer.

"He's an American policeman – Chicago," he said. "A very brilliant man, but occasionally he indulges in fantastic theories. One of his theories is that I killed my uncle."

He opened the door leading into the library, saw the men engaged and closed the door again.

"They're doing some high-class searching. I wonder if they'll find the will? I suppose it was a will. It might have been some other document?" he added inquiringly.

He went to the door and stood there, leaning his head against the broad edge of it. "By the way, I shall want you to stay on and deal with my uncle's papers and books – they'll require cataloguing. The job will last six months, and at the end of that time I will find something for you."

He looked at her for a long time without speaking, and then he said slowly: "If you find that missing document will you oblige me by not reading it, and handing it to me – not to the police? I'll give you fifty thousand pounds if you do this." He smiled. "A lot of money, isn't it? And it would be quite honestly earned."

She gasped. "But, Mr. Tanner…" she stammered.

"I'm serious. And may I ask you not to repeat this to Mr. Terry Weston? You're now in my employ – I hope you won't object to my reminding you – and I'm sure I can count on your loyalty."

He went out, pulling the door to noiselessly.

She sat for a long time, looking at the door blankly. He had meant it…fifty thousand pounds! Then suddenly she remembered something; it was extraordinary that she had not thought of this before. She rang the bell and Danes came in.

"What time did you clear the post-box last night?" she asked.

He thought for a second. "About half-past seven, miss."

There was only one post-box, a large mahogany receptacle that stood on a table just inside the library. All letters except those sent by Eddie Tanner were placed in that box before they were despatched.

"Mr. Decadon rang for me – he just pointed to the box and I took the letters out."

"How many were there?" she asked.

He was not sure; he thought about six. She went over in her mind quickly the correspondence for which she had been responsible.

"There was one long envelope, and the rest were just ordinary…"

"One long envelope?" she said quickly. "Was it in handwriting or typewritten?"

"In handwriting, miss. It was in Mr. Decadon's hand. I know because the ink was still wet and I smudged it a bit with my thumb."

"Do you remember the address to which it was sent?"

Danes put his hand to his forehead and thought hard.

"It was written on the top, miss: 'Personal attention of Mr. Jerrington. Private and confidential.' That's right, miss. I don't remember the address, though."

The mystery was a mystery no longer, "Will you ask Mr. Tanner to come to me if he is in the house" she said.

Ed Tanner was with her in a minute. "Well?" he asked. "Is it about the will?"

For the first time since she had known him he displayed some kind of emotion.

"Yes, I think I know what happened to it. Mr. Decadon must have posted it."

"Posted it?"

"The box was cleared at half-past seven, and Danes said he saw a long envelope which had recently been addressed in Mr. Decadon's writing. It was marked: "For Mr. Jerrington" of Jerrington, Sanders & Graves, Mr. Decadon's lawyers."

"Oh, yes?" He stood for a few seconds fingering his chin, his eyes downcast. "Mr. Jerrington. I know him, naturally. Thank you, Miss Ranger."

She wondered afterwards whether she should not have informed the police, in spite of his warning, and she called up Scotland Yard, but Terry Weston was out.

Mr. George Jerrington, the eminent head of a famous legal firm, was often described by his associates as being a little inhuman. He was sufficiently human, however, to develop a peculiar appendix, and a week before the murder he had gone into a nursing home and had parted with that troublesome and unnecessary thing, with the assistance of the most expensive surgeon in London.

That day he was near enough to convalescence to deal with his personal correspondence, and a telephone message was sent to Lincoln's Inn Fields, to his head clerk, requesting that the most urgent of the letters should be sent to him.

"You'd better take them yourself," said Mr. Jerrington's partner to the clerk. "Who was that in your office half an hour ago?"

"Mr. Decadon's nephew, sir – Mr. Edwin Tanner."

"Oh, yes," said the partner. "A fortunate young man. Decadon died intestate, I understand?"

"I believe so, sir."

"What did he want – Mr. Tanner?"

"I think it was in connection with the estate. I asked him if I he'd see you, but when I told him that Mr. Jerrington was ill he said he would wait. He said he'd sent Mr. Jerrington an urgent personal letter, and I told him Mr. Jerrington would probably attend to that today. I have several such letters to take to him."

The nursing home was at Putney. The clerk, whose name was Smethwick Gould, travelled by bus to the foot of Putney Hill and walked the rest of the way. It was nearly six o'clock, and ordinarily it would have been quite light, but heavy clouds were coming up from the south-west and there was a smell of rain in the air. Most of the cars which passed him had their headlights on.

He had reached the top of the hill and was turning left towards the houses which face Putney Common when a car came abreast of him and a man jumped out. "Are you from Jerrington's?" he said.

Smethwick Gould said that the man spoke with a slightly foreign accent. He wore a big, yellow waterproof coat, the high collar of which reached above the tip of his nose.

"Yes, I'm from Jerrington's," said the clerk.

"Then I'll take that bag from you."

And then Smethwick Gould saw that in the man's hand was an automatic. He stated afterwards that he made a desperate struggle, but the balance of probability is that he handed over the bag without protest. The man in the raincoat jumped into the car and it drove off. With great presence of mind, Gould realised that he had forgotten to note the number of the car. He realised this the moment the number was invisible, but in all probability he would not have been greatly assisted, for a car was afterwards found abandoned on Barnes Common which was proved to have been stolen from Grosvenor Square.

The report of the loss went straight through to Scotland Yard, but did not come to Terry. He was just going out to superintend the Salaman case, and to coach that young man in his conduct, when Leslie phoned through to him and told him what had happened that afternoon.

"I've got a guilty feeling that I should have rung you before."

"Good Lord! That's news!" said Terry. "I'll ring through to Jerrington's right away."

But Messrs. Jerrington were precise people who closed their offices at five o'clock, and he had no satisfaction from them. It was not until he had smuggled himself into Salaman's handsome house that the report of the robbery reached him. He was not particularly interested until he learned that the victim was Mr. Jerrington's head clerk, and then he swore softly to himself, realising what had happened. "Tell me quickly, exactly what happened?"

"I've got the report here, sir," said the officer at the other end of the wire. "Mr. Jerrington has been in a nursing home. He's been operated on for appendicitis, and has seen none of his personal correspondence. As they knew he was making satisfactory progress, letters weren't opened but were kept for him until he was ready to deal with them. This morning they phoned through from the nursing home asking somebody to take out the personal letters, and Mr. Smethwick Gould went out with them. He carried them in a briefcase…"

"And he was held up and robbed on the way," said Terry. "Quick work! All right. Have all the facts ready for me when I get back to the Yard, and tell this Smethwick person that I would like to see him." He was hardly off the line before the phone rang again.

They were in Salaman's beautiful drawing-room. The ceiling was black, the curtains purple, the carpet a dead white. There were green candles in old gold sconces, and large divans. Even the telephone had been specially designed to match the apartment.

Terry did not like the house and he did not like the slim, sallow owner; and liked less the faint scent of incense which hung about the room.

He motioned to Salaman, who took up the phone and lisped an inquiry. Terry waited, listening.

"Yes, I've put the candle in the drawing-room window. You saw it. Where am I to meet you?"

By arrangement, he was repeating every word of the man who was phoning.

"At the top of Park Lane, on the park side. Twenty-five paces from the Marble Arch corner. Yes, I understand. A man will come along wearing a red flower, and I'm to give him the package. Certainly…not at all."

He replaced the receiver and smiled fatuously.

"We've got him!" he said.

Terry did not echo his enthusiasm.

The police had gone when Leslie reached Berkeley Square the next morning, and she was somewhat relieved. She was very uncomfortable, working under their eyes, never knowing at what moment they would come in and fire off some question which, if not embarrassing, was at least difficult to answer.

All the papers that had been taken from the old man's desk had to be filed or destroyed. She had been working half an hour, when Eddie came in, his cool and imperturbable self.

"No luck, I suppose?"

"I'm sure it went to Mr. Jerrington, if you're talking about the will," she said. "Did you get on to him?"

He nodded. "Yes, I called, but Mr. Jerrington is in a nursing home with appendicitis. Apparently all his private papers were stolen yesterday by some hold-up man who robbed his clerk in broad daylight. I read it in the paper."

"That's terribly unfortunate," she said.

"Isn't it?" said he, with that inscrutable smile of his. "This country is becoming so lawless, so unlike the old England I used to know." He looked round. "I think that's a mutual friend of ours, Mr. Terry Weston."

His sharp ears had heard the bell, and he went to the door, intercepting Danes.

"If that's Mr. Weston, show him in here, please. He phoned to say that he was coming," he told the girl. "I hope he isn't being infected with Captain Allerman's suspicion! Good morning, Inspector."

"Good morning."

Terry was bright, but it was a hard brightness, and Leslie was not quite sure that she liked him that way. He was kindly enough to her, and offered her his hand in greeting – a formality he had omitted in dealing with Eddie Tanner.

"We were just discussing the robbery of Mr. Jerrington's private papers," said Eddie.

"I wanted to discuss that too." Terry looked at him. "Rather an extraordinary happening, in all the circumstances."

Eddie Tanner ran his hand over his bald forehead and frowned. "I don't perhaps know all the circumstances, but in any circumstances it was unfortunate."

"You called at the office in the afternoon?"

Mr. Tanner nodded. "Naturally. Mr. Jerrington is my lawyer – or, at least, he acted for my uncle. There are several matters which have to be straightened up, the most urgent being some interest he has in an oilfield in a town called Tacan, which I believe is in Oklahoma." He looked at the girl. "Have you heard about that?"

"No, Mr. Tanner, but I knew very little about Mr. Decadon's private investments."

"The point is" – he frowned deeply, and this seemed to absorb his attention more than the theft of Mr. Smethwick Gould's papers – "Tacan – is there such a place?"

"That's not very important at the moment," began Terry.

Then he saw the real Eddie Tanner. Two cold eyes stared at him. They held neither resentment nor anger, but there was in them a deadly cold that he had never seen in the eyes of man.

"It's important to me."

Leslie was growing uncomfortable in the presence of this unspoken antagonism. "I can easily tell you where Tacan is, Mr. Tanner," she said. "We have a very good gazetteer."

She went into the library, ran her fingers along the shelves and pulled out a big book. As she opened it a paper dropped to the floor. She stooped and picked it up; in another second she came running in to them. "Look!" she said. "The will!"

Terry snatched it from her hand. "Where did you find it?" he asked.

"In a book – in the gazetteer I was looking at."

Terry read quickly. There were half a dozen lines.

"I, Elijah John Decadon, being of sound mind, declare this to be my last will and testament. I leave all of which I die possessed without reservation to Edwin Carl Tanner, the son of my sister, born Elizabeth Decadon, and I hope he will make a good use of his new possessions, a better use than I fear he will make."

It was signed in his own sprawling hand, and by the side were the names, addresses, and occupations of the three witnesses, one of which signatures was her own, and this had been crossed out and initialled by old Decadon.

Terry folded the paper slowly, his eyes still on Eddie Tanner. "Rather a coincidence Miss Ranger was looking in that identical gazetteer at this identical moment," he said slowly. "This, I presume, you will want to send to your lawyers – I don't think you'll lose it." He handed the paper to Eddie. "I congratulate you, Mr. Tanner – so it wasn't necessary to destroy this document after all. It must have been a great surprise to you."

Tanner did not reply. Danes, who saw him come out of the room, thought he was amused.

There was a consultation that afternoon at Scotland Yard, and everybody was wrong except Jiggs Allerman. He had interjected comments from time to time as the discussion proceeded, and when at the end the Assistant Commissioner had asked him for an opinion.

"You don't want an opinion, you want approval," he growled. "I tell you, you people are just crazy. You don't realise what you're up against. If you imagine that this crowd is going to be caught tonight, you've got another guess coming. If they send anybody to collect this envelope, it'll be a pigeon anyway, and if it only ends with the pinching of a man who's earning a dollar for taking a risk he doesn't understand, I'll be glad, and so will you."

There was one man on that board who did not like Jiggs. Detective Inspector Tetley was not particularly popular with anybody, least of all with his peers. He was a man with a remarkably small head and a remarkably generous appreciation of what was in it. Jiggs disliked him the first time he saw him. He hated his little moustache; he disliked his shining hair, and loathed his lack of intelligence.

"What's your solution?" asked Tetley. "I know you American police are clever fellows and, personally speaking, I'd like to have the benefit of your advice, especially as I'm in charge of the show tonight."

"My solution is a fairly simple one," said Jiggs shortly. Take this boy Salaman and put him in prison – in a cell – anywhere these fellows can't get him. If you do that you'll break the jinx. They depend entirely on quick results. If you can hold 'em off Salaman for two or three weeks, they're sunk!"

"You're talking as though this fellow's going to be killed!" said Tetley scornfully. "I'll have twenty officers round him."

"Tell 'em not to get too close," said Jiggs.

Tetley had been given charge of the local arrangements. The trap had been staged in his division, and as the hour approached quite a respectable number of loafers began to appear on the sidewalk. They were working men, city clerks, business men.

"Artistically they're wonderful," said Terry, who inspected them in the station yard before they went out. "But you men have got to realise you may be in a pretty tight corner.

You've been chosen because you understand the use of fire-arms, and because you're single men. Whatever happens, you're not to lose your heads. The moment this man approaches Salaman you're to close on him. There'll be a squad car waiting, with four officers in attendance, and you'll just turn him over to them and your work will be finished. If there's any shooting you'll shoot to kill – this is no wrist-slapping expedition."

He waited on the opposite corner of Park Lane. At three minutes before the hour Salaman arrived in his chauffeur-driven car and stepped down on to the sidewalk. Except for the detectives, there were very few people about, for the point chosen was well away from the bus stop.

Standing reading a newspaper on the kerb, Terry watched.

"Here comes the stool," said Jiggs suddenly.

A middle-aged man, wearing a flaming flower in his buttonhole, was walking from the direction of Piccadilly. Terry saw him stop and look at his watch and then go on. He walked a short way past the spot where he had to meet Salaman, then he turned back and came to a halt within a foot of the position which had been described over the telephone. Salaman had seen him and strolled down to meet him. They saw the man touch his hat and ask Salaman a question, and the young man took an envelope from his pocket and handed it to the messenger. As he did so, the detectives closed. They were within a foot of their terrified prisoner, when the staccato crash of a machine-gun came from somewhere overhead. The little man with the flower in his coat and Salaman went down together. A detective drooped and sank by the railings, and a second a doubled up and fell with his head in the roadway.

"In that block of flats!" yelled Jiggs.

The entrance to the flats was behind them. The elevator door was open.

"Upstairs, quick! We're police officers."

The lift shot up, and even in the brief space of time it took to go from the ground floor to the fourth Terry learned the names of the occupants.

"One empty flat? That's the place. Have you a pass-key?"

By the greatest good fortune he had. But there was no need for a key: the door of the flat was wide open, and even as the men ran into the room they could smell the acrid scent of exploded cordite.

Jiggs ran into the front room. The window was wide open. The room was empty, except for a chair drawn up near the window-sill and the small machine- gun that lay on the floor.

"First blood to green," said Jiggs between his teeth. "I wonder how many of those poor coppers are killed. It doesn't matter about Salaman. I just don't like people who have black ceilings."

Terry went for the liftman, who was also the assistant caretaker. He had admitted nobody to the empty flat, and was quite ignorant of the fact that there was anybody in the building. It was easy, he said, to get an order to view, and in the course of the last two or three days there had been several parties who had made an inspection of the apartment.

There was the usual fire-escape; it was at the end of a short passage leading from the main corridor.

"That's the way they went," said Terry, looking down.

Looking from the window of the flat, he saw a huge crowd surrounding the dead and the dying men, and as he looked an ambulance came up, followed immediately by another. Police whistles were blowing and men in uniform were coming from all directions, while from nowhere had appeared two mounted policemen who were peeling the edge of the crowd.

He sent a man in search of Tetley, and the inspector came, awhile of face and shaking. "That young man's killed, and so is the fellow with the flower, and one of my best sergeants. I had a narrow escape myself."

"You had a narrow escape," said Jiggs, "because you weren't on that side of the road. What made you stay over our side?"

Tetley shot a malevolent look at him. "I was just going over…" he began.

"About two minutes too late," said Jiggs. "What made you stay over on our side? I'd like to know that, Mr. Tetley."

The man turned on him in a fury which was half panic. "Perhaps if you ask the Commissioner tomorrow he'll tell you!" he shouted.

The last of the ambulances had moved away, the crowd was being skilfully dispersed, and already road-sweepers were working at the mess that the shooting had left on the sidewalk.

"This is going to put the cat amongst the pigeons," said Jiggs. "Incidentally, it's going to make London sit up and take notice, and I'm rather wondering how they'll take it."

Terry was silent as they drove back to Scotland Yard in a police car. He was feeling bitterly his own responsibility, though it was not entirely due to his advice or judgment that Salaman had been allowed to walk blindly into a trap that had been set probably since the early morning.

The machine-gun yielded no clue. It was of American make, and of the type which, Jiggs said, was most frequently used by the gangsters of his city.

"That's one to the green," said Jiggs again, "and now it will be the blue's turn. The only hope is that these two bands of brigands won't be satisfied to sit quietly and share the loot."

"By 'the green' you mean the last set of notices, the one Salaman had: there are two gangs working – you're sure of that?"

"Absolutely sure," said Jiggs. "The blue caught old Decadon. The green are the smarter crowd, I think. It's going to be very interesting to see how it all works out." He paused for a moment. "And I hope we'll live to see it!"

A more exhaustive examination of the officials connected with the building brought no result. The empty flat was in the hands of two or three agents; it was the property of a stockbroker who had moved to other premises. None of the estate agents had given the key to a likely tenant, but three of them had within the past two days personally conducted likely tenants through the empty apartment. The last of these, a man and a woman, had inspected the flat early on the morning of the outrage.

"And while they were going through the rooms," said Jiggs, "the front door would be open and anybody could come in."

The hall porter remembered 'a dark-looking man,' carrying a heavy suitcase, which he said had to be personally delivered to a tenant on the floor whence the shots were fired. He had gone up in the elevator, but the lift attendant did not remember his coming down again. It was exactly at the hour when the prospective tenant was making his inspection.

"That's the explanation," Jiggs nodded. "It was easy to get up and down the stairs when the elevator was working and miss seeing the attendant. Probably two of them were in the flat; one was certainly there before the people who were looking the flat over had left the premises."

All London was scoured that night, and particularly that section of London where the alien had his quarters. Fire-arms experts and ballistic authorities examined the machine-gun. Terry Weston, in the course of an inspection of the murder scene, discovered what had been obvious, yet had been missed – that two of the park railings had been neatly painted white for a depth of about four inches from the cross-bar.

"I didn't notice it either," said Jiggs, "and that's the one thing I should have looked for – the choppers had to have a target to make absolutely sure. Those marks on the rails gave them the distance and the direction without fail. Lord! I was mad not to have seen that when we were waiting for Salaman to come along."

Scotland Yard waited in some trepidation for its Press, and there was relief in high quarters when Fleet Street, with singular unanimity, agreed that it was not the moment to blame Scotland Yard, but to devise methods for preventing a recurrence of the outrage. Said the Megaphone:

"We do not yet know the full particulars of what preliminary precautions the police took, and what steps were taken to minimise the danger to this unfortunate gentleman. Until we know this it would be unfair to offer any criticism of Scotland Yard and its system. Neither Scotland Yard nor the public could possibly expect an outrage of this character, committed with cold-blooded ferocity and the reckless employment of machine-guns."

It was generally believed at the time that there were two machine-guns employed, and indeed an erroneous statement to this effect had gone out to the Press.

Early the next morning Terry had a phone message from the last person in the world he expected to hear from. "It's Eddie Tanner speaking. I wonder if you could find time to come round and see me? It's on a purely personal matter, and I'd come to Scotland Yard, but I don't think it's particularly advisable at the moment."

When Terry arrived he found the young man sitting at the very desk where, forty-eight hours before, his uncle had sat, and at which he had been murdered in cold blood. He was smoking a cigarette, and before him was a newspaper.

"Bad business, this," he said, tapping the black headlines with his finger. "You must be having a pretty lively time at Scotland Yard."

Terry was not favourably disposed towards him, but even now could not believe that this man had deliberately shot to death a harmless old man, cold- bloodedly and without compunction. "Do you want to talk about this?" he asked.

"No, it's rather out of my line." Eddie pushed the paper aside. "Miss Ranger will be here in half an hour, and I intend dismissing her."

He waited, but Terry made no comment.

"I've been thinking the matter over, and I've decided that the situation is a little dangerous for her. Within an hour or two of my uncle being killed she was picked up by a gang, who are probably the murderers, and she went through an experience which must have terrified her. Evidently the people who are responsible for this murder" – he tapped the paper again – "aren't very fond of me, and I'm very anxious that her experience shouldn't be repeated. You're a friend of hers – at least, you know her – and I'm anxious to get you to help me."

"In what way?"

Eddie swung round in his swivel chair so that his profile was to Terry Weston. He dropped the end of his cigarette into a water-filled vase and lit another.

"That young lady lives in an out-of-the-way place: rather cheap room, no telephone – a particularly dangerous situation, if these birds still think she can supply them with hot news. I want Miss Ranger to take a flat in the West End, right in the very centre and in a good-class neighbourhood. It's rather a delicate matter to suggest to her, because I'm willing to pay the rent of that flat and naturally, being a charming young lady, she'll kick at the idea. I'm not only willing to pay the rent, but I'll furnish the flat."

"Why?" asked Terry.

The other shrugged.

"It's a small price for a large peace of mind," he smiled. "In other words, I don't want this lady on my mind."

"That's a very generous offer," said Terry, "and I quite see your point of view, although you may have another one at the back of your mind which you haven't given me."

Still smiling, Edwin Tanner shook his head. "I have no arriere pensee. I'm telling you just how I feel. I like this young lady – which doesn't mean that I'm in love with her, or that I should like to be any better acquainted than I am. She's one of the few women I've met in this world whom I would trust, in spite of the fact that she notified you of something which I asked her not to communicate to the police. But I think I understand that. The circumstances were unusual. Anyhow I want, as far as possible, to protect her from her accidental association with me. If you think there's anything behind my very simple suggestion, I can't help it."

"What do you want me to do?" asked Terry.

"Merely to persuade her to accept my suggestion."

"I have no influence with Miss Ranger," said Terry, and again came that quick smile of Eddie's.

"I think you have a greater influence than you imagine and, if this is the case, will you help me?"

"I'll have to think about it," said Terry.

When Leslie arrived, a quarter of an hour later, she found Eddie Tanner sitting on her desk.

"No work today. Miss Ranger." He was almost gay. "You're pleasantly fired."

She looked at him in consternation. "Do you mean you don't want me any more?"

"I mean that there's no more work to do. There's plenty of work," he said, "but I've decided that it's rather dangerous for you to be in my employ any longer."

He told her practically what he had told Terry.

"I've had Terry Weston here this morning," he explained quite frankly, "and I've asked him to help me by adding his influence to mine."

"But I couldn't possibly accept money for..."

Eddie nodded. "I see your point of view, and in fact I've anticipated it. I'm greatly obliged to you that you're not furious with me. But that's exactly how the matter stands. Miss Ranger, and you'd be taking a great load off my mind if you'd see my point of view. I owe you fifty thousand pounds..."

"You owe me fifty thousand pounds?" she gasped.

She had forgotten a promise which she had regarded at the time as a piece of extravagance, not to be seriously considered.

He nodded. "I haven't fifty thousand pounds to give you at the moment, because it will be some considerable time before my uncle's fortune passes into my hands. But I haven't forgotten."

"Mr. Tanner" – she stood squarely before him – "you know exactly what Mr. Weston thinks, and I'm afraid it's what I think – that in some way you secured possession of that will and that you put it in the gazetteer for me to find. As I believe; you found it before I did, that absolves you..."

"It does nothing of the kind," he interrupted, "even supposing Inspector Weston's fantastic theory were well founded. In any circumstances I'm the executor of my uncle's estate, and he left you a thousand pounds, which I shall give to you today. But I want you to let me add to that the service I suggest."

She shook her head.

"I'd even forgotten about the thousand pounds," she said with a faint smile. "That will be ample for me. I promise you this, Mr. Tanner, that I will move to a more central position. In fact, I'd already decided to do that. I have some of my mother's furniture stored, and I shall be able to make myself a comfortable home. I'm very grateful to you all the same," she nodded. "I didn't somehow think it was going to be very easy, and I doubt whether even the influence of Mr. Terry Weston would make me change my mind."

"I respect you for it," said Eddie curtly.

He paid her her salary and that for another week in lieu of notice, with punctilious exactness, and half an hour later she was in her little room, packing in preparation for the move which she had long since regarded as inevitable.

She would not be sorry to leave behind that dreary little home of hers. It was a lonely place and when she returned at night she would sometimes walk for a hundred yards without seeing a soul.

"I shall be sorry to lose you, miss," said the landlady. Yet apparently mingled in her sorrow was a certain satisfaction which made it possible for her to be sprightly, even in the moment of her misfortune – if misfortune it was to lose a single young lady who very rarely had a meal in the house. "The truth is, I've let one room on your floor and I could have let yours. They're coming about it tonight. As a matter of fact, miss, I was going to ask you whether you minded moving upstairs. They're two nice young foreign gentlemen who're studying at the University."

Just about that time quite a number of young Europeans 'studying at the University' were seeking lodgings in the West End.

It was a relief to Leslie to know that her departure would not at any rate bring any gloom to a woman who had always been kindly, if sometimes a little tiresome.

With all the morning before her, she intended to do a little shopping, lunch in the West End, and then go out to the repository where her mother's furniture had been stored since that dreadful day three years before when Leslie had had to face the world alone.

She had been guided by a fussy relative who always appeared on such occasions, and who had induced her to store the goods in a pet repository of his own situated in one of the most inaccessible spots. Leslie did not welcome the prospect of a visit to Rotherhithe. She would, she decided, do the unpleasant task first and leave the shopping, and maybe dinner, till that was completed. In the circumstances she decided on a taxi.

She dived out of the traffic of London Bridge, down the slope into Tooley Street, and the drabness of Rotherhithe came out to meet her. She was not quite sure where the repository was, and stopped the cab to ask a policeman.

"Zaymen's Repository, miss?"

He gave elaborate directions, in which everything seemed to be on the left and nothing on the right.

"You going to claim your property? You're just about in time. They've been advertising for a week. Old Zaymen's been dead two years; young Zaymen..." He lifted his eyes and shrugged his shoulders.

Leslie supposed that young Mr. Zaymen was not all he might be, and began to fear for her furniture. "Some say they've gone broke," said the policeman, "some say they're just selling out, but whichever way it is it can't be right."

She excused herself from his philosophy and directed the taxi onward, and after a lot of searching they came to the repository, which was not on the roadside, as she had expected, but through a labyrinth of small lanes, down one more dirty than any, past walls which seemed to exist for the purpose of giving a resting-place to rusting iron, and eventually they came to a stark-looking warehouse which she dimly remembered having seen before, though in point of fact she had never been in the neighbourhood until that moment.

There was a certain amount of activity. Men were going in and out; there was an uncleanly-looking clerk sitting behind a glass-covered partition, and to him she addressed her request for information, producing the receipt for the furniture and a smaller receipt for the money she had paid from time to time in Zaymen's London office.

The clerk looked at them, scowled at them, held them up to the light, brought them close to his eyes and far away from him.

"You're just in time, young lady. That deposit was going to be sold off tomorrow."

"You'd have been sold off the next day," said Leslie, with spirit.

She was handed over to the care of a young clerk who was beautifully tailored and whose hair was glossy and perfectly brushed. He was very young, very important, and spoke continuously of 'we,' and she presumed he was the younger Zaymen until he admitted he only had a 'position' with the firm. After a while he came down to earth and was quite agreeable as he showed her over the floor and when she had identified her furniture he summoned white-aproned men to remove it in a truck which providentially was there at the moment. "It's a shame" – he almost said 'shime' but corrected himself – "Zaymen's busting up like this, but I suppose they couldn't refuse the offer. It's one of the soundest warehouses on the: river, with a wharf in front, hauling gear, wood-panel walls, fireproofed throughout…"

"In fact a very good warehouse," said Leslie, a little amused.

"It's young Mr. Zaymen." He shook his head and heaved a sigh.

"Is it women or drink?" asked Leslie, and he was rather shocked. Apparently Mr. Zaymen was a gambler. "He's gambled away the old family warehouse with wharfage and haulage in good condition."

"I agree with you it's a shame."

He became more and more gallant. She felt that at any moment he might take off his coat and lay it over a puddle, if there was a puddle, that her feet should not be soiled.

"When I saw you first," he admitted at parting – he gave her a very moist hand – "I thought you were a bit stuck up."

"When I saw you first," she said very gravely, "I thought you were a bit stuck down. And now we're both wrong."

She went round to the wharf, saw her furniture being loaded on to a van, and gave the address to which it should be sent. She was taking rather a wild risk, for the little flat she had applied for had not yet been assigned to her. Tipping the workmen, she was going on, when she heard two men talking. They were American and, as she was passing, she heard the voice of the second man.

"Say, listen, you couldn't compare this with the Hudson. Why, right up by the palisades it's more'n six times as wide."

Her heart leapt almost into her mouth. She did not forget voices, and the voice she heard was that of the man who had told her to get into the car that night when she was wanted at Scotland Yard.

He spoke again – some triviality about the colour of the river – and she was sure. She looked round carefully for she did not want them to recognise her. There were two men; they both wore untidy-looking pullovers; both were dressed in blue dungarees, over which had been pulled heavy gum-boots, knee high.

"Well, boy," said the voice, "let's go and shoot the works, and after we're through you can take Jane and I'll take Christabel and we'll go to the movies."

The second man laughed at this, a short, hard laugh that finished as abruptly as it had begun. They were both of moderate height, she noticed, both lithe, unusual-looking men. They lurched along past the workmen who were loading her furniture, and presently disappeared behind the van. She went back to her taxi, a little uncertain as to what she should do. Though she was confident in her mind that this was the man who had led her into danger that night, she could not be sure. She had once heard an American woman say that all English voices sounded alike, but that she could pick out one voice in a thousand when Americans were speaking. It seemed to Leslie that the reverse held now. All American voices did seem alike, and – only the English had a subtle difference.

Who was Jane, and who was Christabel, she wondered as she got into the cab and went bumping over the uneven surface of the lane back to the main road. Some private and possibly ribald jest of their own that did not bear investigating, she decided.

They had reached the main road, and the taxi driver was waiting for a large lorry to pass, when she heard the chug-chug of a motorcycle, and the rider came immediately abreast of the window. He grabbed the roof of the taxi with his hand and looked in. It was the man she had heard speaking. He gave her a long, swift scrutiny, and she returned his stare. "What do you want?" she asked.

He muttered something, and dropped behind as the taxi moved forward.

There was a possible explanation for his conduct. He might have heard the warehousemen mention her name as her furniture was being loaded and come after her to make sure. But if that were so, there could be no question about the accuracy of her recognition. It was the man who had come to her house the night Mr. Decadon was killed. What was he doing there? Perhaps he was a sailor; he was dressed in the clothes she had seen men wear on tramp steamers, and just at that period the Pool was full of shipping. She wondered if she should call up Terry…she was always thinking of excuses for calling up Terry…

The cab turned down Cannon Street. Near to the junction of Queen Victoria Street she was held up in a block of traffic. Then, to her amazement, she heard her name called. She looked round. A man was standing by the open window, a small-faced man with a black moustache.

He lifted his hat with elaborate politeness.

"You don't know me, young lady, but I know you – Inspector Tetley from Scotland Yard…a friend of Mr. Terry Weston's," he smirked.

Then, without waiting for her to speak: "What have you been doing in this part of the world?"

"I've been down to see my furniture loaded. It was in a repository," she said.

She felt it was not the moment to challenge his right to speak to her without an introduction, or to stand on ceremony of any kind. In a few moments the block would break and her car would move on.

"Where was that, now?" asked Mr. Tetley. "Rotherhithe eh?" when she told him. "That's a nasty place! Didn't see anybody you knew, did you? There's some bad characters around there."

She shook her head. "No, I didn't see anybody I knew. I hardly expected to."

"I don't know," he said, still watching her with his ferret eyes. "There's something queer about Rotherhithe: you're always meeting people you've met before – it's almost a saying."

"It isn't my saying," she said, and at that moment the taxi moved on.

She dimly remembered now having seen the man. He had come to the house once, after Mr. Decadon's death. How odd of him to accost her in the street! She wondered if she would tell Terry…

She heaved a long, impatient sigh. "You're a fool, Leslie Ranger. Keep your mind off policemen."

The taxi set her down in Cavendish Square and she got out. The driver, after the manner of his kind, came down to the pavement to stretch his legs.

"Hullo!" he said. "What's the lark?"

She followed the direction of his eyes. Pasted on the top of the cab was a white circle. When he pulled it off the gum was still wet. He walked round the taxi: there was another white circle behind, and a third on the opposite side.

"They weren't there when we left Rotherhithe," he said. "I wonder if that chap on the bicycle…"

For some reason or other which she could not explain, a cold shiver ran down Leslie Ranger's spine, and for a second she had a panic sense of fear which was inexplicable, and therefore all the more distressing.

When she had successfully negotiated the hire of her flat she was terribly tempted to go into the nearest call box and ring up Terry. There must be some good excuse for ringing him up, and it seemed to her that she had half a dozen.

Chapter IV

TERRY HURRIED BACK to Scotland Yard for the secret conference which was to be held that morning. At that time the Commissioner was Sir Jonathan Goussie, a military man who all his life had lived according to regulations and had succeeded in reaching the highest rank by the careful avoidance or delegation of responsibility. He was a fussy, nervous man, in terror of Press criticism, and just now he had completely lost his head. It was a shocking discovery to his executive that this suave, easy-going, and rather amusing gentleman could so lose his balance and nerve that he was almost incapable of leadership at a critical moment.

He sat at the end of the long table and glowered left and right.

"This is a fine state of affairs!" There was agitation in his voice. "The finest police force in the world, baffled and beaten by a gang of murdering ruffians…"

"Well, sir, what are we going to do about it?"

It was Wembury, Assistant Commissioner, brisk, brusque, who broke in upon the tirade.

"I'm not suggesting that every precaution wasn't taken," said the Commissioner. "Tetley, I'm sure, did everything that ingenuity could suggest."

"I did my best," said Tetley.

He was a favourite with the old man and, though he had no right to be in the meeting of the inner council, in the circumstances Wembury had called him.

"I don't want to make any complaint," he went on, "but there was a lot of interference which there shouldn't have been." He glanced malevolently at Jiggs. "American methods are all very well in their way, but you can't expect American police officers to understand the routine of work in London."

"What interference?" demanded Terry wrathfully. "He gave you every assistance..."

"We don't want any wrangling," said Sir Jonathan testily. "The point is, we've got to find some method by which a recurrence of this ghastly affair can be avoided, and I think Inspector Tetley's suggestion is an excellent one."

Terry looked at Wembury. Wembury looked at him. It was the first news they had had that a system had been devised. "I don't mind any suggestions," said Wembury gruffly, "but I hardly like to have them sprung on me at a meeting. What is Tetley's idea?"

"Mr. Tetley's idea," said Sir Jonathan, "is that we should issue a notice giving an enormous reward for information that will lead to the arrest of the murderers, and that the reward should not, as is usually the case, be confined to people outside the police force."

"That seems fairly original, sir," said Wembury coldly, "but I doubt very much if it's of much value. We shall have to take every case individually and on its merits. Nothing is more certain than that there will be a regular flooding of London with these notices – 'Pay or be killed'."

"One has been received this morning," said Sir Jonathan soberly. "I have it in my pocket." He searched in his pocket and produced a folded sheet. From where he sat Terry saw that it was printed in blue. "It came to a very dear friend of mine, or rather the nephew of a dear friend of mine, and he particularly requested that I should make no announcement whatever to my colleagues, and certainly not to the public, as to who he was."

Terry stared at the old chief, amazed. "Do you mean to say that you're not telling us, sir?"

"I mean to say that I'm not telling you or anybody else," said Sir Jonathan stiffly. "I've practically pledged my word of honour on the telephone that I wouldn't reveal the name of the recipient."

Jiggs sniffed. "Will they keep his name secret at the inquest?" he asked, and Sir Jonathan glowered at him.

"There will be no inquest, sir," he rasped. "If the police do their duty, and if our newly-found allies really are the clever people they're supposed to be..."

"I'm all that," interrupted Jiggs.

Wembury, white with anger, broke in.

"I don't think you quite realise what you're saying, sir. This man, whoever he is, will have to have some form of protection, and we can't protect him unless we know who he is. I must insist on knowing his name and where he lives."

The old soldier sat bolt upright, and in his eyes was a court martial and a firing squad.

"No person insists when I'm in the saddle, sir," he said, and Terry groaned inwardly, for he knew that when Sir Jonathan talked about being 'in the saddle' the situation was hopeless. The conference broke up soon afterwards, with a mysterious hint from the Commissioner that he intended issuing a statement to the Press.

After the party dispersed there was a private conference in the Assistant Commissioner's office.

"We've got to stop that statement going out to the Press until we've seen it," said Wembury. "The old man has never been particularly clever, but now he's gone stark, staring mad. I'm going over to the Home Office to see the Home Secretary, and I'm chancing ignominious dismissal from the service for going behind my superior's back."

His interview with the Home Secretary, however, did not take place. The Minister of State was not in London, though at the Home Office they had had a telegram from him that he was hurrying back to town.

"Perhaps," said the permanent under-secretary, "if you saw Sir Jonathan and had a private talk with him…"

"I'd sooner see Balaam's ass and have a private talk with him," said the exasperated Assistant Commissioner.

Nevertheless, when he returned to the Yard he sought an interview which, however, was refused.

At four o'clock that day the afternoon newspapers carried the Commissioner's 'official statement,' which he had carefully penned at his club during the lunch-hour. This statement will go down to history as the most extraordinary document that has ever been issued from Scotland Yard. It ran:

> *"Two desperate crimes, which may or may not have a connection, have been committed in the Metropolitan police area during the past week, and have followed the receipt of threatening communications in which the writer has demanded a large sum of money, failing which the recipient would be killed. There is reason to believe that the killing of Mr. Salaman at Marble Arch was a direct consequence of one of these threats. The writer of the letter has stated that if any communication is made to the police, directly or indirectly, the person who receives the message will be murdered. Despite this threat, the Commissioner of Police earnestly requests any person who receives such a communication, whether accompanied by threats of murder or otherwise, to forward it immediately to Scotland Yard, and to communicate by telephone with the Assistant Commissioner that the letter has been forwarded. If the threatened person desires to remain anonymous his wishes will be respected. It may be perhaps advisable that the police should know his name, his address, and his movements. In a fight against organised crime it necessarily follows that there must be occasions when the threat will be executed, and the Commissioner is not able to guarantee, either on his own behalf, or on behalf of the Metropolitan police, complete immunity to any person who forwards particulars of these communications, but every effort will be made to afford protection to law-abiding citizens."*

It was signed with the Commissioner's name and all his titles. Jiggs was the first to get a copy of the paper, and he hurried to the Assistant Commissioner's office and found Terry and the big man in conference.

"Read that."

Wembury read it through quickly, and his jaw dropped.

"For the love of Mike!" he said softly.

"You know what that means, don't you?" said Jiggs. "This old boy has told the world that Scotland Yard is unable to protect people whose lives are threatened."

Wembury snatched up the paper and raced along the corridor to the Commissioner's room. He was just coming out, and with him was Inspector Tetley.

"Well, well, well?" he asked.

"It isn't well at all," said Wembury. "Is this your communication to the Press?"

The old man fixed his glasses deliberately and read the paragraph from end to end while Wembury fretted himself hot with impatience.

"Yes, that is my communication."

"I'm taking it to the Home Secretary at once," said Wembury. "You've given murder a licence – told these thugs in so many words that they can go right ahead and that we're not in a position to protect their victims."

"I wrote that after full consideration…" began Sir Jonathan.

The telephone in his room was ringing.

"Answer that, Mr. Tetley," he said and, turning to Wembury: "You understand this is a gross act of insubordination on your part, and it's a matter which must be reported to the highest quarters."

Tetley appeared in the doorway. "It's for you, sir."

The old man went back. His conversation was a short one. Wembury heard him answering, "Yes, sir," and, "No, sir" and knew he was speaking to the Home Secretary. He started some sort of explanation, which was evidently cut short. When he came out of his room he was very white.

"I'm going to the Home Office," he said. "The matter had better remain in abeyance until I return." He never did return. Ten minutes after he was ushered into the room of the Secretary of State he came out again, and the late editions of the newspapers that night carried the bald announcement, without any equivocation, that Sir Jonathan Goussie had been dismissed from his office.

"They didn't even let him resign," said Terry.

"Hell! Why should they?" growled Jiggs. "It's the same thing, ain't it?"

They were having a late tea in Terry's office, and the inspector remembered his conversation with Eddie Tanner that morning, and related the interview.

"Maybe he's genuine," said Jiggs. "There are funny streaks of generosity in Eddie."

Terry shook his head. "I couldn't make myself believe that he killed his uncle in cold blood…" he began.

Jiggs scoffed. "Kill him in cold blood? You don't understand these fellows, boy!" he said. "That's just the way they kill. There's no emotion in it, no hate, no hot blood at all. They treat human beings the same as the stockyard butchers in Chicago treat hogs! Do you hate a fly when you swat it? No, sir! The fact that old man Decadon was his uncle and was old, wouldn't make any difference to Eddie or to any of that crowd. Killing to them is just brushing your coat or putting your tie straight." He thought a moment. "Naturally he wants the girl out of the house. All the other servants will go too. His own crowd's there by now, I'll bet you. Do you know the names of any of the other servants besides…well, she wasn't a servant exactly."

"There's a boy called Danes, an under footman," said Terry after a moment's consideration.

Jiggs reached for the phone and dialled a number. After a while: "I want to talk to Danes, the under-footman – that is Mr. Tanner's house, isn't it?"

He listened for a few seconds. "Is that so?" he said at last, and hung up the receiver. "Danes left this afternoon. What did I tell you?" He took a cigar from his waistcoat pocket, bit off the end and lit it.

"You couldn't expect anything else. Eddie couldn't have that house run by a bunch of servants he knew nothing about."

"He'll have his own crowd in?" suggested Terry.

"Not on your life," chuckled Jiggs. "That'd be too easy. No, he'll get a lot of daily folks in – people who sleep home at night. Maybe he'll have a 'secretary,' but if you go to the house and ask for him you'll find he's just gone out. He'll have a couple of workmen fixing bells and things. They'll be there most of the time, but if you ask for them they'll not be there – they'll just have gone out to lunch. You'll find the only person he hasn't fired is the cook."

"Why?" asked Terry.

"Because she's a daily woman anyway, and lives in the basement and never comes up, and she cooks good stuff. Now, about this young lady you're in love with…"

"I'm not in love with her at all," protested Terry loudly.

"Your ears have gone red," said the calm Jiggs, "which means either that you're in love or you're conscious that you're telling a lie! Anyway, what's her name? Leslie Ranger. There may be a lot in what Eddie said. They might pick her up any night and find out things that she knows without knowing she knows."

"If she told them," said Terry.

Jiggs smiled grimly. "She'd tell 'em all right. You don't know these guys, Terry! You've heard the expression about people stopping at nothing – well, that's them! You look up any old book on the way mediaeval executioners got people to talk, and that won't be the half of it. These birds have improved on Nuremburg – especially with a woman. I could tell you stories that'd make your hair pop out of your head, follicles an' everything! There was a gang in Michigan that was after a member of another gang, and they picked up his girl – a reg'lar redhead and full of fight – and like a fool she said she knew, but she wasn't going to tell where her John was."

He took the cigar out of his mouth and looked at it. "Well, maybe I'd better not tell you. Anyway, she told them! They got her John in a Brooklyn speakeasy. The girl was dead when we found her, but there were a lot of signs. They had no feelings against her, you understand – they just wanted to know. And they hadn't any feelings against the guy they bumped – they just had to kill him, and that's all there was to it."

He thought for a moment, and consulted his cigar again. "Pretty girl, too."

"The one that was killed?" asked Terry.

Jiggs shook his head. "I didn't see her till after she was dead, and she wasn't pretty then! No, this Leslie girl. I've seen her twice – she's lovely. Where's the old boy?"

"The Commissioner? He's gone home. Wembury's seen him, and tried to get him to give the name of the man who's been threatened. All he could find out was that the old man had advised this fellow to keep absolutely quiet and slip away to Scotland tonight."

Jiggs groaned. "Well, there must have been lots of other letters received by people in London. Have you heard about them?"

Terry shook his head. He was uneasy. "No, we haven't had one case reported, and I'm a little worried. Orders have been given to all the men on duty – the uniformed policemen, I mean – to report any house that shows a candle tonight."

Jiggs shook his head. "There'll be no candle. This is a blue assignment."

"There may be green as well," said Terry. "We can't keep track of the phone calls, but we can watch for the candles."

Jiggs got up.

"I'll be changing my hotel from tonight," he said. "I'm a bit too conspicuous and easy to get at, and if any of these guys have got an idea that I'm being useful to Scotland Yard I shall hear from them! If nobody tries to kill me in the next fortnight I'm going to feel mighty insulted!"

He left Scotland Yard and went on foot down Whitehall to his hotel. His hands were in his coat pockets and the cigar between his teeth and the rakish set of his hat contributed to the picture of a man who found life a very amusing experience. But the hand in each pocket gripped an automatic, and under the brim of the down-turned hat which shaded his eyes was a sliver of mirror.

Whitehall was filled with junior Civil Servants homeward bound. Trafalgar Square a whirling roundabout of traffic. He crossed Whitehall where the Square and that thoroughfare meet, and without any warning of his intention suddenly swung himself on to a westward-bound bus. Five minutes later he passed through the door of his hotel. He had not told Terry that he had already changed his place of residence, though he had notified the telephone exchange at Scotland Yard where he could be found.

He went up to the first floor, where his suite was, unlocked the door and, reaching in his hand, switched on the light. The next second he was lying half-stunned on the floor, covered with plaster and the debris of a smashed party wall. The hotel rocked with the crash of the explosion. When he got painfully to his feet he saw the door hanging on its hinges, and clouds of smoke were coming out of the room.

The right hand which had turned on the switch had escaped miraculously. He examined it carefully: there was a scratch or two, but no serious damage. All the lights in the corridor were out. Indeed, for five minutes the whole hotel was in darkness.

He heard shouts below; the loud gong of the fire-alarm was ringing, and voices were coming to him up the stairs.. He took a flat torch from his hip pocket and sent a ray into the room. It was wrecked. Part of the ceiling had fallen in, the windows had been blown into the street. The wreckage of a table was scattered round the room, and pieces of chairs with torn upholstery lay about the floor. Jiggs stared and blinked.

"Pineapples and everything!" he said. The bomb had been placed on the table, and had been connected with the electric light. If Jiggs had gone into the room before he had turned the switch, he must have been killed.

The clang of fire-engines came to him as he walked back along the littered corridor. At the head of the stairs he met the manager, pale, almost speechless. "It was only a bomb," said Jiggs. "Go along and see if anybody's hurt in the other rooms."

Fortunately at this hour of the day the rooms were empty. His own sitting- room was immediately above an hotel cloakroom, the ceiling of which had been blown in but, except for a slight cut, the attendant had been uninjured.

After the firemen had come and extinguished an unimportant blaze Jiggs inspected his own bedroom. The wall had been breached; a two-foot jagged hole showed where the wardrobe had been.

"I shall have very little to pack," said Jiggs philosophically.

He tried to phone Scotland Yard, but the whole telephone system of the hotel was out of action.

A huge crowd had collected in front of the building, and crowds at the moment were fairly dangerous. Jiggs went out the back way, found a call box and acquainted Terry.

"Would you like to be host to a homeless American copper, who has one pair of burnt pyjamas and a mangled tooth-brush?"

Terry gave his address. "I'll come round and pick you up," he said.

"Take the back way," warned Jiggs. "There's a crowd of guns in front."

Here he may have been exaggerating but, as he told Terry later, one gun in the hands of an expert chopper can be as deadly as fifty.

They drove back to Scotland Yard with such of Jiggs' luggage as could be retrieved.

"Pineapples, eh?" said Jiggs as they drove along. "I wondered if they'd use 'em."

"By 'pineapple' you mean 'bomb?'"

"By 'pineapple' I mean 'bomb'," said Jiggs gravely. "It's part of the racketeer's equipment."

Then suddenly he brightened up. "That's a compliment, anyway. These birds think I mean something! Who's in charge?" he asked suddenly.

"Tetley," said Terry. "The Assistant Commissioner brought him into the Yard for special duty. Tetley's a pretty shrewd kind of fellow," he explained, "with a more or less good record. He's too well off to please me, but he may have got it honestly."

"Sure he may," said Jiggs sardonically. "But what he's got now will be nothing to what he'll have this time three months – if he gets right away with it, and that's doubtful."

Later in the evening fragments of the bomb were brought to Scotland Yard to be examined by the experts.

"Good stuff, well made," was Jiggs' verdict. "They've got a factory somewhere in London, but the bomb itself was cast in America. I think your chemists will find that when they start analysing it."

Tetley, who had brought the pieces, made a brief but not particularly illuminating report. Nobody had been seen to enter the room, and three-quarters of an hour before Jiggs return a chambermaid had been in and seen nothing unusual. "Here's a list of all the guests in the hotel," said Tetley, and laid a typewritten paper on the table. "You see, sir, I've divided them into floors – on Mr. Jiggs'..."

"Captain Allerman," said Jiggs.

"I beg your pardon. On Captain Allerman's floor there were Lady Kensil and her maid, Mr. Braydon of Bradford, Mr. Charles Lincoln, the American film actor, and Mr. Walter Harman and family, from Paris."

Jiggs bent over and looked at the list. "And Mr. John Smith of Leeds," he said. "You seem to have forgotten him, Inspector."

Tetley looked round at him. "That's the list that was given to me."

"And Mr. John Smith of Leeds," repeated Jiggs. "I've been on the phone to the manager and got the list of the people on my floor, and it included Mr. John Smith."

"He didn't tell me," said Tetley quickly.

"He not only told you" – Jiggs' tone was deliberate and offensive – "but he also said that he was rather suspicious of Mr. John Smith, who spoke with a curious accent."

There was a dead silence. "Yes, I remember now," said Tetley carelessly. "In fact, he talked so much about him that I forgot to put him down."

He scribbled in the name.

"Did he tell you," Jiggs went on, "that Mr. John Smith was the only person he hadn't seen since the explosion, and that when he opened the door of his room he could find no baggage?"

"Did he?" demanded Wembury when Tetley hesitated.

"No, sir," said the Inspector boldly. "He may have told Captain Allerman that, but he didn't tell me. As a matter of fact, I haven't finished my investigations. I thought you wanted the pieces of the bomb over as quickly as you could get them."

"Go and find John Smith – of Leeds," said Wembury curtly.

Jiggs waited till the door had closed on the inspector.

"I don't want to say anything about the investigating methods of Scotland Yard, Chief," he said, "but it seems to me that that is a piece of information that should have been reported."

Wembury nodded. "I think so," he said.

"Did the Commissioner tell you the name of the man who's been threatened?" asked Terry.

"No – I don't know why, but he flatly refused. When I say I don't know why, I'm not quite telling the truth. The old man has got the old Army code, which is a pretty good code in the mess-room, but not so good at Scotland Yard. Apparently he promised this fellow, or his uncle or whoever it was communicating with him, that the name should not be given, and not even the Secretary of State can compel this stubborn old dev – the late Commissioner to give us any information on the subject."

"That's tough." Jiggs shook his head. He looked down at the table thoughtfully.

"Suppose we get somebody under suspicion, what are the rules at Scotland Yard? Do you treat him gently and ask him a few questions, or do you slap his wrist or anything?"

A glint was in Wembury's eye. "No, we treat them like perfect citizens," he said, "and if we dare ask them a question or two about their antecedents, somebody gets up in Parliament and that's the end of the man who asked the question."

Jiggs nodded slowly. "Is that so? Well, I hope you realise that if you do catch any of this crowd – and you're pretty sure to – you're dealing with the toughest bunch of babies that ever shook hands with the yellow jury that acquitted 'em on a murder charge. If that's the law. Chief, I'm all for breaking it."

Wembury shook his head.

"I'm afraid you can't break it here, Jiggs."

"Maybe I'll find some place where I can," said Jiggs, and nobody protested.

He drove home with Terry and was glad to walk into the cosy flat where Terry lived. It was in a block just off the Marylebone Road. Terry kept no staff, except a woman who came in daily to clean for him. Fortunately there was a spare bed made up, for Terry was expecting a visit from an aunt who occasionally stayed with him when she was in London.

"If auntie comes in the middle of the night she's got to be a loud knocker to wake me," said Jiggs.

"She won't. As a matter of fact, I had a telegram from her; today telling me she's postponed her visit."

Terry yawned. Neither he nor Jiggs had had two hours of consecutive sleep during the past two days.

"Personally," said Jiggs, "I don't believe in sleep. I shut my eyes occasionally as a sort of concession to human practices."

Yet ten minutes later he was in bed, and was asleep when Terry knocked at his door to ask if he wanted anything.

They both slept heavily, so heavily that the consistent ringing of the telephone failed to waken them for ten minutes. It was Jiggs who heard it first, and by the time he was in the passage Terry was out.

"What time is it?" said Jiggs.

"Half-past two," said his host.

"Where's the telephone?"

"In the next room."

Terry followed him and stood by when Jiggs took up the receiver.

"It's probably for me," he said. "I've got a few boys looking around on behalf of the Chicago Police Department." Then "It's Scotland Yard. All right, I'll take the message...Yes, Chief Inspector Weston's here, but it's Captain Allerman speaking."

He listened in silence for a long time, then he looked up. "The name of that feller that the Commissioner was so stuffy about is Sir George Gilsant."

"How do you know?" asked the startled Terry.

"He was picked up by the side of a railway at midnight," said Jiggs, "in his pyjamas, and chock full of slugs."

Terry snatched the phone from him.. "That's all I can tell you, sir," said the operator. "We got a message in just a few minutes ago from the Hertfordshire police. They found him lying on the bank by the railside. He'd evidently been in bed."

"Dead?"

"Oh yes, sir. The Hertfordshire police believe he was on the Scottish express. The body was found half an hour after the train passed, by a platelayer."

"All right," said Terry after a moment's pause. "I'll be down."

Jiggs squatted down in a chair, his elbows on the table, his head in his hands.

"The old man advised him to go to Scotland, eh?" he said savagely. "He went! Who is Sir George Gilsant?" he asked.

As it happened, Terry was in a position to inform him. Sir George was a very wealthy landowner, who had a big interest in a North Country steel corporation. He himself was of foreign extraction, and had been naturalised a few years previous to the war, when his father had taken out papers. He had a house in Aberdeen.

Jiggs nodded. "He might have been safe if he'd got there," he said surprisingly. "I think your old man was every kind of a fool, but if you can get any of these threatened men out of London, into the wide open spaces – if you'll excuse the cinema expression – the gangs aren't going after them – it's too dangerous. Open country roads are easy to watch. But if you try to get away from London in a train you're liable to end in the mortuary. We've got to know these fellows – know their names and where they live – the minute the threatening letter reaches them, and then we can save them. When I say we can, I mean we may," said Jiggs.

He looked at the clock ticking on the mantelpiece. "It's too late for a morning sensation – or is it?"

Terry shook his head. "No; the last editions go at four o'clock. It'll be in the morning papers all right."

He had a bath and dressed, and waited an interminable time till Jiggs was ready.

"You had to wait till a squad car arrived, anyway," said Jiggs.

"We could have taken a taxi," said Terry fretfully.

"While you're talking about taking things, will you take a word of advice, Terry?" Jiggs was very serious. "In no circumstances hire a taxi on the street till this little trouble's through. And if you don't follow my advice, maybe you'll know all about it!"

All Scotland Yard was illuminated as though it were early evening when they reached there. The Assistant Commissioner was in his office, and Terry heard the full story of the murder. It had been compiled by investigators on the spot and by the reports which had been telephoned from Hertford.

Sir George had left his house shortly after ten, accompanied by his valet. He carried two suitcases, and the valet had booked two sleeping- compartments for the ten-thirty to Scotland. They had driven to King's Cross, arriving there about ten minutes past ten, and Sir George had gone straight to his compartment, and – apparently on the advice of the Commissioner – had locked himself in.

The valet's compartment was at the farther end of the train. He had waited till the train started, then knocked at the door and had gone in to assist Sir George to retire for the night. During that period the door was locked. He had left his employer at five minutes to eleven and waited until the door was locked after him.

Between Sir George's sleeping-berth and the next compartment there was a door, which was locked. The next compartment was occupied by an elderly lady, who had booked her compartment in the name of Dearborn. She was apparently an invalid and walked with difficulty and she was attended by a dark and elderly nurse who wore glasses.

After the discovery of the body a telegram had been sent up the line to York, and the station officials and the local police conducted a search of the train. The compartment occupied by the lady was found to be empty. The attendant said that the lady and her nurse had left the train, which had been specially stopped, at Hitchin.

Sir George's compartment was locked on the inside, and so also was the communicating door. The bed in which the unfortunate baronet had slept bore marks of the tragedy. Pillow, sheets and blankets were soaked with blood. There was blood too, on the window-ledge, but the window itself was closed and the blinds drawn. Also, the report stated, the extra blanket which is carried in the rack had been taken down and covered over the bed, so that at first, when the inspecting officers entered the compartment, they saw no sign of the murder.

The Hitchin railway authorities confirmed the fact that the two women had left the train at that station. A big black car was waiting to receive them. The porter on duty was struck by the fact that neither of them carried luggage.

By the time this information reached Scotland Yard it was too late to establish roadblocks. It was not until the next day that any reliable information came through as to the movements of the black car.

Sir Jonathan Groussie was aroused from his bed in the early-hours of the morning and told of the tragedy. He was shocked beyond measure.

"Yes, that was the gentleman who communicated with me," he said. "And perhaps… on consideration…it might have been better if I'd broken my word. It was on my advice he went to Scotland…oh, my God! How dreadful!"

They left him, a shattered old man, and came back to Terry's room as the first light of dawn was showing in the sky.

"Things are certainly moving," said Jiggs. "I wonder what the rake-off will be today."

"Do you think they've sent to other people?" Jiggs nodded. "And that they've paid?"

"Sure they've paid," said Jiggs. "Don't you see the psychology of it? These guys are not asking for a lot of money. They wanted two thousand from Sir George Gilsant, and he could have paid two thousand pounds without remembering that he ever had it. It isn't as though they were asking twenty or fifty thousand, or some colossal sum. They're making reasonable demands – and in two months' time they'll make more reasonable demands. Any man they catch for money will be caught again. That's the art and essence of blackmail. You can always afford to pay once. It's after you've paid about ten times that it becomes monotonous. After this train murder the letters are going out by the hundred."

"But you don't suggest," said Terry hotly, "that Englishmen will submit…"

"Forget all that English stuff, will you?" said Jiggs, scowling at him. "Lose the notion that the English are just godlike supermen that won't react the same as every other nation reacts. We can sit outside and criticise – say they're yeller, and that we wouldn't pay – but our job is to get killed – it isn't their job. Who was the grandest Englishman that ever lived?

Richard Coeur de Lion, wasn't it? And when that Emperor of Austria, or whatever dump it was, said he'd bump him off unless he paid, didn't Mr. Lion G. Heart send home and collect all the rates and taxes and babies' money-boxes and everything to get himself free? Sure he did! People ain't yeller because they want to live, or else we're all that colour, boy!"

When Jiggs said he had a few people scouting round for him he spoke no more than the truth. It is true they were not attached, officially or unofficially, to the Chicago Police Department, but they were recruited from a class with which he was very well acquainted. Jiggs' journey to England had originally been arranged in connection with an international conference of police, to deal with a considerable body of card-sharpers and confidence men which spent its life travelling between the United States and Europe. Jiggs had got in touch with half a dozen right fellows, and was getting useful information from them.

He invited himself to breakfast with one Canary Joe Lieber that morning. Joe lived in good style at a railway station hotel in the Euston Road. It was quiet, a little off the beaten track, and it was the kind of place where he was unlikely to meet anybody with whom he had played cards on his late transatlantic journey.

Lieber was stout, red-faced, slightly bald. He had a sense of humour; but his principal asset lay in the fact that he was well acquainted with the Middle West and its more undesirable citizenry. He looked up as Jiggs walked unannounced into his sitting-room, where he was about to have breakfast.

"Eggs and bacon? That goes for me too, Joe. Anything doing?"

Joe stared at him solemnly. "Seen the morning paper, Jiggs? Put a pineapple on you, didn't they? Is that the same crowd that bumped off that Sir Somebody?"

Jiggs nodded. "It's going to be hot for some of us," he said.

"I guess you'd better count me out as a well of information."

"Cold feet, Joe?" Jiggs pulled up a chair.

"Why, no, but I'd like 'em to stay warm, Jiggs. I didn't know the racket was jigging like it is. You've got a pretty bad bunch here."

"Have you seen anybody?" asked Jiggs.

Joe pursed his lips. "Well, I'm not so sure that I want to tell you anything – I never was a stool – but Eddie Tanner's here, and so is Kerky Smith. You know that, of course?"

Jiggs nodded.

"Any little men?"

"Hick Molasco's here. His sister's married to Kerky."

"She's got his name anyway," said Jiggs. "Anybody else?"

Joe leaned back in his chair. "I'm thinking, Jiggs, whether it's worth while telling you – they're yeller rats, all of 'em, and I'd sooner see 'em in hell than eat candy. But I'm a married man with a large and hungry family." He looked round the room. "Just have a peek outside that door, Jiggs."

A waiter was just coming in in answer to Joe's bell.

"Order what you want," said Joe.

When Jiggs had closed the door on the waiter:

"I don't like them Sicilian-looking waiters," he said. "Sit down."

He leaned across the table and lowered his voice.

"Do you remember Pineapple Pouliski – the guy that took a rap for ten to life in Chi?"

Jiggs nodded.

"I knew him," Joe went on, "because he stood in with the crowd that was working the western ocean twelve – it must be fifteen years ago. Then I heard he'd gone into a racket in Chicago, and met him wearing everything except ear- rings. He was working for the advancement of American labour when the stockyard strike was on..."

"Bombed the State Attorney's house or sump'n'..." Jiggs nodded. "That's what he got it for."

Again Joe looked round then, almost inaudibly: "He's here."

"In this hotel, or in London?"

"In London. It's a funny thing, I saw him in a shop on Oxford Street, buying clothes for his old mother. He didn't see me, but I heard him tell the girl who was serving."

"He didn't see you?" asked Jiggs. His eyes were alight with excitement.

"No, sir." Joe shook his head.

"Can you remember the store on Oxford Street?"

The other pursed his large lips. "No, sir. Rightly it wasn't on Oxford Street, it was just off it. As a matter of fact, I was in there getting something for my wife, one of – um..." He made ineffectual gestures.

"Does it matter?" said Jiggs politely. "You don't remember what he bought?"

"No. They were still handing out stuff to him when I went away."

He could, however, give a fairly accurate description of where the shop was situated.

"You don't know where he's living now?"

"You know all I know, Jiggs," snapped the other, for once coming out of his genial character. "I tell you, I'll be glad not to be in on this racket, because it looks mighty dangerous to me. They're yeller rats – they got my brother-in-law's home with a pineapple because he wouldn't join their plumbing association, and I don't feel very good towards 'em."

Then, inconsequently: "Pineapple was wearing glasses, and there was a yellow taxi with the wheels painted green waiting for him outside." Suddenly he struck himself in the mouth with the flat of his hand. "Shut up, will you?" he growled. "Won't you never learn? At the same time, Jiggs, it mightn't have been his taxi, but there it was with the flag down."

Jiggs went back to Terry's flat and called him on the phone. Briefly he gave the gist of what he had heard, without, however, disclosing the name of his informant.

"You've got a taxi department at Scotland Yard...Public Vehicles, is it? Well, can you get on to the fellow in charge and find if he's heard of such an atrocity as a yellow taxi with green wheels? And listen, Terry, get the Chicago Police Department. Put a transatlantic call in for me, and I'll be there in your bureau – well, office."

He had hung up the telephone, when it started ringing again. He thought that the Scotland Yard operator had forgotten to ring off. He picked up the receiver.

"Hullo! Is that you, Jiggs?"

Allerman had not spoken. "Hullo, Kerky! Thought-readin'?"

"No, sir!" He heard a chuckle from the other end of the wire. "Nothin' mysterious about it. I was trying to get through to you, and maybe I didn't get tangled up with the last part of your talk with little old Scotland Yard. Everything all right in Chicago? Nobody sick, Jiggs?"

"That's just what I'm going to find out," said Jiggs. "How did you know I was here?"

"The operator at Scotland Yard told me," said Kerky. "Wondered if you might like to come and have lunch with me at the Carlton or any place you like. Nothing's too swell for you, Jiggs. I'd like to have you meet my wife too."

"Which one is this?" asked Jiggs rudely.

"Say, listen! If I told her that she'd be so sore! Is it a date?"

"Mark it," said Jiggs.

If there was one thing more certain than another, it was that Scotland Yard's very secretive operator had not given Albuquerque Smith the telephone number. Jiggs took the trouble to inquire when he reached headquarters, and had his views confirmed.

"They're tailing all the time – they knew I was there," said Jiggs thoughtfully.

When he had come out from seeing his friend of the morning, he had noticed the waiter emerging from the room next to the suite occupied by Joe. Jiggs took a bold step. Accompanied by two officers from Scotland Yard, he went back to the hotel. His friend was out, but he saw the dark-faced waiter who had served them that morning. The manager of the hotel was present at the interview, which took place in Joe's sitting-room.

"I'm putting this man under arrest on suspicion, and I want you to take one of these officers to his room," Jiggs said to the manager.

He was drawing a bow at a very large venture. Luck was with him. The waiter, having been at first amused and indifferent, suddenly made a dart for liberty. When he was captured he committed the unpardonable sin from a policeman's point of view; he pulled a gun on the detective who held him. Jiggs knocked it out of his hand, and they put the irons on him.

In his room was a half-finished letter, written in English. It began without any preliminary compliment.

"Jiggs came up to see Canary Joe Lieber and they had a long talk. Joe said something about Pouliski-Pineapple Pouliski. I could not hear; they were talking in a very low voice."

Jiggs read the letter and put it in his pocket. "Don't take that man to the Yard, take him to Mr. Weston's house," he said. "Frisk him first, and then take the irons off him. We don't want to attract any attention."

He walked out arm in arm with his prisoner, and came to Terry's flat without any unusual incident.

"You two boys can wait outside while I talk to this feller," said Jiggs, and a look of alarm came to the dark man's face.

The two officers demurred, but they retired.

"Now, sonny boy," said Jiggs, "I've got a very short time to get the truth from you, but I want to know just where you were sending that letter."

"That I shall not tell," said the man, who called himself Rossi.

"Ever heard of the third degree, kid?" asked Jiggs. "Because you're going to get it. Where was that letter going?"

"I'll see you in hell…" began the man passionately.

Jiggs yanked him on to his feet again by his collar.

"Let's talk as brothers," he said kindly. "I don't want to beat you up. It breaks my heart to do it. But I've got to know just where that letter was going."

The trembling youth thought awhile. "All right," he said sulkily. "It is for a young lady I make these notes. Her name is Miss Leslie Ranger."

Jiggs gaped at him. "For who?" he asked incredulously.

"Miss Leslie Ranger." Then, to Jiggs' astonishment, he gave Leslie's address.

"Do you send it to her?"

"No, mister." The young man shook his head. "A boy comes for it and he takes it to her."

Jiggs heaved a sigh. "Oh, just that! Now, what boy comes for it, and when?"

Here Rossi could tell him nothing except that those were the orders he had received on the night before. He was told by a compatriot on the telephone – Rossi was a Sicilian – to keep an eye on the guest, to note the names of his visitors and to hear, if he possibly could, any conversation between them. The compatriot had invoked the sacred name of a common society, and Rossi had obeyed.

"A very simple little story," said Jiggs. "Now perhaps you'll explain why you carried a gun loaded in every chamber, and why you pulled it on the officer who arrested you? What were you expecting?"

The man was silent here. "Are you going to talk?" asked Jiggs wearily.

Ten minutes later Rossi broke and, after allowing him time to compose himself, Jiggs took him off to Scotland Yard and handed him over to the station sergeant at Cannon Row. He reported to the Assistant Commissioner.

"There's a member of the gang in every big hotel. As a matter of fact, there's one on every floor. This boy Rossi is from New Orleans, of all places in the world. He was doing badly and was tipped off there was good money in England. He reported to the chief of his society in New York and got his assignment right away – there's some arrangement by which countries exchange waiters, and Rossi was put into this particular job. The gunplay was easy to explain. He's served one term, having been sentenced to from one year to twenty for unlawful wounding – he's not a fully-fledged gunman, but he's got the makings."

"What about his passport?"

"It's in order," nodded Jiggs. "No, we've got nothing on him and we can't connect him with anybody in town – doesn't know Eddie Tanner or Kerky or any of them. If he had he'd have spilt it, because he's soft."

Wembury looked at Jiggs suspiciously. "Did you get all this as a result of questions?" he asked.

"More or less," said Jiggs.

Then, suddenly, leaning over the table: "Listen, Chief: you've had five people killed in less than five days, and there's a whole lot of people who are due for the death rap. Are you putting the tender feelings of this wop before the lives of your friends and fellow citizens? Is that the way it goes in England, that you mustn't hurt this kind of dirt?"

"It's a rule, Jiggs," said the Assistant Commissioner. Jiggs nodded.

"Sure it's a rule. Get yourself assassinated like gentlemen, eh? You can't fight machine-guns with pea-shooters, Chief, nor with pillows. I just slapped his wrist and he fell. If he'd got his finger inside the trigger-guard of his Smith-Wesson one of your detectives would either be dead or feeling more hurt than Rossi is."

The argument was unanswerable. "You'd better have a talk with Terry," said Wembury. "I couldn't say any more to you without approving, and that I mustn't do."

Jiggs had hardly been in Terry's office five minutes when the transatlantic call came through. In another second he heard a familiar voice.

"Oh, Hoppy!" he hailed him joyfully. "It's Jiggs speaking, from London, England. Listen – don't waste your time on all that 'sounds like in the next room' stuff. Remember Pineapple Peter Pouliski?…Sure. Isn't he in Joliet?…"

Terry saw him pull a long face.

"Is that so? Have you got a good picture of him?…Yeah, that'll do. Send it down to the Western Union and have 'em telegraph it across. If they haven't got an instrument they'll tell you where you can get it. When did he come out of Joliet?…Only served two years? Poor soul!"

Terry Weston had Inspector Tetley with him when he went up for the preliminary hearing of the inquest on Sir George Gilsant. By a special Home Office order the inquiry had been moved from Hertford to London.

"Life," said Tetley, "is just one darned inquest after another." He fingered his little moustache and grinned expectantly.

"When you say anything funny I'll laugh, Tetley," said Terry. "At the moment it's taking a hell of a lot to amuse me."

"You take things too seriously," said the inspector. "After all, you can't help crimes like this being committed, and the great thing is not to lose your head. If Sir George had taken our advice…"

"By 'our' I presume you mean the Commissioner and yourself?"

Tetley nodded. "We wanted him to go out of town by car."

"Did he tell you – the old man?" Tetley nodded. He was rather proud of himself. "Yes, sir, he told me. In fact, I'm the only person he did tell that it was Sir George who was threatened."

Terry Weston said nothing; he could hardly think about the blunder without wanting something particularly exciting to happen to the late Commissioner.

Tetley was right. He saw before him a ghastly procession of inquests. That on the detectives and Salaman had been adjourned. The coroner who was inquiring into the latest fatality only heard formal evidence of identification, and agreed to an adjournment of a fortnight. Terry stayed behind to talk to him and to make arrangements for future sittings. "I suppose you'll want more than a fortnight, Inspector?"

"It looks as if we'll want years," said Terry ruefully. "Unless we get a lucky break I can't tell you when we shall want the next sitting."

The coroner scratched his chin. "It's a curious business," he said. "I met a man this morning, "a very rich man called Jenner, who's in a terrible state. He shook like a leaf when I talked to him, and it occurred to me that he might have had one of these letters."

"Really?" Terry was interested. "I think I know the man you mean – Turnbull Jenner, the coal man?"

"That's the chap," said the coroner. "He was saying what a disgraceful thing it was that Scotland Yard couldn't give protection to people. He was quoting the Commissioner's letter."

"That will be quoted for a long time," said Terry grimly.

When he came out of the court he saw Tetley speaking very earnestly to a man who was a stranger to him. He was fair enough to be described as an ash blond. His long face and his heavy chin made him memorable to Terry. As they were speaking a third man passed them, turned back and said a few words to the two. He was a round, plump-faced man below middle height; he wore horn-rimmed glasses and was carefully tailored. The two men went off together, and Tetley strolled back towards the courthouse. He was visibly disconcerted to see Terry watching him.

"Hullo, Chief! I've just been talking to those fellows. They wanted to know which was the nearest way to Highgate, and as they seemed foreign I improved the shining moment, so to speak, by asking them who they were."

"I didn't even notice them," said Terry, and he saw a look of relief on the other's face. "You can take the police car back to headquarters, Tetley," he said. "I shall want to see you this evening."

"I thought if you drove me back in your car we might talk things over," began Tetley.

"Go the way I suggest," said Terry, and the Inspector's face went livid with fury.

"You're not talking to a flat-footed copper, you know, Weston," he said. "All this high-hat business…"

"When you speak to me, say 'sir'," said Terry. "Will you remember that, Inspector?"

He left the man so shaken with rage that he could not have spoken even if he had thought of an appropriate answer.

Terry got back to headquarters just before five. He was a very tired man, in no physical condition to undertake any further investigation. He had promised himself that he would seek out Leslie Ranger. He knew she was moving that day, and up to the moment had received no information as to her new address.

Jiggs came in, looking as if he had just woken up and had all the day before him. He could do no more than point to a chair. "Sit down, and don't be energetic. I'm all in."

Jiggs relit the stump of his cigar. "I hear that picture has come through on the television apparatus or whatever you call it – the picture of Pineapple Pouliski. The funny thing that, though I pinched him, I don't remember what he looked like – I'm confusing him with somebody else all the time. How much did they ask from Sir George Gilsant?"

"Two thousand pounds," said Terry, and took up the phone. "That reminds me," he said. "Is the Assistant Commissioner here?…Can I speak to him?"

"He's on his way down to you, sir," said the secretary's voice, and at that moment the Chief came in.

"What are we going to do?" said Terry. "A man named Jenner has been threatened – at least, the coroner thinks so."

Wembury nodded and dropped into a chair.

"That's what's worrying me. I've had a tip about another man who has had a letter of demand and hasn't contacted Scotland Yard. What are we to do? If we start making inquiries we're responsible for the man's death, supposing he's killed. I think we've got to make it a rule, Terry, that we don't move in any of these cases until we are requested to do so by the threatened party. It's an act of cowardice, I admit, but what are we to do? We can't be responsible for the lives of these people, and for the moment I certainly can think of no method of offering them protection. That man you put into Cannon Row, Jiggs, has asked to see a lawyer. He has also complained to the station sergeant and the divisional surgeon that you beat him up."

"I'll talk to him," said Jiggs.

It was at that moment that a messenger came in with a photograph in his hand. "This has come over the wire, sir. The man who brought it is outside."

"Show him in."

The operator was admitted, and carefully stripped the cover from the photograph, which was still a little wet.

"That's the boy," said Jiggs. "Why, how could I forget him! Pineapple Pouliski!"

He handed the photograph across the table to Terry, and the Chief Inspector gasped, for the photograph was the picture of the little man who had spoken to Tetley that afternoon outside the coroner's court!

A Man Called Famous

Rachel Watts

IT'S NOT OFTEN you meet a man whose name is Famous. But on the worst night of my life, here he is, in beige pants and shirtsleeves. He doesn't see me as he gets out of his car, parked on the patch of dirt outside his little house. Across the road the last train rattles past, snaking through the fences and railway reserve between us, and the warehouse I staggered over from. I'm clutching my guts to stop them spilling out and I try to yell out to him but my voice has been ripped out of me. It's too late, the beige bloke is walking to his front door. He's almost inside. I'm torn in half, I'm spilling out, I'm dying.

Shit. I'm dying.

A hideous sound emerges in the night air, a scream like metal on metal, and I realise my mouth is open, it's coming from me. The man turns. My legs stop responding and I stagger into one of those metal fences that make you think of primary schools and pensioners. Blood slips under my hand as I hold on. Just as I start to go under he finally sees me.

He is Famous, he says. Famous for what? He's standing over me, his lips are moving but I can't hear what he's saying. I'm fixated on his brown tie and his ridiculous name.

Honestly, who wears a brown tie?

He's standing over me with a phone in his hand, asking who I am. Who am I?

"Franco."

He's calling an ambulance, maybe the police. I wonder what's left of the scene at the warehouse. Jack's boys, my own pathetic bunch. The gear. The knife. Slick and thick handled. Sliding inside me. Over and over. Police. If Famous calls the police I'm done for. If they don't lock me up Jack's boys will kill me. If they haven't already. My hand reaches out of its own accord and grips him by the forearm. Blood smears his pale skin.

"Gnnf." It's all I can get out. "Drive. Gnuh. Me." He looks me up and down, surveying the urgency of my injuries.

"You need an ambulance." His voice is surprisingly soft.

"Gnnno. No." My teeth are gritted. My fingers dig into his flesh. A meeting of two men, a shared moment of indecision in the dark. A plea. I'm not the praying type, but that's what I'm doing now, clutching onto the stranger. Please. Help me.

Then I'm upright, Famous has his arms around me, half carrying me to the car in a clumsy embrace. The strange vowel sounds keep slipping from my lips. How can he stand himself, driving around in this shitbox Hyundai? My limbs feel far away. Blood smears on the seat fabric. That will never come out. I've made my mark on his life.

Time is slipping. It's getting away from me. I blink and we're in the city, the night-time traffic ebbs around us. Then we're pulling up to a brightly lit hospital. I'm underwater, a team of uniform-clad fish school around me, opening and closing their mouths out of sync with the noises coming out. They bob and weave, flitting in and out of focus. Some of the noises have question marks at the end but I can't focus. My powers of speech have slipped out through the hole in my guts. They draw me further into the fluorescent tunnel, corridors stretch endlessly around me.

Time slips again and I see myself on a hospital bed. I see myself as I am, bleeding guts, staring eyes. Someone hangs a bag of blood up, inserts a line into my desperate vein. I'm pumped full of someone else. I'm sitting in the corner of the room watching myself, the frantic energy of the room is far away as they pump and stick my empty body. Eventually I am gone.

But here I am.

Outside in the waiting room, a man called Famous is sitting in a plastic orange chair with his head in his hands. A doctor approaches him and he deflates as the news is delivered. I catch the words in snippets.

"...next of kin?"

"...only just met him. He was in the street..." Famous is shaking his head. His white shirt is still coated in my blood, drying to a dark crust, his brown tie is askew.

Time passes. I blink and I am alone with Famous again, we're walking across his yard, and into his tiny house together. The first train of the morning rattles by outside.

I don't know why I follow him into the bathroom but I seem unable to stop myself. His tie, shirt, pants drop to the floor horrific and bloody. He steps over the edge of the bath and stands in the steaming shower, curled in on himself, the knuckles of his spine strain against the skin. His body is wracked with guttural tears and I realise it is me he grieves for, and himself, that we are tied together now, bonded, by virtue of that life that slipped from me onto his clothes, his skin. The pulse that was once in me is shared with his and to him it beats a truth. We will die. We will die. We will die. I leave him as he sobs.

I have bigger fish to commune with. And some of them are sharks.

* * *

The warehouse reeks of old motor oil and metal. But underneath it is the scent of blood and fear. Perhaps all abandoned places have this lingering tint of death. Perhaps I only notice it now. All things are happening at once, time has compressed. As I drift around the open space, the dust lingers in sunbeams from the skylights overhead, and behind it layer upon layer of past events. I sift through the past, looking for a specific event, a link to *my* past. And eventually, there it is.

Jack's boys stand opposite my guys, Fitz up front with me, Derek behind us like he was wishing he could be anywhere else. I was thinking about the gear. It all looks so unimportant now. A meeting of men in the dark. From across the gulf of time I recognise the glint in Jack's eyes. He knows he's in control. He always was.

"Franco, mate." His hands are in his pockets. Casual as you like. "Why are we out here in the middle of the night?"

"Got this stuff, you see." The living me doesn't realise how weak he looks. Fitz tries to wipe his sweaty palms on the legs of his jeans surreptitiously. "I can't use it. Figured maybe you could."

Jack bobs his head down to light the cigarette, inhales deeply, and looks at me from under a veil of smoke.

"You got some stuff," he repeats. "Where did this mystery stuff come from then?"

"That's my concern." The jut of my chin. I'd been preparing that line all day.

Across the abyss I watch my fate seal itself, tie itself neatly in string, and arrange for delivery to Famous' door, covered in blood.

"Thing is, *Frank*, it's my business you're fucking with." Jack took one last long drag on the cigarette and dropped it to the concrete floor. "I control the market around here. You know that." He crushed the cigarette butt under his heel.

"We can arrange a deal that's profitable to us both." My voice is starting to grow thin. It's dawning on me, painfully slowly, that this might not end well.

Jack sauntered across the distance between us. His guys shuffled up behind him. Next to me Fitz subconsciously shrank back. This is it. The beginning of the end.

"I've got a better idea, *Frankie*." Jack was so close I could smell the cigarette on his breath. "How about you drop this gear of yours. Go back to moving laptops and old ladies' TVs. And we forget this ever happened."

There was a moment's silence. The scene before me lays fixed. It could still go either way. I watch myself racing through the options. Every nerve ending was firing in my still living body. If I was smart, I would look up at Jack, smile, and agree with his terms. I could go back to TAFE and get that apprenticeship.

But I never have been that smart.

"That would cost me a lot, Jack," I said. If I still had eyes, I would be rolling them.

Jack exhaled a shallow humourless laugh.

"That's a shame, mate," he said.

He turned his shoulders, looking back at the guys behind him, and walked back towards the warehouse exit.

Back when I was alive, this is when things seemed to speed up. But from my vantage point I see the slow inevitability of the guys approaching me, from either side, and grabbing my shoulders. Fitz and Derek hesitate. In front of me, the third bloke approaches. He has a strange smile on his face, like this is the scene in the movie he liked the best. Between his hands glints a blade. Fitz and Derek glance at each other and turn and run. Useless fuckers.

I watch as that third bloke's face splits into a lopsided grin and he shows me the knife. He loves this. He stands close to me, one hand around the back of my neck as though about to plant a kiss on me. His breath on my face in murderous intimacy. He's still smiling as he draws back the blade, he maintains eye contact as he plunges it into the cavity of me.

I'll find him first.

The tableaux, the four men, locked in an embrace is almost beautiful in its sadness. So many wasted lives. But then a circular light bounces around the shadows at the other end of the warehouse. A gust of air disturbs the scene as a door opens.

"Fuck. Rentacop," hisses one of the guys clutching my shoulder. All three of the men let go and turn towards the wobbling torch beam.

They all release me as though on cue, and glance around them, looking for exits.

"Let's go." And they are gone.

I stand there, bleeding and stunned. My hands find their way to the gaping wound of their own accord. I lurch. I flee.

* * *

It's daylight and Famous has dressed and caught a bus into the city. Every item of clothing he owns seems to be a variation of beige. His urge to disappear would be suspicious if it wasn't so clearly sub-conscious. He turns into a side street and approaches a junk shop at a nonchalant pace, still glancing at his phone.

I'm not sure why I'm still here, to be honest. I need to find that guy with the lopsided smile, the one who clearly enjoyed gutting me. I want to see how he lives, a guy who takes life with so much pleasure. And I want to end him. But something keeps me coming back to Famous. This man who tried, and failed, to save me.

Just the other day I was parked around the corner with Derek. Laptops and DVD players in the back of the car. Carefully scoured for identifying marks. We used this shop to offload stuff because it was lax about security. But still, you couldn't be too careful. We arrived early when the shop would be quiet and parked a distance away. Derek always went in, and I waited outside.

I watch Famous fumble with a ring bristling with keys, find the one he's after, and unlock the grilled shop front. He *runs* the shop? How could Derek never have mentioned a bloke called *Famous*?

The interior is where the past comes to die, old furniture and sporting equipment haunts darkened corners. Famous switches on the lights and weaves through tables laden with bric-a-brac to the back of the shop, each footfall exhuming a puff of dust. Hiding behind the counter he pulls out a plain yellow envelope and tips its contents out in front of him. My possessions, handed over by the hospital. A wallet, containing a handful of loose change and no ID. The prepaid phone I used to set up the meeting with Jack. The thumb drive with the details of the gear from that shipment. Some small alarm bell starts to ring in the back of my mind. Famous shouldn't have this.

The shop door opens and closes with a tinkling bell and Famous brushes my worldly possessions off the counter into a drawer below, lifting a blank expression to his customer. And look who it is, my old mate, Derek. Selling more stuff, while my dead body lies unidentified in the morgue. Nice.

"Same deal," Famous says with barely a glance at the iPad in front of him. "Proof of ownership, name and number."

"I don't have a receipt, mate, you know that."

"Means I'll have to give you less for it then."

"That's okay."

I watch as Derek writes a fake name and phone number on a form. The same one he's been using for years. I told him to do that.

Famous counts out a handful of twenty dollar notes onto the counter. He pauses as he tears off the receipt, looks at Derek intently for a moment. He draws in breath to say something, perhaps something about me, the prepaid phone in the drawer in front of him. But he just exhales the thought, all at once, and hands over the cash and handwritten paperwork.

"Find somewhere else, eh?" he says. "Can't keep doing this without proof of purchase."

Derek just nods. The exchange feels habitual and it occurs to me that Famous has been helping Derek out for far too long. That bloke needs to get a damned job.

I can only spend so long in the junk shop. I move, without form, across the city. I search for a man with a lopsided smile and a taste for blood. It doesn't take long.

I find him at the hospital.

* * *

It's my second time here in as many days. This time we make it out of emergency, into the bright, airless corridors upstairs. Mick finds his way to a room with four ageing women laying in four, slim beds. They're quiet, labouring under the strain of life, ill health, faulty anatomy. He stuffs his hands into his pocket as he tiptoes past the hospital beds, and stops at the foot of one by the window. Outside the shadows have grown long and the air is crisp. The woman in the bed is plugged into machines and fluid. She's asleep, her limp face looks made of paper. Mick shuffles his feet and clears his throat. I wanted revenge on this guy. I wanted him to hurt. It seems like that will happen without me doing a thing.

We stand together, strangers, and watch the old woman as the light drains from the sky outside. Eventually she stirs, gazes at Mick confused for a moment, before locking eyes with me. I recoil with a start. Can she see me?

Eventually she clears her throat and looks away.

"What do you want?" She's talking to Mick.

"I… I wanted to see you."

"Well, now you've seen me."

"Is there anything I can do?"

The woman fixes Mick with a cool look. Her teeth are gritted but the flesh of her cheeks sinks. Her skin looks empty.

"It's fucking cancer, Mick."

"But still." Mick swallows and fixes his gaze on the foot of the bed. "Dad said…"

"He shouldn't have said nothing. You've seen me. Go." She straightens the bed clothes around her and folds her arms. The room is unexpectedly cold.

"I'm sorry."

The old woman raises a hand to her sagging face, rubs her eyes, and glances at me before turning to look at Mick. A bag strapped to the side of the bed fills slowly with urine. At the other end of the room someone else moans in their sleep.

"Sorry isn't worth a damn thing," the woman says. "You weren't there when we lost the house. No point being here now. Go."

I leave Mick in the WRX outside the hospital. His face is blank, the colour of wet concrete. The car park is full of the sounds of insects and the sky has grown dark.

* * *

I'm back at the junk shop, watching Famous click his way slowly through a Google search of stabbings in the warehouse district. I don't know why I gravitate back here. There doesn't seem to be any decision making involved, it's like I blink and here I am. Staring at the back of Famous' head, his thinning hair and irksome two finger typing.

He can't Google my full name, he doesn't know it. But he's looking for media reports, crime statistics, with grim, methodical determination.

"Leave it alone, Famous," I whisper. He doesn't hear me, of course. But he pauses, pulls on his jacket, and resumes his search. The chill of death becomes stronger the longer I hang around. I don't feel it but I know it's there. How much longer can I stay?

Famous glances at a missed call on his phone, plays the voicemail on speaker.

"Hello, this is Detective Sergeant Collins from Kensington Detectives, I'm calling about a stabbing victim you may know. Please return my call on 9474 7555 as soon as you can."

A stabbing victim. That's all I am now.

It's late by the time he finally leaves the shop, locks it carefully behind him. And it isn't until he's walking away, me drifting behind him, that I realise. My phone, my thumb drive. He left them in the top drawer behind the counter. The only thing to link him to me. I wonder if in death I could have more power than in life. If I could do good for a change.

* * *

It's dawn. The drawer, the subject of my attention, my ire, for the whole night remains obstinately closed. I can't open it. I have no hands. I tried to force my willpower into it. I tried to harness my desperation to save Famous from his own good deed. He tried to save me. I want to save him.

But I gave up an hour or so ago. I am nothing. Useless, even in death. Why am I still here then? Why can't I just die?

Across the city I know Famous is getting up, showering, eating breakfast. He'll come in here and he'll ring that cop back. He'll do the sensible thing. Surely. Perhaps he doesn't need me to save him.

Outside, the early morning sun is golden and warm, throwing sharp shadows around the streets. One of the shadows, looming around the corner, draws into focus. Derek. Back so soon? And someone's with him. It takes a moment for me to recognise the figure walking next to him. Jack.

Famous. Stay away.

I blink and I'm alongside him on the bus. He's looking blankly out the window. I lean into him. Hear me, damn you. Turn around. Go home. Go anywhere else.

"Mate, you don't look great, eh?" I mutter to him. He can't hear me. No-one can. "Perhaps you should take a sick day."

Famous shivers involuntarily. The morning is full of sparkling light, but my presence casts its own shadow. He pulls his jacket, too warm for this weather, closer to him. The bus is only three stops away from the shop.

"Famous, go home." If cold is all I have to wield, I'll take it. I push my death chill out at him. Cover him in it. "Go home, buddy. Get warm."

He's sunk down into the grimy bus seat. He cups his hands in front of his mouth and blows. The bus is one stop away.

"Famous, I mean it." I'm yelling now. "I don't know what they'll do, but Jack won't stand for loose ends. Your life could be in danger. Go home!"

A wave of fidgeting runs through the bus. A few coughs. They sense me. They don't know what it is, but somewhere, in the back of their minds, they can feel my yelling, my panic. Across the aisle an ancient woman is looking straight at me. I return her dark gaze. She's gripping the bar beside the priority seats tight, her fingers bloodless from the pressure.

The bus lingers at Famous' stop.

The woman leans forward and grabs his forearm as he passes her in the aisle.

"You look terrible, love," she says. Her voice is cracked and dry. "Maybe you should take some rest?"

Famous turns and looks at her but she's not looking at him at all. She's looking at me. I nod.

"Yes, some rest I should think," she continues. "There's been some nasty stuff going around."

* * *

I hung around the shop after Famous got back on the bus going in the other direction. Just to see what Jack and Derek would do. They waited another half an hour or so before giving up. They'll be back. I've got to get Famous to ditch that phone and the thumb drive.

Meanwhile, Famous hasn't moved from the couch. I'm drifting around his house trying to think of a way to get him to get rid of the stuff, when there's a banging at the door. Two cops stand outside, one peers into the depths of the house, the other faces away, staring down the empty street, hands on her hips. This must be Detective Sergeant Collins.

Famous ushers them inside, seats them, with an over-politeness cops must get a lot.

"We know you took him to the hospital and took possession of his personal effects," one of the cops is saying. "What we want to know is why you'd do that if you didn't know him."

I'm interested in that too, to be honest.

"Seemed like the right thing to do," Famous' voice is low, almost guilty.

"The right thing to do?"

"Couldn't let him just bleed to death in the street, could I?"

"Some would."

"I couldn't."

The room steeps in silence for a few moments, as the simplicity of Famous' statement sinks in. He's just a good guy. Who would have thought? It's clearly something these cops don't see often.

"And his personal effects?"

"At my shop, in town. I can take you to get them, if you like."

"Why'd you keep them at all?"

"Not sure, to be honest," Famous' voice is light now, as though a burden has lifted off him. "I thought I might find out who this guy was. Make sure his family knew what happened."

I realise this is the most speaking I've heard Famous do. And he's speaking about me. I feel, somehow, past-tense.

"And did you?"

"Nah, no ID."

"Nothing at all?"

Famous shook his head. He bites his lower lip, fighting emotion.

I feel finished.

They walk out to the cops' car and pile in. I follow, at a distance, but I can still hear them.

"He was still young. It just seems like such a waste, you know?"

"Usually we see these guys a fair bit," Det Sgt Collins says. "Petty crimes, a little shoplifting maybe."

My petty history.

"They have plenty of chances to turn around."

Plenty of chances.

"Before it's too late."

It feels late.

* * *

"You didn't come to work today, Mr…ah… Famous?" The cop is glancing around the shop with an upturned nose. What must it look like to her? Half this stuff is probably stolen.

"Famous is my first name," I say. "And no, I felt awful today, cold chills."

"Something going around."

"Maybe. Feel much better now though."

And I do. Like a weight has lifted. Perhaps it's unloading it all to the cops. The reality of it all, the sadness of it. I had a man bleed out in my arms. A stranger. The last few days my arms have felt weighed down by his blood. Like it was spilling in a trail behind me.

Detective Sergeant Collins takes the things individually in a gloved hand and drops them into ziplock bags.

"Thank you Famous, you've been very helpful," she's handing the bags to her partner, silent and hulking behind her.

She's taking the rest of my details when the shop doorbell rings. All three of us look up. And it's that bloke, who sells an awful lot of iPads. Behind him is a tall guy in a smart jacket. They both notice the cops standing there, notepads in hand, and their faces fall.

"Jack!" Detective Sergeant Collins says. A broad smile lights up her face, a smile a shark might wear. I realise it's really warm in here. "Shopping for a deal are we?"

Underpass

Chris Wheatley

I WAS BACK in the underpass where I'd bitten off Louis Mayer's thumb. It had been Summer then. Now snow lies banked up at the entrance, wet pools seep across the dirty floor and my breath clouds in the cold. Traffic rumbles numbly overhead. Miles of concrete pumping iron blood, squirting black fumes into the air. Wipe your face at the end of a day and you can see the poison. Needles on the floor. Junk food cartons. Just like when I left.

Kid stands silhouetted at the far end. I don't recognise him but as I pass he juts his chin sharp up and "wassup K?" he says.

"You know me?"

He shrugs his skinny shoulders. "Sure K. You want some dope?"

Out in the compound things haven't changed a bit. Two dozen caravans fill the square. Motorway steals the sky on three sides. Chain-link fence. Disused warehouse. Windows like broken teeth. A metal bin charred dark stands in the centre where it's always been. Something wrapped in toilet paper squats in a corner. I wish I could say that it's nice to be back.

A face stares at me from a yellow window before the curtains are pulled shut. I walk over and bang on the door and then bang some more. It opens a crack. The woman inside has a beaten-up face and ash-blonde hair and the voice of a heavy smoker. "What you want?"

"I'm looking for Marie."

"I know you," says the face. She pushes the door open wider. I can see the sharp bones of her hips in the gap between her jogging bottoms and her top. "You're Kenny."

"Yeah."

"I thought you was in the nut-house." She crosses her arms. "No offence."

"Do you know where Marie is?"

I think that she isn't going to answer but then she unfurls a skinny arm and points to another van.

Well I knew that Marie had left the one that we had together, because that was my little brother Ritchie's now. This other was cream-coloured with a dark blue stripe and it wasn't here before. There is a big muddy puddle at the base of its steps. I go to knock on the door but then change my mind and try the handle. It's not locked and the door swings open and I step inside and the first thing I see is Marie, sitting on the edge of a bed, dressed in a pale-pink dressing-gown, one foot raised, a bottle of nail-varnish and a little brush in her hands.

"No, no, no," she says, putting the brush back in the bottle and standing up, looking away and shaking her head.

"How are you?" is all that I can think to say.

She flashes me the briefest of smiles and busies herself around place, looking anywhere but at me. I catch her arm as she hustles past.

"No," she says again.

"No what, Marie?"

She pulls away.

"How have you been?" I ask again.

"You shouldn't have come back," she says.

I take a seat and watch in silence as she bustles around doing nothing.

"I'm old and fat," says Marie, "that's nice for you isn't it."

"You look as good as you ever did."

"That's a nice thing to say." Marie gets out fag-paper and a pouch of tobacco and begins to roll one on the kitchen counter. "I thought you were in the hospital," she says.

"I've been out for a while. I've got a job. It's good to see you," I add, even though I'm not sure that's true.

"You know," she says, lighting the fag from the stove, "Vince runs everything now."

I nod. "I heard."

"He's good to me," she says, breathing smoke into the air. She sighs deeply and half-laughs.

"Marie," I say, "I need to find Ritchie. He sent me a message. He said he's in trouble."

"You know there was a murder here?" she says. "Just over in the warehouse. Cops were everywhere. A TV crew wanted to interview me. I said no. Can you imagine me on TV?"

"Who got killed?"

"Some politician," says Marie. "It made the news."

"Who is Ritchie scared of?" I say. "What's going on?"

"I can't talk to you," says Marie, "I can't. I'm Vince's girl now." She looks me straight in the eyes.

"That's how it is?"

"Yeah," she says, and takes another deep drag on her cigarette, "it's not like you care. You just walk right off and disappear. Well what was I supposed to do?"

"I was ill."

"We're all ill," she says and pulls the dressing-gown tighter around her.

I'm silent for a few seconds.

"It was nice seeing you Marie."

"Kenny," she says, as my hands on the door-handle. "Stay away from Vince. He'll mess you up bad."

Back in the compound I zip up my jacket up against the cold. I know where Vince is. His is the beaten-up old Airstream right at the back. I don't feel ready for that yet. Instead I take the East gate, through the wire, down past the canal and round the corner. Frank's hot-dog van is still there – a dirty-white island in the middle of what used to be a playground, before the council pulled up all the rides and painted parking-lines over the cracked and broken tarmac. The shutter on the van is down but a little smoke wisps up from the chimney, greasy black against the grey sky.

I walk once around the van, counting my foot-steps. Away past the terraced houses, the lights on the tower-blocks are beginning to come on. Tiny squares of yellow light. In the corner of the yard, a little clump of flowers are pushing up through the asphalt. They are tiny and blue and look far too fragile to survive here.

It was fourteen when I bit off Louis' thumb. Louis was a hood from our school. Him and a bunch of his pals jumped Ritchie on his way home. They were laying into him when I came along. That was the first time I got expelled.

Frank opens the door after my second knock. He has lost a little more hair and gained a few more lines on his face, which is as thin and vulture-like as it ever was. A small gold medallion dangles over his white t-shirt.

"Kenny," he says and he slaps me on the shoulder, "where you been, son?"

"I had to go away for a while. I was ill."

"Ill? No? You better now?"

"Yeah, Frank," I say, "I'm better now."

"Well, come in," he says, and he starts fussing around, tidying up magazines and crap. "Sit down. You want some tea?"

Frank lights the stove and puts the kettle on. He flashes me a smile, puts his hands on his hips, stretches and groans, then "cups," he says, opening a cupboard and fishing out a couple of mugs.

"You seem tense, Frank."

He's almost too eager to laugh. "Me? You want sugar, Kenny?"

"Sure."

Frank sets the mugs down on the little table and we sit. I decide to keep quiet and let him squirm a little.

"Kenny," he says, eventually, licking his lips, "I had nothing to do with it."

I take a sip of my tea. It's good. "You had nothing to do with what, Frank?"

"Oh god," says Frank, running his hands over his face. There are smudges of dirt on his white t-shirt. "It's not like the old days," he says, "Vince runs everything now."

"What happened to Ritchie?"

"Kenny…"

"What happened to my brother?"

Frank nods. He looks close to tears. I don't feel a thing.

"Guess you read," he says, "about that politician, Hawksworth, got killed round here?"

"Sure."

"Just over there," he points, "in the warehouse out back."

"What's that got to do with Ritchie?"

Frank looks away. He rubs his knees.

"This isn't easy for me to say."

"Spit it out, Frank."

"Ritchie was seeing Hawksworth."

"Seeing him? You mean for sex?"

"Yeah. Ritchie owes Vince a lot of money."

I take a long look into my cup.

"It don't bother me," says Frank, waving his hands, "you know I think Ritchie's a stand-up guy."

"What did he owe Vince for?"

"Drugs. Football. Horses. Ritchie likes to have fun. You know that."

"How much?"

Frank sighs. "A lot."

"Did Vince make him do it?"

"Nah," says Frank, "nah. But he knew about it."

"Where's Ritchie now?"

"I ain't seen him for days, Kenny, that's the truth."

"Are you lying to me, Frank?"

Frank pulls agitatedly at his knuckles. "Nay," he says, "I wouldn't do that."

I shut the door on my way out. For a while I just stand there, looking up where the sharp corner of the warehouse cuts into the swirling clouds. Then over at the fly-way, its great curving arc alive with noise and headlights. A mammoth slab of concrete smothering the yard like a blanket. Protecting us, Ritchie used to say. Saving us from prying eyes.

There is a light on in Vince's van and the blinds are drawn right up. I knock and without pause I push open the door and go in. Vince sits on a sofa behind a table. He is running through a three-card-monte routine and he barely looks up, although his hand pauses for just an instant. He is as big and as ugly as I remember. He wears a towel draped over his bare shoulders.

"Kenny."

I want to scream at him. I want to pick him up with my bare hands and crush him. "Hello Vince," is all that I say.

"Take a seat. Drink?"

I shake my head.

"Excuse me a moment," says Vince. He types a long message into his phone, watches it for a while and then puts it down carefully upon the table. "What can I do for you Kenny?"

"I'm looking for my brother, Vince. I'm looking for Ritchie."

Vince scratches under his beard and starts to roll a fag. "I ain't seen him in a while."

"That's not what I heard."

"Yeah?" Vince runs his tongue across the fag-paper. "That was a bad business," he says, "that politician fella. Now I don't care what any man does with another. That's his business. But your brother Ritchie, pimping himself out to a man like that. Bringing him here. What was he thinking, eh?"

"Ritchie needed the money. To pay you."

Vince lights the fag. The door opens and a big man comes in. He is a mountain in black leather. Young and shaven-headed with a thick sculpted beard. He takes a seat to the right of Vince and the caravan shifts under his weight.

"You know Barry?" says Vince.

"Where is my brother?"

Vince sniffs. "Okay." He gets up, throws the towel on the sofa and squeezes past Barry. I stand aside to let him pass.

"I lied to you just now," says Vince, as he opens a cupboard and takes out a shirt, "and for that I am truly sorry. But you have to understand," he goes on, "these are difficult times and you're an unpredictable man." He buttons the shirt and the pulls on a heavy leather jacket. "I have to protect my interests."

I say nothing. Vince gestures to the door and him and Barry follow me out into the compound.

"Where are we going?"

"Not far," says Vince. He thrusts his hands into the pockets of his jacket and I follow him and Barry towards the gate. There are rolls of fat on the back on Barry's neck.

"Ritchie owes me lot," says Vince, half-turning his head as we walk, "I was doing him a favour."

The aluminium door of the old warehouse rattles up sharp in the icy air. Inside, the cavernous space is quiet and still. Most of the windows, twenty-feet up, are broken and jagged. Our footsteps echo loudly. We go through another door into a room which is smaller but no less high. Big industrial pipes jut out from the walls. Vince leads us to a patch of brick-work where the wall and the floor are stained a deep dark red. I feel a tight sickness in my stomach.

"Did you kill my brother, Vince?"

Vince looks at me. "I guess we should leave you two to talk," he says, and he and Barry head back to the door. As they leave I hear a sound behind me and when I turn he is there, coming out from behind the pipes.

"Ritchie."

"Hello brother." Ritchie smiles but he looks beaten up and bad.

"What's going on, Ritchie?"

"It's good to see you," he says, "I mean that." There are tears in his eyes and he wipes them away with the backs of his hands. He points to the blood. "That's where Hawksworth died. Right there."

"Tell me."

"Vince knew about me and Hawksworth. I owed him money. I owed him a lot of money, Kenny. They made me bring Hawksworth here. They were only supposed to take pictures. They were planning to blackmail him. It was going to pay off my debt."

"But it didn't happen that way, did it?" I say.

"Hawksworth saw them. He freaked out. He was going to call the cops and then they was all fighting."

"Who killed him?" I say, "was it Barry? Was it Vince?"

Ritchie wipes tears from his eyes. "It was me," he says.

"What?"

"I didn't want to do it. They were screaming at me to pick up the knife. They told me I had to."

"It's okay," I say, as he collapses against me, "it's okay. You didn't mean to do it. It was an accident."

"Vince was going to turn me in, for the reward money." He looks up at me. "I can't do jail, Kenny. I told them if they did that, then I'd finger them too."

"So you sent me a message."

For a while Kenny is silent. "They figure," he begins, "they figure you could take the fall and the money would pay off my debt."

"Why me?"

"They figure you got motive, K, and with your record. Your illness."

Snow is falling outside. Soft shadows against the clouded panes.

"Whose idea was that, Ritchie?" I say.

He pulls away. "They had my stash, Kenny," he says, "I needed it. You know I need it. They didn't give me a shot for three days. Three days."

The door opens. Vince and Barry walk in. Their footsteps echo on the concrete as they move to stand beside us.

Vince rubs his hands together. "So?"

Ritchie looks at me wild-eyed.

"Do we have a deal?" says Vince.

"Yeah," I say, "Yeah, I'll take the fall."

Vince nods. "I have to say, Kenny, you're doing the…"

Vince does not finish that sentence. While he speaks I take out the .38 Colt revolver and I shoot him through the neck. Barry's mouth sags open and I take a single pace towards him and shoot him dead through the heart. Vince slumps to the ground. His hand is on the wound but his blood spurts around it. I kneel beside him. Already he's looking pale. I look him in the eyes until his body falls sideways and his chest is still.

Ritchie is mumbling the same words over and over. I can't make out what they are.

"You should go now, Ritichie," I say.

"Kenny," he says, "Kenny."

"It's all right, brother." I stand up. "It's okay. You can go."

Kenny shakes his head. "Where?"

"Anywhere you like. Just promise me you'll do it right this time."

Ritchie starts to speak but I shout at him. "Go."

From the door he looks back. "I love you," he says, and then he is gone.

For a while I pace up and down the warehouse. When I look at the bodies I feel nothing. Outside in the snow I tilt back my head and look up into the whiteness until it stings my eyes to tears and my face is numb. Somewhere a voice is calling my name.

Marie wears a thin dress and has her fur-coat wrapped around her. She is wearing the beaten-up Ugg Boots I bought her for her thirtieth birthday. Flakes of snow nestle in her hair and she gives me a look that I don't understand.

"Did you really do it?" she says. "I just saw Ritchie. I gave him money."

"He tell you everything?"

There are tears in her eyes now. "I didn't know they was planning to do that."

"It's okay."

"You got to run, Kenny," she takes hold of my jacket. "You got to go."

"No. This way Ritchie is safe."

Marie flings her arms around my neck and nuzzles her cold, wet head against my own.

"You can still go. Nobody will tell the police you were here. You know we don't talk to the cops."

"But Ritiche…"

"Ritchie can look after himself. You have to live."

"Why?"

Marie stands back and looks at me for a long time. The snow falls faster and more densely, impossibly quick, great clumps with barely any space between them. I watch and I watch as it covers Marie, covers her until there is nothing left but the outline of her form, and then not even that.

Maybe she was never there.

I walk away into the cold grey city. A mass of concrete so big it can swallow you up. A creeping thing which will expand forever outward until there is nothing left. We think that we made it but it is the city which makes us.

The old iron arched bridge is decorated with white. The canal is deep and silent like a cold tomb. I hold the gun up under my chin. The metal barrel pushes hard into my flesh. I close my eyes and feel the snow upon my face. Everything is peaceful. None of it matters any more. Now I can understand my life as it really is, an insignificant nothing and the weight of years falls from my shoulders.

I open my eyes and I lower the gun and beneath me the water is beginning to freeze. Great sheets of ice lapping under the gentle waves.

The thrum of the traffic is always here.

How the Bank Was Saved

Victor L. Whitechurch

THORPE HAZELL always looked upon the affair of the Birmingham Bank from a distinctly humorous point of view, declaring that it was really not worth calling a railway mystery or adventure, and that it scarcely called forth any astuteness on his part. And yet there were facts in the case that are, perhaps, worth recording.

The banking firm of Crosbie, Penfold, & Co. was an old-established one in Birmingham, numbering many of the leading manufacturers among its customers. At the time of this story the firm suddenly became aware that they had an enemy, and that this enemy was no other than an exceedingly powerful multi-millionaire of Germanic Jewish origin, named Peter Kinch. His reputation was none of the best in the financial world, and it was rumoured that he would stop at nothing to attain an object.

He had a personal quarrel with the senior partner of the bank – old Mr. Crosbie. Kinch's son had met the latter's daughter abroad, and proposed to her before the girl was old enough to know her own mind. Her father was furious when he heard about it, for the young man bore about the same reputation as his father; and although there were hundreds who looked upon him as a "good catch," old Crosbie came of a Puritan family, and retained its instincts strongly.

Samuel Kinch, who was only unbusinesslike when matters concerned his son, whom he foolishly idolised, went to see Mr. Crosbie on the matter, and, it is said, offered to settle half-a-million on his daughter if the old gentleman would consent to the marriage. This only made him more angry than ever, and he retorted that the girl was not to be sold.

A couple of years had passed since then, and Phyllis Crosbie had forgotten her girlish love, and was engaged to Charlie Penfold, the son of the junior partner – the "Co.," in reality of the firm. But Samuel Kinch had *not* forgotten. Deep down in that keen, financial brain of his was a strong instinct of revenge for injuries, and he had taken the affair as a personal slight.

However, outwardly he seemed to have made it up. He was occasionally in Birmingham on business and in contact with Mr. Crosbie, and he never referred to the subject. Then, one day, he deposited the sum of two hundred thousand pounds with the bank.

"I have so much business in Birmingham," he explained, "that it will be a matter of great convenience if you will hold this money."

Old Crosbie didn't half like it, and proposed keeping it intact in their strong room; but the other partners prevailed upon him to invest it in securities. For some months nothing was heard about it. Then some strange rumours suddenly got about with regard to the bank. People began to ask for their cash, and quite a little "run" was taking place. Suddenly Peter Kinch announced that he wanted his two hundred thousand pounds immediately.

The partners were met in consultation in their private room at the bank, which was not yet opened to the public.

"Yes," said Mr. Crosbie, "he wants every penny of it tomorrow. We must face it."

"Under ordinary circumstances we could have paid easily," said Mr. Penfold senior, "but it's very awkward just now. I can't understand matters."

"I can," said old Mr. Crosbie; "I believe we're the victims of a plot, and that Kinch is working it."

"But his object?" asked Charles Penfold.

"Partly private, perhaps – but there's something else at the bottom of it, and he could well afford to sacrifice his money here altogether if he gained his ends."

"What is it?" asked Charles and his lather simultaneously.

"Railway contracts," replied Mr. Crosbie. "It's a question of cutting German estimates by Hill & Co. and a couple of other firms here. If we were to stop payment there would be a serious lack of ready money, because those three firms do most of their business with us. If they can't be sure of ready money now, they daren't undertake the contracts at the price they could otherwise have done. And in steps the German firm, and the firm in question, gentlemen, is really Samuel Kinch. It's a smart bit of business."

He rose from his seat and took a glance out of the window.

"Look here," he said to the others.

It was ten minutes to ten, the hour when the bank opened, and already five or six people were waiting outside, one of them with a cheque fluttering in his hand, tapping the pavement impatiently with his stick. It was obvious that trouble was ahead.

"H'm," exclaimed Mr. Penfold. "I suppose we can hold out today."

"Yes, for today," replied the senior partner grimly. "We have a fair supply of cash, and I don't think there's any danger. But we must have some more before we open tomorrow. We had better ask Simpson to bring us the securities at once. Also we will telegraph to the Imperial and City, asking them to get the money ready for us. Then, perhaps you, Mr. Charles, and Simpson could go up by the 11.12 train and bring it down this evening?"

The Imperial and City Bank acted as London agents for Crosbie, Penfold, & Co., and it would be their office to raise the necessary funds on the firm's securities. A busy hour was passed in going over these documents and signing transfers. Meanwhile, a steady stream of customers kept coming into the bank, and the cashiers were hard at work paying out money.

Simpson, one of the senior cashiers, who had been selected to accompany Charles Penfold to London, was a particularly smart and level-headed fellow.

"I should like to tell you of a rumour I heard last night, sir," he said to Mr. Crosbie, when the securities had been looked over and packed in a strong leather bag.

"Yes – what is it?"

"Well, sir, we have a powerful enemy, and not over scrupulous…am I right, sir?"

"Quite right. What of that?"

"It would be to his interest to prevent us from getting this money in time, sir, and he might not be particular as to what means he took to do it. One of the juniors was asked a lot of questions about us last night by a suspicious-looking stranger he met – er – well, in a bar. He didn't let out anything, but he told me about it, and just now he saw this same man hanging about the bank."

"Thank you," said Mr. Penfold. "Of course, Charles," he went on, "you will take every precaution. You had better telegraph to Scotland Yard, and ask for a detective to travel back with you this evening."

"I'll do better than that, father. I'll wire to my friend Thorpe Hazell. What he doesn't know about railways isn't worth knowing, and I'll ask him to meet me at the Imperial and

City. He'll probably come back with us, and I'd really rather have him than an ordinary detective. If there's going to be any attempt at robbery on the line, his advice will be the best to act upon, I'm sure."

Thus it came to pass that Thorpe Hazell found himself in consultation with Charles Penfold a little after three o'clock that day in a private room at the Imperial and City Bank, which, as everyone knows, is situated in Throgmorton Street.

"I'm sure we are being carefully watched," said Penfold. "You noticed it, didn't you, Simpson?"

"Distinctly, sir. Not only on the train, but I'm certain a taxi followed us here."

"Well," replied Hazell, "the thing is very obvious. You say you have reason to believe that an attempt is going to be made to rob you of this large sum of money. By the way, what does it consist of and how do you propose to carry it?"

"Mostly of Bank of England notes, but a certain amount of gold. We shall pack it in this bag. If we all three travel with it, it ought to be safe."

"Well, I'm not so sure of that," said Hazell; "from what you tell me, we evidently have a very wily enemy to deal with, and my experience of railway mysteries tells me there is not always safety in numbers. What train did you think of taking?"

"The 4.55 from Paddington. But if you advised it we might travel by another route."

"Quite so. But the enemy might have thought of that, too, and taken steps accordingly. We must be prepared for all emergencies. Now, suppose you tell me exactly why you think this attempt is likely to be made. Is there any ulterior motive besides robbery?"

Penfold explained that there was, telling Hazell the question of the German contracts. The latter's face brightened during the recital.

"Tell me," he said, "suppose your hypothesis is correct and the robbery took place, what would happen?"

"Well, Kinch would know at once, I expect, and would wire to Germany without delay, anticipating the fact that we should have to stop payment tomorrow. He has everything ready, we know."

"Ah, and suppose he wired and put the machinery in motion, and after all you *could* pay tomorrow, what about that?"

"He wouldn't be such a fool. Why, it would cost him a million. Sure to. Perhaps more. When a man like Kinch once makes a slip it's pretty bad for his reputation."

Hazell got up from his chair and slapped Penfold on the shoulder.

"Excellent, my dear chap," he exclaimed; "I thought at first you were only bringing me an ordinary case of prevention of robbery in a train. But this is really likely to be interesting. Quite a little comedy, in fact. That is, if you will place yourself in my hands entirely?"

"Very well," replied Penfold, "but I don't quite see your meaning."

"Ah, you're rather tired and run down, you see. This affair is making you over anxious. Let me recommend a few hours at the seaside. Bournemouth, now, is a capital place. And, by the way, Mr. Simpson," he went on, addressing the cashier, "it's close on half-past three. Not too soon in the afternoon for a cup of tea. There's an A. B. C. fifty yards from the bank. Go and get some tea, my dear sir, and come back in a quarter of an hour's time; and would you mind bringing me a pint of milk in a bottle and a packet of plasmon chocolate? I shall have to dine *en route*."

Penfold stared at him in amazement, but Hazell insisted. As soon as he was out of the room Hazell exclaimed:

"Quick now – see the directors here and get the cash; it ought to be ready now. Have it as much in notes as possible. We must pack that bag before Simpson returns. I'm afraid I'm going to impose on him a little. Ah, and I shall want another bag – mine will do. I brought it with me in case I was out for the night; and we'll ask the people here to lend us some weights, or anything heavy will do."

He emptied the things out of his bag, two of the directors came in with the money a few minutes afterwards, and then Penfold began to see daylight. Meanwhile Hazell was rapidly turning over the leaves of a Bradshaw and jotting down notes on a bit of paper, which he presently handed to Penfold.

"Follow these directions carefully. It's best for you to keep out of the way. Now then, here comes Simpson. Not a word, gentlemen, please!"

"Well, Mr. Simpson," he went on, as the cashier came in, "Mr. Penfold agrees with me that you had better take the money down with me. He's not feeling very well, and he's going for a little holiday. You will have to explain matters to his partners. You and I will start directly, but I'm going to see Mr. Penfold off first. Come along, old fellow, you'll catch the 4.10 to Bournemouth easily."

He took him outside the bank, holding his bag in his hand, hailed a hansom, and, as Penfold got in, said to him in a loud tone of voice:

"Don't you worry, old chap. I'll see this thing through. It's much better for you to keep out of it, because Simpson and I can manage it. I hope you'll find your sister better when you get to Bournemouth; it may not be so bad as the telegram makes out."

He noticed, to his intense delight, that a man who was lounging past dropped his stick on the pavement close by, and stopped to pick it up.

"Good-bye, Penfold – oh, I was nearly forgetting your bag; here you are. Now then, my man," he added, addressing the chauffeur, "Waterloo Station, sharp!"

He had the satisfaction of seeing the man who had dropped the stick hail another hansom, which followed in the wake of Penfold's.

"Ah," he said, "they'll see he takes a ticket for Bournemouth, and they won't suspect anything. Now for a little adventure!"

A quarter of an hour later he was seated in a taxi-cab with Simpson, *en route* for Paddington. The leather bag, heavy with the weight of its contents, lay on the floor in front of them. Once or twice Hazell put his head out of the window and looked behind, laughing softly to himself when he drew it back.

"Now, Mr. Simpson," he said to his companion, presently, "you and I are about to run the gauntlet. Perhaps you may think my conduct a little strange, later, but I must beg of you not to question it."

"Very well," replied Simpson, who had hardly taken his eyes off the precious bag in front of him, "I have every confidence in you, Mr. Hazell."

"That's right. Now, suppose – mind, I only say *suppose* – you and I are attacked on the train tonight, you would defend that bag of money, eh?"

Simpson turned to him in surprise.

"Of course—" he began, but a smile on the other's face stopped him.

"It is a considerable sum, I know," he said, "but not so valuable as a human life – *if* you were threatened, Mr. Simpson, eh?"

Again the smile crept over his face, and puzzled the cashier for a moment.

"*I* should prefer to save my life, I think," went on Hazell. "Let us look at the matter seriously. You are attacked, we'll say, and the odds are too great. The villains get away with the money. Perhaps you are able to stop the train. But the money has disappeared. You would go to Mr. Crosbie when you reached Birmingham, and tell him of this terrible misfortune. You would tell the Police. This fellow, Kinch, if he's at the bottom of it, would, put his little plan in action at once. Dear me! A most `regrettable incident,' as politicians call it. You would throw the whole blame on me. And then – and then – let us suppose that after all the money was at the bank the next morning. What a surprise! Villainy defeated – virtue triumphant. No! Don't ask me any questions. Here we are at Paddington."

A broad grin broke out on Simpson's face as he got out.

"Be careful of the precious bag," said Hazell. "That's right."

The short winter's day was drawing to a close, and darkness had begun to set in. Hazell looked, suspiciously, all round him, and kept close to Simpson, helping him to carry the heavy bag. They took first-class tickets for Birmingham, and tipped the guard to secure them a compartment. On Hazell giving Simpson directions, the latter got in with the bag, and Hazell stood outside on the platform as if on guard.

Presently an old clergyman came along with shuffling step. He was about to get into the same compartment, when Hazell stopped him, telling him it was engaged. He bowed politely, and got into the next one. The carriage was well up the platform and in front of the train, and the majority of the passengers were getting in behind, as is often the case at terminal stations.

A few minutes before the train started a couple of men – strong-looking fellows – came marching up the platform and got into the compartment immediately in front of Simpson. They were dressed rather like farmers, and one of them carried a heavy stick.

The positions of the travellers in this particular carriage were now as follows:

1st compartment – the two men. 2nd compartment – Simpson. 3rd compartment – the old clergyman.

Hazell still stood outside the door on the platform. The hand of the great clock was almost on the moment of departure when he suddenly exclaimed:

"I've forgotten to get a paper. There's just time."

He ran back to the bookstall. At the same moment the old clergyman put his head out of the window and watched him. He bought his paper and started back.

At that exact moment the guard waved his green lamp, the whistle sounded, and the train began very slowly to move.

"Look sharp, sir!"

Then Hazell did a very clumsy thing. He caught his toe in the platform and fell, sprawling.

The next moment he was on his feet, but it was too late to catch his compartment. He made a rush for the next carriage; his keen eyes detected an empty compartment; he opened the door and swung himself into the moving train. Simpson, who had his head out of the window, saw what had happened. At first he felt strangely disconcerted, and then, once more, he broke into a smile.

The first stop was at Oxford. Hazell lit a cigar and threw himself back in his seat, laughing softly to himself.

"They are really a very clumsy lot," he soliloquised, "my reputation is quite at stake in allowing it. Never mind, though."

From time to time he looked out of the window towards the front of the train, but it was not until they had travelled a considerable distance beyond Reading that the comedy he was expecting began to be played.

Then he saw, in the darkness, the door of the compartment in front of Simpson's open, and a figure on the footboard. Darting to the other side and looking out of that window he could just discern someone on that side of the carriage also.

Simpson was sitting in his compartment, wondering what was going to happen. Suddenly there was an awful crashing of glass, and the window on the left-hand side was splintered to bits by a violent blow from a stick from outside. Involuntarily Simpson first started back, and then sprang at the window.

The ruse succeeded admirably, for at the same moment the opposite door was opened and a man sprang in. Before Simpson knew what had happened, he felt himself seized by the collar from behind and dragged back. Then the door with the splintered window opened, and the second villain threw himself upon him. Resistance was out of the question. In three minutes Simpson lay on the seat, his hands and feet tied, and a handkerchief bound over his mouth.

"There," said one of the men, "that little job's done. It's lucky for you my friend, that that clumsy detective isn't in with you, or we might have had to use *this*," and he showed a revolver. "But we shan't hurt you. We're just going to search you to see if you have any notes on you, in case they're not all in the bag."

They set to work, coolly enough, but found nothing.

"Well," went on the man, "now we'll clear out. Sorry to have troubled you," he added, to the cashier, "but you should have taken more care of your property. By George, it's precious heavy!"

"Ready?" asked the other.

"Yes – where are we?"

"Between Cholsey and Didcot."

"Right!"

He gave a sharp tug at the chain of the communication-cord with which every Great Western express is provided inside the carriages. A moment or two later there was a shrieking of the engine whistle and a grinding of the brakes.

As the train slowed down the two men, taking the heavy bag with them, prepared to get out. The one who held the bag was actually on the footboard before the train stopped, and Hazell, who was watching from his window, distinctly saw what happened.

The train came to a standstill on an embankment, and the two robbers jumped and ran for all they were worth, but not before more than one of the passengers had caught a glimpse of them. The guard came running along the train, together with Hazell.

The latter made for Simpson's compartment, and was taken a little aback when he found him lying prostrate, but a couple of seconds sufficed to show he was unhurt. He tore the gag off, and the two of them raised a hue-and-cry that was heard all along the train.

"What is it?" asked the guard.

"Robbery!" shouted Simpson, as they cut his bonds, "thousands of pounds, man."

"Money for a Birmingham bank," explained Hazell. "I was in charge of it with the cashier here, only I nearly got left behind at Paddington and travelled in another compartment. Quick! They mustn't escape!"

"What was the money in?" asked the guard, who thought the men a couple of fools to travel with it as they had done.

"A leather bag – they must have taken it off – there were two of them."

"I saw them running down the embankment," exclaimed a passenger who had joined them, "but I'll swear they were carrying nothing. They vaulted over the fence at the bottom, and each of them used both his hands."

Hazell was standing beside the train and a frown swept over his face. He glanced up quickly at the elderly clergyman, who was looking out of the window.

"Did you see them, sir?" he asked.

"Yes – yes."

"Could you make out if they carried a bag?"

"Oh, yes – I'm sure they did."

"And I'll swear they didn't," said the dogged passenger.

"We'll search the train – sharp, please," said the guard, and he mounted into the old clergyman's compartment at once. But there was nothing there. Nor could anything be discovered in or near the train.

"Now," said the guard, "I'm very sorry gentlemen, but I can't delay the train longer. You should have carried the money in my van. All I can do is to stop at Didcot to let you get out and send a telegram or see the police. That's your affair. It's evident they've made off. Take your seats, please!"

One or two passengers who had started on a chase on the spur of the moment came panting back. Hazell nudged Simpson, and they climbed up into the compartment occupied by the clergyman.

"This is not your carriage," he said mildly, as the train started.

"Oh – so I see," said Hazell. "Never mind. This is a terrible thing – terrible!" and he went on to discuss the robbery.

"You had better wire from Didcot to Mr. Crosbie," he said to Simpson, "see the police there, and then come on to Birmingham by a later train."

"What shall you do?"

"Oh, I think I'll go on. Of course you'll also wire back to London to have the notes stopped. That's all we can do, I think."

An almost imperceptible smile passed over the face of the old clergyman.

"Was it all in notes, may I ask?"

"Oh, no. There was a considerable sum in gold," replied Hazell, who, even for an amateur detective, was strangely communicative.

At Oxford the old clergyman got out for a moment. Hazell saw him hand a paper to an official, and the latter made for the telegraph office. When he came back to the carriage he got into another compartment. Hazell followed him, a sweet smile on his face. The old clergyman grew very grumpy and uneasy.

But Hazell stuck to him like a leech – not only to Birmingham, but all the way to Chester. The old gentleman became more and more uneasy as the train went on. He even told Hazell that he wished to be alone. But Hazell only smiled, and offered excuses. Then he introduced the subject of physical culture, explaining the desirability of lentil and plasmon diet, and giving practical explanation of "nerve training" by holding a piece of paper in front of his face at arm's length and keeping the edge in line with the hat-rack opposite. When they got to Chester he stood about on the platform till the empty train was backed off into a siding.

Then the old gentleman, who had been hovering about the train also, lost his temper, and swore under his breath.

Old Mr. Crosbie and Mr. Penfold, senior, sat in their private room in the bank, with Simpson standing before them. The latter was having a very bad time of it indeed. Questions and rebukes were being hurled at his devoted head by the two partners.

"I cannot understand it at all, can you, Penfold?"

"No," said the latter, "and I'm bound to say I think you have acted in a very strange manner, Simpson. You may go to your place – but there is a detective in the bank, and he has orders to see that you don't leave."

All the papers were full of the robbery that morning. A little crowd had gathered outside the bank waiting for the doors to open. Several Birmingham firms were in consternation. The partners, who had been up all night, looked at each other blankly.

"Can we open?" asked Mr. Crosbie in a hoarse whisper.

The other shook his head.

"We daren't," he groaned.

A few minutes passed in silence. The clock in the office marked seven minutes to the hour. A cab dashed up outside.

The next moment Charles Penfold, fresh and smiling, stood before the partners, opening a bag, and turning out his pockets before their astounded gaze. There was no time for explanation.

Five minutes later the doors of the bank opened, and the foremost of the crowd outside entered, wondering what was about to happen. By common consent they gave way to a coarse-looking man who was forcing his way to the paying-out counter, a smile of triumph on his evil features. For they recognised him as the Nemesis of the bank, Samuel Kinch himself, who had come to take his revenge in person.

He slammed down a cheque upon the counter. The cashier turned it over carelessly to see the indorsement. He did not even ask him to step into the partners' room. He had his instructions.

"You will take it in notes, I suppose, sir?" he asked coolly.

"Yes, if you've got enough," replied Kinch insolently.

"Oh, that's all right, sir."

There was a dead silence, broken only by the rustle and crackling of roll after roll of Bank of England notes as the cashier counted them out and Kinch checked them, with a snarling expression on his face.

Then arose a hum and a buzz. Kinch had been paid. For half-an-hour the paying cashiers were fairly busy, but the tide was beginning to turn, and in an hour's time the receiving cashiers were doing all the work.

The credit of Crosbie, Penfold & Co. was saved, and the tenders for the railway contracts could be delivered without fear of lack of cash for preliminary expenses and raw material.

"One in the eye for old Kinch!" was the verdict of the day.

"Oh, the thing was childish!" said Hazell that evening at the snug little dinner to which old Mr. Crosbie had invited him, but at which he only ate his "plasmon," and partook of seven raw apples – the other partner, Charles Penfold, and Simpson were also present – "I saw that if there was a sham robbery this cunning Samuel Kinch would heap vengeance on himself. So I sent Mr. Charles Penfold here down to Bournemouth, his pockets stuffed with notes, and my own bag stuffed with gold, and slung on the roof of a hansom to avoid suspicion. It would be difficult for them to connect Bournemouth with Birmingham, but we managed to do so by a devious route.

"Then I filled the leather bag with weights and things. Simpson, *of course,* thought we had the money, ha! ha! ha! Oh, *don't* say you didn't, Simpson – don't spoil it. It was a clumsy method of attack, but it answered."

"But what became of that bag?"

"That's just the greatest joke of the whole thing. I was looking out of the window, Simpson, as the beggars got off, and I saw them hand the bag to that sweet old clergyman. The train had hardly stopped before he was out of it. He climbed to the roof of the carriage by the steps at the end, put the bag on the top, and was in at the other side of his compartment in a jiffy. I travelled all the way to Chester to prevent him from laying his hands on that bag, and he was furious. It may be going about the country in that fashion still, for all we know."

"But why prevent him when it was of no value?" asked Mr. Crosbie.

"That was just it. If he had once discovered it was only a sham robbery he would have given the alarm to Kinch – and that would have spoilt all."

"Well, Mr. Hazell. I'm sure the Bank is deeply indebted to you."

"Not at all. It has been a very ludicrous little adventure, and I've thoroughly enjoyed it."

Here he suddenly jumped from his seat, threw himself on his back on the floor, stretching his arms over his head as far as they could reach.

"Good gracious," exclaimed old Mr. Crosbie, "what's the matter? Are you ill?"

"I should be," replied Hazell gravely, "very probably, if I did not take fifty deep breaths in a recumbent position. It is the secret of digesting fruit!"

Lord Arthur Savile's Crime
A Study of Duty

Oscar Wilde

Chapter I

IT WAS LADY WINDERMERE'S last reception before Easter, and Bentinck House was even more crowded than usual. Six Cabinet Ministers had come on from the Speaker's Levée in their stars and ribands, all the pretty women wore their smartest dresses, and at the end of the picture-gallery stood the Princess Sophia of Carlsrühe, a heavy Tartar-looking lady, with tiny black eyes and wonderful emeralds, talking bad French at the top of her voice, and laughing immoderately at everything that was said to her. It was certainly a wonderful medley of people. Gorgeous peeresses chatted affably to violent Radicals, popular preachers brushed coat-tails with eminent sceptics, a perfect bevy of bishops kept following a stout prima-donna from room to room, on the staircase stood several Royal Academicians, disguised as artists, and it was said that at one time the supper-room was absolutely crammed with geniuses. In fact, it was one of Lady Windermere's best nights, and the Princess stayed till nearly half-past eleven.

As soon as she had gone, Lady Windermere returned to the picture-gallery, where a celebrated political economist was solemnly explaining the scientific theory of music to an indignant virtuoso from Hungary, and began to talk to the Duchess of Paisley. She looked wonderfully beautiful with her grand ivory throat, her large blue forget-me-not eyes, and her heavy coils of golden hair. *Or pur* they were – not that pale straw colour that nowadays usurps the gracious name of gold, but such gold as is woven into sunbeams or hidden in strange amber; and they gave to her face something of the frame of a saint, with not a little of the fascination of a sinner. She was a curious psychological study. Early in life she had discovered the important truth that nothing looks so like innocence as an indiscretion; and by a series of reckless escapades, half of them quite harmless, she had acquired all the privileges of a personality. She had more than once changed her husband; indeed, Debrett credits her with three marriages; but as she had never changed her lover, the world had long ago ceased to talk scandal about her. She was now forty years of age, childless, and with that inordinate passion for pleasure which is the secret of remaining young.

Suddenly she looked eagerly round the room, and said, in her clear contralto voice, "Where is my cheiromantist?"

"Your what, Gladys?" exclaimed the Duchess, giving an involuntary start.

"My cheiromantist, Duchess; I can't live without him at present."

"Dear Gladys! you are always so original," murmured the Duchess, trying to remember what a cheiromantist really was, and hoping it was not the same as a cheiropodist.

"He comes to see my hand twice a week regularly," continued Lady Windermere, "and is most interesting about it."

"Good heavens!" said the Duchess to herself, "he is a sort of cheiropodist after all. How very dreadful. I hope he is a foreigner at any rate. It wouldn't be quite so bad then."

"I must certainly introduce him to you."

"Introduce him!" cried the Duchess; "you don't mean to say he is here?" and she began looking about for a small tortoise-shell fan and a very tattered lace shawl, so as to be ready to go at a moment's notice.

"Of course he is here; I would not dream of giving a party without him. He tells me I have a pure psychic hand, and that if my thumb had been the least little bit shorter, I should have been a confirmed pessimist, and gone into a convent."

"Oh, I see!" said the Duchess, feeling very much relieved; "he tells fortunes, I suppose?"

"And misfortunes, too," answered Lady Windermere, "any amount of them. Next year, for instance, I am in great danger, both by land and sea, so I am going to live in a balloon, and draw up my dinner in a basket every evening. It is all written down on my little finger, or on the palm of my hand, I forget which."

"But surely that is tempting Providence, Gladys."

"My dear Duchess, surely Providence can resist temptation by this time. I think every one should have their hands told once a month, so as to know what not to do. Of course, one does it all the same, but it is so pleasant to be warned. Now if some one doesn't go and fetch Mr. Podgers at once, I shall have to go myself."

"Let me go, Lady Windermere," said a tall handsome young man, who was standing by, listening to the conversation with an amused smile.

"Thanks so much, Lord Arthur; but I am afraid you wouldn't recognise him."

"If he is as wonderful as you say, Lady Windermere, I couldn't well miss him. Tell me what he is like, and I'll bring him to you at once."

"Well, he is not a bit like a cheiromantist. I mean he is not mysterious, or esoteric, or romantic-looking. He is a little, stout man, with a funny, bald head, and great gold-rimmed spectacles; something between a family doctor and a country attorney. I'm really very sorry, but it is not my fault. People are so annoying. All my pianists look exactly like poets, and all my poets look exactly like pianists; and I remember last season asking a most dreadful conspirator to dinner, a man who had blown up ever so many people, and always wore a coat of mail, and carried a dagger up his shirt-sleeve; and do you know that when he came he looked just like a nice old clergyman, and cracked jokes all the evening? Of course, he was very amusing, and all that, but I was awfully disappointed; and when I asked him about the coat of mail, he only laughed, and said it was far too cold to wear in England. Ah, here is Mr. Podgers! Now, Mr. Podgers, I want you to tell the Duchess of Paisley's hand. Duchess, you must take your glove off. No, not the left hand, the other."

"Dear Gladys, I really don't think it is quite right," said the Duchess, feebly unbuttoning a rather soiled kid glove.

"Nothing interesting ever is," said Lady Windermere: "*on a fait le monde ainsi*. But I must introduce you. Duchess, this is Mr. Podgers, my pet cheiromantist. Mr. Podgers, this is the Duchess of Paisley, and if you say that she has a larger mountain of the moon than I have, I will never believe in you again."

"I am sure, Gladys, there is nothing of the kind in my hand," said the Duchess gravely.

"Your Grace is quite right," said Mr. Podgers, glancing at the little fat hand with its short square fingers, "the mountain of the moon is not developed. The line of life, however, is excellent. Kindly bend the wrist. Thank you. Three distinct lines on the *rascette!* You will live to a great age, Duchess, and be extremely happy. Ambition – very moderate, line of intellect not exaggerated, line of heart—"

"Now, do be indiscreet, Mr. Podgers," cried Lady Windermere.

"Nothing would give me greater pleasure," said Mr. Podgers, bowing, "if the Duchess ever had been, but I am sorry to say that I see great permanence of affection, combined with a strong sense of duty."

"Pray go on, Mr. Podgers," said the Duchess, looking quite pleased.

"Economy is not the least of your Grace's virtues," continued Mr. Podgers, and Lady Windermere went off into fits of laughter.

"Economy is a very good thing," remarked the Duchess complacently; "when I married Paisley he had eleven castles, and not a single house fit to live in."

"And now he has twelve houses, and not a single castle," cried Lady Windermere.

"Well, my dear," said the Duchess, "I like—"

"Comfort," said Mr. Podgers, "and modern improvements, and hot water laid on in every bedroom. Your Grace is quite right. Comfort is the only thing our civilisation can give us.

"You have told the Duchess's character admirably, Mr. Podgers, and now you must tell Lady Flora's"; and in answer to a nod from the smiling hostess, a tall girl, with sandy Scotch hair, and high shoulder-blades, stepped awkwardly from behind the sofa, and held out a long, bony hand with spatulate fingers.

"Ah, a pianist! I see," said Mr. Podgers, "an excellent pianist, but perhaps hardly a musician. Very reserved, very honest, and with a great love of animals."

"Quite true!" exclaimed the Duchess, turning to Lady Windermere, "absolutely true! Flora keeps two dozen collie dogs at Macloskie, and would turn our town house into a menagerie if her father would let her."

"Well, that is just what I do with my house every Thursday evening," cried Lady Windermere, laughing, "only I like lions better than collie dogs."

"Your one mistake, Lady Windermere," said Mr. Podgers, with a pompous bow.

"If a woman can't make her mistakes charming, she is only a female," was the answer. "But you must read some more hands for us. Come, Sir Thomas, show Mr. Podgers yours"; and a genial-looking old gentleman, in a white waistcoat, came forward, and held out a thick rugged hand, with a very long third finger.

"An adventurous nature; four long voyages in the past, and one to come. Been ship-wrecked three times. No, only twice, but in danger of a shipwreck your next journey. A strong Conservative, very punctual, and with a passion for collecting curiosities. Had a severe illness between the ages sixteen and eighteen. Was left a fortune when about thirty. Great aversion to cats and Radicals."

"Extraordinary!" exclaimed Sir Thomas; "you must really tell my wife's hand, too."

"Your second wife's," said Mr. Podgers quietly, still keeping Sir Thomas's hand in his. "Your second wife's. I shall be charmed"; but Lady Marvel, a melancholy-looking woman, with brown hair and sentimental eyelashes, entirely declined to have her past or her future exposed; and nothing that Lady Windermere could do would induce Monsieur de Koloff, the Russian Ambassador, even to take his gloves off. In fact, many people seemed afraid to face the odd little man with his stereotyped smile, his gold spectacles, and his bright, beady eyes; and when he told poor Lady Fermor, right out before every one, that she did not care a bit for music, but was extremely fond of musicians, it was generally felt that cheiromancy was a most dangerous science, and one that ought not to be encouraged, except in a *tête-à-tête*.

Lord Arthur Savile, however, who did not know anything about Lady Fermor's unfortunate story, and who had been watching Mr. Podgers with a great deal of interest, was filled with an immense curiosity to have his own hand read, and feeling somewhat shy about putting himself forward, crossed over the room to where Lady Windermere was sitting, and, with a charming blush, asked her if she thought Mr. Podgers would mind.

"Of course, he won't mind," said Lady Windermere, "that is what he is here for. All my lions, Lord Arthur, are performing lions, and jump through hoops whenever I ask them. But I must warn you beforehand that I shall tell Sybil everything. She is coming to lunch with me tomorrow, to talk about bonnets, and if Mr. Podgers finds out that you have a bad temper, or a tendency to gout, or a wife living in Bayswater, I shall certainly let her know all about it."

Lord Arthur smiled, and shook his head. "I am not afraid," he answered. "Sybil knows me as well as I know her."

"Ah! I am a little sorry to hear you say that. The proper basis for marriage is a mutual misunderstanding. No, I am not at all cynical, I have merely got experience, which, however, is very much the same thing. Mr. Podgers, Lord Arthur Savile is dying to have his hand read. Don't tell him that he is engaged to one of the most beautiful girls in London, because that appeared in the *Morning Post* a month ago.

"Dear Lady Windermere," cried the Marchioness of Jedburgh, "do let Mr. Podgers stay here a little longer. He has just told me I should go on the stage, and I am so interested."

"If he has told you that, Lady Jedburgh, I shall certainly take him away. Come over at once, Mr. Podgers, and read Lord Arthur's hand."

"Well," said Lady Jedburgh, making a little *moue* as she rose from the sofa, "if I am not to be allowed to go on the stage, I must be allowed to be part of the audience at any rate."

"Of course; we are all going to be part of the audience," said Lady Windermere; "and now, Mr. Podgers, be sure and tell us something nice. Lord Arthur is one of my special favourites."

But when Mr. Podgers saw Lord Arthur's hand he grew curiously pale, and said nothing. A shudder seemed to pass through him, and his great bushy eyebrows twitched convulsively, in an odd, irritating way they had when he was puzzled. Then some huge beads of perspiration broke out on his yellow forehead, like a poisonous dew, and his fat fingers grew cold and clammy.

Lord Arthur did not fail to notice these strange signs of agitation, and, for the first time in his life, he himself felt fear. His impulse was to rush from the room, but he restrained himself. It was better to know the worst, whatever it was, than to be left in this hideous uncertainty.

"I am waiting, Mr. Podgers," he said.

"We are all waiting," cried Lady Windermere, in her quick, impatient manner, but the cheiromantist made no reply.

"I believe Arthur is going on the stage," said Lady Jedburgh, "and that, after your scolding, Mr. Podgers is afraid to tell him so."

Suddenly Mr. Podgers dropped Lord Arthur's right hand, and seized hold of his left, bending down so low to examine it that the gold rims of his spectacles seemed almost to touch the palm. For a moment his face became a white mask of horror, but he soon recovered his *sang-froid,* and looking up at Lady Windermere, said with a forced smile, "It is the hand of a charming young man."

"Of course it is!" answered Lady Windermere, "but will he be a charming husband? That is what I want to know."

"All charming young men are," said Mr. Podgers.

"I don't think a husband should be too fascinating," murmured Lady Jedburgh pensively, "it is so dangerous."

"My dear child, they never are too fascinating," cried Lady Windermere. "But what I want are details. Details are the only things that interest. What is going to happen to Lord Arthur?"

"Well, within the next few months Lord Arthur will go a voyage—"

"Oh yes, his honeymoon, of course!"

"And lose a relative."

"Not his sister, I hope?" said Lady Jedburgh, in a piteous tone of voice.

"Certainly not his sister," answered Mr. Podgers, with a deprecating wave of the hand, "a distant relative merely."

"Well, I am dreadfully disappointed," said Lady Windermere. "I have absolutely nothing to tell Sybil tomorrow. No one cares about distant relatives nowadays. They went out of fashion years ago. However, I suppose she had better have a black silk by her; it always does for church, you know. And now let us go to supper. They are sure to have eaten everything up, but we may find some hot soup. François used to make excellent soup once, but he is so agitated about politics at present, that I never feel quite certain about him. I do wish General Boulanger would keep quiet. Duchess, I am sure you are tired?"

"Not at all, dear Gladys," answered the Duchess, waddling towards the door. "I have enjoyed myself immensely, and the cheiropodist, I mean the cheiromantist, is most interesting. Flora, where can my tortoise-shell fan be? Oh, thank you, Sir Thomas, so much. And my lace shawl, Flora? Oh, thank you, Sir Thomas, very kind, I'm sure"; and the worthy creature finally managed to get downstairs without dropping her scent-bottle more than twice.

All this time Lord Arthur Savile had remained standing by the fireplace, with the same feeling of dread over him, the same sickening sense of coming evil. He smiled sadly at his sister, as she swept past him on Lord Plymdale's arm, looking lovely in her pink brocade and pearls, and he hardly heard Lady Windermere when she called to him to follow her. He thought of Sybil Merton, and the idea that anything could come between them made his eyes dim with tears.

Looking at him, one would have said that Nemesis had stolen the shield of Pallas, and shown him the Gorgon's head. He seemed turned to stone, and his face was like marble in its melancholy. He had lived the delicate and luxurious life of a young man of birth and fortune, a life exquisite in its freedom from sordid care, its beautiful boyish insouciance; and now for the first time he became conscious of the terrible mystery of Destiny, of the awful meaning of Doom.

How mad and monstrous it all seemed! Could it be that written on his hand, in characters that he could not read himself, but that another could decipher, was some fearful secret of sin, some blood-red sign of crime? Was there no escape possible? Were we no better than chessmen, moved by an unseen power, vessels the potter fashions at his fancy, for honour or for shame? His reason revolted against it, and yet he felt that some tragedy was hanging over him, and that he had been suddenly called upon to bear an intolerable burden. Actors are so fortunate. They can choose whether they will appear in tragedy or in comedy, whether they will suffer or make merry, laugh or shed tears. But in real life it is different. Most men and women are forced to perform parts for which they have no qualifications. Our Guildensterns play Hamlet for us, and our Hamlets have to jest like Prince Hal. The world is a stage, but the play is badly cast.

Suddenly Mr. Podgers entered the room. When he saw Lord Arthur he started, and his coarse, fat face became a sort of greenish-yellow colour. The two men's eyes met, and for a moment there was silence.

"The Duchess has left one of her gloves here, Lord Arthur, and has asked me to bring it to her," said Mr. Podgers finally. "Ah, I see it on the sofa! Good evening."

"Mr. Podgers, I must insist on your giving me a straightforward answer to a question I am going to put to you."

"Another time, Lord Arthur, but the Duchess is anxious. I am afraid I must go."

"You shall not go. The Duchess is in no hurry."

"Ladies should not be kept waiting, Lord Arthur," said Mr. Podgers, with his sickly smile. "The fair sex is apt to be impatient."

Lord Arthur's finely-chiselled lips curled in petulant disdain. The poor Duchess seemed to him of very little importance at that moment. He walked across the room to where Mr. Podgers was standing, and held his hand out.

"Tell me what you saw there," he said. "Tell me the truth. I must know it. I am not a child."

Mr. Podgers's eyes blinked behind his gold-rimmed spectacles, and he moved uneasily from one foot to the other, while his fingers played nervously with a flash watch-chain.

"What makes you think that I saw anything in your hand, Lord Arthur, more than I told you?"

"I know you did, and I insist on your telling me what it was. I will pay you. I will give you a cheque for a hundred pounds."

The green eyes flashed for a moment, and then became dull again.

"Guineas?" said Mr. Podgers at last, in a low voice.

"Certainly. I will send you a cheque tomorrow. What is your club?"

"I have no club. That is to say, not just at present. My address is – , but allow me to give you my card"; and producing a bit of gilt-edge pasteboard from his waistcoat pocket, Mr. Podgers handed it, with a low bow, to Lord Arthur, who read on it,

Mr. *SEPTIMUS R. PODGERS*
Professional Cheiromantist
103a West Moon Street

"My hours are from ten to four," murmured Mr. Podgers mechanically, "and I make a reduction for families."

"Be quick," cried Lord Arthur, looking very pale, and holding his hand out.

Mr. Podgers glanced nervously round, and drew the heavy portière across the door.

"It will take a little time, Lord Arthur, you had better sit down."

"Be quick, sir," cried Lord Arthur again, stamping his foot angrily on the polished floor.

Mr. Podgers smiled, drew from his breast-pocket a small magnifying glass, and wiped it carefully with his handkerchief.

"I am quite ready," he said.

Chapter II

TEN MINUTES LATER, with face blanched by terror, and eyes wild with grief, Lord Arthur Savile rushed from Bentinck House, crushing his way through the crowd of fur-coated footmen that stood round the large striped awning, and seeming not to see or hear anything. The night was bitter cold, and the gas-lamps round the square flared and flickered in the keen wind; but his hands were hot with fever, and his forehead burned like fire. On and on he went, almost with the gait of a drunken man. A policeman looked curiously at him as he passed, and a beggar, who slouched from an archway to ask for alms, grew frightened, seeing misery greater than his own. Once he stopped under a lamp, and looked at his hands. He thought he could detect the stain of blood already upon them, and a faint cry broke from his trembling lips.

Murder! that is what the cheiromantist had seen there. Murder! The very night seemed to know it, and the desolate wind to howl it in his ear. The dark corners of the streets were full of it. It grinned at him from the roofs of the houses.

First he came to the Park, whose sombre woodland seemed to fascinate him. He leaned wearily up against the railings, cooling his brow against the wet metal, and listening to the tremulous silence of the trees. "Murder! murder!" he kept repeating, as though iteration could dim the horror of the word. The sound of his own voice made him shudder, yet he almost hoped that Echo might hear him, and wake the slumbering city from its dreams. He felt a mad desire to stop the casual passer-by, and tell him everything.

Then he wandered across Oxford Street into narrow, shameful alleys. Two women with painted faces mocked at him as he went by. From a dark courtyard came a sound of oaths and blows, followed by shrill screams, and, huddled upon a damp door-step, he saw the crook-backed forms of poverty and eld. A strange pity came over him. Were these children of sin and misery predestined to their end, as he to his? Were they, like him, merely the puppets of a monstrous show?

And yet it was not the mystery, but the comedy of suffering that struck him; its absolute uselessness, its grotesque want of meaning. How incoherent everything seemed! How lacking in all harmony! He was amazed at the discord between the shallow optimism of the day, and the real facts of existence. He was still very young.

After a time he found himself in front of Marylebone Church. The silent roadway looked like a long riband of polished silver, flecked here and there by the dark arabesques of waving shadows. Far into the distance curved the line of flickering gas-lamps, and outside a little walled-in house stood a solitary hansom, the driver asleep inside. He walked hastily in the direction of Portland Place, now and then looking round, as though he feared that he was being followed. At the corner of Rich Street stood two men, reading a small bill upon a hoarding. An odd feeling of curiosity stirred him, and he crossed over. As he came near, the word "Murder," printed in black letters, met his eye. He started, and a deep flush came into his cheek. It was an advertisement offering a reward for any information leading to the arrest of a man of medium height, between thirty and forty years of age, wearing a billy-cock hat, a black coat, and check trousers, and with a scar upon his right cheek. He read it over and over again, and wondered if the wretched man would be caught, and how he had been scarred. Perhaps, some day, his own name might be placarded on the walls of London. Some day, perhaps, a price would be set on his head also.

The thought made him sick with horror. He turned on his heel, and hurried on into the night.

Where he went he hardly knew. He had a dim memory of wandering through a labyrinth of sordid houses, of being lost in a giant web of sombre streets, and it was bright dawn when he found himself at last in Piccadilly Circus. As he strolled home towards Belgrave Square, he met the great waggons on their way to Covent Garden. The white-smocked carters, with their pleasant sunburnt faces and coarse curly hair, strode sturdily on, cracking their whips, and calling out now and then to each other; on the back of a huge grey horse, the leader of a jangling team, sat a chubby boy, with a bunch of primroses in his battered hat, keeping tight hold of the mane with his little hands, and laughing; and the great piles of vegetables looked like masses of jade against the morning sky, like masses of green jade against the pink petals of some marvellous rose. Lord Arthur felt curiously affected, he could not tell why. There was something in the dawn's delicate loveliness that seemed to him inexpressibly pathetic, and he thought of all the days that break in beauty, and that set in storm. These rustics, too, with their rough, good-humoured voices, and their nonchalant ways, what a strange London they saw! A London free from the sin of night and the smoke of day, a pallid, ghost-like city, a desolate town of tombs! He wondered what they thought of it, and whether they knew anything of its splendour and its shame, of its fierce, fiery-coloured joys, and its horrible hunger, of all it makes and mars from morn to eve. Probably it was to them merely a mart where they brought their fruits to sell, and where they tarried for a few hours at most, leaving the streets still silent, the houses still asleep. It gave him pleasure to watch them as they went by. Rude as they were, with their heavy, hob-nailed shoes, and their awkward gait, they brought a little of a ready with them. He felt that they had lived with Nature, and that she had taught them peace. He envied them all that they did not know.

By the time he had reached Belgrave Square the sky was a faint blue, and the birds were beginning to twitter in the gardens.

Chapter III

WHEN LORD ARTHUR woke it was twelve o'clock, and the midday sun was streaming through the ivory-silk curtains of his room. He got up and looked out of the window. A dim haze of heat was hanging over the great city, and the roofs of the houses were like dull silver. In the flickering green of the square below some children were flitting about like white butterflies, and the pavement was crowded with people on their way to the Park. Never had life seemed lovelier to him, never had the things of evil seemed more remote.

Then his valet brought him a cup of chocolate on a tray. After he had drunk it, he drew aside a heavy *portière* of peach-coloured plush, and passed into the bathroom. The light stole softly from above, through thin slabs of transparent onyx, and the water in the marble tank glimmered like a moonstone. He plunged hastily in, till the cool ripples touched throat and hair, and then dipped his head right under, as though he would have wiped away the stain of some shameful memory. When he stepped out he felt almost at peace. The exquisite physical conditions of the moment had dominated him, as indeed often happens in the case of very finely-wrought natures, for the senses, like fire, can purify as well as destroy.

After breakfast, he flung himself down on a divan, and lit a cigarette. On the mantel-shelf, framed in dainty old brocade, stood a large photograph of Sybil Merton, as he had seen her first at Lady Noel's ball. The small, exquisitely-shaped head drooped slightly to one side, as though the thin, reed-like throat could hardly bear the burden of so much beauty;

the lips were slightly parted, and seemed made for sweet music; and all the tender purity of girlhood looked out in wonder from the dreaming eyes. With her soft, clinging dress of *crêpe-de-chine,* and her large leaf-shaped fan, she looked like one of those delicate little figures men find in the olive-woods near Tanagra; and there was a touch of Greek grace in her pose and attitude. Yet she was not *petite.* She was simply perfectly proportioned – a rare thing in an age when so many women are either over life-size or insignificant.

Now as Lord Arthur looked at her, he was filled with the terrible pity that is born of love. He felt that to marry her, with the doom of murder hanging over his head, would be a betrayal like that of Judas, a sin worse than any the Borgia had ever dreamed of. What happiness could there be for them, when at any moment he might be called upon to carry out the awful prophecy written in his hand? What manner of life would be theirs while Fate still held this fearful fortune in the scales? The marriage must be postponed, at all costs. Of this he was quite resolved. Ardently though he loved the girl, and the mere touch of her fingers, when they sat together, made each nerve of his body thrill with exquisite joy, he recognised none the less clearly where his duty lay, and was fully conscious of the fact that he had no right to marry until he had committed the murder. This done, he could stand before the altar with Sybil Merton, and give his life into her hands without terror of wrongdoing. This done, he could take her to his arms, knowing that she would never have to blush for him, never have to hang her head in shame. But done it must be first; and the sooner the better for both.

Many men in his position would have preferred the primrose path of dalliance to the steep heights of duty; but Lord Arthur was too conscientious to set pleasure above principle. There was more than mere passion in his love; and Sybil was to him a symbol of all that is good and noble. For a moment he had a natural repugnance against what he was asked to do, but it soon passed away. His heart told him that it was not a sin, but a sacrifice; his reason reminded him that there was no other course open. He had to choose between living for himself and living for others, and terrible though the task laid upon him undoubtedly was, yet he knew that he must not suffer selfishness to triumph over love. Sooner or later we are all called upon to decide on the same issue – of us all, the same question is asked. To Lord Arthur it came early in life – before his nature had been spoiled by the calculating cynicism of middle-age, or his heart corroded by the shallow, fashionable egotism of our day, and he felt no hesitation about doing his duty. Fortunately also, for him, he was no mere dreamer, or idle dilettante. Had he been so, he would have hesitated, like Hamlet, and let irresolution mar his purpose. But he was essentially practical. Life to him meant action, rather than thought. He had that rarest of all things, common sense.

The wild, turbid feelings of the previous night had by this time completely passed away, and it was almost with a sense of shame that he looked back upon his mad wanderings from street to street, his fierce emotional agony. The very sincerity of his sufferings made them seem unreal to him now. He wondered how he could have been so foolish as to rant and rave about the inevitable. The only question that seemed to trouble him was, whom to make away with; for he was not blind to the fact that murder, like the religions of the Pagan world, requires a victim as well as a priest. Not being a genius, he had no enemies, and indeed he felt that this was not the time for the gratification of any personal pique or dislike, the mission in which he was engaged being one of great and grave solemnity. He accordingly made out a list of his friends and relatives on a sheet of notepaper, and after careful consideration, decided in favour of Lady Clementina Beauchamp, a dear old lady who lived in Curzon Street, and was his own second cousin by his mother's side. He had always been very fond of Lady Clem, as every one called her, and as he was very wealthy himself, having come into all Lord Rugby's property when he came of age, there was no possibility of his deriving any vulgar monetary advantage by her death. In fact, the more he thought over the matter, the more she seemed to him to be just the right person, and, feeling that any delay would be unfair to Sybil, he determined to make his arrangements at once.

The first thing to be done was, of course, to settle with the cheiromantist; so he sat down at a small Sheraton writing-table that stood near the window, drew a cheque for £105, payable to the order of Mr. Septimus Podgers, and, enclosing it in an envelope, told his valet to take it to West Moon Street. He then telephoned to the stables for his hansom, and dressed to go out. As he was leaving the room he looked back at Sybil Merton's photograph, and swore that, come what may, he would never let her know what he was doing for her sake, but would keep the secret of his self-sacrifice hidden always in his heart.

On his way to the Buckingham, he stopped at a florist's, and sent Sybil a beautiful basket of narcissus, with lovely white petals and staring pheasants' eyes, and on arriving at the club, went straight to the library, rang the bell, and ordered the waiter to bring him a lemon-and-soda, and a book on Toxicology. He had fully decided that poison was the best means to adopt in this troublesome business. Anything like personal violence was extremely distasteful to him, and besides, he was very anxious not to murder Lady Clementina in any way that might attract public attention, as he hated the idea of being lionised at Lady Windermere's, or seeing his name figuring in the paragraphs of vulgar society – newspapers. He had also to think of Sybil's father and mother, who were rather old-fashioned people, and might possibly object to the marriage if there was anything like a scandal, though he felt certain that if he told them the whole facts of the case they would be the very first to appreciate the motives that had actuated him. He had every reason, then, to decide in favour of poison. It was safe, sure, and quiet, and did away with any necessity for painful scenes, to which, like most Englishmen, he had a rooted objection.

Of the science of poisons, however, he knew absolutely nothing, and as the waiter seemed quite unable to find anything in the library but *Ruff's Guide* and *Bailey's Magazine,* he examined the book-shelves himself, and finally came across a handsomely-bound edition of the *Pharmacopoeia,* and a copy of Erskine's *Toxicology,* edited by Sir Mathew Reid, the President of the Royal College of Physicians, and one of the oldest members of the Buckingham, having been elected in mistake for somebody else; a *contretemps* that so enraged the Committee, that when the real man came up they black-balled him unanimously. Lord Arthur was a good deal puzzled at the technical terms used in both books, and had begun to regret that he had not paid more attention to his classics at Oxford, when in the second volume of Erskine, he found a very interesting and complete account of the properties of aconitine, written in fairly clear English. It seemed to him to be exactly the poison he wanted. It was swift – indeed, almost immediate, in its effect – perfectly painless, and when taken in the form of a gelatine capsule, the mode recommended by Sir Mathew, not by any means unpalatable. He accordingly made a note, upon his shirt-cuff, of the amount necessary for a fatal dose, put the books back in their places, and strolled up St. James's Street, to Pestle and Humbey's, the great chemists. Mr. Pestle, who always attended personally on the aristocracy, was a good deal surprised at the order, and in a very deferential manner murmured something about a medical certificate being necessary. However, as soon as Lord Arthur explained to him that it was for a large Norwegian mastiff that he was obliged to get rid of, as it showed signs of incipient rabies, and had already bitten the coachman twice in the calf of the leg, he expressed himself as being perfectly satisfied, complimented Lord Arthur on his wonderful knowledge of Toxicology, and had the prescription made up immediately.

Lord Arthur put the capsule into a pretty little silver *bonbonnière* that he saw in a shop window in Bond Street, threw away Pestle and Hambey's ugly pill-box, and drove off at once to Lady Clementina's.

"Well, *monsieur le mauvais sujet,*" cried the old lady, as he entered the room, "why haven't you been to see me all this time?"

"My dear Lady Clem, I never have a moment to myself," said Lord Arthur, smiling.

"I suppose you mean that you go about all day long with Miss Sybil Merton, buying *chiffons* and talking nonsense? I cannot understand why people make such a fuss about being married. In my day we never dreamed of billing and cooing in public, or in private for that matter."

"I assure you I have not seen Sybil for twenty-four hours, Lady Clem. As far as I can make out, she belongs entirely to her milliners."

"Of course; that is the only reason you come to see an ugly old woman like myself. I wonder you men don't take warning. *On a fait des folies pour moi,* and here I am, a poor rheumatic creature, with a false front and a bad temper. Why, if it were not for dear Lady Jansen, who sends me all the worst French novels she can find, I don't think I could get through the day. Doctors are no use at all, except to get fees out of one. They can't even cure my heartburn."

"I have brought you a cure for that, Lady Clem," said Lord Arthur gravely. "It is a wonderful thing, invented by an American."

"I don't think I like American inventions, Arthur. I am quite sure I don't. I read some American novels lately, and they were quite nonsensical."

"Oh, but there is no nonsense at all about this, Lady Clem! I assure you it is a perfect cure. You must promise to try it"; and Lord Arthur brought the little box out of his pocket, and handed it to her.

"Well, the box is charming, Arthur. Is it really a present? That is very sweet of you. And is this the wonderful medicine? It looks like a *bonbon.* I'll take it at once."

"Good heavens! Lady Clem," cried Lord Arthur, catching hold of her hand, "you mustn't do anything of the kind. It is a homoeopathic medicine, and if you take it without having heartburn, it might do you no end of harm. Wait till you have an attack, and take it then. You will be astonished at the result."

"I should like to take it now," said Lady Clementina, holding up to the light the little transparent capsule, with its floating bubble of liquid aconitine. I am sure it is delicious. The fact is that, though I hate doctors, I love medicines. However, I'll keep it till my next attack."

"And when will that be?" asked Lord Arthur eagerly. "Will it be soon?"

"I hope not for a week. I had a very bad time yesterday morning with it. But one never knows."

"You are sure to have one before the end of the month then, Lady Clem?"

"I am afraid so. But how sympathetic you are today, Arthur! Really, Sybil has done you a great deal of good. And now you must run away, for I am dining with some very dull people, who won't talk scandal, and I know that if I don't get my sleep now I shall never be able to keep awake during dinner. Good-bye, Arthur, give my love to Sybil, and thank you so much for the American medicine."

"You won't forget to take it, Lady Clem, will you?" said Lord Arthur, rising from his seat.

"Of course I won't, you silly boy. I think it is most kind of you to think of me, and I shall write and tell you if I want any more."

Lord Arthur left the house in high spirits, and with a feeling of immense relief.

That night he had an interview with Sybil Merton. He told her how he had been suddenly placed in a position of terrible difficulty, from which neither honour nor duty would allow him to recede. He told her that the marriage must be put off for the present, as until he had got rid of his fearful entanglements, he was not a free man. He implored her to trust him, and not to have any doubts about the future. Everything would come right, but patience was necessary.

The scene took place in the conservatory of Mr. Merton's house, in Park Lane, where Lord Arthur had dined as usual. Sybil had never seemed more happy, and for a moment Lord Arthur had been tempted to play the coward's part, to write to Lady Clementina for the pill, and to let the marriage go on as if there was no such person as Mr. Podgers in the world. His better nature, however, soon asserted itself, and even when Sybil flung herself weeping into his arms, he did not falter. The beauty that stirred his senses had touched his conscience also. He felt that to wreck so fair a life for the sake of a few months' pleasure would be a wrong thing to do.

He stayed with Sybil till nearly midnight, comforting her and being comforted in turn, and early the next morning he left for Venice, after writing a manly, firm letter to Mr. Merton about the necessary postponement of the marriage.

Chapter IV

IN VENICE he met his brother, Lord Surbiton, who happened to have come over from Corfu in his yacht. The two young men spent a delightful fortnight together. In the morning they rode on the Lido, or glided up and down the green canals in their long black gondola; in the afternoon they usually entertained visitors on the yacht; and in the evening they dined at Florian's, and smoked innumerable cigarettes on the Piazza. Yet somehow Lord Arthur was not happy. Every day he studied the obituary column in the Times, expecting to see a notice of Lady Clementina's death, but every day he was disappointed. He began to be afraid that some accident had happened to her, and often regretted that he had prevented her taking the aconitine when she had been so anxious to try its effect. Sybil's letters, too, though full of love, and trust, and tenderness, were often very sad in their tone, and sometimes he used to think that he was parted from her for ever.

After a fortnight Lord Surbiton got bored with Venice, and determined to run down the coast to Ravenna, as he heard that there was some capital cock-shooting in the Pinetum. Lord Arthur at first refused absolutely to come, but Surbiton, of whom he was extremely fond, finally persuaded him that if he stayed at Danieli's by himself he would be moped to death, and on the morning of the 15th they started, with a strong nor'-east wind blowing, and a rather choppy sea. The sport was excellent, and the free, open-air life brought the colour back to Lord Arthur's cheek, but about the 22nd he became anxious about Lady Clementina, and, in spite of Surbiton's remonstrances, came back to Venice by train.

As he stepped out of his gondola on to the hotel steps, the proprietor came forward to meet him with a sheaf of telegrams. Lord Arthur snatched them out of his hand, and tore them open. Everything had been successful. Lady Clementina had died quite suddenly on the night of the 17th!

His first thought was for Sybil, and he sent her off a telegram announcing his immediate return to London. He then ordered his valet to pack his things for the night mail, sent his gondoliers about five times their proper fare, and ran up to his sitting-room with a light step and a buoyant heart. There he found three letters waiting for him. One was from Sybil herself, full of sympathy and condolence. The others were from his mother, and from Lady Clementina's solicitor. It seemed that the old lady had dined with the Duchess that very night, had delighted every one by her wit and *esprit,* but had gone home somewhat early, complaining of heartburn. In the morning she was found dead in her bed, having apparently suffered no pain. Sir Mathew Reid had been sent for at once, but, of course, there was nothing to be done, and she was to be buried on the 22nd at Beauchamp Chalcote. A few days before she died she had made her will, and left Lord Arthur her little house in Curzon Street, and all her furniture, personal effects, and pictures, with the exception of her collection of miniatures, which was to go to her sister, Lady Margaret Rufford, and her amethyst necklace, which Sybil Merton was to have. The property was not of much value; but Mr. Mansfield, the solicitor, was extremely anxious for Lord Arthur to return at once, if possible, as there were a great many bills to be paid, and Lady Clementina had never kept any regular accounts.

Lord Arthur was very much touched by Lady Clementina's kind remembrance of him, and felt that Mr. Podgers had a great deal to answer for. His love of Sybil, however, dominated every other emotion, and the consciousness that he had done his duty gave him peace and comfort. When he arrived at Charing Cross, he felt perfectly happy.

The Mertons received him very kindly. Sybil made him promise that he would never again allow anything to come between them, and the marriage was fixed for the 7th June. Life seemed to him once more bright and beautiful, and all his old gladness came back to him again.

One day, however, as he was going over the house in Curzon Street, in company with Lady Clementina's solicitor and Sybil herself, burning packages of faded letters, and turning out drawers of odd rubbish, the young girl suddenly gave a little cry of delight.

"What have you found, Sybil?" said Lord Arthur, looking up from his work, and smiling.

"This lovely little silver *bonbonnière,* Arthur. Isn't it quaint and Dutch? Do give it to me! I know amethysts won't become me till I am over eighty."

It was the box that had held the aconitine.

Lord Arthur started, and a faint blush came into his cheek. He had almost entirely forgotten what he had done, and it seemed to him a curious coincidence that Sybil, for whose sake he had gone through all that terrible anxiety, should have been the first to remind him of it.

"Of course you can have it, Sybil. I gave it to poor Lady Clem myself."

"Oh! thank you, Arthur; and may I have the *bonbon* too? I had no notion that Lady Clementina liked sweets. I thought she was far too intellectual."

Lord Arthur grew deadly pale, and a horrible idea crossed his mind.

"*Bonbon,* Sybil? What do you mean?" he said in a slow, hoarse voice.

"There is one in it, that is all. It looks quite old and dusty, and I have not the slightest intention of eating it. What is the matter, Arthur? How white you look!"

Lord Arthur rushed across the room, and seized the box. Inside it was the amber-coloured capsule, with its poison-bubble. Lady Clementina had died a natural death after all!

The shock of the discovery was almost too much for him. He flung the capsule into the fire, and sank on the sofa with a cry of despair.

Chapter V

MR. MERTON was a good deal distressed at the second postponement of the marriage, and Lady Julia, who had already ordered her dress for the wedding, did all in her power to make Sybil break off the match. Dearly, however, as Sybil loved her mother, she had given her whole life into Lord Arthur's hands, and nothing that Lady Julia could say could make her waver in her faith. As for Lord Arthur himself, it took him days to get over his terrible disappointment, and for a time his nerves were completely unstrung. His excellent common sense, however, soon asserted itself, and his sound, practical mind did not leave him long in doubt about what to do. Poison having proved a complete failure, dynamite, or some other form of explosive, was obviously the proper thing to try.

He accordingly looked again over the list of his friends and relatives, and, after careful consideration, determined to blow up his uncle, the Dean of Chichester. The Dean, who was a man of great culture and learning, was extremely fond of clocks, and had a wonderful collection of timepieces, ranging from the fifteenth century to the present day, and it seemed to Lord Arthur that this hobby of the good Dean's offered him an excellent opportunity for carrying out his scheme. Where to procure an explosive machine was, of course, quite another matter. The London Directory gave him no information on the point, and he felt that there was very little use in going to Scotland Yard about it, as they never seemed to know anything about the movements of the dynamite faction till after an explosion had taken place, and not much even then.

Suddenly he thought of his friend Rouvaloff, a young Russian of very revolutionary tendencies, whom he had met at Lady Windermere's in the winter. Count Rouvaloff was supposed to be writing a life of Peter the Great, and to have come over to England for the purpose of studying the documents relating to that Tsar's residence in this country as a ship carpenter; but it was generally suspected that he was a Nihilist agent, and there was no doubt that the Russian Embassy did not look with any favour upon his presence in London. Lord Arthur felt that he was just the man for his purpose, and drove down one morning to his lodgings in Bloomsbury, to ask his advice and assistance.

"So you are taking up politics seriously?" said Count Rouvaloff, when Lord Arthur had told him the object of his mission; but Lord Arthur, who hated swagger of any kind, felt bound to admit to him that he had not the slightest interest in social questions, and simply wanted the explosive machine for a purely family matter, in which no one was concerned but himself.

Count Rouvaloff looked at him for some moments in amazement, and then seeing that he was quite serious, wrote an address on a piece of paper, initialled it, and handed it to him across the table.

"Scotland Yard would give a good deal to know this address, my dear fellow."

"They shan't have it," cried Lord Arthur, laughing; and after shaking the young Russian warmly by the hand he ran downstairs, examined the paper, and told the coachman to drive to Soho Square.

There he dismissed him, and strolled down Greek Street, till he came to a place called Bayle's Court. He passed under the archway, and found himself in a curious cul-de-sac, that was apparently occupied by a French Laundry, as a perfect network of clothes-lines was stretched across from house to house, and there was a flutter of white linen in the morning air. He walked right to the end, and knocked at a little green house. After some delay, during which every window in the court became a blurred mass of peering faces, the door was opened by a rather rough-looking foreigner, who asked him in very bad English what his business was. Lord Arthur handed him the paper Count Rouvaloff had given him. When the man saw it he bowed, and invited Lord Arthur into a very shabby front parlour on the ground floor, and in a few moments Herr Winckelkopf, as he was called in England, bustled into the room, with a very wine-stained napkin round his neck, and a fork in his left hand.

"Count Rouvaloff has given me an introduction to you," said Lord Arthur, bowing, "and I am anxious to have a short interview with you on a matter of business. My name is Smith, Mr. Robert Smith, and I want you to supply me with an explosive clock."

"Charmed to meet you, Lord Arthur," said the genial little German, laughing. "Don't look so alarmed, it is my duty to know everybody, and I remember seeing you one evening at Lady Windermere's. I hope her ladyship is quite well. Do you mind sitting with me while I finish my breakfast? There is an excellent pâté, and my friends are kind enough to say that my Rhine wine is better than any they get at the German Embassy," and before Lord Arthur had got over his surprise at being recognised, he found himself seated in the back-room, sipping the most delicious Marcobrünner out of a pale yellow hock-glass marked with the Imperial monogram, and chatting in the friendliest manner possible to the famous conspirator.

"Explosive clocks," said Herr Winckelkopf, "are not very good things for foreign exportation, as, even if they succeed in passing the Custom House, the train service is so irregular, that they usually go off before they have reached their proper destination. If, however, you want one for home use, I can supply you with an excellent article, and guarantee that you will he satisfied with the result. May I ask for whom it is intended? If it is for the police, or for any one connected with Scotland Yard, I am afraid I cannot do anything for you. The English detectives are really our best friends, and I have always found that by relying on their stupidity, we can do exactly what we like. I could not spare one of them."

"I assure you," said Lord Arthur, "that it has nothing to do with the police at all. In fact, the clock is intended for the Dean of Chichester."

"Dear me! I had no idea that you felt so strongly about religion, Lord Arthur. Few young men do nowadays."

"I am afraid you overrate me, Herr Winckelkopf," said Lord Arthur, blushing. "The fact is, I really know nothing about theology."

"It is a purely private matter then?"

"Purely private."

Herr Winckelkopf shrugged his shoulders, and left the room, returning in a few minutes with a round cake of dynamite about the size of a penny, and a pretty little French clock, surmounted by an ormolu figure of Liberty trampling on the hydra of Despotism.

Lord Arthur's face brightened up when he saw it. "That is just what I want," he cried, "and now tell me how it goes off."

"Ah! there is my secret," answered Herr Winckelkopf, contemplating his invention with a justifiable look of pride; "let me know when you wish it to explode, and I will set the machine to the moment."

"Well, today is Tuesday, and if you could send it off at once—"

"That is impossible; I have a great deal of important work on hand for some friends of mine in Moscow. Still, I might send it off tomorrow."

"Oh, it will be quite time enough!" said Lord Arthur politely, "if it is delivered tomorrow night or Thursday morning. For the moment of the explosion, say Friday at noon exactly. The Dean is always at home at that hour."

"Friday, at noon," repeated Herr Winckelkopf, and he made a note to that effect in a large ledger that was lying on a bureau near the fireplace.

"And now," said Lord Arthur, rising from his seat, "pray let me know how much I am in your debt."

"It is such a small matter, Lord Arthur, that I do not care to make any charge. The dynamite comes to seven and sixpence, the clock will be three pounds ten, and the carriage about five shillings. I am only too pleased to oblige any friend of Count Rouvaloff's."

"But your trouble, Herr Winckelkopf?"

"Oh, that is nothing! It is a pleasure to me. I do not work for money; I live entirely for my art."

Lord Arthur laid down £4, 2s. 6d. on the table, thanked the little German for his kindness, and, having succeeded in declining an invitation to meet some Anarchists at a meat-tea on the following Saturday, left the house and went off to the Park.

For the next two days he was in a state of the greatest excitement, and on Friday at twelve o'clock he drove down to the Buckingham to wait for news. All the afternoon the stolid hall-porter kept posting up telegrams from various parts of the country giving the results of horse-races, the verdicts in divorce suits, the state of the weather, and the like, while the tape ticked out wearisome details about an all-night sitting in the House of Commons, and a small panic on the Stock Exchange. At four o'clock the evening papers came in, and Lord Arthur disappeared into the library with the Pall Mall, the St. James's, the Globe, and the Echo, to the immense indignation of Colonel Goodchild, who wanted to read the reports of a speech he had delivered that morning at the Mansion House, on the subject of South African Missions, and the advisability of having black Bishops in every province, and for some reason or other had a strong prejudice against the Evening News. None of the papers, however, contained even the slightest allusion to Chichester, and Lord Arthur felt that the attempt must have failed. It was a terrible blow to him, and for a time he was quite unnerved. Herr Winckelkopf, whom he went to see the next day was full of elaborate apologies, and offered to supply him with another clock free of charge, or with a case of nitro-glycerine bombs at cost price. But he had lost all faith in explosives, and Herr Winckelkopf himself acknowledged that everything is so adulterated nowadays, that even dynamite can hardly be got in a pure condition. The little German, however, while admitting that something must have gone wrong with the machinery, was not without hope that the clock might still go off, and instanced the case of a barometer that he had once sent to the military Governor at Odessa, which, though timed to explode in ten days, had not done so for something like three months. It was quite true that when it did go off, it merely succeeded in blowing a housemaid to atoms, the Governor having gone out of town six weeks before, but at least it showed that dynamite, as a destructive force, was, when under the control of machinery, a powerful, though a somewhat unpunctual agent. Lord Arthur was a little consoled by this reflection, but even here he was destined to disappointment, for two days afterwards, as he was going upstairs, the Duchess called him into her boudoir, and showed him a letter she had just received from the Deanery.

"Jane writes charming letters," said the Duchess; "you must really read her last. It is quite as good as the novels Mudie sends us."

Lord Arthur seized the letter from her hand. It ran as follows:

The Deanery,
Chichester,
27th May.

My Dearest Aunt,

Thank you so much for the flannel for the Dorcas Society, and also for the gingham. I quite agree with you that it is nonsense their wanting to wear pretty things, but everybody is so Radical and irreligious nowadays, that it is difficult to make them see that they should not try and dress like the upper classes. I am sure I don't know what we are coming to. As papa has often said in his sermons, we live in an age of unbelief.

We have had great fun over a clock that an unknown admirer sent papa last Thursday. It arrived in a wooden box from London, carriage paid, and papa feels it must have been sent by some one who had read his remarkable sermon, 'Is Licence Liberty?' for on the top of the clock was a figure of a woman, with what papa said was the cap of Liberty on her head. I didn't think it very becoming myself, but papa said it was historical, so I suppose it is all right. Parker unpacked it, and papa put it on the mantelpiece in the library, and we were all sitting there on Friday morning, when just as the clock struck twelve, we heard a whirring noise, a little puff of smoke came from the pedestal of the figure, and the goddess of Liberty fell off, and broke her nose on the fender! Maria was quite alarmed, but it looked so ridiculous, that James and I went off into fits of laughter, and even papa was amused. When we examined it, we found it was a sort of alarum clock, and that, if you set it to a particular hour, and put some gunpowder and a cap under a little hammer, it went off whenever you wanted. Papa said it must not remain in the library, as it made a noise, so Reggie carried it away to the schoolroom, and does nothing but have small explosions all day long. Do you think Arthur would like one for a wedding present? I suppose they are quite fashionable in London. Papa says they should do a great deal of good, as they show that Liberty can't last, but must fall down. Papa says Liberty was invented at the time of the French Revolution. How awful it seems!

I have now to go to the Dorcas, where I will read them your most instructive letter. How true, dear aunt, your idea is, that in their rank of life they should wear what is unbecoming. I must say it is absurd, their anxiety about dress, when there are so many more important things in this world, and in the next. I am so glad your flowered poplin turned out so well, and that your lace was not torn. I am wearing my yellow satin, that you so kindly gave me, at the Bishop's on Wednesday, and think it will look all right. Would you have bows or not? Jennings says that every one wears bows now, and that the underskirt should be frilled. Reggie has just had another explosion, and papa has ordered the clock to be sent to the stables. I don't think papa likes it so much as he did at first, though he is very flattered at being sent such a pretty and ingenious toy. It shows that people read his sermons, and profit by them.

Papa sends his love, in which James, and Reggie, and Maria all unite, and, hoping that Uncle Cecil's gout is better, believe me, dear aunt, ever your affectionate niece,

Jane Percy.

PS. – Do tell me about the bows. Jennings insists they are the fashion.

Lord Arthur looked so serious and unhappy over the letter, that the Duchess went into fits of laughter.

"My dear Arthur," she cried, "I shall never show you a young lady's letter again! But what shall I say about the clock? I think it is a capital invention, and I should like to have one myself."

"I don't think much of them," said Lord Arthur, with a sad smile, and, after kissing his mother, he left the room.

When he got upstairs, he flung himself on a sofa, and his eyes filled with tears. He had done his best to commit this murder, but on both occasions he had failed, and through no fault of his own. He had tried to do his duty, but it seemed as if Destiny herself had turned traitor. He was oppressed with the sense of the barrenness of good intentions, of the futility of trying to be fine. Perhaps, it would be better to break off the marriage altogether. Sybil would suffer, it is true, but suffering could not really mar a nature so noble as hers. As for himself, what did it matter? There is always some war in which a man can die, some cause to which a man can give his life, and as life had no pleasure for him, so death had no terror. Let Destiny work out his doom. He would not stir to help her.

At half-past seven he dressed, and went down to the club. Surbiton was there with a party of young men, and he was obliged to dine with them. Their trivial conversation and idle jests did not interest him, and as soon as coffee was brought he left them, inventing some engagement in order to get away. As he was going out of the club, the hall-porter handed him a letter. It was from Herr Winckelkopf, asking him to call down the next evening, and look at an explosive umbrella, that went off as soon as it was opened. It was the very latest invention, and had just arrived from Geneva. He tore the letter up into fragments. He had made up his mind not to try any more experiments. Then he wandered down to the Thames Embankment, and sat for hours by the river. The moon peered through a mane of tawny clouds, as if it were a lion's eye, and innumerable stars spangled the hollow vault, like gold dust powdered on a purple dome. Now and then a barge swung out into the turbid stream, and floated away with the tide, and the railway signals changed from green to scarlet as the trains ran shrieking across the bridge. After some time, twelve o'clock boomed from the tall tower at Westminster, and at each stroke of the sonorous bell the night seemed to tremble. Then the railway lights went out, one solitary lamp left gleaming like a large ruby on a giant mast, and the roar of the city became fainter.

At two o'clock he got up, and strolled towards Blackfriars. How unreal everything looked! How like a strange dream! The houses on the other side of the river seemed built out of darkness. One would have said that silver and shadow had fashioned the world anew. The huge dome of St. Paul's loomed like a bubble through the dusky air.

As he approached Cleopatra's Needle he saw a man leaning over the parapet, and as he came nearer the man looked up, the gas-light falling full upon his face.

It was Mr. Podgers, the cheiromantist! No one could mistake the fat, flabby face, the gold-rimmed spectacles, the sickly feeble smile, the sensual mouth.

Lord Arthur stopped. A brilliant idea flashed across him, and he stole softly up behind. In a moment he had seized Mr. Podgers by the legs, and flung him into the Thames. There was a coarse oath, a heavy splash, and all was still. Lord Arthur looked anxiously over, but could see nothing of the cheiromantist but a tall hat, pirouetting in an eddy of moonlit water. After a time it also sank, and no trace of Mr. Podgers was visible. Once he thought that he caught sight of the bulky misshapen figure striking out for the staircase by the bridge, and a horrible feeling of failure came over him, but it turned out to be merely a reflection, and when the moon shone out from behind a cloud it passed away. At last he seemed to have realised the decree of destiny. He heaved a deep sigh of relief, and Sybil's name came to his lips.

"Have you dropped anything, sir?" said a voice behind him suddenly.

He turned round, and saw a policeman with a bull's-eye lantern.

"Nothing of importance, sergeant," he answered, smiling, and hailing a passing hansom, he jumped in, and told the man to drive to Belgrave Square.

For the next few days he alternated between hope and fear. There were moments when he almost expected Mr. Podgers to walk into the room, and yet at other times he felt that Fate could not be so unjust to him. Twice he went to the cheiromantist's address in West Moon Street, but he could not bring himself to ring the bell. He longed for certainty, and was afraid of it.

Finally it came. He was sitting in the smoking-room of the club having tea, and listening rather wearily to Surbiton's account of the last comic song at the Gaiety, when the waiter came in with the evening papers. He took up the *St. James's,* and was listlessly turning over its pages, when this strange heading caught his eye:

Suicide of a Cheiromantist.

He turned pale with excitement, and began to read. The paragraph ran as follows:

> *Yesterday morning, at seven o'clock, the body of Mr. Septimus R. Podgers, the eminent cheiromantist, was washed on shore at Greenwich, just in front of the Ship Hotel. The unfortunate gentleman had been missing for some days, and considerable anxiety for his safety had been felt in cheiromantic circles. It is supposed that he committed suicide under the influence of a temporary mental derangement, caused by overwork, and a verdict to that effect was returned this afternoon by the coroner's jury. Mr. Podgers had just completed an elaborate treatise on the subject of the Human Hand, that will shortly be published, when it will no doubt attract much attention. The deceased was sixty-five years of age, and does not seem to have left any relations.*

Lord Arthur rushed out of the club with the paper still in his hand, to the immense amazement of the hall-porter, who tried in vain to stop him, and drove at once to Park Lane. Sybil saw him from the window, and something told her that he was the bearer of good news. She ran down to meet him, and, when she saw his face, she knew that all was well.

"My dear Sybil," cried Lord Arthur, "let us be married tomorrow!"

"You foolish boy! Why, the cake is not even ordered!" said Sybil, laughing through her tears.

Chapter VI

WHEN THE WEDDING took place, some three weeks later, St. Peter's was crowded with a perfect mob of smart people. The service was read in the most impressive manner by the Dean of Chichester, and everybody agreed that they had never seen a handsomer couple than the bride and bridegroom. They were more than handsome, however – they were happy. Never for a single moment did Lord Arthur regret all that he had suffered for Sybil's sake, while she, on her side, gave him the best things a woman can give to any man – worship, tenderness, and love. For them romance was not killed by reality. They always felt young.

Some years afterwards, when two beautiful children had been born to them, Lady Windermere came down on a visit to Alton Priory, a lovely old place, that had been the Duke's wedding present to his son; and one afternoon as she was sitting with Lady Arthur under a lime-tree in the garden, watching the little boy and girl as they played up and down the rose-walk, like fitful sunbeams, she suddenly took her hostess's hand in hers, and said, "Are you happy, Sybil?"

"Dear Lady Windermere, of course I am happy. Aren't you?"

"I have no time to be happy, Sybil. I always like the last person who is introduced to me; but, as a rule, as soon as I know people I get tired of them."

"Don't your lions satisfy you, Lady Windermere?"

"Oh dear, no! lions are only good for one season. As soon as their manes are cut, they are the dullest creatures going. Besides, they behave very badly, if you are really nice to them. Do you remember that horrid Mr. Podgers? He was a dreadful impostor. Of course, I didn't mind that at all, and even when he wanted to borrow money I forgave him, but I could not stand his making love to me. He has really made me hate cheiromancy. I go in for telepathy now. It is much more amusing."

"You mustn't say anything against cheiromancy here, Lady Windermere; it is the only subject that Arthur does not like people to chaff about. I assure you he is quite serious over it."

"You don't mean to say that he believes in it, Sybil?"

"Ask him, Lady Windermere, here he is"; and Lord Arthur came up the garden with a large bunch of yellow roses in his hand, and his two children dancing round him.

"Lord Arthur?"

"Yes, Lady Windermere."

"You don't mean to say that you believe in cheiromancy?"

"Of course I do," said the young man, smiling.

"But why?"

"Because I owe to it all the happiness of my life," he murmured, throwing himself into a wicker chair.

"My dear Lord Arthur, what do you owe to it?"

"Sybil," he answered, handing his wife the roses, and looking into her violet eyes.

"What nonsense!" cried Lady Windermere. "I never heard such nonsense in all my life."

Biographies & Sources

Stacy Aumonier

Miss Bracegirdle Does Her Duty

(First Published in *The Strand Magazine*, 1921)

A British writer of six novels, eighty-five short stories and many essays, Stacy Aumonier (1877–1928) was known for his humour, and often mistakenly credited as 'Stacey' Aumonier. His talent lay in short story writing in the main, as he was a master of being gripping from the very first sentence, and keeping a reader hooked. His short story 'Miss Bracegirdle Does Her Duty' is considered one of his best, and appeared on *Alfred Hitchcock Presents* in 1958. He is also known for the stories 'The Octave of Jealousy' and 'Two of Those Women' and his work is included in numerous anthologies that collect the best of British short stories.

Robert Barr

The Absent-Minded Coterie

(Originally Published in *The Triumphs of Eugène Valmont*, 1906)

A Scottish-Canadian short story writer, Robert Barr (1849–1912) was born in Glasgow before his family emigrated to Toronto, where he grew up and became a teacher and then worked for the newspaper *Detroit Free Press* until 1881 when he moved to London, to establish a weekly English edition. He later founded *The Idler*, collaborating with Jerome K. Jerome, and became known as a successful novelist, publishing a book a year. He continued to write short stories however, becoming known for two Sherlock Holmes parodies. The first of these was 'The Adventures of Sherlaw Kombs' which was published in *The Idler* in 1892 and led to Barr becoming good friends with Arthur Conan Doyle.

T.J. Berg

Mickey's Ghost

(First Publication)

T.J. Berg is a molecular and cellular biologist working and writing in Sweden. She is a graduate of the Odyssey Writing Workshop. Her short fiction has appeared in *Talebones* (for which it received an honorable mention in *The Year's Best Fantasy and Horror*), *Tales of the Unanticipated*, *Electric Velocipede*, *Daily Science Fiction*, *Caledonia Dreamin'*, *Sensorama*, and *Thirty Years of Rain*, and is upcoming in *New Myths*, *Tales of Terror*, and *Diabolical Plots*. When not writing or doing science, she can be found stravaigin the world, cooking, or hiking. She can be found on the web at www.infinity-press.com.

Judi Calhoun

Hungry Coyote

(Originally Published as an Alternative Version on the *Crimson Streets* webzine, 2016)

As a child, Judi Calhoun became intrigued with plotting amazing stories. Armed with art supplies, she designed paper doll characters, hand-painted backgrounds, fostered schemes and fashioned scenes: all fodder for her Smith Corona manuscripts. Since then, her work has appeared in numerous e-zines and printed periodicals such as Plaidswede's Pulp & Murder Mystery Newsroom Crime Florilegium series – 'The Haunted Coach', 'Wail Song', 'Murder at the Monitor'; John Greenleaf Whittier Inspired Collection by Haverhill House: 'Exposed for Murder, & Cultivar Wars'; and the highly esteemed *Appalachian* journal literary piece 'My Time Is Short'; plus many more. Find out more about Judi's work at www.judicalhoun.com.

Ramsey Campbell
See How They Run
(Originally Published in Monsters in Our Midst, edited by Robert Bloch and [uncredited] Martin H. Greenberg. Copyright © 1993 by Ramsey Campbell.)
Ramsey Campbell has been given more awards than any other writer in the field, including the Grand Master Award of the World Horror Convention, the Lifetime Achievement Award of the Horror Writers Association, the Living Legend Award of the International Horror Guild and the World Fantasy Lifetime Achievement Award. In 2015 he was made an Honorary Fellow of Liverpool John Moores University for outstanding services to literature. Among his novels available from Flame Tree Press are *Thirteen Days by Sunset Beach* and *Think Yourself Lucky*.

Irvin S. Cobb
The Escape of Mr. Trimm
(First Published in *The Escape of Mr. Trimm and Other Plights*, 1909)
An Occurrence Up A Side Street
(First Published in *The Escape of Mr. Trimm and Other Plights*, 1909)
Irvin Shrewsbury Cobb (1876–1944) was an American author, editor and columnist who was originally from Kentucky but then in 1904 relocated to New York, where he lived for the rest of his life. He wrote for the *New York World* newspaper as one of their highest paid employees, having worked his way up from his first job with the *Paducah Daily News* when he was seventeen. He is best known for his short story collection Old Judge Priest (1915) and his humorous Speaking of Operations (1916). Several of his stories were adapted in silent films, and his Judge Priest stories were adapted by film director John Ford.

Wilkie Collins
The Traveler's Story of a Terribly Strange Bed
(Originally Published in *After Dark*, Smith, Elder & Co., 1856)
William Wilkie Collins (1824–1889) was born in London's Marylebone and he lived there almost consistently for 65 years. Writing over 30 major books, 100 articles, short stories and essays and a dozen or more plays, he is best known for *The Moonstone* and *The Woman in White*. He was good friends with novelist Charles Dickens with whom he collaborated as well as took inspiration from to help write novels like *The Lighthouse* and *The Frozen Deep*. Finally becoming internationally reputable in the 1860s, Collins truly showed himself as the master of his craft as he wrote many profitable novels in less than a decade and earned himself the title of a successful English novelist, playwright and author of short stories.

Fyodor Dostoevsky
Crime and Punishment (Part I)
(Originally Published in 1866)
Fyodor Mikhailovich Dostoevsky (1821–81) was a prolific writer and philosopher from Russia, who produced eleven novels, three novellas and numerous short stories and other works. He began writing from an early age and briefly worked as a translator, before he wrote his first novel *Poor Folk*, which opened up opportunities for him in St. Petersburg. He was arrested in 1849 for belonging to a literary group that discussed banned books, and

spent four years in a prison camp, followed by six years of military service. Despite this, he built a career as a successful journalist in the years following his release and became one of the most highly regarded and most widely read Russian writers.

Arthur Conan Doyle
The Adventure of the Abbey Grange
(Originally Published in *The Return of Sherlock Holmes*, 1904)
The Adventure of the Red Circle
(Originally Published in *His Last Bow*, 1911)
Arthur Conan Doyle (1859–1930) was born in Edinburgh, Scotland. As a medical student he was so impressed by his professor's powers of deduction that he was inspired to create the illustrious and much-loved figure Sherlock Holmes. Holmes is known for his keen power of observation and logical reasoning, which often astounds his companion Dr. Watson. Whatever the subject or character, Doyle's vibrant and remarkable writing has breathed life into all of his stories, engaging readers throughout the decades.

Meg Elison
Ripping
(First Publication)
Meg Elison is the author of *The Book of the Unnamed Midwife*, Tiptree recommendation, Audie Award finalist and winner of the Philip K. Dick Award. Her sequel, *The Book of Etta*, was published in February 2017, and the third and final book in the series comes out in April of 2019. She has also been published in *Fantasy & Science Fiction*, *Shimmer*, *McSweeney's*, *Catapult*, and many other places. Elison is a high school dropout and a graduate of UC Berkeley. She lives in Oakland, CA and writes like she's running out of time.

E.W. Hornung
Nine Points of the Law
(Original Published in *The Amateur Cracksman*, 1899)
The Raffles Relics
(Original Published in *A Thief in the Night*, 1905)
Ernest William Hornung (1866–1921) was born in Middlesborough, England. As a young adult he spent time in Australia, a setting which would inspire his later novels, before eventually settling in London. His marriage to Constance Doyle led to him becoming the brother-in-law of Arthur Conan Doyle. Echoing his brother-in-law's gift for characterisation, Hornung's most famous character creation, Raffles the gentleman thief, has often been considered the criminal parallel to Conan Doyle's Sherlock. Hornung wrote several stories in his series based around the illicit exploits of the memorable Raffles and his companion 'Bunny', which would go on to inspire stage and screen adaptations.

Fergus Hume
The Mystery of a Hansom Cab (chapters I–IX)
(Originally Published in 1886)
Fergus Hume (1859–1932) was born in England but emigrated to Dunedin, New Zealand when he was just three years old and later lived in Melbourne, Australia. He began writing after being influenced by the popular novelist Émile Gaboriau, who inspired him to write his first novel *The Mystery of the Hansom Cab*. It was set in Melbourne, and was applauded

for its descriptions of poverty, becoming the best-selling mystery novel of the Victorian era and inspiring Arthur Conan Doyle to write *A Study in Scarlet*. Hume's later work included Professor Brankel's Secret and Madame Midas. He moved to England in 1888 where he lived in the countryside for the rest of his life.

Rich Larson
A Scattered Body
(Originally Published in *The Cadaverine*, 2013)
Rich Larson was born in Galmi, Niger, has studied in Rhode Island and worked in the south of Spain, and now lives in Ottawa, Canada. He is the author of Annex and Cypher, as well as over a hundred short stories – some of the best of which can be found in his collection *Tomorrow Factory*. His award-winning work has been translated into Polish, Czech, French, Italian, Vietnamese and Chinese. Besides writing, he enjoys travelling, learning languages, playing soccer, watching basketball, shooting pool, and dancing kizomba.

Maurice Leblanc
The Escape of Arsène Lupin
(Originally Published in *Arsène Lupin, Gentleman Burglar*, 1907)
Born in Rouen, France, Maurice Leblanc (1864–1941) dropped his law studies in favour of a literary career, publishing his first novel, *Une Femme*, in 1887. His fame is largely due to his Arsène Lupin series of stories. 'The Arrest of Arsène Lupin' was the first story to feature the roguish gentleman criminal, appearing in 1905 as a commissioned piece for a new journal. The character was an instant success, and the thief-turned-detective went on to appear in over 60 Leblanc's works. Some of the Lupin tales even feature a parodied Sherlock Holmes, with Lupin invariably outwitting his English rival.

Jack London
When the World Was Young
(Originally Published in *The Night Born*, 1913)
Winged Blackmail
(Originally Published in *The Night Born*, 1913)
Jack London (1876–1916) was born as John Griffith Chaney in California, America. As a young man he went to work in the Klondike during the Gold Rush, which became the setting for two of his best-known novels, *White Fang* and *The Call of the Wild*. However it is his short stories which have often received wider critical acclaim. Coming from a working-class background, London was a keen social activist and wrote several stories and articles from a socialist standpoint. It is thought that he is one of the first fiction authors to have enjoyed prosperity and worldwide fame from his writings alone.

C.L. McDaniel
Wet Work
(First Publication)
C.L. McDaniel is a teacher, actor, and author living in Berlin, Germany. His writings include the indie urban fantasy series *The Caleb Ride Chronicles* and the play *Voices Through the Wall*, which was featured in a segment of the BBC Radio program *The Strand*. He co-starred in the 2017 film *Weather House*, and the young adult podcast *Cast of Wonders* published his short story 'And Flights of Skuhwiggle' in July 2018.

Dan Micklethwaite

Sirens

(First Publication)

Dan Micklethwaite writes stories in a shed in West Yorkshire. His work has previously appeared in Flame Tree Publishing's *Swords & Steam* anthology, and more recently in *Beneath Ceaseless Skies*, NewMyths.com, and Third Flatiron's *Terra! Tara! Terror!* collection. His debut novel, *The Less than Perfect Legend of Donna Creosote*, was published by the award-winning UK publisher Bluemoose Books, and shortlisted for the Guardian's Not the Booker Prize in 2016. Follow him on twitter @Dan_M_writer for further updates and info.

Trixie Nisbet

Breaking News

(First Publication)

Despite her apparent knowledge of urban crime, blackmail and murder, Trixie Nisbet wishes it to be known that 'Breaking News' came entirely from her imagination. She lives in a peaceful town on the South coast of England near Brighton and has had over forty stories printed, mostly in women's magazines, in the UK, Australia and South Africa. She has also won several national short story competitions, without having to resort to urban crime, blackmail or murder – honest.

Thana Niveau

From Hell to Eternity

(Originally Published in *From Hell to Eternity*, 2012, and won first place in the 2010 Whitechapel's Society contest)

Thana Niveau is a horror and science fiction writer. Originally from the States, she now lives in the UK, in a Victorian seaside town between Bristol and Wales. She is the author of the short story collections *Octoberland*, *Unquiet Waters*, and *From Hell to Eternity*, as well as the novel *House of Frozen Screams*. Her work has been reprinted in *Best New Horror* and *Best British Horror*. She has twice been nominated for the British Fantasy award – for her debut collection *From Hell to Eternity* and her story 'Death Walks En Pointe'.

Baroness Orczy

The Regent's Park Murder

(Originally Published in *The Old Man in the Corner*, 1908)

Baroness Emma Orczy (1865–1947) was born in Tarnaörs, Heves County, Hungary. She spent her childhood in Budapest, Brussels and Paris before moving to London when she was 14. After her marriage to a young illustrator, she worked as a translator and illustrator to supplement their low income. Baroness Orczy's first novel, *The Emperor's Candlesticks*, was a failure but her later novels faired better. She is most famous for the play 'The Scarlet Pimpernel', which she wrote with her husband. She went on to write a novelization of it, as well as many sequels and other works of mystery fiction and adventure romances.

Josh Pachter

The Dilmun Exchange

(Copyright © 1984 by Josh Pachter. Originally Published in *Ellery Queen's Mystery Magazine*, reprinted with the permission of the author)

Josh Pachter's short fiction appears regularly in *Ellery Queen's Mystery Magazine* and many other periodicals and anthologies. He recently co-edited *Amsterdam Noir* (Akashic Books) and *The Misadventures of Ellery Queen* (Wildside Press) and edited *The Man Who Read Mysteries* (Crippen & Landru). He also translates fiction and nonfiction from Dutch and Flemish to English. An American native, Pachter lives in Virginia, where he teaches interpersonal communication and film appreciation at Northern Virginia Community College. This is his third contribution to Flame Tree's Gothic Fantasy series, with previous appearances in *Crime & Mystery* and *Agents & Spies*.

Michael Penncavage
The Gauntlet
(First Publication)
Michael Penncavage's fiction can be found in over 100 magazines and anthologies from 7 different countries, such as *Alfred Hitchcock Mystery Magazine* (USA), *Here and Now* (England), *Tenebres* (France), *Crime Factory* (Australia), *Reaktor* (Estonia), *Speculative Mystery* (South Africa), and *Visionarium* (Austria). His other stories include 'The Cost of Doing Business', which won the Derringer Award for best mystery; 'The Converts', which was filmed as a short movie; and 'The Landlord', which was adapted into a play. Michael has been an Associate Editor for *Space and Time Magazine* as well as the Editor of the horror/suspense anthology *Tales from a Darker State*.

Melville Davisson Post
The End of the Road
(Originally Published in *The Sleuth of St. James's Square,* 1920)
American author Melville Davisson Post (1869–1930) was known for the character Sir Henry Marquis of Scotland Yard in his short story collection *The Sleuth of St. James's Square*. His other characters included the well-known lawyers Randolph Mason and Colonel Braxton, and the detectives Sir Henry Marquis and Monsieur Jonquelle. He wrote a vast amount of novels in his lifetime, which were almost all crime fiction, totalling over two hundred titles.

Jennifer Quail
A Father's Child
(First Publication)
Jennifer Quail lives in Michigan and usually writes romance whether she wants to or not, but also writes mystery, suspense and fantasy. Her work has appeared in the anthology *A Kiss and a Promise*, *Spark Magazine*, and *Dreams of Decadence*. Her urban fantasy novels *Strange Roads* and *The Demon That is Dreaming* are available on Amazon. In her embarrassing student days, she was selected to perform her poetry with beat composer David Amram. Updates, blogs, and the odd recipe are on her website: authorjenniferquail.com.

Zandra Renwick
Lovely Young Losers
(Originally Published in *Alfred Hitchcock's Mystery Magazine*, 2014)
Under various mashups of her full name, Zandra Renwick's fiction has been translated

into nine languages, adapted to stage and audio, and optioned for television. She spent formative years in Austin, Copenhagen, and Toronto wearing ripped fishnets and sneaking into punk clubs. She currently splits her time between an urban swamp in Texas and Ottawa's historic Timberhouse, a heritage residence in the heart of Canada's capital city. More online at zandrarenwick.com or on Twitter @zandrarenwick.

K.W. Roberts

Someone's Out There

(First Publication)

K.W. Roberts lived near Chicago for three years where a loud but dysfunctional rock band in which he played guitar struggled with little success, prompting a move to Boulder, Colorado, where he has found much greater happiness climbing rocks and mountains. While he has idolised Wilkie Collins and Agatha Christie since getting introduced to crime fiction in college, the idea of trying such a story himself never occurred to him. He does, however, plan to write many more. He feels it is about time he got published.

Leo X. Robertson

Mr. Sleepy

(First Publication)

Leo X. Robertson is a Scottish process engineer, currently living on the island of Stord in Norway. He has work published by or forthcoming in *Helios Quarterly*, *Expanded Horizons*, *Unnerving Magazine* and *PULP Literature*, among others. Leo's stories often draw influence from true crime. On his walks to and from work, he listens to the *NoSleep*, *My Favorite Murder* and *LetsNotMeet* podcasts – which, while assisting with his fiction, make it tougher to sleep at night.

Christopher P. Semtner

Foreword: Urban Crime Short Stories

Christopher P. Semtner is an internationally exhibited artist, author, and curator living in Virginia. The curator of the Edgar Allan Poe Museum in Richmond, Virginia, he has served as author, co-author or editor of several books including the History Press title *Edgar Allan Poe's Richmond: The Raven in the River City*. He has created museum exhibits on Poe in the Comics, Poe's Mysterious Death and Poe in the Movies. *The New York Times* called the exhibit he curated for the Library of Virginia, Poe: Man, Myth, or Monster, 'provocative' and 'a playful, robust exhibit.'

David Tallerman

Step Light

(Originally Published in *Alfred Hitchcock's Mystery Magazine*, 2016)

David Tallerman is the author of the Flame Tree Press thriller *The Bad Neighbour*, ongoing YA fantasy series *The Black River Chronicles*, the *Tales of Easie Damasco* trilogy, and the novella *Patchwerk*. His comics work includes the absurdist steampunk graphic novel *Endangered Weapon B: Mechanimal Science*, with Bob Molesworth. David's short fiction has appeared in around eighty markets, including *Clarkesworld*, *Nightmare*, *Lightspeed*, and *Beneath Ceaseless Skies*. A number of his best dark fantasy and horror stories were gathered together in his debut collection *The Sign in the Moonlight and Other Stories*. He can be found online at davidtallerman.co.uk.

Salinda Tyson
My Jack
(First Publication)
Born in Pennsylvania, Salinda was a long-time resident of Northern California, and currently lives in North Carolina. Her fiction appears in *Third Flatiron* anthologies, *Abyss & Apex* magazine, and the *Shadows in Salem* anthology. She began writing due to a keen interest in crime, and this is her first crime story to be published. Currently she volunteers as a docent at North Carolina's Museum of History. There she enjoys provoking curiosity about the past and consideration of how the present evolved from the past...and keeps on evolving.

Edgar Wallace
When the Gangs Came to London
(Originally Published by John Long Ltd., London, 1932)
Edgar Wallace (1875–1932) was born illegitimately to an actress, and adopted by a London fishmonger and his wife. On leaving school at the age of 12, he took up many jobs, including selling newspapers. This foreshadowed his later career as a war correspondent for such periodicals as the Daily Mail after he had enrolled in the army. He later turned to writing stories inspired by his time in Africa, and was incredibly prolific over a large number of genres and formats. Wallace is credited as being one of the first writers of detective fiction whose protagonists were policemen as opposed to amateur sleuths.

Rachel Watts
A Man Called Famous
(First Publication)
Rachel Watts is an author and former journalist from Perth, Western Australia. Her essays and fiction have been published by *Westerly, Island, Kill Your Darlings, Tincture* and more. Her young-adult climate change novella *Survival* was released in March 2018. She writes speculative and literary fiction with a focus on memory, gender, violence and the environment. She finds joy running creative writing workshops for adults and teens. You can find her at wattswrites.com and @watts_writes.

Chris Wheatley
Underpass
(First Publication)
Chris Wheatley splits his time between Oxford and Cambridge. He is a freelance journalist, writer and musician, with two previously published short stories and many non-fiction articles. Chris has an enduring love for the works of Dashiell Hammett, Raymond Chandler, Chester Himes and Cornell Woolrich. He has just completed his first full-length crime novel and is forever indebted to the advice and encouragement of his wife, his son and his mother, without whom he would never have come so far.

Victor L. Whitechurch
How the Bank Was Saved
(Originally Published in *Stories of the Railway*, 1912)
Victor Lorenzo Whitechurch (1868–1933) was a clergyman, educated at Chichester

Theological College in England. He was also a fiction writer, best-known for characters such as the vegetarian, fitness fanatic and detective Thorpe Hazell; and spy Ivan Koravitch. Whitechurch wrote several stories inspired by his clerical vocation, however he was also a railway enthusiast, as evidenced by his many railway mysteries featuring the detective Godfrey Page and later better developed with his Thorpe Hazell stories. The eccentric nature of Hazell was intended as a contrast to Sherlock Holmes.

Oscar Wilde
Lord Arthur Savile's Crime
(Originally Published in *The Court and Society Review*, 1887)
Oscar Wilde (1854–1900) was born in Dublin, Ireland, and was a successful author, poet, philosopher and playwright with an impressive gift for language. With several acclaimed works including his novel *The Picture of Dorian Gray* and the play *The Importance of Being Earnest*, Wilde was known for his biting wit and flamboyant personality in the Victorian era. He was famously imprisoned on homosexual charges, an imprisonment that proved disastrous to his health. He continued to write while in prison, and following his release he left for France and spent his remaining days in exile, essentially in poverty. 'The Canterville Ghost' was the first of Wilde's stories to be published, and has remained an ever-popular story that has since been adapted to many mediums.

FLAME TREE PUBLISHING
Short Story Series
New & Classic Writing

Flame Tree's Gothic Fantasy books offer a carefully curated series of new titles, each with combinations of original and classic writing:

*Chilling Horror • Chilling Ghost • Science Fiction
Murder Mayhem • Crime & Mystery • Swords & Steam
Dystopia Utopia • Supernatural Horror • Lost Worlds
Time Travel • Heroic Fantasy • Pirates & Ghosts
Agents & Spies • Endless Apocalypse • Alien Invasion
Robots & AI • Lost Souls • Haunted House
Cosy Crime • American Gothic*

Also, new companion titles offer rich collections of classic fiction, myths and tales in the gothic fantasy tradition:

*H.G. Wells • Lovecraft • Sherlock Holmes
Edgar Allan Poe • Bram Stoker • Mary Shelley
African Myths & Tales • Celtic Myths & Tales
Chinese Myths & Tales • Norse Myths & Tales
Greek Myths & Tales • Irish Fairy Tales
King Arthur & The Knights of the Round Table
Alice's Adventures in Wonderland • The Divine Comedy
The Wonderful Wizard of Oz • The Age of Queen Victoria • Brothers Grimm*

Available from all good bookstores, worldwide, and online at
flametreepublishing.com

See our new fiction imprint
FLAME TREE PRESS | FICTION WITHOUT FRONTIERS
New and original writing in Horror, Crime, SF and Fantasy

And join our monthly newsletter with offers and more stories:
FLAME TREE FICTION NEWSLETTER
flametreepress.com

GOTHIC FANTASY

For our books, calendars, blog
and latest special offers please see:
flametreepublishing.com